Stories for
Christmas
by
Charles Dickens

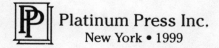

Platinum Press Inc.
New York • 1999

Publishers Note:

The first collected Edition of Dicken's contribu-
tions to the Christmas numbers of *Household
Words*' and *'All the Year Round*' was issued in
the 'Charles Dickens' Edition of his works in
1871, under the general title of Christmas Stories
from *'Household Words*' and *'All the Year
Round*'. The present Edition includes, in addi-
tion, the following five stories: *'A Christmas
Tree*', *'The Poor Relation's Story*', *'The Child's
Story*', *'The Schoolboy's Story*', and *'Nobody's
Story*', which originally appeared in Reprinted
Pieces.

Every attempt has been made to provide an
authentic facsimile edition. As the original manuscript (more than 100 years old) was used for
reproduction, the type quality reflects this.

Platinum Press Inc.
311 Crossways Park Drive Woodbury, NY 11797
ISBN 1-879582-41-4

Printed in USA

Introduction

Rather more than a hundred years ago, in a rotting London warehouse that drooped above the Thames at Hungerford Stairs, an undersized and undernourished wretch of a boy named Charles Dickens was drearily employed in pasting labels on pots of blacking. First he would cover the pots with oiled paper and blue paper, tying them neatly, clipping the edges; then he would stick on his labels. The task was monotonous, interminable. The filth and litter of decay surrounded him, and from the cellars of the building rose the constant squeaking and scrabbling of great gray rats. At night when his work was finished he would go home to a miserable lodging where he supped on bread and cheese. And every Sunday without fail he spent within the gloomy confines of the Marshalsea prison where, according to the quaint custom of the time, his father, who had been committed for debt, was living with his wife, several children, and a visiting maid who served them. The boy was only ten years old, and it is small wonder he was forlorn. "No words can express the secret agony of my soul," he wrote long afterwards referring to that time. "The deep remembrance of the sense I had of being utterly neglected and hopeless; of the shame I felt in my position; of the misery that it was to my young heart to believe that, day by day, what I had learned, and thought, and delighted in, and raised my fancy and my emulation up by, was passing away from me, never to be brought back any more; cannot be written."

INTRODUCTION

Gone was the house at Portsea, with its small front garden, where he had been born on the seventh of February, 1812. Gone was the pleasant house in Chatham, with gardens back and front, to which his father John Dickens, a naval paymaster's clerk, had removed him at a tender age; and gone was the little upstairs room of that house where he had found the magic library consisting of "Roderick Random," "Peregrine Pickle," "Humphry Clinker," "Tom Jones," "The Vicar of Wakefield," "Don Quixote," "Gil Blas," and "Robinson Crusoe"; where his imagination had taken wing, and he had felt within himself the first faint stirrings of literary genius and ambition. These things he had lost. He was, in his own phrase, cast away. The future was black, black as the contents of the pots he labelled. The most optimistic and kindest of prophets, watching that child of ten slaving for his six paltry shillings a week, could scarcely have reassured him. What, indeed, had he to live for? Yet—and this is the miracle—within another fifteen or sixteen years that same Charles Dickens was to be the most popular author of the English-reading world; for thirty years or so he was to move among men as one of the great ones of the earth; and when he died, in the June of 1870, he was to lie in Westminster Abbey, flanked by the monuments of Shakespeare and Dryden, and confronting the monument of Chaucer.

It is a "success story" to delight a twentieth century magazine editor; such a story as life itself consents to write but seldom. It is the story of a man whose pulse beat with the pulse of his generation, whose ideals were identical with those of his age, whose taste was the taste of the many; but of a man who was also, unlike the multitude, a supremely articulate genius—a man who could speak for millions as well as to them. Chesterton caught the truth in an epigram when he said: "Dickens did not write what the people wanted. Dickens wanted what the people wanted." And, satisfying himself, he satisfied a host; and their children after them, and their children's children. The readers whom he did not and does not satisfy are those with interests aloof from the common interests of mankind, with sentiments unresponsive to stimuli that stir the majority. Nor does he command the suffrage of those to whom ideas are more precious than rubies, of those who delight chiefly in sweet sessions of well-ordered thought; for as one of his votaries, Sir Arthur Quiller-Couch, has publicly confessed, "Dickens' world was not a world of ideas at all, but a city 'full of folk.' Compared with the world as Carlyle saw it, or Clough, or Martineau, or Newman, or Arnold, it is void of ideas, if not entirely unintellectual." Nor, again, will the connoisseurs who distinguish fine writing from merely efficient prose, and value only the former, turn to Dickens for delectation. He wrote from his heart, not from his brain; from the heart that had almost broken in the blacking warehouse by the Thames. And the manner of his writing was far less to him than the matter of it: so long as his tale was told, so long as it was understood, and moved or amused his readers as he wished them to be entertained or affected, he was content. It is in such a spirit that all the greatest writers have written; the "fine writing" of the greatest is always a by-product; it simply happens that in this by-product Dickens was not rich.

Nowhere, perhaps, does the man's heart beat more plainly to the public view than in the "Christmas Books," those little books that he composed in such breathing-spaces as his great novels left him. "A Christmas Carol" was written during those trying days when the comparative failure of the early parts of "Chuzzlewit" was bothering its author mightily. Much hope attended this first Christmas story, and hope was justified by the sale of six thousand copies on the day of publication; but Dickens was disappointed by the margin of profit shown. In following years he would have to do better, and he did; for "The Chimes" outsold the

INTRODUCTION

"Carol," and "The Cricket on the Hearth" doubled the sale of its predecessors. All of which would suggest that these stories were written to sell, which they indubitably were; but they were also sent into the world with a message meant to imbue their readers with what Dickens sincerely believed to be the true "Christmas Spirit,"—a spirit ennobling to the individual and to society at large. Dickens believed in the mission of these little books, and Jeffrey spoke for a multitude that shared that faith when he told the author of the "Carol" that he should be happy, "for you may be sure you have done more good by this little publication, fostered more kindly feelings, and prompted more positive acts of beneficence, than can be traced to all the pulpits and confessionals in Christendon since Christmas, 1842." If some of us demur at what we consider the excessive sentimentality of these tales, we must admit that this sentimentality is quintessentially Dickensian, and that we are simply incapable of enjoying the sentiment of Dickens in undiluted purity. But we need not feel guilty, for numberless hands will reach for the cup we put aside.

CONTENTS

PART I

A CHRISTMAS CAROL

THE CHIMES

THE CRICKET ON THE HEARTH

PART II

FROM "HOUSEHOLD WORDS"

FROM "ALL THE YEAR ROUND"

PART I

A CHRISTMAS CAROL

IN PROSE

BEING

A GHOST STORY OF CHRISTMAS

A CHRISTMAS CAROL

Stave One

MARLEY'S GHOST

MARLEY was dead, to begin with. There is no doubt whatever about that. The register of his burial was signed by the clergyman, the clerk, the undertaker, and the chief mourner. Scrooge signed it. And Scrooge's name was good upon 'Change, for anything he chose to put his hand to.

Old Marley was as dead as a door-nail.

Mind! I don't mean to say that I know, of my own knowledge, what there is particularly dead about a door-nail. I might have been inclined, myself, to regard a coffin-nail as the deadest piece of ironmongery in the trade. But the wisdom of our ancestors is in the simile; and my unhallowed hands shall not disturb it, or the Country's done for. You will therefore permit me to repeat, emphatically, that Marley was as dead as a door-nail.

Scrooge knew he was dead? Of course he did. How could it be otherwise? Scrooge and he were partners for I don't know how many years. Scrooge was his sole executor, his sole administrator, his sole assign, his sole residuary legatee, his sole friend, and sole mourner. And even Scrooge was not so dreadfully cut up by the sad event, but that he was an excellent man of business on the very day of the funeral, and solemnised it with an undoubted bargain.

The mention of Marley's funeral brings me back to the point I started from. There is no doubt that Marley was dead. This must be distinctly understood, or nothing wonderful can come of the story I am going to relate. If we were not perfectly convinced that Hamlet's Father died before the play began, there would be nothing more remarkable in his taking a stroll at night, in an easterly wind, upon his own ramparts, than there would be in any other middle-aged gentleman rashly turning out after dark in a breezy spot—say Saint Paul's Churchyard for instance—literally to astonish his son's weak mind.

Scrooge never painted out Old Marley's name. There it stood, years afterwards, above the warehouse door: Scrooge and Marley. The firm was known as Scrooge and Marley. Sometimes people new to the business called Scrooge Scrooge, and sometimes Marley, but he answered to both names. It was all the same to him.

Oh! But he was a tight-fisted hand at the grindstone, Scrooge! a squeezing, wrenching, grasping, scraping, clutching, covetous, old sinner! Hard and sharp as flint, from which no steel had ever struck out generous fire; secret, and self-contained, and solitary as an oyster. The cold within him froze his old features, nipped his pointed nose, shrivelled his cheek, stiffened his gait; made his eyes red, his thin lips blue; and spoke out shrewdly in his grating voice. A frosty rime was on his head, and on his eyebrows, and his wiry chin. He carried his own low temperature always about with him; he iced his office in the dog-days; and didn't thaw it one degree at Christmas.

External heat and cold had little influence on Scrooge. No warmth could warm, no wintry weather chill him. No wind that blew was bitterer than he, no falling snow was more intent upon its purpose,

no pelting rain less open to entreaty. Foul weather didn't know where to have him. The heaviest rain, and snow, and hail, and sleet, could boast of the advantage over him in only one respect. They often 'came down' handsomely, and Scrooge never did.

Nobody ever stopped him in the street to say, with gladsome looks, 'My dear Scrooge, how are you? When will you come to see me?' No beggars implored him to bestow a trifle, no children asked him what it was o'clock, no man or woman ever once in all his life inquired the way to such and such a place, of Scrooge. Even the blind men's dogs appeared to know him; and when they saw him coming on, would tug their owners into doorways and up courts; and then would wag their tails as though they said, 'No eye at all is better than an evil eye, dark master!'

But what did Scrooge care! It was the very thing he liked. To edge his way along the crowded paths of life, warning all human sympathy to keep its distance, was what the knowing ones call 'nuts' to Scrooge.

Once upon a time—of all the good days in the year, on Christmas Eve—old Scrooge sat busy in his counting-house. It was cold, bleak, biting weather: foggy withal: and he could hear the people in the court outside, go wheezing up and down, beating their hands upon their breasts, and stamping their feet upon the pavement stones to warm them. The city clocks had only just gone three, but it was quite dark already— it had not been light all day—and candles were flaring in the windows of the neighbouring offices, like ruddy smears upon the palpable brown air. The fog came pouring in at every chink and keyhole, and was so dense without, that although the court was of the narrowest, the houses opposite were mere phantoms. To see the dingy cloud come drooping down, obscur-

ing everything, one might have thought that Nature lived hard by, and was brewing on a large scale.

The door of Scrooge's counting-house was open that he might keep his eye upon his clerk, who in a dismal little cell beyond, a sort of tank, was copying letters. Scrooge had a very small fire, but the clerk's fire was so very much smaller that it looked like one coal. But he couldn't replenish it, for Scrooge kept the coal-box in his own room; and so surely as the clerk came in with the shovel, the master predicted that it would be necessary for them to part. Wherefore the clerk put on his white comforter, and tried to warm himself at the candle; in which effort, not being a man of a strong imagination, he failed.

'A merry Christmas, uncle! God save you!' cried a cheerful voice. It was the voice of Scrooge's nephew, who came upon him so quickly that this was the first intimation he had of his approach.

'Bah!' said Scrooge, 'Humbug!'

He had so heated himself with rapid walking in the fog and frost, this nephew of Scrooge's, that he was all in a glow; his face was ruddy and handsome; his eyes sparkled, and his breath smoked again.

'Christmas a humbug, uncle!' said Scrooge's nephew. 'You don't mean that, I am sure?'

'I do,' said Scrooge. 'Merry Christmas! What right have you to be merry? What reason have you to be merry? You 're poor enough.'

'Come, then,' returned the nephew gaily. 'What right have you to be dismal? What reason have you to be morose? You 're rich enough.'

Scrooge having no better answer ready on the spur of the moment, said 'Bah!' again; and followed it up with 'Humbug.'

'Don't be cross, uncle!' said the nephew.

'What else can I be,' returned the uncle, 'when I

live in such a world of fools as this? Merry Christmas! Out upon merry Christmas! What's Christmas time to you but a time for paying bills without money; a time for finding yourself a year older, but not an hour richer; a time for balancing your books and having every item in 'em through a round dozen of months presented dead against you? If I could work my will,' said Scrooge indignantly, 'every idiot who goes about with "Merry Christmas" on his lips, should be boiled with his own pudding, and buried with a stake of holly through his heart. He should!'

'Uncle!' pleaded the nephew.

'Nephew!' returned the uncle, sternly, 'keep Christmas in your own way, and let me keep it in mine.'

'Keep it!' repeated Scrooge's nephew. 'But you don't keep it.'

'Let me leave it alone, then,' said Scrooge. 'Much good may it do you! Much good it has ever done you!'

'There are many things from which I might have derived good, by which I have not profited, I dare say,' returned the nephew. 'Christmas among the rest. But I am sure I have always thought of Christmas time, when it has come round—apart from the veneration due to its sacred name and origin, if anything belonging to it can be apart from that—as a good time; a kind, forgiving, charitable, pleasant time: the only time I know of, in the long calendar of the year, when men and women seem by one consent to open their shut-up hearts freely, and to think of people below them as if they really were fellow-passengers to the grave, and not another race of creatures bound on other journeys. And therefore, uncle, though it has never put a scrap of gold or silver in my pocket, I believe that it *has* done me good, and *will* do me good; and I say, God bless it!'

The clerk in the Tank involuntarily applauded. Becoming immediately sensible of the impropriety, he poked the fire, and extinguished the last frail spark for ever.

'Let me hear another sound from *you*,' said Scrooge, 'and you'll keep your Christmas by losing your situation! You're quite a powerful speaker, sir,' he added, turning to his nephew. 'I wonder you don't go into Parliament.'

'Don't be angry, uncle. Come! Dine with us to-morrow.'

Scrooge said that he would see him—yes, indeed he did. He went the whole length of the expression, and said that he would see him in that extremity first.

'But why?' cried Scrooge's nephew. 'Why?'

'Why did you get married?' said Scrooge.

'Because I fell in love.'

'Because you fell in love!' growled Scrooge, as if that were the only one thing in the world more ridiculous than a merry Christmas. 'Good afternoon!'

'Nay, uncle, but you never came to see me before that happened. Why give it as a reason for not coming now?'

'Good afternoon,' said Scrooge.

'I want nothing from you; I ask nothing of you; why cannot we be friends?'

'Good afternoon,' said Scrooge.

'I am sorry, with all my heart, to find you so resolute. We have never had any quarrel, to which I have been a party. But I have made the trial in homage to Christmas, and I'll keep my Christmas humour to the last. So A Merry Christmas, uncle!'

'Good afternoon,' said Scrooge.

'And A Happy New Year!'

'Good afternoon,' said Scrooge.

His nephew left the room without an angry word,

notwithstanding. He stopped at the outer door to bestow the greetings of the season on the clerk, who, cold as he was, was warmer than Scrooge; for he returned them cordially.

'There's another fellow,' muttered Scrooge; who overheard him: 'my clerk, with fifteen shillings a week, and a wife and family, talking about a merry Christmas. I'll retire to Bedlam.'

This lunatic, in letting Scrooge's nephew out, had let two other people in. They were portly gentlemen, pleasant to behold, and now stood, with their hats off, in Scrooge's office. They had books and papers in their hands, and bowed to him.

'Scrooge and Marley's, I believe,' said one of the gentlemen, referring to his list. 'Have I the pleasure of addressing Mr. Scrooge, or Mr. Marley?'

'Mr. Marley has been dead these seven years,' Scrooge replied. 'He died seven years ago, this very night.'

'We have no doubt his liberality is well represented by his surviving partner,' said the gentleman, presenting his credentials.

It certainly was; for they had been two kindred spirits. At the ominous word 'liberality,' Scrooge frowned, and shook his head, and handed the credentials back.

'At this festive season of the year, Mr. Scrooge,' said the gentleman, taking up a pen, 'it is more than usually desirable that we should make some slight provision for the Poor and destitute, who suffer greatly at the present time. Many thousands are in want of common necessaries; hundreds of thousands are in want of common comforts, sir.'

'Are there no prisons?' asked Scrooge.

'Plenty of prisons,' said the gentleman, laying down the pen again.

'And the Union workhouses?' demanded Scrooge. 'Are they still in operation?'

'They are. Still,' returned the gentleman, 'I wish I could say they were not.'

'The Treadmill and the Poor Law are in full vigour, then?' said Scrooge.

'Both very busy, sir.'

'Oh! I was afraid, from what you said at first, that something had occurred to stop them in their useful course,' said Scrooge. 'I'm very glad to hear it.'

'Under the impression that they scarcely furnish Christian cheer of mind or body to the multitude,' returned the gentleman, 'a few of us are endeavouring to raise a fund to buy the Poor some meat and drink, and means of warmth. We choose this time, because it is a time, of all others, when Want is keenly felt, and Abundance rejoices. What shall I put you down for?'

'Nothing!' Scrooge replied.

'You wish to be anonymous?'

'I wish to be left alone,' said Scrooge. 'Since you ask me what I wish, gentlemen, that is my answer. I don't make merry myself at Christmas and I can't afford to make idle people merry. I help to support the establishments I have mentioned—they cost enough; and those who are badly off must go there.'

'Many can't go there; and many would rather die.'

'If they would rather die,' said Scrooge, 'they had better do it, and decrease the surplus population. Besides—excuse me—I don't know that.'

'But you might know it,' observed the gentleman.

'It's not my business,' Scrooge returned. 'It's enough for a man to understand his own business, and not to interfere with other people's. Mine occupies me constantly. Good afternoon, gentlemen!'

Seeing clearly that it would be useless

their point, the gentlemen withdrew. Scrooge resumed his labours with an improved opinion of himself, and in a more facetious temper than was usual with him.

Meanwhile the fog and darkness thickened so, that people ran about with flaring links, proffering their services to go before horses in carriages, and conduct them on their way. The ancient tower of a church, whose gruff old bell was always peeping slily down at Scrooge out of a gothic window in the wall, became invisible, and struck the hours and quarters in the clouds, with tremulous vibrations afterwards as if its teeth were chattering in its frozen head up there. The cold became intense. In the main street at the corner of the court, some labourers were repairing the gas-pipes, and had lighted a great fire in a brazier, round which a party of ragged men and boys were gathered: warming their hands and winking their eyes before the blaze in rapture. The water-plug being left in solitude, its overflowings sullenly congealed, and turned to misanthropic ice. The brightness of the shops where holly sprigs and berries crackled in the lamp heat of the windows, made pale faces ruddy as they passed. Poulterers' and grocers' trades became a splendid joke; a glorious pageant, with which it was next to impossible to believe that such dull principles as bargain and sale had anything to do. The Lord Mayor, in the stronghold of the mighty Mansion House, gave orders to his fifty cooks and butlers to keep Christmas as a Lord Mayor's household should; and even the little tailor, whom he had fined five shillings on the previous Monday for being drunk and bloodthirsty in the streets, stirred up to-morrow's pudding in his garret, while his lean wife and the baby sallied out to buy the beef.

Foggier yet, and colder! Piercing, searching, bit-

ing cold.   If the good Saint Dunstan had but nipped
the Evil Spirit's nose with a touch of such weather
as that, instead of using his familiar weapons, then
indeed he would have roared to lusty purpose.   The
owner of one scant young nose, gnawed and mumbled
by the hungry cold as bones are gnawed by dogs,
stooped down at Scrooge's keyhole to regale him with
a Christmas carol: but at the first sound of

'God bless you, merry gentleman!
May nothing you dismay!'

Scrooge seized the ruler with such energy of action,
that the singer fled in terror, leaving the keyhole to
the fog and even more congenial frost.

At length the hour of shutting up the counting-
house arrived.   With an ill-will Scrooge dismounted
from his stool, and tacitly admitted the fact to the
expectant clerk in the Tank, who instantly snuffed
his candle out, and put on his hat.

'You'll want all day to-morrow, I suppose?' said
Scrooge.

'If quite convenient, sir.'

'It's not convenient,' said Scrooge, 'and it's not
fair. If I was to stop half-a-crown for it, you'd
think yourself ill-used, I'll be bound?'

The clerk smiled faintly.

'And yet,' said Scrooge, 'you don't think *me* ill-
used, when I pay a day's wages for no work.'

The clerk observed that it was only once a year.

'A poor excuse for picking a man's pocket every
twenty-fifth of December!' said Scrooge, buttoning
his great-coat to the chin.   'But I suppose you must
have the whole day.   Be here all the earlier next
morning.'

The clerk promised that he would; and Scrooge
walked out with a growl.   The office was closed in a

twinkling, and the clerk, with the long ends of his white comforter dangling below his waist (for he boasted no great-coat), went down a slide on Corn-hill, at the end of a lane of boys, twenty times, in honour of its being Christmas Eve, and then ran home to Camden Town as hard as he could pelt, to play at blindman's-bluff.

Scrooge took his melancholy dinner in his usual melancholy tavern; and having read all the news-papers, and beguiled the rest of the evening with his banker's-book, went home to bed. He lived in chambers which had once belonged to his deceased partner. They were a gloomy suite of rooms, in a lowering pile of building up a yard, where it had so little business to be, that one could scarcely help fancying it must have run there when it was a young house, playing at hide-and-seek with other houses, and forgotten the way out again. It was old enough now, and dreary enough, for nobody lived in it but Scrooge, the other rooms being all let out as offices. The yard was so dark that even Scrooge, who knew its every stone, was fain to grope with his hands. The fog and frost so hung about the black old gate-way of the house, that it seemed as if the Genius of the Weather sat in mournful meditation on the threshold.

Now, it is a fact, that there was nothing at all par-ticular about the knocker on the door, except that it was very large. It is also a fact, that Scrooge had seen it, night and morning, during his whole residence in that place; also that Scrooge had as little of what is called fancy about him as any man in the city of London, even including—which is a bold word—the corporation, aldermen, and livery. Let it also be borne in mind that Scrooge had not bestowed one thought on Marley, since his last mention of his seven-

years' dead partner that afternoon. And then let any man explain to me, if he can, how it happened that Scrooge, having his key in the lock of the door, saw in the knocker, without its undergoing any intermediate process of change—not a knocker, but Marley's face.

Marley's face. It was not in impenetrable shadow as the other objects in the yard were, but had a dismal light about it, like a bad lobster in a dark cellar. It was not angry or ferocious, but looked at Scrooge as Marley used to look: with ghostly spectacles turned up on its ghostly forehead. The hair was curiously stirred, as if by breath or hot air; and, though the eyes were wide open, they were perfectly motionless. That, and its livid colour, made it horrible; but its horror seemed to be in spite of the face and beyond its control, rather than a part of its own expression.

As Scrooge looked fixedly at this phenomenon, it was a knocker again.

To say that he was not startled, or that his blood was not conscious of a terrible sensation to which it had been a stranger from infancy, would be untrue. But he put his hand upon the key he had relinquished, turned it sturdily, walked in, and lighted his candle.

He *did* pause, with a moment's irresolution, before he shut the door; and he *did* look cautiously behind it first, as if he half-expected to be terrified with the sight of Marley's pigtail sticking out into the hall. But there was nothing on the back of the door, except the screws and nuts that held the knocker on, so he said 'Pooh, pooh!' and closed it with a bang.

The sound resounded through the house like thunder. Every room above, and every cask in the wine-merchant's cellars below, appeared to have a separate

peal of echoes of its own.   Scrooge was not a man to be frightened by echoes.   He fastened the door, and walked across the hall, and up the stairs; slowly too; trimming his candle as he went.

You may talk vaguely about driving a coach-and-six up a good old flight of stairs, or through a bad young Act of Parliament; but I mean to say you might have got a hearse up that staircase, and taken it broadwise, with the splinter-bar towards the wall and the door towards the balustrades: and done it easy.   There was plenty of width for that, and room to spare; which is perhaps the reason why Scrooge thought he saw a locomotive hearse going on before him in the gloom.   Half a dozen gas-lamps out of the street wouldn't have lighted the entry too well, so you may suppose that it was pretty dark with Scrooge's dip.

Up Scrooge went, not caring a button for that. Darkness is cheap, and Scrooge liked it.   But before he shut his heavy door, he walked through his rooms to see that all was right.   He had just enough recollection of the face to desire to do that.

Sitting-room, bedroom, lumber-room.   All as they should be.   Nobody under the table, nobody under the sofa; a small fire in the grate; spoon and basin ready; and the little saucepan of gruel (Scrooge had a cold in his head) upon the hob.   Nobody under the bed; nobody in the closet; nobody in his dressing-gown, which was hanging up in a suspicious attitude against the wall.   Lumber-room as usual.   Old fire-guards, old shoes, two fish-baskets, washing-stand on three legs, and a poker.

Quite satisfied, he closed his door, and locked himself in; double-locked himself in, which was not his custom.   Thus secured against surprise, he took off

his cravat; put on his dressing-gown and slippers, and his nightcap; and sat down before the fire to take his gruel.

It was a very low fire indeed; nothing on such a bitter night. He was obliged to sit close to it, and brood over it, before he could extract the least sensation of warmth from such a handful of fuel. The fireplace was an old one, built by some Dutch merchant long ago, and paved all round with quaint Dutch tiles, designed to illustrate the Scriptures. There were Cains and Abels, Pharaohs' daughters, Queens of Sheba, Angelic messengers descending through the air on clouds like feather-beds, Abrahams, Belshazzars, Apostles putting off to sea in butter-boats, hundreds of figures to attract his thoughts; and yet that face of Marley, seven years dead, came like the ancient Prophet's rod, and swallowed up the whole. If each smooth tile had been a blank at first, with power to shape some picture on its surface from the disjointed fragments of his thoughts, there would have been a copy of old Marley's head on every one.

'Humbug!' said Scrooge; and walked across the room.

After several turns, he sat down again. As he threw his head back in the chair, his glance happened to rest upon a bell, a disused bell, that hung in the room, and communicated for some purpose now forgotten with a chamber in the highest story of the building. It was with great astonishment, and with a strange, inexplicable dread, that as he looked, he saw this bell begin to swing. It swung so softly in the outset that it scarcely made a sound; but soon it rang out loudly, and so did every bell in the house.

This might have lasted half a minute, or a minute, but it seemed an hour. The bells ceased as they had begun, together. They were succeeded by a clank-

ing noise, deep down below; as if some person were dragging a heavy chain over the casks in the wine merchant's cellar. Scrooge then remembered to have heard that ghosts in haunted houses were described as dragging chains.

The cellar-door flew open with a booming sound, and then he heard the noise much louder, on the floors below; then coming up the stairs; then coming straight towards his door.

'It's humbug still!' said Scrooge. 'I won't believe it.'

His colour changed though, when, without a pause, it came on through the heavy door, and passed into the room before his eyes. Upon its coming in, the dying flame leaped up, as though it cried 'I know him; Marley's Ghost!' and fell again.

The same face: the very same. Marley in his pig-tail, usual waistcoat, tights and boots; the tassels on the latter bristling, like his pigtail, and his coat-skirts, and the hair upon his head. The chain he drew was clasped about his middle. It was long, and wound about him like a tail; and it was made (for Scrooge observed it closely) of cash-boxes, keys, padlocks, ledgers, deeds, and heavy purses wrought in steel. His body was transparent; so that Scrooge, observing him, and looking through his waistcoat, could see the two buttons on his coat behind.

Scrooge had often heard it said that Marley had no bowels, but he had never believed it until now.

No, nor did he believe it even now. Though he looked the phantom through and through, and saw it standing before him; though he felt the chilling influence of its death-cold eyes; and marked the very texture of the folded kerchief bound about its head and chin, which wrapper he had not observed before; he was still incredulous, and fought against his senses.

'How now!' said Scrooge, caustic and cold as ever. 'What do you want with me?'

'Much!'—Marley's voice, no doubt about it.

'Who are you?'

'Ask me who I *was*.'

'Who *were* you then?' said Scrooge, raising his voice. 'You're particular, for a shade.' He was going to say '*to* a shade,' but substituted this, as more appropriate.

'In life I was your partner, Jacob Marley.'

'Can you—can you sit down?' asked Scrooge, looking doubtfully at him.

'I can.'

'Do it, then.'

Scrooge asked the question, because he didn't know whether a ghost so transparent might find himself in a condition to take a chair; and felt that in the event of its being impossible, it might involve the necessity of an embarrassing explanation. But the ghost sat down on the opposite side of the fireplace, as if he were quite used to it.

'You don't believe in me,' observed the Ghost.

'I don't, said Scrooge.

'What evidence would you have of my reality beyond that of your senses?'

'I don't know,' said Scrooge.

'Why do you doubt your senses?'

'Because,' said Scrooge, 'a little thing affects them. A slight disorder of the stomach makes them cheats. You may be an undigested bit of beef, a blot of mustard, a crumb of cheese, a fragment of an underdone potato. There's more of gravy than of grave about you, whatever you are!'

Scrooge was not much in the habit of cracking jokes, nor did he feel, in his heart, by any means waggish then. The truth is, that he tried to be

smart, as a means of distracting his own attention, and keeping down his terror; for the spectre's voice disturbed the very marrow in his bones.

To sit, staring at those fixed glazed eyes, in silence for a moment, would play, Scrooge felt, the very deuce with him. There was something very awful, too, in the spectre's being provided with an infernal atmosphere of its own. Scrooge could not feel it himself, but this was clearly the case; for though the Ghost sat perfectly motionless, its hair, and skirts, and tassels, were still agitated as by the hot vapour from an oven.

'You see this toothpick?' said Scrooge, returning quickly to the charge, for the reason just assigned; and wishing, though it were only for a second, to divert the vision's stony gaze from himself.

'I do,' replied the Ghost.

'You are not looking at it,' said Scrooge.

'But I see it,' said the Ghost, 'notwithstanding.'

'Well!' returned Scrooge, 'I have but to swallow this, and be for the rest of my days persecuted by a legion of goblins, all of my own creation. Humbug, I tell you! humbug!'

At this the spirit raised a frightful cry, and shook its chain with such a dismal and appalling noise, that Scrooge held on tight to his chair, to save himself from falling in a swoon. But how much greater was his horror, when the phantom taking off the bandage round its head, as if it were too warm to wear indoors, its lower jaw dropped down upon its breast!

Scrooge fell upon his knees, and clasped his hands before his face.

'Mercy!' he said. 'Dreadful apparition, why do you trouble me?'

'Man of the worldly mind!' replied the Ghost, 'do you believe in me or not?'

'I do,' said Scrooge. 'I must. But why do spirits walk the earth, and why do they come to me?'

'It is required of every man,' the Ghost returned, 'that the spirit within him should walk abroad among his fellowmen, and travel far and wide; and if that spirit goes not forth in life, it is condemned to do so after death. It is doomed to wander through the world—oh, woe is me!—and witness what it cannot share, but might have shared on earth, and turned to happiness!'

Again the spectre raised a cry, and shook its chain and wrung its shadowy hands.

'You are fettered,' said Scrooge, trembling. 'Tell me why?'

'I wear the chain I forged in life,' replied the Ghost. 'I made it link by link, and yard by yard; I girded it on of my own free will, and of my own free will I wore it. Is its pattern strange to *you?*'

Scrooge trembled more and more.

'Or would you know,' pursued the Ghost, 'the weight and length of the strong coil you bear yourself? It was full as heavy and as long as this, seven Christmas Eves ago. You have laboured on it, since. It is a ponderous chain!'

Scrooge glanced about him on the floor, in the expectation of finding himself surrounded by some fifty or sixty fathoms of iron cable: but he could see nothing.

'Jacob,' he said, imploringly. 'Old Jacob Marley, tell me more. Speak comfort to me, Jacob!'

'I have none to give,' the Ghost replied. 'It comes from other regions, Ebenezer Scrooge, and is conveyed by other ministers, to other kinds of men. Nor can I tell you what I would. A very little more, is all permitted to me. I cannot rest, I cannot stay, I cannot linger anywhere. My spirit never walked be-

yond our counting-house—mark me!—in life my
spirit never roved beyond the narrow limits of our
money-changing hole; and weary journeys lie before
me!'

It was a habit with Scrooge, whenever he became
thoughtful, to put his hands in his breeches pockets.
Pondering on what the Ghost had said, he did so now,
but without lifting up his eyes, or getting off his
knees.

'You must have been very slow about it, Jacob,'
Scrooge observed, in a business-like manner, though
with humility and deference.

'Slow!' the Ghost repeated.

'Seven years dead,' mused Scrooge. 'And travelling all the time!'

'The whole time,' said the Ghost. 'No rest, no
peace. Incessant torture of remorse.'

'You travel fast?' said Scrooge.

'On the wings of the wind,' replied the Ghost.

'You might have got over a great quantity of
ground in seven years,' said Scrooge.

The Ghost, on hearing this, set up another cry, and
clanked its chain so hideously in the dead silence of
the night, that the Ward would have been justified in
indicting it for a nuisance.

'Oh! captive, bound, and double-ironed,' cried the
phantom, 'not to know, that ages of incessant labour,
by immortal creatures, for this earth must pass into
eternity before the good of which it is susceptible is
all developed. Not to know that any Christian spirit
working kindly in its little sphere, whatever it may
be, will find its mortal life too short for its vast
means of usefulness. Not to know that no space of
regret can make amends for one life's opportunity
misused! Yet such was I! Oh! such was I!'

'But you were always a good man of business

Jacob,' faltered Scrooge, who now began to apply this to himself.

'Business!' cried the Ghost, wringing its hands again. 'Mankind was my business. The common welfare was my business; charity, mercy, forbearance, and benevolence, were, all, my business. The dealings of my trade were but a drop of water in the comprehensive ocean of my business!'

It held up its chain at arm's length, as if that were the cause of all its unavailing grief, and flung it heavily upon the ground again.

'At this time of the rolling year,' the spectre said, 'I suffer most. Why did I walk through crowds of fellow-beings with my eyes turned down, and never raise them to that blessed Star which led the Wise Men to a poor abode! Were there no poor homes to which its light would have conducted *me!*'

Scrooge was very much dismayed to hear the spectre going on at this rate, and began to quake exceedingly.

'Hear me!' cried the Ghost. 'My time is nearly gone.'

'I will,' said Scrooge. 'But don't be hard upon me! Don't be flowery, Jacob! Pray!'

'How it is that I appear before you in a shape that you can see, I may not tell. I have sat invisible beside you many and many a day.'

It was not an agreeable idea. Scrooge shivered, and wiped the perspiration from his brow.

'That is no light part of my penance,' pursued the Ghost. 'I am here to-night to warn you, that you have yet a chance and hope of escaping my fate. A chance and hope of my procuring, Ebenezer.'

'You were always a good friend to me,' said Scrooge. 'Thank 'ee!'

'You will be haunted,' resumed the Ghost, 'by Three Spirits.'

Scrooge's countenance fell almost as low as the Ghost's had done.

'Is that the chance and hope you mentioned, Jacob?' he demanded, in a faltering voice.

'It is.'

'I—I think I'd rather not,' said Scrooge.

'Without their visits,' said the Ghost, 'you cannot hope to shun the path I tread. Expect the first to-morrow, when the bell tolls One.'

'Couldn't I take 'em all at once, and have it over, Jacob?' hinted Scrooge.

'Expect the second on the next night at the same hour. The third upon the next night when the last stroke of Twelve has ceased to vibrate. Look to see me no more; and look that, for your own sake, you remember what has passed between us!'

When it had said these words, the spectre took its wrapper from the table, and bound it round its head, as before. Scrooge knew this, by the smart sound its teeth made, when the jaws were brought together by the bandage. He ventured to raise his eyes again, and found his supernatural visitor confronting him in an erect attitude, with its chain wound over and about its arm.

The apparition walked backward from him; and at every step it took, the window raised itself a little, so that when the spectre reached it, it was wide open.

It beckoned Scrooge to approach, which he did. When they were within two paces of each other, Marley's Ghost held up its hand, warning him to come no nearer. Scrooge stopped.

Not so much in obedience, as in surprise and fear: for on the raising of the hand, he became sensible of

confused noises in the air; incoherent sounds of lamentation and regret; wailings inexpressibly sorrowful and self-accusatory. The spectre, after listening for a moment, joined in the mournful dirge; and floated out upon the bleak, dark night.

Scrooge followed to the window: desperate in his curiosity. He looked out.

The air was filled with phantoms, wandering hither and thither in restless haste, and moaning as they went. Every one of them wore chains like Marley's Ghost; some few (they might be guilty governments) were linked together; none were free. Many had been personally known to Scrooge in their lives. He had been quite familiar with one old ghost, in a white waistcoat, with a monstrous iron safe attached to its ankle, who cried piteously at being unable to assist a wretched woman with an infant, whom it saw below, upon a door-step. The misery with them all was, clearly, that they sought to interfere, for good, in human matters, and had lost the power for ever.

Whether these creatures faded into mist, or mist enshrouded them, he could not tell. But they and their spirit voices faded together; and the night became as it had been when he walked home.

Scrooge closed the window, and examined the door by which the Ghost had entered. It was double-locked, as he had locked it with his own hands, and the bolts were undisturbed. He tried to say 'Humbug!' but stopped at the first syllable. And being, from the emotion he had undergone, or the fatigues of the day, or his glimpse of the Invisible World, or the dull conversation of the Ghost, or the lateness of the hour, much in need of repose; went straight to bed, without undressing, and fell asleep upon the instant.

Stave Two

THE FIRST OF THE THREE SPIRITS

WHEN Scrooge awoke, it was so dark, that looking out of bed, he could scarcely distinguish the transparent window from the opaque walls of his chamber. He was endeavouring to pierce the darkness with his ferret eyes, when the chimes of a neighbouring church struck the four quarters. So he listened for the hour.

To his great astonishment the heavy bell went on from six to seven and from seven to eight, and regularly up to twelve; then stopped. Twelve! It was past two when he went to bed. The clock was wrong. An icicle must have got into the works. Twelve!

He touched the spring of his repeater, to correct this most preposterous clock. Its rapid little pulse beat twelve; and stopped.

'Why, it isn't possible,' said Scrooge, 'that I can have slept through a whole day and far into another night. It isn't possible that anything has happened to the sun, and this is twelve at noon!'

The idea being an alarming one, he scrambled out of bed, and groped his way to the window. He was obliged to rub the frost off with the sleeve of his dressing-gown before he could see anything; and could see very little then. All he could make out, was, that it was still very foggy and extremely cold, and that there was no noise of people running to and fro, and making a great stir, as there unquestionably would have been if night had beaten off bright day, and taken possession of the world. This was a great relief, because 'three days after sight of this First of Exchange pay to Mr. Ebenezer Scrooge or his order,'

and so forth, would have become a mere United States security if there were no days to count by.

Scrooge went to bed again, and thought, and thought, and thought it over and over and over, and could make nothing of it. The more he thought, the more perplexed he was; and the more he endeavoured not to think, the more he thought.

Marley's Ghost bothered him exceedingly. Every time he resolved within himself, after mature inquiry, that it was all a dream, his mind flew back again, like a strong spring released, to its first position, and presented the same problem to be worked all through, 'Was it a dream or not?'

Scrooge lay in this state until the chime had gone three quarters more, when he remembered, on a sudden, that the Ghost had warned him of a visitation when the bell tolled one. He resolved to lie awake until the hour was passed; and, considering that he could no more go to sleep than go to Heaven, this was perhaps the wisest resolution in his power.

The quarter was so long, that he was more than once convinced he must have sunk into a doze unconsciously, and missed the clock. At length it broke upon his listening ear.

'Ding, dong!'

'A quarter past,' said Scrooge, counting.

'Ding, dong!'

'Half-past!' said Scrooge.

'Ding, dong!'

'A quarter to it,' said Scrooge.

'Ding, dong!'

'The hour itself,' said Scrooge, triumphantly, 'and nothing else!'

He spoke before the hour bell sounded, which it now did with a deep, dull, hollow, melancholy ONE.

Light flashed up in the room upon the instant, and the curtains of his bed were drawn.

The curtains of his bed were drawn aside, I tell you, by a hand. Not the curtains at his feet, nor the curtains at his back, but those to which his face was addressed. The curtains of his bed were drawn aside; and Scrooge, starting up into a half-recumbent attitude, found himself face to face with the unearthly visitor who drew them: as close to it as I am now to you, and I am standing in the spirit at your elbow.

It was a strange figure—like a child: yet not so like a child as like an old man, viewed through some supernatural medium, which gave him the appearance of having receded from the view, and being diminished to a child's proportions. Its hair, which hung about its neck and down its back, was white as if with age; and yet the face had not a wrinkle in it, and the tenderest bloom was on the skin. The arms were very long and muscular; the hands the same, as if its hold were of uncommon strength. Its legs and feet, most delicately formed, were, like those upper members, bare. It wore a tunic of the purest white; and round its waist was bound a lustrous belt, the sheen of which was beautiful. It held a branch of fresh green holly in its hand; and, in singular contradiction of that wintry emblem, had its dress trimmed with summer flowers. But the strangest thing about it was, that from the crown of its head there sprung a bright clear jet of light, by which all this was visible; and which was doubtless the occasion of its using, in its duller moments, a great extinguisher for a cap, which it now held under its arm.

Even this, though, when Scrooge looked at it with increasing steadiness, was *not* its strangest quality. For as its belt sparkled and glittered now in one part

and now in another, and what was light one instant, at another time was dark, so the figure itself fluctuated in its distinctness: being now a thing with one arm, now with one leg, now with twenty legs, now a pair of legs without a head, now a head without a body: of which dissolving parts, no outline would be visible in the dense gloom wherein they melted away. And in the very wonder of this, it would be itself again; distinct and clear as ever.

'Are you the Spirit, sir, whose coming was foretold to me?' asked Scrooge.

'I am!'

The voice was soft and gentle. Singularly low, as if instead of being so close beside him, it were at a distance.

'Who, and what are you?' Scrooge demanded.

'I am the Ghost of Christmas Past.'

'Long Past?' inquired Scrooge: observant of its dwarfish stature.

'No. Your past.'

Perhaps, Scrooge could not have told anybody why, if anybody could have asked him; but he had a special desire to see the Spirit in his cap; and begged him to be covered.

'What!' exclaimed the Ghost, 'would you so soon put out, with worldly hands, the light I give? Is it not enough that you are one of those whose passions made this cap, and forced me through whole trains of years to wear it low upon my brow!'

Scrooge reverently disclaimed all intention to offend or any knowledge of having wilfully 'bonneted' the Spirit at any period of his life. He then made bold to inquire what business brought him there.

'Your welfare!' said the Ghost.

Scrooge expressed himself much obliged, but could not help thinking that a night of unbroken rest would

have been more conducive to that end. The Spirit must have heard him thinking, for it said immediately:

'Your reclamation, then. Take heed!'

It put out its strong hand as it spoke, and clasped him gently by the arm.

'Rise! and walk with me!'

It would have been in vain for Scrooge to plead that the weather and the hour were not adapted to pedestrian purposes; that bed was warm, and the thermometer a long way below freezing; that he was clad but lightly in his slippers, dressing-gown, and nightcap; and that he had a cold upon him at that time. The grasp, though gentle as a woman's hand, was not to be resisted. He rose: but finding that the Spirit made towards the window, clasped his robe in supplication.

'I am a mortal,' Scrooge remonstrated, 'and liable to fall.'

'Bear but a touch of my hand *there*,' said the Spirit, laying it upon his heart, 'and you shall be upheld in more than this!'

As the words were spoken, they passed through the wall, and stood upon an open country road, with fields on either hand. The city had entirely vanished. Not a vestige of it was to be seen. The darkness and the mist had vanished with it, for it was a clear, cold, winter day, with snow upon the ground.

'Good Heaven!' said Scrooge, clasping his hands together, as he looked about him. 'I was bred in this place. I was a boy here!'

The Spirit gazed upon him mildly. Its gentle touch, though it had been light and instantaneous, appeared still present to the old man's sense of feeling. He was conscious of a thousand odours floating in the air, each one connected with a thousand

thoughts, and hopes, and joys, and cares long, long, forgotten!

'Your lip is trembling,' said the Ghost. 'And what is that upon your cheek?'

Scrooge muttered, with an unusual catching in his voice, that it was a pimple; and begged the Ghost to lead him where he would.

'You recollect the way?' inquired the Spirit.

'Remember it?' cried Scrooge with fervour; 'I could walk it blindfold.'

'Strange to have forgotten it for so many years!' observed the Ghost. 'Let us go on.'

They walked along the road, Scrooge recognising every gate, and post, and tree; until a little market-town appeared in the distance, with its bridge, its church, and winding river. Some shaggy ponies now were seen trotting towards them with boys upon their backs, who called to other boys in country gigs and carts, driven by farmers. All these boys were in great spirits, and shouted to each other, until the broad fields were so full of merry music, that the crisp air laughed to hear it.

'These are but shadows of the things that have been,' said the Ghost. 'They have no consciousness of us.'

The jocund travellers came on; and as they came, Scrooge knew and named them every one. Why was he rejoiced beyond all bounds to see them! Why did his cold eye glisten, and his heart leap up as they went past! Why was he filled with gladness when he heard them give each other Merry Christmas, as they parted at cross-roads and by-ways, for their several homes! What was merry Christmas to Scrooge? Out upon merry Christmas! What good had it ever done to him?

'The school is not quite deserted,' said the Ghost.

'A solitary child, neglected by his friends, is left there still.'

Scrooge said he knew it. And he sobbed

They left the high-road, by a well-remembered lane, and soon approached a mansion of dull red brick, with a little weathercock-surmounted cupola, on the roof, and a bell hanging in it. It was a large house, but one of broken fortunes; for the spacious offices were little used, their walls were damp and mossy, their windows broken, and their gates decayed. Fowls clucked and strutted in the stables; and the coach-houses and sheds were overrun with grass. Nor was it more retentive of its ancient state, within; for entering the dreary hall, and glancing through the open doors of many rooms, they found them poorly furnished, cold, and vast. There was an earthy savour in the air, a chilly bareness in the place. which associated itself somehow with too much getting up by candle-light, and not too much to eat.

They went, the Ghost and Scrooge, across the hall, to a door at the back of the house. It opened before them, and disclosed a long, bare, melancholy room, made barer still by lines of plain deal forms and desks. At one of these a lonely boy was reading near a feeble fire: and Scrooge sat down upon a form, and wept to see his poor forgotten self as he used to be.

Not a latent echo in the house, not a squeak and scuffle from the mice behind the panelling, not a drip from the half-thawed water-spout in the dull yard behind, not a sigh among the leafless boughs of one despondent poplar, not the idle swinging of an empty store-house door, no, not a clicking in the fire, but fell upon the heart of Scrooge with a softening influence, and gave a freer passage to his tears.

The Spirit touched him on the arm, and pointed to his younger self, intent upon his reading. Sud-

denly a man, in foreign garments: wonderfully real and distinct to look at: stood outside the window, with an axe stuck in his belt, and leading by the bridle an ass laden with wood.

'Why, it's Ali Baba!' Scrooge exclaimed in ecstasy. 'It's dear old honest Ali Baba! Yes, yes, I know! One Christmas time, when yonder solitary child was left here all alone, he *did* come, for the first time, just like that. Poor boy! And Valentine,' said Scrooge, 'and his wild brother, Orson; there they go! And what's his name, who was put down in his drawers, asleep, at the Gate of Damascus; don't you see him! And the Sultan's Groom turned upside down by the Genii; there he is upon his head! Serve him right. I'm glad of it. What business had *he* to be married to the Princess!'

To hear Scrooge expending all the earnestness of his nature on such subjects, in a most extraordinary voice between laughing and crying; and to see his heightened and excited face; would have been a surprise to his business friends in the city, indeed.

'There's the Parrot!' cried Scrooge. 'Green body and yellow tail, with a thing like a lettuce growing out of the top of his head; there he is! Poor Robin Crusoe, he called him, when he came home again after sailing round the island. "Poor Robin Crusoe, where have you been, Robin Crusoe?" The man thought he was dreaming, but he wasn't. It was the Parrot, you know. There goes Friday, running for his life to the little creek! Halloa! Hoop! Halloo!'

Then, with a rapidity of transition very foreign to his usual character, he said, in pity for his former self, 'Poor boy!' and cried again.

'I wish,' Scrooge muttered, putting his hand in his pocket, and looking about him, after drying his eyes with his cuff: 'but it's too late now.'

'What is the matter?' asked the Spirit.

'Nothing,' said Scrooge. 'Nothing. There was a boy singing a Christmas Carol at my door last night. I should like to have given him something: that 's all.'

The Ghost smiled thoughtfully, and waved its hand: saying as it did so, 'Let us see another Christmas!'

Scrooge's former self grew larger at the words, and the room became a little darker and more dirty. The panels shrunk, the windows cracked; fragments of plaster fell out of the ceiling, and the naked laths were shown instead; but how all this was brought about, Scrooge knew no more than you do. He only knew that it was quite correct; that everything had happened so; that there he was, alone again, when all the other boys had gone home for the jolly holidays.

He was not reading now, but walking up and down despairingly. Scrooge looked at the Ghost, and with a mournful shaking of his head, glanced anxiously towards the door.

It opened; and a little girl, much younger than the boy came darting in, and putting her arms about his neck, and often kissing him, addressed him as her 'Dear, dear brother.'

'I have come to bring you home, dear brother!' said the child, clapping her tiny hands, and bending down to laugh. 'To bring you home, home, home!'

'Home, little Fan?' returned the boy.

'Yes!' said the child, brimful of glee. 'Home, for good and all. Home, for ever and ever. Father is so much kinder than he used to be, that home 's like Heaven! He spoke so gently to me one dear night when I was going to bed, that I was not afraid to ask him once more if you might come home; and he said Yes, you should; and sent me in a coach to bring you. And you 're to be a man!' said the child, open-

ing her eyes, 'and are never to come back here; but first, we 're to be together all the Christmas long, and have the merriest time in all the world.'

'You 're quite a woman, little Fan!' exclaimed the boy.

She clapped her hands and laughed, and tried to touch his head; but being too little, laughed again, and stood on tiptoe to embrace him. Then she began to drag him, in her childish eagerness, towards the door; and he, nothing loth to go, accompanied her.

A terrible voice in the hall cried, 'Bring down Master Scrooge's box, there!' and in the hall appeared the schoolmaster himself, who glared on Master Scrooge with a ferocious condescension, and threw him into a dreadful state of mind by shaking hands with him. He then conveyed him and his sister into the veriest old well of a shivering best-parlour that ever was seen, where the maps upon the wall, and the celestial and terrestrial globes in the windows, were waxy with cold. Here he produced a decanter of curiously light wine, and a block of curiously heavy cake, and administered instalments of those dainties to the young people: at the same time, sending out a meagre servant to offer a glass of 'something' to the postboy, who answered that he thanked the gentleman, but if it was the same tap as he had tasted before, he had rather not. Master Scrooge's trunk being by this time tied on to the top of the chaise, the children bade the schoolmaster good-bye right willingly; and getting into it, drove gaily down the garden-sweep: the quick wheels dashing the hoarfrost and snow from off the dark leaves of the evergreens like spray.

'Always a delicate creature, whom a breath might have withered,' said the Ghost. 'But she had a large heart!'

'So she had,' cried Scrooge. 'You're right. I will not gainsay it, Spirit. God forbid!'

'She died a woman,' said the Ghost, 'and had, as I think, children.'

'One child,' Scrooge returned.

'True,' said the Ghost. 'Your nephew!'

Scrooge seemed uneasy in his mind; and answered briefly, 'Yes.'

Although they had but that moment left the school behind them, they were now in the busy thoroughfares of a city, where shadowy passengers passed and repassed; where shadowy carts and coaches battled for the way, and all the strife and tumult of a real city were. It was made plain enough, by the dressing of the shops, that here too it was Christmas time again; but it was evening, and the streets were lighted up.

The Ghost stopped at a certain warehouse door, and asked Scrooge if he knew it.

'Know it!' said Scrooge. 'Was I apprenticed here!'

They went in. At sight of an old gentleman in a Welsh wig, sitting behind such a high desk, that if he had been two inches taller he must have knocked his head against the ceiling, Scrooge cried in great excitement:

'Why, it's old Fezziwig! Bless his heart; it's Fezziwig alive again!'

Old Fezziwig laid down his pen, and looked up at the clock, which pointed to the hour of seven. He rubbed his hands; adjusted his capacious waistcoat; laughed all over himself, from his shoes to his organ of benevolence; and called out in a comfortable, oily, rich, fat, jovial voice:

'Yo ho, there! Ebenezer! Dick!'

Scrooge's former self, now grown a young man,

came briskly in, accompanied by his fellow-'prentice.

'Dick Wilkins, to be sure!' said Scrooge to the Ghost. 'Bless me, yes. There he is. He was very much attached to me, was Dick. Poor Dick! Dear, dear!'

'Yo ho, my boys!' said Fezziwig. 'No more work to-night. Christmas Eve, Dick. Christmas, Ebenezer! Let's have the shutters up,' cried old Fezziwig, with a sharp clap of his hands, 'before a man can say Jack Robinson!'

You wouldn't believe how those two fellows went at it! They charged into the street with the shutters—one, two, three—had 'em up in their places—four, five, six—barred 'em and pinned 'em—seven, eight, nine—and came back before you could have got to twelve, panting like racehorses.

'Hilli-ho!' cried old Fezziwig, skipping down from the high desk, with wonderful agility. 'Clear away, my lads, and let's have lots of room here! Hilli-ho, Dick! Chirrup, Ebenezer!'

Clear away! There was nothing they wouldn't have cleared away, or couldn't have cleared away, with old Fezziwig looking on. It was done in a minute. Every movable was packed off, as if it were dismissed from public life for evermore; the floor was swept and watered, the lamps were trimmed, fuel was heaped upon the fire; and the warehouse was as snug, and warm, and dry, and bright a ball-room, as you would desire to see upon a winter's night.

In came a fiddler with a music-book, and went up to the lofty desk, and made an orchestra of it, and tuned like fifty stomach-aches. In came Mrs. Fezziwig, one vast substantial smile. In came the three Miss Fezziwigs, beaming and loveable. In came the six young followers whose hearts they broke. In

came all the young men and women employed in the business. In came the housemaid, with her cousin, the baker. In came the cook, with her brother's particular friend, the milkman. In came the boy from over the way, who was suspected of not having board enough from his master; trying to hide himself behind the girl from next door but one, who was proved to have had her ears pulled by her mistress. In they all came, one after another; some shyly, some boldly, some gracefully, some awkwardly, some pushing, some pulling; in they all came, anyhow and everyhow. Away they all went, twenty couple at once; hands half round and back again the other way; down the middle and up again; round and round in various stages of affectionate grouping; old top couple always turning up in the wrong place; new top couple starting off again, as soon as they got there; all top couples at last, and not a bottom one to help them! When this result was brought about, old Fezziwig, clapping his hands to stop the dance, cried out, 'Well done!' and the fiddler plunged his hot face into a pot of porter, especially provided for that purpose. But scorning rest, upon his reappearance, he instantly began again, though there were no dancers yet, as if the other fiddler had been carried home, exhausted, on a shutter, and he were a bran-new man resolved to beat him out of sight, or perish.

There were more dances, and there were forfeits, and more dances, and there was cake, and there was negus, and there was a great piece of Cold Roast, and there was a great piece of Cold Boiled, and there were mince-pies, and plenty of beer. But the great effect of the evening came after the Roast and Boiled, when the fiddler (an artful dog, mind! The sort of man who knew his business better than

you or I could have told it him!) struck up 'Sir Roger de Coverley.' Then old Fezziwig stood out to dance with Mrs. Fezziwig. Top couple, too; with a good stiff piece of work cut out for them; three or four and twenty pair of partners; people who were not to be trifled with; people who *would* dance, and had no notion of walking.

But if they had been twice as many—ah, four times —old Fezziwig would have been a match for them, and so would Mrs. Fezziwig. As to *her*, she was worthy to be his partner in every sense of the term. If that's not high praise, tell me higher, and I'll use it. A positive light appeared to issue from Fezziwig's calves. They shone in every part of the dance like moons. You couldn't have predicted, at any given time, what would have become of them next. And when old Fezziwig and Mrs. Fezziwig had gone all through the dance; advance and retire, both hands to your partner, bow and curtsey, corkscrew, thread-the-needle, and back again to your place; Fezziwig 'cut'—cut so deftly, that he appeared to wink with his legs, and came upon his feet again without a stagger.

When the clock struck eleven, this domestic ball broke up. Mr. and Mrs. Fezziwig took their stations, one on either side of the door, and shaking hands with every person individually as he or she went out, wished him or her a Merry Christmas. When everybody had retired but the two 'prentices, they did the same to them; and thus the cheerful voices died away, and the lads were left to their beds; which were under a counter in the back-shop.

During the whole of this time, Scrooge had acted like a man out of his wits. His heart and soul were in the scene, and with his former self. He corroborated everything, remembered everything, enjoyed

everything, and underwent the strangest agitation. It was not until now, when the bright faces of his former self and Dick were turned from them, that he remembered the Ghost, and became conscious that it was looking full upon him, while the light upon its head burnt very clear.

'A small matter,' said the Ghost, 'to make these silly folks so full of gratitude.'

'Small!' echoed Scrooge.

The Spirit signed to him to listen to the two apprentices, who were pouring out their hearts in praise of Fezziwig: and when he had done so, said,

'Why! Is it not? He has spent but a few pounds of your mortal money: three or four perhaps. Is that so much that he deserves this praise?'

'It isn't that,' said Scrooge, heated by the remark, and speaking unconsciously like his former, not his latter, self. 'It isn't that, Spirit. He has the power to render us happy or unhappy; to make our service light or burdensome; a pleasure or a toil. Say that his power lies in words and looks; in things so slight and insignificant that it is impossible to add and count 'em up: what then? The happiness he gives, is quite as great as if it cost a fortune.'

He felt the Spirit's glance, and stopped.

'What is the matter?' asked the Ghost.

'Nothing particular,' said Scrooge.

'Something, I think?' the Ghost insisted.

'No,' said Scrooge, 'No. I should like to be able to say a word or two to my clerk just now. That's all.'

His former self turned down the lamps as he gave utterance to the wish; and Scrooge and the Ghost again stood side by side in the open air.

'My time grows short,' observed the Spirit. 'Quick!'

This was not addressed to Scrooge, or to any one whom he could see, but it produced an immediate effect. For again Scrooge saw himself. He was older now; a man in the prime of life. His face had not the harsh and rigid lines of later years; but it had begun to wear the signs of care and avarice. There was an eager, greedy, restless motion in the eye, which showed the passion that had taken root, and where the shadow of the growing tree would fall.

He was not alone, but sat by the side of a fair young girl in a mourning-dress: in whose eyes there were tears, which sparkled in the light that shone out of the Ghost of Christmas Past.

'It matters little,' she said, softly. 'To you, very little. Another idol has displaced me; and if it can cheer and comfort you in time to come, as I would have tried to do, I have no just cause to grieve.'

'What Idol has displaced you?' he rejoined.

'A golden one.'

'This is the even-handed dealing of the world!' he said. 'There is nothing on which it is so hard as poverty; and there is nothing it professes to condemn with such severity as the pursuit of wealth!'

'You fear the world too much,' she answered, gently. 'All your other hopes have merged into the hope of being beyond the chance of its sordid reproach. I have seen your nobler aspirations fall off one by one, until the master-passion, Gain, engrosses you. Have I not?'

'What then?' he retorted. 'Even if I have grown so much wiser, what then? I am not changed towards you.'

She shook her head.

'Am I?'

'Our contract is an old one. It was made when we were both poor and content to be so, until, in good

season, we could improve our worldly fortune by our patient industry. You *are* changed. When it was made, you were another man.'

'I was a boy,' he said impatiently.

'Your own feeling tells you that you were not what you are,' she returned. 'I am. That which promised happiness when we were one in heart, is fraught with misery now that we are two. How often and how keenly I have thought of this, I will not say. It is enough that I *have* thought of it, and can release you.'

'Have I ever sought release?'

'In words. No. Never.'

'In what, then?'

'In a changed nature; in an altered spirit; in another atmosphere of life; another Hope as its great end. In everything that made my love of any worth or value in your sight. If this had never been between us,' said the girl, looking mildly, but with steadiness, upon him; 'tell me, would you seek me out and try to win me now? Ah, no!'

He seemed to yield to the justice of this supposition, in spite of himself. But he said with a struggle, 'You think not.'

'I would gladly think otherwise if I could,' she answered, 'Heaven knows! When *I* have learned a Truth like this, I know how strong and irresistible it must be. But if you were free to-day, to-morrow, yesterday, can even I believe that you would choose a dowerless girl—you who, in your very confidence with her, weigh everything by Gain: or, choosing her, if for a moment you were false enough to your one guiding principle to do so, do I not know that your repentance and regret would surely follow? I do; and I release you. With a full heart, for the love of him you once were.'

He was about to speak; but with her head turned from him, she resumed.

'You may—the memory of what is past half makes me hope you will—have pain in this. A very, very brief time, and you will dismiss the recollection of it, gladly, as an unprofitable dream, from which it happened well that you awoke. May you be happy in the life you have chosen!'

She left him, and they parted.

'Spirit!' said Scrooge, 'show me no more! Conduct me home. Why do you delight to torture me?'

'One shadow more!' exclaimed the Ghost.

'No more!' cried Scrooge. 'No more. I don't wish to see it. Show me no more!'

But the relentless Ghost pinioned him in both his arms, and forced him to observe what happened next.

They were in another scene and place; a room, not very large or handsome, but full of comfort. Near to the winter fire sat a beautiful young girl, so like that last that Scrooge believed it was the same, until he saw *her*, now a comely matron, sitting opposite her daughter. The noise in this room was perfectly tumultuous, for there were more children there, than Scrooge in his agitated state of mind could count; and, unlike the celebrated herd in the poem, they were not forty children conducting themselves like one, but every child was conducting itself like forty. The consequences were uproarious beyond belief; but no one seemed to care; on the contrary, the mother and daughter laughed heartily, and enjoyed it very much; and the latter, soon beginning to mingle in the sports, got pillaged by the young brigands most ruthlessly. What would I not have given to be one of them! Though I never could have been so rude, no, no! I wouldn't for the wealth of all the world have crushed that braided hair, and

torn it down; and for the precious little shoe, I wouldn't have plucked it off, God bless my soul! to save my life. As to measuring her waist in sport, as they did, bold young brood, I couldn't have done it; I should have expected my arm to have grown round it for a punishment, and never come straight again. And yet I should have dearly liked, I own, to have touched her lips; to have questioned her, that she might have opened them; to have looked upon the lashes of her downcast eyes, and never raised a blush; to have let loose waves of hair, an inch of which would be a keepsake beyond price: in short, I should have liked, I do confess, to have had the lightest license of a child, and yet to have been man enough to know its value.

But now a knocking at the door was heard, and such a rush immediately ensued that she with laughing face and plundered dress was borne towards it in the centre of a flushed and boisterous group, just in time to greet the father, who came home attended by a man laden with Christmas toys and presents. Then the shouting and the struggling, and the onslaught that was made on the defenceless porter! The scaling him with chairs for ladders to drive into his pockets, despoil him of brown-paper parcels, hold on tight by his cravat, hug him round his neck, pommel his back, and kick his legs in irrepressible affection! The shouts of wonder and delight with which the development of every package was received! The terrible announcement that the baby had been taken in the act of putting a doll's frying-pan into his mouth, and was more than suspected of having swallowed a fictitious turkey, glued on a wooden platter! The immense relief of finding this a false alarm! The joy, and gratitude, and ecstasy! They are all indescribable alike. It is enough that by de-

grees the children and their emotions got out of the parlour and by one stair at a time, up to the top of the house; where they went to bed, and so subsided.

And now Scrooge looked on more attentively than ever, when the master of the house, having his daughter leaning fondly on him, sat down with her and her mother at his own fireside; and when he thought that such another creature, quite as graceful and as full of promise, might have called him father, and been a spring-time in the haggard winter of his life, his sight grew very dim indeed.

'Belle,' said the husband, turning to his wife with a smile, 'I saw an old friend of yours this afternoon.'

'Who was it?'

'Guess!'

'How can I? Tut, don't I know?' she added in the same breath, laughing as he laughed. 'Mr. Scrooge.'

'Mr. Scrooge it was. I passed his office window; and as it was not shut up, and he had a candle inside, I could scarcely help seeing him. His partner lies upon the point of death, I hear; and there he sat alone. Quite alone in the world, I do believe.'

'Spirit!' said Scrooge in a broken voice, 'remove me from this place.'

'I told you these were shadows of the things that have been,' said the Ghost. 'That they are what they are, do not blame me!'

'Remove me!' Scrooge exclaimed, 'I cannot bear it!'

He turned upon the Ghost, and seeing that it looked upon him with a face, in which in some strange way there were fragments of all the faces it had shown him, wrestled with it.

'Leave me! Take me back. Haunt me no longer!'

In the struggle, if that can be called a struggle in which the Ghost with no visible resistance on its own part was undisturbed by any effort of its adversary, Scrooge observed that its light was burning high and bright; and dimly connecting that with its influence over him, he seized the extinguisher-cap, and by a sudden action pressed it down upon its head.

The Spirit dropped beneath it, so that the extinguisher covered its whole form; but though Scrooge pressed it down with all his force, he could not hide the light, which streamed from under it, in an unbroken flood upon the ground.

He was conscious of being exhausted, and overcome by an irresistible drowsiness; and, further, of being in his own bedroom. He gave the cap a parting squeeze, in which his hand relaxed; and had barely time to reel to bed, before he sank into a heavy sleep.

Stave Three

THE SECOND OF THE THREE SPIRITS

Awaking in the middle of a prodigiously tough snore, and sitting up in bed to get his thoughts together, Scrooge had no occasion to be told that the bell was again upon the stroke of One. He felt that he was restored to consciousness in the right nick of time, for the especial purpose of holding a conference with the second messenger despatched to him through Jacob Marley's intervention. But, finding that he turned uncomfortably cold when he

began to wonder which of his curtains this new spectre would draw back, he put them every one aside with his own hands, and lying down again, established a sharp look-out all round the bed. For, he wished to challenge the Spirit on the moment of its appearance, and did not wish to be taken by surprise, and made nervous.

Gentlemen of the free-and-easy sort, who plume themselves on being acquainted with a move or two, and being usually equal to the time-of-day, express the wide range of their capacity for adventure by observing that they are good for anything from pitch-and-toss to manslaughter; between which opposite extremes, no doubt, there lies a tolerably wide and comprehensive range of subjects. Without venturing for Scrooge quite as hardily as this, I don't mind calling on you to believe that he was ready for a good broad field of strange appearances, and that nothing between a baby and rhinoceros would have astonished him very much.

Now, being prepared for almost anything, he was not by any means prepared for nothing; and, consequently, when the Bell struck One, and no shape appeared, he was taken with a violent fit of trembling. Five minutes, ten minutes, a quarter of an hour went by, yet nothing came. All this time, he lay upon his bed, the very core and centre of a blaze of ruddy light, which streamed upon it when the clock proclaimed the hour; and which, being only light, was more alarming than a dozen ghosts, as he was powerless to make out what it meant, or would be at; and was sometimes apprehensive that he might be at that very moment an interesting case of spontaneous combustion, without having the consolation of knowing it. At last, however, he began to think—as you or I would have thought at first; for it is always the

person not in the predicament who knows what ought to have been done in it, and would unquestionably have done it too—at last, I say, he began to think that the source and secret of this ghostly light might be in the adjoining room, from whence, on further tracing it, it seemed to shine. This idea taking full possession of his mind, he got up softly and shuffled in his slippers to the door.

The moment Scrooge's hand was on the lock, a strange voice called him by his name, and bade him enter. He obeyed.

It was his own room. There was no doubt about that. But it had undergone a surprising transformation. The walls and ceiling were so hung with living green, that it looked a perfect grove; from every part of which, bright gleaming berries glistened. The crisp leaves of holly, mistletoe, and ivy reflected back the light, as if so many little mirrors had been scattered there; and such a mighty blaze went roaring up the chimney, as that dull petrifaction of a hearth had never known in Scrooge's time, or Marley's, or for many and many a winter season gone. Heaped up on the floor, to form a kind of throne, were turkeys, geese, game, poultry, brawn, great joints of meat, sucking-pigs, long wreaths of sausages, mince-pies, plum-puddings, barrels of oysters, red-hot chestnuts, cherry-cheeked apples, juicy oranges, luscious pears, immense twelfth-cakes, and seething bowls of punch, that made the chamber dim with their delicious steam. In easy state upon this couch, there sat a jolly Giant, glorious to see; who bore a glowing torch, in shape not unlike Plenty's horn, and held it up, high up, to shed its light on Scrooge, as he came peeping round the door.

'Come in!' exclaimed the Ghost. 'Come in! and know me better, man!'

Scrooge entered timidly, and hung his head before this Spirit. He was not the dogged Scrooge he had been; and though the Spirit's eyes were clear and kind, he did not like to meet them.

'I am the Ghost of Christmas Present,' said the Spirit. 'Look upon me!'

Scrooge reverently did so. It was clothed in one simple green robe, or mantle, bordered with white fur. This garment hung so loosely on the figure, that its capacious breast was bare, as if disdaining to be warded or concealed by any artifice. Its feet, observable beneath the ample folds of the garment, were also bare; and on its head it wore no other covering than a holly wreath, set here and there with shining icicles. Its dark brown curls were long and free; free as its genial face, its sparkling eye, its open hand, its cheery voice, its unconstrained demeanour, and its joyful air. Girded round its middle was an antique scabbard; but no sword was in it, and the ancient sheath was eaten up with rust.

'You have never seen the like of me before!' exclaimed the Spirit.

'Never,' Scrooge made answer to it.

'Have never walked forth with the younger members of my family; meaning (for I am very young) my elder brothers born in these later years?' pursued the Phantom.

'I don't think I have,' said Scrooge. 'I am afraid I have not. Have you had many brothers, Spirit?'

'More than eighteen hundred,' said the Ghost.

'A tremendous family to provide for!' muttered Scrooge.

The Ghost of Christmas Present rose.

'Spirit,' said Scrooge submissively, 'conduct me where you will. I went forth last night on compulsion, and I learnt a lesson which is working now.

To-night, if you have aught to teach me, let me profit by it.'

'Touch my robe!'

Scrooge did as he was told, and held it fast.

Holly, mistletoe, red berries, ivy, turkeys, geese, game, poultry, brawn, meat, pigs, sausages, oysters, pies, puddings, fruit, and punch, all vanished instantly. So did the room, the fire, the ruddy glow, the hour of night, and they stood in the city streets on Christmas morning where (for the weather was severe) the people made a rough, but brisk and not unpleasant kind of music, in scraping the snow from the pavement in front of their dwellings, and from the tops of their houses, whence it was mad delight to the boys to see it come plumping down into the road below, and splitting into artificial little snow-storms.

The house fronts looked black enough, and the windows blacker, contrasting with the smooth white sheet of snow upon the roofs, and with the dirtier snow upon the ground; which last deposit had been ploughed up in deep furrows by the heavy wheels of carts and waggons; furrows that crossed and re-crossed each other hundreds of times where the great streets branched off; and made intricate channels, hard to trace in the thick yellow mud and ice water. The sky was gloomy, and the shortest streets were choked up with a dingy mist, half thawed half frozen, whose heavier particles descended in a shower of sooty atoms, as if all the chimneys in Great Britain had, by one consent, caught fire, and were blazing away to their dear hearts' content. There was nothing very cheerful in the climate or the town, and yet was there an air of cheerfulness abroad that the clearest summer air and brightest summer sun might have endeavoured to diffuse in vain.

For, the people who were shovelling away on the house-tops were jovial and full of glee; calling out to one another from the parapets, and now and then exchanging a facetious snowball—better-natured missile far than many a wordy jest—laughing heartily if it went right and not less heartily if it went wrong. The poulterers' shops were still half open, and the fruiterers' were radiant in their glory. There were great, round, pot-bellied baskets of chestnuts, shaped like the waistcoats of jolly old gentlemen, lolling at the doors, and tumbling out into the street in their apoplectic opulence. There were ruddy, brown-faced- broad-girthed Spanish Onions, shining in the fatness of their growth like Spanish Friars, and winking from their shelves in wanton slyness at the girls as they went by, and glanced demurely at the hung-up mistletoe. There were pears and apples, clustered high in blooming pyramids; there were bunches of grapes, made, in the shopkeepers' benevolence, to dangle from conspicuous hooks, that people's mouths might water gratis as they passed; there were piles of filberts, mossy and brown, recalling, in their fragrance, ancient walks among the woods, and pleasant shufflings ankle deep through withered leaves; there were Norfolk Biffins, squab and swarthy, setting off the yellow of the oranges and lemons, and, in the great compactness of their juicy persons, urgently entreating and beseeching to be carried home in paper bags and eaten after dinner. The very gold and silver fish, set forth among these choice fruits in a bowl, though members of a dull and stagnant-blooded race, appeared to know that there was something going on; and, to a fish, went gasping round and round their little world in slow and passionless excitement.

The Grocers'! oh the Grocers'! nearly closed, with

perhaps two shutters down, or one; but through those gaps such glimpses! It was not alone that the scales descending on the counter made a merry sound, or that the twine and roller parted company so briskly, or that the canisters were rattled up and down like juggling tricks, or even that the blended scents of tea and coffee were so grateful to the nose, or even that the raisins were so plentiful and rare, the almonds so extremely white, the sticks of cinnamon so long and straight, the other spices so delicious, the candied fruits so caked and spotted with molten sugar as to make the coldest lookers-on feel faint and subsequently bilious. Nor was it that the figs were moist and pulpy, or that the French plums blushed in modest tartness from their highly-decorated boxes, or that everything was good to eat and in its Christmas dress; but the customers were all so hurried and so eager in the hopeful promise of the day, that they tumbled up against each other at the door, crashing their wicker baskets wildly, and left their purchases upon the counter, and came running back to fetch them, and committed hundreds of the like mistakes, in the best humour possible; while the Grocer and his people were so frank and fresh that the polished hearts with which they fastened their aprons behind might have been their own, worn outside for general inspection, and for Christmas daws to peck at if they chose.

But soon the steeples called good people all, to church and chapel, and away they came, flocking through the streets in their best clothes, and with their gayest faces. And at the same time there emerged from scores of by-streets, lanes, and nameless turnings, innumerable people, carrying their dinners to the bakers' shops. The sight of these poor revellers appeared to interest the Spirit very much,

for he stood with Scrooge beside him in a baker's doorway, and taking off the covers as their bearers passed, sprinkled incense on their dinners from his torch.   And it was a very uncommon kind of torch, for once or twice when there were angry words between some dinner-carriers who had jostled each other, he shed a few drops of water on them from it, and their good humour was restored directly.   For they said, it was a shame to quarrel upon Christmas Day.   And so it was!   God love it, so it was!

In time the bells ceased, and the bakers were shut up; and yet there was a genial shadowing forth of all these dinners and the progress of their cooking, in the thawed blotch of wet above each baker's oven; where the pavement smoked as if its stones were cooking too.

'Is there a peculiar flavour in what you sprinkle from your torch?' asked Scrooge.

'There is.   My own.'

'Would it apply to any kind of dinner on this day?' asked Scrooge.

'To any kindly given.   To a poor one most.'

'Why to a poor one most?' asked Scrooge.

'Because it needs it most.'

'Spirit,' said Scrooge, after a moment's thought, 'I wonder you, of all the beings in the many worlds about us, should desire to cramp these people's opportunities of innocent enjoyment.'

'I!' cried the Spirit.

'You would deprive them of their means of dining every seventh day, often the only day on which they can be said to dine at all,' said Scrooge.   'Wouldn't you?'

'I!' cried the Spirit.

'You seek to close these places on the Seventh Day?' said Scrooge.   'And it comes to the same thing.'

'*I* seek!' exclaimed the Spirit.

'Forgive me if I am wrong. It has been done in your name, or at least in that of your family,' said Scrooge.

'There are some upon this earth of yours,' returned the Spirit, 'who lay claim to know us, and who do their deeds of passion, pride, ill-will, hatred, envy, bigotry, and selfishness in our name, who are as strange to us and all our kith and kin, as if they had never lived. Remember that, and charge their doings on themselves, not us.'

Scrooge promised that he would; and they went on, invisible, as they had been before, into the suburbs of the town. It was a remarkable quality of the Ghost (which Scrooge had observed at the baker's), that notwithstanding his gigantic size, he could accommodate himself to any place with ease; and that he stood beneath a low roof quite as gracefully and like a supernatural creature, as it was possible he could have done in any lofty hall.

And perhaps it was the pleasure the good Spirit had in showing off this power of his, or else it was his own kind, generous, hearty nature, and his sympathy with all poor men, that led him straight to Scrooge's clerk's; for there he went, and took Scrooge with him, holding to his robe; and on the threshold of the door the Spirit smiled, and stopped to bless Bob Cratchit's dwelling with the sprinklings of his torch. Think of that! Bob had but fifteen 'Bob' a week himself; he pocketed on Saturdays but fifteen copies of his Christian name; and yet the Ghost of Christmas Present blessed his four-roomed house!

Then up rose Mrs. Cratchit, Cratchit's wife, dressed out but poorly in a twice-turned gown, but brave in ribbons, which are cheap and make a goodly show for sixpence; and she laid the cloth, assisted

by Belinda Cratchit, second of her daughters, also brave in ribbons; while Master Peter Cratchit plunged a fork into the saucepan of potatoes, and getting the corners of his monstrous shirt collar (Bob's private property, conferred upon his son and heir in honour of the day) into his mouth, rejoiced to find himself so gallantly attired, and yearned to show his linen in the fashionable Parks.   And now two smaller Cratchits, boy and girl, came tearing in, screaming that outside the baker's they had smelt the goose, and known it for their own; and basking in luxurious thoughts of sage and onion, these young Cratchits danced about the table, and exalted Master Peter Cratchit to the skies, while he (not proud, although his collars nearly choked him) blew the fire, until the slow potatoes bubbling up, knocked loudly at the saucepan-lid to be let out and peeled.

'What has ever got your precious father then?' said Mrs. Cratchit. 'And your brother, Tiny Tim! And Martha warn't as late last Christmas Day by half an hour?'

'Here 's Martha, mother!' said a girl, appearing as she spoke.

'Here 's Martha, mother!' cried the two young Cratchits. 'Hurrah! There 's *such* a goose, Martha!'

'Why, bless your heart alive, my dear, how late you are!' said Mrs. Cratchit, kissing her a dozen times, and taking off her shawl and bonnet for her with officious zeal.

'We 'd a deal of work to finish up last night,' replied the girl, 'and had to clear away this morning, mother!'

'Well! Never mind so long as you are come,' said Mrs. Cratchit. 'Sit ye down before the fire, my dear, and have a warm, Lord bless ye!'

'No, no! There's father coming,' cried the two young Cratchits, who were everywhere at once. 'Hide, Martha, hide!'

So Martha hid herself, and in came little Bob, the father, with at least three feet of comforter exclusive of the fringe, hanging down before him; and his threadbare clothes darned up and brushed, to look seasonable; and Tiny Tim upon his shoulder. Alas for Tiny Tim, he bore a little crutch, and had his limbs supported by an iron frame!

'Why, where's our Martha?' cried Bob Cratchit, looking round.

'Not coming,' said Mrs. Cratchit.

'Not coming!' said Bob, with a sudden declension in his high spirits; for he had been Tim's blood horse all the way from church, and had come home rampant. 'Not coming upon Christmas Day!'

Martha didn't like to see him disappointed, if it were only in joke; so she came out prematurely from behind the closet door, and ran into his arms, while the two young Cratchits hustled Tiny Tim, and bore him off into the wash-house, that he might hear the pudding singing in the copper.

'And how did little Tim behave?' asked Mrs Cratchit, when she had rallied Bob on his credulity, and Bob had hugged his daughter to his heart's content.

'As good as gold,' said Bob, 'and better. Somehow he gets thoughtful, sitting by himself so much, and thinks the strangest things you ever heard. He told me, coming home, that he hoped the people saw him in the church, because he was a cripple, and it might be pleasant to them to remember upon Christmas Day, who made lame beggars walk, and blind men see.'

Bob's voice was tremulous when he told them this

and trembled more when he said that Tiny Tim was growing strong and hearty.

His active little crutch was heard upon the floor, and back came Tiny Tim before another word was spoken, escorted by his brother and sister to his stool before the fire; and while Bob, turning up his cuffs— as if, poor fellow, they were capable of being made more shabby—compounded some hot mixture in a jug with gin and lemons, and stirred it round and round and put it on the hob to simmer; Master Peter, and the two ubiquitous young Cratchits, went to fetch the goose, with which they soon returned in high procession.

Such a bustle ensued that you might have thought a goose the rarest of all birds; a feathered phenomenon, to which a black swan was a matter of course— and in truth it was something very iike it in that house. Mrs. Cratchit made the gravy (ready beforehand in a little saucepan) hissing hot; Master Peter mashed the potatoes with incredible vigour; Miss Belinda sweetened up the apple-sauce; Martha dusted the hot plates; Bob took Tiny Tim beside him in a tiny corner at the table; the two young Cratchits set chairs for everybody, not forgetting themselves, and mounting guard upon their posts, crammed spoons into their mouths, lest they should shriek for goose before their turn came to be helped. At last the dishes were set on, and grace was said. It was succeeded by a breathless pause, as Mrs. Cratchit, looking slowly all along the carving-knife, prepared to plunge it in the breast; but when she did, and when the long expected gush of stuffing issued forth, one murmur of delight arose all round the board, and even Tiny Tim, excited by the two young Cratchits, beat on the table with the handle of his knife, and feebly cried Hurrah!

There never was such a goose. Bob said he didn't believe there ever was such a goose cooked. Its tenderness and flavour, size and cheapness, were the themes of universal admiration. Eked out by apple sauce and mashed potatoes, it was a sufficient dinner for the whole family: indeed, as Mrs. Cratchit said with great delight (surveying one small atom of a bone upon the dish), they hadn't ate it all at last! Yet every one had had enough, and the youngest Cratchits in particular, were steeped in sage and onion to the eyebrows. But now, the plates being changed by Miss Belinda, Mrs. Cratchit left the room alone—too nervous to bear witnesses—to take the pudding up and bring it in.

Suppose it should not be done enough! Suppose it should break in turning out! Suppose somebody should have got over the wall of the back-yard, and stolen it, while they were merry with the goose—a supposition at which the two young Cratchits became livid! All sorts of horrors were supposed.

Hallo! A great deal of steam! The pudding was out of the copper. A smell like a washing-day! That was the cloth. A smell like an eating-house and a pastrycook's next door to each other, with a laundress's next door to that! That was the pudding! In half a minute Mrs. Cratchit entered— flushed, but smiling proudly—with the pudding, like a speckled cannon-ball, so hard and firm, blazing in half of half-a-quartern of ignited brandy, and bedight with Christmas holly stuck into the top.

Oh, a wonderful pudding! Bob Cratchit said, and calmly too, that he regarded it as the greatest success achieved by Mrs. Cratchit since their marriage. Mrs. Cratchit said that now the weight was off her mind, she would confess she had had her doubts about the quantity of flour. Everybody had something to say

about it, but nobody said or thought it was at all a small pudding for a large family. It would have been flat heresy to do so. Any Cratchit would have blushed to hint at such a thing.

At last the dinner was all done, the cloth was cleared, the hearth swept, and the fire made up. The compound in the jug being tasted, and considered perfect, apples and oranges were put upon the table, and a shovel-full of chestnuts on the fire. Then all the Cratchit family drew round the hearth, in what Bob Cratchit called a circle, meaning half a one; and at Bob Cratchit's elbow stood the family display of glass. Two tumblers, and a custard-cup without a handle.

These held the hot stuff from the jug, however, as well as golden goblets would have done; and Bob served it out with beaming looks, while the chestnuts on the fire sputtered and cracked noisily. Then Bob proposed:

'A Merry Christmas to us all, my dears. God bless us!'

Which all the family re-echoed.

'God bless us every one!' said Tiny Tim, the last of all.

He sat very close to his father's side upon his little stool. Bob held his withered little hand in his, as if he loved the child, and wished to keep him by his side, and dreaded that he might be taken from him.

'Spirit,' said Scrooge, with an interest he had never felt before, 'tell me if Tiny Tim will live.'

'I see a vacant seat,' replied the Ghost, 'in the poor chimney-corner, and a crutch without an owner, carefully preserved. If these shadows remain un-altered by the Future, the child will die.'

'No, no,' said Scrooge. 'Oh, no, kind Spirit! say he will be spared.'

'If these shadows remain unaltered by the Future, none other of my race,' returned the Ghost, 'will find him here. What then? If he be like to die, he had better do it, and decrease the surplus population.'

Scrooge hung his head to hear his own words quoted by the Spirit, and was overcome with penitence and grief.

'Man,' said the Ghost, 'if man you be in heart, not adamant, forbear that wicked cant until you have discovered What the surplus is, and Where it is. Will you decide what men shall live, what men shall die? It may be, that in the sight of Heaven, you are more worthless and less fit to live than millions like this poor man's child. Oh God! to hear the Insect on the leaf pronouncing on the too much life among his hungry brothers in the dust!'

Scrooge bent before the Ghost's rebuke, and trembling cast his eyes upon the ground. But he raised them speedily, on hearing his own name.

'Mr. Scrooge!' said Bob; 'I'll give you Mr. Scrooge, the Founder of the Feast!'

'The Founder of the Feast indeed!' cried Mrs. Cratchit, reddening. 'I wish I had him here. I'd give him a piece of my mind to feast upon, and I hope he'd have a good appetite for it.'

'My dear,' said Bob, 'the children! Christmas Day.'

'It should be Christmas Day, I am sure,' said she, 'on which one drinks the health of such an odious, stingy, hard, unfeeling man as Mr. Scrooge. You know he is, Robert! Nobody knows it better than you do, poor fellow?'

'My dear,' was Bob's mild answer, 'Christmas Day.'

'I'll drink his health for your sake and the Day's,' said Mrs. Cratchit, 'not for his. Long life to him! A merry Christmas and a happy new year! He'll

be very merry and very happy, I have no doubt!'

The children drank the toast after her. It was the
first of their proceedings which had no heartiness.
Tiny Tim drank it last of all, but he didn't care twopence for it. Scrooge was the Ogre of the family.
The mention of his name cast a dark shadow on the
party, which was not dispelled for full five minutes.

After it had passed away, they were ten times
merrier than before, from the mere relief of Scrooge
the Baleful being done with. Bob Cratchit told
them how he had a situation in his eye for Master
Peter, which would bring in, if obtained, full five-
and-sixpence weekly. The two young Cratchits
laughed tremendously at the idea of Peter's being a
man of business; and Peter himself looked thoughtfully at the fire from between his collars, as if he were
deliberating what particular investments he should
favour when he came into the receipt of that bewildering income. Martha, who was a poor apprentice at
a milliner's, then told them what kind of work she had
to do, and how many hours she worked at a stretch,
and how she meant to lie abed to-morrow morning
for a good long rest; to-morrow being a holiday she
passed at home. Also how she had seen a countess
and a lord some days before, and how the lord 'was
much about as tall as Peter'; at which Peter pulled
up his collars so high that you couldn't have seen his
head if you had been there. All this time the chestnuts and the jug went round and round; and by and
by they had a song, about a lost child travelling in the
snow, from Tiny Tim, who had a plaintive little voice,
and sang it very well indeed.

There was nothing of high mark in this. They
were not a handsome family; they were not well
dressed; their shoes were far from being water-proof;
their clothes were scanty; and Peter might have

known, and very likely did, the inside of a pawn-broker's. But, they were happy, grateful, pleased with one another, and contented with the time; and when they faded, and looked happier yet in the bright sprinklings of the Spirit's torch at parting, Scrooge had his eye upon them, and especially on Tiny Tim, until the last.

By this time it was getting dark, and snowing pretty heavily; and as Scrooge and the Spirit went along the streets, the brightness of the roaring fires in kitchens, parlours, and all sorts of rooms, was wonderful. Here, the flickering of the blaze showed preparations for a cosy dinner, with hot plates baking through and through before the fire, and deep red curtains, ready to be drawn to shut out cold and darkness. There all the children of the house were running out into the snow to meet their married sisters, brothers, cousins, uncles, aunts, and be the first to greet them. Here, again, were shadows on the window-blind of guests assembling; and there a group of handsome girls, all hooded and fur-booted, and all chattering at once, tripped lightly off to some near neighbour's house; where, woe upon the single man who saw them enter—artful witches, well they knew it—in a glow!

But, if you had judged from the numbers of people on their way to friendly gatherings, you might have thought that no one was at home to give them welcome when they got there, instead of every house expecting company, and piling up its fires half-chimney high. Blessings on it, how the Ghost exulted. How it bared its breadth of breast, and opened its capacious palm, and floated on, outpouring, with a generous hand, its bright and harmless mirth on everything within its reach! The very lamplighter, who ran on before, dotting the dusky street with specks

of light, and who was dressed to spend the evening somewhere, laughed out loudly as the Spirit passed, though little kenned the lamplighter that he had any company but Christmas!

And now, without a word of warning from the Ghost, they stood upon a bleak and desert moor, where monstrous masses of rude stone were cast about, as though it were the burial-place of giants; and water spread itself wheresoever it listed, or would have done so, but for the frost that held it prisoner; and nothing grew but moss and furze, and coarse rank grass. Down in the west the setting sun had left a streak of fiery red, which glared upon the desolation for an instant, like a sullen eye, and frowning lower, lower, lower yet, was lost in the thick gloom of darkest night.

'What place is this?' asked Scrooge.

'A place where Miners live, who labour in the bowels of the earth,' returned the Spirit. 'But they know me. See!'

A light shone from the window of a hut, and swiftly they advanced towards it. Passing through the wall of mud and stone, they found a cheerful company assembled round a glowing fire. An old, old man and woman, with their children and their children's children, and another generation beyond that, all decked out gaily in their holiday attire. The old man, in a voice that seldom rose above the howling of the wind upon the barren waste, was singing them a Christmas song—it had been a very old song when he was a boy—and from time to time they all joined in the chorus. So surely as they raised their voices, the old man got quite blithe and loud; and so surely as they stopped, his vigour sank again.

The Spirit did not tarry here, but bade Scrooge hold his robe, and passing on above the moor, sped—

whither? Not to sea? To sea. To Scrooge's horror, looking back, he saw the last of the land, a frightful range of rocks, behind them; and his ears were deafened by the thundering of water, as it rolled and roared, and raged among the dreadful caverns it had worn, and fiercely tried to undermine the earth.

Built upon a dismal reef of sunken rocks, some league or so from shore, on which the waters chafed and dashed, the wild year through, there stood a solitary lighthouse. Great heaps of sea-weed clung to its base, and storm-birds—born of the wind one might suppose, as sea-weed of the water—rose and fell about it, like the waves they skimmed.

But even here, two men who watched the light had made a fire, that through the loophole in the thick stone wall shed out a ray of brightness on the awful sea. Joining their horny hands over the rough table at which they sat, they wished each other Merry Christmas in their can of grog; and one of them: the elder, too, with his face all damaged and scarred with hard weather, as the figure-head of an old ship might be: struck up a sturdy song that was like a Gale in itself.

Again the Ghost sped on, above the black and heaving sea—on, on—until, being far away, as he told Scrooge, from any shore, they lighted on a ship. They stood beside the helmsman at the wheel, the look-out in the bow, the officers who had the watch; dark, ghostly figures in their several stations; but every man among them hummed a Christmas tune, or had a Christmas thought, or spoke below his breath to his companion of some by-gone Christmas Day, with homeward hopes belonging to it. And every man on board, waking or sleeping, good or bad, had had a kinder word for another on that day than on any day in the year; and had shared to some extent in

its festivities; and had remembered those he cared for at a distance, and had known that they delighted to remember him.

It was a great surprise to Scrooge, while listening to the moaning of the wind, and thinking what a solemn thing it was to move on through the lonely darkness over an unknown abyss, whose depths were secrets as profound as Death: it was a great surprise to Scrooge, while thus engaged, to hear a hearty laugh. It was a much greater surprise to Scrooge to recognise it as his own nephew's and to find himself in a bright, dry, gleaming room, with the Spirit standing smiling by his side, and looking at that same nephew with approving affability!

'Ha, ha!' laughed Scrooge's nephew. 'Ha, ha, ha!'

If you should happen, by any unlikely chance, to know a man more blest in a laugh than Scrooge's nephew, all I can say is, I should like to know him too. Introduce him to me, and I'll cultivate his acquaintance.

It is a fair, even-handed, noble adjustment of things, that while there is infection in disease and sorrow, there is nothing in the world so irresistibly contagious as laughter and good-humour. When Scrooge's nephew laughed in this way: holding his sides, rolling his head, and twisting his face into the most extravagant contortions: Scrooge's niece, by marriage, laughed as heartily as he. And their assembled friends being not a bit behindhand, roared out lustily.

'Ha, ha! Ha, ha, ha, ha!'

'He said that Christmas was a humbug, as I live!' cried Scrooge's nephew. 'He believed it too!'

'More shame for him, Fred!' said Scrooge's niece, indignantly. Bless those women; they never do anything by halves. They are always in earnest.

She was very pretty: exceedingly pretty. With a dimpled, surprised-looking, capital face; a ripe little mouth, that seemed made to be kissed—as no doubt it was; all kinds of good little dots about her chin, that melted into one another when she laughed; and the sunniest pair of eyes you ever saw in any little creature's head. Altogether she was what you would have called provoking, you know; but satisfactory, too. Oh, perfectly satisfactory.

'He 's a comical old fellow,' said Scrooge's nephew, 'that 's the truth; and not so pleasant as he might be. However, his offences carry their own punishment, and I have nothing to say against him.'

'I 'm sure he is very rich, Fred,' hinted Scrooge's niece. 'At least you always tell *me* so.'

'What of that, my dear!' said Scrooge's nephew. 'His wealth is of no use to him. He don't do any good with it. He don't make himself comfortable with it. He hasn't the satisfaction of thinking —ha, ha, ha!—that he is ever going to benefit Us with it.'

'I have no patience with him,' observed Scrooge's niece. Scrooge's niece's sisters, and all the other ladies, expressed the same opinion.

'Oh, I have!' said Scrooge's nephew. 'I am sorry for him; I couldn't be angry with him if I tried. Who suffers by his ill whims! Himself, always. Here, he takes it into his head to dislike us, and he won't come and dine with us. What 's the consequence? He don't lose much of a dinner.'

'Indeed, I think he loses a very good dinner,' interrupted Scrooge's niece. Everybody else said the same, and they must be allowed to have been competent judges, because they had just had dinner; and, with the dessert upon the table, were clustered round the fire, by lamplight.

'Well! I'm very glad to hear it,' said Scrooge's nephew, 'because I haven't great faith in these young housekeepers. What do *you* say, Topper?'

Topper had clearly got his eye upon one of Scrooge's niece's sisters, for he answered that a bachelor was a wretched outcast, who had no right to express an opinion on the subject. Whereat Scrooge's niece's sister—the plump one with the lace tucker: not the one with the roses—blushed.

'Do go on, Fred,' said Scrooge's niece, clapping her hands. 'He never finishes what he begins to say! He is such a ridiculous fellow!'

Scrooge's nephew revelled in another laugh, and as it was impossible to keep the infection off; though the plump sister tried hard to do it with aromatic vinegar: his example was unanimously followed.

'I was only going to say,' said Scrooge's nephew, 'that the consequence of his taking a dislike to us, and not making merry with us, is, as I think, that he loses some pleasant moments, which could do him no harm. I am sure he loses pleasanter companions than he can find in his own thoughts, either in his mouldy old office, or his dusty chambers. I mean to give him the same chance every year, whether he likes it or not, for I pity him. He may rail at Christmas till he dies, but he can't help thinking better of it—I defy him—if he finds me going there, in good temper, year after year, and saying "Uncle Scrooge, how are you?" If it only puts him in the vein to leave his poor clerk fifty pounds, *that's* something; and I think I shook him yesterday.'

It was their turn to laugh now at the notion of his shaking Scrooge. But being thoroughly good-natured, and not much caring what they laughed at, so that they laughed at any rate, he encouraged them in their merriment, and passed the bottle joyously.

After tea, they had some music. For they were a musical family, and knew what they were about, when they sung a Glee or Catch, I can assure you: especially Topper, who could growl away in the bass like a good one, and never swell the large veins in his forehead, or get red in the face over it. Scrooge's niece played well upon the harp; and played among other tunes a simple little air (a mere nothing; you might learn to whistle it in two minutes), which had been familiar to the child who fetched Scrooge from the boarding-school, as he had been reminded by the Ghost of Christmas Past. When this strain of music sounded, all the things that Ghost had shown him, came upon his mind; he softened more and more; and thought that if he could have listened to it often, years ago, he might have cultivated the kindnesses of life for his own happiness with his own hands, without resorting to the sexton's spade that buried Jacob Marley.

But they didn't devote the whole evening to music. After a while they played at forfeits; for it is good to be children sometimes, and never better than at Christmas, when its mighty Founder was a child himself. Stop! There was first a game at blind-man's buff. Of course there was. And I no more believe Topper was really blind than I believe he had eyes in his boots. My opinion is, that it was a done thing between him and Scrooge's nephew: and that the Ghost of Christmas Present knew it. The way he went after that plump sister in the lace tucker, was an outrage on the credulity of human nature. Knocking down the fire-irons, tumbling over the chairs, bumping against the piano, smothering himself among the curtains, wherever she went, there went he! He always knew where the plump sister was. He wouldn't catch anybody else. If you had fallen up against

him (as some of them did), on purpose, he would have made a feint of endeavouring to seize you, which would have been an affront to your understanding, and would instantly have sidled off in the direction of the plump sister. She often cried out that it wasn't fair; and it really was not. But when at last, he caught her; when, in spite of all her silken rustlings, and her rapid flutterings past him, he got her into a corner, whence there was no escape; then his conduct was the most execrable. For his pretending not to know her; his pretending that it was necessary to touch her head-dress, and further to assure himself of her identity by pressing a certain ring upon her finger, and a certain chain about her neck; was vile, monstrous! No doubt she told him her opinion of it, when, another blind man being in office, they were so very confidential together, behind the curtains.

Scrooge's niece was not one of the blind-man's buff party, but was made comfortable with a large chair and a footstool, in a snug corner, where the Ghost and Scrooge were close behind her. But she joined in the forfeits, and loved her love to admiration with all the letters of the alphabet. Likewise at the game of How, When, and Where, she was very great, and to the secret joy of Scrooge's nephew, beat her sisters hollow: though they were sharp girls too, as Topper could have told you. There might have been twenty people there, young and old, but they all played, and so did Scrooge; for wholly forgetting in the interest he had in what was going on, that his voice made no sound in their ears, he sometimes came out with his guess quite loud, and very often guessed quite right, too; for the sharpest needle, best Whitechapel, warranted not to cut in the eye, was not sharper than Scrooge; blunt as he took it in his head to be.

The Ghost was greatly pleased to find him in this

mood, and looked upon him with such favour, that he begged like a boy to be allowed to stay until the guests departed. But this the Spirit said could not be done.

'Here is a new game,' said Scrooge. 'One half-hour, Spirit, only one!'

It is a Game called Yes and No, where Scrooge's nephew had to think of something, and the rest must find out what; he only answering to their questions yes or no, as the case was. The brisk fire of questioning to which he was exposed, elicited from him that he was thinking of an animal, a live animal, rather a disagreeable animal, a savage animal, an animal, that growled and grunted sometimes, and talked sometimes, and lived in London, and walked about the streets, and wasn't made a show of, and wasn't led by anybody, and didn't live in a menagerie, and was never killed in a market, and was not a horse, or an ass, or a cow, or a bull, or a tiger, or a dog, or a pig, or a cat, or a bear. At every fresh question that was put to him, this nephew burst into a fresh roar of laughter; and was so inexpressibly tickled, that he was obliged to get up off the sofa and stamp. At last the plump sister, falling into a similar state, cried out:

'I have found it out! I know what it is, Fred! I know what it is!'

'What is it?' cried Fred.

'It's your Uncle Scro-o-o-o-oge!'

Which it certainly was. Admiration was the universal sentiment, though some objected that the reply to 'Is it a bear?' ought to have been 'Yes'; inasmuch as an answer in the negative was sufficient to have diverted their thoughts from Mr. Scrooge, supposing they had ever had any tendency that way.

'He has given us plenty of merriment, I am sure,' said Fred, 'and it would be ungrateful not to drink

his health. Here is a glass of mulled wine ready to our hand at the moment; and I say, "Uncle Scrooge!"'

'Well! Uncle Scrooge!' they cried.

'A merry Christmas and a Happy New Year to the old man, whatever he is!' said Scrooge's nephew. 'He wouldn't take it from me, but may he have it, nevertheless. Uncle Scrooge!'

Uncle Scrooge had imperceptibly become so gay and light of heart, that he would have pledged the unconscious company in return, and thanked them in an inaudible speech, if the Ghost had given him time. But the whole scene passed off in the breath of the last word spoken by his nephew; and he and the Spirit were again upon their travels.

Much they saw, and far they went, and many homes they visited, but always with a happy end. The Spirit stood beside sick-beds, and they were cheerful; on foreign lands, and they were close at home; by struggling men, and they were patient in their greater hope; by poverty, and it was rich. In almshouse, hospital, and jail, in misery's every refuge, where vain man in his little brief authority had not made fast the door, and barred the Spirit out, he left his blessing, and taught Scrooge his precepts.

It was a long night, if it were only a night; but Scrooge had his doubts of this, because the Christmas Holidays appeared to be condensed into the space of time they passed together. It was strange, too, that while Scrooge remained unaltered in his outward form, the Ghost grew older, clearly older. Scrooge had observed this change, but never spoke of it, until they left a children's Twelfth Night party, when, looking at the Spirit as they stood together in an open place, he noticed that its hair was grey.

'Are spirits' lives so short?' asked Scrooge.

'My life upon this globe, is very brief,' replied the Ghost. 'It ends to-night.'

'To-night!' cried Scrooge.

'To-night at midnight. Hark! The time is draw-ing near.'

The chimes were ringing the three quarters past eleven at that moment.

'Forgive me if I am not justified in what I ask,' said Scrooge, looking intently at the Spirit's robe, 'but I see something strange, and not belonging to yourself, protruding from your skirts. Is it a foot or a claw?'

'It might be a claw, for the flesh there is upon it,' was the Spirit's sorrowful reply. 'Look here.'

From the foldings of its robe, it brought two chil-dren; wretched, abject, frightful, hideous, miserable. They knelt down at its feet, and clung upon the out-side of its garment.

'Oh, Man! look here. Look, look, down here!' ex-claimed the Ghost.

They were a boy and girl. Yellow, meagre, ragged, scowling, wolfish; but prostrate, too, in their humility. Where graceful youth should have filled their features out, and touched them with its freshest tints, a stale and shrivelled hand, like that of age, had pinched, and twisted them, and pulled them into shreds. Where angels might have sat enthroned, devils lurked, and glared out menacing. No change, no degradation, no perversion of humanity, in any grade, through all the mysteries of wonderful crea-tion, has monsters half so horrible and dread.

Scrooge started back, appalled. Having them shown to him in this way, he tried to say they were fine children, but the words choked themselves, rather than be parties to a lie of such enormous magnitude.

'Spirit! are they yours?' Scrooge could say no more.

'They are Man's,' said the Spirit, looking down upon them. 'And they cling to me, appealing from their fathers. This boy is Ignorance. This girl is Want. Beware them both, and all of their degree, but most of all beware this boy, for on his brow I see that written which is Doom, unless the writing be erased. Deny it!' cried the Spirit, stretching out its hand towards the city. 'Slander those who tell it ye! Admit it for your factious purposes, and make it worse. And abide the end!'

'Have they no refuge or resource?' cried Scrooge.

'Are there no prisons?' said the Spirit, turning on him for the last time with his own words. 'Are there no workhouses?'

The bell struck twelve.

Scrooge looked about him for the Ghost, and saw it not. As the last stroke ceased to vibrate, he remembered the prediction of old Jacob Marley, and lifting up his eyes, beheld a solemn Phantom, draped and hooded, coming, like a mist along the ground, towards him.

Stave Four

THE LAST OF THE SPIRITS

The Phantom slowly, gravely, silently approached. When it came near him, Scrooge bent down upon his knee; for in the very air through which this Spirit moved it seemed to scatter gloom and mystery.

It was shrouded in a deep black garment, which concealed its head, its face, its form, and left nothing of it visible save one outstretched hand. But for this it would have been difficult to detach its figure from

the night, and separate it from the darkness by which it was surrounded.

He felt that it was tall and stately when it came beside him, and that its mysterious presence filled him with a solemn dread. He knew no more, for the Spirit neither spoke nor moved.

'I am in the presence of the Ghost of Christmas Yet to Come?' said Scrooge.

The Spirit answered not, but pointed onward with its hand.

'You are about to show me shadows of the things that have not happened, but will happen in the time before us,' Scrooge pursued. 'Is that so, Spirit?'

The upper portion of the garment was contracted for an instant in its folds, as if the Spirit had inclined its head. That was the only answer he received.

Although well used to ghostly company by this time, Scrooge feared the silent shape so much that his legs trembled beneath him, and he found that he could hardly stand when he prepared to follow it. The Spirit paused a moment, as observing his condition, and giving him time to recover.

But Scrooge was all the worse for this. It thrilled him with a vague uncertain horror, to know that behind the dusky shroud, there were ghostly eyes intently fixed upon him, while he, though he stretched his own to the utmost, could see nothing but a spectral hand and one great heap of black.

'Ghost of the Future!' he exclaimed, 'I fear you more than any spectre I have seen. But as I know your purpose is to do me good, and as I hope to live to be another man from what I was, I am prepared to bear you company, and do it with a thankful heart. Will you not speak to me?'

It gave him no reply. The hand was pointed straight before them.

'Lead on!' said Scrooge. 'Lead on! The night is waning fast, and it is precious time to me, I know. Lead on, Spirit!'

The Phantom moved away as it had come towards him. Scrooge followed in the shadow of its dress, which bore him up, he thought, and carried him along.

They scarcely seemed to enter the city; for the city rather seemed to spring up about them, and encompass them of its own act. But there they were, in the heart of it; on 'Change, amongst the merchants; who hurried up and down, and chinked the money in their pockets, and conversed in groups, and looked at their watches, and trifled thoughtfully with their great gold seals; and so forth, as Scrooge had seen them often.

The Spirit stopped beside one little knot of business men. Observing that the hand was pointed to them, Scrooge advanced to listen to their talk.

'No,' said a great fat man with a monstrous chin, 'I don't know much about it, either way. I only know he's dead.'

'When did he die?' inquired another.

'Last night, I believe.'

'Why, what was the matter with him?' asked a third, taking a vast quantity of snuff out of a very large snuff-box. 'I thought he'd never die.'

'God knows,' said the first, with a yawn.

'What has he done with his money?' asked a red-faced gentleman with a pendulous excrescence on the end of his nose, that shook like the gills of a turkey-cock.

'I haven't heard,' said the man with the large chin, yawning again. 'Left it to his company, perhaps. He hasn't left it to *me*. That's all I know'.

This pleasantry was received with a general laugh.

'It's likely to be a very cheap funeral,' said the same speaker; 'for upon my life I don't know of any,

body to go to it. Suppose we make up a party and volunteer?'

'I don't mind going if a lunch is provided,' observed the gentleman with the excrescence on his nose. 'But I must be fed, if I make one.'

Another laugh.

'Well, I am the most disinterested among you, after all,' said the first speaker, 'for I never wear black gloves, and I never eat lunch. But I'll offer to go, if anybody else will. When I come to think of it, I'm not at all sure that I wasn't his most particular friend; for we used to stop and speak whenever we met. Bye, bye!'

Speakers and listeners strolled away, and mixed with other groups. Scrooge knew the men, and looked towards the Spirit for an explanation.

The Phantom glided on into a street. Its finger pointed to two persons meeting. Scrooge listened again, thinking that the explanation might lie here.

He knew these men, also, perfectly. They were men of business: very wealthy, and of great importance. He had made a point always of standing well in their esteem: in a business point of view, that is; strictly in a business point of view.

'How are you?' said one.

'How are you?' returned the other.

'Well!' said the first. 'Old Scratch has got his own at last, hey?'

'So I am told,' returned the second. 'Cold, isn't it?'

'Seasonable for Christmas time. You're not a skater, I suppose?'

'No. No. Something else to think of, Good morning!'

Not another word. That was their meeting, their conversation, and their parting.

Scrooge was at first inclined to be surprised that the Spirit should attach importance to conversations apparently so trivial; but feeling assured that they must have some hidden purpose, he set himself to consider what it was likely to be. They could scarcely be supposed to have any bearing on the death of Jacob, his old partner, for that was Past, and this Ghost's province was the Future. Nor could he think of any one immediately connected with himself, to whom he could apply them. But nothing doubting that to whomsoever they applied they had some latent moral for his own improvement, he resolved to treasure up every word he heard, and everything he saw; and especially to observe the shadow of himself when it appeared. For he had an expectation that the conduct of his future self would give him the clue he missed, and would render the solution of these riddles easy.

He looked about in that very place for his own image; but another man stood in his accustomed corner, and though the clock pointed to his usual time of day for being there, he saw no likeness of himself among the multitudes that poured in through the Porch. It gave him little surprise, however; for he had been revolving in his mind a change of life, and thought and hoped he saw his new-born resolutions carried out in this.

Quiet and dark, beside him stood the Phantom, with its outstretched hand. When he roused himself from his thoughtful quest, he fancied from the turn of the hand, and its situation in reference to himself, that the Unseen Eyes were looking at him keenly. It made him shudder, and feel very cold.

They left the busy scene, and went into an obscure part of the town, where Scrooge had never penetrated before, although he recognised its situation, and its

bad repute.   The ways were foul and narrow; the shops and houses wretched; the people, half-naked, drunken, slipshod, ugly.   Alleys and archways, like so many cesspools, disgorged their offences of smell, and dirt, and life, upon the straggling streets; and the whole quarter reeked with crime, with filth, and misery.

Far in this den of infamous resort, there was a low-browed, beetling shop, below a pent-house roof, where iron, old rags, bottles, bones, and greasy offal, were bought.   Upon the floor within, were piled up heaps of rusty keys, nails, chains, hinges, files, scales, weights, and refuse iron of all kinds.   Secrets that few would like to scrutinise were bred and hidden in mountains of unseemly rags, masses of corrupted fat, and sepulchres of bones.   Sitting in among the wares he dealt in, by a charcoal stove, made of old bricks, was a grey-haired rascal, nearly seventy years of age; who had screened himself from the cold air without, by a frousy curtaining of miscellaneous tatters, hung upon a line; and smoked his pipe in all the luxury of calm retirement.

Scrooge and the Phantom came into the presence of this man, just as a woman with a heavy bundle slunk into the shop.   But she had scarcely entered, when another woman, similarly laden, came in too; and she was closely followed by a man in faded black, who was no less startled by the sight of them, than they had been upon the recognition of each other. After a short period of blank astonishment, in which the old man with the pipe had joined them, they all three burst into a laugh.

'Let the charwoman alone to be the first!' cried she who had entered first.   'Let the laundress alone to be the second; and let the undertaker's man alone to be the third.   Look here, old Joe, here's a chance!

If we haven't all three met here without meaning it!'

'You couldn't have met in a better place,' said old Joe, removing his pipe from his mouth. 'Come into the parlour. You were made free of it long ago, you know; and the other two an't strangers. Stop till I shut the door of the shop. Ah! How it skreeks! There an't such a rusty bit of metal in the place as its own hinges, I believe; and I'm sure there's no such old bones here, as mine. Ha, ha! We're all suitable to our calling, we're well matched. Come into the parlour. Come into the parlour.'

The parlour was the space behind the screen of rags. The old man raked the fire together with an old stair-rod, and having trimmed his smoky lamp (for it was night), with the stem of his pipe, put it in his mouth again.

While he did this, the woman who had already spoken threw her bundle on the floor, and sat down in a flaunting manner on a stool; crossing her elbows on her knees, and looking with a bold defiance at the other two.

'What odds then! What odds, Mrs. Dilber?' said the woman. 'Every person has a right to take care of themselves. *He* always did.'

'That's true, indeed!' said the laundress. 'No man more so.'

'Why then, don't stand staring as if you was afraid, woman; who's the wiser? We're not going to pick holes in each other's coats, I suppose?'

'No, indeed!' said Mrs. Dilber and the man together. 'We should hope not.'

'Very well, then!' cried the woman. 'That's enough. Who's the worse for the loss of a few things like these? Not a dead man, I suppose.'

'No, indeed,' said Mrs. Dilber, laughing.

'If he wanted to keep 'em after he was dead, a

wicked old screw,' pursued the woman, 'why wasn't he natural in his lifetime? If he had been, he 'd have had somebody to look after him when he was struck with Death, instead of lying gasping out his last there, alone by himself.'

'It 's the truest word that ever was spoke,' said Mrs. Dilber. 'It 's a judgment on him.'

'I wish it was a little heavier judgment,' replied the woman; 'and it should have been, you may depend upon it, if I could have laid my hands on anything else. Open that bundle, old Joe, and let me know the value of it. Speak out plain. I 'm not afraid to be the first, nor afraid for them to see it. We knew pretty well that we were helping ourselves, before we met here, I believe. It 's no sin. Open the bundle, Joe.'

But the gallantry of her friends would not allow of this; and the man in faded black, mounting the breach first, produced *his* plunder. It was not extensive. A seal or two, a pencil-case, a pair of sleeve-buttons, and a brooch of no great value, were all. They were severally examined and appraised by old Joe, who chalked the sums he was disposed to give for each, upon the wall, and added them up into a total when he found there was nothing more to come.

'That 's your account,' said Joe, 'and I wouldn't give another sixpence, if I was to be boiled for not doing it. Who 's next?'

Mrs. Dilber was next. Sheets and towels, a little wearing apparel, two old-fashioned silver teaspoons, a pair of sugar-tongs, and a few boots. Her account was stated on the wall in the same manner.

'I always give too much to ladies. It 's a weakness of mine, and that 's the way I ruin myself,' said old Joe. 'That 's your account. If you asked me for another penny, and made it an open question, I 'd

repent of being so liberal and knock off half-a-
crown.'

'And now undo *my* bundle, Joe,' said the first
woman.

Joe went down on his knees for the greater convenience of opening it, and having unfastened a great
many knots, dragged out a large and heavy roll of
some dark stuff.

'What do you call this?' said Joe.   'Bed-curtains!'

'Ah!' returned the woman, laughing and leaning
forward on her crossed arms.   'Bed-curtains!'

'You don't mean to say you took 'em down, rings
and all, with him lying there?' said Joe.

'Yes I do,' replied the woman.   'Why not?'

'You were born to make your fortune,' said Joe,
'and you 'll certainly do it.'

'I certainly shan't hold my hand, when I can get
anything in it by reaching it out, for the sake of such
a man as He was, I promise you, Joe,' returned the
woman coolly.   'Don't drop that oil upon the blankets, now.'

'His blankets?' asked Joe.

'Whose else's do you think?' replied the woman.
'He isn't likely to take cold without 'em, I dare say.'

'I hope he didn't die of anything catching? Eh?'
said old Joe, stopping in his work, and looking up.

'Don't you be afraid of that,' returned the woman.
'I an't so found of his company that I 'd loiter about
him for such things, if he did.   Ah! you may look
through that shirt till your eyes ache; but you won't
find a hole in it, nor a threadbare place.   It 's the best
he had, and a fine one too.   They 'd have wasted it, if
it hadn't been for me.'

'What do you call wasting of it?' asked old Joe.

'Putting it on him to be buried in, to be sure,' replied the woman with a laugh.   'Somebody was fool

enough to do it, but I took it off again. If calico an't good enough for such a purpose, it isn't good enough for anything. It's quite as becoming to the body. He can't look uglier than he did in that one.'

Scrooge listened to this dialogue in horror. As they sat grouped about their spoil, in the scanty light afforded by the old man's lamp, he viewed them with a detestation and disgust, which could hardly have been greater, though they had been obscene demons, marketing the corpse itself.

'Ha, ha!' laughed the same woman, when old Joe, producing a flannel bag with money in it, told out their several gains upon the ground. 'This is the end of it, you see! He frightened every one away from him when he was alive, to profit us when he was dead! Ha, ha, ha!'

'Spirit!' said Scrooge, shuddering from head to foot. 'I see, I see. The case of this unhappy man might be my own. My life tends that way, now. Merciful Heaven, what is this!'

He recoiled in terror, for the scene had changed, and now he almost touched a bed: a bare, uncurtained bed: on which, beneath a ragged sheet, there lay a something covered up, which, though it was dumb, announced itself in awful language.

The room was very dark, too dark to be observed with any accuracy, though Scrooge glanced round it in obedience to a secret impulse, anxious to know what kind of room it was. A pale light, rising in the outer air, fell straight upon the bed; and on it, plundered and bereft, unwatched, unwept, uncared for, was the body of this man.

Scrooge glanced towards the Phantom. Its steady hand was pointed to the head. The cover was so carelessly adjusted that the slightest raising of it, the motion of a finger upon Scrooge's part, would have

disclosed the face. He thought of it, felt how easy it would be to do, and longed to do it; but had no more power to withdraw the veil than to dismiss the spectre at his side.

Oh cold, cold, rigid, dreadful Death, set up thine altar here, and dress it with such terrors as thou hast at thy command: for this is thy dominion! But of the loved, revered, and honoured head, thou canst not turn one hair to thy dread purposes, or make one feature odious. It is not that the hand is heavy and will fall down when released; it is not that the heart and pulse are still; but that the hand WAS open, generous, and true; the heart brave, warm, and tender; and the pulse a man's. Strike, Shadow, strike! And see his good deeds springing from the wound, to sow the world with life immortal!

No voice pronounced these words in Scrooge's ears, and yet he heard them when he looked upon the bed. He thought, if this man could be raised up now, what would be his foremost thoughts? Avarice, hard-dealing, griping cares? They have brought him to a rich end, truly!

He lay, in the dark empty house, with not a man, a woman, or a child, to say that he was kind to me in this or that, and for the memory of one kind word I will be kind to him. A cat was tearing at the door, and there was a sound of gnawing rats beneath the hearth-stone. What *they* wanted in the room of death, and why they were so restless and disturbed, Scrooge did not dare to think.

'Spirit!' he said, 'this is a fearful place. In leaving it, I shall not leave its lesson, trust me. Let us go!'

Still the Ghost pointed with an unmoved finger to the head.

'I understand you,' Scrooge returned, 'and I would

do it, if I could. But I have not the power, Spirit. I have not the power.'

Again it seemed to look upon him.

'If there is any person in the town, who feels emotion caused by this man's death,' said Scrooge quite agonised, 'show that person to me, Spirit, I beseech you!'

The Phantom spread its dark robe before him for a moment, like a wing; and withdrawing it, revealed a room by daylight, where a mother and her children were.

She was expecting some one, and with anxious eagerness; for she walked up and down the room; started at every sound; looked out from the window; glanced at the clock; tried, but in vain, to work with her needle; and could hardly bear the voices of the children in their play.

At length the long-expected knock was heard. She hurried to the door, and met her husband; a man whose face was careworn and depressed, though he was young. There was a remarkable expression in it now; a kind of serious delight of which he felt ashamed, and which he struggled to repress.

He sat down to the dinner that had been hoarding for him by the fire; and when she asked him faintly what news (which was not until after a long silence), he appeared embarrassed how to answer.

'Is it good,' she said, 'or bad?'—to help him.

'Bad,' he answered.

'We are quite ruined?'

'No. There is hope yet, Caroline.'

'If *he* relents,' she said, amazed, 'there is! Nothing is past hope if such a miracle has happened.'

'He is past relenting,' said her husband. 'He is dead.'

She was a mild and patient creature if her face

spoke truth; but she was thankful in her soul to hear it, and she said so, with clasped hands. She prayed forgiveness the next moment, and was sorry; but the first was the emotion of her heart.

'What the half-drunken woman whom I told you of last night, said to me, when I tried to see him and obtain a week's delay; and what I thought was a mere excuse to avoid me; turns out to have been quite true. He was not only very ill, but dying, then.'

'To whom will our debt be transferred?'

'I don't know. But before that time we shall be ready with the money; and even though we were not, it would be a bad fortune indeed to find so merciless a creditor in his successor. We may sleep to-night with light hearts, Caroline!'

Yes. Soften it as they would, their hearts were lighter. The children's faces, hushed and clustered round to hear what they so little understood, were brighter; and it was a happier house for this man's death! The only emotion that the Ghost could show him, caused by the event, was one of pleasure.

'Let me see some tenderness connected with a death,' said Scrooge; 'or that dark chamber, Spirit, which we left just now, will be for ever present to me.'

The Ghost conducted him through several streets familiar to his feet; and as they went along, Scrooge looked here and there to find himself, but nowhere was he to be seen. They entered poor Bob Cratchit's house; the dwelling he had visited before; and found the mother and the children seated round the fire.

Quiet. Very quiet. The noisy little Cratchits were as still as statues in one corner, and sat looking up at Peter, who had a book before him. The mother and her daughters were engaged in sewing. But surely they were very quiet!

' "And He took a child and set him in the midst of them." '

Where had Scrooge heard those words? He had not dreamed them. The boy must have read them out, as he and the Spirit crossed the threshold. Why did he not go on?

The mother laid her work upon the table, and put her hand up to her face.

'The colour hurts my eyes,' she said.

The colour? Ah, poor Tiny Tim!

'They 're better now again,' said Cratchit's wife. 'It makes them weak by candlelight; and I wouldn't show weak eyes to your father when he comes home, for the world. It must be near his time.'

'Past it rather,' Peter answered, shutting up his book. 'But I think he has walked a little slower than he used, these few last evenings, mother.'

They were very quiet again. At last she said, and in a steady, cheerful voice, that only faltered once:

'I have known him walk with—I have known him walk with Tiny Tim upon his shoulder, very fast indeed.'

'And so have I,' cried Peter. 'Often.'

'And so have I,' exclaimed another. So had all.

'But he was very light to carry,' she resumed, intent upon her work, 'and his father loved him so, that it was no trouble: no trouble. And there is your father at the door!'

She hurried out to meet him; and little Bob in his comforter—he had need of it, poor fellow—came in. His tea was ready for him on the hob, and they all tried who should help him to it most. Then the two young Cratchits got upon his knees and laid, each child a little cheek, against his face, as if they said, 'Don't mind it, father! Don't be grieved!'

Bob was very cheerful with them, and spoke pleasantly to all the family. He looked at the work upon the table, and praised the industry and speed of Mrs. Cratchit and the girls. They would be done long before Sunday, he said.

'Sunday! You went to-day, then, Robert?' said his wife.

'Yes, my dear,' returned Bob. 'I wish you could have gone. It would have done you good to see how green a place it is. But you'll see it often. I promised him that I would walk there on a Sunday. My little, little child!' cried Bob. 'My little child!'

He broke down all at once. He couldn't help it. If he could have helped it, he and his child would have been farther apart perhaps than they were.

He left the room, and went upstairs into the room above, which was lighted cheerfully, and hung with Christmas. There was a chair set close beside the child, and there were signs of some one having been there, lately. Poor Bob sat down in it, and when he had thought a little and composed himself, he kissed the little face. He was reconciled to what had happened, and went down again quite happy.

They drew about the fire, and talked; the girls and mother working still. Bob told them of the extraordinary kindness of Mr. Scrooge's nephew, whom he had scarcely seen but once, and who, meeting him in the street that day, and seeing that he looked a little—'just a little down you know,' said Bob, inquired what had happened to distress him. 'On which,' said Bob, 'for he is the pleasantest-spoken gentleman you ever heard, I told him. "I am heartily sorry for it, Mr. Cratchit," he said, "and heartily sorry for your good wife." By the bye, how he ever knew *that,* I don't know.'

'Knew what, my dear?'

'Why, that you were a good wife,' replied Bob.
'Everybody knows that!' said Peter.

'Very well observed, my boy!' cried Bob. 'I hope
they do. "Heartily sorry," he said, "for your good
wife. If I can be of service to you in any way," he
said, giving me his card, "that's where I live. Pray
come to me." Now it wasn't,' cried Bob, 'for the
sake of anything he might be able to do for us, so
much as for his kind way, that this was quite delightful. It really seemed as if he had known our Tiny
Tim, and felt with us.'

'I'm sure he's a good soul!' said Mrs. Cratchit.

'You would be surer of it, my dear,' returned Bob,
'if you saw and spoke to him. I shouldn't be at all
surprised—mark what I say!—if he got Peter a
better situation.'

'Only hear that, Peter,' said Mrs. Cratchit.

'And then,' cried one of the girls, 'Peter will be
keeping company with some one, and setting up for
himself.'

'Get along with you!' retorted Peter, grinning.

'It's just as likely as not,' said Bob, 'one of these
days; though there's plenty of time for that, my dear.
But however and whenever we part from one another,
I am sure we shall none of us forget poor Tiny Tim
—shall we—or this first parting that there was among
us?'

'Never, father!' cried they all.

'And I know,' said Bob, 'I know, my dears, that
when we recollect how patient and how mild he was;
although he was a little, little child; we shall not
quarrel easily among ourselves, and forget poor Tiny
Tim in doing it.'

'No, never, father!' they all cried again.

'I am very happy,' said little Bob, 'I am very
happy!'

Mrs. Cratchit kissed him, his daughters kissed him, the two young Cratchits kissed him, and Peter and himself shook hands. Spirit of Tiny Tim, thy childish essence was from God!

'Spectre,' said Scrooge, 'something informs me that our parting moment is at hand. I know it, but I know not how. Tell me what man that was whom we saw lying dead?'

'The Ghost of Christmas Yet To Come conveyed him, as before—though at a different time, he thought: indeed, there seemed no order in these latter visions, save that they were in the Future—into the resorts of business men, but showed him not himself. Indeed, the Spirit did not stay for anything, but went straight on, as to the end just now desired, until besought by Scrooge to tarry for a moment.

'This court,' said Scrooge, 'through which we hurry now, is where my place of occupation is, and has been for a length of time. I see the house. Let me behold what I shall be, in days to come!'

The Spirit stopped; the hand was pointed elsewhere.

'The house is yonder,' Scrooge exclaimed. 'Why do you point away?'

The inexorable finger underwent no change.

Scrooge hastened to the window of his office, and looked in. It was an office still, but not his. The furniture was not the same, and the figure in the chair was not himself. The Phantom pointed as before.

He joined it once again, and wondering why and whither he had gone, accompanied it until they reached an iron gate. He paused to look round before entering.

A churchyard. Here, then, the wretched man whose name he had now to learn, lay underneath the ground. It was a worthy place. Walled in by

houses; overrun by grass and weeds, the growth of vegetation's death, not life; choked up with too much burying; fat with repleted appetite. A worthy place!

The Spirit stood among the graves, and pointed down to One. He advanced towards it trembling. The Phantom was exactly as it had been, but he dreaded that he saw new meaning in its solemn shape.

'Before I draw nearer to that stone to which you point,' said Scrooge, 'answer me one question. Are these the shadows of the things that Will be, or are they shadows of things that May be, only?'

Still the Ghost pointed downward to the grave by which it stood.

'Men's courses will foreshadow certain ends, to which, if persevered in, they must lead,' said Scrooge. 'But if the courses be departed from, the ends will change. Say it is thus with what you show me?'

The Spirit was immovable as ever.

Scrooge crept towards it, trembling as he went; and following the finger, read upon the stone of the neglected grave his own name, EBENEZER SCROOGE.

'Am *I* that man who lay upon the bed?' he cried, upon his knees.

The finger pointed from the grave to him, and back again.

'No, Spirit! Oh no, no!'

The finger still was there.

'Spirit!' he cried, tight clutching at its robe, 'hear me! I am not the man I was. I will not be the man I must have been but for this intercourse. Why show me this, if I am past all hope!'

For the first time the hand appeared to shake.

'Good Spirit,' he pursued, as down upon the ground he fell before it: 'Your nature intercedes for

me, and pities me.   Assure me that I yet may change
these shadows you have shown me, by an altered life!'

The kind hand trembled.

'I will honour Christmas in my heart, and try to
keep it all the year.   I will live in the Past, the
Present, and the Future.   The Spirits of all Three
shall strive within me.   I will not shut out the lessons
that they teach.   Oh, tell me I may sponge away the
writing on this stone!'

In his agony, he caught the spectral hand.   It
sought to free itself, but he was strong in his entreaty,
and detained it.   The Spirit, stronger yet, repulsed
him.

Holding up his hands in a last prayer to have his
fate reversed, he saw an alteration in the Phantom's
hood and dress.   It shrunk, collapsed, and dwindled
down into a bedpost.

Stave Five

THE END OF IT

Yes! and the bedpost was his own.   The bed was his
own, the room was his own.   Best and happiest of all,
the Time before him was his own, to make amends in!

'I will live in the Past, the Present, and the
Future!' Scrooge repeated, as he scrambled out of
bed.   'The Spirits of all Three shall strive within
me.   Oh Jacob Marley!   Heaven, and the Christmas Time be praised for this!   I say it on my knees,
old Jacob, on my knees!'

He was so fluttered and so glowing with his good
intentions, that his broken voice would scarcely
answer to his call.   He had been sobbing violently in

his conflict with the Spirit, and his face was wet with tears.

'They are not torn down,' cried Scrooge, folding one of his bed-curtains in his arms, 'they are not torn down, rings and all. They are here—I am here—the shadows of the things that would have been, may be dispelled. They will be. I know they will!'

His hands were busy with his garments all this time; turning them inside out, putting them on upside down, tearing them, mislaying them, making them parties to every kind of extravagance.

'I don't know what to do!' cried Scrooge, laughing and crying in the same breath; and making a perfect Laocoön of himself with his stockings. 'I am as light as a feather, I am as happy as an angel, I am as merry as a schoolboy. I am as giddy as a drunken man. A merry Christmas to everybody! A happy New Year to all the world. Hallo here! Whoop! Hallo!'

He had frisked into the sitting-room, and was now standing there: perfectly winded.

'There's the saucepan that the gruel was in!' cried Scrooge, starting off again, and going round the fireplace. 'There's the door, by which the Ghost of Jacob Marley entered! There's the corner where the Ghost of Christmas Present, sat! There's the window where I saw the wandering Spirits! It's all right, it's all true, it all happened. Ha, ha, ha!'

Really, for a man who had been out of practice for so many years, it was a splendid laugh, a most illustrious laugh. The father of a long, long line of brilliant laughs!

'I don't know what day of the month it is!' said Scrooge. 'I don't know how long I've been among the Spirits. I don't know anything. I'm quite a

baby. Never mind. I don't care. I'd rather be a baby. Hallo! Whoop! Hallo here!'

He was checked in his transports by the churches ringing out the lustiest peals he had ever heard. Clash, clang, hammer; ding, dong, bell. Bell, dong, ding; hammer, clang, clash! Oh, glorious, glorious!

Running to the window, he opened it and put out his head. No fog, no mist; clear, bright, jovial, stirring, cold; cold, piping for the blood to dance to; Golden sunlight; Heavenly sky; sweet fresh air; merry bells. Oh, glorious. Glorious!

'What's to-day?' cried Scrooge, calling downward to a boy in Sunday clothes, who perhaps had loitered in to look about him.

'Eh?' returned the boy, with all his might of wonder.

'What's to-day, my fine fellow?' said Scrooge.

'To-day!' replied the boy. 'Why, CHRISTMAS DAY.'

'It's Christmas Day!' said Scrooge to himself. 'I haven't missed it. The Spirits have done it all in one night. They can do anything they like. Of course they can. Of course they can. Hallo, my fine fellow!'

'Hallo!' returned the boy.

'Do you know the Poulterer's, in the next street but one, at the corner?' Scrooge inquired.

'I should hope I did,' replied the lad.

'An intelligent boy!' said Scrooge. 'A remarkable boy! Do you know whether they've sold the prize Turkey that was hanging up there?—Not the little prize Turkey: the big one?'

'What, the one as big as me?' returned the boy.

'What a delightful boy!' said Scrooge. 'It's a pleasure to talk to him. Yes, my buck!'

'It's hanging there now,' replied the boy.

'Is it?' said Scrooge.   'Go and buy it.'

'Walk-ER!' exclaimed the boy.

'No, no,' said Scrooge, 'I am in earnest.   Go and buy it, and tell 'em to bring it here, that I may give them the direction where to take it.   Come back with the man, and I 'll give you a shilling.   Come back with him in less than five minutes and I 'll give you half-a-crown!'

The boy was off like a shot.   He must have had a steady hand at a trigger who could have got a shot off half so fast.

'I 'll send it to Bob Cratchit's!' whispered Scrooge, rubbing his hands, and splitting with a laugh.   'He shan't know who sends it.   It 's twice the size of Tiny Tim.   Joe Miller never made such a joke as sending it to Bob's will be!'

The hand in which he wrote the address was not a steady one, but write it he did, somehow, and went downstairs to open the street door, ready for the coming of the poulterer's man.   As he stood there, waiting his arrival, the knocker caught his eye.

'I shall love it, as long as I live!' cried Scrooge, patting it with his hand.   'I scarcely ever looked at it before.   What an honest expression it has in its face!   It 's a wonderful knocker!—Here 's the Turkey.   Hallo!   Whoop!   How are you!   Merry Christmas!'

It *was* a Turkey!   He could never have stood upon his legs, that bird.   He would have snapped 'em short off in a minute, like sticks of sealing-wax.

'Why, it 's impossible to carry that to Camden Town,' said Scrooge.   'You must have a cab.'

The chuckle with which he said this, and the chuckle with which he paid for the Turkey, and the chuckle with which he paid for the cab, and the chuckle with which he recompensed the boy, were only to be ex-

ceeded by the chuckle with which he sat down breathless in his chair again, and chuckled till he cried.

Shaving was not an easy task, for his hand continued to shake very much; and shaving requires attention, even when you don't dance while you are at it. But if he had cut the end of his nose off, he would have put a piece of sticking-plaister over it, and been quite satisfied.

He dressed himself 'all in his best,' and at last got out into the streets. The people were by this time pouring forth, as he had seen them with the Ghost of Christmas Present; and walking with his hands behind him, Scrooge regarded every one with a delighted smile. He looked so irresistibly pleasant, in a word, that three or four good-humoured fellows said, 'Good-morning, sir! A merry Christmas to you!' And Scrooge said often afterwards, that of all the blithe sounds he had ever heard, those were the blithest in his ears.

He had not gone far, when coming on towards him he beheld the portly gentleman, who had walked into his counting-house the day before, and said, 'Scrooge and Marley's, I believe?' It sent a pang across his heart to think how this old gentleman would look upon him when they met; but he knew what path lay straight before him, and he took it.

'My dear sir,' said Scrooge, quickening his pace, and taking the old gentleman by both his hands. 'How do you do? I hope you succeeded yesterday. It was very kind of you. A merry Christmas to you, sir!'

'Mr. Scrooge?'

'Yes,' said Scrooge. 'That is my name, and I fear it may not be pleasant to you. Allow me to ask your pardon. And will you have the goodness'—here Scrooge whispered in his ear.

'Lord bless me!' cried the gentleman, as if his breath were taken away. 'My dear Mr. Scrooge, are you serious?'

'If you please,' said Scrooge. 'Not a farthing less. A great many back-payments are included in it, I assure you. Will you do me that favour?'

'My dear sir,' said the other, shaking hands with him. 'I don't know what to say to such munifi—'

'Don't say anything, please,' retorted Scrooge. 'Come and see me. Will you come and see me?'

'I will!' cried the old gentleman. And it was clear he meant to do it.

'Thank 'ee,' said Scrooge. 'I am much obliged to you. I thank you fifty times. Bless you!'

He went to church, and walked about the streets, and watched the people hurrying to and fro, and patted children on the head, and questioned beggars, and looked down into the kitchens of houses, and up to the windows, and found that everything could yield him pleasure. He had never dreamed that any walk —that anything—could give him so much happiness. In the afternoon he turned his steps towards his nephew's house.

He passed the door a dozen times, before he had the courage to go up and knock. But he made a dash, and did it:

'Is your master at home, my dear? said Scrooge to the girl. Nice girl! Very.

'Yes, sir.'

'Where is he, my love?' said Scrooge.

'He's in the dining-room, sir, along with mistress. I'll show you upstairs, if you please.'

'Thank 'ee. He knows me,' said Scrooge, with his hand already on the dining-room lock. 'I'll go in here, my dear.'

He turned it gently, and sidled his face in round

the door. They were looking at the table (which was spread out in great array); for these young housekeepers are always nervous on such points, and like to see that everything is right.

'Fred!' said Scrooge.

Dear heart alive, how his niece by marriage started! Scrooge had forgotten, for the moment, about her sitting in the corner with the footstool, or he wouldn't have done it, on any account.

'Why bless my soul!' cried Fred, 'who's that?'

'It's I. Your uncle Scrooge. I have come to dinner. Will you let me in, Fred?'

Let him in! It is a mercy he didn't shake his arm off. He was at home in five minutes. Nothing could be heartier. His niece looked just the same. So did Topper when *he* came. So did the plump sister, when *she* came. So did every one when *they* came. Wonderful party, wonderful games, wonderful unanimity, won-der-ful happiness!

But he was early at the office next morning. Oh, he was early there. If he could only be there first, and catch Bob Cratchit coming late! That was the thing he had set his heart upon.

And he did it; yes he did! The clock struck nine. No Bob. A quarter past. No Bob. He was full eighteen minutes and a half behind his time. Scrooge sat with his door wide open, that he might see him come into the Tank.

His hat was off, before he opened the door; his comforter too. He was on his stool in a jiffy; driving away with his pen, as if he were trying to overtake nine o'clock.

'Hallo!' growled Scrooge, in his accustomed voice, as near as he could feign it. 'What do you mean by coming here at this time of day?'

'I am very sorry, sir,' said Bob. 'I *am* behind my time.'

'You are?' repeated Scrooge. 'Yes. I think you are. Step this way, sir, if you please.'

'It 's only once a year, sir,' pleaded Bob, appearing from the Tank. 'It shall not be repeated. I was making rather merry yesterday, sir.'

'Now, I 'll tell you what, my friend,' said Scrooge, 'I am not going to stand this sort of thing any longer. And therefore,' he continued, leaping from his stool, and giving Bob such a dig in the waistcoat that he staggered back into the Tank again: 'and therefore I am about to raise your salary!'

Bob trembled, and got a little nearer to the ruler. He had a momentary idea of knocking Scrooge down with it, holding him, and calling to the people in the court for help and a strait-waistcoat.

'A merry Christmas, Bob!' said Scrooge, with an earnestness that could not be mistaken, as he clapped him on the back. 'A merrier Christmas, Bob, my good fellow, than I have given you for many a year! I 'll raise your salary, and endeavour to assist your struggling family, and we will discuss your affairs this very afternoon, over a Christmas bowl of smoking bishop, Bob! Make up the fires, and buy another coal-scuttle before you dot another i, Bob Cratchit!'

Scrooge was better than his word. He did it all, and infinitely more; and to Tiny Tim, who did NOT die, he was a second father. He became as good a friend, as good a master, and as good a man, as the good old city knew, or any other good old city, town, or borough, in the good old world. Some people laughed to see the alteration in him, but he let them laugh, and little heeded them; for he was wise enough

to know that nothing ever happened on this globe, for good, at which some people did not have their fill of laughter in the outset; and knowing that such as these would be blind anyway, he thought it quite as well that they should wrinkle up their eyes in grins, as have the malady in less attractive forms. His own heart laughed: and that was quite enough for him.

He had no further intercourse with Spirits, but lived upon the Total Abstinence Principle, ever afterwards; and it was always said of him, that he knew how to keep Christmas well, if any man alive possessed the knowledge. May that be truly said of us, and all of us! And so, as Tiny Tim observed, God bless Us, Every One!

THE CHIMES

A GOBLIN STORY OF
SOME BELLS THAT RANG
AN OLD YEAR OUT AND
A NEW YEAR IN

THE CHIMES

First Quarter

THERE are not many people—and as it is desirable
that a story-teller and a story-reader should establish
a mutual understanding as soon as possible, I beg it
to be noticed that I confine this observation neither to
young people nor to little people, but extend it
to all conditions of people: little and big, young
and old: yet growing up, or already growing
down again—there are not, I say, many people who
would care to sleep in a church. I don't mean at
sermon-time in warm weather (when the thing has
actually been done, once or twice), but in the night,
and alone. A great multitude of persons will be
violently astonished, I know, by this position, in the
broad bold Day. But it applies to Night. It must
be argued by night, and I will undertake to maintain
it successfully on any gusty winter's night appointed
for the purpose, with any one opponent chosen from
the rest, who will meet me singly in an old churchyard, before an old church-door; and will previously
empower me to lock him in, if needful to his satisfaction, until morning.

For the night-wind has a dismal trick of wandering round and round a building of that sort, and
moaning as it goes; and of trying, with its unseen
hand, the windows and the doors; and seeking out
some crevices by which to enter. And when it has
got in; as one not finding what it seeks, whatever that

103

may be, it wails and howls to issue forth again: and not content with stalking through the aisles, and gliding round and round the pillars, and tempting the deep organ, soars up to the roof, and strives to rend the rafters: then flings itself despairingly upon the stones below, and passes, muttering, into the vaults. Anon, it comes up stealthily, and creeps along the walls, seeming to read, in whispers, the Inscriptions sacred to the Dead. At some of these, it breaks out shrilly, as with laughter; and at others, moans and cries as if it were lamenting. It has a ghostly sound too, lingering within the altar; where it seems to chaunt, in its wild way, of Wrong and Murder done, and false Gods worshipped, in defiance of the Tables of the Law, which look so fair and smooth, but are so flawed and broken. Ugh! Heaven preserve us, sitting snugly round the fire! It has an awful voice, that wind at Midnight, singing in a church!

But, high up in the steeple! There the foul blast roars and whistles! High up in the steeple, where it is free to come and go through many an airy arch and loophole, and to twist and twine itself about the giddy stair, and twirl the groaning weathercock, and make the very tower shake and shiver! High up in the steeple, where the belfry is, and iron rails are ragged with rust, and sheets of lead and copper, shrivelled by the changing weather, crackle and heave beneath the unaccustomed tread; and birds stuff shabby nests into corners of old oaken joists and beams; and dust grows old and grey; and speckled spiders, indolent and fat with long security, swing idly to and fro in the vibration of the bells, and never loose their hold upon their thread-spun castles in the air, or climb up sailor-like in quick alarm, or drop upon the ground and ply a score of nimble legs to save one life! High up in the steeple of an old

church, far above the light and murmur of the town and far below the flying clouds that shadow it, is the wild and dreary place at night: and high up in the steeple of an old church, dwelt the Chimes I tell of.

They were old Chimes, trust me. Centuries ago, these Bells had been baptized by bishops: so many centuries ago, that the register of their baptism was lost long, long before the memory of man, and no one knew their names. They had had their Godfathers and Godmothers, these Bells (for my own part, by the way, I would rather incur the responsibility of being Godfather to a Bell than a Boy), and had their silver mugs no doubt, besides. But Time had mowed down their sponsors, and Henry the Eighth had melted down their mugs; and they now hung, name-less and mugless, in the church-tower.

Not speechless, though. Far from it. They had clear, loud, lusty, sounding voices, had these Bells; and far and wide they might be heard upon the wind. Much too sturdy Chimes were they, to be dependent on the pleasure of the wind, moreover; for, fighting gallantly against it when it took an adverse whim, they would pour their cheerful notes into a listening ear right royally; and bent on being heard, on stormy nights, by some poor mother watching a sick child, or some lone wife whose husband was at sea, they had been sometimes known to beat a blustering Nor'-Wester; aye, 'all to fits,' as Toby Veck said;—for though they chose to call him Trotty Veck, his name was Toby, and nobody could make it anything else either (except Tobias) without a special act of parlia-ment; he having been as lawfully christened in his day as the Bells had been in theirs, though with not quite so much of solemnity or public rejoicing.

For my part, I confess myself of Toby Veck's belief, for I am sure he had opportunities enough of

forming a correct one. And whatever Toby Veck said, I say. And I take my stand by Toby Veck, although he *did* stand all day long (and weary work it was) just outside the church-door. In fact he was a ticket-porter, Toby Veck, and waited there for jobs.

And a breezy, goose-skinned, blue-nosed, red-eyed, stony-toed, tooth-chattering place it was, to wait in, in the winter-time, as Toby Veck well knew. The wind came tearing round the corner—especially the east wind—as if it had sallied forth, express, from the confines of the earth, to have a blow at Toby. And oftentimes it seemed to come upon him sooner than it had expected, for bouncing round the corner, and passing Toby, it would suddenly wheel round again, as if it cried 'Why, here he is!' Incontinently his little white apron would be caught up over his head like a naughty boy's garments, and his feeble little cane would be seen to wrestle and struggle unavailingly in his hand, and his legs would undergo tremendous agitation, and Toby himself all aslant, and facing now in this direction, now in that, would be so banged and buffeted, and touzled, and worried, and hustled, and lifted off his feet, as to render it a state of things but one degree removed from a positive miracle, that he wasn't carried up bodily into the air as a colony of frogs or snails or other very portable creatures sometimes are, and rained down again, to the great astonishment of the natives, on some strange corner of the world where ticket-porters are unknown.

But, windy weather, in spite of its using him so roughly, was, after all, a sort of holiday for Toby. That's the fact. He didn't seem to wait so long for sixpence in the wind, as at other times; the having to fight with that boisterous element took off his attention, and quite freshened him up, when he was

getting hungry and low-spirited. A hard frost too, or a fall of snow, was an Event; and it seemed to do him good, somehow or other—it would have been hard to say in what respect though, Toby! So wind and frost and snow, and perhaps a good stiff storm of hail, were Toby Veck's red-letter days.

Wet weather was the worst; the cold, damp, clammy wet, that wrapped him up like a moist great-coat—the only kind of great-coat Toby owned, or could have added to his comfort by dispensing with. Wet days, when the rain came slowly, thickly, obstinately down; when the streets's throat, like his own, was choked with mist; when smoking umbrellas passed and re-passed, spinning round and round like so many teetotums, as they knocked against each other on the crowded footway, throwing off a little whirlpool of uncomfortable sprinklings; when gutters brawled and waterspouts were full and noisy; when the wet from the projecting stones and ledges of the church fell drip, drip, drip, on Toby, making the wisp of straw on which he stood mere mud in no time; those were the days that tried him. Then indeed, you might see Toby looking anxiously out from his shelter in an angle of the church wall— such a meagre shelter that in summer time it never cast a shadow thicker than a good-sized walking-stick upon the sunny pavement—with a disconsolate and lengthened face. But coming out, a minute afterwards, to warm himself by exercise, and trotting up and down some dozen times, he would brighten even then, and go back more brightly to his niche.

They called him Trotty from his pace, which meant speed if it didn't make it. He could have Walked faster perhaps; most likely; but rob him of his trot, and Toby would have taken to his bed and died. It bespattered him with mud in dirty weather;

it cost him a world of trouble; he could have walked with infinitely greater ease; but that was one reason for his clinging to it so tenaciously. A weak, small, spare old man, he was a very Hercules, this Toby, in his good intentions. He loved to earn his money. He delighted to believe—Toby was very poor, and couldn't well afford to part with a delight—that he was worth his salt. With a shilling or an eighteen-penny message or small parcel in hand, his courage, always high, rose higher. As he trotted on, he would call out to fast Postmen ahead of him, to get out of the way; devoutly believing that in the natural course of things he must inevitably overtake and run them down; and he had perfect faith—not often tested—in his being able to carry anything that man could lift.

Thus, even when he came out of his nook to warm himself on a wet day, Toby trotted. Making, with his leaky shoes, a crooked line of slushy footprints in the mire; and blowing on his chilly hands and rubbing them against each other, poorly defended from the searching cold by threadbare mufflers of grey worsted, with a private apartment only for the thumb, and a common room or tap for the rest of the fingers; Toby, with his knees bent and his cane beneath his arm, still trotted. Falling out into the road to look up at the belfry when the Chimes resounded, Toby trotted still.

He made this last excursion several times a day, for they were company to him; and when he heard their voices, he had an interest in glancing at their lodging-place, and thinking how they were moved, and what hammers beat upon them. Perhaps he was the more curious about these Bells, because there were points of resemblance between themselves and him. They hung there, in all weathers, with the wind and

rain driving in upon them; facing only the outsides
of all those houses; never getting any nearer to the
blazing fires that gleamed and shone upon the windows, or came puffing out of the chimney tops; and
incapable of participation in any of the good things
that were constantly being handed, through the street
doors and the area railings, to prodigious cooks.
Faces came and went at many windows: sometimes
pretty faces, youthful faces, pleasant faces: sometimes the reverse: but Toby knew no more (though
he often speculated on these trifles, standing idle in the
streets) whence they came, or where they went, or
whether, when the lips moved, one kind word was said
of him in all the year, than did the Chimes themselves.

Toby was not a casuist—that he knew of, at least—
and I don't mean to say that when he began to take
to the Bells, and to knit up his first rough acquaintance with them into something of a closer and more
delicate woof, he passed through these considerations
one by one, or held any formal review or great field-
day in his thoughts. But what I mean to say, and
do say is, that as the functions of Toby's body, his
digestive organs for example, did of their own cunning, and by a great many operations of which he
was altogether ignorant, and the knowledge of which
would have astonished him very much, arrive at a certain end; so his mental faculties, without his privity
or concurrence, set all these wheels and springs in
motion, with a thousand others, when they worked to
bring about his liking for the Bells.

And though I had said his love, I would not have
recalled the word, though it would scarcely have expressed his complicated feeling. For, being but a
simple man, he invested them with a strange and
solemn character. They were so mysterious, often
heard and never seen; so high up, so far off, so full of

such a deep strong melody, that he regarded them with a species of awe; and sometimes when he looked up at the dark arched windows in the tower, he half expected to be beckoned to by something which was not a Bell, and yet was what he had heard so often sounding in the Chimes.   For all this, Toby scouted with indignation a certain flying rumour that the Chimes were haunted, as implying the possibility of their being connected with any Evil thing.   In short, they were very often in his ears, and very often in his thoughts, but always in his good opinion; and he very often got such a crick in his neck by staring with his mouth wide open, at the steeple where they hung, that he was fain to take an extra trot or two, after-wards, to cure it.

The very thing he was in the act of doing one cold day, when the last drowsy sound of Twelve o'clock, just struck, was humming like a melodious monster of a Bee, and not by any means a busy bee, all through the steeple!

'Dinner-time, eh!' said Toby, trotting up and down before the church.   'Ah!'

Toby's nose was very red, and his eyelids were very red, and he winked very much, and his shoulders were very near his ears, and his legs were very stiff, and altogether he was evidently a long way upon the frosty side of cool.

'Dinner-time, eh!' repeated Toby, using his right-hand muffler like an infantine boxing-glove, and punishing his chest for being cold.   'Ah-h-h-h!'

He took a silent trot, after that, for a minute or two.

'There's nothing,' said Toby, breaking forth afresh—but here he stopped short in his trot, and with a face of great interest and some alarm, felt his nose carefully all the way up.   It was but a little way

(not being much of a nose) and he had soon finished.

'I thought it was gone,' said Toby, trotting off again. 'It's all right, however. I am sure I couldn't blame it if it was to go. It has a precious hard service of it in the bitter weather, and precious little to look forward to; for I don't take snuff myself. It's a good deal tried, poor creetur, at the best of times; for when it *does* get hold of a pleasant whiff or so (which an't too often), it's generally from somebody else's dinner, a-coming home from the baker's.'

The reflection reminded him of that other reflection, which he had left unfinished.

'There's nothing,' said Toby, 'more regular in its coming round than dinner-time, and nothing less regular in its coming round than dinner. That's the great difference between 'em. It's took me a long time to find it out. I wonder whether it would be worth any gentleman's while, now, to buy that observation for the Papers; or the Parliament!'

Toby was only joking, for he gravely shook his head in self-depreciation.

'Why! Lord!' said Toby. 'The Papers is full of obserwations as it is; and so's the Parliament. Here's last week's paper, now'; taking a very dirty one from his pocket, and holding it from him at arm's length; 'full of obserwations! Full of obserwations! I like to know the news as well as any man,' said Toby, slowly; folding it a little smaller, and putting it in his pocket again: but it almost goes against the grain with me to read a paper now. It frightens me almost. I don't know what we poor people are coming to. Lord send we may be coming to something better in the New Year nigh upon us!'

'Why, father, father!' said a pleasant voice, hard by.

But Toby, not hearing it, continued to trot backwards and forwards; musing as he went, and talking
to himself.

'It seems as if we can't go right, or do right, or be
righted,' said Toby. 'I hadn't much schooling, myself, when I was young; and I can't make out whether
we have any business on the face of the earth, or not.
Sometimes I think we must have—a little; and sometimes I think we must be intruding. I get so puzzled
sometimes that I am not even able to make up my
mind whether there is any good at all in us, or whether
we are born bad. We seem to be dreadful things;
we seem to give a deal of trouble; we are always being
complained of and guarded against. One way or
other, we fill the papers. Talk of a New Year!'
said Toby, mournfully. 'I can bear up as well as
another man at most times; better than a good many,
for I am as strong as a lion, and all men an't; but
supposing it should really be that we have no right
to a New Year—supposing we really *are* intruding—'

'Why, father, father!' said the pleasant voice again.

Toby heard it this time; started; stopped; and
shortening his sight, which had been directed a long
way off as seeking for enlightenment in the very
heart of the approaching year, found himself face
to face with his own child, and looking close into
her eyes.

Bright eyes they were. Eyes that would bear a
world of looking in, before their depth was fathomed.
Dark eyes, that reflected back the eyes which searched
them; not flashingly, or at the owner's will, but with
a clear, calm, honest, patient radiance, claiming kindred with that light which Heaven called into being.
Eyes that were beautiful and true, and beaming with
Hope. With Hope so young and fresh; with Hope

so buoyant, vigorous, and bright, despite the twenty
years of work and poverty on which they had looked;
that they became a voice to Trotty Veck, and said:
'I think we have some business here—a little!'

Trotty kissed the lips belonging to the eyes, and
squeezed the blooming face between his hands.

'Why, Pet,' said Trotty. 'What's to do? I
didn't expect you to-day, Meg.'

'Neither did I expect to come, father,' cried the
girl, nodding her head and smiling as she spoke.
'But here I am! And not alone; not alone!'

'Why you don't mean to say,' observed Trotty,
looking curiously at a covered basket which she carried
in her hand, 'that you—'

'Smell it, father dear,' said Meg. 'Only smell it!'

Trotty was going to lift up the cover at once, in a
great hurry, when she gaily interposed her hand.

'No, no, no,' said Meg, with the glee of a child.
'Lengthen it out a little. Let me just lift up the
corner; just the lit-tle ti-ny cor-ner, you know,' said
Meg, suiting the action to the word with the utmost
gentleness, and speaking very softly, as if she were
afraid of being overheard by something inside the
basket; 'there. Now. What's that?'

Toby took the shortest possible sniff at the edge of
the basket, and cried out in a rapture:

'Why, it's hot!'

'It's burning hot!' cried Meg. 'Ha, ha, ha! It's
scalding hot!'

'Ha, ha, ha!' roared Toby, with a sort of kick.
'It's scalding hot.'

'But what is it, father?' said Meg. 'Come. You
haven't guessed what it is. And you must guess
what it is. I can't think of taking it out, till you
guess what it is. Don't be in such a hurry! Wait a
minute! A little bit more of the cover. Now guess!'

Meg was in a perfect fright lest he should guess right too soon; shrinking away, as she held the basket towards him; curling up her pretty shoulders; stopping her ear with her hand, as if by so doing she could keep the right word out of Toby's lips; and laughing softly the whole time.

Meanwhile Toby, putting a hand on each knee, bent down his nose to the basket, and took a long inspiration at the lid; the grin upon his withered face expanding in the process, as if he were inhaling laughing gas.

'Ah! It's very nice,' said Toby. 'It an't—I suppose it an't Polonies?'

'No, no, no!' cried Meg, delighted. 'Nothing like Polonies!'

'No,' said Toby, after another sniff. 'It's—it's mellower than Polonies. It's very nice. It improves every moment. It's too decided for Trotters. An't it?'

Meg was in an ecstasy. He could not have gone wider of the mark than Trotters—except Polonies.

'Liver?' said Toby, communing with himself. 'No. There's a mildness about it that don't answer to liver. Pettitoes? No. It an't faint enough for pettitoes. It wants the stringiness of Cocks' heads. And I know it an't sausages. I'll tell you what it is. It's chitterlings!'

'No, it an't!' cried Meg, in a burst of delight. 'No, it an't!'

'Why, what am I a-thinking of!' said Toby, suddenly recovering a position as near the perpendicular as it was possible for him to assume. 'I shall forget my own name next. It's tripe!'

Tripe it was; and Meg, in high joy, protested he should say, in half a minute more, it was the best tripe ever stewed.

'And so,' said Meg, busying herself exultingly with the basket, 'I 'll lay the cloth at once, father; for I have brought the tripe in a basin, and tied the basin up in a pocket-handkerchief; and if I like to be proud for once, and spread that for a cloth, and call it a cloth, there 's no law to prevent me; is there, father?'

'Not that I know of, my dear,' said Toby. 'But they 're always a-bringing up some new law or other.'

'And according to what I was reading you in the paper the other day, father; what the Judge said, you know; we poor people are supposed to know them all. Ha, ha! What a mistake! My goodness me, how clever they think us!'

'Yes, my dear,' cried Trotty; 'and they 'd be very fond of any one of us that *did* know 'em all. He 'd grow fat upon the work he 'd get, that man, and be popular with the gentle-folks in his neighbourhood. Very much so!'

'He 'd eat his dinner with an appetite, whoever he was, if it smelt like this,' said Meg, cheerfully. 'Make haste, for there 's a hot potato besides, and half a pint of fresh-drawn beer in a bottle. Where will you dine, father? On the Post, or on the Steps? Dear, dear, how grand we are. Two places to choose from!'

'The steps to-day, my Pet,' said Trotty. 'Steps in dry weather. Post in wet. There 's a greater conveniency in the steps at all times, because of the sitting down; but they 're rheumatic in the damp.'

'Then here,' said Meg, clapping her hands, after a moment's bustle; 'here it is, all ready! And beautiful it looks! Come, father. Come!'

Since his discovery of the contents of the basket, Trotty had been standing looking at her—and had been speaking too—in an abstracted manner, which showed that though she was the object of his thoughts

and eyes, to the exclusion even of tripe, he neither saw
nor thought about her as she was at that moment, but
had before him some imaginary rough sketch or
drama of her future life. Roused, now, by her cheerful summons, he shook off a melancholy shake of the
head which was just coming upon him, and trotted to
her side. As he was stooping to sit down, the Chimes
rang.

'Amen!' said Trotty, pulling off his hat and looking up towards them.

'Amen to the Bells, father?' cried Meg.

'They broke in like a grace, my dear,' said Trotty,
taking his seat. 'They 'd say a good one, I am sure,
if they could. Many 's the kind thing they say to
me.'

'The Bells do, father!' laughed Meg, as she
set the basin, and a knife and fork, before him.
'Well!'

'Seem to, my Pet,' said Trotty, falling to with
great vigour. 'And where 's the difference? If I
hear 'em, what does it matter whether they speak it
or not? Why bless you, my dear,' said Toby, pointing at the tower with his fork, and becoming more
animated under the influence of dinner, 'how often
have I heard them bells say "Toby Veck, Toby Veck,
keep a good heart, Toby! Toby Veck, Toby Veck,
keep a good heart, Toby!" A million times?
More!'

'Well, I never!' cried Meg.

She had, though—over and over again. For it
was Toby's constant topic.

'When things is very bad,' said Trotty; 'very bad
indeed, I mean; almost at the worst; then it 's "Toby
Veck, Toby Veck, job coming soon, Toby! Toby
Veck, Toby Veck, job coming soon, Toby!" That
way.'

'And it comes—at last, father,' said Meg, with a touch of sadness in her pleasant voice.

'Always,' answered the unconscious Toby. 'Never fails.'

While this discourse was holding, Trotty made no pause in his attack upon the savoury meat before him, but cut and ate, and cut and drank, and cut and chewed, and dodged about, from tripe to hot potato, and from hot potato back again to tripe, with an unctuous and unflagging relish. But happening now to look all round the street—in case anybody should be beckoning from any door or window, for a porter—his eyes, in coming back again, encountered Meg: sitting opposite to him, with her arms folded: and only busy in watching his progress with a smile of happiness.

'Why, Lord forgive me!' said Trotty, dropping his knife and fork. 'My dove! Meg! why didn't you tell me what a beast I was?'

'Father?'

'Sitting here,' said Trotty, in penitent explanation, 'cramming, and stuffing, and gorging myself; and you before me there, never so much as breaking your precious fast, nor wanting to, when—'

'But I have broken it, father,' interposed his daughter, laughing, 'all to bits. I have had my dinner.'

'Nonsense,' said Trotty. 'Two dinners in one day! It an't possible! You might as well tell me that two New Year's days will come together, or that I have had a gold head all my life, and never changed it.'

'I have had my dinner, father, for all that,' said Meg, coming nearer to him. 'And if you'll go on with yours, I'll tell you how and where; and how your dinner came to be bought; and—and something else besides.'

Toby still appeared incredulous; but she looked into his face with her clear eyes, and laying her hand upon his shoulder, motioned him to go on while the meat was hot. So Trotty took up his knife and fork again, and went to work. But much more slowly than before, and shaking his head, as if he were not at all pleased with himself.

'I had my dinner, father,' said Meg, after a little hesitation, 'with—with Richard. His dinner-time was early; and as he brought his dinner with him when he came to see me, we—we had it together, father.'

Trotty took a little beer, and smacked his lips. Then he said 'Oh!'—because she waited.

'And Richard says, father—' Meg resumed. Then stopped.

'What does Richard say, Meg?' asked Toby.

'Richard says, father—' Another stoppage.

'Richard 's a long time saying it,' said Toby.

'He says then, father,' Meg continued, lifting up her eyes at last, and speaking in a tremble, but quite plainly; 'another year is nearly gone, and where is the use of waiting on from year to year, when it is so unlikely we shall ever be better off than we are now? He says we are poor now, father, and we shall be poor then, but we are young now, and years will make us old before we know it. He says that if we wait: people in our condition: until we see our way quite clearly, the way will be a narrow one indeed— the common way—the Grave, father.'

A bolder man than Trotty Veck must needs have drawn upon his boldness largely, to deny it. Trotty held his peace.

'And how hard, father, to grow old, and die, and think we might have cheered and helped each other! How hard in all our lives to love each other; and to

grieve, apart, to see each other working, changing, growing old and grey. Even if I got the better of it, and forgot him (which I never could), oh father dear, how hard to have a heart so full as mine is now, and live to have it slowly drained out every drop, without the recollection of one happy moment of a woman's life, to stay behind and comfort me, and make me better!'

Trotty sat quite still. Meg dried her eyes, and said more gaily: that is to say, with here a laugh, and there a sob, and here a laugh and sob together:

'So Richard says, father; as his work was yesterday made certain for some time to come, and as I love him, and have loved him full three years—ah! longer than that, if he knew it!—will I marry him on New Year's Day; the best and happiest day, he says, in the whole year, and one that is almost sure to bring good fortune with it. 'It's a short notice, father —isn't it?—but I haven't my fortune to be settled, or my wedding dresses to be made, like the great ladies, father, have I? And he said so much, and said it in his way; so strong and earnest, and all the time so kind and gentle; that I said I'd come and talk to you, father. And as they paid the money for that work of mine this morning (unexpectedly, I am sure!) and as you have fared very poorly for a whole week, and as I couldn't help wishing there should be something to make this day a sort of holiday to you as well as a dear and happy day to me, father, I made a little treat and brought it to surprise you.'

'And see how he leaves it cooling on the step!' said another voice.

It was the voice of this same Richard, who had come upon them unobserved, and stood before the father and daughter; looking down upon them with

a face as glowing as the iron on which his stout sledge-hammer daily rung. A handsome, well-made, powerful youngster he was; with eyes that sparkled like the red-hot droppings from a furnace fire; black hair that curled about his swarthy temples rarely; and a smile—a smile that bore out Meg's eulogium on his style of conversation.

'See how he leaves it cooling on the step!' said Richard. 'Meg don't know what he likes. Not she!'

Trotty, all action and enthusiasm, immediately reached up his hand to Richard, and was going to address him in a great hurry, when the house-door opened without any warning, and a footman very nearly put his foot into the tripe.

'Out of the vays here, will you! You must always go and be a-settin' on our steps, must you! You can't go and give a turn to none of the neighbours never, can't you! *Will* you clear the road, or won't you?'

Strictly speaking, the last question was irrelevant, as they had already done it.

'What's the matter, what's the matter!' said the gentleman for whom the door was opened; coming out of the house at that kind of light-heavy pace —that peculiar compromise between a walk and a jog-trot—with which a gentleman upon the smooth down-hill of life, wearing creaking boots, a watch-chain, and clean linen, *may* come out of his house: not only without any abatement of his dignity, but with an expression of having important and wealthy engagements elsewhere. 'What's the matter! What's the matter!'

'You're always a-being begged, and prayed, upon your bended knees you are,' said the footman with great emphasis to Trotty Veck, 'to let our door-steps

be. Why don't you let 'em be? CAN'T you let 'em be?'

'There! That 'll do, that 'll do!' said the gentle-man. 'Halloa there! Porter!' beckoning with his head to Trotty Veck. 'Come here. What 's that? Your dinner?'

'Yes, sir,' said Trotty, leaving it behind him in a corner.

'Don't leave it there,' exclaimed the gentleman. 'Bring it here, bring it here. So! This is your dinner, is it?'

'Yes, sir,' repeated Trotty, looking with a fixed eye and a watery mouth, at the piece of tripe he had reserved for a last delicious tit-bit; which the gentleman was now turning over and over on the end of the fork.

Two other gentlemen had come out with him. One was a low-spirited gentleman of middle age, of a meagre habit, and a disconsolate face; who kept his hands continually in the pockets of his scanty pepper-and-salt trousers, very large and dog's-eared from that custom; and was not particularly well brushed or washed. The other, a full-sized, sleek, well-conditioned gentleman, in a blue coat with bright buttons, and a white cravat. This gentleman had a very red face, as if an undue proportion of the blood in his body were squeezed up into his head; which perhaps accounted for his having also the ap-pearance of being rather cold about the heart.

He who had Toby's meat upon the fork, called to the first one by the name of Filer; and they both drew near together. Mr. Filer being exceedingly short-sighted, was obliged to go so close to the remnant of Toby's dinner before he could make out what it was, that Toby's heart leaped up into his mouth. But Mr. Filer didn't eat it.

'This is a description of animal food, Alderman,' said Filer, making little punches in it, with a pencil-case, 'commonly known to the labouring population of this country, by the name of tripe.'

The Alderman laughed, and winked; for he was a merry fellow, Alderman Cute. Oh, and a sly fellow too! A knowing fellow. Up to everything. Not to be imposed upon. Deep in the people's hearts! He knew them, Cute did. I believe you!

'But who eats tripe?' said Mr. Filer, looking round. 'Tripe is without an exception the least economical, and the most wasteful article of consumption that the markets of this country can by possibility produce. The loss upon a pound of tripe has been found to be, in the boiling, seven-eighths of a fifth more than the loss upon a pound of any other animal substance whatever. Tripe is more expensive, properly understood, than the hothouse pine-apple. Taking into account the number of animals slaughtered yearly within the bills of mortality alone; and forming a low estimate of the quantity of tripe which the carcasses of those animals, reasonably well butchered, would yield; I find that the waste on that amount of tripe, if boiled, would victual a garrison of five hundred men for five months of thirty-one days each, and a February over. The Waste, the Waste!'

Trotty stood aghast, and his legs shook under him. He seemed to have starved a garrison of five hundred men with his own hand.

'Who eats tripe?' said Mr. Filer, warmly. 'Who eats tripe?'

Trotty made a miserable bow.

'You do, do you?' said Mr. Filer. 'Then I'll tell you something. You snatch your tripe, my friend, out of the mouths of widows and orphans.'

'I hope not, sir,' said Trotty, faintly. 'I'd sooner die of want!'

'Divide the amount of tripe before mentioned, Alderman,' said Mr. Filer, 'by the estimated number of existing widows and orphans, and the result will be one pennyweight of tripe to each. Not a grain is left for that man. Consequently, he's a robber.'

Trotty was so shocked, that it gave him no concern to see the Alderman finish the tripe himself. It was a relief to get rid of it, anyhow.

'And what do you say?' asked the Alderman, jocosely, of the red-faced gentleman in the blue coat. 'You have heard friend Filer. What do *you* say?'

'What's it possible to say?' returned the gentleman. 'What *is* to be said? Who can take any interest in a fellow like this,' meaning Trotty; 'in such degenerate times as these? Look at him! What an object! The good old times, the grand old times, the great old times! *Those* were the times for a bold peasantry, and all that sort of thing. Those were the times for every sort of thing, in fact. There's nothing now-a-days. Ah!' sighed the red-faced gentleman, 'The good old times, the good old times!'

The gentleman didn't specify what particular times he alluded to; nor did he say whether he objected to the present times, from a disinterested consciousness that they had done nothing very remarkable in producing himself.

'The good old times, the good old times,' repeated the gentleman. 'What times they were! They were the only times. It's of no use talking about any other times, or discussing what the people are in *these* times. You don't call these, times, do you? I don't. Look into Strutt's Costumes, and see what a Porter

used to be, in any of the good old English reigns.'

'He hadn't, in his very best circumstances, a shirt to his back, or a stocking to his foot; and there was scarcely a vegetable in all England for him to put into his mouth,' said Mr. Filer. 'I can prove it, by tables.'

But still the red-faced gentleman extolled the good old times, the grand old times, the great old times. No matter what anybody else said, he still went turning round and round in one set form of words concerning them; as a poor squirrel turns and turns in its revolving cage; touching the mechanism, and trick of which, it has probably quite as distinct perceptions, as ever this red-faced gentleman had of his deceased Millennium.

It is possible that poor Trotty's faith in these very vague Old Times was not entirely destroyed, for he felt vague enough, at that moment. One thing, however, was plain to him, in the midst of his distress; to wit, that however these gentlemen might differ in details, his misgivings of that morning, and of many other mornings, were well founded. 'No, no. We can't go right or do right,' thought Trotty in despair. 'There is no good in us. We are born bad!'

But Trotty had a father's heart within him; which had somehow got into his breast in spite of this decree; and he could not bear that Meg, in the blush of her brief joy, should have her fortune read by these wise gentlemen. 'God help her,' thought poor Trotty. 'She will know it soon enough.'

He anxiously signed, therefore, to the young smith, to take her away. But he was so busy, talking to her softly at a little distance, that he only became conscious of this desire, simultaneously with Alderman Cute. Now, the Alderman had not yet had his

say, but *he* was a philosopher, too—practical, though!
Oh, very practical—and, as he had no idea of losing
any portion of his audience, he cried 'Stop!'

'Now, you know,' said the Alderman, addressing
his two friends, with a self-complacent smile upon
his face which was habitual to him, 'I am a plain
man, and a practical man; and I go to work in a
plain practical way. That's my way. There is not
the least mystery or difficulty in dealing with this
sort of people if you only understand 'em, and can
talk to 'em in their own manner. Now, you Porter!
Don't you ever tell me, or anybody else, my friend,
that you haven't always enough to eat, and of the
best; because I know better. I have tasted your
tripe, you know, and you can't "chaff" me. You
understand what "chaff" means, eh? That's the
right word, isn't it? Ha, ha, ha! Lord bless you,'
said the Alderman, turning to his friends again, 'it's
the easiest thing on earth to deal with this sort of
people, if you understand 'em.'

Famous man for the common people, Alderman
Cute! Never out of temper with them! Easy,
affable, joking, knowing gentleman!

'You see, my friend,' pursued the Alderman,
'there's a great deal of nonsense talked about Want
—"hard up," you know; that's the phrase, isn't it?
ha! ha! ha!—and I intend to Put it Down. There's
a certain amount of cant in vogue about Starvation,
and I mean to Put it Down. That's all! Lord
bless you,' said the Alderman, turning to his friends
again, 'you may Put Down anything among this
sort of people, if you only know the way to set about
it.'

Trotty took Meg's hand and drew it through his
arm. He didn't seem to know what he was doing
though.

'Your daughter, eh?' said the Alderman, chucking her familiarly under the chin.

Always affable with the working classes, Alderman Cute! Knew what pleased them! Not a bit of pride!

'Where 's her mother?' asked that worthy gentleman.

'Dead,' said Toby. 'Her mother got up linen; and was called to Heaven when She was born.'

'Not to get up linen *there*, I suppose,' remarked the Alderman pleasantly.

Toby might or might not have been able to separate his wife in Heaven from her old pursuits. But query: If Mrs. Alderman Cute had gone to Heaven, would Mr. Alderman Cute have pictured her as holding any state or station there?

'And you 're making love to her, are you?' said Cute to the young smith.

'Yes,' returned Richard quickly, for he was nettled by the question. 'And we are going to be married on New Year's Day.'

'What do you mean!' cried Filer sharply. 'Married!'

'Why, yes, we 're thinking of it, Master,' said Richard. 'We 're rather in a hurry, you see, in case it should be Put Down first.'

'Ah!' cried Filer, with a groan. 'Put *that* down indeed, Alderman, and you 'll do something. Married! Married!! The ignorance of the first principles of political economy on the part of these people; their improvidence; their wickedness; is, by Heavens! enough to—Now look at that couple, will you!'

Well? They were worth looking at. And marriage seemed as reasonable and fair a deed as they need have in contemplation.

'A man may live to be as old as Methusaleh,' said

Mr. Filer, 'and may labour all his life for the benefit
of such people as those; and may heap up facts on
figures, facts on figures, facts on figures, mountains
high and dry; and he can no more hope to persuade
'em that they have no right or business to be married, than he can hope to persuade 'em that they
have no earthly right or business to be born. And
that we know they haven't. We reduced it to a
mathematical certainty long ago!'

Alderman Cute was mightily diverted, and laid his
right forefinger on the side of his nose, as much as
to say to both his friends, 'Observe me, will you!
Keep your eye on the practical man!'—and called
Meg to him.

'Come here, my girl!' said Alderman Cute.

The young blood of her lover had been mounting, wrathfully, within the last few minutes; and he
was indisposed to let her come. But, setting a
constraint upon himself, he came forward with a
stride as Meg approached, and stood beside her.
Trotty kept her hand within his arm still, but looked
from face to face as wildly as a sleeper in a dream.

'Now, I'm going to give you a word or two of
good advice, my girl,' said the Alderman, in his nice
easy way. 'It's my place to give advice, you know,
because I'm a Justice. You know I'm a Justice,
don't you?'

Meg timidly said, 'Yes.' But everybody knew
Alderman Cute was a Justice! Oh dear, so active
a Justice always! Who such a mote of brightness
in the public eye, as Cute!

'You are going to be married, you say,' pursued
the Alderman. 'Very unbecoming and indelicate in
one of your sex! But never mind that. After you
are married, you'll quarrel with your husband and
come to be a distressed wife. You may think not;

but you will, because I tell you so. Now, I give you fair warning, that I have made up my mind to Put distressed wives Down. So, don't be brought before me. You 'll have children—boys. Those boys will grow up bad, of course, and run wild in the streets, without shoes and stockings. Mind, my young friend! I 'll convict 'em summarily, every one, for I am determined to Put boys without shoes and stockings, Down. Perhaps your husband will die young (most likely) and leave you with a baby. Then you 'll be turned out of doors, and wander up and down the streets. Now, don't wander near me, my dear, for I am resolved to Put all wandering mothers Down. All young mothers, of all sorts and kinds, it 's my determination to Put Down. Don't think to plead illness as an excuse with me; or babies as an excuse with me; for all sick persons and young children (I hope you know the church-service, but I 'm afraid not) I am determined to Put Down. And if you attempt, desperately, and ungratefully, and impiously, and fraudulently attempt, to drown yourself, or hang yourself, I 'll have no pity for you, for I have made up my mind to Put all suicide Down! If there is one thing,' said the Alderman, with his self-satisfied smile, 'on which I can be said to have made up my mind more than on another, it is to Put suicide Down. So don't try it on. That 's the phrase, isn't it? Ha, ha! now we understand each other.'

Toby knew not whether to be agonised or glad, to see that Meg had turned a deadly white, and dropped her lover's hand.

'And as for you, you dull dog,' said the Alderman, turning with even increased cheerfulness and urbanity to the young smith, 'what are you thinking of being married for? What do you want to be married for,

you silly fellow? If I was a fine, young, strapping chap like you, I should be ashamed of being milksop enough to pin myself to a woman's apron-strings! Why, she 'll be an old woman before you 're a middle-aged man! And a pretty figure you 'll cut then, with a draggle-tailed wife and a crowd of squalling children crying after you wherever you go!'

O, he knew how to banter the common people, Alderman Cute!

'There! Go along with you,' said the Alderman, 'and repent. Don't make such a fool of yourself as to get married on New Year's Day. You 'll think very differently of it, long before next New Year's Day; a trim young fellow like you, with all the girls looking after you. There! Go along with you!'

They went along. Not arm in arm, or hand in hand, or interchanging bright glances; but, she in tears; he, gloomy and down-looking. Were these the hearts that had so lately made old Toby's leap up from its faintness? No, no. The Alderman (a blessing on his head!) had Put *them* Down.

'As you happen to be here,' said the Alderman to Toby, 'you shall carry a letter for me. Can you be quick? You 're an old man.'

Toby, who had been looking after Meg, quite stupidly, made shift to murmur out that he was very quick, and very strong.

'How old are you?' inquired the Alderman.

'I 'm over sixty, sir,' said Toby.

'O! This man 's a great deal past the average, you know,' cried Mr. Filer, breaking in as if his patience would bear some trying, but this really was carrying matters a little too far.

'I feel I 'm intruding, sir,' said Toby. 'I—I misdoubted it this morning. Oh dear me!'

The Alderman cut him short by giving him the

letter from his pocket. Toby would have got a
shilling too; but Mr. Filer clearly showing that in
that case he would rob a certain given number of
persons of ninepence-halfpenny a-piece, he only got
sixpence; and thought himself very well off to get
that.

Then the Alderman gave an arm to each of his
friends, and walked off in high feather; but, he immediately came hurrying back alone, as if he had
forgotten something.

'Porter!' said the Alderman.

'Sir!' said Toby.

'Take care of that daughter of yours. She's
much too handsome.'

'Even her good looks are stolen from somebody or
other I suppose,' thought Toby, looking at the sixpence in his hand, and thinking of the tripe. 'She's
been and robbed five hundred ladies of a bloom a-
piece, I shouldn't wonder. It's very dreadful!'

'She's much too handsome, my man,' repeated the
Alderman. 'The chances are, that she'll come to no
good, I clearly see. Observe what I say. Take care
of her!' With which, he hurried off again.

'Wrong every way. Wrong every way!' said
Trotty, clasping his hands. 'Born bad. No business
here!'

The Chimes came clashing in upon him as he said
the words. Full, loud, and sounding—but with no
encouragement. No, not a drop.

'The tune's changed,' cried the old man, as he
listened. 'There's not a word of all that fancy in
it. Why should there be? I have no business with
the New Year nor with the old one neither. Let
me die!'

Still the Bells, pealing forth their changes, made
the very air spin. Put 'em down, Put 'em down!

Good old Times, Good old Times! Facts and Figures, Facts and Figures! Put 'em down, Put 'em down. If they said anything they said this, until the brain of Toby reeled.

He pressed his bewildered head between his hands, as if to keep it from splitting asunder. A well-timed action, as it happened; for finding the letter in one of them, and being by that means reminded of his charge, he fell, mechanically, into his usual trot, and trotted off.

The Second Quarter

THE letter Toby had received from Alderman Cute, was addressed to a great man in the great district of the town. The greatest district of the town. It must have been the greatest district of the town, because it was commonly called 'the world' by its inhabitants.

The letter positively seemed heavier in Toby's hand, than another letter. Not because the Alderman had sealed it with a very large coat of arms and no end of wax, but because of the weighty name on the superscription, and the ponderous amount of gold and silver with which it was associated.

'How different from us!' thought Toby, in all simplicity and earnestness, as he looked at the direction. 'Divide the lively turtles in the bills of mortality, by the number of gentlefolks able to buy 'em; and whose share does he take but his own! As to snatching tripe from anybody's mouth—he'd scorn it!'

With the involuntary homage due to such an exalted character, Toby interposed a corner of his apron between the letter and his fingers.

'His children,' said Trotty, and a mist rose before his eyes; 'his daughters—Gentlemen may win their hearts and marry them; they may be happy wives and mothers; they may be handsome like my darling M—e—'

He couldn't finish the name. The final letter swelled in his throat, to the size of the whole alphabet.

'Never mind,' thought Trotty. 'I know what I mean. That's more than enough for me.' And with this consolatory rumination, trotted on.

It was a hard frost, that day. The air was bracing, crisp, and clear. The wintry sun, though powerless for warmth, looked brightly down upon the ice it was too weak to melt, and set a radiant glory there. At other times, Trotty might have learned a poor man's lesson from the wintry sun; but, he was past that, now.

The Year was Old, that day. The patient Year had lived through the reproaches and misuses of its slanderers, and faithfully performed its work. Spring, summer, autumn, winter. It had laboured through the destined round, and now laid down its weary head to die. Shut out from hope, high impulse, active happiness, itself, but active messenger of many joys to others, it made appeal in its decline to have its toiling days and patient hours remembered, and to die in peace. Trotty might have read a poor man's allegory in the fading year; but he was past that, now.

And only he? Or has the like appeal been ever made, by seventy years at once upon an English labourer's head, and made in vain!

The streets were full of motion, and the shops were decked out gaily. The New Year, like an Infant Heir to the whole world, was waited for, with

welcomes, presents, and rejoicings. There were
books and toys for the New Year, glittering trinkets
for the New Year, dresses for the New Year,
schemes of fortune for the New Year; new inventions to beguile it. Its life was parcelled out in al-
manacks and pocket-books; the coming of its moons,
and stars, and tides, was known beforehand to the
moment; all the workings of its seasons in their days
and nights, were calculated with as much precision
as Mr. Filer could work sums in men and women.

The New Year, the New Year. Everywhere the
New Year! The Old Year was already looked upon
as dead; and its effects were selling cheap, like some
drowned mariner's aboard ship. Its patterns were
Last Year's, and going at a sacrifice, before its
breath was gone. Its treasures were mere dirt, beside the riches of its unborn successor!

Trotty had no portion, to his thinking, in the New
Year or the Old.

'Put 'em down, Put 'em down! Facts and Figures, Facts and Figures! Good old Times, Good
old Times! Put 'em down, Put 'em down!'—his trot
went to that measure, and would fit itself to nothing else.

But, even that one, melancholy as it was, brought
him, in due time, to the end of his journey. To
the mansion of Sir Joseph Bowley, Member of
Parliament.

The door was opened by a Porter. Such a Porter!
Not of Toby's order. Quite another thing. His
place was the ticket though; not Toby's.

This Porter underwent some hard panting before
he could speak; having breathed himself by coming
incautiously out of his chair, without first taking
time to think about it and compose his mind. When

he had found his voice—which it took him a long
time to do, for it was a long way off, and hidden
under a load of meat—he said in a fat whisper,

'Who 's it from?'

Toby told him.

'You 're to take it in, yourself,' said the Porter,
pointing to a room at the end of a long passage,
opening from the hall. 'Everything goes straight
in, on this day of the year. You 're not a bit too
soon: for, the carriage is at the door now, and they
have only come to town for a couple of hours, a'
purpose.'

Toby wiped his feet (which were quite dry already)
with great care, and took the way pointed out to
him; observing as he went that it was an awfully
grand house, but hushed and covered up, as if the
family were in the country. Knocking at the room-
door, he was told to enter from within; and doing
so found himself in a spacious library, where, at a
table strewn with files and papers, were a stately lady
in a bonnet; and a not very stately gentleman in
black who wrote from her dictation; while another,
and an older, and a much statelier gentleman, whose
hat and cane were on the table, walked up and down,
with one hand in his breast, and looked complacently
from time to time at his own picture—a full length;
a very full length—hanging over the fireplace.

'What is this?' said the last-named gentleman.
'Mr. Fish, will you have the goodness to attend?'

Mr. Fish begged pardon, and taking the letter
from Toby, handed it, with great respect.

'From Alderman Cute, Sir Joseph.'

'Is this all? Have you nothing else, Porter?' inquired Sir Joseph.

Toby replied in the negative.

'You have no bill or demand upon me—my name

is Bowley, Sir Joseph Bowley—of any kind from anybody, have you?' said Sir Joseph. 'If you have, present it. There is a cheque-book by the side of Mr. Fish. I allow nothing to be carried into the New Year. Every description of account is settled in this house at the close of the old one. So that if death was to—to—'

'To cut,' suggested Mr. Fish.

'To sever, sir,' returned Sir Joseph, with great asperity, 'the cord of existence—my affairs would be found, I hope, in a state of preparation.'

'My dear Sir Joseph!' said the lady, who was greatly younger than the gentleman. 'How shocking!'

'My lady Bowley,' returned Sir Joseph, floundering now and then, as in the great depth of his observations, 'at this season of the year we should think of—of—ourselves. We should look into our—our accounts. We should feel that every return of so eventful a period in human transactions, involves a matter of deep moment between a man and his—and his banker.'

Sir Joseph delivered these words as if he felt the full morality of what he was saying; and desired that even Trotty should have an opportunity of being improved by such discourse. Possibly he had this end before him in still forbearing to break the seal of the letter, and in telling Trotty to wait where he was, a minute.

'You were desiring Mr. Fish to say, my lady—' observed Sir Joseph.

'Mr. Fish has said that, I believe,' returned his lady, glancing at the letter. 'But, upon my word, Sir Joseph, I don't think I can let it go after all. It is so very dear.'

'What is dear?' inquired Sir Joseph.

'That Charity, my love. They only allow two votes for a subscription of five pounds. Really monstrous!'

'My lady Bowley,' returned Sir Joseph, 'you surprise me. Is the luxury of feeling in proportion to the number of votes; or is it, to a rightly constituted mind, in proportion to the number of applicants, and the wholesome state of mind to which their canvassing reduces them? Is there no excitement of the purest kind in having two votes to dispose of among fifty people?'

'Not to me, I acknowledge,' replied the lady. 'It bores one. Besides, one can't oblige one's acquaintance. But you are the Poor Man's Friend, you know, Sir Joseph. You think otherwise.'

'I *am* the Poor Man's Friend,' observed Sir Joseph, glancing at the poor man present. 'As such I may be taunted. As such I have been taunted. But I ask no other title.'

'Bless him for a noble gentleman!' thought Trotty.

'I don't agree with Cute here, for instance,' said Sir Joseph, holding out the letter. 'I don't agree with the Filer party. I don't agree with any party. My friend the Poor Man, has no business with anything of that sort, and nothing of that sort has any business with him. My friend the Poor Man, in my district, is my business. No man or body of men has any right to interfere between my friend and me. That is the ground I take. I assume a—a paternal character towards my friend. I say, "My good fellow, I will treat you paternally." '

Toby listened with great gravity, and began to feel more comfortable.

'Your only business, my good fellow,' pursued Sir Joseph, looking abstractedly at Toby; 'your only

business in life is with me. You needn't trouble yourself to think about anything. I will think for you; I know what is good for you; I am your perpetual parent. Such is the dispensation of an all-wise Providence! Now, the design of your creation is—not that you should swill, and guzzle, and associate your enjoyments, brutally, with food'; Toby thought remorsefully of the tripe; 'but that you should feel the Dignity of Labour. Go forth erect into the cheerful morning air, and—and stop there. Live hard and temperately, be respectful, exercise your self-denial, bring up your family on next to nothing, pay your rent as regularly as the clock strikes, be punctual in your dealings (I set you a good example; you will find Mr. Fish, my confidential secretary, with a cash-box before him at all times); and you may trust to me to be your Friend and Father.'

'Nice children, indeed, Sir Joseph!' said the lady, with a shudder. 'Rheumatisms, and fevers, and crooked legs, and asthmas, and all kinds of horrors!'

'My lady,' returned Sir Joseph, with solemnity, 'not the less am I the Poor Man's Friend and Father. Not the less shall he receive encouragement at my hands. Every quarter-day he will be put in communication with Mr. Fish. Every New Year's Day, myself and friends will drink his health. Once every year, myself and friends will address him with the deepest feeling. Once in his life, he may even perhaps receive; in public, in the presence of the gentry; a Trifle from a Friend. And when, upheld no more by these stimulants, and the Dignity of Labour, he sinks into his comfortable grave, then my lady'— here Sir Joseph blew his nose—'I will be a Friend and a Father—on the same terms—to his children.'

Toby was greatly moved.

'O! You have a thankful family, Sir Joseph!' cried his wife.

'My lady,' said Sir Joseph, quite majestically, 'Ingratitude is known to be the sin of that class. I expect no other return.'

'Ah! Born bad!' thought Toby. 'Nothing melts us.'

'What man can do, *I* do,' pursued Sir Joseph. 'I do my duty as the Poor Man's Friend and Father; and I endeavour to educate his mind, by inculcating on all occasions the one great moral lesson which that class requires. That is, entire Dependence on myself. They have no business whatever with—with themselves. If wicked and designing persons tell them otherwise, and they become impatient and discontented, and are guilty of insubordinate conduct and black-hearted ingratitude; which is undoubtedly the case; I am their Friend and Father still. It is so Ordained. It is in the nature of things.'

With that great sentiment, he opened the Alderman's letter; and read it.

'Very polite and attentive, I am sure!' exclaimed Sir Joseph. 'My lady, the Alderman is so obliging as to remind me that he has had "the distinguished honour"—he is very good—of meeting me at the house of our mutual friend Deedles, the banker; and he does me the favour to inquire whether it will be agreeable to me to have Will Fern put down.'

'*Most* agreeable!' replied my Lady Bowley. 'The worst man among them! He has been committing a robbery, I hope?'

'Why no,' said Sir Joseph, referring to the letter. 'Not quite. Very near. Not quite. He came up to London, it seems, to look for employment (trying to better himself—that's his story), and being

found at night asleep in a shed, was taken into custody, and carried next morning before the Alderman. The Alderman observes (very properly) that he is determined to put this sort of thing down; and that if it will be agreeable to me to have Will Fern put down, he will be happy to begin with him.'

'Let him be made an example of, by all means,' returned the lady. 'Last winter, when I introduced pinking and eyelet-holing among the men and boys in the village, as a nice evening employment, and had the lines,

> O let us love our occupations,
> Bless the squire and his relations,
> Live upon our daily rations,
> And always know our proper stations,

set to music on the new system, for them to sing the while; this very Fern—I see him now—touched that hat of his, and said, "I humbly ask your pardon, my lady, but *an't* I something different from a great girl?" I expected it, of course; who can expect anything but insolence and ingratitude from that class of people! That is not to the purpose, however. Sir Joseph! Make an example of him!'

'Hem!' coughed Sir Joseph. 'Mr. Fish, if you'll have the goodness to attend—'

Mr. Fish immediately seized his pen, and wrote from Sir Joseph's dictation.

'Private. My dear Sir. I am very much indebted to you for your courtesy in the matter of the man William Fern, of whom, I regret to add, I can say nothing favourable. I have uniformly considered myself in the light of his Friend and Father, but have been repaid (a common case I grieve to say) with ingratitude, and constant opposition to my plans. He is a turbulent and rebellious spirit. His character

will not bear investigation. Nothing will persuade him to be happy when he might. Under these
circumstances, it appears to me, I own, that when he
comes before you again (as you informed me he
promised to do to-morrow, pending your inquiries,
and I think he may be so far relied upon), his com-
mittal for some short term as a Vagabond, would
be a service to society, and would be a salutary example in a country where—for the sake of those who
are, through good and evil report, the Friends and
Fathers of the Poor, as well as with a view to that,
generally speaking, misguided class themselves—examples are greatly needed. And I am,' and so forth.

'It appears,' remarked Sir Joseph when he had
signed this letter, and Mr. Fish was sealing it, 'as if
this were Ordained: really. At the close of the year,
I wind up my account and strike my balance, even
with William Fern!'

Trotty, who had long ago relapsed, and was very
low-spirited, stepped forward with a rueful face to
take the letter.

'With my compliments and thanks,' said Sir
Joseph. 'Stop!'

'Stop!' echoed Mr. Fish.

'You have heard, perhaps,' said Sir Joseph,
oracularly, 'certain remarks into which I have been
led respecting the solemn period of time at which
we have arrived, and the duty imposed upon us of
settling our affairs, and being prepared. You have
observed that I don't shelter myself behind my
superior standing in society, but that Mr. Fish—that
gentleman—has a cheque-book at his elbow, and is
in fact here, to enable me to turn over a perfectly
new leaf, and enter on the epoch before us with a
clean account. Now, my friend, can you lay your

hand upon your heart, and say, that you also have made preparations for a New Year?'

'I am afraid, sir,' stammered Trotty, looking meekly at him, 'that I am a—a—little behind-hand with the world.'

'Behind-hand with the world!' repeated Sir Joseph Bowley, in a tone of terrible distinctness.

'I am afraid, sir,' faltered Trotty, 'that there's a matter of ten or twelve shillings owing to Mrs. Chickenstalker.'

'To Mrs. Chickenstalker!' repeated Sir Joseph, in the same tone as before.

'A shop, sir,' exclaimed Toby, 'in the general line. Also a—a little money on account of rent. A very little, sir. It oughtn't to be owing, I know, but we have been hard put to it, indeed!'

Sir Joseph looked at his lady, and at Mr. Fish, and at Trotty, one after another, twice all round. He then made a despondent gesture with both hands at once, as if he gave the thing up altogether.

'How a man, even among this improvident and impracticable race; an old man; a man grown grey; can look a New Year in the face, with his affairs in this condition; how he can lie down on his bed at night, and get up again in the morning, and—There!' he said, turning his back on Trotty. 'Take the letter. Take the letter!'

'I heartily wish it was otherwise, sir,' said Trotty, anxious to excuse himself. 'We have been tried very hard.'

Sir Joseph still repeating 'Take the letter, take the letter!' and Mr. Fish not only saying the same thing, but giving additional force to the request by motioning the bearer to the door, he had nothing for it but to make his bow and leave the house. And

in the street, poor Trotty pulled his worn old hat
down on his head, to hide the grief he felt at getting
no hold on the New Year, anywhere.

He didn't even lift his hat to look up at the Bell
tower when he came to the old church on his return.
He halted there a moment, from habit: and knew
that it was growing dark, and that the steeple rose
above him, indistinct and faint, in the murky air.   He
knew, too, that the Chimes would ring immediately;
and that they sounded to his fancy, at such a time,
like voices in the clouds.   But he only made the
more haste to deliver the Alderman's letter, and get
out of the way before they began; for he dreaded
to hear them tagging 'Friends and Fathers, Friends
and Fathers,' to the burden they had rung out last.

Toby discharged himself of his commission, therefore, with all possible speed, and set off trotting homeward.   But what with his pace, which was at best an
awkward one in the street; and what with his hat,
which didn't improve it; he trotted against somebody
in less than no time, and was sent staggering out
into the road.

'I beg your pardon, I 'm sure!' said Trotty, pulling
up his hat in great confusion, and between the hat
and the torn lining, fixing his head into a kind of
bee-hive.   'I hope I haven't hurt you.'

As to hurting anybody, Toby was not such an
absolute Samson, but that he was much more likely
to be hurt himself: and indeed, he had flown out
into the road, like a shuttlecock.   He had such an
opinion of his own strength, however, that he was in
real concern for the other party: and said again,

'I hope I haven't hurt you?'

The man against whom he had run; a sun-
browned, sinewy, country-looking man, with grizzled
hair. and a rough chin: stared at him for a moment,

as if he suspected him to be in jest. But, satisfied of his good faith, he answered:

'No, friend. You have not hurt me.'

'Nor the child, I hope?' said Trotty.

'Nor the child,' returned the man. 'I thank you kindly.'

As he said so, he glanced at a little girl he carried in his arms, asleep: and shading her face with the long end of the poor handkerchief he wore about his throat, went slowly on.

The tone in which he said 'I thank you kindly,' penetrated Trotty's heart. He was so jaded and foot-sore, and so soiled with travel, and looked about him so forlorn and strange, that it was a comfort to him to be able to thank any one: no matter for how little. Toby stood gazing after him as he plodded wearily away, with the child's arm clinging round his neck.

At the figure in the worn shoes—now the very shade and ghost of shoes—rough leather leggings, common frock, and broad slouched hat, Trotty stood gazing, blind to the whole street. And at the child's arm, clinging round its neck.

Before he merged into the darkness the traveller stopped; and looking round, and seeing Trotty standing there yet, seemed undecided whether to return or go on. After doing first the one and then the other, he came back, and Trotty went half way to meet him.

'You can tell me, perhaps,' said the man with a faint smile, 'and if you can I am sure you will, and I'd rather ask you than another—where Alderman Cute lives.'

'Close at hand,' replied Toby. 'I'll show you his house with pleasure.'

'I was to have gone to him elsewhere to-morrow,' said the man, accompanying Toby, 'but I'm uneasy

under suspicion, and want to clear myself, and to be free to go and seek my bread—I don't know where. So, maybe he 'll forgive my going to his house to-night.'

'It 's impossible,' cried Toby with a start, 'that your name 's Fern!'

'Eh!' cried the other, turning on him in astonishment.

'Fern! Will Fern!' said Trotty.

'That 's my name,' replied the other.

'Why then,' cried Trotty, seizing him by the arm, and looking cautiously round, 'for Heaven's sake don't go to him! Don't go to him! He 'll put you down as sure as ever you were born. Here! come up this alley, and I 'll tell you what I mean. Don't go to *him*.'

His new acquaintance looked as if he thought him mad; but he bore him company nevertheless. When they were shrouded from observation, Trotty told him what he knew, and what character he had received, and all about it.

The subject of his history listened to it with a calmness that surprised him. He did not contradict or interrupt it, once. He nodded his head now and then— more in corroboration of an old and worn-out story, it appeared, than in refutation of it; and once or twice threw back his hat, and passed his freckled hand over a brow, where every furrow he had ploughed seemed to have set its image in little. But he did no more.

'It 's true enough in the main,' he said, 'master, I could sift grain from husk here and there, but let it be as 'tis. What odds? I have gone against his plans; to my misfortun'. I can't help it; I should do the like to-morrow. As to character, them gentlefolks will search and search, and pry and pry, and have it as free from spot or speck in us, afore they 'll help us to a

dry good word!—Well! I hope they don't lose good
opinion as easy as we do, or their lives is strict indeed, and hardly worth the keeping. For myself,
master, I never took with that hand'—holding it before him—'what wasn't my own; and never held it
back from work, however hard, or poorly paid. Whoever can deny it, let him chop it off! But when work
won't maintain me like a human creetur; when my
living is so bad, that I am Hungry, out of doors and
in; when I see a whole working life begin that way,
go on that way, and end that way, without a chance
or change; then I say to the gentlefolks "Keep away
from me! Let my cottage be. My doors is dark
enough without your darkening of 'em more. Don't
look for me to come up into the Park to help the show
when there's a Birthday, or a fine Speechmaking, or
what not. Act your Plays and Games without me,
and be welcome to 'em, and enjoy 'em. We've nowt
to do with one another. I'm best let alone!"'

Seeing that the child in his arms had opened her
eyes, and was looking about her in wonder, he
checked himself to say a word or two of foolish prat-
tle in her ear, and stand her on the ground beside him.
Then slowly winding one of her long tresses round
and round his rough forefinger like a ring, while she
hung about his dusty leg, he said to Trotty:

'I'm not a cross-grained man by natur', I believe;
and easy satisfied, I'm sure. I bear no ill-will
against none of 'em. I only want to live like one of
the Almighty's creeturs. I can't—I don't—and so
there's a pit dug between me, and them that can and
do. There's others like me. You might tell 'em off
by hundreds and by thousands, sooner than by ones.'

Trotty knew he spoke the Truth in this, and shook
his head to signify as much.

'I've got a bad name this way,' said Fern; 'and I'm

not likely, I 'm afeared, to get a better. 'Tan't lawful to be out of sorts, and I AM out of sorts, though
God knows I 'd sooner bear a cheerful spirit if I
could. Well! I don't know as this Alderman could
hurt *me* much by sending me to gaol; but without a
friend to speak a word for me, he might do it; and
you see—!' pointing downward with his finger, at the
child.

'She has a beautiful face,' said Trotty.

'Why yes!' replied the other in a low voice, as he
gently turned it up with both his hands towards his
own, and looked upon it steadfastly. 'I 've thought
so, many times. I 've thought so, when my hearth
was very cold, and cupboard very bare. I thought
so t' other night, when we were taken like two thieves.
But they—they shouldn't try the little face too often,
should they, Lilian? That 's hardly fair upon a
man!'

He sunk his voice so low, and gazed upon her with
an air so stern and strange, that Toby, to divert the
current of his thoughts, inquired if his wife were
living.

'I never had one,' he returned, shaking his head.
'She 's my brother's child: a orphan. Nine year old,
though you 'd hardly think it; but she 's tired and
worn out now. They 'd have taken care on her, the
Union—eight-and-twenty mile away from where we
live—between four walls (as they took care of my old
father when he couldn't work no more, though he
didn't trouble 'em long); but I took her instead, and
she 's lived with me ever since. Her mother had a
friend once, in London here. We are trying to find
her, and to find work too; but it 's a large place.
Never mind. More room for us to walk about in
Lilly!'

Meeting the child's eyes with a smile which melted Toby more than tears, he shook him by the hand.

'I don't so much as know your name,' he said, 'but I 've opened my heart free to you, for I 'm thankful to you; with good reason. I 'll take your advice, and keep clear of this—'

'Justice,' suggested Toby.

'Ah!' he said. 'If that 's the name they give him This Justice. And to-morrow will try whether there 's better fortun' to be met with, somewheres near London. Good-night. A Happy New Year!'

'Stay!' cried Trotty, catching at his hand, as he relaxed his grip. 'Stay! The New Year never can be happy to me, if we part like this. The New Year never can be happy to me, if I see the child and you, go wandering away, you don't know where, without a shelter for your heads. Come home with me! I 'm a poor man, living in a poor place; but I can give you lodging for one night and never miss it. Come home with me! Here! I 'll take her!' cried Trotty, lifting up the child. 'A pretty one! I 'd carry twenty times her weight, and never know I 'd got it. Tell me if I go too quick for you. I 'm very fast. I always was!' Trotty said this, taking about six of his trotting paces to one stride of his fatigued companion; and with his thin legs quivering again, beneath the load he bore.

'Why, she 's as light,' said Trotty, trotting in his speech as well as in his gait; for he couldn't bear to be thanked, and dreaded a moment's pause; 'as light as a feather. Lighter than a Peacock's feather—a great deal lighter. Here we are, and here we go! Round this first turning to the right, Uncle Will, and past the pump, and sharp off up the passage to the left, right opposite the public-house. Here we are

and here we go! Cross over, Uncle Will, and mind
the kidney pieman at the corner! Here we are and
here we go! Down the Mews here, Uncle Will, and
stop at the black door, with "T. Veck, Ticket Porter"
wrote upon a board; and here we are and here we go,
and here we are indeed, my precious Meg, surprising
you!'

With which words Trotty, in a breathless state, set
the child down before his daughter in the middle of
the floor. The little visitor looked once at Meg; and
doubting nothing in that face, but trusting everything she saw there; ran into her arms.

'Here we are and here we go!' cried Trotty, running round the room, and choking audibly. 'Here,
Uncle Will, here's a fire you know! Why don't you
come to the fire? Oh here we are and here we go!
Meg, my precious darling, where's the kettle? Here
it is and here it goes, and it'll bile in no time!'

Trotty really had picked up the kettle somewhere
or other in the course of his wild career, and now put
it on the fire; while Meg, seating the child in a warm
corner, knelt down on the ground before her, and
pulled off her shoes, and dried her wet feet on a cloth.
Ay, and she laughed at Trotty too—so pleasantly, so
cheerfully, that Trotty could have blessed her where
she kneeled; for he had seen that, when they entered,
she was sitting by the fire in tears.

'Why, father!' said Meg. 'You're crazy to-night,
I think. I don't know what the Bells would say to
that. Poor little feet. How cold they are!'

'Oh, they're warmer now!' exclaimed the child.
'They're quite warm now!'

'No, no, no,' said Meg. 'We haven't rubbed 'em
half enough. We're so busy. So busy! And when
they're done, we'll brush out the damp hair; and
when that's done, we'll bring some colour to the poor

pale face with fresh water; and when that's done, we'll be so gay, and brisk, and happy—!'

The child, in a burst of sobbing, clasped her round the neck; caressed her fair cheek with its hand; and said, 'Oh Meg! oh dear Meg!'

Toby's blessing could have done no more. Who could do more!

'Why, father!' cried Meg, after a pause.

'Here I am and here I go, my dear!' said Trotty.

'Good Gracious me!' cried Meg. 'He's crazy! He's put the dear child's bonnet on the kettle, and hung the lid behind the door!'

'I didn't go for to do it, my love,' said Trotty, hastily repairing this mistake. 'Meg, my dear?'

Meg looked towards him and saw that he had elaborately stationed himself behind the chair of their male visitor, where with many mysterious gestures he was holding up the sixpence he had earned.

'I see, my dear,' said Trotty, 'as I was coming in, half an ounce of tea lying somewhere on the stairs; and I'm pretty sure there was a bit of bacon too. As I don't remember where it was exactly, I'll go myself and try to find 'em.'

With this inscrutable artifice, Toby withdrew to purchase the viands he had spoken of, for ready money, at Mrs. Chickenstalker's; and presently came back, pretending he had not been able to find them, at first, in the dark.

'But here they are at last,' said Trotty, setting out the tea-things, 'all correct! I was pretty sure it was tea, and a rasher. So it is, Meg, my pet, if you'll just make the tea, while your unworthy father toasts the bacon, we shall be ready, immediate. It's a curious circumstance,' said Trotty, proceeding in his cookery, with the assistance of the toasting-fork, 'curious, but well known to my friends, that I never

care, myself, for rashers, nor for tea. I like to see other people enjoy 'em,' said Trotty, speaking very loud, to impress the fact upon his guest, 'but to me, as food, they 're disagreeable.'

Yet Trotty sniffed the savour of the hissing bacon —ah!—as if he liked it; and when he poured the boiling water in the tea-pot, looked lovingly down into the depths of that snug cauldron, and suffered the fragrant steam to curl about his nose, and wreathe his head and face in a thick cloud. However, for all this, he neither ate nor drank, except at the very beginning, a mere morsel for form's sake, which he appeared to eat with infinite relish, but declared was perfectly uninteresting to him.

No. Trotty's occupation was, to see Will Fern and Lilian eat and drink; and so was Meg's. And never did spectators at a city dinner or court banquet find such high delight in seeing others feast: although it were a monarch or a pope: as those two did, in looking on that night. Meg smiled at Trotty, Trotty laughed at Meg. Meg shook her head, and made belief to clap her hands, applauding Trotty; Trotty conveyed, in dumb-show, unintelligible narratives of how and when and where he had found their visitors, to Meg; and they were happy. Very happy.

'Although,' thought Trotty, sorrowfully, as he watched Meg's face; 'that match is broken off, I see!'

'Now, I 'll tell you what,' said Trotty after tea. 'The little one, she sleeps with Meg, I know.'

'With good Meg!' cried the child, caressing her. 'With Meg.'

'That 's right,' said Trotty. 'And I shouldn't wonder if she kiss Meg's father, won't she? I 'm Meg's father.'

Mightily delighted Trotty was, when the child went

timidly towards him, and having kissed him, fell back upon Meg again.

'She 's as sensible as Solomon,' said Trotty. 'Here we come and here we—no, we don't—I don't mean that—I—what was I saying, Meg, my precious?'

Meg looked towards their guest, who leaned upon her chair, and with his face turned from her, fondled the child's head, half hidden in her lap.

'To be sure,' said Toby. 'To be sure! I don't know what I 'm rambling on about, to-night. My wits are wool-gathering, I think. Will Fern, you come along with me. You 're tired to death, and broken down for want of rest. You come along with me.'

The man still played with the child's curls, still leaned upon Meg's chair, still turned away his face. He didn't speak, but in his rough coarse fingers, clenching and expanding in the fair hair of the child, there was an eloquence that said enough.

'Yes, yes,' said Trotty, answering unconsciously what he saw expressed in his daughter's face. 'Take her with you, Meg. Get her to bed. There! Now, Will, I 'll show you where you lie. It 's not much of a place: only a loft; but, having a loft, I always say, is one of the great conveniences of living in a mews; and till this coach-house and stable gets a better let, we live here cheap. There 's plenty of sweet hay up there, belonging to a neighbour; and it 's as clean as hands, and Meg, can make it. Cheer up! Don't give way. A new heart for a New Year, always!'

The hand released from the child's hair, had fallen, trembling, into Trotty's hand. So Trotty, talking without intermission, led him out as tenderly and easily as if he had been a child himself.

Returning before Meg, he listened for an instant

at the door of her little chamber; an adjoining room. The child was murmuring a simple Prayer before lying down to sleep; and when she had remembered Meg's name, 'Dearly, Dearly'—so her words ran—Trotty heard her stop and ask for his.

It was some short time before the foolish little old fellow could compose himself to mend the fire, and draw his chair to the warm hearth. But, when he had done so, and had trimmed the light, he took his newspaper from his pocket, and began to read. Carelessly at first, and skimming up and down the columns; but with an earnest and a sad attention, very soon.

For this same dreaded paper re-directed Trotty's thoughts into the channel they had taken all that day, and which the days' events had so marked out and shaped. His interest in the two wanderers had set him on another course of thinking, and a happier one, for the time; but being alone again, and reading of the crimes and violences of the people, he relapsed into his former train.

In this mood, he came to an account (and it was not the first he had ever read) of a woman who had laid her desperate hands not only on her own life but on that of her young child. A crime so terrible, and so revolting to his soul, dilated with the love of Meg, that he let the journal drop, and fell back in his chair, appalled!

'Unnatural and cruel!' Toby cried. 'Unnatural and cruel! None but people who were bad at heart, born bad, who had no business on the earth, could do such deeds. It 's too true, all I 've heard to-day; too just, too full of proof. We 're Bad!'

The Chimes took up the words so suddenly—burst out so loud, and clear, and sonorous—that the Bells seemed to strike him in his chair.

And what was that they said?

'Toby Veck, Toby Veck, waiting for you Toby! Toby Veck, Toby Veck, waiting for you Toby! Come and see us, come and see us, Drag him to us, drag him to us, Haunt and hunt him, haunt and hunt him, Break his slumbers, break his slumbers! Toby Veck Toby Veck, door open wide Toby, Toby Veck Toby Veck, door open wide Toby—' then fiercely back to their impetuous strain again, and ringing in the very bricks and plaster on the walls.

Toby listened. Fancy, fancy! His remorse for having run away from them that afternoon! No, no. Nothing of the kind. Again, again, and yet a dozen times again. 'Haunt and hunt him, haunt and hunt him, Drag him to us, drag him to us!' Deafening the whole town!

'Meg,' said Trotty softly: tapping at her door. 'Do you hear anything?'

'I hear the Bells, father. Surely they 're very loud to-night.'

'Is she asleep?' said Toby, making an excuse for peeping in.

'So peacefully and happily! I can't leave her yet though, father. Look how she holds my hand!'

'Meg,' whispered Trotty. 'Listen to the Bells!'

She listened, with her face towards him all the time. But it underwent no change. She didn't understand them.

Trotty withdrew, resumed his seat by the fire, and once more listened by himself. He remained here a little time.

It was impossible to bear it; their energy was dreadful.

'If the tower-door is really open,' said Toby, hastily laying aside his apron, but never thinking of his hat,

'what 's to hinder me from going up into the steeple and satisfying myself? If it 's shut, I don't want any other satisfaction.   That 's enough.'

He was pretty certain as he slipped out quietly into the street that he should find it shut and locked, for he knew the door well, and had so rarely seen it open, that he couldn't reckon above three times in all. It was a low arched portal, outside the church, in a dark nook behind a column; and had such great iron hinges, and such a monstrous lock, that there was much more hinge and lock than door.

But what was his astonishment when, coming bare-headed to the church; and putting his hand into this dark nook, with a certain misgiving that it might be unexpectedly seized, and a shivering propensity to draw it back again; he found that the door, which opened outwards, actually stood ajar!

He thought, on the first surprise, of going back; or of getting a light, or a companion; but his courage aided him immediately, and he determined to ascend alone.

'What have I to fear?' said Trotty.   'It 's a church! Besides, the ringers may be there, and have forgotten to shut the door.'

So he went in, feeling his way as he went, like a blind man; for it was very dark.   And very quiet, for the Chimes were silent.

The dust from the street had blown into the recess; and lying there, heaped up, made it so soft and velvet-like to the foot, that there was something startling, even in that.   The narrow stair was so close to the door, too, that he stumbled at the very first; and shutting the door upon himself, by striking it with his foot, and causing it to rebound back heavily, he couldn't open it again.

'This was another reason, however, for going on. Trotty groped his way, and went on. Up, up, up, and round, and round; and up, up, up; higher, higher, higher up!

It was a disagreeable staircase for that groping work; so low and narrow, that his groping hand was always touching something; and it often felt so like a man or ghostly figure standing up erect and making room for him to pass without discovery, that he would rub the smooth wall upward searching for its face, and downward searching for its feet, while a chill tingling crept all over him. Twice or thrice, a door or niche broke the monotonous surface; and then it seemed a gap as wide as the whole church; and he felt on the brink of an abyss, and going to tumble head-long down, until he found the wall again.

Still up, up, up; and round and round, and up, up, up; higher, higher, higher up!

At length, the dull and stifling atmosphere began to freshen: presently to feel quite windy: presently it blew so strong, that he could hardly keep his legs. But, he got to an arched window in the tower, breast high, and holding tight, looked down upon the house-tops, on the smoking chimneys, on the blurr and blotch of lights (towards the place where Meg was wondering where he was and calling to him perhaps), all kneaded up together in a leaven of mist and darkness.

This was the belfry, where the ringers came. He had caught hold of one of the frayed ropes which hung down through apertures in the oaken roof. At first he started, thinking it was hair; then trembled at the very thought of waking the deep Bell. The Bells themselves were higher. Higher, Trotty, in his fascination, or in working out the spell upon him,

groped his way. By ladders now, and toilsomely, for it was steep, and not too certain holding for the feet.

Up, up, up; and climb and clamber; up, up, up; higher, higher, higher up!

Until, ascending through the floor, and pausing with his head just raised above its beams, he came among the Bells. It was barely possible to make out their great shapes in the gloom; but there they were. Shadowy, and dark, and dumb.

A heavy sense of dread and loneliness fell instantly upon him, as he climbed into this airy nest of stone and metal. His head went round and round. He listened, and then raised a wild 'Holloa!'

Holloa! was mournfully protracted by the echoes.

Giddy, confused, and out of breath, and frightened, Toby looked about him vacantly, and sunk down in a swoon.

Third Quarter

BLACK are the brooding clouds and troubled the deep waters, when the Sea of Thought, first heaving from a calm, gives up its Dead. Monsters uncouth and wild, arise in premature, imperfect resurrection; the several parts and shapes of different things are joined and mixed by chance; and when, and how, and by what wonderful degrees, each separates from each, and every sense and object of the mind resumes its usual form and lives again, no man—though every man is every day the casket of this type of the Great Mystery—can tell.

So, when and how the darkness of the night-black steeple changed to shining light; when and how the solitary tower was peopled with a myriad figures;

when and how the whispered 'Haunt and hunt him,' breathing monotonously through his sleep or swoon, became a voice exclaiming in the waking ears of Trotty, 'Break his slumbers'; when and how he ceased to have a sluggish and confused idea that such things were, companioning a host of others that were not; there are no dates or means to tell. But, awake and standing on his feet upon the boards where he had lately lain, he saw this Goblin Sight.

He saw the tower, whither his charmed footsteps had brought him, swarming with dwarf phantoms, spirits, elfin creatures of the Bells. He saw them leaping, flying, dropping, pouring from the Bells without a pause. He saw them, round him on the ground; above him, in the air; clambering from him, by the ropes below; looking down upon him, from the massive iron-girded beams; peeping in upon him, through the chinks and loopholes in the walls; spreading away and away from him in enlarging circles, as the water ripples give way to a huge stone that suddenly comes plashing in among them. He saw them, of all aspects and all shapes. He saw them ugly, handsome, crippled, exquisitely formed. He saw them young, he saw them old, he saw them kind, he saw them cruel, he saw them merry, he saw them grim; he saw them dance, and heard them sing; he saw them tear their hair, and heard them howl. He saw the air thick with them. He saw them come and go, incessantly. He saw them riding downward, soaring upward, sailing off afar, perching near at hand, all restless and all violently active. Stone, and brick, and slate, and tile, became transparent to him as to them. He saw them *in* the houses, busy at the sleepers' beds. He saw them soothing people in their dreams; he saw them beating them with knotted whips; he saw them yelling in their ears; he saw them playing softest

music on their pillows; he saw them cheering some with the songs of birds and the perfume of flowers; he saw them flashing awful faces on the troubled rest of others, from enchanted mirrors which they carried in their hands.

He saw these creatures, not only among sleeping men but waking also, active in pursuits irreconcilable with one another, and possessing or assuming natures the most opposite. He saw one buckling on innumerable wings to increase his speed; another loading himself with chains and weights, to retard his. He saw some putting the hands of clocks forward, some putting the hands of clocks backward, some endeavouring to stop the clock entirely. He saw them representing, here a marriage ceremony, there a funeral; in this chamber an election, in that a ball; he saw, everywhere, restless and untiring motion.

Bewildered by the host of shifting and extraordinary figures, as well as by the uproar of the Bells, which all this while were ringing, Trotty clung to a wooden pillar for support, and turned his white face here and there, in mute and stunned astonishment.

As he gazed, the Chimes stopped. Instantaneous change! The whole swarm fainted! their forms collapsed, their speed deserted them; they sought to fly, but in the act of falling died and melted into air. No fresh supply succeeded them. One straggler leaped down pretty briskly from the surface of the Great Bell, and alighted on his feet, but he was dead and gone before he could turn round. Some few of the late company who had gambolled in the tower, remained there, spinning over and over a little longer; but these became at every turn more faint, and few, and feeble, and soon went the way of the rest. The last of all was one small hunchback, who had got into an echoing corner, where he twirled and twirled, and

floated by himself a long time; showing such perseverance, that at last he dwindled to a leg and even to
a foot, before he finally retired; but he vanished in
the end, and then the tower was silent.

Then and not before, did Trotty see in every Bell
a bearded figure of the bulk and stature of the Bell—
incomprehensibly, a figure and the Bell itself.
Gigantic, grave, and darkly watchful of him, as he
stood rooted to the ground.

Mysterious and awful figures! Resting on nothing; poised in the night air of the tower, with their
draped and hooded heads merged in the dim roof; motionless and shadowy. Shadowy and dark, although
he saw them by some light belonging to themselves—
none else was there—each with its muffled hand upon
its goblin mouth.

He could not plunge down wildly through the opening in the floor; for all power of motion had deserted
him. Otherwise he would have done so—aye, would
have thrown himself, headforemost, from the steeple-
top, rather than have seen them watching him with
eyes that would have waked and watched although
the pupils had been taken out.

Again, again, the dread and terror of the lonely
place, and of the wild and fearful night that reigned
there, touched him like a spectral hand. His distance
from all help; the long, dark, winding, ghost-be-
leaguered way that lay between him and the earth on
which men lived; his being high, high, high, up there,
where it had made him dizzy to see the birds fly in
the day; cut off from all good people, who at such an
hour were safe at home and sleeping in their beds;
all this struck coldly through him, not as a reflection
but a bodily sensation. Meantime his eyes and
thoughts and fears, were fixed upon the watchful
figures; which, rendered unlike any figures of this

world by the deep gloom and shade enwrapping and enfolding them, as well as by their looks and forms and supernatural hovering above the floor, were nevertheless as plainly to be seen as were the stalwart oaken frames, cross-pieces, bars and beams, set up there to support the Bells. These hemmed them, in a very forest of hewn timber; from the entanglements, intricacies, and depths of which, as from among the boughs of a dead wood blighted for their phantom use, they kept their darksome and unwinking watch.

A blast of air—how cold and shrill!—came moaning through the tower. As it died away, the Great Bell, or the Goblin of the Great Bell, spoke.

'What visitor is this?' it said. The voice was low and deep, and Trotty fancied that it sounded in the other figures as well.

'I thought my name was called by the Chimes!' said Trotty, raising his hands in an attitude of supplication. 'I hardly know why I am here, or how I came. I have listened to the Chimes these many years. They have cheered me often.'

'And you have thanked them?' said the Bell.

'A thousand times!' cried Trotty.

'How?'

'I am a poor man,' faltered Trotty, 'and could only thank them in words.'

'And always so?' inquired the Goblin of the Bell. 'Have you never done us wrong in words?'

'No!' cried Trotty eagerly.

'Never done us foul, and false, and wicked wrong, in words?' pursued the Goblin of the Bell.

Trotty was about to answer, 'Never!' But he stopped, and was confused.

'The voice of Time,' said the Phantom, 'cries to man, Advance! Time is for his advancement and

improvement; for his greater worth, his greater happiness, his better life; his progress onward to that goal within its knowledge and its view, and set there, in the period when Time and He began. Ages of darkness, wickedness, and violence, have come and gone—millions uncountable, have suffered, lived, and died—to point the way before him. Who seeks to turn him back, or stay him on his course, arrests a mighty engine which will strike the meddler dead; and be the fiercer and the wilder, ever, for its momentary check!'

'I never did so to my knowledge, sir,' said Trotty. 'It was quite by accident if I did. I wouldn't go to do it, I'm sure.'

'Who puts into the mouth of Time, or of its servants,' said the Goblin of the Bell, 'a cry of lamentation for days which have had their trial and their failure, and have left deep traces of it which the blind may see—a cry that only serves the present time, by showing men how much it needs their help when any ears can listen to regrets for such a past—who does this, does a wrong. And you have done that wrong, to us, the Chimes.'

Trotty's first excess of fear was gone. But he had felt tenderly and gratefully towards the Bells, as you have seen; and when he heard himself arraigned as one who had offended them so weightily, his heart was touched with penitence and grief.

'If you knew,' said Trotty, clasping his hands earnestly—'or perhaps you do know—if you know how often you have kept me company; how often you have cheered me up when I've been low; how you were quite the plaything of my little daughter Meg (almost the only one she ever had) when first her mother died, and she and me were left alone; you won't bear malice for a hasty word!'

'Who hears in us, the Chimes, one note bespeaking disregard, or stern regard, of any hope, or joy, or pain, or sorrow, of the many-sorrowed throng; who hears us make response to any creed that gauges human passions and affections, as it gauges the amount of miserable food on which humanity may pine and wither; does us wrong. That wrong you have done us!' said the Bell.

'I have!' said Trotty. 'Oh forgive me!'

'Who hears us echo the dull vermin of the earth: the Putters Down of crushed and broken natures, formed to be raised up higher than such maggots of the time can crawl or can conceive,' pursued the Goblin of the Bell; 'who does so, does us wrong. And you have done us wrong!'

'Not meaning it,' said Trotty. 'In my ignorance. Not meaning it!'

'Lastly, and most of all,' pursued the Bell. 'Who turns his back upon the fallen and disfigured of his kind; abandons them as vile; and does not trace and track with pitying eyes the unfenced precipice by which they fell from good—grasping in their fall some tufts and shreds of that lost soil, and clinging to them still when bruised and dying in the gulf below; does wrong to Heaven and man, to time and to eternity. And you have done that wrong!'

'Spare me,' cried Trotty, falling on his knees; 'for Mercy's sake!'

'Listen!' said the Shadow.

'Listen!' cried the other Shadows.

'Listen!' said a clear and childlike voice, which Trotty thought he recognised as having heard before.

The organ sounded faintly in the church below. Swelling by degrees, the melody ascended to the roof, and filled the choir and nave. Expanding more and more, it rose up, up; up, up; higher, higher, higher

up; awakening agitated hearts within the burly piles of oak, the hollow bells, the iron-bound doors, the stairs of solid stone; until the tower walls were insufficient to contain it, and it soared into the sky.

No wonder that an old man's breast could not contain a sound so vast and mighty. It broke from that weak prison in a rush of tears; and Trotty put his hands before his face.

'Listen!' said the Shadow.

'Listen!' said the other Shadows.

'Listen!' said the child's voice.

A solemn strain of blended voices, rose into the tower.

It was a very low and mournful strain—a Dirge—and as he listened, Trotty heard his child among the singers.

'She is dead!' exclaimed the old man. 'Meg is dead! Her spirit calls to me. I hear it!'

'The Spirit of your child bewails the dead, and mingles with the dead—dead hopes, dead fancies, dead imaginings of youth,' returned the Bell, 'but she is living. Learn from her life, a living truth. Learn from the creature dearest to your heart, how bad the bad are born. See every bud and leaf plucked one by one from off the fairest stem, and know how bare and wretched it may be. Follow her! To desperation!'

Each of the shadowy figures stretched its right arm forth, and pointed downward.

'The Spirit of the Chimes is your companion,' said the figure. 'Go! It stands behind you!'

Trotty turned, and saw—the child! The child Will Fern had carried in the street; the child whom Meg had watched, but now, asleep.

'I carried her myself, to-night,' said Trotty. 'In these arms!'

'Show him what he calls himself,' said the dark figures, one and all.

The tower opened at his feet. He looked down, and beheld his own form, lying at the bottom, on the outside: crushed and motionless.

'No more a living man!' cried Trotty. 'Dead!'

'Dead!' said the figures all together.

'Gracious Heaven! And the New Year—'

'Past,' said the figures.

'What!' he cried, shuddering. 'I missed my way, and coming on the outside of this tower in the dark, fell down—a year ago?'

'Nine years ago!' replied the figures.

As they gave the answer, they recalled their outstretched hands; and where their figures had been, there the Bells were.

And they rung; their time being come again. And once again, vast multitudes of phantoms sprung into existence; once again, were incoherently engaged, as they had been before; once again, faded on the stopping of the Chimes; and dwindled into nothing.

'What are these?' he asked his guide. 'If I am not mad, what are these?'

'Spirits of the Bells. Their sound upon the air,' returned the child. 'They take such shapes and occupations as the hopes and thoughts of mortals, and the recollections they have stored up, give them.'

'And you,' said Trotty wildly. 'What are you?'

'Hush, hush!' returned the child. 'Look here!'

In a poor, mean room: working at the same kind of embroidery which he had often, often seen before her; Meg, his own dear daughter, was presented to his view. He made no effort to imprint his kisses on her face; he did not strive to clasp her to his loving heart; he knew that such endearments were, for him, no more. But, he held his trembling breath, and

brushed away the blinding tears, that he might look upon her; that he might only see her.

Ah! Changed. Changed. The light of the clear eye, how dimmed. The bloom, how faded from the cheek. Beautiful she was, as she had ever been, but Hope, Hope, Hope, oh where was the fresh Hope that had spoken to him like a voice!

She looked up from her work, at a companion. Following her eyes, the old man started back.

In the woman grown, he recognised her at a glance. In the long silken hair, he saw the self-same curls; around the lips, the child's expression lingering still. See! In the eyes, now turned inquiringly on Meg, there shone the very look that scanned those features when he brought her home!

Then what was this, beside him!

Looking with awe into its face, he saw a something reigning there: a lofty something, undefined and indistinct, which made it hardly more than a remembrance of that child—as yonder figure might be—yet it was the same: the same: and wore the dress.

Hark. They were speaking!

'Meg,' said Lilian, hesitating. 'How often you raise your head from your work to look at me!'

'Are my looks so altered, that they frighten you?' asked Meg.

'Nay, dear! But you smile at that, yourself! Why not smile, when you look at me, Meg?'

'I do so. Do I not?' she answered: smiling on her.

'Now you do,' said Lilian, 'but not usually. When you think I'm busy, and don't see you, you look so anxious and so doubtful, that I hardly like to raise my eyes. There is little cause for smiling in this hard and toilsome life, but you were once so cheerful.'

'Am I not now!' cried Meg, speaking in a tone of strange alarm, and rising to embrace her. 'Do I

make our weary life more weary to you, Lilian!'

'You have been the only thing that made it life,'
said Lilian, fervently kissing her; 'sometimes the only
thing that made me care to live so, Meg. Such work,
such work! So many hours, so many days, so many
long, long nights of hopeless, cheerless, never-ending
work—not to heap up riches, not to live grandly or
gaily, not to live upon enough, however coarse; but to
earn bare bread: to scrape together just enough to
toil upon, and want upon, and keep alive in us the
consciousness of our hard fate! Oh Meg, Meg!' she
raised her voice and twined her arms about her as she
spoke, like one in pain. 'How can the cruel world go
round, and bear to look upon such lives!'

'Lilly!' said Meg, soothing her, and putting back
her hair from her wet face. 'Why Lilly! You!
So pretty and so young!'

'Oh Meg!' she interrupted, holding her at arm's-
length, and looking in her face imploringly. 'The
worst of all, the worst of all! Strike me old, Meg!
Wither me, and shrivel me, and free me from the
dreadful thoughts that tempt me in my youth!'

Trotty turned to look upon his guide. But, the
Spirit of the child had taken flight. Was gone.

Neither did he himself remain in the same place;
for, Sir Joseph Bowley, Friend and Father of the
Poor, held a great festivity at Bowley Hall, in honour of the natal day of Lady Bowley. And as Lady
Bowley had been born on New Year's Day (which
the local newspapers considered an especial pointing
of the finger of Providence to number One, as Lady
Bowley's destined figure in Creation), it was on a
New Year's Day that this festivity took place.

Bowley Hall was full of visitors. The red-faced
gentleman was there, Mr. Filer was there, the great
Alderman Cute was there—Alderman Cute had a

sympathetic feeling with great people, and had considerably improved his acquaintance with Sir Joseph
Bowley on the strength of his attentive letter: indeed
had become quite a friend of the family since then—
and many guests were there. Trotty's ghost was
there, wandering about, poor phantom, drearily; and
looking for its guide.

There was to be a great dinner in the Great Hall.
At which Sir Joseph Bowley, in his celebrated character of Friend and Father of the Poor, was to make
his great speech. Certain plum-puddings were to be
eaten by his Friends and Children in another Hall
first; and, at a given signal, Friends and Children
flocking in among their Friends and Fathers, were to
form a family assemblage, with not one manly eye
therein unmoistened by emotion.

But, there was more than this to happen. Even
more than this. Sir Joseph Bowley, Baronet and
Member of Parliament, was to play a match at skittles
—real skittles—with his tenants!

'Which quite reminds me,' said Alderman Cute, 'of
the days of old King Hal, stout King Hal, bluff
King Hal. Ah. Fine character!'

'Very,' said Mr. Filer, dryly. 'For marrying
women and murdering 'em. Considerably more than
the average number of wives by the bye.'

'You'll marry the beautiful ladies, and not murder
'em, eh?' said Alderman Cute to the heir of Bowley,
aged twelve. 'Sweet boy! We shall have this little
gentleman in Parliament now,' said the Alderman,
holding him by the shoulders, and looking as reflect-
ive as he could, 'before we know where we are. We
shall hear of his successes at the poll; his speeches in
the House; his overtures from Governments; his brilliant achievements of all kinds; ah! we shall make our
little orations about him in the Common Council. I 'll

be bound; before we have time to look about us!'

'Oh, the difference of shoes and stockings!' Trotty thought. But his heart yearned towards the child, for the love of those same shoeless and stockingless boys, predestined (by the Alderman) to turn out bad, who might have been the children of poor Meg.

'Richard,' moaned Trotty, roaming among the company, to and fro; 'where is he? I can't find Richard! Where is Richard?'

Not likely to be there, if still alive! But Trotty's grief and solitude confused him; and he still went wandering among the gallant company, looking for his guide, and saying, 'Where is Richard? Show me Richard!'

He was wandering thus, when he encountered Mr. Fish, the confidential Secretary: in great agitation.

'Bless my heart and soul!' cried Mr. Fish. 'Where's Alderman Cute? Has anybody seen the Alderman?'

Seen the Alderman? Oh dear! Who could ever help seeing the Alderman? He was so considerate, so affable, he bore so much in mind the natural desires of folks to see him, that if he had a fault, it was the being constantly On View. And wherever the great people were, there, to be sure, attracted by the kindred sympathy between great souls, was Cute.

Several voices cried that he was in the circle round Sir Joseph. Mr. Fish made way there; found him; and took him secretly into a window near at hand. Trotty joined them. Not of his own accord. He felt that his steps were led in that direction.

'My dear Alderman Cute,' said Mr. Fish. 'A little more this way. The most dreadful circumstance has occurred. I have this moment received the intelligence. I think it will be best not to acquaint Sir Joseph with it till the day is over. You understand

Sir Joseph, and will give me your opinion. The most frightful and deplorable event!'

'Fish!' returned the Alderman. 'Fish! My good fellow, what is the matter? Nothing revolutionary, I hope! No—no attempted interference with the magistrates?'

'Deedles, the banker,' gasped the Secretary. 'Deedles Brothers—who was to have been here to-day—high in office in the Goldsmiths' Company—'

'Not stopped!' exclaimed the Alderman. 'It can't be!'

'Shot himself!'

'Good God!'

'Put a double-barrelled pistol to his mouth, in his own counting-house,' said Mr. Fish, 'and blew his brains out. No motive. Princely circumstances!'

'Circumstances!' exclaimed the Alderman. 'A man of noble fortune. One of the most respectable of men. Suicide, Mr. Fish! By his own hand!'

'This very morning,' returned Mr. Fish.

'Oh the brain, the brain!' exclaimed the pious Alderman, lifting up his hands. 'Oh the nerves, the nerves; the mysteries of this machine called Man! Oh the little that unhinges it: poor creatures that we are! Perhaps a dinner, Mr. Fish. Perhaps the conduct of his son, who, I have heard, ran very wild, and was in the habit of drawing bills upon him without the least authority! A most respectable man. One of the most respectable men I ever knew! A lamentable instance, Mr. Fish. A public calamity! I shall make a point of wearing the deepest mourning. A most respectable man! But there is One above. We must submit, Mr. Fish. We must submit!'

What, Alderman! No word of Putting Down? Remember, Justice, your high moral boast and pride. Come, Alderman! Balance those scales. Throw me

into this, the empty one, no dinner, and Nature's
founts in some poor woman, dried by starving misery
and rendered obdurate to claims for which her off-
spring *has* authority in holy mother Eve.   Weigh me
the two, you Daniel, going to judgment, when your
day shall come!   Weigh them, in the eyes of suffering thousands, audience (not unmindful) of the grim
farce you play.   Or supposing that you strayed from
your five wits—it 's not so far to go, but that it might
be—and laid hands upon that throat of yours, warning your fellows (if you have a fellow) how they
croak their comfortable wickedness to raving heads
and stricken hearts.   What then?'

The words rose up in Trotty's breast, as if they had
been spoken by some other voice within him.   Alderman Cute pledged himself to Mr. Fish that he would
assist him in breaking the melancholy catastrophe to
Sir Joseph when the day was over.   Then, before
they parted, wringing Mr. Fish's hand in bitterness
of soul, he said, 'The most respectable of men!'   And
added that he hardly knew (not even he), why such
afflictions were allowed on earth.

'It 's almost enough to make one think, if one didn't
know better,' said Alderman Cute, 'that at times some
motion of a capsizing nature was going on in things,
which affected the general economy of the social fab-
ric.   Deedles Brothers!'

The skittle-playing came off with immense success.
Sir Joseph knocked the pins about quite skilfully;
Master Bowley took an innings at a shorter distance
also; and everybody said that now, when a Baronet
and the Son of a Baronet played at skittles, the country was coming round again, as fast as it could come.

At its proper time, the Banquet was served up.
Trotty involuntarily repaired to the Hall with the
rest, for he felt himself conducted thither by some

stronger impulse than his own free will. The sight was gay in the extreme; the ladies were very handsome; the visitors delighted, cheerful, and good-tempered. When the lower doors were opened, and the people flocked in, in their rustic dresses, the beauty of the spectacle was at its height; but Trotty only murmured more and more, 'Where is Richard! He should help and comfort her! I can't see Richard!'

There had been some speeches made; and Lady Bowley's health had been proposed; and Sir Joseph Bowley had returned thanks, and had made his great speech, showing by various pieces of evidence that he was the born Friend and Father, and so forth; and had given as a Toast, his Friends and Children, and the Dignity of Labour; when a slight disturbance at the bottom of the Hall attracted Toby's notice. After some confusion, noise, and opposition, one man broke through the rest, and stood forward by himself.

Not Richard. No. But one whom he had thought of, and had looked for, many times. In a scantier supply of light, he might have doubted the identity of that worn man, so old, and grey, and bent; but with a blaze of lamps upon his gnarled and knotted head, he knew Will Fern as soon as he stepped forth.

'What is this!' exclaimed Sir Joseph, rising. 'Who gave this man admittance? This is a criminal from prison! Mr. Fish, sir, *will* you have the goodness—'

'A minute!' said Will Fern. 'A minute! My Lady, you was born on this day along with a New Year. Get me a minute's leave to speak.'

She made some intercession for him. Sir Joseph took his seat again, with native dignity.

The ragged visitor—for he was miserably dressed —looked round upon the company, and made his homage to them with a humble bow.

'Gentlefolks!' he said. 'You 've drunk the Labourer. Look at me!'

'Just come from jail,' said Mr. Fish.

'Just come from jail,' said Will. 'And neither for the first time, nor the second, nor the third, nor yet the fourth.'

Mr. Filer was heard to remark testily, that four times was over the average; and he ought to be ashamed of himself.

'Gentlefolks!' repeated Will Fern. 'Look at me! You see I 'm at the worst. Beyond all hurt or harm; beyond your help; for the time when your kind words or kind actions could have done ME good,'—he struck his hand upon his breast, and shook his head, 'is gone, with the scent of last year's beans or clover on the air. Let me say a word for these,' pointing to the labouring people in the Hall; 'and when you 're met together, hear the real Truth spoke out for once.'

'There 's not a man here,' said the host, 'who would have him for a spokesman.'

'Like enough, Sir Joseph. I believe it. Not the less true, perhaps, is what I say. Perhaps that 's a proof on it. Gentlefolks, I 've lived many a year in this place. You may see the cottage from the sunk fence over yonder. I 've seen the ladies draw it in their books, a hundred times. It looks well in a picter, I 've heerd say; but there an't weather in picters, and maybe 'tis fitter for that, than for a place to live in. Well! I lived there. How hard—how bitter hard, I lived there, I won't say. Any day in the year, and every day, you can judge for your own selves.'

He spoke as he had spoken on the night when Trotty found him in the street. His voice was deeper and more husky, and had a trembling in it now and then; but he never raised it passionately. and

seldom lifted it above the firm stern level of the homely facts he stated.

' 'Tis harder than you think for, gentlefolks, to grow up decent, commonly decent, in such a place. That I growed up a man and not a brute, says something for me—as I was then. As I am now, there's nothing can be said for me or done for me. I 'm past it.'

'I am glad this man has entered,' observed Sir Joseph, looking round serenely. 'Don't disturb him. It appears to be Ordained. He is an example: a living example. I hope and trust, and confidently expect, that it will not be lost upon my Friends here.'

'I dragged on,' said Fern, after a moment's silence, 'somehow. Neither me nor any other man knows how; but so heavy, that I couldn't put a cheerful face upon it, or make believe that I was anything but what I was. Now, gentlemen—you gentlemen that sits at Sessions—when you see a man with discontent writ on his face, you says to one another, "He's suspicious. I has my doubts," says you, "about Will Fern. Watch that fellow!" I don't say, gentlemen, it an't quite nat'ral, but I say 'tis so; and from that hour, whatever Will Fern does, or lets alone—all one—it goes against him.'

Alderman Cute stuck his thumbs in his waistcoat-pockets, and leaning back in his chair, and smiling, winked at a neighbouring chandelier. As much as to say, 'Of course! I told you so. The common cry! Lord bless you, we are up to all this sort of thing—myself and human nature.'

'Now, gentlemen,' said Will Fern, holding out his hands, and flushing for an instant in his haggard face, 'see how your laws are made to trap and hunt us when we 're brought to this. I tries to live elsewhere. And I 'm a vagabond. To jail with him! I comes back

here. I goes a-nutting in your woods, and breaks—
who don't?—a limber branch or two. To jail with
him! One of your keepers sees me in the broad day,
near my own patch of garden, with a gun. To jail
with him! I has a nat'ral angry word with that man,
when I'm free again! To jail with him! I cuts a
stick. To jail with him! I eats a rotten apple or a
turnip. To jail with him! It's twenty mile away;
and coming back I begs a trifle on the road. To jail
with him! At last, the constable, the keeper—anybody—finds me anywhere, a-doing anything. To
jail with him, for he's a vagrant, and a jail-bird
known; and the jail's the only home he's got.'

The Alderman nodded sagaciously, as who should
say, 'A very good home too!'

'Do I say this to serve MY cause!' cried Fern.
'Who can give me back my liberty, who can give me
back my good name, who can give me back my innocent niece? Not all the Lords and Ladies in wide
England. But gentlemen, gentlemen, dealing with
other men like me, begin at the right end. Give
us, in mercy, better homes when we're a-lying in
our cradles; give us better food when we're a-work-
ing for our lives; give us kinder laws to bring
us back when we're a-going wrong; and don't set
Jail, Jail, Jail, afore us, everywhere we turn.
There an't a condescension you can show the
Labourer then, that he won't take, as ready and as
grateful as a man can be; for, he has a patient, peaceful, willing heart. But you must put his rightful
spirit in him first; for, whether he's a wreck and ruin
such as me, or is like one of them that stand here
now, his spirit is divided from you at this time.
Bring it back, gentlefolks, bring it back! Bring
it back, afore the day comes when even his Bible
changes in his altered mind, and the words seem

to him to read, as they have sometimes read in my
own eyes—in Jail: "Whither thou goest, I can Not
go; where thou lodgest, I do Not lodge; thy people
are Not my people; Nor thy God my God!" '

A sudden stir and agitation took place in the Hall.
Trotty thought at first, that several had risen to eject
the man; and hence this change in its appearance.
But, another moment showed him that the room and
all the company had vanished from his sight, and that
his daughter was again before him, seated at her
work. But in a poorer, meaner garret than before;
and with no Lilian by her side.

The frame at which she had worked, was put away
upon a shelf and covered up. The chair in which
she had sat, was turned against the wall. A history
was written in these little things, and in Meg's grief-
worn face. Oh! who could fail to read it!

Meg strained her eyes upon her work until it was
too dark to see the threads; and when the night closed
in, she lighted her feeble candle and worked on. Still
her old father was invisible about her; looking down
upon her; loving her—how dearly loving her!—and
talking to her in a tender voice about the old times,
and the Bells. Though he knew, poor Trotty,
though he knew she could not hear him.

A great part of the evening had worn away, when
a knock came at her door. She opened it. A man
was on the threshold. A slouching, moody, drunken
sloven, wasted by intemperance and vice, and with his
matted hair and unshorn beard in wild disorder; but,
with some traces on him, too, of having been a man
of good proportion and good features in his youth.

He stopped until he had her leave to enter; and
she, retiring a pace or two from the open door, silently
and sorrowfully looked upon him. Trotty had his
wish. He saw Richard.

'May I come in, Margaret?'

'Yes! Come in. Come in!'

It was well that Trotty knew him before he spoke; for with any doubt remaining on his mind, the harsh discordant voice would have persuaded him that it was not Richard but some other man.

There were but two chairs in the room. She gave him hers, and stood at some short distance from him, waiting to hear what he had to say.

He sat, however, staring vacantly at the floor; with a lustreless and stupid smile. A spectacle of such deep degradation, of such abject hopelessness, of such a miserable downfall, that she put her hands before her face and turned away, lest he should see how much it moved her.

Roused by the rustling of her dress, or some such trifling sound, he lifted his head, and began to speak as if there had been no pause since he entered.

'Still at work, Margaret? You work late.'

'I generally do.'

'And early?'

'And early.'

'So she said. She said you never tired; or never owned that you tired. Not all the time you lived together. Nor even when you fainted, between work and fasting. But I told you that, the last time I came.'

'You did,' she answered. 'And I implored you to tell me nothing more; and you made me a solemn promise, Richard, that you never would.'

'A solemn promise,' he repeated, with a drivelling laugh and vacant stare. 'A solemn promise. To be sure. A solemn promise!' Awakening, as it were, after a time; in the same manner as before; he said with sudden animation:

'How can I help it, Margaret? What am I to do? She has been to me again!'

'Again!' cried Meg, clasping her hands. 'O, does she think of me so often! Has she been again!'

'Twenty times again,' said Richard. 'Margaret, she haunts me. She comes behind me in the street, and thrusts it in my hand. I hear her foot upon the ashes when I 'm at my work (ha, ha! that an't often), and before I can turn my head, her voice is in my ear, saying, "Richard, don't look round. For Heaven's love, give her this!" She brings it where I live; she sends it in letters; she taps at the window and lays it on the sill. What *can* I do? Look at it!'

He held out in his hand a little purse, and chinked the money it enclosed.

'Hide it,' said Meg. 'Hide it! When she comes again, tell her, Richard, that I love her in my soul. That I never lie down to sleep, but I bless her, and pray for her. That, in my solitary work, I never cease to have her in my thoughts. That she is with me, night and day. That if I died to-morrow, I would remember her with my last breath. But, that I cannot look upon it!'

He slowly recalled his hand, and crushing the purse together, said with a kind of drowsy thoughtfulness:

'I told her so. I told her so, as plain as words could speak. I 've taken this gift back and left it at her door, a dozen times since then. But when she came at last, and stood before me, face to face, what could I do?'

'You saw her!' exclaimed Meg. 'You saw her! O Lilian, my sweet girl! O, Lilian, Lilian!'

'I saw her,' he went on to say, not answering, but engaged in the same slow pursuit of his own thoughts.

'There she stood: trembling! "How does she look, Richard? Does she ever speak of me? Is she thinner? My old place at the table: what's in my old place? And the frame she taught me our old work on—has she burnt it, Richard!" There she was. I heard her say it.'

Meg checked her sobs, and with the tears streaming from her eyes, bent over him to listen. Not to lose a breath.

With his arms resting on his knees; and stooping forward in his chair, as if what he said were written on the ground in some half legible character, which it was his occupation to decipher and connect; he went on.

' "Richard, I have fallen very low; and you may guess how much I have suffered in having this sent back, when I can bear to bring it in my hand to you. But you loved her once, even in my memory, dearly. Others stepped in between you; fears, and jealousies, and doubts, and vanities, estranged you from her; but you did love her, even in my memory!" I suppose I did,' he said, interrupting himself for a moment. 'I did! That's neither here nor there. "O Richard, if you ever did: if you have any memory for what is gone and lost, take it to her once more. Once more! Tell her how I laid my head upon your shoulder, where her own head might have lain, and was so humble to you, Richard. Tell her that you looked into my face, and saw the beauty which she used to praise, all gone: all gone: and in its place, a poor, wan, hollow cheek, that she would weep to see. Tell her everything, and take it back, and she will not refuse again. She will not have the heart!" '

So he sat musing, and repeating the last words until he woke again, and rose.

'You won't take it, Margaret?'

She shook her head, and motioned an entreaty to him to leave her.

'Good-night, Margaret.'

'Good-night!'

He turned to look upon her; struck by her sorrow, and perhaps by the pity for himself which trembled in her voice. It was a quick and rapid action; and for the moment some flash of his old bearing kindled in his form. In the next he went as he had come. Nor did this glimmer of a quenched fire seem to light him to a quicker sense of his debasement.

In any mood, in any grief, in any torture of the mind or body, Meg's work must be done. She sat down to her task, and plied it. Night, midnight. Still she worked.

She had a meagre fire, the night being very cold; and rose at intervals to mend it. The Chimes rang half-past twelve while she was thus engaged; and when they ceased she heard a gentle knocking at the door. Before she could so much as wonder who was there, at that unusual hour, it opened.

O Youth and Beauty, happy as ye should be, look at this. O Youth and Beauty, blest and blessing all within your reach, and working out the ends of your Beneficent Creator, look at this!

She saw the entering figure; screamed its name; cried 'Lilian!'

It was swift, and fell upon its knees before her: clinging to her dress.

'Up, dear! Up! Lilian! My own dearest!'

'Never more, Meg; never more! Here! Here! Close to you, holding to you, feeling your dear breath upon my face!'

'Sweet Lilian! Darling Lilian! Child of my heart—no mother's love can be more tender—lay your head upon my breast!'

'Never more, Meg. Never more! When I first looked into your face, you knelt before me. On my knees before you, let me die. Let it be here!'

'You have come back. My Treasure! We will live together, work together, hope together, die together!'

'Ah! Kiss my lips, Meg; fold your arms about me; press me to your bosom; look kindly on me; but don't raise me. Let it be here. Let me see the last of your dear face upon my knees!'

O Youth and Beauty, happy as ye should be, look at this! O Youth and Beauty, working out the ends of your Beneficent Creator, look at this!

'Forgive me, Meg! So dear, so dear! Forgive me! I know you do, I see you do, but say so, Meg!'

She said so, with her lips on Lilian's cheek. And with her arms twined round—she knew it now—a broken heart.

'His blessing on you, dearest love. Kiss me once more! He suffered her to sit beside His feet, and dry them with her hair. O Meg, what Mercy and Compassion!'

As she died, the Spirit of the child returning, innocent and radiant, touched the old man with its hand, and beckoned him away.

Fourth Quarter

SOME new remembrance of the ghostly figures in the Bell; some faint impression of the ringing of the Chimes; some giddy consciousness of having seen the swarm of phantoms reproduced and reproduced until the recollection of them lost itself in the confusion of their numbers; some hurried knowledge, how conveyed to him he knew not, that more years

had passed; and Trotty, with the Spirit of the child attending him, stood looking on at mortal company.

Fat company, rosy-cheeked company, comfortable company. They were but two, but they were red enough for ten. They sat before a bright fire, with a small low table between them; and unless the fragrance of hot tea and muffins lingered longer in that room than in most others, the table had seen service very lately. But all the cups and saucers being clean, and in their proper places in the corner-cupboard; and the brass toasting-fork hanging in its usual nook and spreading its four idle fingers out as if it wanted to be measured for a glove; there remained no other visible tokens of the meal just finished, than such as purred and washed their whiskers in the person of the basking cat, and glistened in the gracious, not to say the greasy, faces of her patrons.

This cosy couple (married, evidently) had made a fair division of the fire between them, and sat looking at the glowing sparks that dropped into the grate; now nodding off into a doze; now waking up again when some hot fragment, larger than the rest, came rattling down, as if the fire were coming with it.

It was in no danger of sudden extinction, however; for it gleamed not only in the little room, and on the panes of window-glass in the door, and on the curtain half drawn across them, but in the little shop beyond. A little shop, quite crammed and choked with the abundance of its stock; a perfectly voracious little shop, with a maw as accommodating and full as any shark's. Cheese, butter, firewood, soap, pickles, matches, bacon, table-beer, peg-tops, sweetmeats, boys' kites, bird-seed, cold ham, birch brooms, hearth-stones, salt, vinegar, blacking, red-herrings, stationery, lard, mushroom-ketchup, staylaces, loaves of bread, shuttlecocks, eggs, and slate pencil; everything was

fish that came to the net of this greedy little shop, and all articles were in its net. How many other kinds of petty merchandise were there, it would be difficult to say; but balls of packthread, ropes of onions, pounds of candles, cabbage-nets, and brushes, hung in bunches from the ceiling, like extraordinary fruit; while various odd canisters emitting aromatic smells, established the veracity of the inscription over the outer door, which informed the public that the keeper of this little shop was a licensed dealer in tea, coffee, tobacco, pepper, and snuff.

Glancing at such of these articles as were visible in the shining of the blaze, and the less cheerful radiance of two smoky lamps which burnt but dimly in the shop itself, as though its plethora sat heavy on their lungs; and glancing, then, at one of the two faces by the parlour-fire; Trotty had small difficulty in recognising in the stout old lady, Mrs. Chicken-stalker: always inclined to corpulency, even in the days when he had known her as established in the general line, and having a small balance against him in her books.

The features of her companion were less easy to him. The great broad chin, with creases in it large enough to hide a finger in; the astonished eyes, that seemed to expostulate with themselves for sinking deeper and deeper into the yielding fat of the soft face; the nose afflicted with that disordered action of its functions which is generally termed The Snuffles; the short thick throat and labouring chest, with other beauties of the like description; though calculated to impress the memory, Trotty could at first allot to nobody he had ever known: and yet he had some recollection of them too. At length, in Mrs. Chicken-stalker's partner in the general line, and in the crooked and eccentric line of life, he recognised the

former porter of Sir Joseph Bowley; an apoplectic innocent, who had connected himself in Trotty's mind
with Mrs. Chickenstalker years ago, by giving him
admission to the mansion where he had confessed his
obligations to that lady, and drawn on his unlucky
head such grave reproach.

Trotty had little interest in a change like this, after
the changes he had seen; but association is very strong
sometimes; and he looked involuntarily behind the
parlour-door, where the accounts of credit customers
were usually kept in chalk.   There was no record of
his name.   Some names were there, but they were
strange to him, and infinitely fewer than of old; from
which he argued that the porter was an advocate of
ready money transactions, and on coming into the
business had looked pretty sharp after the Chickenstalker defaulters.

So desolate was Trotty, and so mournful for the
youth and promise of his blighted child, that it was a
sorrow to him, even to have no place in Mrs. Chickenstalker's ledger.

'What sort of a night is it, Anne?' inquired the
former porter of Sir Joseph Bowley, stretching out
his legs before the fire, and rubbing as much of them
as his short arms could reach; with an air that added,
'Here I am if it's bad, and I don't want to go out if
it's good.'

'Blowing and sleeting hard,' returned his wife; 'and
threatening snow.   Dark.   And very cold.'

'I'm glad to think we had muffins,' said the former
porter, in the tone of one who had set his conscience
at rest.   'It's a sort of night that's meant for
muffins.   Likewise crumpets.   Also Sally Lunns.'

The former porter mentioned each successive kind
of eatable, as if he were musingly summing up his
good actions.   After which he rubbed his fat legs as

before, and jerking them at the knees to get the fire upon the yet unroasted parts, laughed as if somebody had tickled him.

'You're in spirits, Tugby, my dear,' observed his wife.

The firm was Tugby, late Chickenstalker.

'No,' said Tugby. 'No. Not particular. I'm a little elewated. The muffins came so pat!'

With that he chuckled until he was black in the face; and had so much ado to become any other colour, that his fat legs took the strangest excursions into the air. Nor were they reduced to anything like decorum until Mrs. Tugby had thumped him violently on the back, and shaken him as if he were a great bottle.

'Good gracious, goodness, lord-a-mercy bless and save the man!' cried Mrs. Tugby, in great terror. 'What's he doing?'

Mr. Tugby wiped his eyes, and faintly repeated that he found himself a little elewated.

'Then don't be so again, that's a dear good soul,' said Mrs. Tugby, 'if you don't want to frighten me to death, with your struggling and fighting!'

Mr. Tugby said he wouldn't; but, his whole existence was a fight, in which, if any judgment might be founded on the constantly-increasing shortness of his breath, and the deepening purple of his face, he was always getting the worst of it.

'So it's blowing, and sleeting, and threatening snow; and it's dark, and very cold, is it, my dear?' said Mr. Tugby, looking at the fire, and reverting to the cream and marrow of his temporary elevation.

'Hard weather indeed,' returned his wife, shaking her head.

'Aye, aye! Years,' said Mr. Tugby, 'are like Christians in that respect. Some of 'em die hard:

some of 'em die easy. This one hasn't many days to
run, and is making a fight for it. I like him all the
better. There's a customer, my love!'

Attentive to the rattling door, Mrs. Tugby had
already risen.

'Now then!' said that lady, passing out into the little
shop. 'What's wanted? Oh! I beg your pardon,
sir, I'm sure. I didn't think it was you.'

She made this apology to a gentleman in black,
who, with his wristbands tucked up, and his hat
cocked loungingly on one side, and his hands in his
pockets, sat down astride on the table-beer barrel, and
nodded in return.

'This is a bad business upstairs, Mrs. Tugby,' said
the gentleman. 'The man can't live.'

'Not the back-attic can't!' cried Tugby, coming out
into the shop to join the conference.

'The back-attic, Mr. Tugby,' said the gentleman,
'is coming downstairs fast, and will be below the
basement very soon.'

Looking by turns at Tugby and his wife, he
sounded the barrel with his knuckles for the depth of
beer, and having found it, played a tune upon the
empty part.

'The back-attic, Mr. Tugby,' said the gentleman:
Tugby having stood in silent consternation for some
time: 'is Going.'

'Then,' said Tugby, turning to his wife, 'he must
Go, you know, before he's Gone.'

'I don't think you can move him,' said the gentleman, shaking his head. 'I wouldn't take the responsibility of saying it could be done, myself. You had
better leave him where he is. He can't live long.'

'It's the only subject,' said Tugby, bringing the
butter-scale down upon the counter with a crash, by
weighing his fist on it, 'that we've ever had a word

upon; she and me; and look what it comes to! He 's going to die here, after all. Going to die upon the premises. Going to die in our house!'

'And where should he have died, Tugby?' cried his wife.

'In the workhouse,' he returned. 'What are work-houses made for?'

'Not for that,' said Mrs. Tugby, with great energy. 'Not for that! Neither did I marry you for that. Don't think it, Tugby. I won't have it. I won't allow it. I 'd be separated first, and never see your face again. When my widow's name stood over that door, as it did for many years: this house being known as Mrs. Chickenstalker's far and wide, and never known but to its honest credit and its good report: when my widow's name stood over that door, Tugby, I knew him as a handsome, steady, manly, independent youth; I knew her as the sweetest-looking, sweetest-tempered girl, eyes ever saw; I knew her father (poor old creetur, he fell down from the steeple walking in his sleep, and killed himself), for the simplest, hard-est-working, childest-hearted man, that ever drew the breath of life; and when I turn them out of house and home, may angels turn me out of Heaven. As they would! And serve me right!'

Her old face, which had been a plump and dimpled one before the changes which had come to pass, seemed to shine out of her as she said these words; and when she dried her eyes, and shook her head and her handkerchief at Tugby, with an expression of firmness which it was quite clear was not to be easily resisted, Trotty said, 'Bless her! Bless her!'

Then he listened, with a panting heart, for what should follow. Knowing nothing yet, but that they spoke of Meg.

If Tugby had been a little elevated in the parlour,

he more than balanced that account by being not a little depressed in the shop, where he now stood staring at his wife, without attempting a reply; secretly conveying, however—either in a fit of abstraction or as a precautionary measure—all the money from the till into his own pockets, as he looked at her.

The gentleman upon the table-beer cask, who appeared to be some authorised medical attendant upon the poor, was far too well accustomed, evidently, to little differences of opinion between man and wife, to interpose any remark in this instance. He sat softly whistling, and turning little drops of beer out of the tap upon the ground, until there was a perfect calm: when he raised his head, and said to Mrs. Tugby, late Chickenstalker:

'There 's something interesting about the woman, even now. How did she come to marry him?'

'Why that,' said Mrs. Tugby, taking a seat near him, 'is not the least cruel part of her story, sir. You see they kept company, she and Richard, many years ago. When they were a young and beautiful couple, everything was settled, and they were to have been married on a New Year's Day. But, somehow, Richard got it into his head, through what the gentlemen told him, that he might do better, and that he 'd soon repent it, and that she wasn't good enough for him, and that a young man of spirit had no business to be married. And the gentlemen frightened her, and made her melancholy, and timid of his deserting her, and of her children coming to the gallows, and of its being wicked to be man and wife, and a good deal more of it. And in short, they lingered and lingered, and their trust in one another was broken, and so at last was the match. But the fault was his. She would have married him, sir, joyfully. I 've seen her heart swell, many times afterwards, when

he passed her in a proud and careless way; and never did a woman grieve more truly for a man, than she for Richard when he first went wrong.'

'Oh! he went wrong, did he?' said the gentleman, pulling out the vent-peg of the table-beer, and trying to peep down into the barrel through the hole.

'Well, sir, I don't know that he rightly understood himself, you see. I think his mind was troubled by their having broke with one another; and that but for being ashamed before the gentlemen, and perhaps for being uncertain too, how she might take it, he 'd have gone through any suffering or trial to have had Meg's promise and Meg's hand again. That 's my belief. He never said so; more 's the pity! He took to drinking, idling, bad companions: all the fine resources that were to be so much better for him than the Home he might have had. He lost his looks, his character, his health, his strength, his friends, his work: everything!'

'He didn't lose everything, Mrs. Tugby,' returned the gentleman, 'because he gained a wife; and I want to know how he gained her.'

'I 'm coming to it, sir, in a moment. This went on for years and years; he sinking lower and lower; she enduring, poor thing, miseries enough to wear her life away. At last, he was so cast down, and cast out, that no one would employ or notice him; and doors were shut upon him, go where he would. Applying from place to place, and door to door; and coming for the hundredth time to one gentleman who had often and often tried him (he was a good workman to the very end); that gentleman, who knew his history, said, "I believe you are incorrigible; there is only one person in the world who has a chance of reclaiming you; ask me to trust you no more, until she

tries to do it." Something like that, in his anger and vexation.'

'Ah!' said the gentleman. 'Well?'

'Well, sir, he went to her, and kneeled to her; said it was so: said it ever had been so; and made a prayer to her to save him.'

'And she?—Don't distress yourself, Mrs. Tugby.'

'She came to me that night to ask me about living here. "What he was once to me," she said, "is buried in a grave, side by side with what I was to him. But I have thought of this; and I will make the trial. In the hope of saving him; for the love of the light-hearted girl (you remember her) who was to have been married on a New Year's Day; and for the love of her Richard." And she said he had come to her from Lilian, and Lilian had trusted to him, and she never could forget that. So they were married; and when they came home here, and I saw them, I hoped that such prophecies as parted them when they were young, may not often fulfil themselves as they did in this case, or I wouldn't be the makers of them for a Mine of Gold.'

The gentleman got off the cask, and stretched himself, observing:

'I suppose he used her ill, as soon as they were married?'

'I don't think he ever did that,' said Mrs. Tugby, shaking her head, and wiping her eyes. 'He went on better for a short time; but, his habits were too old and strong to be got rid of; he soon fell back a little; and was falling fast back, when his illness came so strong upon him. I think he has always felt for her. I am sure he has. I have seen him, in his crying fits and tremblings, try to kiss her hand; and I have heard him call her "Meg," and say it was her

nineteenth birthday. There he has been lying, now, these weeks and months. Between him and her baby, she has not been able to do her own work; and by not being able to be regular, she has lost it, even if she could have done it. How they have lived, I hardly know!'

'*I* know,' muttered Mr. Tugby; looking at the till, and round the shop, and at his wife; and rolling his head with immense intelligence. 'Like Fighting Cocks!'

He was interrupted by a cry—a sound of lamentation—from the upper story of the house. The gentleman moved hurriedly to the door.

'My friend,' he said, looking back, 'you needn't discuss whether he shall be removed or not. He has spared you that trouble, I believe.'

Saying so, he ran upstairs, followed by Mrs. Tugby; while Mr. Tugby panted and grumbled after them at leisure: being rendered more than commonly short-winded by the weight of the till, in which there had been an inconvenient quantity of copper. Trotty, with the child beside him, floated up the staircase like mere air.

'Follow her! Follow her! Follow her!' He heard the ghostly voices in the Bells repeat their words as he ascended. 'Learn it, from the creature dearest to your heart!'

It was over. It was over. And this was she, her father's pride and joy! This haggard, wretched woman, weeping by the bed, if it deserved that name, and pressing to her breast, and hanging down her head upon, an infant. Who can tell how spare, how sickly, and how poor an infant! Who can tell how dear!

'Thank God!' cried Trotty, holding up his folded hands. 'O, God be thanked! She loves her child!'

The gentleman, not otherwise hard-hearted or indifferent to such scenes, than that he saw them every day, and knew that they were figures of no moment in the Filer sums—mere scratches in the working of these calculations—laid his hand upon the heart that beat no more, and listened for the breath, and said, 'His pain is over. It's better as it is!' Mrs. Tugby tried to comfort her with kindness. Mr. Tugby tried philosophy.

'Come, come!' he said, with his hands in his pockets, 'you mustn't give way, you know. That won't do. You must fight up. What would have become of me if *I* had given way when I was porter, and we had as many as six runaway carriage-doubles at our door in one night! But, I fell back upon my strength of mind, and didn't open it!'

Again Trotty heard the voices, saying, 'Follow her!' He turned towards his guide, and saw it rising from him, passing through the air. 'Follow her!' it said. And vanished.

He hovered round her; sat down at her feet; looked up into her face for one trace of her old self; listened for one note of her old pleasant voice. He flitted round the child: so wan, so prematurely old, so dreadful in its gravity, so plaintive in its feeble, mournful, miserable wail. He almost worshipped it. He clung to it as her only safeguard; as the last unbroken link that bound her to endurance. He set his father's hope and trust on the frail baby; watched her every look upon it as she held it in her arms; and cried a thousand times, 'She loves it! God be thanked, she loves it!'

He saw the woman tend her in the night; return to her when her grudging husband was asleep, and all was still; encourage her, shed tears with her, set nourishment before her. He saw the day come, and the

night again; the day, the night; the time go by; the house of death relieved of death; the room left to herself and to the child; he heard it moan and cry; he saw it harass her, and tire her out, and when she slumbered in exhaustion, drag her back to consciousness, and hold her with its little hands upon the rack; but she was constant to it, gentle with it, patient with it. Patient! Was its loving mother in her inmost heart and soul, and had its Being knitted up with hers as when she carried it unborn.

All this time, she was in want: languishing away, in dire and pining want. With the baby in her arms, she wandered here and there, in quest of occupation; and with its thin face lying in her lap, and looking up in hers, did any work for any wretched sum; a day and night of labour for as many farthings as there were figures on the dial. If she had quarrelled with it; if she had neglected it; if she had looked upon it with a moment's hate; if, in the frenzy of an instant, she had struck it! No. His comfort was, She loved it always.

She told no one of her extremity, and wandered abroad in the day lest she should be questioned by her only friend: for any help she received from her hands, occasioned fresh disputes between the good woman and her husband; and it was new bitterness to be the daily cause of strife and discord, where she owed so much.

She loved it still. She loved it more and more. But a change fell on the aspect of her love. One night.

She was singing faintly to it in its sleep, and walking to and fro to hush it, when her door was softly opened, and a man looked in.

'For the last time,' he said.

'William Fern!'

'For the last time.'

He listened like a man pursued: and spoke in whispers.

'Margaret, my race is nearly run. I couldn't finish it, without a parting word with you. Without one grateful word.'

'What have you done?' she asked: regarding him with terror.

He looked at her, but gave no answer.

After a short silence, he made a gesture with his hand, as if he set her question by; as if he brushed it aside; and said:

'It's long ago, Margaret, now; but that night is as fresh in my memory as ever 'twas. We little thought, then,' he added, looking round, 'that we should ever meet like this. Your child, Margaret? Let me have it in my arms. Let me hold your child.'

He put his hat upon the floor, and took it. And he trembled as he took it, from head to foot.

'Is it a girl?'

'Yes.'

He put his hand before its little face.

'See how weak I'm grown, Margaret, when I want the courage to look at it! Let her be, a moment. I won't hurt her. It's long ago, but—What's her name?'

'Margaret,' she answered, quickly.

'I'm glad of that,' he said. 'I'm glad of that!'

He seemed to breathe more freely; and after pausing for an instant, took away his hand, and looked upon the infant's face. But covered it again, immediately.

'Margaret!' he said; and gave her back the child. 'It's Lilian's.'

'Lilian's!'

'I held the same face in my arms when Lilian's mother died and left her.'

'When Lilian's mother died and left her!' she repeated, wildly.

'How shrill you speak! Why do you fix your eyes upon me so? Margaret!'

She sunk down in a chair, and pressed the infant to her breast, and wept over it. Sometimes, she released it from her embrace, to look anxiously in its face: then strained it to her bosom again. At those times, when she gazed upon it, then it was that something fierce and terrible began to mingle with her love. Then it was that her old father quailed.

'Follow her!' was sounded through the house. 'Learn it, from the creature dearest to your heart!'

'Margaret,' said Fern, bending over her, and kissing her upon the brow: 'I thank you for the last time. Good-night. Good-bye! Put your hand in mine, and tell me you'll forget me from this hour, and try to think the end of me was here.'

'What have you done?' she asked again.

'There'll be a Fire to-night,' he said, removing from her. 'There'll be Fires this winter-time, to light the dark nights, East, West, North, and South. When you see the distant sky red, they'll be blazing. When you see the distant sky red, think of me no more; or, if you do, remember what a Hell was lighted up inside of me, and think you see its flames reflected in the clouds. Good-night. Good-bye!'

She called to him; but he was gone. She sat down stupefied, until her infant roused her to a sense of hunger, cold, and darkness. She paced the room with it the livelong night, hushing it and soothing it. She said at intervals, 'Like Lilian, when her mother died and left her!' Why was her step so quick, her

eye so wild, her love so fierce and terrible, whenever she repeated those words?

'But, it is Love,' said Trotty. 'It is Love. She 'll never cease to love it. My poor Meg!'

She dressed the child next morning with unusual care—ah, vain expenditure of care upon such squalid robes!—and once more tried to find some means of life. It was the last day of the Old Year. She tried till night, and never broke her fast. She tried in vain.

She mingled with an abject crowd, who tarried in the snow, until it pleased some officer appointed to dispense the public charity (the lawful charity; not that once preached upon a Mount), to call them in, and question them, and say to this one, 'Go to such a place,' to that one, 'Come next week'; to make a football of another wretch, and pass him here and there, from hand to hand, from house to house, until he wearied and lay down to die; or started up and robbed, and so became a higher sort of criminal, whose claims allowed of no delay. Here, too, she failed.

She loved her child, and wished to have it lying on her breast. And that was quite enough.

It was night: a bleak, dark, cutting night: when, pressing the child close to her for warmth, she arrived outside the house she called her home. She was so faint and giddy, that she saw no one standing in the doorway until she was close upon it, and about to enter. Then she recognised the master of the house, who had so disposed himself—with his person it was not difficult—as to fill up the whole entry.

'O!' he said softly. 'You have come back?'

She looked at the child, and shook her head.

'Don't you think you have lived here long enough without paying any rent? Don't you think that,

without any money, you've been a pretty constant customer at this shop, now?' said Mr. Tugby.

She repeated the same mute appeal.

'Suppose you try and deal somewhere else,' he said. 'And suppose you provide yourself with another lodging. Come! Don't you think you could manage it?'

She said in a low voice, that it was very late. To-morrow.

'Now I see what you want,' said Tugby; 'and what you mean. You know there are two parties in this house about you, and you delight in setting 'em by the ears. I don't want any quarrels; I'm speaking softly to avoid a quarrel; but if you don't go away, I'll speak out loud, and you shall cause words high enough to please you. But you shan't come in. That I am determined.'

She put her hair back with her hand, and looked in a sudden manner at the sky, and the dark lowering distance.

'This is the last night of an Old Year, and I won't carry ill-blood and quarrellings and disturbances into a New One, to please you nor anybody else,' said Tugby, who was quite a retail Friend and Father. 'I wonder you an't ashamed of yourself, to carry such practices into a New Year. If you haven't any business in the world, but to be always giving way, and always making disturbances between man and wife, you'd be better out of it. Go along with you.'

'Follow her! To desperation!'

Again the old man heard the voices. Looking up, he saw the figures hovering in the air, and pointing where she went, down the dark street.

'She loves it!' he exclaimed, in agonised entreaty for her. 'Chimes! she loves it still!'

'Follow her!' The shadows swept upon the track she had taken, like a cloud.

He joined in the pursuit; he kept close to her; he looked into her face. He saw the same fierce and terrible expression mingling with her love, and kindling in her eyes. He heard her say, 'Like Lilian! To be changed like Lilian!' and her speed redoubled.

O, for something to awaken her! For any sight, or sound, or scent, to call up tender recollections in a brain on fire! For any gentle image of the Past, to rise before her!

'I was her father! I was her father!' cried the old man, stretching out his hands to the dark shadows flying on above. 'Have mercy on her, and on me! Where does she go? Turn her back! I was her father!'

But they only pointed to her, as she hurried on; and said, 'To desperation! Learn it from the creature dearest to your heart!'

A hundred voices echoed it. The air was made of breath expended in those words. He seemed to take them in, at every gasp he drew. They were everywhere, and not to be escaped. And still she hurried on; the same light in her eyes, the same words in her mouth, 'Like Lilian! To be changed like Lilian!'

All at once she stopped.

'Now, turn her back!' exclaimed the old man, tearing his white hair. 'My child! Meg! Turn her back! Great Father, turn her back!'

In her own scanty shawl, she wrapped the baby warm. With her fevered hands, she smoothed its limbs, composed its face, arranged its mean attire. In her wasted arms she folded it, as though she never would resign it more. And with her dry lips, kissed it in a final pang, and last long agony of Love.

Putting its tiny hand up to her neck, and holding it there, within her dress, next to her distracted heart,

she set its sleeping face against her: closely, steadily, against her: and sped onward to the River.

To the rolling River, swift and dim, where Winter Night sat brooding like the last dark thoughts of many who had sought a refuge there before her. Where scattered lights upon the banks gleamed sullen, red, and dull, as torches that were burning there, to show the way to Death. Where no abode of living people cast its shadow, on the deep, impenetrable, melancholy shade.

To the River! To that portal of Eternity, her desperate footsteps tended with the swiftness of its rapid waters running to the sea. He tried to touch her as she passed him, going down to its dark level; but, the wild distempered form, the fierce and terrible love, the desperation that had left all human check or hold behind, swept by him like the wind.

He followed her. She paused a moment on the brink, before the dreadful plunge. He fell down on his knees, and in a shriek addressed the figures in the Bells now hovering above them.

'I have learnt it!' cried the old man. 'From the creature dearest to my heart! O, save her, save her!'

He could wind his fingers in her dress; could hold it! As the words escaped his lips, he felt his sense of touch return, and knew that he detained her.

The figures looked down steadfastly upon him.

'I have learnt it!' cried the old man. 'O, have mercy on me in this hour, if, in my love for her, so young and good, I slandered Nature in the breasts of mothers rendered desperate! Pity my presumption, wickedness, and ignorance, and save her.'

He felt his hold relaxing. They were silent still.

'Have mercy on her!' he exclaimed, 'as one in whom this dreadful crime has sprung from Love perverted; from the strongest, deepest Love we fallen creatures

know! Think what her misery must have been, when such seed bears such fruit! Heaven meant her to be good. There is no loving mother on the earth who might not come to this, if such a life had gone before. O, have mercy on my child, who, even at this pass, means mercy to her own, and dies herself, and perils her immortal soul, to save it!'

She was in his arms. He held her now. His strength was like a giant's.

'I see the Spirit of the Chimes among you!' cried the old man, singling out the child, and speaking in some inspiration, which their looks conveyed to him. 'I know that our inheritance is held in store for us by Time. I know there is a sea of Time to rise one day, before which all who wrong us or oppress us will be swept away like leaves. I see it, on the flow! I know that we must trust and hope, and neither doubt ourselves, nor doubt the good in one another. I have learnt it from the creature dearest to my heart. I clasp her in my arms again. O Spirits, merciful and good, I take your lesson to my breast along with her! O Spirits, merciful and good, I am grateful!'

He might have said more; but, the Bells, the old familiar Bells, his own dear, constant, steady friends, the Chimes, began to ring the joy-peals for a New Year: so lustily, so merrily, so happily, so gaily, that he leapt upon his feet, and broke the spell that bound him.

'And whatever you do, father,' said Meg, 'don't eat tripe again, without asking some doctor whether it's likely to agree with you; for how you *have* been going on, Good gracious!'

She was working with her needle, at the little table by the fire: dressing her simple gown with ribbons for her wedding. So quietly happy, so blooming and

youthful, so full of beautiful promise, that he uttered a great cry as if it were an Angel in his house; then flew to clasp her in his arms.

But, he caught his feet in the newspaper, which had fallen on the hearth; and somebody came rushing in between them.

'No!' cried the voice of this same somebody; a generous and jolly voice it was! 'Not even you. Not even you. The first kiss of Meg in the New Year is mine. Mine! I have been waiting outside the house, this hour, to hear the Bells and claim it. Meg, my precious prize, a happy year! A life of happy years, my darling wife!'

And Richard smothered her with kisses.

You never in all your life saw anything like Trotty after this. I don't care where you have lived or what you have seen; you never in all your life saw anything at all approaching him! He sat down in his chair and beat his knees and cried; he sat down in his chair and beat his knees and laughed; he sat down in his chair and beat his knees and laughed and cried together; he got out of his chair and hugged Meg; he got out of his chair and hugged Richard; he got out of his chair and hugged them both at once; he kept running up to Meg, and squeezing her fresh face between his hands and kissing it, going from her backwards not to lose sight of it, and running up again like a figure in a magic lantern; and whatever he did, he was constantly sitting himself down in this chair, and never stopping in it for one single moment; being—that's the truth—beside himself with joy.

'And to-morrow's your wedding-day, my pet!' cried Trotty. 'Your real, happy wedding-day!'

'To-day!' cried Richard, shaking hands with him. 'To-day. The Chimes are ringing in the New Year. Hear them!'

They WERE ringing! Bless their sturdy hearts, they WERE ringing! Great Bells as they were; melodious, deep-mouthed, noble Bells; cast in no common metal; made by no common founder; when had they ever chimed like that before!

'But, to-day, my pet,' said Trotty. 'You and Richard had some words to-day.'

'Because he's such a bad fellow, father,' said Meg. 'An't you, Richard! Such a headstrong, violent man! He'd have made no more of speaking his mind to that great Alderman, and putting *him* down I don't know where, than he would of—'

'—Kissing Meg,' suggested Richard. Doing it too!

'No. Not a bit more,' said Meg. 'But I wouldn't let him, father. Where would have been the use!'

'Richard my boy!' cried Trotty. 'You was turned up Trumps originally; and Trumps you must be, till you die! But, you were crying by the fire to-night, my pet, when I came home! Why did you cry by the fire?'

'I was thinking of the years we've passed together, father. Only that. And thinking that you might miss me, and be lonely.'

Trotty was backing off to that extraordinary chair again, when the child who had been awakened by the noise, came running in half-dressed.

'Why, here she is!' cried Trotty, catching her up. 'Here's little Lilian! Ha ha ha! Here we are and here we go! O here we are and here we go again! And here we are and here we go! and Uncle Will too!' Stopping in his trot to greet him heartily. 'O, Uncle Will, the vision that I've had to-night, through lodging you! O, Uncle Will, the obligations that you've laid me under, by your coming, my good friend!'

Before Will Fern could make the least reply, a band of music burst into the room, attended by a lot of neighbours, screaming 'A Happy New Year, Meg!' 'A Happy Wedding!' 'Many of 'em!' and other fragmentary good wishes of that sort. The Drum (who was a private friend of Trotty's) then stepped forward, and said:

'Trotty Veck, my boy! It's got about, that your daughter is going to be married to-morrow. There an't a soul that knows you that don't wish you well, or that knows her and don't wish her well. Or that knows you both, and don't wish you both all the happiness the New Year can bring. And here we are, to play it in and dance it in, accordingly.'

Which was received with a general shout. The Drum was rather drunk, by the bye; but, never mind.

'What a happiness it is, I'm sure,' said Trotty, 'to be so esteemed! How kind and neighbourly you are! It's all along of my dear daughter. She deserves it!'

They were ready for a dance in half a second (Meg and Richard at the top); and the Drum was on the very brink of leathering away with all his power; when a combination of prodigious sounds was heard outside, and a good-humoured comely woman of some fifty years of age, or thereabouts, came running in, attended by a man bearing a stone pitcher of terrific size, and closely followed by the marrow-bones and cleavers, and the bells; not *the* Bells, but a portable collection on a frame.

Trotty said, 'It's Mrs. Chickenstalker!' And sat down and beat his knees again.

'Married, and not tell me, Meg!' cried the good woman. 'Never! I couldn't rest on the last night of the Old Year without coming to wish you joy. I couldn't have done it, Meg. Not if I had been

bedridden. So here I am; and as it's New Year's Eve, and the Eve of your wedding too, my dear, I had a little flip made and brought it with me.'

Mrs. Chickenstalker's notion of a little flip, did honour to her character. The pitcher steamed and smoked and reeked like a volcano; and the man who had carried it, was faint.

'Mrs. Tugby!' said Trotty, who had been going round and round her, in an ecstasy.—'I *should* say, Chickenstalker—Bless your heart and soul! A happy New Year, and many of 'em! Mrs. Tugby,' said Trotty when he had saluted her;—'I *should* say, Chickenstalker—This is William Fern and Lilian.'

The worthy dame, to his surprise, turned very pale and very red.

'Not Lilian Fern whose mother died in Dorsetshire!' said she.

Her uncle answered 'Yes,' and meeting hastily, they exchanged some hurried words together; of which the upshot was, that Mrs. Chickenstalker shook him by both hands; saluted Trotty on his cheek again of her own free will; and took the child to her capacious breast.

'Will Fern!' said Trotty, pulling on his right-hand muffler. 'Not the friend you was hoping to find?'

'Ay!' returned Will, putting a hand on each of Trotty's shoulders. 'And like to prove a'most as good a friend, if that can be, as one I found.'

'O!' said Trotty. 'Please to play up there. Will you have the goodness!'

To the music of the band, the bells, the marrow-bones and cleavers, all at once; and while the Chimes were yet in lusty operation out of doors; Trotty, making Meg and Richard second couple, led off Mrs. Chickenstalker down the dance, and danced it in a

step unknown before or since; founded on his own peculiar trot.

Had Trotty dreamed? Or, are his joys and sorrows, and the actors in them, but a dream; himself a dream; the teller of this tale a dreamer, waking but now? If it be so, O listener, dear to him in all his visions, try to bear in mind the stern realities from which these shadows come; and in your sphere—none is too wide, and none too limited for such an end—endeavour to correct, improve, and soften them. So may the New Year be a happy one to you, happy to many more whose happiness depends on you! So may each year be happier than the last, and not the meanest of our brethren or sisterhood debarred their rightful share, in what our Great Creator formed them to enjoy.

THE CRICKET ON THE HEARTH
A FAIRY TALE OF HOME

TO
LORD JEFFREY
this little Story is inscribed, with the affection
and attachment of his Friend
THE AUTHOR
December, 1845

THE CRICKET ON THE HEARTH

Chirp the First

THE kettle began it! Don't tell me what Mrs. Peerybingle said. I know better. Mrs. Peerybingle may leave it on record to the end of time that she couldn't say which of them began it; but, I say the kettle did. I ought to know, I hope! The kettle began it, full five minutes by the little waxy-faced Dutch clock in the corner, before the Cricket uttered a chirp.

As if the clock hadn't finished striking, and the convulsive little Haymaker at the top of it, jerking away right and left with a scythe in front of a Moorish Palace, hadn't mowed down half an acre of imaginary grass before the Cricket joined in at all!

Why, I am not naturally positive. Every one knows that. I wouldn't set my own opinion against the opinion of Mrs. Peerybingle, unless I were quite sure, on any account whatever. Nothing should induce me. But, this is a question of fact. And the fact is, that the kettle began it, at least five minutes before the Cricket gave any sign of being in existence. Contradict me, and I'll say ten.

Let me narrate exactly how it happened. I should have proceeded to do so in my very first word, but for this plain consideration—if I am to tell a story I must begin at the beginning; and how is it possible to begin at the beginning, without beginning at the kettle?

It appeared as if there were a sort of match, or trial of skill, you must understand, between the kettle and the Cricket. And this is what led to it, and how it came about.

Mrs. Peerybingle, going out into the raw twilight, and clicking over the wet stones in a pair of pattens that worked innumerable rough impressions of the first proposition in Euclid all about the yard—Mrs. Peerybingle filled the kettle at the water-butt. Presently returning, less the pattens (and a good deal less, for they were tall and Mrs. Peerybingle was but short), she set the kettle on the fire. In doing which she lost her temper, or mislaid it for an instant; for, the water being uncomfortably cold, and in that slippy, slushy, sleety sort of state wherein it seems to penetrate through every kind of substance, patten rings included—had laid hold of Mrs. Peerybingle's toes, and even splashed her legs. And when we rather plume ourselves (with reason too) upon our legs, and keep ourselves particularly neat in point of stockings, we find this for the moment, hard to bear.

Besides, the kettle was aggravating and obstinate. It wouldn't allow itself to be adjusted on the top bar; it wouldn't hear of accommodating itself kindly to the knobs of coal; it *would* lean forward with a drunken air, and dribble, a very Idiot of a kettle, on the hearth. It was quarrelsome, and hissed and spluttered morosely at the fire. To sum up all, the lid, resisting Mrs. Peerybingle's fingers, first of all turned topsy-turvy, and then, with an ingenious pertinacity deserving of a better cause, dived sideways in—down to the very bottom of the kettle. And the hull of the Royal George has never made

half the monstrous resistance to coming out of the
water, which the lid of that kettle employed against
Mrs. Peerybingle, before she got it up again.

It looked sullen and pig-headed enough, even then;
carrying its handle with an air of defiance, and
cocking its spout pertly and mockingly at Mrs.
Peerybingle, as if it said, 'I won't boil. Nothing
shall induce me!'

But, Mrs. Peerybingle, with restored good humour,
dusted her chubby little hands against each other,
and sat down before the kettle, laughing. Meantime, the jolly blaze uprose and fell, flashing and
gleaming on the little Haymaker at the top of the
Dutch clock, until one might have thought he stood
stock still before the Moorish Palace, and nothing was
in motion but the flame.

He was on the move, however; and had his spasms,
two to the second, all right and regular. But, his
sufferings when the clock was going to strike, were
frightful to behold; and, when a Cuckoo looked out
of a trap-door in the Palace, and gave note six times,
it shook him, each time, like a spectral voice—or like
a something wiry, plucking at his legs.

It was not until a violent commotion and a whir-
ring noise among the weights and ropes below him
had quite subsided, that this terrified Haymaker became himself again. Nor was he startled without
reason; for these rattling, bony skeletons of clocks
are very disconcerting in their operation, and I
wonder very much how any set of men, but most of
all how Dutchmen, can have had a liking to invent
them. There is a popular belief that Dutchmen love
broad cases and much clothing for their own lower
selves; and they might know better than to leave their
clocks so very lank and unprotected, surely.

Now it was, you observe, that the kettle began to

spend the evening. Now it was, that the kettle, growing mellow and musical, began to have irrepressible gurglings in its throat, and to indulge in short vocal snorts, which it checked in the bud, as if it hadn't quite made up its mind yet, to be good company. Now it was, that after two or three such vain attempts to stifle its convivial sentiments, it threw off all moroseness, all reserve, and burst into a stream of song so cosy and hilarious, as never maudlin nightingale yet formed the least idea of.

So plain too! Bless you, you might have understood it like a book—better than some books you and I could name, perhaps. With its warm breath gushing forth in a light cloud which merrily and gracefully ascended a few feet, then hung about the chimney-corner as its own domestic Heaven, it trolled its song with that strong energy of cheerfulness, that its iron body hummed and stirred upon the fire; and the lid itself, the recently rebellious lid—such is the influence of a bright example—performed a sort of jig, and clattered like a deaf and dumb young cymbal that had never known the use of its twin brother.

That this song of the kettle's was a song of invitation and welcome to somebody out of doors: to somebody at that moment coming on, towards the snug small home and the crisp fire: there is no doubt whatever. Mrs. Peerybingle knew it, perfectly, as she sat musing before the hearth. It's a dark night, sang the kettle, and the rotten leaves are lying by the way; and, above, all is mist and darkness, and, below, all is mire and clay; and there's only one relief in all the sad and murky air; and I don't know that it is one, for it's nothing but a glare; of deep and angry crimson, where the sun and wind together; set a brand upon the clouds for being guilty of such weather; and the wildest open country is a long dull streak

THE CRICKET ON THE HEARTH 213

of black; and there's hoar-frost on the finger-post, and thaw upon the track; and the ice it isn't water, and the water isn't free; and you couldn't say that anything is what it ought to be; but he's coming, coming, coming!—

And here, if you like, the Cricket DID chime in! with a Chirrup, Chirrup, Chirrup of such magnitude, by way of chorus; with a voice so astoundingly disproportionate to its size, as compared with the kettle; (size! you couldn't see it!) that if it had then and there burst itself like an overcharged gun, if it had fallen a victim on the spot, and chirruped its little body into fifty pieces, it would have seemed a natural and inevitable consequence, for which it had expressly laboured.

The kettle had had the last of its solo performance. It persevered with undiminished ardour; but the Cricket took first fiddle and kept it. Good Heaven, how it chirped! Its shrill, sharp, piercing voice resounded through the house, and seemed to twinkle in the outer darkness like a star. There was an indescribable little trill and tremble in it, at its loudest, which suggested its being carried off its legs, and made to leap again, by its own intense enthusiasm. Yet they went very well together, the Cricket and the kettle. The burden of the song was still the same; and louder, louder, louder still, they sang it in their emulation.

The fair little listener—for fair she was, and young: though something of what is called the dumpling shape; but I don't myself object to that—lighted a candle, glanced at the Haymaker on the top of the clock, who was getting in a pretty average crop of minutes; and looked out of the window, where she saw nothing, owing to the darkness, but her own face imaged in the glass. And my opinion is (and so

would yours have been), that she might have looked a long way, and seen nothing half so agreeable. When she came back, and sat down in her former seat, the Cricket and the kettle were still keeping it up, with a perfect fury of competition. The kettle's weak side clearly being, that he didn't know when he was beat.

There was all the excitement of a race about it. Chirp, chirp, chirp! Cricket a mile ahead. Hum, hum, hum—m—m! Kettle making play in the distance, like a great top. Chirp, chirp, chirp! Cricket round the corner. Hum, hum, hum—m—m! Kettle sticking to him in his own way; no idea of giving in. Chirp, chirp, chirp! Cricket fresher than ever. Hum, hum, hum—m—m! Kettle slow and steady. Chirp, chirp, chirp! Cricket going in to finish him. Hum, hum, hum—m—m! Kettle not to be finished. Until at last they got so jumbled together, in the hurry-skurry, helter-skelter, of the match, that whether the kettle chirped and the Cricket hummed, or the Cricket chirped and the kettle hummed, or they both chirped and both hummed, it would have taken a clearer head than yours or mine to have decided with anything like certainty. But, of this, there is no doubt: that, the kettle and the Cricket, at one and the same moment, and by some power of amalgamation best known to themselves, sent, each, his fireside song of comfort streaming into a ray of the candle that shone out through the window, and a long way down the lane. And this light, bursting on a certain person who, on the instant, approached towards it through the gloom, expressed the whole thing to him, literally in a twinkling, and cried, 'Welcome home, old fellow! Welcome home, my boy!'

This end attained, the kettle, being dead beat, boiled over, and was taken off the fire. Mrs. Peerybingle then went running to the door, where, what with the wheels of a cart, the tramp of a horse, the voice of a man, the tearing in and out of an excited dog, and the surprising and mysterious appearance of a baby, there was soon the very What 's-his-name to pay.

Where the baby came from, or how Mrs. Peerybingle got hold of it in that flash of time, *I* don't know. But a live baby there was, in Mrs. Peerybingle's arms; and a pretty tolerable amount of pride she seemed to have in it, when she was drawn gently to the fire, by a sturdy figure of a man, much taller and much older than herself, who had to stoop a long way down, to kiss her. But she was worth the trouble. Six foot six, with the lumbago, might have done it.

'Oh goodness, John!' said Mrs. P. 'What a state you are in with the weather!'

He was something the worse for it, undeniably. The thick mist hung in clots upon his eyelashes like candied thaw; and between the fog and fire together, there were rainbows in his very whiskers.

'Why, you see, Dot,' John made answer, slowly, as he unrolled a shawl from about his throat; and warmed his hands; 'it—it an't exactly summer weather. So, no wonder.'

'I wish you wouldn't call me Dot, John. I don't like it,' said Mrs. Peerybingle: pouting in a way that clearly showed she *did* like it, very much.

'Why what else are you?' returned John, looking down upon her with a smile, and giving her waist as light a squeeze as his huge hand and arm could give. 'A dot and'—here he glanced at the baby—'a dot and

carry—I won't say it, for fear I should spoil it; but I was very near a joke. I don't know as ever I was nearer.'

He was often near to something or other very clever, by his own account: this lumbering, slow, honest John; this John so heavy, but so light of spirit; so rough upon the surface, but so gentle at the core; so dull without, so quick within; so stolid, but so good! Oh Mother Nature, give thy children the true poetry of heart that hid itself in this poor Carrier's breast—he was but a Carrier by the way—and we can bear to have them talking prose, and leading lives of prose; and bear to bless thee for their company!

It was pleasant to see Dot, with her little figure, and her baby in her arms: a very doll of a baby: glancing with a coquettish thoughtfulness at the fire, and inclining her delicate little head just enough on one side to let it rest in an odd, half-natural, half-affected, wholly nestling and agreeable manner, on the great rugged figure of the Carrier. It was pleasant to see him, with his tender awkwardness, endeavouring to adapt his rude support to her slight need, and make his burly middle-age a leaning-staff not inappropriate to her blooming youth. It was pleasant to observe how Tilly Slowboy, waiting in the background for the baby, took especial cognizance (though in her earliest teens) of this grouping; and stood with her mouth and eyes wide open, and her head thrust forward, taking it in as if it were air. Nor was it less agreeable to observe how John the Carrier, reference being made by Dot to the aforesaid baby, checked his hand when on the point of touching the infant, as if he thought he might crack it; and bending down, surveyed it from a safe distance, with a kind of puzzled pride, such as an amiable

mastiff might be supposed to show, if he found himself, one day, the father of a young canary.

'An't he beautiful, John? Don't he look precious in his sleep?'

'Very precious,' said John. 'Very much so. He generally *is* asleep, an't he?'

'Lor, John! Good gracious no!'

'Oh,' said John, pondering. 'I thought his eyes was generally shut. Halloa!'

'Goodness, John, how you startle one!'

'It an't right for him to turn 'em up in that way!' said the astonished Carrier, 'is it? See how he's winking with both of 'em at once! And look at his mouth! Why he's gasping like a gold and silver fish!'

'You don't deserve to be a father, you don't,' said Dot, with all the dignity of an experienced matron. 'But how should you know what little complaints children are troubled with, John! You wouldn't so much as know their names, you stupid fellow.' And when she had turned the baby over on her left arm, and had slapped its back as a restorative, she pinched her husband's ear, laughing.

'No,' said John, pulling off his outer coat. 'It's very true, Dot. I don't know much about it. I only know that I've been fighting pretty stiffly with the wind to-night. It's been blowing north-east, straight into the cart, the whole way home.'

'Poor old man, so it has!' cried Mrs. Peerybingle, instantly becoming very active. 'Here! Take the precious darling, Tilly, while I make myself of some use. Bless it, I could smother it with kissing it, I could! Hie then, good dog! Hie Boxer, boy! Only let me make the tea first, John; and then I'll help you with the parcels, like a busy bee. "How doth the little"—and all the rest of it. you know,

John. Did you ever learn "how doth the little," when you went to school, John?'

'Not to quite know it,' John returned. 'I was very near it once. But I should only have spoilt it, I dare say.'

'Ha ha,' laughed Dot. She had the blithest little laugh you ever heard. 'What a dear old darling of a dunce you are, John, to be sure!'

Not at all disputing this position, John went out to see that the boy with the lantern, which had been dancing to and fro before the door and window, like a Will of the Wisp, took due care of the horse; who was fatter than you would quite believe, if I gave you his measure, and so old that his birthday was lost in the mists of antiquity. Boxer, feeling that his attentions were due to the family in general, and must be impartially distributed, dashed in and out with bewildering inconstancy; now, describing a circle of short barks round the horse, where he was being rubbed down at the stable-door; now, feigning to make savage rushes at his mistress, and facetiously bringing himself to sudden stops; now, eliciting a shriek from Tilly Slowboy, in the low nursing-chair near the fire, by the unexpected application of his moist nose to her countenance; now, exhibiting an obtrusive interest in the baby; now, going round and round upon the hearth, and lying down as if he had established himself for the night; now, getting up again, and taking that nothing of a fag-end of a tail of his, out into the weather, as if he had just remembered an appointment, and was off, at a round trot, to keep it.

'There! There 's the teapot, ready on the hob!' said Dot; as briskly busy as a child at play at keeping house. 'And there 's the cold knuckle of ham; and there 's the butter; and there 's the crusty loaf, and

all! Here's the clothes-basket for the small parcels, John, if you've got any there—where are you, John? Don't let the dear child fall under the grate, Tilly, whatever you do!'

It may be noted of Miss Slowboy, in spite of her rejecting the caution with some vivacity, that she had a rare and surprising talent for getting this baby into difficulties: and had several times imperilled its short life, in a quiet way peculiarly her own. She was of a spare and straight shape, this young lady, insomuch that her garments appeared to be in constant danger of sliding off those sharp pegs, her shoulders, on which they were loosely hung. Her costume was remarkable for the partial development, on all possible occasions, of some flannel vestment of a singular structure; also for affording glimpses, in the region of the back, of a corset, or pair of stays, in colour a dead-green. Being always in a state of gaping admiration at everything, and absorbed, besides, in the perpetual contemplation of her mistress's perfections and the baby's, Miss Slowboy, in her little errors of judgment, may be said to have done equal honour to her head and to her heart; and though these did less honour to the baby's head, which they were the occasional means of bringing into contact with deal doors, dressers, stair-rails, bedposts, and other foreign substances, still they were the honest results of Tilly Slowboy's constant astonishment at finding herself so kindly treated, and installed in such a comfortable home. For, the maternal and paternal Slowboy were alike unknown to Fame, and Tilly had been bred by public charity, a foundling; which word, though only differing from fondling by one vowel's length, is very different in meaning, and expresses quite another thing.

To have seen little Mrs. Peerybingle come back

with her husband, tugging at the clothes-basket, and
making the most strenuous exertions to do nothing
at all (for he carried it), would have amused you
almost as much as it amused him.   It may have entertained the Cricket too, for anything I know; but,
certainly, it now began to chirp again, vehemently.

'Heyday!' said John, in his slow way. 'It's
merrier than ever, to-night, I think.'

'And it's sure to bring us good fortune, John! It
always has done so. To have a Cricket on the
Hearth, is the luckiest thing in all the world!'

John looked at her as if he had very nearly got
the thought into his head, that she was his Cricket
in chief, and he quite agreed with her.   But, it was
probably one of his narrow escapes, for he said nothing.

'The first time I heard its cheerful little note, John,
was on that night when you brought me home—
when you brought me to my new home here; its
little mistress. Nearly a year ago. You recollect,
John?'

O yes. John remembered. I should think so!

'Its chirp was such a welcome to me! It seemed
so full of promise and encouragement. It seemed
to say, you would be kind and gentle with me, and
would not expect (I had a fear of that, John, then)
to find an old head on the shoulders of your foolish
little wife.'

John thoughtfully patted one of the shoulders,
and then the head, as though he would have said
No, no; he had had no such expectation; he had been
quite content to take them as they were. And really
he had reason. They were very comely.

'It spoke the truth, John, when it seemed to say
so; for you have ever been, I am sure, the best, the
most considerate, the most affectionate of husbands

to me. This has been a happy home, John; and I love the Cricket for its sake!'

'Why so do I then,' said the Carrier. 'So do I, Dot.'

'I love it for the many times I have heard it, and the many thoughts its harmless music has given me. Sometimes, in the twilight, when I have felt a little solitary and down-hearted, John—before baby was here to keep me company and make the house gay —when I have thought how lonely you would be if I should die; how lonely I should be if I could know that you had lost me, dear; its Chirp, Chirp, Chirp upon the hearth, has seemed to tell me of another little voice, so sweet, so very dear to me, before whose coming sound my trouble vanished like a dream. And when I used to fear—I did fear once, John, I was very young you know—that ours might prove to be an ill-assorted marriage, I being such a child, and you more like my guardian than my husband; and that you might not, however hard you tried, be able to learn to love me, as you hoped and prayed you might; its Chirp, Chirp, Chirp has cheered me up again, and filled me with new trust and confidence. I was thinking of these things to-night, dear, when I sat expecting you; and I love the Cricket for their sake!'

'And so do I,' repeated John. 'But Dot? *I* hope and pray that I might learn to love you? How you talk! I had learnt that, long before I brought you here, to be the Cricket's little mistress, Dot!'

She laid her hand, an instant, on his arm, and looked up at him with an agitated face, as if she would have told him something. Next moment she was down upon her knees before the basket, speaking in a sprightly voice, and busy with the parcels.

'There are not many of them to-night, John, but

I saw some goods behind the cart, just now; and though they give more trouble, perhaps, still they pay as well; so we have no reason to grumble, have we? Besides, you have been delivering, I dare say, as you came along?'

'Oh yes,' John said. 'A good many.'

'Why what's this round box? Heart alive, John, it's a wedding-cake!'

'Leave a woman alone to find out that,' said John, admiringly. 'Now a man would never have thought of it. Whereas, it's my belief that if you was to pack a wedding-cake up in a tea-chest, or a turn-up bedstead, or a pickled salmon keg, or any unlikely thing, a woman would be sure to find it out directly. Yes; I called for it at the pastry-cook's.'

'And it weighs I don't know what—whole hundred-weights!' cried Dot, making a great demonstration of trying to lift it. 'Whose is it, John? Where is it going?'

'Read the writing on the other side,' said John.

'Why, John! My Goodness, John!'

'Ah! who'd have thought it!' John returned.

'You never mean to say,' pursued Dot, sitting on the floor and shaking her head at him, 'that it's Gruff and Tackleton the toy-maker!'

John nodded.

Mrs. Peerybingle nodded also, fifty times at least. Not in assent—in dumb and pitying amazement; screwing up her lips the while with all their little force (they were never made for screwing up; I am clear of that), and looking the good Carrier through and through, in her abstraction. Miss Slowboy, in the mean time, who had a mechanical power of reproducing scraps of current conversation for the delectation of the baby, with all the sense struck out of them, and all the nouns changed into the plural

number, inquired aloud of that young creature, Was it Gruffs and Tackletons the toymakers then, and Would it call at Pastry-cooks for wedding-cakes, and Did its mothers know the boxes when its fathers brought them homes; and so on.

'And that is really to come about!' said Dot. 'Why, she and I were girls at school together, John.'

He might have been thinking of her, or nearly thinking of her, perhaps, as she was in that same school time. He looked upon her with a thoughtful pleasure, but he made no answer.

'And he's as old! As unlike her!—Why, how many years older than you, is Gruff and Tackleton, John?'

'How many more cups of tea shall I drink to-night at one sitting, than Gruff and Tackleton ever took in four, I wonder!' replied John, good-humouredly, as he drew a chair to the round table, and began at the cold ham. 'As to eating, I eat but little; but, that little I enjoy, Dot.'

Even this, his usual sentiment at meal times, one of his innocent delusions (for his appetite was always obstinate, and flatly contradicted him), awoke no smile in the face of his little wife, who stood among the parcels, pushing the cake-box slowly from her with her foot, and never once looked, though her eyes were cast down too, upon the dainty shoe she generally was so mindful of. Absorbed in thought, she stood there, heedless alike of the tea and John (although he called to her, and rapped the table with his knife to startle her), until he rose and touched her on the arm; when she looked at him for a moment, and hurried to her place behind the teaboard, laughing at her negligence. But, not as she had laughed before. The manner and the music were quite changed.

The Cricket, too, had stopped. Somehow the room was not so cheerful as it had been. Nothing like it.

'So, these are all the parcels, are they, John?' she said, breaking a long silence, which the honest Carrier had devoted to the practical illustration of one part of his favourite sentiment—certainly enjoying what he ate, if it couldn't be admitted that he ate but little. 'So these are all the parcels; are they, John?'

'That's all,' said John. 'Why—no—I—' laying down his knife and fork, and taking a long breath. 'I declare—I've clean forgotten the old gentleman!'

'The old gentleman?'

'In the cart,' said John. 'He was asleep, among the straw, the last time I saw him. I've very nearly remembered him, twice, since I came in; but, he went out of my head again. Holloa! Yahip there! Rouse up! That's my hearty!'

John said these latter words outside the door, whither he had hurried with the candle in his hand.

Miss Slowboy, conscious of some mysterious reference to The Old Gentleman, and connecting in her mystified imagination certain associations of a religious nature with the phrase, was so disturbed, that hastily rising from the low chair by the fire to seek protection near the skirts of her mistress, and coming into contact as she crossed the doorway with an ancient Stranger, she instinctively made a charge or butt at him with the only offensive instrument within her reach. This instrument happening to be the baby, great commotion and alarm ensued, which the sagacity of Boxer rather tended to increase; for, that good dog, more thoughtful than its master, had, it seemed, been watching the old gentleman in his

sleep, lest he should walk off with a few young poplar trees that were tied up behind the cart; and he still attended on him very closely, worrying his gaiters in fact, and making dead sets at the buttons.

'You 're such an undeniable good sleeper, sir,' said John, when tranquillity was restored; in the mean time the old gentleman had stood, bareheaded and motionless, in the centre of the room; 'that I have half a mind to ask you where the other six are— only that would be a joke, and I know I should spoil it. Very near though,' murmured the Carrier, with a chuckle; 'very near!'

The Stranger, who had long white hair, good features, singularly bold and well defined for an old man, and dark, bright, penetrating eyes, looked round with a smile, and saluted the Carrier's wife by gravely inclining his head.

His garb was very quaint and odd—a long, long way behind the time. Its hue was brown, all over. In his hand he held a great brown club or walking-stick; and striking this upon the floor, it fell asunder, and became a chair. On which he sat down, quite composedly.

'There!' said the Carrier, turning to his wife. 'That 's the way I found him, sitting by the road-side! Upright as a milestone. And almost as deaf.'

'Sitting in the open air, John!'

'In the open air,' replied the Carrier, 'just at dusk. "Carriage Paid," he said; and gave me eighteen-pence. Then he got in. And there he is.'

'He 's going, John, I think!'

Not at all. He was only going to speak.

'If you please, I was to be left till called for,' said the Stranger, mildly. 'Don't mind me.'

With that, he took a pair of spectacles from one

of his large pockets, and a book from another, and leisurely began to read. Making no more of Boxer than if he had been a house lamb!

The Carrier and his wife exchanged a look of perplexity. The Stranger raised his head; and glancing from the latter to the former, said,

'Your daughter, my good friend?'

'Wife,' returned John.

'Niece?' said the Stranger.

'Wife,' roared John.

'Indeed?' observed the Stranger. 'Surely? Very young!'

He quietly turned over, and resumed his reading. But, before he could have read two lines, he again interrupted himself to say:

'Baby, yours?'

John gave him a gigantic nod; equivalent to an answer in the affirmative, delivered through a speaking trumpet.

'Girl?'

'Bo-o-oy!' roared John.

'Also very young, eh?'

Mrs. Peerybingle instantly struck in. 'Two months and three da-ays! Vaccinated just six weeks ago-o! Took very fine-ly! Considered, by the doctor, a remarkably beautiful chi-ild! Equal to the general run of children at five months o-old! Takes notice, in a way quite won-der-ful! May seem impossible to you, but feels his legs al-ready!'

Here the breathless little mother, who had been shrieking these short sentences into the old man's ear, until her pretty face was crimsoned, held up the Baby before him as a stubborn and triumphant fact; while Tilly Slowboy, with a melodious cry of 'Ketcher, Ketcher'—which sounded like some unknown words, adapted to a popular Sneeze—performed some cow-

like gambols round that all-unconscious Innocent.

'Hark! He's called for, sure enough,' said John. 'There's somebody at the door. Open it, Tilly.'

Before she could reach it, however, it was opened from without; being a primitive sort of door, with a latch, that any one could lift if he chose—and a good many people did choose, for all kinds of neighbours liked to have a cheerful word or two with the Carrier, though he was no great talker himself. Being opened, it gave admission to a little, meagre, thoughtful, dingy-faced man, who seemed to have made himself a great-coat from the sack-cloth covering of some old box; for, when he turned to shut the door, and keep the weather out, he disclosed upon the back of that garment, the inscription G & T in large black capitals. Also the word GLASS in bold characters.

'Good-evening John!' said the little man. 'Good-evening Mum. Good-evening Tilly. Good-evening Unbeknown! How's Baby Mum? Boxer's pretty well I hope?'

'All thriving, Caleb,' replied Dot. 'I am sure you need only look at the dear child, for one, to know that.'

'And I'm sure I need only look at you for another,' said Caleb.

He didn't look at her though; he had a wandering and thoughtful eye which seemed to be always projecting itself into some other time and place, no matter what he said; a description which will equally apply to his voice.

'Or at John for another,' said Caleb. 'Or at Tilly, as far as that goes. Or certainly at Boxer.'

'Busy just now, Caleb?' asked the Carrier.

'Why, pretty well, John,' he returned, with the distraught air of a man who was casting about for the

Philosopher's stone, at least. 'Pretty much so. There's rather a run on Noah's Arks at present. I could have wished to improve upon the Family, but I don't see how it's to be done at the price. It would be a satisfaction to one's mind, to make it clearer which was Shems and Hams, and which was Wives. Flies an't on that scale neither, as compared with elephants you know! Ah! well! Have you got anything in the parcel line for me, John?'

The Carrier put his hand into a pocket of the coat he had taken off; and brought out, carefully preserved in moss and paper, a tiny flower-pot.

'There it is!' he said, adjusting it with great care. 'Not so much as a leaf damaged. Full of buds!'

Caleb's dull eye brightened, as he took it and thanked him.

'Dear, Caleb,' said the Carrier. 'Very dear at this season.'

'Never mind that. It would be cheap to me, whatever it cost,' returned the little man. 'Anything else, John?'

'A small box,' replied the Carrier. 'Here you are!'

'"For Caleb Plummer,"' said the little man, spelling out the direction. '"With Cash." With Cash, John. I don't think it's for me.'

'With Care,' returned the Carrier, looking over his shoulder. 'Where do you make out cash?'

'Oh! To be sure!' said Caleb. 'It's all right. With care! Yes, yes; that's mine. It might have been with cash, indeed, if my dear Boy in the Golden South Americas had lived, John. You loved him like a son; didn't you? You needn't say you did. I know, of course. "Caleb Plummer. With care." Yes, yes, it's all right. It's a box of dolls' eyes for my daughter's work. I wish it was her own sight in a box. John.'

'I wish it was, or could be!' cried the Carrier.

'Thank 'ee,' said the little man. 'You speak very hearty. To think that she should never see the Dolls —and them a-staring at her, so bold, all day long! That's where it cuts. What's the damage, John?'

'I'll damage you,' said John, 'if you inquire. Dot! Very near?'

'Well! it's like you to say so,' observed the little man. 'It's your kind way. Let me see. I think that's all.'

'I think not,' said the Carrier. 'Try again.'

'Something for our Governor, eh?' said Caleb, after pondering a little while. 'To be sure. That's what I came for; but my head's so running on them Arks and things! He hasn't been here, has he?'

'Not he,' returned the Carrier. 'He's too busy, courting.'

'He's coming round though,' said Caleb; 'for he told me to keep on the near side of the road going home, and it was ten to one he'd take me up. I had better go, by the bye.—You couldn't have the goodness to let me pinch Boxer's tail, Mum, for half a moment, could you?'

'Why, Caleb! what a question!'

'Oh never mind, Mum,' said the little man. 'He mightn't like it perhaps. There's a small order just come in, for barking dogs; and I should wish to go as close to Natur' as I could, for sixpence. That's all. Never mind, Mum.'

It happened opportunely, that Boxer, without receiving the proposed stimulus, began to bark with great zeal. But, as this implied the approach of some new visitor, Caleb, postponing his study from the life to a more convenient season, shouldered the round box, and took a hurried leave. He might have

spared himself the trouble, for he met the visitor upon the threshold.

'Oh! You are here, are you? Wait a bit. I 'll take you home. John Peerybingle, my service to you. More of my service to your pretty wife. Handsomer every day! Better too, if possible! And younger,' mused the speaker, in a low voice; 'that 's the Devil of it!'

'I should be astonished at your paying compliments, Mr. Tackleton,' said Dot, not with the best grace in the world; 'but for your condition.'

'You know all about it then?'

'I have got myself to believe it, somehow,' said Dot.

'After a hard struggle, I suppose?'

'Very.'

Tackleton the Toy-merchant, pretty generally known as Gruff and Tackleton—for that was the firm, though Gruff had been bought out long ago; only leaving his name, and as some said his nature, according to its Dictionary meaning, in the business —Tackleton the Toy-merchant, was a man whose vocation had been quite misunderstood by his Parents and Guardians. If they had made him a Money Lender, or a sharp Attorney, or a Sheriff's Officer, or a Broker, he might have sown his discontented oats in his youth, and, after having had the full run of himself in ill-natured transactions, might have turned out amiable, at last, for the sake of a little freshness and novelty. But, cramped and chafing in the peaceable pursuit of toy-making, he was a domestic Ogre, who had been living on children all his life, and was their implacable enemy. He despised all toys; wouldn't have bought one for the world; delighted, in his malice, to insinuate grim expressions into the faces of brown-paper farmers who drove pigs to market, bellmen who advertised lost lawyers' con-

sciences, moveable old ladies who darned stockings or carved pies; and other like samples of his stock-in-trade. In appalling masks; hideous, hairy, red-eyed Jacks in Boxes; Vampire Kites; demoniacal Tumblers who wouldn't lie down, and were perpetually flying forward, to stare infants out of countenance; his soul perfectly revelled. They were his only relief, and safety-valve. He was great in such inventions. Anything suggestive of a Pony-nightmare, was delicious to him. He had even lost money (and he took to that toy very kindly) by getting up Goblin slides for magic-lanterns, whereon the Powers of Darkness were depicted as a sort of supernatural shell-fish, with human faces. In intensifying the portraiture of Giants, he had sunk quite a little capital; and, though no painter himself, he could indicate, for the instruction of his artists, with a piece of chalk, a certain furtive leer for the countenances of those monsters, which was safe to destroy the peace of mind of any young gentleman between the ages of six and eleven, for the whole Christmas or Midsummer Vacation.

What he was in toys, he was (as most men are) in other things. You may easily suppose, therefore, that within the great green cape, which reached down to the calves of his legs, there was buttoned up to the chin an uncommonly pleasant fellow; and that he was about as choice a spirit, and as agreeable a companion, as ever stood in a pair of bull-headed looking boots with mahogany-coloured tops.

Still, Tackleton, the toy-merchant, was going to be married. In spite of all this, he was going to be married. And to a young wife too, a beautiful young wife.

He didn't look much like a bridegroom, as he stood in the Carrier's kitchen, with a twist in his dry face,

and a screw in his body, and his hat jerked over the bridge of his nose, and his hands tucked down into the bottoms of his pockets, and his whole sarcastic ill-conditioned self peering out of one little corner of one little eye, like the concentrated essence of any number of ravens. But, a Bridegroom he designed to be.

'In three days' time. Next Thursday. The last day of the first month in the year. That's my wedding day,' said Tackleton.

Did I mention that he had always one eye wide open, and one eye nearly shut; and that the one eye nearly shut, was always the expressive eye? I don't think I did.

'That's my wedding-day!' said Tackleton, rattling his money.

'Why, it's our wedding-day too,' exclaimed the Carrier.

'Ha ha!' laughed Tackleton. 'Odd! You're just such another couple. Just!'

The indignation of Dot at this presumptuous assertion is not to be described. What next? His imagination would compass the possibility of just such another Baby, perhaps. The man was mad.

'I say! A word with you,' murmured Tackleton, nudging the Carrier with his elbow, and taking him a little apart. 'You'll come to the wedding? We're in the same boat, you know.'

'How in the same boat?' inquired the Carrier.

'A little disparity, you know'; said Tackleton, with another nudge. 'Come and spend an evening with us, beforehand.'

'Why?' demanded John, astonished at this pressing hospitality.

'Why?' returned the other. 'That's a new way of receiving an invitation. Why, for pleasure— sociability, you know, and all that!'

'I thought you were never sociable,' said John, in his plain way.

'Tchah! It's of no use to be anything but free with you I see,' said Tackleton. 'Why, then, the truth is you have a—what tea-drinking people call a sort of a comfortable appearance together, you and your wife. We know better, you know, but—'

'No, we don't know better,' interposed John. 'What are you talking about?'

'Well! We *don't* know better, then,' said Tackleton. 'We'll agree that we don't. As you like; what does it matter? I was going to say, as you have that sort of appearance, your company will produce a favourable effect on Mrs. Tackleton that will be. And, though I don't think your good lady's very friendly to me, in this matter, still she can't help herself from falling into my views, for there's a compactness and cosiness of appearance about her that always tells, even in an indifferent case. You'll say you'll come?'

'We have arranged to keep our Wedding-Day (as far as that goes) at home,' said John. 'We have made the promise to ourselves these six months. We think, you see, that home—'

'Bah! what's home?' cried Tackleton. 'Four walls and a ceiling! (why don't you kill that Cricket! *I* would! I always do. I hate their noise). There are four walls and a ceiling at my house. Come to me!'

'You kill your Crickets, eh?' said John.

'Scrunch 'em, sir,' returned the other, setting his heel heavily on the floor. 'You'll say you'll come? It's as much your interest as mine, you know, that the women should persuade each other that they're quiet and contented, and couldn't be better off. I know their way. Whatever one woman says, another

woman is determined to clinch, always.   There's that spirit of emulation among 'em, sir, that if your wife says to my wife, "I'm the happiest woman in the world, and mine's the best husband in the world, and I dote on him," my wife will say the same to yours, or more, and half believe it.'

Do you mean to say she don't, then?' asked the Carrier.

'Don't!' cried Tackleton, with a short, sharp laugh. 'Don't what?'

The Carrier had some faint idea of adding, 'dote upon you.'   But, happening to meet the half-closed eye, as it twinkled upon him over the turned-up collar of the cape, which was within an ace of poking it out, he felt it such an unlikely part and parcel of anything to be doted on, that he substituted, 'that she don't believe it?'

'Ah you dog!   You're joking,' said Tackleton.

But the Carrier, though slow to understand the full drift of his meaning, eyed him in such a serious manner, that he was obliged to be a little more explanatory.

'I have the humour,' said Tackleton: holding up the fingers of his left hand, and tapping the forefinger, to imply 'there I am, Tackleton to wit': 'I have the humour, sir, to marry a young wife, and a pretty wife': here he rapped his little finger, to express the Bride; not sparingly, but sharply; with a sense of power.   'I'm able to gratify that humour and I do. It's my whim.   But—now look there!'

He pointed to where Dot was sitting, thoughtfully, before the fire; leaning her dimpled chin upon her hand, and watching the bright blaze.   The Carrier looked at her, and then at him, and then at her, and then at him again.

'She honours and obeys, no doubt, you know,' said

Tackleton; 'and that, as I am not a man of sentiment, is quite enough for *me*. But do you think there's anything more in it?'

'I think,' observed the Carrier, 'that I should chuck any man out of window, who said there wasn't.'

'Exactly so,' returned the other with an unusual alacrity of assent. 'To be sure! Doubtless you would. Of course. I'm certain of it. Good-night. Pleasant dreams!'

The Carrier was puzzled, and made uncomfortable and uncertain, in spite of himself. He couldn't help showing it, in his manner.

'Good-night, my dear friend!' said Tackleton, compassionately. 'I'm off. We're exactly alike, in reality, I see. You won't give us to-morrow evening? Well! Next day you go out visiting, I know. I'll meet you there, and bring my wife that is to be. It'll do her good. You're agreeable? Thank 'ee. What's that!'

It was a loud cry from the Carrier's wife: a loud, sharp, sudden cry, that made the room ring, like a glass vessel. She had risen from her seat, and stood like one transfixed by terror and surprise. The Stranger had advanced towards the fire to warm himself, and stood within a short stride of her chair. But quite still.

'Dot!' cried the Carrier. 'Mary! Darling! What's the matter?'

They were all about her in a moment. Caleb, who had been dozing on the cake-box, in the first imperfect recovery of his suspended presence of mind, seized Miss Slowboy by the hair of her head, but immediately apologised.

'Mary!' exclaimed the Carrier, supporting her in his arms. 'Are you ill! What is it? Tell me, dear!'

She only answered by beating her hands together,

and falling into a wild fit of laughter. Then, sinking from his grasp upon the ground, she covered her face with her apron, and wept bitterly. And then she laughed again, and then she cried again, and then she said how cold it was, and suffered him to lead her to the fire, where she sat down as before. The old man standing, as before, quite still.

'I'm better, John,' she said. 'I'm quite well now —I—'

'John!' But John was on the other side of her. Why turn her face towards the strange old gentleman, as if addressing him! Was her brain wandering?

'Only a fancy, John dear—a kind of shock—a something coming suddenly before my eyes—I don't know what it was. It's quite gone, quite gone.'

'I'm glad it's gone,' muttered Tackleton, turning the expressive eye all round the room. 'I wonder where it's gone, and what it was. Humph! Caleb, come here! Who's that with the grey hair?'

'I don't know, sir,' returned Caleb in a whisper. 'Never see him before, in all my life. A beautiful figure for a nut-cracker; quite a new model. With a screw-jaw opening down into his waistcoat, he'd be lovely.'

'Not ugly enough,' said Tackleton.

'Or for a firebox, either,' observed Caleb, in deep contemplation, 'what a model! Unscrew his head to put the matches in; turn him heels up'ards for the light; and what a firebox for a gentleman's mantelshelf, just as he stands!'

'Not half ugly enough,' said Tackleton. 'Nothing in him at all! Come! Bring that box! All right now, I hope!'

'Oh quite gone! Quite gone!' said the little woman, waving him hurriedly away. 'Good-night!'

'Good-night,' said Tackleton. 'Good-night, John Peerybingle! Take care how you carry that box, Caleb. Let it fall, and I'll murder you! Dark as pitch, and weather worse than ever, eh? Good-night!'

So, with another sharp look round the room, he went out at the door; followed by Caleb with the wedding-cake on his head.

The Carrier had been so much astounded by his little wife, and so busily engaged in soothing and tending her, that he had scarcely been conscious of the Stranger's presence, until now, when he again stood there, their only guest.

'He don't belong to them, you see,' said John. 'I must give him a hint to go.'

'I beg your pardon, friend,' said the old gentleman, advancing to him; 'the more so, as I fear your wife has not been well; but the Attendant whom my infirmity,' he touched his ears and shook his head, 'renders almost indispensable, not having arrived, I fear there must be some mistake. The bad night which made the shelter of your comfortable cart (may I never have a worse!) so acceptable, is still as bad as ever. Would you, in your kindness, suffer me to rent a bed here?'

'Yes, yes,' cried Dot. 'Yes! Certainly!'

'Oh!' said the Carrier, surprised by the rapidity of this consent. 'Well! I don't object; but still I'm not quite sure that—'

'Hush!' she interrupted. 'Dear John!'

'Why, he's stone deaf,' urged John.

'I know he is, but—Yes sir, certainly. Yes! certainly! I'll make him up a bed, directly, John.'

As she hurried off to do it, the flutter of her spirits, and the agitation of her manner, were so strange, that the Carrier stood looking after her, quite confounded.

'Did its mothers make it up a Bed then!' cried Miss Slowboy to the Baby; 'and did its hair grow brown and curly, when its caps was lifted off, and frighten it, a precious Pets, a-sitting by the fires!'

With that unaccountable attraction of the mind to trifles, which is often incidental to a state of doubt and confusion, the Carrier, as he walked slowly to and fro, found himself mentally repeating even these absurd words, many times. So many times that he got them by heart, and was still conning them over and over, like a lesson, when Tilly, after administering as much friction to the little bald head with her hand as she thought wholesome (according to the practice of nurses), had once more tied the Baby's cap on.

'And frighten it a precious Pets, a-sitting by the fires. What frightened Dot, I wonder!' mused the Carrier, pacing to and fro.

He scouted, from his heart, the insinuations of the Toy-merchant, and yet they filled him with a vague, indefinite uneasiness. For, Tackleton was quick and sly; and he had that painful sense, himself, of being a man of slow perception, that a broken hint was always worrying to him. He certainly had no intention in his mind of linking anything that Tackleton had said, with the unusual conduct of his wife, but the two subjects of reflection came into his mind together, and he could not keep them asunder.

The bed was soon made ready; and the visitor, declining all refreshment but a cup of tea, retired. Then, Dot—quite well again, she said, quite well again—arranged the great chair in the chimney-corner for her husband; filled his pipe and gave it him; and took her usual little stool beside him on the hearth.

She always *would* sit on that little stool. I think

she must have had a kind of notion that it was a coaxing, wheedling, little stool.

She was, out and out, the very best filler of a pipe, I should say, in the four quarters of the globe. To see her put that chubby little finger in the bowl, and then blow down the pipe to clear the tube, and, when she had done so, affect to think that there was really something in the tube, and blow a dozen times, and hold it to her eye like a telescope, with a most provoking twist in her capital little face, as she looked down it, was quite a brilliant thing. As to the tobacco, she was perfect mistress of the subject: and her lighting of the pipe, with a wisp of paper, when the Carrier had it in his mouth—going so very near his nose, and yet not scorching it—was Art, high Art.

And the Cricket and the kettle, turning up again, acknowledged it! The bright fire, blazing up again, acknowledged it! The little Mower on the clock in his unheeded work acknowledged it! The Carrier, in his smoothing forehead and expanding face, acknowledged it, the readiest of all.

And as he soberly and thoughtfully puffed at his old pipe, and as the Dutch clock ticked, and as the red fire gleamed, and as the Cricket chirped; that Genius of his Hearth and Home (for such the Cricket was) came out, in fairy shape, into the room, and summoned many forms of Home about him. Dots of all ages, and all sizes, filled the chamber. Dots who were merry children, running on before him gathering flowers, in the fields; coy Dots, half shrinking from, half yielding to, the pleading of his own rough image; newly-married Dots, alighting at the door, and taking wondering possession of the household keys; motherly little Dots, attended by fictitious Slowboys, bearing babies to be christened; matronly Dots, still young and blooming, watching Dots of

daughters, as they danced at rustic balls; fat Dots, encircled and beset by troops of rosy grand-children; withered Dots, who leaned on sticks, and tottered as they crept along. Old Carriers too, appeared, with blind old Boxers lying at their feet; and newer carts with younger drivers ('Peerybingle Brothers' on the tilt); and sick old Carriers, tended by the gentlest hands; and graves of dead and gone old Carriers, green in the churchyard. And as the Cricket showed him all these things—he saw them plainly, though his eyes were fixed upon the fire—the Carrier's heart grew light and happy, and he thanked his Household Gods with all his might, and cared no more for Gruff and Tackleton than you do.

But, what was that young figure of a man, which the same Fairy Cricket set so near Her stool, and which remained there, singly and alone? Why did it linger still, so near her, with its arm upon the chimney-piece, ever repeating 'Married! and not to me!'

O Dot! O failing Dot! There is no place for it in all your husband's visions; why has its shadow fallen on his hearth!

Chirp the Second

CALEB PLUMMER and his Blind Daughter lived all alone by themselves, as the Story-books say—and my blessing, with yours to back it I hope, on the Story-books, for saying anything in this workaday world! —Caleb Plummer and his Blind Daughter lived all alone by themselves, in a little cracked nutshell of a wooden house, which was, in truth, no better than a pimple on the prominent red-brick nose of Gruff and Tackleton. The premises of Gruff and Tackleton

were the great feature of the street; but you might have knocked down Caleb Plummer's dwelling with a hammer or two, and carried off the pieces in a cart.

If any one had done the dwelling-house of Caleb Plummer the honour to miss it after such an inroad, it would have been, no doubt, to commend its demolition as a vast improvement. It stuck to the premises of Gruff and Tackleton, like a barnacle to a ship's keel, or a snail to a door, or a little bunch of toadstools to the stem of a tree. But, it was the germ from which the full-grown trunk of Gruff and Tackleton had sprung; and, under its crazy roof, the Gruff before last, had, in a small way, made toys for a generation of old boys and girls, who had played with them, and found them out, and broken them, and gone to sleep.

I have said that Caleb and his poor Blind Daughter lived here. I should have said that Caleb lived here, and his poor Blind Daughter somewhere else— in an enchanted home of Caleb's furnishing, where scarcity and shabbiness were not, and trouble never entered. Caleb was no sorcerer, but in the only magic art that still remains to us, the magic of devoted, deathless love, Nature had been the mistress of his study; and from her teaching, all the wonder came.

The Blind Girl never knew that ceilings were discoloured, walls blotched and bare of plaster here and there, high crevices unstopped, and widening every day, beams mouldering and tending downward. The Blind Girl never knew that iron was rusting, wood rotting, paper peeling off; the size, and shape, and true proportion of the dwelling, withering away. The Blind Girl never knew that ugly shapes of delf and earthenware were on the board; that sorrow and faint-heartedness were in the house; that Caleb's scanty hairs were turning greyer and more grey, be-

fore her sightless face. The Blind Girl never knew
they had a master, cold, exacting, and uninterested—
never knew that Tackleton was Tackleton in short;
but lived in the belief of an eccentric humourist who
loved to have his jest with them, and who while he
was the Guardian Angel of their lives, disdained to
hear one word of thankfulness.

And all was Caleb's doing; all the doing of her
simple father! But he too had a Cricket on his
Hearth; and listening sadly to its music when the
motherless Blind Child was very young, that Spirit
had inspired him with the thought that even her great
deprivation might be almost changed into a blessing,
and the girl made happy by these little means. For
all the Cricket tribe are potent Spirits, even though
the people who hold converse with them do not know
it (which is frequently the case); and there are not
in the unseen world, voices more gentle and more true,
that may be so implicitly relied on, or that are so certain to give none but tenderest counsel, as the Voices
in which the Spirits of the Fireside and the Hearth
address themselves to human kind.

Caleb and his daughter were at work together in
their usual working-room, which served them for
their ordinary living-room as well; and a strange place
it was. There were houses in it, finished and unfinished, for Dolls of all stations in life. Suburban
tenements for Dolls of moderate means; kitchens and
single apartments for Dolls of the lower classes;
capital town residences for Dolls of high estate.
Some of these establishments were already furnished
according to estimate, with a view to the convenience
of Dolls of limited income; others, could be fitted on
the most expensive scale, at a moment's notice, from
whole shelves of chairs and tables, sofas, bedsteads,
and upholstery. The nobility and gentry, and public

in general, for whose accommodation these tenements were designed, lay, here and there, in baskets, staring straight up at the ceiling; but, in denoting their degrees in society, and confining them to their respective stations (which experience shows to be lamentably difficult in real life), the makers of these Dolls had far improved on Nature, who is often froward and perverse; for, they, not resting on such arbitrary marks as satin, cotton-print, and bits of rag, had superadded striking personal differences which allowed of no mistake. Thus, the Doll-lady of distinction had wax limbs of perfect symmetry; but, only she and her compeers. The next grade in the social scale being made of leather, and the next of coarse linen stuff. As to the common-people, they had just so many matches out of tinder-boxes, for their arms and legs, and there they were—established in their sphere at once, beyond the possibility of getting out of it.

There were various other samples of his handicraft, besides Dolls, in Caleb Plummer's room. There were Noah's Arks, in which the Birds and Beasts were an uncommonly tight fit, I assure you; though they could be crammed in, anyhow, at the roof, and rattled and shaken into the smallest compass. By a bold poetical licence, most of these Noah's Arks had knockers on the doors; inconsistent appendages, perhaps, as suggestive of morning callers and a Postman, yet a pleasant finish to the outside of the building. There were scores of melancholy little carts which, when the wheels went round, performed most doleful music. Many small fiddles, drums, and other instruments of torture; no end of cannon, shields, swords, spears, and guns. There were little tumblers in red breeches, incessantly swarming up high obstacles of red-tape, and coming down, head first, on the other side; and there were innumerable old gentle-

men of respectable, not to say venerable, appearance, insanely flying over horizontal pegs, inserted, for the purpose, in their own street doors. There were beasts of all sorts; horses, in particular, of every breed, from the spotted barrel on four pegs, with a small tippet for a mane, to the thoroughbred rocker on his highest mettle. As it would have been hard to count the dozens upon dozens of grotesque figures that were ever ready to commit all sorts of absurdities on the turning of a handle, so it would have been no easy task to mention any human folly, vice, or weakness, that had not its type, immediate or remote, in Caleb Plummer's room. And not in an exaggerated form, for very little handles will move men and women to as strange performances, as any Toy was ever made to undertake.

In the midst of all these objects, Caleb and his daughter sat at work. The Blind Girl busy as a Doll's dressmaker; Caleb painting and glazing the four-pair front of a desirable family mansion.

The care imprinted in the lines of Caleb's face, and his absorbed and dreamy manner, which would have sat well on some alchemist or abstruse student, were at first sight an odd contrast to his occupation, and the trivialities about him. But, trivial things, invented and pursued for bread, become very serious matters of fact; and, apart from this consideration, I am not at all prepared to say, myself, that if Caleb had been a Lord Chamberlain, or a Member of Parliament, or a lawyer, or even a great speculator, he would have dealt in toys one whit less whimsical, while I have a very great doubt whether they would have been as harmless.

'So you were out in the rain last night, father, in your beautiful new great-coat,' said Caleb's daughter.

'In my beautiful new great-coat,' answered Caleb, glancing towards a clothes-line in the room, on which the sack-cloth garment previously described, was carefully hung up to dry.

'How glad I am you bought it, father!'

'And of such a tailor, too,' said Caleb. 'Quite a fashionable tailor. It's too good for me.'

The Blind Girl rested from her work, and laughed with delight. 'Too good, father! What can be too good for you?'

'I'm half ashamed to wear it though,' said Caleb, watching the effect of what he said, upon her brightening face; 'upon my word! When I hear the boys and people say behind me, "Halloa! Here's a swell!" I don't know which way to look. And when the beggar wouldn't go away last night; and when I said I was a very common man, said "No, your Honour! Bless your Honour, don't say that!" I was quite ashamed. I really felt as if I hadn't a right to wear it.'

Happy Blind Girl! How merry she was, in her exultation!

'I see you, father,' she said, clasping her hands, 'as plainly, as if I had the eyes I never want when you are with me. A blue coat—'

'Bright blue,' said Caleb.

'Yes, yes! Bright blue!' exclaimed the girl, turning up her radiant face; 'the colour I can just remember in the blessed sky! You told me it was blue before! A bright blue coat—'

'Made loose to the figure,' suggested Caleb.

'Made loose to the figure!' cried the Blind Girl, laughing heartily; 'and in it, you, dear father, with your merry eye, your smiling face, your free step, and your dark hair—looking so young and handsome!'

'Halloa! Halloa!' said Caleb. 'I shall be vain, presently!'

'I think you are, already,' cried the Blind Girl, pointing at him, in her glee. 'I know you, father! Ha, ha, ha! I've found you out, you see!'

How different the picture in her mind, from Caleb, as he sat observing her! She had spoken of his free step. She was right in that. For years and years, he had never once crossed that threshold at his own slow pace, but with a footfall counterfeited for her ear; and never had he, when his heart was heaviest, forgotten the light tread that was to render hers so cheerful and courageous!

Heaven knows! But I think Caleb's vague bewilderment of manner may have half originated in his having confused himself about himself and everything around him, for the love of his Blind Daughter. How could the little man be otherwise than bewildered, after labouring for so many years to destroy his own identity, and that of all the objects that had any bearing on it!

'There we are,' said Caleb, falling back a pace or two to form the better judgment of his work; 'as near the real thing as sixpenn'orth of halfpence is to sixpence. What a pity that the whole front of the house opens at once! If there was only a staircase in it, now, and regular doors to the rooms to go in at! But that's the worst of my calling, I'm always deluding myself, and swindling myself.'

'You are speaking quite softly. You are not tired, father?'

'Tired!' echoed Caleb, with a great burst of animation, 'what should tire me, Bertha? *I* was never tired. What does it mean?'

To give the greater force to his words, he checked himself in an involuntary imitation of two half-

length stretching and yawning figures on the mantel-shelf, who were represented as in one eternal state of weariness from the waist upwards; and hummed a fragment of a song. It was a Bacchanalian song, something about a Sparkling Bowl. He sang it with an assumption of a Devil-may-care voice, that made his face a thousand times more meagre and more thoughtful than ever.

'What! You're singing, are you?' said Tackleton, putting his head in at the door. 'Go it! *I* can't sing.'

Nobody would have suspected him of it. He hadn't what is generally termed a singing face, by any means.

'I can't afford to sing,' said Tackleton. 'I'm glad *you* can. I hope you can afford to work too. Hardly time for both, I should think?'

'If you could only see him, Bertha, how he's winking at me!' whispered Caleb. 'Such a man to joke! you'd think, if you didn't know him, he was in earnest—wouldn't you now?'

The Blind Girl smiled and nodded.

'The bird that can sing and won't sing, must be made to sing, they say,' grumbled Tackleton. 'What about the owl that can't sing, and oughtn't to sing, and will sing; is there anything that *he* should be made to do?'

'The extent to which he's winking at this moment!' whispered Caleb to his daughter. 'O, my gracious!'

'Always merry and light-hearted with us!' cried the smiling Bertha.

'O, you're there, are you?' answered Tackleton. 'Poor Idiot!'

He really did believe she was an Idiot; and he founded the belief, I can't say whether consciously or not, upon her being fond of him.

'Well! and being there,—how are you?' said Tackleton, in his grudging way.

'Oh! well; quite well. And as happy as even you can wish me to be. As happy as you would make the whole world, if you could!'

'Poor Idiot!' muttered Tackleton. 'No gleam of reason. Not a gleam!'

The Blind Girl took his hand and kissed it; held it for a moment in her own two hands; and laid her cheek against it tenderly, before releasing it. There was such unspeakable affection and such fervent gratitude in the act, that Tackleton himself was moved to say, in a milder growl than usual:

'What 's the matter now?'

'I stood it close beside my pillow when I went to sleep last night, and remembered it in my dreams. And when the day broke, and the glorious red sun—the *red* sun, father?'

'Red in the mornings and the evenings, Bertha,' said poor Caleb, with a woeful glance at his employer.

'When it rose, and the bright light I almost fear to strike myself against in walking, came into the room, I turned the little tree towards it, and blessed Heaven for making things so precious, and blessed you for sending them to cheer me!'

'Bedlam broke loose!' said Tackleton under his breath. 'We shall arrive at the strait-waistcoat and mufflers soon. We 're getting on!'

Caleb, with his hands hooked loosely in each other, stared vacantly before him while his daughter spoke, as if he really were uncertain (I believe he was) whether Tackleton had done anything to deserve her thanks, or not. If he could have been a perfectly free agent, at that moment, required, on pain of death, to kick the Toy-merchant, or fall at his feet, according to his merits, I believe it would have been

an even chance which course he would have taken.
Yet, Caleb knew that with his own hands he had
brought the little rose-tree home for her, so carefully,
and that with his own lips he had forged the innocent
deception which should help to keep her from suspecting how much, how very much, he every day denied
himself, that she might be the happier.

'Bertha!' said Tackleton, assuming, for the nonce,
a little cordiality. 'Come here.'

'Oh! I can come straight to you! You needn't
guide me!' she rejoined.

'Shall I tell you a secret, Bertha?'

'If you will!' she answered, eagerly.

How bright the darkened face! How adorned
with light, the listening head!

'This is the day on which little what 's-her-name, the
spoilt child, Peerybingle's wife, pays her regular
visit to you—makes her fantastic Pic-Nic here; an't
it?' said Tackleton, with a strong expression of dis-
taste for the whole concern.

'Yes,' replied Bertha. 'This is the day.'

'I thought so,' said Tackleton. 'I should like to
join the party.'

'Do you hear that, father!' cried the Blind Girl in
an ecstasy.

'Yes, yes, I hear it,' murmured Caleb, with the fixed
look of a sleep-walker; 'but I don't believe it. It 's
one of my lies, I 've no doubt.'

'You see I—I want to bring the Peerybingles a little more into company with May Fielding,' said Tackleton. 'I am going to be married to May.'

'Married!' cried the Blind Girl, starting from him.

'She 's such a con-founded Idiot,' muttered Tackleton, 'that I was afraid she 'd never comprehend me.
Ah, Bertha! Married! Church, parson, clerk,
beadle, glass-coach, bells, breakfast, bride-cake, fa-

vours, marrow-bones, cleavers, and all the rest of the tom-foolery. A wedding, you know; a wedding. Don't you know what a wedding is?'

'I know,' replied the Blind Girl, in a gentle tone. 'I understand!'

'Do you?' muttered Tackleton. 'It's more than I expected. Well! On that account I want to join the party, and to bring May and her mother. I'll send in a little something or other, before the afternoon. A cold leg of mutton, or some comfortable trifle of that sort. You'll expect me?'

'Yes,' she answered.

She had drooped her head, and turned away; and so stood, with her hands crossed, musing.

'I don't think you will,' muttered Tackleton, looking at her; 'for you seem to have forgotten all about it already. Caleb!'

'I may venture to say I'm here, I suppose,' thought Caleb. 'Sir!'

'Take care she don't forget what I've been saying to her.'

'*She* never forgets,' returned Caleb. 'It's one of the few things she an't clever in.'

'Every man thinks his own geese swans,' observed the Toy-merchant, with a shrug. 'Poor devil!'

Having delivered himself of which remark, with infinite contempt, old Gruff and Tackleton withdrew.

Bertha remained where he had left her, lost in meditation. The gaiety had vanished from her downcast face, and it was very sad. Three or four times, she shook her head, as if bewailing some remembrance or some loss; but, her sorrowful reflections found no vent in words.

It was not until Caleb had been occupied, some time, in yoking a team of horses to a wagon by the summary process of nailing the harness to the vital

parts of their bodies, that she drew near to his working-stool, and sitting down beside him, said:

'Father, I am lonely in the dark. I want my eyes, my patient, willing eyes.'

'Here they are,' said Caleb. 'Always ready. They are more yours than mine, Bertha, any hour in the four-and-twenty. What shall your eyes do for you, dear?'

'Look round the room, father.'

'All right,' said Caleb. 'No sooner said than done, Bertha.'

'Tell me about it.'

'It's much the same as usual,' said Caleb. 'Homely, but very snug. The gay colours on the walls; the bright flowers on the plates and dishes; the shining wood, where there are beams or panels; the general cheerfulness and neatness of the building; make it very pretty.'

Cheerful and neat it was wherever Bertha's hands could busy themselves. But nowhere else, were cheerfulness and neatness possible, in the old crazy shed which Caleb's fancy so transformed.

'You have your working dress on, and are not so gallant as when you wear the handsome coat?' said Bertha, touching him.

'Not quite so gallant,' answered Caleb. 'Pretty brisk though.'

'Father,' said the Blind Girl, drawing close to his side, and stealing one arm round his neck, 'tell me something about May. She is very fair?'

'She is indeed,' said Caleb. And she was indeed. It was quite a rare thing to Caleb, not to have to draw on his invention.

'Her hair is dark,' said Bertha, pensively, 'darker than mine. Her voice is sweet and musical, I know. I have often loved to hear it. Her shape—'

'There's not a Doll's in all the room to equal it,' said Caleb. 'And her eyes!'—

He stopped; for Bertha had drawn closer round his neck, and, from the arm that clung about him, came a warning pressure which he understood too well.

He coughed a moment, hammered for a moment, and then fell back upon the song about the sparkling bowl; his infallible resource in all such difficulties.

'Our friend, father, our benefactor. I am never tired you know of hearing about him.—Now, was I ever?' she said, hastily.

'Of course not,' answered Caleb, 'and with reason.'

'Ah! With how much reason!' cried the Blind Girl. With such fervency, that Caleb, though his motives were so pure, could not endure to meet her face; but dropped his eyes, as if she could have read in them his innocent deceit.

'Then, tell me again about him, dear father,' said Bertha. 'Many times again! His face is benevolent, kind, and tender. Honest and true, I am sure it is. The manly heart that tries to cloak all favours with a show of roughness and unwillingness, beats in its every look and glance.'

'And makes it noble,' added Caleb, in his quiet desperation.

'And makes it noble!' cried the Blind Girl. 'He is older than May, father.'

'Ye-es,' said Caleb, reluctantly. 'He's a little older than May. But that don't signify.'

'Oh father, yes! To be his patient companion in infirmity and age; to be his gentle nurse in sickness, and his constant friend in suffering and sorrow; to know no weariness in working for his sake; to watch him, tend him, sit beside his bed and talk to him awake, and pray for him asleep; what privileges these would

be! What opportunities for proving all her truth and devotion to him! Would she do all this, dear father?'

'No doubt of it,' said Caleb.

'I love her, father; I can love her from my soul!' exclaimed the Blind Girl. And saying so, she laid her poor blind face on Caleb's shoulder, and so wept and wept, that he was almost sorry to have brought that tearful happiness upon her.

In the mean time, there had been a pretty sharp commotion at John Peerybingle's, for, little Mrs. Peerybingle naturally couldn't think of going anywhere without the Baby; and to get the Baby under weigh, took time. Not that there was much of the Baby, speaking of it as a thing of weight and measure, but, there was a vast deal to do about and about it, and it all had to be done by easy stages. For instance, when the Baby was got, by hook and by crook, to a certain point of dressing, and you might have rationally supposed that another touch or two would finish him off, and turn him out a tip-top Baby challenging the world, he was unexpectedly extinguished in a flannel cap, and hustled off to bed; where he simmered (so to speak) between two blankets for the best part of an hour. From this state of inaction he was then recalled, shining very much and roaring violently, to partake of—well? I would rather say, if you 'll permit me to speak generally—of a slight repast. After which, he went to sleep again. Mrs. Peerybingle took advantage of this interval, to make herself as smart in a small way as ever you saw anybody in all your life; and, during the same short truce, Miss Slowboy insinuated herself into a spencer of a fashion so surprising and ingenious, that it had no connection with herself, or anything else in the universe, but was a shrunken, dog's-

eared, independent fact, pursuing its lonely course without the least regard to anybody. By this time, the Baby, being all alive again, was invested, by the united efforts of Mrs. Peerybingle and Miss Slowboy, with a cream-coloured mantle for its body, and a sort of nankeen raised-pie for its head; and so in course of time they all three got down to the door, where the old horse had already taken more than the full value of his day's toll out of the Turnpike Trust, by tearing up the road with his impatient autographs; and whence Boxer might be dimly seen in the remote perspective, standing looking back, and tempting him to come on without orders.

As to a chair, or anything of that kind for helping Mrs. Peerybingle into the cart, you know very little of John, if you think *that* was necessary. Before you could have seen him lift her from the ground, there she was in her place, fresh and rosy, saying, 'John! How *can* you! Think of Tilly!'

If I might be allowed to mention a young lady's legs, on any terms, I would observe of Miss Slowboy's that there was a fatality about them which rendered them singularly liable to be grazed; and that she never effected the smallest ascent or descent, without recording the circumstance upon them with a notch, as Robinson Crusoe marked the days upon his wooden calendar. But as this might be considered ungenteel, I'll think of it.

'John? You've got the basket with the Veal and Ham-Pie and things, and the bottles of Beer?' said Dot. 'If you haven't, you must turn round again, this very minute.'

'You're a nice little article,' returned the Carrier, 'to be talking about turning round, after keeping me a full quarter of an hour behind my time.'

'I am sorry for it, John,' said Dot in a great bustle, 'but I really could not think of going to Bertha's— I would not do it, John, on any account—without the Veal and Ham-Pie and things, and the bottles of Beer. Way!'

This monosyllable was addressed to the horse, who didn't mind it at all.

'Oh *do* way, John!' said Mrs. Peerybingle. 'Please!'

'It 'll be time enough to do that,' returned John, 'when I begin to leave things behind me. The basket 's here, safe enough.'

'What a hard-hearted monster you must be, John, not to have said so, at once, and save me such a turn! I declared I wouldn't go to Bertha's without the Veal and Ham-Pie and things, and the bottles of Beer, for any money. Regularly once a fortnight ever since we have been married, John, have we made our little Pic-Nic there. If anything was to go wrong with it, I should almost think we were never to be lucky again.'

'It was a kind thought in the first instance,' said the Carrier: 'and I honour you for it, little woman.'

'My dear John,' replied Dot, turning very red, 'Don't talk about honouring *me*. Good Gracious!'

By the bye—' observed the Carrier. 'That old gentleman,'—

Again so visibly, and instantly embarrassed!

'He 's an odd fish,' said the Carrier, looking straight along the road before them. 'I can't make him out. I don't believe there 's any harm in him.'

'None at all. I 'm—I 'm sure there 's none at all.'

'Yes,' said the Carrier, with his eyes attracted to her face by the great earnestness of her manner. 'I am glad you feel so certain of it. because it 's a confirma-

tion to me. It 's curious that he should have taken it into his head to ask leave to go on lodging with us; an't it? Things come about so strangely.'

'So very strangely,' she rejoined in a low voice, scarcely audible.

'However, he 's a good-natured old gentleman,' said John, 'and pays as a gentleman, and I think his word is to be relied upon, like a gentleman's. I had quite a long talk with him this morning: he can hear me better already, he says, as he gets more used to my voice. He told me a great deal about himself, and I told him a good deal about myself, and a rare lot of questions he asked me. I gave him information about my having two beats, you know, in my business; one day to the right from our house and back again; another day to the left from our house and back again (for he 's a stranger and don't know the names of places about here); and he seemed quite pleased. "Why, then I shall be returning home to-night your way," he says, "when I thought you 'd be coming in an exactly opposite direction. That 's capital! I may trouble you for another lift perhaps, but I 'll engage not to fall so sound asleep again." He *was* sound asleep, sure-ly!—Dot! what are you thinking of?'

'Thinking of, John? I—I was listening to you.'

'O! That 's all right!' said the honest Carrier. 'I was afraid, from the look of your face, that I had gone rambling on so long, as to set you thinking about something else. I was very near it, I 'll be bound.'

Dot making no reply, they jogged on, for some little time, in silence. But, it was not easy to remain silent very long in John Peerybingle's cart, for, everybody on the road had something to say. Though it might only be 'How are you!' and indeed it was very often nothing else, still, to give that back

again in the right spirit of cordiality, required, not merely a nod and a smile, but as wholesome an action of the lungs withal, as a long-winded Parliamentary speech. Sometimes, passengers on foot, or horseback, plodded on a little way beside the cart, for the express purpose of having a chat; and then there was a great deal to be said, on both sides.

Then, Boxer gave occasion to more good-natured recognitions of, and by, the Carrier, than half a dozen Christians could have done! Everybody knew him, all along the road—especially the fowls and pigs, who when they saw him approaching, with his body all on one side, and his ears pricked up inquisitively, and that knob of a tail making the most of itself in the air, immediately withdrew into remote back settlements, without waiting for the honour of a nearer acquaintance. He had business everywhere; going down all the turnings, looking into all the wells, bolting in and out of all the cottages, dashing into the midst of all the Dame-Schools, fluttering all the pigeons, magnifying the tails of all the cats, and trotting into the public-houses like a regular customer. Wherever he went, somebody or other might have been heard to cry, 'Halloa! Here's Boxer!' and out came that somebody forthwith, accompanied by at least two or three other somebodies, to give John Peerybingle and his pretty wife, Good-Day.

The packages and parcels for the errand cart, were numerous; and there were many stoppages to take them in and give them out, which were not by any means the worst parts of the journey. Some people were so full of expectation about their parcels, and other people were so full of wonder about their parcels, and other people were so full of inexhaustible directions about their parcels, and John had such a lively interest in all the parcels, that it was as good as a play.

Likewise, there were articles to carry, which required to be considered and discussed, and in reference to the adjustment and disposition of which, councils had to be holden by the Carrier and the senders: at which Boxer usually assisted, in short fits of the closest attention, and long fits of tearing round and round the assembled sages and barking himself hoarse. Of all these little incidents, Dot was the amused and open-eyed spectatress from her chair in the cart; and as she sat there, looking on—a charming little portrait framed to admiration by the tilt—there was no lack of nudgings and glancings and whisperings and envyings among the younger men. And this delighted John the Carrier, beyond measure; for he was proud to have his little wife admired, knowing that she didn't mind it—that, if anything, she rather liked it perhaps.

The trip was a little foggy, to be sure, in the January weather; and was raw and cold. But who cared for such trifles? Not Dot, decidedly. Not Tilly Slowboy, for she deemed sitting in a cart, on any terms, to be the highest point of human joys; the crowning circumstance of earthly hopes. Not the Baby, I'll be sworn; for it's not in Baby nature to be warmer or more sound asleep, though its capacity is great in both respects, than that blessed young Peerybingle was, all the way.

You couldn't see very far in the fog, of course: but you could see a great deal! It's astonishing how much you may see, in a thicker fog than that, if you will only take the trouble to look for it. Why, even to sit watching for the Fairy-rings in the fields, and for the patches of hoar-frost still lingering in the shade, near hedges and by trees, was a pleasant occupation: to make no mention of the unexpected shapes in which the trees themselves came starting out of the

mist, and glided into it again. The hedges were tangled and bare, and waved a multitude of blighted garlands in the wind; but, there was no discouragement in this. It was agreeable to contemplate; for, it made the fireside warmer in possession, and the summer greener in expectancy. The river looked chilly; but it was in motion, and moving at a good pace— which was a great point. The canal was rather slow and torpid; that must be admitted. Never mind. It would freeze the sooner when the frost set fairly in, and then there would be skating, and sliding; and the heavy old barges, frozen up somewhere near a wharf, would smoke their rusty iron chimney pipes all day, and have a lazy time of it.

In one place, there was a great mound of weeds or stubble burning; and they watched the fire, so white in the day time, flaring through the fog, with only here and there a dash of red in it, until, in consequence as she observed of the smoke 'getting up her nose,' Miss Slowboy choked—she could do anything of that sort, on the smallest provocation—and woke the Baby, who wouldn't go to sleep again. But, Boxer, who was in advance some quarter of a mile or so, had already passed the outposts of the town, and gained the corner of the street where Caleb and his daughter lived; and long before they had reached the door, he and the Blind Girl were on the pavement waiting to receive them.

Boxer, by the way, made certain delicate distinctions of his own, in his communication with Bertha, which persuade me fully that he knew her to be blind. He never sought to attract her attention by looking at her, as he often did with other people, but touched her invariably. What experience he could ever have had of blind people or blind dogs, I don't know. He had never lived with a blind master; nor had Mr.

Boxer the elder, nor Mrs. Boxer, nor any of his respectable family on either side, ever been visited with blindness, that I am aware of.   He may have found it out for himself, perhaps, but he had got hold of it somehow; and therefore he had hold of Bertha too, by the skirt, and kept hold, until Mrs. Peerybingle and the Baby, and Miss Slowboy, and the basket, were all got safely within doors.

May Fielding was already come; and so was her mother—a little querulous chip of an old lady with a peevish face, who, in right of having preserved a waist like a bedpost, was supposed to be a most transcendent figure; and who, in consequence of having once been better off, or of labouring under an impression that she might have been, if something had happened which never did happen, and seemed to have never been particularly likely to come to pass—but it's all the same—was very genteel and patronising indeed.   Gruff and Tackleton was also there, doing the agreeable, with the evident sensation of being as perfectly at home, and as unquestionably in his own element, as a fresh young salmon on the top of the Great Pyramid.

'May! My dear old friend!' cried Dot, running up to meet her.   'What a happiness to see you.'

Her old friend was, to the full, as hearty and as glad as she; and it really was, if you'll believe me, quite a pleasant sight to see them embrace.   Tackleton was a man of taste, beyond all question.   May was very pretty.

You know sometimes, when you are used to a pretty face, how, when it comes into contact and comparison with another pretty face, it seems for the moment to be homely and faded, and hardly to deserve the high opinion you have had of it.   Now, this was

not at all the case, either with Dot or May; for May's face set off Dot's, and Dot's face set off May's, so naturally and agreeably, that, as John Peerybingle was very near saying when he came into the room, they ought to have been born sisters—which was the only improvement you could have suggested.

Tackleton had brought his leg of mutton, and, wonderful to relate, a tart besides—but we don't mind a little dissipation when our brides are in the case; we don't get married every day—and in addition to these dainties, there were the Veal and Ham-Pie, and 'things,' as Mrs. Peerybingle called them; which were chiefly nuts and oranges, and cakes, and such small deer. When the repast was set forth on the board, flanked by Caleb's contribution, which was a great wooden bowl of smoking potatoes (he was prohibited, by solemn compact, from producing any other viands), Tackleton led his intended mother-in-law to the post of honour. For the better gracing of this place at the high festival, the majestic old soul had adorned herself with a cap, calculated to inspire the thoughtless with sentiments of awe. She also wore her gloves. But let us be genteel, or die!

Caleb sat next his daughter; Dot and her old schoolfellow were side by side; the good Carrier took care of the bottom of the table. Miss Slowboy was isolated, for the time being, from every article of furniture but the chair she sat on, that she might have nothing else to knock the Baby's head against.

As Tilly stared about her at the dolls and toys, they stared at her and at the company. The venerable old gentlemen at the street-doors (who were all in full action) showed especial interest in the party, pausing occasionally before leaping, as if they were listening to the conversation, and then plunging wildly over

and over, a great many times, without halting for breath—as in a frantic state of delight with the whole proceedings.

Certainly, if these old gentlemen were inclined to have a fiendish joy in the contemplation of Tackleton's discomfiture, they had good reason to be satisfied. Tackleton couldn't get on at all; and the more cheerful his intended bride became in Dot's society, the less he liked it, though he had brought them together for that purpose. For he was a regular dog in the manger, was Tackleton; and when they laughed and he couldn't, he took it into his head, immediately, that they must be laughing at him.

'Ah May!' said Dot. 'Dear, dear, what changes! To talk of those merry school-days makes one young again.'

'Why, you an't particularly old, at any time; are you?' said Tackleton.

'Look at my sober plodding husband there,' returned Dot. 'He adds twenty years to my age at least. Don't you, John?'

'Forty,' John replied.

'How many *you* 'll add to May's, I 'm sure I don't know,' said Dot, laughing. 'But she can't be much less than a hundred years of age on her next birthday.'

'Ha ha!' laughed Tackleton. Hollow as a drum, that laugh though. And he looked as if he could have twisted Dot's neck, comfortably.

'Dear dear!' said Dot. 'Only to remember how we used to talk, at school, about the husbands we would choose. I don't know how young, and how handsome, and how gay, and how lively, mine was not to be! And as to May's—Ah dear! I don't know whether to laugh or cry, when I think what silly girls we were.'

May seemed to know which to do; for the colour flushed into her face, and tears stood in her eyes.

'Even the very persons themselves — real live young men—were fixed on sometimes,' said Dot. 'We little thought how things would come about. I never fixed on John I'm sure; I never so much as thought of him. And if I had told you, you were ever to be married to Mr. Tackleton, why you'd have slapped me. Wouldn't you, May?'

Though May didn't say yes, she certainly didn't say no, or express no, by any means.

Tackleton laughed—quite shouted, he laughed so loud. John Peerybingle laughed too, in his ordinary good-natured and contented manner; but his was a mere whisper of a laugh, to Tackleton's.

'You couldn't help yourselves, for all that. You couldn't resist us, you see,' said Tackleton. 'Here we are! Here we are! Where are your gay young bridegrooms now!'

'Some of them are dead,' said Dot; 'and some of them forgotten. Some of them, if they could stand among us at this moment, would not believe we were the same creatures; would not believe that what they saw and heard was real, and we *could* forget them so. No! they would not believe one word of it!'

'Why, Dot!' exclaimed the Carrier. 'Little woman!'

She had spoken with such earnestness and fire, that she stood in need of some recalling to herself, without doubt. Her husband's check was very gentle, for he merely interfered, as he supposed, to shield old Tackleton; but it proved effectual, for she stopped, and said no more. There was an uncommon agitation, even in her silence, which the wary Tackleton, who had brought his half-shut eye to bear upon her, noted closely, and remembered to some purpose too.

May uttered no word, good or bad, but sat quite still, with her eyes cast down, and made no sign of interest in what had passed. The good lady her mother now interposed, observing, in the first instance, that girls were girls, and byegones byegones, and that so long as young people were young and thoughtless, they would probably conduct themselves like young and thoughtless persons: with two or three other positions of a no less sound and incontrovertible character. She then remarked, in a devout spirit, that she thanked Heaven she had always found in her daughter May, a dutiful and obedient child; for which she took no credit to herself, though she had every reason to believe it was entirely owing to herself. With regard to Mr. Tackleton she said, That he was in a moral point of view an undeniable individual, and That he was in an eligible point of view a son-in-law to be desired, no one in their senses could doubt. (She was very emphatic here.) With regard to the family into which he was so soon about, after some solicitation, to be admitted, she believed Mr. Tackleton knew that, although reduced in purse, it had some pretensions to gentility; and if certain circumstances, not wholly unconnected, she would go so far as to say, with the Indigo Trade, but to which she would not more particularly refer, had happened differently, it might perhaps have been in possession of wealth. She then remarked that she would not allude to the past, and would not mention that her daughter had for some time rejected the suit of Mr. Tackleton; and that she would not say a great many other things which she did say, at great length. Finally, she delivered it as the general result of her observation and experience, that those marriages in which there was least of what was romantically and sillily called love, were always

the happiest; and that she anticipated the greatest possible amount of bliss—not rapturous bliss; but the solid, steady-going article—from the approaching nuptials. She concluded by informing the company that to-morrow was the day she had lived for, expressly; and that when it was over, she would desire nothing better than to be packed up and disposed of, in any genteel place of burial.

As these remarks were quite unanswerable—which is the happy property of all remarks that are sufficiently wide of the purpose—they changed the current of the conversation, and diverted the general attention to the Veal and Ham-Pie, the cold mutton, the potatoes, and the tart. In order that the bottled beer might not be slighted, John Peerybingle proposed To-morrow: the Wedding-Day; and called upon them to drink a bumper to it, before he proceeded on his journey

For you ought to know that he only rested there, and gave the old horse a bait. He had to go some four or five miles farther on; and when he returned in the evening, he called for Dot, and took another rest on his way home. This was the order of the day on all the Pic-Nic occasions, and had been, ever since their institution.

There were two persons present, beside the bride and bridegroom elect, who did but indifferent honour to the toast. One of these was Dot, too flushed and discomposed to adapt herself to any small occurrence of the moment; the other, Bertha, who rose up hurriedly, before the rest, and left the table.

'Good-bye!' said stout John Peerybingle, pulling on his dreadnought coat. 'I shall be back at the old time. Good-bye all!'

'Good-bye, John,' returned Caleb.

He seemed to say it by rote, and to wave his hand

in the same unconscious manner; for he stood observing Bertha with an anxious wondering face, that never altered its expression.

'Good-bye, young shaver!' said the jolly Carrier, bending down to kiss the child; which Tilly Slowboy, now intent upon her knife and fork, had deposited asleep (and strange to say, without damage) in a little cot of Bertha's furnishing; 'good-bye! Time will come, I suppose, when *you*'ll turn out into the cold, my little friend, and leave your old father to enjoy his pipe and his rheumatics in the chimney-corner; eh? Where's Dot?'

'I'm here, John!' she said, starting.

'Come, come!' returned the Carrier, clapping his sounding hands. 'Where's the pipe?'

'I quite forgot the pipe, John.'

Forgot the pipe! Was such a wonder ever heard of! She! Forgot the pipe!

'I'll—I'll fill it directly. It's soon done.'

But it was not so soon done, either. It lay in the usual place—the Carrier's dreadnought pocket—with the little pouch, her own work, from which she was used to fill it; but her hand shook so, that she entangled it (and yet her hand was small enough to have come out easily, I am sure), and bungled terribly. The filling of the pipe and lighting it, those little offices in which I have commended her discretion, were vilely done, from first to last. During the whole process, Tackleton stood looking on maliciously with the half-closed eye; which, whenever it met hers —or caught it, for it can hardly be said to have ever met another eye: rather being a kind of trap to snatch it up—augmented her confusion in a most remarkable degree.

'Why, what a clumsy Dot you are, this afternoon!'

said John. 'I could have done it better myself, I verily believe!'

With these good-natured words, he strode away, and presently was heard, in company with Boxer, and the old horse, and the cart, making lively music down the road. What time the dreamy Caleb still stood, watching his blind daughter, with the same expression on his face.

'Bertha!' said Caleb, softly. 'What has happened? How changed you are, my darling, in a few hours— since this morning. *You* silent and dull all day! What is it? Tell me!'

'Oh father, father!' cried the Blind Girl, bursting into tears. 'Oh my hard, hard fate!'

Caleb drew his hand across his eyes before he answered her.

'But think how cheerful and how happy you have been, Bertha! How good, and how much loved, by many people.'

'That strikes me to the heart, dear father! Always so mindful of me! Always so kind to me!'

Caleb was very much perplexed to understand her.

'To be—to be blind, Bertha, my poor dear,' he faltered, 'is a great affliction; but—'

'I have never felt it!' cried the Blind Girl. 'I have never felt it, in its fulness. Never! I have sometimes wished that I could see you, or could see him —only once, dear father, only for one little minute— that I might know what it is I treasure up,' she laid her hands upon her breast, 'and hold here! That I might be sure and have it right! And sometimes (but then I was a child) I have wept in my prayers at night, to think that when your images ascended from my heart to Heaven, they might not be the true resemblance of yourselves. But I have never had these

feelings long. They have passed away and left me tranquil and contented.'

'And they will again,' said Caleb.

'But father! Oh my good, gentle father, bear with me, if I am wicked!' said the Blind Girl. 'This is not the sorrow that so weighs me down!'

Her father could not choose but let his moist eyes overflow; she was so earnest and pathetic, but he did not understand her, yet.

'Bring her to me,' said Bertha. 'I cannot hold it closed and shut within myself. Bring her to me, father!'

She knew he hesitated, and said, 'May. Bring May!'

May heard the mention of her name, and coming quietly towards her, touched her on the arm. The Blind Girl turned immediately, and held her by both hands.

'Look into my face, Dear heart, Sweet heart!' said Bertha. 'Read it with your beautiful eyes, and tell me if the truth is written on it.'

'Dear Bertha, Yes!'

The Blind Girl still, upturning the blank sightless face, down which the tears were coursing fast, addressed her in these words:

'There is not, in my soul, a wish or thought that is not for your good, bright May! There is not, in my soul, a grateful recollection stronger than the deep remembrance which is stored there, of the many many times when, in the full pride of sight and beauty, you have had consideration for Blind Bertha, even, when we two were children, or when Bertha was as much a child as ever blindness can be! Every blessing on your head! Light upon your happy course! Not the less, my dear May'; and she drew towards her, in a closer grasp; 'not the less, my bird, because,

to-day, the knowledge that you are to be His wife has wrung my heart almost to breaking! Father, May, Mary! oh forgive me that it is so, for the sake of all he has done to relieve the weariness of my dark life: and for the sake of the belief you have in me, when I call Heaven to witness that I could not wish him married to a wife more worthy of his goodness!'

While speaking, she had released May Fielding's hands, and clasped her garments in an attitude of mingled supplication and love. Sinking lower and lower down, as she proceeded in her strange confession, she dropped at last at the feet of her friend, and hid her blind face in the folds of her dress.

'Great Power!' exclaimed her father, smitten at one blow with the truth, 'have I deceived her from her cradle, but to break her heart at last!'

It was well for all of them that Dot, that beaming, useful, busy little Dot—for such she was, whatever faults she had, and however you may learn to hate her, in good time—it was well for all of them, I say, that she was there: or where this would have ended, it were hard to tell. But Dot, recovering her self-possession, interposed, before May could reply, or Caleb say another word.

'Come come, dear Bertha! come away with me! Give her your arm, May. So! How composed she is, you see, already; and how good it is of her to mind us,' said the cheery little woman, kissing her upon the forehead. 'Come away, dear Bertha. Come! and here's her good father will come with her; won't you, Caleb? To—be—sure!'

Well, well! she was a noble little Dot in such things, and it must have been an obdurate nature that could have withstood her influence. When she had got poor Caleb and his Bertha away, that they might comfort and console each other, as she knew they only

could, she presently came bouncing back,—the saying is, as fresh as any daisy; *I* say fresher—to mount guard over that bridling little piece of consequence in the cap and gloves, and prevent the dear old creature from making discoveries.

'So bring me the precious Baby, Tilly,' said she, drawing a chair to the fire; 'and while I have it in my lap, here's Mrs. Fielding, Tilly, will tell me all about the management of Babies, and put me right in twenty points where I'm as wrong as can be. Won't you, Mrs. Fielding?'

Not even the Welsh Giant, who according to the popular expression, was so 'slow' as to perform a fatal surgical operation upon himself, in emulation of a juggling-trick achieved by his arch-enemy at break-fast-time; not even he fell half so readily into the snare prepared for him, as the old lady did into this artful pitfall. The fact of Tackleton having walked out; and furthermore, of two or three people having been talking together at a distance, for two minutes, leaving her to her own resources; was quite enough to have put her on her dignity, and the bewailment of that mysterious convulsion in the Indigo trade, for four-and-twenty hours. But this becoming deference to her experience, on the part of the young mother, was so irresistible, that after a short affectation of humility, she began to enlighten her with the best grace in the world; and sitting bolt upright before the wicked Dot, she did, in half an hour, deliver more infallible domestic recipes and precepts, than would (if acted on) have utterly destroyed and done up that Young Peerybingle, though he had been an Infant Samson.

To change the theme, Dot did a little needlework—she carried the contents of a whole workbox in her

pocket; however she contrived it, I don't know—then did a little nursing; then a little more needlework; then had a little whispering chat with May, while the old lady dozed; and so in little bits of bustle, which was quite her manner always, found it a very short afternoon. Then, as it grew dark, and as it was a solemn part of this Institution of the Pic-Nic that she should perform all Bertha's household tasks, she trimmed the fire, and swept the hearth, and set the tea-board out, and drew the curtain, and lighted a candle. Then she played an air or two on a rude kind of harp, which Caleb had contrived for Bertha, and played them very well; for Nature had made her delicate little ear as choice a one for music as it would have been for jewels, if she had had any to wear. By this time it was the established hour for having tea; and Tackleton came back again, to share the meal, and spend the evening.

Caleb and Bertha had returned some time before, and Caleb had sat down to his afternoon's work. But he couldn't settle to it, poor fellow, being anxious and remorseful for his daughter. It was touching to see him sitting idle on his working-stool, regarding her so wistfully, and always saying in his face, 'Have I deceived her from her cradle, but to break her heart!'

When it was night, and tea was done, and Dot had nothing more to do in washing up the cups and saucers; in a word—for I must come to it, and there is no use in putting it off—when the time drew nigh for expecting the Carrier's return in every sound of distant wheels, her manner changed again, her colour came and went, and she was very restless. Not as good wives are, when listening for their husbands. No, no, no. It was another sort of restlessness from that.

Wheels heard. A horse's feet. The barking of a dog. The gradual approach of all the sounds. The scratching paw of Boxer at the door!

'Whose step is that!' cried Bertha, starting up.

'Whose step?' returned the Carrier, standing in the portal, with his brown face ruddy as a winter berry from the keen night air. 'Why, mine.'

'The other step,' said Bertha. 'The man's tread behind you!'

'She is not to be deceived,' observed the Carrier, laughing. 'Come along, sir. You'll be welcome, never fear!'

He spoke in a loud tone; and as he spoke, the deaf old gentleman entered.

He's not so much a stranger, that you haven't seen him once, Caleb,' said the Carrier. 'You give him house-room till we go?'

'Oh surely, John, and take it as an honour.'

'He's the best company on earth, to talk secrets in,' said John. 'I have reasonable good lungs, but he tries 'em, I can tell you. Sit down, sir. All friends here, and glad to see you!'

When he had imparted this assurance, in a voice that amply corroborated what he had said about his lungs, he added in his natural tone, 'A chair in the chimney-corner, and leave to sit quite silent and look pleasantly about him, is all he cares for. He's easily pleased.'

Bertha had been listening intently. She called Caleb to her side, when he had set the chair, and asked him, in a low voice, to describe their visitor. When he had done so (truly now: with scrupulous fidelity), she moved, for the first time since he had come in, and sighed, and seemed to have no further interest concerning him.

The Carrier was in high spirits, good fellow that he was, and fonder of his little wife than ever.

'A clumsy Dot she was, this afternoon!' he said, encircling her with his rough arm, as she stood, removed from the rest; 'and yet I like her somehow. See yonder, Dot!'

He pointed to the old man. She looked down. I think she trembled.

'He's—ha ha ha!—he's full of admiration for you!' said the Carrier. 'Talked of nothing else, the whole way here. Why, he's a brave old boy. I like him for it!'

'I wish he had had a better subject, John'; she said, with an uneasy glance about the room. At Tackleton especially.

'A better subject!' cried the jovial John. 'There's no such thing. Come, off with the great-coat, off with the thick shawl, off with the heavy wrappers! and a cosy half-hour by the fire! My humble service, Mistress. A game at cribbage, you and I? That's hearty. The cards and board, Dot. And a glass of beer here, if there's any left, small wife!'

His challenge was addressed to the old lady, who accepting it with gracious readiness, they were soon engaged upon the game. At first, the Carrier looked about him sometimes, with a smile, or now and then called Dot to peep over his shoulder at his hand, and advise him on some knotty point. But his adversary being a rigid disciplinarian, and subject to an occasional weakness in respect of pegging more than she was entitled to, required such vigilance on his part, as left him neither eyes nor ears to spare. Thus, his whole attention gradually became absorbed upon the cards; and he thought of nothing else, until a hand upon his shoulder restored him to a consciousness of Tackleton.

'I am sorry to disturb you—but a word, directly.'

'I'm going to deal,' returned the Carrier. 'It's a crisis.'

'It is,' said Tackleton. 'Come here, man!'

There was that in his pale face which made the other rise immediately, and ask him, in a hurry, what the matter was.

'Hush! John Peerybingle,' said Tackleton. 'I am sorry for this. I am indeed. I have been afraid of it. I have suspected it from the first.'

'What is it?' asked the Carrier, with a frightened aspect.

'Hush! I'll show you, if you'll come with me.'

The Carrier accompanied him, without another word. They went across a yard, where the stars were shining, and by a little side-door, into Tackleton's own counting-house, where there was a glass window, commanding the ware-room, which was closed for the night. There was no light in the counting-house itself, but there were lamps in the long narrow ware-room; and consequently the window was bright.

'A moment!' said Tackleton. 'Can you bear to look through that window, do you think?'

'Why not?' returned the Carrier.

'A moment more,' said Tackleton. 'Don't commit any violence. It's of no use. It's dangerous too. You're a strong-made man; and you might do murder before you know it.'

The Carrier looked him in the face, and recoiled a step as if he had been struck. In one stride he was at the window, and he saw—

Oh Shadow on the Hearth! Oh truthful Cricket! Oh perfidious Wife!

He saw her, with the old man—old no longer, but erect and gallant—bearing in his hand the false white hair that had won his way into their desolate

and miserable home. He saw her listening to him, as he bent his head to whisper in her ear; and suffering him to clasp her round the waist, as they moved slowly down the dim wooden gallery towards the door by which they had entered it. He saw them stop, and saw her turn—to have the face, the face he loved so, so presented to his view!—and saw her, with her own hands, adjust the lie upon his head, laughing, as she did it, at his unsuspicious nature!

He clenched his strong right hand at first, as if it would have beaten down a lion. But opening it immediately again, he spread it out before the eyes of Tackleton (for he was tender of her, even then), and so, as they passed out, fell down upon a desk, and was as weak as any infant.

He was wrapped up to the chin, and busy with his horse and parcels, when she came into the room, prepared for going home.

'Now John, dear! Good night May! Good night Bertha!'

Could she kiss them? Could she be blithe and cheerful in her parting? Could she venture to reveal her face to them without a blush? Yes. Tackleton observed her closely, and she did all this.

Tilly was hushing the Baby, and she crossed and re-crossed Tackleton, a dozen times, repeating drowsily:

'Did the knowledge that it was to be its wifes, then, wring its hearts almost to breaking; and did its fathers deceive it from its cradles but to break its hearts at last!'

'Now Tilly, give me the Baby! Good-night, Mr. Tackleton. Where's John, for goodness' sake?'

'He's going to walk, beside the horse's head,' said Tackleton; who helped her to her seat.

'My dear John. Walk? To-night?'

The muffled figure of her husband made a hasty sign in the affirmative; and the false stranger and the little nurse being in their places, the old horse moved off. Boxer, the unconscious Boxer, running on before, running back, running round and round the cart, and barking as triumphantly and merrily as ever.

When Tackleton had gone off likewise, escorting May and her mother home, poor Caleb sat down by the fire beside his daughter; anxious and remorseful at the core; and still saying in his wistful contemplation of her, 'Have I deceived her from her cradle, but to break her heart at last!'

The toys that had been set in motion for the Baby, had all stopped, and run down, long ago. In the faint light and silence, the imperturbably calm dolls, the agitated rocking-horses with distended eyes and nostrils, the old gentlemen at the street-doors, standing half doubled up upon their failing knees and ankles, the wry-faced nut-crackers, the very Beasts upon their way into the Ark, in twos, like a Boarding School out walking, might have been imagined to be stricken motionless with fantastic wonder, at Dot being false, or Tackleton beloved, under any combination of circumstances.

Chirp the Third

THE Dutch clock in the corner struck Ten, when the Carrier sat down by his fireside. So troubled and grief-worn, that he seemed to scare the Cuckoo, who, having cut his ten melodious announcements as short as possible, plunged back into the Moorish Palace again, and clapped his little door behind him,

as if the unwonted spectacle were too much for his feelings.

If the little Haymaker had been armed with the sharpest of scythes, and had cut at every stroke into the Carrier's heart, he never could have gashed and wounded it, as Dot had done.

It was a heart so full of love for her; so bound up and held together by innumerable threads of winning remembrance, spun from the daily working of her many qualities of endearment; it was a heart in which she had enshrined herself so gently and so closely; a heart so single and so earnest in its Truth, so strong in right, so weak in wrong; that it could cherish neither passion nor revenge at first, and had only room to hold the broken image of its Idol.

But, slowly, slowly, as the Carrier sat brooding on his hearth, now cold and dark, other and fiercer thoughts began to rise within him, as an angry wind comes rising in the night. The Stranger was beneath his outraged roof. Three steps would take him to his chamber-door. One blow would beat it in. 'You might do murder before you know it,' Tackleton had said. How could it be murder, if he gave the villain time to grapple with him hand to hand! He was the younger man.

It was an ill-timed thought, bad for the dark mood of his mind. It was an angry thought, goading him to some avenging act, that should change the cheerful house into a haunted place which lonely travellers would dread to pass by night; and where the timid would see shadows struggling in the ruined windows when the moon was dim, and hear wild noises in the stormy weather.

He was the younger man! Yes, yes; some lover

who had won the heart that *he* had never touched. Some lover of her early choice, of whom she had thought and dreamed, for whom she had pined and pined, when he had fancied her so happy by his side. O agony to think of it!

She had been above-stairs with the Baby, getting it to bed. As he sat brooding on the hearth, she came close beside him, without his knowledge—in the turning of the rack of his great misery, he lost all other sounds—and put her little stool at his feet. He only knew it, when he felt her hand upon his own, and saw her looking up into his face.

With wonder? No. It was his first impression, and he was fain to look at her again, to set it right. No, not with wonder. With an eager and inquiring look; but not with wonder. At first it was alarmed and serious; then, it changed into a strange, wild, dreadful smile of recognition of his thoughts; then, there was nothing but her clasped hands on her brow, and her bent head, and falling hair.

Though the power of Omnipotence had been his to wield at that moment, he had too much of its diviner property of Mercy in his breast, to have turned one feather's weight of it against her. But he could not bear to see her crouching down upon the little seat where he had often looked on her, with love and pride, so innocent and gay; and, when she rose and left him, sobbing as she went, he felt it a relief to have the vacant place beside him rather than her so long cherished presence. This in itself was anguish keener than all, reminding him how desolate he was become, and how the great bond of his life was rent asunder.

The more he felt this, and the more he knew he could have better borne to see her lying prematurely

dead before him with their little child upon her breast, the higher and the stronger rose his wrath against his enemy. He looked about him for a weapon.

There was a gun, hanging on the wall. He took it down, and moved a pace or two towards the door of the perfidious Stranger's room. He knew the gun was loaded. Some shadowy idea that it was just to shoot this man like a wild beast, seized him, and dilated in his mind until it grew into a monstrous demon in complete possession of him, casting out all milder thoughts and setting up its undivided empire.

That phrase is wrong. Not casting out his milder thoughts, but artfully transforming them. Changing them into scourges to drive him on. Turning water into blood, love into hate, gentleness into blind ferocity. Her image, sorrowing, humbled, but still pleading to his tenderness and mercy with resistless power, never left his mind; but, staying there, it urged him to the door; raised the weapon to his shoulder; fitted and nerved his finger to the trigger; and cried 'Kill him! In his bed!'

He reversed the gun to beat the stock upon the door; he already held it lifted in the air; some indistinct design was in his thoughts of calling out to him to fly, for God's sake, by the window—

When, suddenly, the struggling fire illumined the whole chimney with a glow of light; and the Cricket on the Hearth began to Chirp!

No sound he could have heard, no human voice, not even hers, could so have moved and softened him. The artless words in which she had told him of her love for this same Cricket, were once more freshly spoken; her trembling, earnest manner at the moment, was again before him; her pleasant voice—O what a voice it was, for making house-

hold music at the fireside of an honest man!—thrilled through and through his better nature, and awoke it into life and action.

He recoiled from the door, like a man walking in his sleep, awakened from a frightful dream; and put the gun aside. Clasping his hands before his face, he then sat down again beside the fire, and found relief in tears.

The Cricket on the Hearth came out into the room, and stood in Fairy shape before him.

' "I love it," ' said the Fairy Voice, repeating what he well remembered, ' "for the many times I have heard it, and the many thoughts its harmless music has given me." '

'She said so!' cried the Carrier. 'True!'

' "This has been a happy home, John; and I love the Cricket for its sake!" '

'It has been, Heaven knows,' returned the Carrier. 'She made it happy, always,—until now.'

'So gracefully sweet-tempered; so domestic, joyful, busy, and light-hearted!' said the Voice.

'Otherwise I never could have loved her as I did,' returned the Carrier.

The Voice, correcting him, said 'do.'

The Carrier repeated 'as I did.' But not firmly. His faltering tongue resisted his control, and would speak in its own way, for itself and him.

The Figure, in an attitude of invocation, raised its hand and said:

'Upon your own hearth—'

'The hearth she has blighted,' interposed the Carrier.

'The hearth she has—how often!—blessed and brightened,' said the Cricket; 'the hearth which, but for her, were only a few stones and bricks and rusty bars, but which has been through her, the Altar of

your Home; on which you have nightly sacrificed some petty passion, selfishness, or care, and offered up the homage of a tranquil mind, a trusting nature, and an overflowing heart; so that the smoke from this poor chimney has gone upward with a better fragance than the richest incense that is burnt before the richest shrines in all the gaudy temples of this world!—Upon your own hearth; in its quiet sanctuary; surrounded by its gentle influences and associations; hear her! Hear me! Hear everything that speaks the language of your hearth and home!'

'And pleads for her?' inquired the Carrier.

'All things that speak the language of your hearth and home, *must* plead for her!' returned the Cricket. 'For they speak the truth.'

And while the Carrier, with his head upon his hands, continued to sit meditating in his chair, the Presence stood beside him, suggesting his reflections by its power, and presenting them before him, as in a glass or picture. It was not a solitary Presence. From the hearthstone, from the chimney, from the clock, the pipe, the kettle, and the cradle; from the floor, the walls, the ceiling, and the stairs; from the cart without, and the cupboard within, and the household implements; from every thing and every place with which she had ever been familiar, and with which she had ever entwined one recollection of herself in her unhappy husband's mind; Fairies came trooping forth. Not to stand beside him as the Cricket did, but to busy and bestir themselves. To do all honour to her image. To pull him by the skirts, and point to it when it appeared. To cluster round it, and embrace it, and strew flowers for it to tread on. To try to crown its fair head with their tiny hands. To show that they were fond of it and loved it; and that there was not one ugly, wicked, or accusatory

creature to claim knowledge of it—none but their playful and approving selves.

His thoughts were constant to her image. It was always there.

She sat plying her needle, before the fire, and singing to herself. Such a blithe, thriving, steady little Dot! The fairy figures turned upon him all at once, by one consent, with one prodigious concentrated stare, and seemed to say 'Is this the light wife you are mourning for!'

There were sounds of gaiety outside, musical instruments, and noisy tongues, and laughter. A crowd of young merrymakers came pouring in, among whom were May Fielding and a score of pretty girls. Dot was the fairest of them all; as young as any of them too. They came to summon her to join their party. It was a dance. If ever little foot were made for dancing, hers was, surely. But she laughed, and shook her head, and pointed to her cookery on the fire, and her table ready spread: with an exulting defiance that rendered her more charming than she was before. And so she merrily dismissed them, nodding to her would-be partners, one by one, as they passed, but with a comical indifference, enough to make them go and drown themselves immediately if they were her admirers—and they must have been so, more or less; they couldn't help it. And yet indifference was not her character. O no! For presently, there came a certain Carrier to the door; and bless her what a welcome she bestowed upon him!

Again the staring figures turned upon him all at once, and seemed to say 'Is this the wife who has forsaken you!'

A shadow fell upon the mirror or the picture: call it what you will. A great shadow of the Stranger,

as he first stood underneath their roof; covering its surface, and blotting out all other objects. But the nimble Fairies worked like bees to clear it off again. And Dot again was there. Still bright and beautiful.

Rocking her little Baby in its cradle, singing to it softly, and resting her head upon a shoulder which had its counterpart in the musing figure by which the Fairy Cricket stood.

The night—I mean the real night: not going by Fairy clocks—was wearing now; and in this stage of the Carrier's thoughts, the moon burst out, and shone brightly in the sky. Perhaps some calm and quiet light had risen also, in his mind; and he could think more soberly of what had happened.

Although the shadow of the Stranger fell at intervals upon the glass—always distinct, and big, and thoroughly defined—it never fell so darkly as at first. Whenever it appeared, the Fairies uttered a general cry of consternation, and plied their little arms and legs, with inconceivable activity, to rub it out. And whenever they got at Dot again, and showed her to him once more, bright and beautiful, they cheered in the most inspiring manner.

They never showed her, otherwise than beautiful and bright, for they were Household Spirits to whom falsehood is annihilation; and being so, what Dot was there for them, but the one active, beaming, pleasant little creature who had been the light and sun of the Carrier's Home!

The Fairies were prodigiously excited when they showed her, with the Baby, gossiping among a knot of sage old matrons, and affecting to be wondrous old and matronly herself, and leaning in a staid demure old way upon her husband's arm, attempting—she! such a bud of a little woman—to convey

the idea of having abjured the vanities of the world in general, and of being the sort of person to whom it was no novelty at all to be a mother; yet in the same breath, they showed her, laughing at the Carrier for being awkward, and pulling up his shirt-collar to make him smart, and mincing merrily about that very room to teach him how to dance!

They turned, and stared immensely at him when they showed her with the Blind Girl; for, though she carried cheerfulness and animation with her wheresoever she went, she bore those influences into Caleb Plummer's home, heaped up and running over. The Blind Girl's love for her, and trust in her, and gratitude to her; her own good busy way of setting Bertha's thanks aside; her dexterous little arts for filling up each moment of the visit in doing something useful to the house, and really working hard while feigning to make holiday; her bountiful provision of those standing delicacies, the Veal and Ham-Pie and the bottles of Beer; her radiant little face arriving at the door, and taking leave; the wonderful expression in her whole self, from her neat foot to the crown of her head, of being a part of the establishment—a something necessary to it, which it couldn't be without; all this the Fairies revelled in, and loved her for. And once again they looked upon him all at once, appealingly, and seemed to say, while some among them nestled in her dress and fondled her, 'Is this the wife who has betrayed your confidence!'

More than once, or twice, or thrice, in the long thoughtful night, they showed her to him sitting on her favourite seat, with her bent head, her hands clasped on her brow, her falling hair. As he had seen her last. And when they found her thus, they neither turned nor looked upon him, but gathered

close round her, and comforted and kissed her, and pressed on one another to show sympathy and kindness to her, and forgot him altogether.

Thus the night passed. The moon went down; the stars grew pale; the cold day broke; the sun rose. The Carrier still sat, musing in the chimney corner. He had sat there, with his head upon his hands, all night. All night the faithful Cricket had been Chirp, Chirp, Chirping on the Hearth. All night he had listened to its voice. All night the household Fairies had been busy with him. All night she had been amiable and blameless in the glass, except when that one shadow fell upon it.

He rose up when it was broad day, and washed and dressed himself. He couldn't go about his customary cheerful avocations—he wanted spirit for them—but it mattered the less, that it was Tackleton's wedding-day, and he had arranged to make his rounds by proxy. He thought to have gone merrily to church with Dot. But such plans were at an end. It was their own wedding-day too. Ah! how little he had looked for such a close to such a year!

The Carrier had expected that Tackleton would pay him an early visit; and he was right. He had not walked to and fro before his own door, many minutes, when he saw the Toy-merchant coming in his chaise along the road. As the chaise drew nearer, he perceived that Tackleton was dressed out sprucely for his marriage, and that he had decorated his horse's head with flowers and favours.

The horse looked much more like a bridegroom than Tackleton, whose half-closed eye was more disagreeably expressive than ever. But the Carrier took little heed of this. His thoughts had other occupation.

'John Peerybingle!' said Tackleton, with an air

of condolence. 'My good fellow, how do you find yourself this morning?'

'I have had but a poor night, Master Tackleton,' returned the Carrier shaking his head: 'for I have been a good deal disturbed in my mind. But it's over now! Can you spare me half an hour or so, for some private talk?'

'I came on purpose,' returned Tackleton, alighting. 'Never mind the horse. He'll stand quiet enough, with the reins over this post, if you'll give him a mouthful of hay.'

The Carrier having brought it from his stable, and set it before him, they turned into the house.

'You are not married before noon?' he said, 'I think?'

'No,' answered Tackleton. 'Plenty of time. Plenty of time.'

When they entered the kitchen, Tilly Slowboy was rapping at the Stranger's door; which was only removed from it by a few steps. One of her very red eyes (for Tilly had been crying all night long, because her mistress cried) was at the keyhole; and she was knocking very loud; and seemed frightened.

'If you please I can't make nobody hear,' said Tilly, looking round. 'I hope nobody an't gone and been and died if you please!'

This philanthropic wish, Miss Slowboy emphasised with various new raps and kicks at the door; which led to no result whatever.

'Shall I go?' said Tackleton. 'It's curious.'

The Carrier, who had turned his face from the door, signed to him to go if he would.

So Tackleton went to Tilly Slowboy's relief; and he too kicked and knocked; and he too failed to get the least reply. But he thought of trying the handle of the door; and as it opened easily, he peeped

in, looked in, went in, and soon came running out again.

'John Peerybingle,' said Tackleton, in his ear. 'I hope there has been nothing—nothing rash in the night?'

The Carrier turned upon him quickly.

'Because he's gone!' said Tackleton; 'and the window's open. I don't see any marks—to be sure it's almost on a level with the garden: but I was afraid there might have been some—some scuffle. Eh?'

He nearly shut up the expressive eye altogether; he looked at him so hard. And he gave his eye, and his face, and his whole person, a sharp twist. As if he would have screwed the truth out of him.

'Make yourself easy,' said the Carrier. 'He went into that room last night, without harm in word or deed from me, and no one has entered it since. He is away of his own free will. I'd go out gladly at that door, and beg my bread from house to house, for life, if I could so change the past, that he had never come. But he has come and gone. And I have done with him!'

'Oh!—Well, I think he has got off pretty easy,' said Tackleton, taking a chair.

The sneer was lost upon the Carrier, who sat down too, and shaded his face with his hand, for some little time, before proceeding.

'You showed me last night,' he said at length, 'my wife; my wife that I love; secretly—'

'And tenderly,' insinuated Tackleton.

'Conniving at that man's disguise, and giving him opportunities of meeting her alone. I think there's no sight I wouldn't have rather seen than that. I think there's no man in the world I wouldn't have rather had to show it me.'

'I confess to having had my suspicions always,' said Tackleton. 'And that has made me objectionable here, I know.'

'But as you did show it me,' pursued the Carrier, not minding him; 'and as you saw her, my wife, my wife that I love'—his voice, and eye, and hand, grew steadier and firmer as he repeated these words: evidently in pursuance of a steadfast purpose—'as you saw her at this disadvantage, it is right and just that you should also see with my eyes, and look into my breast, and know what my mind is, upon the subject. For it's settled,' said the Carrier, regarding him attentively. 'And nothing can shake it now.'

Tackleton muttered a few general words of assent, about its being necessary to vindicate something or other; but he was overawed by the manner of his companion. Plain and unpolished as it was, it had a something dignified and noble in it, which nothing but the soul of generous honour dwelling in the man could have imparted.

'I am a plain, rough man,' pursued the Carrier, 'with very little to recommend me. I am not a clever man, as you very well know. I am not a young man. I loved my little Dot, because I had seen her grow up, from a child, in her father's house; because I knew how precious she was; because she had been my life, for years and years. There's many men I can't compare with, who never could have loved my little Dot like me, I think!'

He paused, and softly beat the ground a short time with his foot, before resuming.

'I often thought that though I wasn't good enough for her, I should make her a kind husband, and perhaps know her value better than another; and in this way I reconciled it to myself, and came to think it

might be possible that we should be married. And in the end it came, and we *were* married.'

'Hah!' said Tackleton, with a significant shake of the head.

'I had studied myself; I had had experience of myself; I knew how much I loved her, and how happy I should be,' pursued the Carrier. 'But I had not—I feel it now—sufficiently considered her.'

'To be sure,' said Tackleton. 'Giddiness, frivolity, fickleness, love of admiration! Not considered! All left out of sight! Hah!'

'You had best not interrupt me,' said the Carrier, with some sternness, 'till you understand me; and you 're wide of doing so. If, yesterday, I 'd have struck that man down at a blow, who dared to breathe a word against her, to-day I 'd set my foot upon his face, if he was my brother!'

The Toy-merchant gazed at him in astonishment. He went on in a softer tone:

'Did I consider,' said the Carrier, 'that I took her —at her age, and with her beauty—from her young companions, and the many scenes of which she was the ornament; in which she was the brightest little star that ever shone, to shut her up from day to day in my dull house, and keep my tedious company? Did I consider how little suited I was to her sprightly humour, and how wearisome a plodding man like me must be, to one of her quick spirit? Did I consider that it was no merit in me, or claim in me, that I loved her, when everybody must, who knew her? Never. I took advantage of her hopeful nature and her cheerful disposition; and I married her. I wish I never had! For her sake; not for mine!'

The Toy-merchant gazed at him, without winking. Even the half-shut eye was open now.

'Heaven bless her!' said the Carrier, 'for the cheerful constancy with which she tried to keep the knowledge of this from me! And Heaven help me, that, in my slow mind, I have not found it out before! Poor child! Poor Dot! *I* not to find it out, who have seen her eyes fill with tears, when such a marriage as our own was spoken of! I, who have seen the secret trembling on her lips a hundred times, and never suspected it till last night! Poor girl! That I could ever hope she would be fond of me! That I could ever believe she was!'

'She made a show of it,' said Tackleton. 'She made such a show of it, that to tell you the truth it was the origin of my misgivings.'

And here he asserted the superiority of May Fielding, who certainly made no sort of show of being fond of *him*.

'She has tried,' said the poor Carrier, with greater emotion than he had exhibited yet; 'I only now begin to know how hard she has tried, to be my dutiful and zealous wife. How good she has been; how much she has done; how brave and strong a heart she has; let the happiness I have known under this roof bear witness! It will be some help and comfort to me, when I am here alone.'

'Here alone?' said Tackleton. 'Oh! Then you do mean to take some notice of this?'

'I mean,' returned the Carrier, 'to do her the greatest kindness, and make her the best reparation, in my power. I can release her from the daily pain of an unequal marriage, and the struggle to conceal it. She shall be as free as I can render her.'

'Make *her* reparation!' exclaimed Tackleton, twisting and turning his great ears with his hands. 'There must be something wrong here. You didn't say that, of course.'

The Carrier set his grip upon the collar of the Toy-merchant, and shook him like a reed.

'Listen to me!' he said. 'And take care that you hear me right. Listen to me. Do I speak plainly?'

'Very plainly indeed,' answered Tackleton.

'As if I meant it?'

'Very much as if you meant it.'

'I sat upon that hearth, last night, all night,' exclaimed the Carrier. 'On the spot where she has often sat beside me, with her sweet face looking into mine. I called up her whole life, day by day. I had her dear self, in its every passage, in review before me. And upon my soul she is innocent, if there is One to judge the innocent and guilty!'

Staunch Cricket on the Hearth! Loyal household Fairies!

'Passion and distrust have left me!' said the Carrier; 'and nothing but my grief remains. In an unhappy moment some old lover, better suited to her tastes and years than I; forsaken, perhaps, for me, against her will; returned. In an unhappy moment, taken by surprise, and wanting time to think of what she did, she made herself a party to his treachery, by concealing it. Last night she saw him, in the interview we witnessed. It was wrong. But otherwise than this she is innocent if there is truth on earth!'

'If that is your opinion—' Tackleton began.

'So let her go!' pursued the Carrier. 'Go, with my blessing for the many happy hours she has given me, and my forgiveness for any pang she has caused me. Let her go, and have the peace of mind I wish her. She 'll never hate me. She 'll learn to like me better, when I 'm not a drag upon her, and she wears the chain I have riveted, more lightly. This is the day on which I took her, with so little thought for

her enjoyment, from her home. To-day she shall return to it, and I will trouble her no more. Her father and mother will be here to-day—we had made a little plan for keeping it together—and they shall take her home. I can trust her, there, or anywhere. She leaves me without blame, and she will live so I am sure. If I should die—I may perhaps while she is still young; I have lost some courage in a few hours—she 'll find that I remembered her, and loved her to the last! This is the end of what you showed me. Now, it 's over!'

'O no, John, not over. Do not say it 's over yet! Not quite yet. I have heard your noble words. I could not steal away, pretending to be ignorant of what has affected me with such deep gratitude. Do not say it 's over, till the clock has struck again!'

She had entered shortly after Tackleton, and had remained there. She never looked at Tackleton, but fixed her eyes upon her husband. But she kept away from him, setting as wide a space as possible between them; and though she spoke with most impassioned earnestness, she went no nearer to him even then. How different in this from her old self!

'No hand can make the clock which will strike again for me the hours that are gone,' replied the Carrier, with a faint smile. 'But let it be so, if you will, my dear. It will strike soon. It 's of little matter what we say. I 'd try to please you in a harder case than that.'

'Well!' muttered Tackleton. 'I must be off, for when the clock strikes again, it 'll be necessary for me to be upon my way to church. Good-morning, John Peerybingle. I 'm sorry to be deprived of the pleasure of your company. Sorry for the loss, and the occasion of it too!'

'I have spoken plainly?' said the Carrier, accompanying him to the door.

'Oh quite!'

'And you 'll remember what I have said?'

'Why, if you compel me to make the observation,' said Tackleton, previously taking the precaution of getting into his chaise; 'I must say that it was so very unexpected, that I 'm far from being likely to forget it.'

'The better for us both,' returned the Carrier. 'Good-bye. I give you joy!'

'I wish I could give it to *you*,' said Tackleton. 'As I can't; thank 'ee. Between ourselves, (as I told you before, eh?) I don't much think I shall have the less joy in my married life, because May hasn't been too officious about me, and too demonstrative. Good-bye! Take care of yourself.'

The Carrier stood looking after him until he was smaller in the distance than his horse's flowers and favours near at hand; and then, with a deep sigh, went strolling like a restless, broken man, among some neighbouring elms; unwilling to return until the clock was on the eve of striking.

His little wife, being left alone, sobbed piteously; but often dried her eyes and checked herself, to say how good he was, how excellent he was! and once or twice she laughed; so heartily, triumphantly, and incoherently (still crying all the time), that Tilly was quite horrified.

'Ow if you please don't!' said Tilly. 'It 's enough to dead and bury the Baby, so it is if you please.'

'Will you bring him sometimes, to see his father, Tilly,' inquired her mistress, drying her eyes; 'when I can't live here, and have gone to my old home?'

'Ow if you please don't!' cried Tilly, throwing

back her head, and bursting out into a howl—she looked at the moment uncommonly like Boxer; 'Ow if you please don't!   Ow, what has everybody gone and been and done with everybody, making everybody else so wretched!   Ow-w-w-w!'

The soft-hearted Slowboy trailed off at this juncture, into such a deplorable howl, the more tremendous from its long suppression, that she must infallibly have awakened the Baby, and frightened him into something serious (probably convulsions), if her eyes had not encountered Caleb Plummer, leading in his daughter.   This spectacle restoring her to a sense of the proprieties, she stood for some few moments silent, with her mouth wide open; and then, posting off to the bed on which the Baby lay asleep, danced in a weird, Saint Vitus manner on the floor, and at the same time rummaged with her face and head among the bedclothes, apparently deriving much relief from those extraordinary operations.

'Mary!' said Bertha.   'Not at the marriage!'

'I told her you would not be there mum,' whispered Caleb.   'I heard as much last night.   Bless you,' said the little man, taking her tenderly by both hands, '*I* don't care for what they say.   *I* don't believe them. There an't much of me, but that little should be torn to pieces sooner than I'd trust a word against you!'

He put his arms about her and hugged her, as a child might have hugged one of his own dolls.

'Bertha couldn't stay at home this morning,' said Caleb.   'She was afraid, I know, to hear the bells ring, and couldn't trust herself to be so near them on their wedding-day.   So we started in good time, and came here.   I have been thinking of what I have done,' said Caleb, after a moment's pause; 'I have been blaming myself till I hardly knew what

to do or where to turn, for the distress of mind I have caused her; and I 've come to the conclusion that I 'd better, if you 'll stay with me, mum, the while, tell her the truth. You 'll stay with me the while?' he inquired, trembling from head to foot. 'I don't know what effect it may have upon her; I don't know what she 'll think of me; I don't know that she 'll ever care for her poor father afterwards. But it 's best for her that she should be undeceived, and I must bear the consequences as I deserve!'

'Mary,' said Bertha, 'where is your hand! Ah! Here it is; here it is!' pressing it to her lips, with a smile, and drawing it through her arm. 'I heard them speaking softly among themselves, last night, of some blame against you. They were wrong.'

The Carrier's Wife was silent. Caleb answered for her.

'They were wrong,' he said.

'I knew it!' cried Bertha, proudly. 'I told them so. I scorned to hear a word! Blame *her* with justice!' she pressed the hand between her own, and the soft cheek against her face. 'No! I am not so blind as that.'

Her father went on one side of her, while Dot remained upon the other: holding her hand.

'I know you all,' said Bertha, 'better than you think. But none so well as her. Not even you, father. There is nothing half so real and so true about me, as she is. If I could be restored to sight this instant, and not a word were spoken, I could choose her from a crowd! My sister!'

'Bertha, my dear!' said Caleb, 'I have something on my mind I want to tell you, while we three are alone. Hear me kindly! I have a confession to make to you, my darling.'

'A confession, father?'

'I have wandered from the truth and lost myself, my child,' said Caleb, with a pitiable expression in his bewildered face. 'I have wandered from the truth, intending to be kind to you; and have been cruel.'

She turned her wonder-stricken face towards him, and repeated 'Cruel!'

'He accuses himself too strongly, Bertha,' said Dot. 'You 'll say so, presently. You 'll be the first to tell him so.'

'He cruel to me!' cried Bertha, with a smile of incredulity.

'Not meaning it, my child,' said Caleb. 'But I have been; though I never suspected it, till yesterday. My dear blind daughter, hear me and forgive me! The world you live in, heart of mine, doesn't exist as I have represented it. The eyes you have trusted in, have been false to you.'

She turned her wonder-stricken face towards him still; but drew back, and clung closer to her friend.

'Your road in life was rough, my poor one,' said Caleb, 'and I meant to smooth it for you. I have altered objects, changed the characters of people, invented many things that never have been, to make you happier. I have had concealments from you, put deceptions on you, God forgive me! and surrounded you with fancies.'

'But living people are not fancies!' she said hurriedly, and turning very pale, and still retiring from him. 'You can't change them.'

'I have done so, Bertha,' pleaded Caleb. 'There is one person that you know, my dove—'

'Oh father! why do you say, I know?' she answered, in a term of keen reproach. 'What and whom do *I* know! I who have no leader! I so miserably blind!'

In the anguish of her heart, she stretched out her hands, as if she were groping her way; then spread them, in a manner most forlorn and sad, upon her face.

'The marriage that takes place to-day,' said Caleb, 'is with a stern, sordid, grinding man. A hard master to you and me, my dear, for many years. Ugly in his looks, and in his nature. Cold and callous always. Unlike what I have painted him to you in everything, my child. In everything.'

'Oh why,' cried the Blind Girl, tortured, as it seemed, almost beyond endurance, 'why did you ever do this! Why did you ever fill my heart so full, and then come in like Death, and tear away the objects of my love! O Heaven, how blind I am! How helpless and alone!'

Her afflicted father hung his head, and offered no reply but in his penitence and sorrow.

She had been but a short time in this passion of regret, when the Cricket on the Hearth, unheard by all but her, began to chirp. Not merrily, but in a low, faint, sorrowing way. It was so mournful that her tears began to flow; and when the Presence which had been beside the Carrier all night, appeared behind her, pointing to her father, they fell down like rain.

She heard the Cricket-voice more plainly soon, and was conscious, through her blindness, of the Presence hovering about her father.

'Mary,' said the Blind Girl, 'tell me what my home is. What it truly is.'

'It is a poor place, Bertha; very poor and bare indeed. The house will scarcely keep out wind and rain another winter. It is as roughly shielded from the weather, Bertha,' Dot continued in a low, clear voice, 'as your poor father in his sack-cloth coat.'

The Blind Girl, greatly agitated, rose, and led the Carrier's little wife aside.

'Those presents that I took such care of; that came almost at my wish, and were so dearly welcome to me,' she said, trembling; 'where did they come from? Did you send them?'

'No.'

'Who then?'

Dot saw she knew, already, and was silent. The Blind Girl spread her hands before her face again. But in quite another manner now.

'Dear Mary, a moment. One moment? More this way. Speak softly to me. You are true, I know. You 'd not deceive me now; would you?'

'No, Bertha, indeed!'

'No, I am sure you would not. You have too much pity for me. Mary, look across the room to where we were just now—to where my father is— my father, so compassionate and loving to me—and tell me what you see.'

'I see,' said Dot, who understood her well, 'an old man sitting in a chair, and leaning sorrowfully on the back, with his face resting on his hand. As if his child should comfort him, Bertha.'

'Yes, yes. She will. Go on.'

'He is an old man, worn with care and work. He is a spare, dejected, thoughtful, grey-haired man. I see him now, despondent and bowed down, and striving against nothing. But, Bertha, I have seen him many times before, and striving hard in many ways for one great sacred object. And I honour his grey head, and bless him!'

The Blind Girl broke away from her; and throwing herself upon her knees before him, took the grey head to her breast.

'It is my sight restored. It is my sight!' she cried.

'I have been blind, and now my eyes are open. I never knew him! To think I might have died, and never truly seen the father who has been so loving to me!'

There were no words for Caleb's emotion.

'There is not a gallant figure on this earth,' exclaimed the Blind Girl, holding him in her embrace, 'that I would love so dearly, and would cherish so devotedly, as this! The greyer, and more worn, the dearer, father! Never let them say I am blind again. There's not a furrow in his face, there's not a hair upon his head, that shall be forgotten in my prayers and thanks to Heaven!'

Caleb managed to articulate 'My Bertha!'

'And in my blindness, I believed him,' said the girl, caressing him with tears of exquisite affection, 'to be so different! And having him beside me, day by day, so mindful of me always, never dreamed of this!'

'The fresh smart father in the blue coat, Bertha,' said poor Caleb. 'He's gone!'

'Nothing is gone,' she answered. 'Dearest father, no! Everything is here—in you. The father that I loved so well: the father that I never loved enough, and never knew; the benefactor whom I first began to reverence and love, because he had such sympathy for me; All are here in you. Nothing is dead to me. The soul of all that was most dear to me is here—here, with the worn face, and the grey head. And I am NOT blind, father, any longer!'

Dot's whole attention had been concentrated, during this discourse, upon the father and daughter; but looking, now, towards the little Haymaker in the Moorish meadow, she saw that the clock was within a few minutes of striking, and fell, immediately, into a nervous and excited state.

'Father,' said Bertha, hesitating. 'Mary.'

'Yes my dear,' returned Caleb. 'Here she is.'

'There is no change in *her*. You never told me anything of *her* that was not true?'

'I should have done it my dear, I am afraid,' returned Caleb, 'if I could have made her better than she was. But I must have changed her for the worse, if I had changed her at all. Nothing could improve her, Bertha.'

Confident as the Blind Girl had been when she asked the question, her delight and pride in the reply and her renewed embrace of Dot, were charming to behold.

'More changes than you think for, may happen though, my dear,' said Dot. 'Changes for the better, I mean; changes for great joy to some of us. You mustn't let them startle you too much, if any such should ever happen, and affect you. Are those wheels upon the road? You 've a quick ear, Bertha. Are they wheels?'

'Yes. Coming very fast.'

'I—I—I know you have a quick ear,' said Dot, placing her hand upon her heart, and evidently talking on, as fast as she could, to hide its palpitating state, 'because I have noticed it often, and because you were so quick to find out that strange step last night. Though why you should have said, as I very well recollect you did say, Bertha, "Whose step is that!" and why you should have taken any greater observation of it than of any other step, I don't know. Though as I said just now, there are great changes in the world: great changes: and we can't do better than prepare ourselves to be surprised at hardly anything.'

Caleb wondered what this meant; perceiving that she spoke to him, no less than to his daughter. He saw her, with astonishment, so fluttered and dis-

tressed that she could scarcely breathe; and holding to a chair, to save herself from falling.

'They are wheels indeed!' she panted. 'Coming nearer! Nearer! Very close! And now you hear them stopping at the garden-gate! And now you hear a step outside the door—the same step, Bertha, is it not!—and now!'—

She uttered a wild cry of uncontrollable delight; and running up to Caleb put her hands upon his eyes, as a young man rushed into the room, and flinging away his hat into the air, came sweeping down upon them.

'Is it over?' cried Dot.

'Yes!'

'Happily over?'

'Yes!'

'Do you recollect the voice, dear Caleb? Did you ever hear the like of it before?' cried Dot.

'If my boy in the Golden South Americas was alive'—said Caleb, trembling.

'He is alive!' shrieked Dot, removing her hands from his eyes, and clapping them in ecstasy; 'look at him! See where he stands before you, healthy and strong! Your own dear son! Your own dear living, loving brother, Bertha!'

All honour to the little creature for her transports! All honour to her tears and laughter, when the three were locked in one another's arms! All honour to the heartiness with which she met the sunburnt sailor-fellow, with his dark streaming hair, half way, and never turned her rosy little mouth aside, but suffered him to kiss it, freely, and to press her to his bounding heart!

And honour to the Cuckoo too—why not!—for bursting out of the trap-door in the Moorish Palace like a housebreaker, and hiccoughing twelve times on

the assembled company, as if he had got drunk for joy!

The Carrier, entering, started back. And well he might, to find himself in such good company.

'Look, John!' said Caleb, exultingly, 'look here! My own boy from the Golden South Americas! My own son! Him that you fitted out, and sent away yourself! Him that you were always such a friend to!'

The Carrier advanced to seize him by the hand; but, recoiling, as some feature in his face awakened a remembrance of the Deaf Man in the Cart, said:

'Edward! Was it you?'

'Now tell him all!' cried Dot. 'Tell him all, Edward; and don't spare me, for nothing shall make me spare myself in his eyes, ever again.'

'I was the man,' said Edward.

'And could you steal, disguised, into the house of your old friend?' rejoined the Carrier. 'There was a frank boy once—how many years is it, Caleb, since we heard that he was dead, and had it proved, we thought?—who never would have done that.'

'There was a generous friend of mine, once; more a father to me than a friend'; said Edward, 'who never would have judged me, or any other man, unheard. You were he. So I am certain you will hear me now.'

The Carrier, with a troubled glance at Dot, who still kept far away from him, replied 'Well! that's but fair. I will.'

'You must know that when I left here, a boy,' said Edward, 'I was in love, and my love was returned. She was a very young girl, who perhaps (you may tell me) didn't know her own mind. But I knew mine, and I had a passion for her.'

'You had!' exclaimed the Carrier. 'You!'

'Indeed I had,' returned the other. 'And she re-turned it. I have ever since believed she did, and now I am sure she did.'

'Heaven help me!' said the Carrier. 'This is worse than all.'

'Constant to her,' said Edward, 'and returning, full of hope, after many hardships and perils, to redeem my part of our old contract, I heard, twenty miles away, that she was false to me; that she had forgotten me; and had bestowed herself upon another and a richer man. I had no mind to reproach her; but I wished to see her, and to prove beyond dispute that this was true. I hoped she might have been forced into it, against her own desire and recollection. It would be small comfort, but it would be some, I thought, and on I came. That I might have the truth, the real truth; observing freely for myself, and judging for myself, without obstruction on the one hand, or presenting my own influence (if I had any) before her, on the other; I dressed myself unlike my-self—you know how; and waited on the road—you know where. You had no suspicion of me; neither had—had she,' pointing to Dot, 'until I whispered in her ear at that fireside, and she so nearly betrayed me.'

'But when she knew that Edward was alive, and had come back,' sobbed Dot, now speaking for her-self, as she had burned to do, all through this narra-tive; 'and when she knew his purpose, she advised him by all means to keep his secret close; for his old friend John Peerybingle was much too open in his nature, and too clumsy in all artifice—being a clumsy man in general,' said Dot, half laughing and half crying —'to keep it for him. And when she—that's me, John,' sobbed the little woman—'told him all, and how his sweetheart had believed him to be dead; and how she had at last been over-persuaded by her mother into

a marriage which the silly, dear old thing called advantageous; and when she—that's me again, John—told him they were not yet married (though close upon it), and that it would be nothing but a sacrifice if it went on, for there was no love on her side; and when he went nearly mad with joy to hear it; then she—that's me again—said she would go between them, as she had often done before in old times, John, and would sound his sweetheart and be sure that what she—me again, John—said and thought was right. And it was right, John! And they were brought together, John. And they were married, John, an hour ago! And here's the Bride! And Gruff and Tackleton may die a bachelor! And I'm a happy little woman, May, God bless you!'

She was an irresistible little woman, if that be anything to the purpose; and never so completely irresistible as in her present transports. There never were congratulations so endearing and delicious, as those she lavished on herself and on the Bride.

Amid the tumult of emotions in his breast, the honest Carrier had stood, confounded. Flying, now, towards her, Dot stretched out her hand to stop him, and retreated as before.

'No John, no! Hear all! Don't love me any more, John, till you've heard every word I have to say. It was wrong to have a secret from you, John. I'm very sorry. I didn't think it any harm, till I came and sat down by you on the little stool last night. But when I knew by what was written in your face, that you had seen me walking in the gallery with Edward, and when I knew what you thought, I felt how giddy and how wrong it was. But oh, dear John, how could you, could you, think so!'

Little woman, how she sobbed again! John Peery-

bingle would have caught her in his arms.   But no;
she wouldn't let him.

'Don't love me yet, please John!   Not for a long
time yet!   When I was sad about this intended marriage, dear, it was because I remembered May and
Edward such young lovers; and knew that her heart
was far away from Tackleton.   You believe that,
now.   Don't you John?'

John was going to make another rush at this appeal; but she stopped him again.

'No; keep there, please John!   When I laugh at
you, as I sometimes do, John, and call you clumsy
and a dear old goose, and names of that sort, it's because I love you John, so well, and take such pleasure
in your ways, and wouldn't see you altered in the
least respect to have you made a King to-morrow.'

'Hooroar!' said Caleb with unusual vigour.   'My
opinion!'

'And when I speak of people being middle-aged,
and steady, John, and pretend that we are a humdrum
couple, going on in a jog-trot sort of way, it's only
because I'm such a silly little thing, John, that I like,
sometimes, to act a kind of Play with Baby, and all
that: and make believe.'

She saw that he was coming; and stopped him
again.   But she was very nearly too late.

'No, don't love me for another minute or two, if
you please John!   What I want most to tell you, I
have kept to the last.   My dear, good, generous John,
when we were talking the other night about the
Cricket, I had it on my lips to say, that at first I did
not love you quite so dearly as I do now; that when I
first came home here, I was half afraid I mightn't
learn to love you every bit as well as I hoped and
prayed I might—being so very young, John!   But,

dear John, every day and hour I loved you more and more. And if I could have loved you better than I do, the noble words I heard you say this morning, would have made me. But I can't. All the affection that I had (it was a great deal John) I gave you, as you well deserve, long, long ago, and I have no more left to give. Now, my dear husband, take me to your heart again! That's my home, John; and never, never think of sending me to any other!'

You never will derive so much delight from seeing a glorious little woman in the arms of a third party, as you would have felt if you had seen Dot run into the Carrier's embrace. It was the most complete, unmitigated, soul-fraught little piece of earnestness that ever you beheld in all your days.

You may be sure the Carrier was in a state of perfect rapture; and you may be sure Dot was likewise; and you may be sure they all were, inclusive of Miss Slowboy, who wept copiously for joy, and wishing to include her young charge in the general interchange of congratulations, handed round the Baby to everybody in succession, as if it were something to drink.

But, now, the sound of wheels was heard again outside the door; and somebody exclaimed that Gruff and Tackleton was coming back. Speedily that worthy gentleman appeared, looking warm and flustered.

'Why, what the Devil's this, John Peerybingle!' said Tackleton. 'There's some mistake. I appointed Mrs. Tackleton to meet me at the church, and I'll swear I passed her on the road, on her way here. Oh! here she is! I beg your pardon, sir; I haven't the pleasure of knowing you; but if you can do me the favour to spare this young lady, she has rather a particular engagement this morning.'

'But I can't spare her,' returned Edward. 'I couldn't think of it.'

'What do you mean, you vagabond?' said Tackleton.

'I mean, that as I can make allowance for your being vexed,' returned the other, with a smile, 'I am as deaf to harsh discourse this morning, as I was to all discourse last night.'

The look that Tackleton bestowed upon him, and the start he gave!

'I am sorry, sir,' said Edward, holding out May's left hand, and especially the third finger; 'that the young lady can't accompany you to church; but as she has been there once, this morning, perhaps you 'll excuse her.'

Tackleton looked hard at the third finger, and took a little piece of silver paper, apparently containing a ring, from his waistcoat-pocket.

'Miss Slowboy,' said Tackleton. 'Will you have the kindness to throw that in the fire? Thank 'ee.'

'It was a previous engagement, quite an old engagement, that prevented my wife from keeping her appointment with you, I assure you,' said Edward.

'Mr. Tackleton will do me the justice to acknowledge that I revealed it to him faithfully; and that I told him, many times, I never could forget it,' said May, blushing.

'Oh certainly!' said Tackleton. 'Oh to be sure. Oh it 's all right. It 's quite correct. Mrs. Edward Plummer, I infer?'

'That 's the name,' returned the bridegroom.

'Ah, I shouldn't have known you, sir,' said Tackleton, scrutinising his face narrowly, and making a low bow. 'I give you joy, sir!'

'Thank 'ee.'

'Mrs. Peerybingle,' said Tackleton, turning suddenly to where she stood with her husband; 'I am sorry. You haven't done me a very great kindness, but, upon my life I am sorry. You are better than I thought you. John Peerybingle, I am sorry. You understand me; that's enough. It's quite correct, ladies and gentlemen all, and perfectly satisfactory. Good-morning!'

With these words he carried it off, and carried himself off too: merely stopping at the door, to take the flowers and favours from his horse's head, and to kick that animal once, in the ribs, as a means of informing him that there was a screw loose in his arrangements.

Of course it became a serious duty now, to make such a day of it, as should mark these events for a high Feast and Festival in the Peerybingle Calendar for evermore. Accordingly, Dot went to work to produce such an entertainment, as should reflect undying honour on the house and on every one concerned; and in a very short space of time, she was up to her dimpled elbows in flour, and whitening the Carrier's coat, every time he came near her, by stopping him to give him a kiss. That good fellow washed the greens, and peeled the turnips, and broke the plates, and upset iron pots full of cold water on the fire, and made himself useful in all sorts of ways: while a couple of professional assistants, hastily called in from somewhere in the neighbourhood, as on a point of life or death, ran against each other in all the doorways and round all the corners, and everybody tumbled over Tilly Slowboy and the Baby, everywhere. Tilly never came out in such force before. Her ubiquity was the theme of general admiration. She was a stumbling-block in the passage at five-and-twenty minutes past two; a man-trap in the kitchen

at half-past two precisely; and a pitfall in the garret at five-and-twenty minutes to three. The Baby's head was, as it were, a test and touchstone for every description of matter,—animal, vegetable, and mineral. Nothing was in use that day that didn't come, at some time or other, into close acquaintance with it.

Then, there was a great Expedition set on foot to go and find out Mrs. Fielding; and to be dismally penitent to that excellent gentlewoman; and to bring her back, by force, if needful, to be happy and forgiving. And when the Expedition first discovered her, she would listen to no terms at all, but said, an unspeakable number of times, that ever she should have lived to see the day! and couldn't be got to say anything else, except, 'Now carry me to the grave': which seemed absurd, on account of her not being dead, or anything at all like it. After a time, she lapsed into a state of dreadful calmness, and observed, that when that unfortunate train of circumstances had occurred in the Indigo Trade, she had foreseen that she would be exposed, during her whole life, to every species of insult and contumely; and that she was glad to find it was the case; and begged they wouldn't trouble themselves about her,—for what was she? oh, dear! a nobody!—but would forget that such a being lived, and would take their course in life without her. From this bitterly sarcastic mood, she passed into an angry one, in which she gave vent to the remarkable expression that the worm would turn if trodden on; and, after that, she yielded to a soft regret, and said, if they had only given her their confidence, what might she not have had it in her power to suggest! Taking advantage of this crisis in her feelings, the Expedition embraced her, and she very soon had her gloves on, and was on her way to John Peerybingle's in

state of unimpeachable gentility; with a paper parcel at her side containing a cap of state, almost as tall, and quite as stiff, as a mitre.

Then, there were Dot's father and mother to come, in another little chaise; and they were behind their time; and fears were entertained; and there was much looking out for them down the road; and Mrs. Fielding always would look in the wrong and morally impossible direction; and being apprised thereof, hoped she might take the liberty of looking where she pleased. At last they came: a chubby little couple, jogging along in a snug and comfortable little way that quite belonged to the Dot family; and Dot and her mother, side by side, were wonderful to see. They were so like each other.

Then, Dot's mother had to renew her acquaintance with May's mother; and May's mother always stood on her gentility; and Dot's mother never stood on anything but her active little feet. And old Dot—so to call Dot's father, I forgot it wasn't his right name, but never mind—took liberties, and shook hands at first sight, and seemed to think a cap but so much starch and muslin, and didn't defer himself at all to the Indigo Trade, but said there was no help for it now; and in Mrs. Fielding's summing up, was a good-natured kind of man—but coarse, my dear.

I wouldn't have missed Dot, doing the honours in her wedding-gown, my benison on her bright face! for any money. No! nor the good Carrier, so jovial and so ruddy, at the bottom of the table. Nor the brown, fresh, sailor-fellow, and his handsome wife. Nor any one among them. To have missed the dinner would have been to miss as jolly and as stout a meal as man need eat; and to have missed the overflowing cups in which they drank The Wedding-Day, would have been the greatest miss of all.

After dinner, Caleb sang the song about the Spark-ling Bowl. As I 'm a living man, hoping to keep so, for a year or two, he sang it through.

And, by the bye, a most unlooked-for incident oc-curred, just as he finished the last verse.

There was a tap at the door; and a man came stag-gering in, without saying with your leave, or by your leave, with something heavy on his head. Setting this down in the middle of the table, symmetrically in the centre of the nuts and apples, he said:

'Mr. Tackleton's compliments, and as he hasn't got no use for the cake himself, p'raps you 'll eat it.'

And with those words, he walked off.

There was some surprise among the company, as you may imagine. Mrs. Fielding, being a lady of infinite discernment, suggested that the cake was poisoned, and related a narrative of a cake, which, within her knowledge, had turned a seminary for young ladies, blue. But she was overruled by ac-clamation; and the cake was cut by May, with much ceremony and rejoicing.

I don't think any one had tasted it, when there came another tap at the door, and the same man ap-peared again, having under his arm a vast brown-paper parcel.

'Mr. Tackleton's compliments, and he 's sent a few toys for the Babby. They ain't ugly.'

After the delivery of which expressions, he retired again.

The whole party would have experienced great difficulty in finding words for their astonishment, even if they had had ample time to seek them. But, they had none at all; for, the messenger had scarcely shut the door behind him, when there came another tap, and Tackleton himself walked in.

'Mrs. Peerybingle!' said the Toy-merchant, hat in

hand. 'I 'm sorry. I 'm more sorry than I was this morning. I have had time to think of it. John Peerybingle! I 'm sour by disposition; but I can't help being sweetened, more or less, by coming face to face with such a man as you. Caleb! This unconscious little nurse gave me a broken hint last night of which I have found the thread. I blush to think how easily I might have bound you and your daughter to me, and what a miserable idiot I was, when I took her for one! Friends, one and all, my house is very lonely to-night. I have not so much as a Cricket on my Hearth. I have scared them all away. Be gracious to me; let me join this happy party!'

He was at home in five minutes. You never saw such a fellow. What *had* he been doing with himself all his life, never to have known, before, his great capacity of being jovial! Or what had the fairies been doing with him, to have effected such a change!

'John! you won't send me home this evening; will you?' whispered Dot.

He had been very near it though!

There wanted but one living creature to make the party complete; and, in the twinkling of an eye, there he was, very thirsty with hard running, and engaged in hopeless endeavours to squeeze his head into a narrow pitcher. He had gone with the cart to its journey's end, very much disgusted with the absence of his master, and stupendously rebellious to the Deputy. After lingering about the stable for some little time, vainly attempting to incite the old horse to the mutinous act of returning on his own account, he had walked into the tap-room and laid himself down before the fire. But suddenly yielding to the conviction that the Deputy was a humbug, and must be abandoned, he had got up again, turned tail, and come home.

There was a dance in the evening. With which general mention of that recreation, I should have left it alone, if I had not some reason to suppose that it was quite an original dance, and one of a most uncommon figure. It was formed in an odd way; in this way.

Edward, that sailor-fellow—a good free dashing sort of a fellow he was—had been telling them various marvels concerning parrots, and mines, and Mexicans, and gold dust, when all at once he took it in his head to jump up from his seat and propose a dance; for Bertha's harp was there, and she had such a hand upon it as you seldom hear. Dot (sly little piece of affectation when she chose) said her dancing days were over; *I* think because the Carrier was smoking his pipe, and she liked sitting by him, best. Mrs. Fielding had no choice, of course, but to say *her* dancing days were over, after that; and everybody said the same, except May; May was ready.

So, May and Edward get up, amid great applause, to dance alone; and Bertha plays her liveliest tune.

Well! if you 'll believe me, they have not been dancing five minutes, when suddenly the Carrier flings his pipe away, takes Dot round the waist, dashes out into the room, and starts off with her, toe and heel, quite wonderfully. Tackleton no sooner sees this, than he skims across to Mrs. Fielding, takes her round the waist, and follows suit. Old Dot no sooner sees this, than up he is, all alive, whisks off Mrs. Dot in the middle of the dance, and is the foremost there. Caleb no sooner sees this, than he clutches Tilly Slowboy by both hands and goes off at score; Miss Slowboy, firm in the belief that diving hotly in among the other couples, and effecting any number of concussions with them, is your only principle of footing it.

Hark! how the Cricket joins the music with its Chirp, Chirp, Chirp; and how the kettle hums!

* * * * * * *

But what is this! Even as I listen to them, blithely, and turn towards Dot, for one last glimpse of a little figure very pleasant to me, she and the rest have vanished into air, and I am left alone. A Cricket sings upon the Hearth; a broken child's-toy lies upon the ground; and nothing else remains.

PART II

CHRISTMAS STORIES

FROM

'HOUSEHOLD WORDS'

A CHRISTMAS TREE

[1850]

A CHRISTMAS TREE

I HAVE been looking on, this evening, at a merry company of children assembled round that pretty German
toy, a Christmas Tree. The tree was planted in the
middle of a great round table, and towered high above
their heads. It was brilliantly lighted by a multitude
of little tapers; and everywhere sparkled and glittered
with bright objects. There were rosy-cheeked dolls,
hiding behind the green leaves; and there were real
watches (with movable hands, at least, and an endless
capacity of being wound up) dangling from innumerable twigs; there were French-polished tables, chairs,
bedsteads, wardrobes, eight-day clocks, and various
other articles of domestic furniture (wonderfully
made, in tin, at Wolverhampton), perched among the
boughs, as if in preparation for some fairy housekeeping; there were jolly, broad-faced little men,
much more agreeable in appearance than many real
men—and no wonder, for their heads took off, and
showed them to be full of sugar-plums; there were
fiddles and drums; there were tambourines, books,
work-boxes, paint-boxes, sweetmeat-boxes, peep-show
boxes, and all kinds of boxes; there were trinkets for
the elder girls, far brighter than any grown-up gold
and jewels; there were baskets and pincushions in all
devices; there were guns, swords, and banners; there
were witches standing in enchanted rings of paste-
board, to tell fortunes; there were teetotums, hum-
ming-tops, needle-cases, pen-wipers, smelling-bottles,

3

conversation-cards, bouquet-holders; real fruit, made artificially dazzling with gold leaf; imitation apples, pears, and walnuts, crammed with surprises; in short, as a pretty child, before me, delightedly whispered to another pretty child, her bosom friend, 'There was everything, and more.' This motley collection of odd objects, clustering on the tree like magic fruit, and flashing back the bright looks directed towards it from every side—some of the diamond-eyes admiring it were hardly on a level with the table, and a few were languishing in timid wonder on the bosoms of pretty mothers, aunts, and nurses—made a lively realisation of the fancies of childhood; and set me thinking how all the trees that grow and all the things that come into existence on the earth, have their wild adornments at that well-remembered time.

Being now at home again, and alone, the only person in the house awake, my thoughts are drawn back, by a fascination which I do not care to resist, to my own childhood. I begin to consider, what do we all remember best upon the branches of the Christmas Tree of our own young Christmas days, by which we climbed to real life.

Straight, in the middle of the room, cramped in the freedom of its growth by no encircling walls or soon-reached ceiling, a shadowy tree arises; and, looking up into the dreamy brightness of its top—for I observe in this tree the singular property that it appears to grow downward towards the earth—I look into my youngest Christmas recollections!

All toys at first, I find. Up yonder, among the green holly and red berries, is the Tumbler with his hands in his pockets, who wouldn't lie down, but whenever he was put upon the floor, persisted in rolling his fat body about, until he rolled himself still, and brought those lobster eyes of his to bear upon me—

when I affected to laugh very much, but in my heart of hearts was extremely doubtful of him. Close beside him is that infernal snuff-box, out of which there sprang a demoniacal Counsellor in a black gown, with an obnoxious head of hair, and a red cloth mouth, wide open, who was not to be endured on any terms, but could not be put away either; for he used suddenly, in a highly magnified state, to fly out of Mammoth Snuff-boxes in dreams, when least expected. Nor is the frog with cobbler's wax on his tail, far off; for there was no knowing where he wouldn't jump; and when he flew over the candle, and came upon one's hand with that spotted back—red on a green ground—he was horrible. The cardboard lady in a blue-silk skirt, who was stood up against the candlestick to dance, and whom I see on the same branch, was milder, and was beautiful; but I can't say as much for the larger cardboard man, who used to be hung against the wall and pulled by a string; there was a sinister expression in that nose of his; and when he got his legs round his neck (which he very often did), he was ghastly, and not a creature to be alone with.

When did that dreadful Mask first look at me? Who put it on, and why was I so frightened that the sight of it is an era in my life? It is not a hideous visage in itself; it is even meant to be droll; why then were its stolid features so intolerable? Surely not because it hid the wearer's face. An apron would have done as much; and though I should have preferred even the apron away, it would not have been absolutely insupportable, like the mask. Was it the immovability of the mask? The doll's face was immovable, but I was not afraid of *her*. Perhaps that fixed and set change coming over a real face, infused into my quickened heart some remote suggestion and

dread of the universal change that is to come on every face, and make it still? Nothing reconciled me to it. No drummers, from whom proceeded a melancholy chirping on the turning of a handle; no regiment of soldiers, with a mute band, taken out of a box, and fitted, one by one, upon a stiff and lazy little set of lazy-tongs; no old woman, made of wires and a brown-paper composition, cutting up a pie for two small children; could give me a permanent comfort, for a long time. Nor was it any satisfaction to be shown the Mask, and see that it was made of paper, or to have it locked up and be assured that no one wore it. The mere recollection of that fixed face, the mere knowledge of its existence anywhere, was sufficient to awake me in the night all perspiration and horror, with, 'O I know it's coming! O the mask!'

I never wondered what the dear old donkey with the panniers—there he is! was made of, then! His hide was real to the touch, I recollect. And the great black horse with the round red spots all over him— the horse that I could even get upon—I never wondered what had brought him to that strange condition, or thought that such a horse was not commonly seen at Newmarket. The four horses of no colour, next to him, that went into the waggon of cheeses, and could be taken out and stabled under the piano, appear to have bits of fur-tippet for their tails, and other bits for their manes, and to stand on pegs instead of legs, but it was not so when they were brought home for a Christmas present. They were all right, then; neither was their harness unceremoniously nailed into their chests, as appears to be the case now. The tinkling works of the music-cart, I *did* find out, to be made of quill tooth-picks and wire; and I always thought that little tumbler in his shirt sleeves, perpetually swarm-

ing up one side of a wooden frame, and coming down, head foremost, on the other, rather a weak-minded person—though good-natured; but the Jacob's Ladder, next him, made of little squares of red wood, that went flapping and clattering over one another, each developing a different picture, and the whole enlivened by small bells, was a mighty marvel and a great delight.

Ah! The Doll's house!—of which I was not proprietor, but where I visited. I don't admire the Houses of Parliament half so much as that stone-fronted mansion with real glass windows, and door-steps, and a real balcony—greener than I ever see now, except at watering places; and even they afford but a poor imitation. And though it *did* open all at once, the entire house-front (which was a blow, I admit, as cancelling the fiction of a staircase), it was but to shut it up again, and I could believe. Even open, there were three distinct rooms in it: a sitting-room and bed-room, elegantly furnished, and best of all, a kitchen, with uncommonly soft fire-irons, a plentiful assortment of diminutive utensils—oh, the warming-pan!—and a tin man-cook in profile, who was always going to fry two fish. What Barmecide justice have I done to the noble feasts wherein the set of wooden platters figured, each with its own peculiar delicacy, as a ham or turkey, glued tight on to it, and garnished with something green, which I recollect as moss! Could all the Temperance Societies of these later days, united, give me such a tea-drinking as I have had through the means of yonder little set of blue crockery, which really would hold liquid (it ran out of the small wooden cask, I recollect, and tasted of matches), and which made tea, nectar. And if the two legs of the ineffectual little sugar-tongs did tumble over one another, and want purpose, like Punch's

hands, what does it matter? And if I did once shriek out, as a poisoned child, and strike the fashionable company with consternation, by reason of having drunk a little teaspoon, inadvertently dissolved in too hot tea, I was never the worse for it, except by a powder!

Upon the next branches of the tree, lower down, hard by the green roller and miniature gardening-tools, how thick the books begin to hang. Thin books, in themselves, at first, but many of them, and with deliciously smooth covers of bright red or green. What fat black letters to begin with! 'A was an archer, and shot at a frog.' Of course he was. He was an apple-pie also, and there he is! He was a good many things in his time, was A, and so were most of his friends, except X, who had so little versatility, that I never knew him to get beyond Xerxes or Xantippe—like Y, who was always confined to a Yacht or a Yew Tree; and Z condemned for ever to be a Zebra or a Zany. But, now, the very tree itself changes, and becomes a bean-stalk—the marvellous bean-stalk up which Jack climbed to the Giant's house! And now, those dreadfully interesting, double-headed giants, with their clubs over their shoulders, begin to stride along the boughs in a perfect throng, dragging knights and ladies home for dinner by the hair of their heads. And Jack—how noble, with his sword of sharpness, and his shoes of swiftness! Again those old meditations come upon me as I gaze up at him; and I debate within myself whether there was more than one Jack (which I am loth to believe possible), or only one genuine original admirable Jack, who achieved all the recorded exploits.

Good for Christmas-time is the ruddy colour of the cloak, in which—the tree making a forest of itself for her to trip through, with her basket—Little Red Rid-

ing-Hood comes to me one Christmas Eve to give me information of the cruelty and treachery of that dissembling Wolf who ate her grandmother, without making any impression on his appetite, and then ate her, after making that ferocious joke about his teeth. She was my first love. I felt that if I could have married Little Red Riding-Hood, I should have known perfect bliss. But, it was not to be; and there was nothing for it but to look out the Wolf in the Noah's Ark there, and put him late in the procession on the table, as a monster who was to be degraded. O the wonderful Noah's Ark! It was not found seaworthy when put in a washing-tub, and the animals were crammed in at the roof, and needed to have their legs well shaken down before they could be got in, even there—and then, ten to one but they began to tumble out at the door, which was but imperfectly fastened with a wire latch—but what was *that* against it! Consider the noble fly, a size or two smaller than the elephant: the lady-bird, the butterfly—all triumphs of art! Consider the goose, whose feet were so small, and whose balance was so indifferent, that he usually tumbled forward, and knocked down all the animal creation. Consider Noah and his family, like idiotic tobacco-stoppers; and how the leopard stuck to warm little fingers; and how the tails of the larger animals used gradually to resolve themselves into frayed bits of string!

Hush! Again a forest, and somebody up in a tree—not Robin Hood, not Valentine, not the Yellow Dwarf (I have passed him and all Mother Bunch's wonders, without mention), but an Eastern King with a glittering scimitar and turban. By Allah! two Eastern Kings, for I see another, looking over his shoulder! Down upon the grass, at the tree's foot, lies the full length of a coal-black Giant, stretched

asleep, with his head in a lady's lap; and near them is a glass box, fastened with four locks of shining steel, in which he keeps the lady prisoner when he is awake. I see the four keys at his girdle now. The lady makes signs to the two kings in the tree, who softly descend. It is the setting-in of the bright Arabian Nights.

Oh, now all common things become uncommon and enchanted to me. All lamps are wonderful; all rings are talismans. Common flower-pots are full of treasure, with a little earth scattered on the top; trees are for Ali Baba to hide in; beef-steaks are to throw down into the Valley of Diamonds, that the precious stones may stick to them, and be carried by the eagles to their nests, whence the traders, with loud cries, will scare them. Tarts are made, according to the recipe of the Vizier's son of Bussorah, who turned pastrycook after he was set down in his drawers at the gate of Damascus; cobblers are all Mustaphas, and in the habit of sewing up people cut into four pieces, to whom they are taken blindfold.

Any iron ring let into stone is the entrance to a cave which only waits for the magician, and the little fire, and the necromancy, that will make the earth shake. All the dates imported come from the same tree as that unlucky date, with whose shell the merchant knocked out the eye of the genie's invisible son. All olives are of the stock of that fresh fruit, concerning which the Commander of the Faithful overheard the boy conduct the fictitious trial of the fraudulent olive merchant; all apples are akin to the apple purchased (with two others) from the Sultan's gardener for three sequins, and which the tall black slave stole from the child. All dogs are associated with the dog, really a transformed man, who jumped upon the baker's counter, and put his paw on the piece of bad money. All

rice recalls the rice which the awful lady, who was a ghoule, could only peck by grains, because of her nightly feasts in the burial-place. My very rocking-horse,—there he is, with his nostrils turned completely inside-out, indicative of Blood!—should have a peg in his neck, by virtue thereof to fly away with me, as the wooden horse did with the Prince of Persia, in the sight of all his father's Court.

Yes, on every object that I recognise among those upper branches of my Christmas Tree, I see this fairy light! When I wake in bed, at daybreak, on the cold, dark, winter mornings, the white snow dimly beheld, outside, through the frost on the window-pane, I hear Dinarzade. 'Sister, sister, if you are yet awake, I pray you finish the history of the Young King of the Black Islands.' Scheherazade replies, 'If my lord the Sultan will suffer me to live another day, sister, I will not only finish that, but tell you a more wonderful story yet.' Then, the gracious Sultan goes out, giving no orders for the execution, and we all three breathe again.

At this height of my tree I begin to see, cowering among the leaves—it may be born of turkey, or of pudding, or mince pie, or of these many fancies, jumbled with Robinson Crusoe on his desert island, Philip Quarll among the monkeys, Sandford and Merton with Mr. Barlow, Mother Bunch, and the Mask—or it may be the result of indigestion, assisted by imagination and over-doctoring—a prodigious nightmare. It is so exceedingly indistinct, that I don't know why it's frightful—but I know it is. I can only make out that it is an immense array of shapeless things, which appear to be planted on a vast exaggeration of the lazy-tongs that used to bear the toy soldiers, and to be slowly coming close to my eyes, and receding to an immeasurable distance. When it comes closest, it

is worse. In connection with it I descry remembrances of winter nights incredibly long; of being sent
early to bed, as a punishment for some small offence,
and waking in two hours, with a sensation of having
been asleep two nights; of the laden hopelessness of
morning ever dawning; and the oppression of a
weight of remorse.

And now, I see a wonderful row of little lights rise
smoothly out of the ground, before a vast green curtain. Now, a bell rings—a magic bell, which still
sounds in my ears unlike all other bells—and music
plays, amidst a buzz of voices, and a fragrant smell of
orange-peel and oil. Anon, the magic bell commands
the music to cease, and the great green curtain rolls
itself up majestically, and The Play begins! The
devoted dog of Montargis avenges the death of his
master, foully murdered in the Forest of Bondy; and
a humorous Peasant with a red nose and a very little
hat, whom I take from this hour forth to my bosom as
a friend (I think he was a Waiter or an Hostler at a
village Inn, but many years have passed since he and
I have met), remarks that the sassigassity of that dog
is indeed surprising; and evermore this jocular conceit
will live in my remembrance fresh and unfading, over-
topping all possible jokes, unto the end of time. Or
now, I learn with bitter tears how poor Jane Shore,
dressed all in white, and with her brown hair hanging
down, went starving through the streets; or how
George Barnwell killed the worthiest uncle that ever
man had, and was afterwards so sorry for it that he
ought to have been let off. Comes swift to comfort
me, the Pantomime—stupendous Phenomenon!—
when clowns are shot from loaded mortars into the
great chandelier, bright constellation that it is; when
Harlequins, covered all over with scales of pure gold,
twist and sparkle, like amazing fish; when Pantaloon

(whom I deem it no irreverence to compare in my own mind to my grandfather) puts red-hot pokers in his pocket, and cries 'Here's somebody coming!' or taxes the Clown with petty larceny, by saying, 'Now, I sawed you do it!' when Everything is capable, with the greatest ease, of being changed into Anything; and 'Nothing is, but thinking makes it so.' Now, too, I perceive my first experience of the dreary sensation —often to return in after-life—of being unable, next day, to get back to the dull, settled world; of wanting to live for ever in the bright atmosphere I have quitted; of doting on the little Fairy, with the wand like a celestial Barber's Pole, and pining for a Fairy immortality along with her. Ah, she comes back, in many shapes, as my eye wanders down the branches of my Christmas Tree, and goes as often, and has never yet stayed by me!

Out of this delight springs the toy-theatre,— there it is, with its familiar proscenium, and ladies in feathers, in the boxes!—and all its attendant occupation with paste and glue, and gum, and water colours, in the getting-up of The Miller and his Men, and Elizabeth, or the Exile of Siberia. In spite of a few besetting accidents and failures (particularly an unreasonable disposition in the respectable Kelmar, and some others, to become faint in the legs, and double up, at exciting points of the drama), a teeming world of fancies so suggestive and all-embracing, that, far below it on my Christmas Tree, I see dark, dirty, real Theatres in the day-time, adorned with these associations as with the freshest garlands of the rarest flowers, and charming me yet.

But hark! The Waits are playing, and they break my childish sleep! What images do I associate with the Christmas music as I see them set forth on the Christmas Tree? Known before all the others, keep-

ing far apart from all the others, they gather round
my little bed. An angel, speaking to a group of
shepherds in a field; some travellers, with eyes up-
lifted, following a star; a baby in a manger; a child
in a spacious temple, talking with grave men; a
solemn figure, with a mild and beautiful face, raising
a dead girl by the hand; again, near a city gate, calling back the son of a widow, on his bier, to life; a
crowd of people looking through the opened roof
of a chamber where he sits, and letting down a sick
person on a bed, with ropes; the same, in a tempest,
walking on the water to a ship; again, on a sea-shore,
teaching a great multitude; again, with a child upon
his knee, and other children round; again, restoring
sight to the blind, speech to the dumb, hearing to the
deaf, health to the sick, strength to the lame, knowledge to the ignorant; again, dying upon a Cross,
watched by armed soldiers, a thick darkness coming
on, the earth beginning to shake, and only one voice
heard, 'Forgive them, for they know not what they
do.'

Still, on the lower and maturer branches of the
Tree, Christmas associations cluster thick. School-
books shut up; Ovid and Virgil silenced; the Rule of
Three, with its cool impertinent inquiries, long disposed of; Terence and Plautus acted no more, in an
arena of huddled desks and forms, all chipped, and
notched, and inked; cricket-bats, stumps, and balls,
left higher up, with the smell of trodden grass and
the softened noise of shouts in the evening air; the
tree is still fresh, still gay. If I no more come home
at Christmas-time, there will be boys and girls (thank
Heaven!) while the World lasts; and they do! Yonder they dance and play upon the branches of my
Tree, God bless them, merrily, and my heart dances
and plays too!

And I *do* come home at Christmas. We all do, or we all should. We all come home, or ought to come home, for a short holiday—the longer, the better—from the great boarding-school, where we are for ever working at our arithmetical slates, to take, and give a rest. As to going a visiting, where can we not go, if we will; where have we not been, when we would; starting our fancy from our Christmas Tree!

Away into the winter prospect. There are many such upon the tree! On, by low-lying, misty grounds, through fens and fogs, up long hills, winding dark as caverns between thick plantations, almost shutting out the sparkling stars; so, out on broad heights, until we stop at last, with sudden silence, at an avenue. The gate-bell has a deep, half-awful sound in the frosty air; the gate swings open on its hinges; and, as we drive up to a great house, the glancing lights grow larger in the windows, and the opposing rows of trees seem to fall solemnly back on either side, to give us place. At intervals, all day, a frightened hare has shot across this whitened turf; or the distant clatter of a herd of deer trampling the hard frost, has, for the minute, crushed the silence too. Their watchful eyes beneath the fern may be shining now, if we could see them, like the icy dewdrops on the leaves; but they are still, and all is still. And so, the lights growing larger, and the trees falling back before us, and closing up again behind us, as if to forbid retreat, we come to the house.

There is probably a smell of roasted chestnuts and other good comfortable things all the time, for we are telling Winter Stories—Ghost Stories, or more shame for us—round the Christmas fire; and we have never stirred, except to draw a little nearer to it. But, no matter for that. We came to the house, and it is an old house, full of great chimneys where wood is burnt

on ancient dogs upon the hearth, and grim portraits (some of them with grim legends, too) lower distrustfully from the oaken panels of the walls. We are a middle-aged nobleman, and we make a generous supper with our host and hostess and their guests—it being Christmas-time, and the old house full of company—and then we go to bed. Our room is a very old room. It is hung with tapestry. We don't like the portrait of a cavalier in green, over the fire-place. There are great black beams in the ceiling, and there is a great black bedstead, supported at the foot by two great black figures, who seem to have come off a couple of tombs in the old baronial church in the park, for our particular accommodation. But, we are not a superstitious nobleman, and we don't mind. Well! we dismiss our servant, lock the door, and sit before the fire in our dressing-gown, musing about a great many things. At length we go to bed. Well! we can't sleep. We toss and tumble, and can't sleep. The embers on the hearth burn fitfully and make the room look ghostly. We can't help peeping out over the counterpane, at the two black figures and the cavalier—that wicked-looking cavalier—in green. In the flickering light they seem to advance and retire: which, though we are not by any means a superstitious nobleman, is not agreeable. Well! we get nervous—more and more nervous. We say 'This is very foolish, but we can't stand this; we 'll pretend to be ill, and knock up somebody.' Well! we are just going to do it, when the locked door opens, and there comes in a young woman, deadly pale, and with long fair hair, who glides to the fire, and sits down in the chair we have left there, wringing her hands. Then, we notice that her clothes are wet. Our tongue cleaves to the roof of our mouth, and we can't speak; but, we observe her accurately. Her clothes are wet; her

long hair is dabbled with moist mud; she is dressed in the fashion of two hundred years ago; and she has at her girdle a bunch of rusty keys. Well! there she sits, and we can't even faint, we are in such a state about it. Presently she gets up, and tries all the locks in the room with the rusty keys, which won't fit one of them; then, she fixes her eyes on the portrait of the cavalier in green, and says, in a low, terrible voice, 'The stags know it!' After that, she wrings her hands again, passes the bedside, and goes out at the door. We hurry on our dressing-gown, seize our pistols (we always travel with pistols), and are following, when we find the door locked. We turn the key, look out into the dark gallery; no one there. We wander away, and try to find our servant. Can't be done. We pace the gallery till daybreak; then return to our deserted room, fall asleep, and are awakened by our servant (nothing ever haunts *him*) and the shining sun. Well! we make a wretched breakfast, and all the company say we look queer. After breakfast, we go over the house with our host, and then we take him to the portrait of the cavalier in green, and then it all comes out. He was false to a young housekeeper once attached to that family, and famous for her beauty, who drowned herself in a pond, and whose body was discovered, after a long time, because the stags refused to drink of the water. Since which, it has been whispered that she traverses the house at midnight (but goes especially to that room where the cavalier in green was wont to sleep), trying the old locks with the rusty keys. Well! we tell our host of what we have seen, and a shade comes over his features, and he begs it may be hushed up; and so it is. But, it's all true; and we said so, before we died (we are dead now) to many responsible people.

There is no end to the old houses, with resounding galleries, and dismal state-bedchambers, and haunted wings shut up for many years, through which we may ramble, with an agreeable creeping up our back, and encounter any number of ghosts, but (it is worthy of remark perhaps) reducible to a very few general types and classes; for, ghosts have little originality, and 'walk' in a beaten track.   Thus, it comes to pass, that a certain room in a certain old hall, where a certain bad lord, baronet, knight, or gentleman, shot himself, has certain planks in the floor from which the blood *will not* be taken out.   You may scrape and scrape, as the present owner has done, or plane and plane, as his father did, or scrub and scrub, as his grandfather did, or burn and burn with strong acids, as his great-grandfather did, but, there the blood will still be— no redder and no paler—no more and no less—always just the same.   Thus, in such another house there is a haunted door, that never will keep open; or another door that never will keep shut; or a haunted sound of a spinning-wheel, or a hammer, or a footstep, or a cry, or a sigh, or a horse's tramp, or the rattling of a chain. Or else, there is a turret-clock, which, at the midnight hour, strikes thirteen when the head of the family is going to die; or a shadowy, immovable black carriage which at such a time is always seen by somebody, waiting near the great gates in the stable-yard.   Or thus, it came to pass how Lady Mary went to pay a visit at a large wild house in the Scottish Highlands, and, being fatigued with her long journey, retired to bed early, and innocently said, next morning, at the break-fast-table, 'How odd, to have so late a party last night, in this remote place, and not to tell me of it, before I went to bed!'   Then, every one asked Lady Mary what she meant?   Then, Lady Mary replied, 'Why, all night long, the carriages were driving round and

round the terrace, underneath my window!' Then, the owner of the house turned pale, and so did his Lady, and Charles Macdoodle of Macdoodle signed to Lady Mary to say no more, and every one was silent. After breakfast, Charles Macdoodle told Lady Mary that it was a tradition in the family that those rumbling carriages on the terrace betokened death. And so it proved, for, two months afterwards, the Lady of the mansion died. And Lady Mary, who was a Maid of Honour at Court, often told this story to the old Queen Charlotte; by this token that the old King always said, 'Eh, eh? What, what? Ghosts, ghosts? No such thing, no such thing!' And never left off saying so, until he went to bed.

Or, a friend of somebody's whom most of us know, when he was a young man at college, had a particular friend, with whom he made the compact that, if it were possible for the Spirit to return to this earth after its separation from the body, he of the twain who first died, should reappear to the other. In course of time, this compact was forgotten by our friend; the two young men having progressed in life, and taken diverging paths that were wide asunder. But, one night, many years afterwards, our friend being in the North of England, and staying for the night in an inn, on the Yorkshire Moors, happened to look out of bed; and there, in the moonlight, leaning on a bureau near the window, steadfastly regarding him, saw his old college friend! The appearance being solemnly addressed, replied, in a kind of whisper, but very audibly, 'Do not come near me. I am dead. I am here to redeem my promise. I come from another world, but may not disclose its secrets!' Then, the whole form becoming paler, melted, as it were, into the moonlight, and faded away.

Or, there was the daughter of the first occupier of the picturesque Elizabethan house, so famous in our neighbourhood. You have heard about her? No! Why, *She* went out one summer evening at twilight, when she was a beautiful girl, just seventeen years of age, to gather flowers in the garden; and presently came running, terrified, into the hall to her father, saying, 'Oh, dear father, I have met myself!' He took her in his arms, and told her it was fancy, but she said, 'Oh no! I met myself in the broad walk, and I was pale and gathering withered flowers, and I turned my head, and held them up!' And, that night, she died; and a picture of her story was begun, though never finished, and they say it is somewhere in the house to this day, with its face to the wall.

Or, the uncle of my brother's wife was riding home on horseback, one mellow evening at sunset, when in a green lane close to his own house, he saw a man standing before him, in the very centre of a narrow way. 'Why does that man in the cloak stand there!' he thought. 'Does he want me to ride over him?' But the figure never moved. He felt a strange sensation at seeing it so still, but slackened his trot and rode forward. When he was so close to it, as almost to touch it with his stirrup, his horse shied, and the figure glided up the bank, in a curious, unearthly manner—backward, and without seeming to use its feet—and was gone. The uncle of my brother's wife, exclaiming, 'Good Heaven! It's my cousin Harry, from Bombay!' put spurs to his horse, which was suddenly in a profuse sweat, and, wondering at such strange behaviour, dashed round to the front of his house. There, he saw the same figure, just passing in at the long French window of the drawing-room, opening on the ground. He threw his bridle to a servant, and hastened in after it. His sister was sit-

ting there, alone. 'Alice, where's my cousin Harry?' 'Your cousin Harry, John?' 'Yes. From Bombay. I met him in the lane just now, and saw him enter here, this instant.' Not a creature had been seen by any one; and in that hour and minute, as it afterwards appeared, this cousin died in India.

Or, it was a certain sensible old maiden lady, who died at ninety-nine, and retained her faculties to the last, who really did see the Orphan Boy; a story which has often been incorrectly told, but, of which the real truth is this—because it is, in fact, a story belonging to our family—and she was a connexion of our family. When she was about forty years of age, and still an uncommonly fine woman (her lover died young, which was the reason why she never married, though she had many offers), she went to stay at a place in Kent, which her brother, an Indian-Merchant, had newly bought. There was a story that this place had once been held in trust by the guardian of a young boy; who was himself the next heir, and who killed the young boy by harsh and cruel treatment. She knew nothing of that. It has been said that there was a Cage in her bedroom in which the guardian used to put the boy. There was no such thing. There was only a closet. She went to bed, made no alarm whatever in the night, and in the morning said composedly to her maid when she came in, 'Who is the pretty forlorn-looking child who has been peeping out of that closet all night?' The maid replied by giving a loud scream, and instantly decamping. She was surprised; but she was a woman of remarkable strength of mind, and she dressed herself and went downstairs, and closeted herself with her brother. 'Now, Walter,' she said, 'I have been disturbed all night by a pretty, forlorn-looking boy, who has been constantly peeping out of that closet in my room,

which I can't open. This is some trick.' 'I am afraid not, Charlotte,' said he, 'for it is the legend of the house. It is the Orphan Boy. What did he do?' 'He opened the door softly,' said she, 'and peeped out. Sometimes, he came a step or two into the room. Then, I called to him, to encourage him, and he shrunk, and shuddered, and crept in again, and shut the door.' 'The closet has no communication, Charlotte,' said her brother, 'with any other part of the house, and it's nailed up.' This was undeniably true, and it took two carpenters a whole forenoon to get it open, for examination. Then, she was satisfied that she had seen the Orphan Boy. But, the wild and terrible part of the story is, that he was also seen by three of her brother's sons, in succession, who all died young. On the occasion of each child being taken ill, he came home in a heat, twelve hours before, and said, Oh, Mamma, he had been playing under a particular oak tree, in a certain meadow, with a strange boy—a pretty, forlorn-looking boy, who was very timid, and made signs! From fatal experience, the parents came to know that this was the Orphan Boy, and that the course of that child whom he chose for his little playmate was surely run.

Legion is the name of the German castles, where we sit up alone to wait for the Spectre—where we are shown into a room, made comparatively cheerful for our reception—where we glance round at the shadows, thrown on the blank walls by the crackling fire—where we feel very lonely when the village inn-keeper and his pretty daughter have retired, after laying down a fresh store of wood upon the hearth, and setting forth on the small table such supper-cheer as a cold roast capon, bread, grapes, and a flask of old Rhine wine—where the reverberating doors close on

their retreat, one after another, like so many peals of sullen thunder—and where, about the small hours of the night, we come into the knowledge of divers supernatural mysteries. Legion is the name of the haunted German students, in whose society we draw yet nearer to the fire, while the schoolboy in the corner opens his eyes wide and round, and flies off the footstool he has chosen for his seat, when the door accidentally blows open. Vast is the crop of such fruit, shining on our Christmas Tree; in blossom, almost at the very top; ripening all down the boughs!

Among the later toys and fancies hanging there— as idle often and less pure—be the images once associated with the sweet old Waits, the softened music in the night, ever unalterable! Encircled by the social thoughts of Christmas-time, still let the benignant figure of my childhood stand unchanged! In every cheerful image and suggestion that the season brings, may the bright star that rested above the poor roof, be the star of all the Christian World! A moment's pause, O vanishing tree, of which the lower boughs are dark to me as yet, and let me look once more! I know there are blank spaces on thy branches, where eyes that I have loved have shone and smiled; from which they are departed. But, far above, I see the raiser of the dead girl, and the Widow's Son; and God is good! If Age be hiding for me in the unseen portion of thy downward growth, O may I, with a grey head, turn a child's heart to that figure yet, and a child's trustfulness and confidence!

Now, the tree is decorated with bright merriment, and song, and dance, and cheerfulness. And they are welcome. Innocent and welcome be they ever held, beneath the branches of the Christmas Tree, which cast no gloomy shadow! But, as it sinks into

the ground, I hear a whisper going through the leaves. 'This, in commemoration of the law of love and kindness, mercy and compassion. This, in remembrance of Me!'

WHAT CHRISTMAS IS AS WE GROW OLDER

[1851]

WHAT CHRISTMAS IS AS WE GROW OLDER

TIME was, with most of us, when Christmas Day encircling all our limited world like a magic ring, left nothing out for us to miss or seek; bound together all our home enjoyments, affections, and hopes; grouped everything and every one around the Christmas fire; and made the little picture shining in our bright young eyes, complete.

Time came, perhaps, all so soon, when our thoughts overleaped that narrow boundary; when there was some one (very dear, we thought then, very beautiful, and absolutely perfect) wanting to the fulness of our happiness; when we were wanting too (or we thought so, which did just as well) at the Christmas hearth by which that some one sat; and when we intertwined with every wreath and garland of our life that some one's name.

That was the time for the bright visionary Christmases which have long arisen from us to show faintly, after summer rain, in the palest edges of the rainbow! That was the time for the beatified enjoyment of the things that were to be, and never were, and yet the things that were so real in our resolute hope that it would be hard to say, now, what realities achieved since, have been stronger!

What! Did that Christmas never really come when we and the priceless pearl who was our young choice were received, after the happiest of totally impossible

27

marriages, by the two united families previously at daggers-drawn on our account? When brothers and sisters-in-law who had always been rather cool to us before our relationship was effected, perfectly doted on us, and when fathers and mothers overwhelmed us with unlimited incomes? Was that Christmas dinner never really eaten, after which we arose, and generously and eloquently rendered honour to our late rival, present in the company, then and there exchanging friendship and forgiveness, and founding an attachment, not to be surpassed in Greek or Roman story, which subsisted until death? Has that same rival long ceased to care for that same priceless pearl, and married for money, and become usurious? Above all, do we really know, now, that we should probably have been miserable if we had won and worn the pearl, and that we are better without her?

That Christmas when we had recently achieved so much fame; when we had been carried in triumph somewhere, for doing something great and good; when we had won an honoured and ennobled name, and arrived and were received at home in a shower of tears of joy; is it possible that *that* Christmas has not come yet?

And is our life here, at the best, so constituted that, pausing as we advance at such a noticeable mile-stone in the track as this great birthday, we look back on the things that never were, as naturally and full as gravely as on the things that have been and are gone, or have been and still are? If it be so, and so it seems to be, must we come to the conclusion that life is little better than a dream, and little worth the loves and strivings that we crowd into it?

No! Far be such miscalled philosophy from us, dear Reader, on Christmas Day! Nearer and closer to our hearts be the Christmas spirit, which is the spirit

of active usefulness, perseverance, cheerful discharge of duty, kindness and forbearance! It is in the last virtues especially, that we are, or should be, strengthened by the unaccomplished visions of our youth; for, who shall say that they are not our teachers to deal gently even with the impalpable nothings of the earth!

Therefore, as we grow older, let us be more thankful that the circle of our Christmas associations and of the lessons that they bring, expands! Let us welcome every one of them, and summon them to take their places by the Christmas hearth.

Welcome, old aspirations, glittering creatures of an ardent fancy, to your shelter underneath the holly! We know you, and have not outlived you yet. Welcome, old projects and old loves, however fleeting, to your nooks among the steadier lights that burn around us. Welcome, all that was ever real to our hearts; and for the earnestness that made you real, thanks to Heaven! Do we build no Christmas castles in the clouds now? Let our thoughts, fluttering like butterflies among these flowers of children, bear witness! Before this boy, there stretches out a Future, brighter than we ever looked on in our old romantic time, but bright with honour and with truth. Around this little head on which the sunny curls lie heaped, the graces sport, as prettily, as airily, as when there was no scythe within the reach of Time to shear away the curls of our first-love. Upon another girl's face near it—placider but smiling bright—a quiet and contented little face, we see Home fairly written. Shining from the word, as rays shine from a star, we see how, when our graves are old, other hopes than ours are young, other hearts than ours are moved; how other ways are smoothed; how other happiness blooms, ripens, and decays—no, not decays, for other homes

and other bands of children, not yet in being nor for
ages yet to be, arise, and bloom and ripen to the end
of all!

Welcome, everything! Welcome, alike what has
been, and what never was, and what we hope may be,
to your shelter underneath the holly, to your places
round the Christmas fire, where what is sits open-
hearted! In yonder shadow, do we see obtruding
furtively upon the blaze, an enemy's face? By
Christmas Day we do forgive him! If the injury he
has done us may admit of such companionship, let
him come here and take his place. If otherwise, unhappily, let him go hence, assured that we will never
injure nor accuse him.

On this day we shut out Nothing!

'Pause,' says a low voice. 'Nothing? Think!'

'On Christmas Day, we will shut out from our fireside, Nothing.'

'Not the shadow of a vast City where the withered
leaves are lying deep?' the voice replies. 'Not the
shadow that darkens the whole globe? Not the
shadow of the City of the Dead?'

Not even that. Of all days in the year, we will
turn our faces towards that City upon Christmas Day,
and from its silent hosts bring those we loved, among
us. City of the Dead, in the blessed name wherein we
are gathered together at this time, and in the Presence
that is here among us according to the promise, we
will receive, and not dismiss, thy people who are dear
to us!

Yes. We can look upon these children angels that
alight, so solemnly, so beautifully among the living
children by the fire, and can bear to think how they
departed from us. Entertaining angels unawares, as
the Patriarchs did, the playful children are unconscious of their guests; but we can see them—can see

a radiant arm around one favourite neck, as if there were a tempting of that child away. Among the celestial figures there is one, a poor mis-shapen boy on earth, of a glorious beauty now, of whom his dying mother said it grieved her much to leave him here, alone, for so many years as it was likely would elapse before he came to her—being such a little child. But he went quickly, and was laid upon her breast, and in her hand she leads him.

There was a gallant boy, who fell, far away, upon a burning sand beneath a burning sun, and said, 'Tell them at home, with my last love, how much I could have wished to kiss them once, but that I died contented and had done my duty!' Or there was another, over whom they read the words, 'Therefore we commit his body to the deep,' and so consigned him to the lonely ocean and sailed on. Or there was another, who lay down to his rest in the dark shadow of great forests, and, on earth, awoke no more. O shall they not, from sand and sea and forest, be brought home at such a time!

There was a dear girl—almost a woman—never to be one—who made a mourning Christmas in a house of joy, and went her trackless way to the silent City. Do we recollect her, worn out, faintly whispering what could not be heard, and falling into that last sleep for weariness? O look upon her now! O look upon her beauty, her serenity, her changeless youth, her happiness! The daughter of Jairus was recalled to life, to die; but she, more blest, has heard the same voice, saying unto her, 'Arise for ever!'

We had a friend who was our friend from early days, with whom we often pictured the changes that were to come upon our lives, and merrily imagined how we would speak, and walk, and think, and talk, when we came to be old. His destined habitation in

the City of the Dead received him in his prime.   Shall
he be shut out from our Christmas remembrance?
Would his love have so excluded us?   Lost friend,
lost child, lost parent, sister, brother, husband, wife,
we will not so discard you!   You shall hold your
cherished places in our Christmas hearts, and by our
Christmas fires; and in the season of immortal hope,
and on the birthday of immortal mercy, we will shut
out Nothing!

The winter sun goes down over town and village;
on the sea it makes a rosy path, as if the Sacred
tread were fresh upon the water.   A few more moments, and it sinks, and night comes on, and lights
begin to sparkle in the prospect.   On the hill-side beyond the shapelessly-diffused town, and in the quiet
keeping of the trees that gird the village steeple, remembrances are cut in stone, planted in common
flowers, growing in grass, entwined with lowly bram-
bles around many a mound of earth.   In town and
village, there are doors and windows closed against
the weather, there are flaming logs heaped high, there
are joyful faces, there is healthy music of voices.   Be
all ungentleness and harm excluded from the temples
of the Household Gods, but be those remembrances
admitted with tender encouragement!   They are of
the time and all its comforting and peaceful reassur-
ances; and of the history that re-united even upon
earth the living and the dead; and of the broad beneficence and goodness that too many men have tried
to tear to narrow shreds.

THE POOR RELATION'S STORY

[1852]

THE POOR RELATION'S STORY

HE was very reluctant to take precedence of so many respected members of the family, by beginning the round of stories they were to relate as they sat in a goodly circle by the Christmas fire; and he modestly suggested that it would be more correct if 'John our esteemed host' (whose health he begged to drink) would have the kindness to begin. For as to himself, he said, he was so little used to lead the way that really— But as they all cried out here, that he must begin, and agreed with one voice that he might, could, would, and should begin, he left off rubbing his hands, and took his legs out from under his arm-chair, and did begin.

I have no doubt (said the poor relation) that I shall surprise the assembled members of our family, and particularly John our esteemed host to whom we are so much indebted for the great hospitality with which he has this day entertained us, by the confession I am going to make. But, if you do me the honour to be surprised at anything that falls from a person so unimportant in the family as I am, I can only say that I shall be scrupulously accurate in all I relate.

I am not what I am supposed to be. I am quite another thing. Perhaps before I go further, I had better glance at what I *am* supposed to be.

It is supposed, unless I mistake—the assembled members of our family will correct me if I do, which is very likely (here the poor relation looked mildly
35

about him for contradiction) ; that I am nobody's
enemy but my own. That I never met with any particular success in anything. That I failed in business
because I was unbusiness-like and credulous—in not
being prepared for the interested designs of my partner. That I failed in love, because I was ridiculously
trustful—in thinking it impossible that Christiana
could deceive me. That I failed in my expectations
from my uncle Chill, on account of not being as sharp
as he could have wished in worldly matters. That,
through life, I have been rather put upon and disappointed in a general way. That I am at present a
bachelor of between fifty-nine and sixty years of age,
living on a limited income in the form of a quarterly
allowance, to which I see that John our esteemed host
wishes me to make no further allusion.

The supposition as to my present pursuits and habits
is to the following effect.

I live in a lodging in the Clapham Road—a very
clean back room, in a very respectable house—where I
am expected not to be at home in the day-time, unless
poorly; and which I usually leave in the morning at
nine o'clock, on pretence of going to business. I take
my breakfast—my roll and butter, and my half-pint
of coffee—at the old-established coffee-shop near
Westminster Bridge; and then I go into the City—I
don't know why—and sit in Garraway's Coffee
House, and on 'Change, and walk about, and look
into a few offices and counting-houses where some of
my relations or acquaintance are so good as to toler-
ate me, and where I stand by the fire if the weather
happens to be cold. I get through the day in this way
until five o'clock, and then I dine: at a cost, on the
average, of one and threepence. Having still a little
money to spend on my evening's entertainment, I
look into the old-established coffee-shop as I go home,

and take my cup of tea, and perhaps my bit of toast. So, as the large hand of the clock makes its way round to the morning hour again, I make my way round to the Clapham Road again, and go to bed when I get to my lodging—fire being expensive, and being objected to by the family on account of its giving trouble and making a dirt.

Sometimes, one of my relations or acquaintances is so obliging as to ask me to dinner. Those are holiday occasions, and then I generally walk in the Park. I am a solitary man, and seldom walk with anybody. Not that I am avoided because I am shabby; for I am not at all shabby, having always a very good suit of black on (or rather Oxford mixture, which has the appearance of black and wears much better); but I have got into a habit of speaking low, and being rather silent, and my spirits are not high, and I am sensible that I am not an attractive companion.

The only exception to this general rule is the child of my first cousin, Little Frank. I have a particular affection for that child, and he takes very kindly to me. He is a diffident boy by nature; and in a crowd he is soon run over, as I may say, and forgotten. He and I, however, get on exceedingly well. I have a fancy that the poor child will in time succeed to my peculiar position in the family. We talk but little; still, we understand each other. We walk about, hand in hand; and without much speaking he knows what I mean, and I know what he means. When he was very little indeed, I used to take him to the windows of the toy-shops, and show him the toys inside. It is surprising how soon he found out that I would have made him a great many presents if I had been in circumstances to do it.

Little Frank and I go and look at the outside of the Monument—he is very fond of the Monument—

and at the Bridges, and at all the sights that are free. On two of my birthdays, we have dined on à-la-mode beef, and gone at half-price to the play, and been deeply interested. I was once walking with him in Lombard Street, which we often visit on account of my having mentioned to him that there are great riches there—he is very fond of Lombard Street— when a gentleman said to me as he passed by, 'Sir, your little son has dropped his glove.' I assure you, if you will excuse my remarking on so trivial a circumstance, this accidental mention of the child as mine, quite touched my heart and brought the foolish tears into my eyes.

When Little Frank is sent to school in the country, I shall be very much at a loss what to do with myself, but I have the intention of walking down there once a month and seeing him on a half holiday. I am told he will then be at play upon the Heath; and if my visits should be objected to, as unsettling the child, I can see him from a distance without his seeing me, and walk back again. His mother comes of a highly genteel family, and rather disapproves, I am aware, of our being too much together. I know that I am not calculated to improve his retiring disposition; but I think he would miss me beyond the feeling of the moment if we were wholly separated.

When I die in the Clapham Road, I shall not leave much more in this world than I shall take out of it; but, I happen to have a miniature of a bright-faced boy, with a curling head, and an open shirt-frill waving down his bosom (my mother had it taken for me, but I can't believe that it was ever like), which will be worth nothing to sell, and which I shall beg may be given to Frank. I have written my dear boy a little letter with it, in which I have told him that I felt very sorry to part from him, though bound to confess that

I knew no reason why I should remain here. I have given him some short advice, the best in my power, to take warning of the consequences of being nobody's enemy but his own; and I have endeavoured to comfort him for what I fear he will consider a bereavement, by pointing out to him, that I was only a superfluous something to every one but him; and that having by some means failed to find a place in this great assembly, I am better out of it.

Such (said the poor relation, clearing his throat and beginning to speak a little louder) is the general impression about me. Now, it is a remarkable circumstance which forms the aim and purpose of my story, that this is all wrong. This is not my life, and these are not my habits. I do not even live in the Clapham Road. Comparatively speaking, I am very seldom there. I reside, mostly, in a—I am almost ashamed to say the word, it sounds so full of pretension—in a Castle. I do not mean that it is an old baronial habitation, but still it is a building always known to every one by the name of a Castle. In it, I preserve the particulars of my history; they run thus:

It was when I first took John Spatter (who had been my clerk) into partnership, and when I was still a young man of not more than five-and-twenty, residing in the house of my uncle Chill, from whom I had considerable expectations, that I ventured to propose to Christiana. I had loved Christiana a long time. She was very beautiful, and very winning in all respects. I rather mistrusted her widowed mother, who I feared was of a plotting and mercenary turn of mind; but, I thought as well of her as I could, for Christiana's sake. I never had loved any one but Christiana, and she had been all the world, and O far more than all the world, to me, from our childhood!

Christiana accepted me with her mother's consent,

and I was rendered very happy indeed. My life at my uncle Chill's was of a spare dull kind, and my garret chamber was as dull, and bare, and cold, as an upper prison room in some stern northern fortress. But, having Christiana's love, I wanted nothing upon earth. I would not have changed my lot with any human being.

Avarice was, unhappily, my uncle Chill's master-vice. Though he was rich, he pinched, and scraped, and clutched, and lived miserably. As Christiana had no fortune, I was for some time a little fearful of confessing our engagement to him; but, at length I wrote him a letter, saying how it all truly was. I put it into his hand one night, on going to bed.

As I came downstairs next morning, shivering in the cold December air; colder in my uncle's unwarmed house than in the street, where the winter sun did sometimes shine, and which was at all events enlivened by cheerful faces and voices passing along; I carried a heavy heart towards the long low breakfast-room in which my uncle sat. It was a large room with a small fire, and there was a great bay window in it which the rain had marked in the night as if with the tears of houseless people. It stared upon a raw yard, with a cracked stone pavement, and some rusted iron railings half uprooted, whence an ugly out-building that had once been a dissecting-room (in the time of the great surgeon who had mortgaged the house to my uncle), stared at it.

We rose so early always, that at that time of the year we breakfasted by candle-light. When I went into the room, my uncle was so contracted by the cold, and so huddled together in his chair behind the one dim candle, that I did not see him until I was close to the table.

As I held out my hand to him, he caught up his stick (being infirm, he always walked about the house with a stick), and made a blow at me, and said, 'You fool!'

'Uncle,' I returned, 'I didn't expect you to be so angry as this.' Nor had I expected it, though he was a hard and angry old man.

'You didn't expect!' said he; 'when did you ever expect? When did you ever calculate, or look forward, you contemptible dog?'

'These are hard words, uncle!'

'Hard words? Feathers, to pelt such an idiot as you with,' said he. 'Here! Betsy Snap! Look at him!'

Betsy Snap was a withered, hard-favoured, yellow old woman—our only domestic—always employed, at this time of the morning, in rubbing my uncle's legs. As my uncle adjured her to look at me, he put his lean grip on the crown of her head, she kneeling beside him, and turned her face towards me. An involuntary thought connecting them both with the Dissecting Room, as it must often have been in the surgeon's time, passed across my mind in the midst of my anxiety.

'Look at the snivelling milksop!' said my uncle. 'Look at the baby! This is the gentleman who, people say, is nobody's enemy but his own. This is the gentleman who can't say no. This is the gentleman who was making such large profits in his business that he must needs take a partner, t' other day. This is the gentleman who is going to marry a wife without a penny, and who falls into the hands of Jezabels who are speculating on my death!'

I knew, now, how great my uncle's rage was; for nothing short of his being almost beside himself would

have induced him to utter that concluding word, which he held in such repugnance that it was never spoken or hinted at before him on any account.

'On my death,' he repeated, as if he were defying me by defying his own abhorrence of the word. 'On my death—death—Death! But I 'll spoil the speculation. Eat your last under this roof, you feeble wretch, and may it choke you!'

You may suppose that I had not much appetite for the breakfast to which I was bidden in these terms; but, I took my accustomed seat. I saw that I was repudiated henceforth by my uncle; still I could bear that very well, possessing Christiana's heart.

He emptied his basin of bread and milk as usual, only that he took it on his knees with his chair turned away from the table where I sat. When he had done, he carefully snuffed out the candle; and the cold, slate-coloured, miserable day looked in upon us.

'Now, Mr. Michael,' said he, 'before we part, I should like to have a word with these ladies in your presence.'

'As you will, sir,' I returned; 'but you deceive yourself, and wrong us, cruelly, if you suppose that there is any feeling at stake in this contract but pure, disinterested, faithful love.'

To this, he only replied, 'You lie!' and not one other word.

We went, through half-thawed snow and half-frozen rain, to the house where Christiana and her mother lived. My uncle knew them very well. They were sitting at their breakfast, and were surprised to see us at that hour.

'Your servant, ma'am,' said my uncle to the mother. 'You divine the purpose of my visit, I dare say, ma'am. I understand there is a world of pure, disinterested, faithful love cooped up here. I am happy

to bring it all it wants, to make it complete. I bring you your son-in-law, ma'am—and you, your husband, miss. The gentleman is a perfect stranger to me, but I wish him joy of his wise bargain.'

He snarled at me as he went out, and I never saw him again.

It is altogether a mistake (continued the poor relation) to suppose that my dear Christiana, over-persuaded and influenced by her mother, married a rich man, the dirt from whose carriage wheels is often, in these changed times, thrown upon me as she rides by. No, no. She married me.

The way we came to be married rather sooner than we intended, was this. I took a frugal lodging and was saving and planning for her sake, when, one day, she spoke to me with great earnestness, and said:

'My dear Michael, I have given you my heart. I have said that I loved you, and I have pledged myself to be your wife. I am as much yours through all changes of good and evil as if we had been married on the day when such words passed between us. I know you well, and know that if we should be separated and our union broken off, your whole life would be shadowed, and all that might, even now, be stronger in your character for the conflict with the world would then be weakened to the shadow of what it is!'

'God help me, Christiana!' said I. 'You speak the truth.'

'Michael!' said she, putting her hand in mine, in all maidenly devotion, 'let us keep apart no longer. It is but for me to say that I can live contented upon such means as you have, and I well know you are happy. I say so from my heart. Strive no more alone; let us strive together. My dear Michael, it is

not right that I should keep secret from you what
you do not suspect, but what distresses my whole life.
My mother: without considering that what you have
lost, you have lost for me, and on the assurance of
my faith: sets her heart on riches, and urges another
suit upon me, to my misery. I cannot bear this, for
to bear it is to be untrue to you. I would rather share
your struggles than look on. I want no better home
than you can give me. I know that you will aspire
and labour with a higher courage if I am wholly
yours, and let it be so when you will!'

I was blest indeed, that day, and a new world
opened to me. We were married in a very little
while, and I took my wife to our happy home. That
was the beginning of the residence I have spoken of;
the Castle we have ever since inhabited together, dates
from that time. All our children have been born in it.
Our first child—now married—was a little girl, whom
we called Christiana. Her son is so like Little Frank,
that I hardly know which is which.

The current impression as to my partner's dealings
with me is also quite erroneous. He did not begin
to treat me coldly, as a poor simpleton, when my uncle
and I so fatally quarrelled; nor did he afterwards
gradually possess himself of our business and edge
me out. On the contrary, he behaved to me with the
utmost good faith and honour.

Matters between us took this turn:—On the day
of my separation from my uncle, and even before
the arrival at our counting-house of my trunks (which
he sent after me, *not* carriage paid), I went down to
our room of business, on our little wharf, overlooking
the river; and there I told John Spatter what had happened. John did not say, in reply, that rich old rela-
tives were palpable facts, and that love and sentiment

were moonshine and fiction. He addressed me thus:

'Michael,' said John, 'we were at school together, and I generally had the knack of getting on better than you, and making a higher reputation.'

'You had, John,' I returned.

'Although,' said John, 'I borrowed your books and lost them; borrowed your pocket-money, and never repaid it; got you to buy my damaged knives at a higher price than I had given for them new; and to own to the windows that I had broken.'

'All not worth mentioning, John Spatter,' said I, 'but certainly true.'

'When you were first established in this infant business, which promises to thrive so well,' pursued John, 'I came to you, in my search for almost any employment, and you made me your clerk.'

'Still not worth mentioning, my dear John Spatter,' said I; 'still, equally true.'

'And finding that I had a good head for business, and that I was really useful *to* the business, you did not like to retain me in that capacity, and thought it an act of justice soon to make me your partner.'

'Still less worth mentioning than any of those other little circumstances you have recalled, John Spatter,' said I; 'for I was, and am, sensible of your merits and my deficiencies.'

'Now, my good friend,' said John, drawing my arm through his, as he had had a habit of doing at school; while two vessels outside the windows of our counting-house—which were shaped like the stern windows of a ship—went lightly down the river with the tide, as John and I might then be sailing away in company, and in trust and confidence, on our voyage of life; 'let there, under these friendly circumstances, be a right understanding between us. You are too easy, Michael. You are nobody's enemy but your

own. If I were to give you that damaging character among our connexion, with a shrug, and a shake of the head, and a sigh; and if I were further to abuse the trust you place in me—'

'But you never will abuse it at all, John,' I observed.

'Never!' said he; 'but I am putting a case—I say, and if I were further to abuse that trust by keeping this piece of our common affairs in the dark, and this other piece in the light, and again this other piece in the twilight, and so on, I should strengthen my strength, and weaken your weakness, day by day, until at last I found myself on the high road to fortune, and you left behind on some bare common, a hopeless number of miles out of the way.'

'Exactly so,' said I.

'To prevent this, Michael,' said John Spatter, 'or the remotest chance of this, there must be perfect openness between us. Nothing must be concealed, and we must have but one interest.'

'My dear John Spatter,' I assured him, 'that is precisely what I mean.'

'And when you are too easy,' pursued John, his face glowing with friendship, 'you must allow me to prevent that imperfection in your nature from being taken advantage of, by any one; you must not expect me to humour it—'

'My dear John Spatter,' I interrupted, 'I *don't* expect you to humour it. I want to correct it.'

'And I, too,' said John.

'Exactly so!' cried I. 'We both have the same end in view; and, honourably seeking it, and fully trusting one another, and having but one interest, ours will be a prosperous and happy partnership.'

'I am sure of it!' returned John Spatter. And we shook hands most affectionately.

I took John home to my Castle, and we had a very happy day. Our partnership throve well. My friend and partner supplied what I wanted, as I had foreseen that he would; and by improving both the business and myself, amply acknowledged any little rise in life to which I had helped him.

I am not (said the poor relation, looking at the fire as he slowly rubbed his hands) very rich, for I never cared to be that; but I have enough, and am above all moderate wants and anxieties. My Castle is not a splendid place, but it is very comfortable, and it has a warm and cheerful air, and is quite a picture of Home.

Our eldest girl, who is very like her mother, married John Spatter's eldest son. Our two families are closely united in other ties of attachment. It is very pleasant of an evening, when we are all assembled together—which frequently happens—and when John and I talk over old times, and the one interest there has always been between us.

I really do not know, in my Castle, what loneliness is. Some of our children or grandchildren are always about it, and the young voices of my descendants are delightful—O, how delightful!—to me to hear. My dearest and most devoted wife, ever faithful, ever loving, ever helpful and sustaining and consoling, is the priceless blessing of my house; from whom all its other blessings spring. We are rather a musical family, and when Christiana sees me, at any time, a little weary or depressed, she steals to the piano and sings a gentle air she used to sing when we were first betrothed. So weak a man am I, that I cannot bear to hear it from any other source. They played it once, at the Theatre, when I was there with Little Frank; and the child said wondering, 'Cousin Michael,

whose hot tears are these that have fallen on my hand!'

Such is my Castle, and such are the real particulars of my life therein preserved. I often take Little Frank home there. He is very welcome to my grand-children, and they play together. At this time of the year—the Christmas and New Year time—I am seldom out of my Castle. For, the associations of the season seem to hold me there, and the precepts of the season seem to teach me that it is well to be there.

'And the Castle is—' observed a grave. kind voice among the company.

'Yes. My Castle,' said the poor relation, shaking his head as he still looked at the fire, 'is in the Air. John our esteemed host suggests its situation accu-rately. My Castle is in the Air! I have done. Will you be so good as to pass the story?'

THE CHILD'S STORY

[1852]

THE CHILD'S STORY

ONCE upon a time, a good many years ago, there was a traveller, and he set out upon a journey. It was a magic journey, and was to seem very long when he began it, and very short when he got half way through.

He travelled along a rather dark path for some little time, without meeting anything, until at last he came to a beautiful child. So he said to the child, 'What do you do here?' And the child said, 'I am always at play. Come and play with me!'

So, he played with that child, the whole day long, and they were very merry. The sky was so blue, the sun was so bright, the water was so sparkling, the leaves were so green, the flowers were so lovely, and they heard such singing-birds and saw so many but-terflies, that everything was beautiful. This was in fine weather. When it rained, they loved to watch the falling drops, and to smell the fresh scents. When it blew, it was delightful to listen to the wind, and fancy what it said, as it came rushing from its home—where was that, they wondered!—whistling and howling, driving the clouds before it, bending the trees, rumbling in the chimneys, shaking the house, and making the sea roar in fury. But, when it snowed, that was best of all; for, they liked nothing so well as to look up at the white flakes falling fast and thick, like down from the breasts of millions of white birds; and to see how smooth and deep the drift was; and to listen to the hush upon the paths and roads.

They had plenty of the finest toys in the world, and the most astonishing picture-books: all about scimitars and slippers and turbans, and dwarfs and giants and genii and fairies, and blue-beards and bean-stalks and riches and caverns and forests and Valentines and Orsons: and all new and all true.

But, one day, of a sudden, the traveller lost the child. He called to him over and over again, but got no answer. So, he went upon his road, and went on for a little while without meeting anything, until at last he came to a handsome boy. So, he said to the boy, 'What do you do here?' And the boy said, 'I am always learning. Come and learn with me.'

So he learned with that boy about Jupiter and Juno, and the Greeks and the Romans, and I don't know what, and learned more than I could tell—or he either, for he soon forgot a great deal of it. But, they were not always learning; they had the merriest games that ever were played. They rowed upon the river in summer, and skated on the ice in winter; they were active afoot, and active on horseback, at cricket, and all games at ball; at prisoners' base, hare and hounds, follow my leader, and more sports than I can think of; nobody could beat them. They had holidays too, and Twelfth cakes, and parties where they danced till midnight, and real Theatres where they saw palaces of real gold and silver rise out of the real earth, and saw all the wonders of the world at once. As to friends, they had such dear friends and so many of them, that I want the time to reckon them up. They were all young, like the handsome boy, and were never to be strange to one another all their lives through.

Still, one day, in the midst of all these pleasures, the traveller lost the boy as he had lost the child, and, after calling to him in vain, went on upon his journey.

So he went on for a little while without seeing anything, until at last he came to a young man. So, he
said to the young man, 'What do you do here?' And
the young man said, 'I am always in love. Come and
love with me.'

So, he went away with that young man, and presently they came to one of the prettiest girls that ever
was seen—just like Fanny in the corner there—and
she had eyes like Fanny, and hair like Fanny, and
dimples like Fanny's, and she laughed and coloured
just as Fanny does while I am talking about her. So,
the young man fell in love directly—just as Somebody I won't mention, the first time he came here,
did with Fanny. Well! he was teased sometimes—
just as Somebody used to be by Fanny; and they
quarrelled sometimes—just as Somebody and Fanny
used to quarrel; and they made it up, and sat in the
dark, and wrote letters every day, and never were
happy asunder, and were always looking out for one
another and pretending not to, and were engaged at
Christmas-time, and sat close to one another by the
fire, and were going to be married very soon—all exactly like Somebody I won't mention, and Fanny!

But, the traveller lost them one day, as he had lost
the rest of his friends, and, after calling to them
to come back, which they never did, went on upon
his journey. So, he went on for a little while without seeing anything, until at last he came to a middle-
aged gentleman. So, he said to the gentleman,
'What are you doing here?' And his answer was, 'I
am always busy. Come and be busy with me!'

So, he began to be very busy with that gentleman,
and they went on through the wood together. The
whole journey was through a wood, only it had been
open and green at first, like a wood in spring; and
now began to be thick and dark, like a wood in sum-

mer; some of the little trees that had come out earliest, were even turning brown. The gentleman was not alone, but had a lady of about the same age with him, who was his Wife; and they had children, who were with them too. So, they all went on together through the wood, cutting down the trees, and making a path through the branches and the fallen leaves, and carrying burdens, and working hard.

Sometimes, they came to a long green avenue that opened into deeper woods. Then they would hear a very little, distant voice crying, 'Father, father, I am another child! Stop for me!' And presently they would see a very little figure, growing larger as it came along, running to join them. When it came up, they all crowded round it, and kissed and welcomed it; and then they all went on together.

Sometimes, they came to several avenues at once, and then they all stood still, and one of the children said, 'Father, I am going to sea,' and another said, 'Father, I am going to India,' and another, 'Father, I am going to seek my fortune where I can,' and another, 'Father, I am going to Heaven!' So, with many tears at parting, they went, solitary, down those avenues, each child upon its way; and the child who went to Heaven, rose into the golden air and vanished.

Whenever these partings happened, the traveller looked at the gentleman, and saw him glance up at the sky above the trees, where the day was beginning to decline, and the sunset to come on. He saw, too, that his hair was turning grey. But, they never could rest long, for they had their journey to perform, and it was necessary for them to be always busy.

At last, there had been so many partings that there were no children left, and only the traveller, the gentleman, and the lady, went upon their way in company. And now the wood was yellow; and now

brown; and the leaves, even of the forest trees, began to fall.

So, they came to an avenue that was darker than the rest, and were pressing forward on their journey without looking down it when the lady stopped.

'My husband,' said the lady. 'I am called.'

They listened, and they heard a voice a long way down the avenue, say, 'Mother, mother!'

It was the voice of the first child who had said, 'I am going to Heaven!' and the father said, 'I pray not yet. The sunset is very near. I pray not yet!'

But, the voice cried, 'Mother, mother!' without minding him, though his hair was now quite white, and tears were on his face.

Then, the mother, who was already drawn into the shade of the dark avenue and moving away with her arms still round his neck, kissed him, and said, 'My dearest, I am summoned, and I go!' And she was gone. And the traveller and he were left alone together.

And they went on and on together, until they came to very near the end of the wood: so near, that they could see the sunset shining red before them through the trees.

Yet, once more, while he broke his way among the branches, the traveller lost his friend. He called and called, but there was no reply, and when he passed out of the wood, and saw the peaceful sun going down upon a wide purple prospect, he came to an old man sitting on a fallen tree. So, he said to the old man, 'What do you do here?' And the old man said with a calm smile, 'I am always remembering. Come and remember with me!'

So the traveller sat down by the side of that old man, face to face with the serene sunset; and all his friends came softly back and stood around him. The

beautiful child, the handsome boy, the young man in love, the father, mother, and children: every one of them was there, and he had lost nothing.   So, he loved them all, and was kind and forbearing with them all, and was always pleased to watch them all, and they all honoured and loved him.   And I think the traveller must be yourself, dear Grandfather, because this is what you do to us, and what we do to you.

THE SCHOOLBOY'S STORY

[1853]

THE SCHOOLBOY'S STORY

BEING rather young at present—I am getting on in years, but still I am rather young—I have no particular adventures of my own to fall back upon. It wouldn't much interest anybody here, I suppose, to know what a screw the Reverend is, or what a griffin *she* is, or how they do stick it into parents—particularly hair-cutting, and medical attendance. One of our fellows was charged in his half's account twelve and sixpence for two pills—tolerably profitable at six and threepence a-piece, I should think—and he never took them either, but put them up the sleeve of his jacket.

As to the beef, it's shameful. It's *not* beef. Regular beef isn't veins. You can chew regular beef. Besides which, there's gravy to regular beef, and you never see a drop to ours. Another of our fellows went home ill, and heard the family doctor tell his father that he couldn't account for his complaint unless it was the beer. Of course it was the beer, and well it might be!

However, beef and Old Cheeseman are two different things. So is beer. It was Old Cheeseman I meant to tell about; not the manner in which our fellows get their constitutions destroyed for the sake of profit.

Why, look at the pie-crust alone. There's no flakiness in it. It's solid—like damp lead. Then our fellows get nightmares, and are bolstered for calling out and waking other fellows. Who can wonder!

59

Old Cheeseman one night walked in his sleep, put his hat on over his night-cap, got hold of a fishing-rod and a cricket-bat, and went down into the parlour, where they naturally thought from his appearance he was a Ghost.   Why, he never would have done that if his meals had been wholesome.   When we all begin to walk in our sleeps, I suppose they'll be sorry for it.

Old Cheeseman wasn't second Latin Master then; he was a fellow himself.   He was first brought there, very small, in a post-chaise, by a woman who was always taking snuff and shaking him—and that was the most he remembered about it.   He never went home for the holidays.   His accounts (he never learnt any extras) were sent to a Bank, and the Bank paid them; and he had a brown suit twice a-year, and went into boots at twelve.   They were always too big for him, too.

In the Midsummer holidays, some of our fellows who lived within walking distance, used to come back and climb the trees outside the playground wall, on purpose to look at Old Cheeseman reading there by himself.   He was always as mild as the tea—and *that's* pretty mild, I should hope!—so when they whistled to him, he looked up and nodded; and when they said, 'Halloa, Old Cheeseman, what have you had for dinner?' he said, 'Boiled mutton'; and when they said, 'An't it solitary, Old Cheeseman?' he said, 'It is a little dull sometimes': and then they said, 'Well, good-bye, Old Cheeseman!' and climbed down again. Of course it was imposing on Old Cheeseman to give him nothing but boiled mutton through a whole Vacation, but that was just like the system.   When they didn't give him boiled mutton, they gave him rice pudding, pretending it was a treat.   And saved the butcher.

So Old Cheeseman went on.   The holidays brought

ʌim into other trouble besides the loneliness; because when the fellows began to come back, not wanting to, he was always glad to see them; which was aggravating when they were not at all glad to see him, and so he got his head knocked against walls, and that was the way his nose bled. But he was a favourite in general. Once a subscription was raised for him; and, to keep up his spirits, he was presented before the holidays with two white mice, a rabbit, a pigeon, and a beautiful puppy. Old Cheeseman cried about it—especially soon afterwards, when they all ate one another.

Of course Old Cheeseman used to be called by the names of all sorts of cheeses—Double Glo'sterman, Family Cheshireman, Dutchman, North Wiltshireman, and all that. But he never minded it. And I don't mean to say he was old in point of years—because he wasn't—only he was called from the first, Old Cheeseman.

At last, Old Cheeseman was made second Latin Master. He was brought in one morning at the beginning of a new half, and presented to the school in that capacity as 'Mr. Cheeseman.' Then our fellows all agreed that Old Cheeseman was a spy, and a deserter, who had gone over to the enemy's camp, and sold himself for gold. It was no excuse for him that he had sold himself for very little gold—two pound ten a quarter and his washing, as was reported. It was decided by a Parliament which sat about it, that Old Cheeseman's mercenary motives could alone be taken into account, and that he had 'coined our blood for drachmas.' The Parliament took the expression out of the quarrel scene between Brutus and Cassius.

When it was settled in this strong way that Old Cheeseman was a tremendous traitor, who had wormed himself into our fellows' secrets on purpose to get

himself into favour by giving up everything he knew, all courageous fellows were invited to come forward and enrol themselves in a Society for making a set against him.   The President of the Society was First Boy, named Bob Tarter.   His father was in the West Indies, and he owned, himself, that his father was worth Millions.   He had great power among our fellows, and he wrote a parody, beginning—

> 'Who made believe to be so meek
> That we could hardly hear him speak,
> Yet turned out an Informing Sneak?
>   Old Cheeseman.'

—and on in that way through more than a dozen verses, which he used to go and sing, every morning, close by the new master's desk. He trained one of the low boys, too, a rosy-cheeked little Brass who didn't care what he did, to go up to him with his Latin Grammar one morning, and say it so: *Nominativus pronominum* —Old Cheeseman, *raro exprimitur*—was never suspected, *nisi distinctionis*—of being an informer, *aut emphasis gratiâ*—until he proved one. *Ut*—for instance, *Vos damnastis*—when he sold the boys. *Quasi*—as though, *dicat*—he should say, *Prætærea nemo*—I'm a Judas!   All this produced a great effect on Old Cheeseman.   He had never had much hair; but what he had, began to get thinner and thinner every day.   He grew paler and more worn; and sometimes of an evening he was seen sitting at his desk with a precious long snuff to his candle, and his hands before his face, crying.   But no member of the Society could pity him, even if he felt inclined, because the President said it was Old Cheeseman's conscience.

So Old Cheeseman went on, and didn't he lead a

miserable life! Of course the Reverend turned up his nose at him, and of course *she* did—because both of them always do that at all the masters—but he suffered from the fellows most, and he suffered from them constantly. He never told about it, that the Society could find out; but he got no credit for that, because the President said it was Old Cheeseman's cowardice.

He had only one friend in the world, and that one was almost as powerless as he was, for it was only Jane. Jane was a sort of wardrobe woman to our fellows, and took care of the boxes. She had come at first, I believe, as a kind of apprentice—some of our fellows say from a Charity, but *I* don't know—and after her time was out, had stopped at so much a year. So little a year, perhaps I ought to say, for it is far more likely. However, she had put some pounds in the Savings' Bank, and she was a very nice young woman. She was not quite pretty; but she had a very frank, honest, bright face, and all our fellows were fond of her. She was uncommonly neat and cheerful, and uncommonly comfortable and kind. And if anything was the matter with a fellow's mother, he always went and showed the letter to Jane.

Jane was Old Cheeseman's friend. The more the Society went against him, the more Jane stood by him. She used to give him a good-humoured look out of her still-room window, sometimes, that seemed to set him up for the day. She used to pass out of the orchard and the kitchen garden (always kept locked, I believe you!) through the playground, when she might have gone the other way, only to give a turn of her head, as much as to say 'Keep up your spirits!' to Old Cheeseman. His slip of a room was so fresh and orderly that it was well known who looked after it while he was at his desk; and when our fellows

saw a smoking hot dumpling on his plate at dinner, they knew with indignation who had sent it up.

Under these circumstances, the Society resolved, after a quantity of meeting and debating, that Jane should be requested to cut Old Cheeseman dead; and that if she refused, she must be sent to Coventry herself. So a deputation, headed by the President, was appointed to wait on Jane, and inform her of the vote the Society had been under the painful necessity of passing. She was very much respected for all her good qualities, and there was a story about her having once waylaid the Reverend in his own study, and got a fellow off from severe punishment, of her own kind comfortable heart. So the deputation didn't much like the job. However, they went up, and the President told Jane all about it. Upon which Jane turned very red, burst into tears, informed the President and the deputation, in a way not at all like her usual way, that they were a parcel of malicious young savages, and turned the whole respected body out of the room. Consequently it was entered in the Society's book (kept in astronomical cypher for fear of detection), that all communication with Jane was interdicted: and the President addressed the members on this convincing instance of Old Cheeseman's undermining.

But Jane was as true to Old Cheeseman as Old Cheeseman was false to our fellows—in their opinion, at all events—and steadily continued to be his only friend. It was a great exasperation to the Society, because Jane was as much a loss to them as she was a gain to him; and being more inveterate against him than ever, they treated him worse than ever. At last, one morning, his desk stood empty, his room was peeped into, and found to be vacant, and a whisper went about among the pale faces of our fellows that

Old Cheeseman, unable to bear it any longer, had got up early and drowned hmself.

The mysterious looks of the other masters after breakfast, and the evident fact that Old Cheeseman was not expected, confirmed the Society in this opinion. Some began to discuss whether the President was liable to hanging or only transportation for life, and the President's face showed a great anxiety to know which. However, he said that a jury of his country should find him game; and that in his address he should put it to them to lay their hands upon their hearts and say whether they as Britons approved of informers, and how they thought they would like it themselves. Some of the Society considered that he had better run away until he found a forest where he might change clothes with a woodcutter, and stain his face with blackberries; but the majority believed that if he stood his ground, his father—belonging as he did to the West Indies, and being worth millions— could buy him off.

All our fellows' hearts beat fast when the Reverend came in, and made a sort of a Roman, or a Field Marshal, of himself with the ruler; as he always did before delivering an address. But their fears were nothing to their astonishment when he came out with the story that Old Cheeseman, 'so long our respected friend and fellow-pilgrim in the pleasant plains of knowledge,' he called him—O yes! I dare say! Much of that!—was the orphan child of a disinherited young lady who had married against her father's wish, and whose young husband had died, and who had died of sorrow herself, and whose unfortunate baby (Old Cheeseman) had been brought up at the cost of a grandfather who would never consent to see it, baby, boy, or man: which grandfather was now dead, and

serve him right—that's *my* putting in—and which grandfather's large property, there being no will, was now, and all of a sudden and for ever, Old Cheeseman's! Our so long respected friend and fellow-pilgrim in the pleasant plains of knowledge, the Reverend wound up a lot of bothering quotations by saying, would 'come among us once more' that day fortnight, when he desired to take leave of us himself, in a more particular manner. With these words, he stared severely round at our fellows, and went solemnly out.

There was precious consternation among the members of the Society, now. Lots of them wanted to resign, and lots more began to try to make out that they had never belonged to it. However, the President stuck up, and said that they must stand or fall together, and that if a breach was made it should be over his body—which was meant to encourage the Society: but it didn't. The President further said, he would consider the position in which they stood, and would give them his best opinion and advice in a few days. This was eagerly looked for, as he knew a good deal of the world on account of his father's being in the West Indies.

After days and days of hard thinking, and drawing armies all over his slate, the President called our fellows together, and made the matter clear. He said it was plain that when Old Cheeseman came on the appointed day, his first revenge would be to impeach the Society, and have it flogged all round. After witnessing with joy the torture of his enemies, and gloating over the cries which agony would extort from them, the probability was that he would invite the Reverend, on pretence of conversation, into a private room—say the parlour into which Parents were shown, where the two great globes were which were

never used—and would there reproach him with the various frauds and oppressions he had endured at his hands. At the close of his observations he would make a signal to a Prizefighter concealed in the passage, who would then appear and pitch into the Reverend, till he was left insensible. Old Cheeseman would then make Jane a present of from five to ten pounds, and would leave the establishment in fiendish triumph.

The President explained that against the parlour part, or the Jane part, of these arrangements he had nothing to say; but, on the part of the Society, he counselled deadly resistance. With this view he recommended that all available desks should be filled with stones, and that the first word of the complaint should be the signal to every fellow to let fly at Old Cheeseman. The bold advice put the Society in better spirits, and was unanimously taken. A post about Old Cheeseman's size was put up in the playground, and all our fellows practised at it till it was dinted all over.

When the day came, and Places were called, every fellow sat down in a tremble. There had been much discussing and disputing as to how Old Cheeseman would come; but it was the general opinion that he would appear in a sort of triumphal car drawn by four horses, with two livery servants in front, and the Prizefighter in disguise up behind. So, all our fellows sat listening for the sound of wheels. But no wheels were heard, for Old Cheeseman walked after all, and came into the school without any preparation. Pretty much as he used to be, only dressed in black.

'Gentlemen,' said the Reverend, presenting him, 'our so long respected friend and fellow-pilgrim in the pleasant plains of knowledge, is desirous to offer a word or two. Attention, gentlemen, one and all!'

Every fellow stole his hand into his desk and looked at the President. The President was all ready, and taking aim at Old Cheeseman with his eyes.

What did Old Cheeseman then, but walk up to his old desk, look round him with a queer smile as if there was a tear in his eye, and begin in a quavering, mild voice, 'My dear companions and old friends!'

Every fellow's hand came out of his desk, and the President suddenly began to cry.

'My dear companions and old friends,' said Old Cheeseman, 'you have heard of my good fortune. I have passed so many years under this roof—my entire life so far, I may say—that I hope you have been glad to hear of it for my sake. I could never enjoy it without exchanging congratulations with you. If we have ever misunderstood one another at all, pray, my dear boys, let us forgive and forget. I have a great tenderness for you, and I am sure you return it. I want in the fulness of a grateful heart to shake hands with you every one. I have come back to do it, if you please, my dear boys.'

Since the President had begun to cry, several other fellows had broken out here and there: but now, when Old Cheeseman began with him as first boy, laid his left hand affectionately on his shoulder and gave him his right; and when the President said 'Indeed, I don't deserve it, sir; upon my honour I don't'; there was sobbing and crying all over the school. Every other fellow said he didn't deserve it, much in the same way; but Old Cheeseman, not minding that a bit, went cheerfully round to every boy, and wound up with every master—finishing off the Reverend last.

Then a snivelling little chap in a corner, who was always under some punishment or other, set up a shrill cry of 'Success to Old Cheeseman! Hooray!' The Reverend glared upon him, and said, '*Mr.* Cheeseman,

sir.' But, Old Cheeseman protesting that he liked his old name a great deal better than his new one, all our fellows took up the cry; and, for I don't know how many minutes, there was such a thundering of feet and hands, and such a roaring of Old Cheeseman, as never was heard.

After that, there was a spread in the dining-room of the most magnificent kind. Fowls, tongues, preserves, fruits, confectionaries, jellies, neguses, barley-sugar temples, trifles, crackers—eat all you can and pocket what you like—all at Old Cheeseman's expense. After that, speeches, whole holiday, double and treble sets of all manners of things for all manners of games, donkeys, pony-chaises and drive yourself, dinner for all the masters at the Seven Bells (twenty pounds a-head our fellows estimated it at), an annual holiday and feast fixed for that day every year, and another on Old Cheeseman's birthday—Reverend bound down before the fellows to allow it, so that he could never back out—all at Old Cheeseman's expense.

And didn't our fellows go down in a body and cheer outside the Seven Bells? O no!

But there's something else besides. Don't look at the next story-teller, for there's more yet. Next day, it was resolved that the Society should make it up with Jane, and then be dissolved. What do you think of Jane being gone, though! 'What? Gone for ever?' said our fellows, with long faces. 'Yes, to be sure,' was all the answer they could get. None of the people about the house would say anything more. At length, the first boy took upon himself to ask the Reverend whether our old friend Jane was really gone? The Reverend (he has got a daughter at home—turn-up nose, and red) replied severely, 'Yes, sir, Miss Pitt is gone.' The idea of calling Jane,

Miss Pitt! Some said she had been sent away in disgrace for taking money from Old Cheeseman; others said she had gone into Old Cheeseman's service at a rise of ten pounds a year. All that our fellows knew, was, she was gone.

It was two or three months afterwards, when, one afternoon, an open carriage stopped at the cricket field, just outside bounds, with a lady and gentleman in it, who looked at the game a long time and stood up to see it played. Nobody thought much about them, until the same little snivelling chap came in, against all rules, from the post where he was Scout, and said, 'It's Jane!' Both Elevens forgot the game directly, and ran crowding round the carriage. It *was* Jane! In such a bonnet! And if you'll believe me, Jane was married to Old Cheeseman.

It soon became quite a regular thing when our fellows were hard at it in the playground, to see a carriage at the low part of the wall where it joins the high part, and a lady and gentleman standing up in it, looking over. The gentleman was always Old Cheeseman, and the lady was always Jane.

The first time I ever saw them, I saw them in that way. There had been a good many changes among our fellows then, and it had turned out that Bob Tarter's father wasn't worth Millions! He wasn't worth anything. Bob had gone for a soldier, and Old Cheeseman had purchased his discharge. But that's not the carriage. The carriage stopped, and all our fellows stopped as soon as it was seen.

'So you have never sent me to Coventry after all!' said the lady, laughing, as our fellows swarmed up the wall to shake hands with her. 'Are you never going to do it?'

'Never! never! never!' on all sides.

I didn't understand what she meant then, but of

course I do now.   I was very much pleased with her face though, and with her good way, and I couldn't help looking at her—and at him too—with all our fellows clustering so joyfully about them.

They soon took notice of me as a new boy, so I thought I might as well swarm up the wall myself, and shake hands with them as the rest did.   I was quite as glad to see them as the rest were, and was quite as familiar with them in a moment.

'Only a fortnight now,' said Old Cheeseman, 'to the holidays.   Who stops?   Anybody?'

A good many fingers pointed at me, and a good many voices cried 'He does!'   For it was the year when you were all away; and rather low I was about it, I can tell you.

'Oh!' said Old Cheeseman.   'But it's solitary here in the holiday time.   He had better come to us.'

So I went to their delightful house, and was as happy as I could possibly be.   They understand how to conduct themselves towards boys, *they* do.   When they take a boy to the play, for instance, they *do* take him.   They don't go in after it's begun, or come out before it's over.   They know how to bring a boy up, too.   Look at their own!   Though he is very little as yet, what a capital boy he is!   Why, my next favourite to Mrs. Cheeseman and Old Cheeseman, is young Cheeseman.

So, now I have told you all I know about Old Cheeseman.   And it's not much after all, I am afraid.   Is it?

NOBODY'S STORY

[1854]

NOBODY'S STORY

HE lived on the bank of a mighty river, broad and deep, which was always silently rolling on to a vast undiscovered ocean. It had rolled on, ever since the world began. It had changed its course sometimes, and turned into new channels, leaving its old ways dry and barren; but it had ever been upon the flow, and ever was to flow until time should be no more. Against its strong, unfathomable stream, nothing made head. No living creature, no flower, no leaf, no particle of animate or inanimate existence, ever strayed back from the undiscovered ocean. The tide of the river set resistlessly towards it; and the tide never stopped, any more than the earth stops in its circling round the sun.

He lived in a busy place, and he worked very hard to live. He had no hope of ever being rich enough to live a month without hard work, but he was quite content, GOD knows, to labour with a cheerful will. He was one of an immense family, all of whose sons and daughters gained their daily bread by daily work, prolonged from their rising up betimes until their lying down at night. Beyond this destiny he had no prospect, and he sought none.

There was over-much drumming, trumpeting, and speech-making, in the neighbourhood where he dwelt; but he had nothing to do with that. Such clash and uproar came from the Bigwig family, at the unaccountable proceedings of which race, he marvelled much. They set up the strangest statues, in iron,

75

marble, bronze, and brass, before his door; and darkened his house with the legs and tails of uncouth images of horses.   He wondered what it all meant, smiled in a rough good-humoured way he had, and kept at his hard work.

The Bigwig family (composed of all the stateliest people thereabouts, and all the noisiest) had undertaken to save him the trouble of thinking for himself, and to manage him and his affairs.   'Why truly,' said he, 'I have little time upon my hands; and if you will be so good as to take care of me, in return for the money I pay over'—for the Bigwig family were not above his money—'I shall be relieved and much obliged, considering that you know best.'   Hence the drumming, trumpeting, and speech-making, and the ugly images of horses which he was expected to fall down and worship.

'I don't understand all this,' said he, rubbing his furrowed brow confusedly.   'But it *has* a meaning, maybe, if I could find it out.'

'It means,' returned the Bigwig family, suspecting something of what he said, 'honour and glory in the highest, to the highest merit.'

'Oh!' said he.   And he was glad to hear that.

But, when he looked among the images in iron, marble, bronze, and brass, he failed to find a rather meritorious countryman of his, once the son of a Warwickshire wooldealer, or any single countryman whomsoever of that kind.   He could find none of the men whose knowledge had rescued him and his children from terrific and disfiguring disease, whose boldness had raised his forefathers from the condition of serfs, whose wise fancy had opened a new and high existence to the humblest, whose skill had filled the working man's world with accumulated wonders.

Whereas, he did find others whom he knew no good of, and even others whom he knew much ill of.

'Humph!' said he. 'I don't quite understand it.'

So, he went home, and sat down by his fireside to get it out of his mind.

Now, his fireside was a bare one, all hemmed in by blackened streets; but it was a precious place to him. The hands of his wife were hardened with toil, and she was old before her time; but she was dear to him. His children, stunted in their growth, bore traces of unwholesome nurture; but they had beauty in his sight. Above all other things, it was an earnest desire of this man's soul that his children should be taught. 'If I am sometimes misled,' said he, 'for want of knowledge, at least let them know better, and avoid my mistakes. If it is hard to me to reap the harvest of pleasure and instruction that is stored in books, let it be easier to them.'

But, the Bigwig family broke out into violent family quarrels concerning what it was lawful to teach to this man's children. Some of the family insisted on such a thing being primary and indispensable above all other things; and others of the family insisted on such another thing being primary and indispensable above all other things; and the Bigwig family, rent into factions, wrote pamphlets, held convocations, delivered charges, orations, and all varieties of discourses; impounded one another in courts Lay and courts Ecclesiastical; threw dirt, exchanged pummelings, and fell together by the ears in unintelligible animosity. Meanwhile, this man, in his short evening snatches at his fireside, saw the demon Ignorance arise there, and take his children to itself. He saw his daughter perverted into a heavy, slatternly drudge; he saw his son go moping down the ways of

low sensuality, to brutality and crime; he saw the dawning light of intelligence in the eyes of his babies so changing into cunning and suspicion, that he could have rather wished them idiots.

'I don't understand this any the better,' said he; 'but I think it cannot be right. Nay, by the clouded Heaven above me, I protest against this as my wrong!'

Becoming peaceable again (for his passion was usually short-lived, and his nature kind), he looked about him on his Sundays and holidays, and he saw how much monotony and weariness there was, and thence how drunkenness arose with all its train of ruin. Then he appealed to the Bigwig family, and said, 'We are a labouring people, and I have a glimmering suspicion in me that labouring people of whatever condition were made—by a higher intelligence than yours, as I poorly understand it—to be in need of mental refreshment and recreation. See what we fall into, when we rest without it. Come! Amuse me harmlessly, show me something, give me an escape!'

But, here the Bigwig family fell into a state of uproar absolutely deafening. When some few voices were faintly heard, proposing to show him the wonders of the world, the greatness of creation, the mighty changes of time, the workings of nature and the beauties of art— to show him these things, that is to say, at any period of his life when he could look upon them—there arose among the Bigwigs such roaring and raving, such pulpiting and petitioning, such maundering and memorialising, such name-calling and dirt-throwing, such a shrill wind of parliamentary questioning and feeble replying—where 'I dare not' waited on 'I would'—that the poor fellow stood aghast, staring wildly around.

'Have 1 provoked all this,' said he, with his hands to his affrighted ears, 'by what was meant to be an innocent request, plainly arising out of my familiar experience, and the common knowledge of all men who choose to open their eyes? I don't understand, and I am not understood. What is to come of such a state of things!'

He was bending over his work, often asking himself the question, when the news began to spread that a pestilence had appeared among the labourers, and ~as slaying them by thousands. Going forth to look about him, he soon found this to be true. The dying and the dead were mingled in the close and tainted houses among which his life was passed. New poison was distilled into the always murky, always sickening air. The robust and the weak, old age and infancy, the father and the mother, all were stricken down alike.

What means of flight had he? He remained there, where he was, and saw those who were dearest to him die. A kind preacher came to him, and would have said some prayers to soften his heart in his gloom, but he replied:

'O what avails it, missionary, to come to me, a man condemned to residence in this fœtid place, where every sense bestowed upon me for my delight becomes a torment, and where every minute of my numbered days is new mire added to the heap under which I lie oppressed! But, give me my first glimpse of Heaven, through a little of its light and air; give me pure water; help me to be clean; lighten this heavy atmosphere and heavy life, in which our spirits sink, and we become the indifferent and callous creatures you too often see us; gently and kindly take the bodies of those who die among us, out of the small room where we grow to be so familiar with the awful

change that even ITS sanctity is lost to us; and Teacher, then I will hear—none know better than you, how willingly—of Him whose thoughts were so much with the poor, and who had compassion for all human sorrow!'

He was at work again, solitary and sad, when his Master came and stood near to him dressed in black. He, also, had suffered heavily. His young wife, his beautiful and good young wife, was dead; so, too, his only child.

'Master, 'tis hard to bear—I know it—but be comforted. I would give you comfort, if I could.'

The Master thanked him from his heart, but, said he, 'O you labouring men! The calamity began among you. If you had but lived more healthily and decently, I should not be the widowed and bereft mourner that I am this day.'

'Master,' returned the other, shaking his head, 'I have begun to understand a little that most calamities will come from us, as this one did, and that none will stop at our poor doors, until we are united with that great squabbling family yonder, to do the things that are right. We cannot live healthily and decently, unless they who undertook to manage us provide the means. We cannot be instructed unless they will teach us; we cannot be rationally amused, unless they will amuse us; we cannot but have some false gods of our own, while they set up so many of theirs in all the public places. The evil consequences of imperfect instruction, the evil consequences of pernicious neglect, the evil consequences of unnatural restraint and the denial of humanising enjoyments, will all come from us, and none of them will stop with us. They will spread far and wide. They always do; they always have done—just like the pestilence. I understand so much, I think, at last.'

But the Master said again, 'O you labouring men! How seldom do we ever hear of you, except in connection with some trouble!'

'Master,' he replied, 'I am Nobody, and little likely to be heard of (nor yet much wanted to be heard of, perhaps), except when there *is* some trouble. But it never begins with me, and it never can end with me. As sure as Death, it comes down to me and it goes up from me.'

There was so much reason in what he said, that the Bigwig family, getting wind of it, and being horribly frightened by the late desolation, resolved to unite with him to do the things that were right—at all events, so far as the said things were associated with the direct prevention, humanly speaking, of another pestilence. But, as their fear wore off, which it soon began to do, they resumed their falling out among themselves, and did nothing. Consequently the scourge appeared again—low down as before—and spread avengingly upward as before, and carried off vast numbers of the brawlers. But not a man among them ever admitted, if in the least degree he ever perceived, that he had anything to do with it.

So Nobody lived and died in the old, old, old way; and this, in the main, is the whole of Nobody's story.

Had he no name, you ask? Perhaps it was Legion. It matters little what his name was. Let us call him Legion.

If you were ever in the Belgian villages near the field of Waterloo, you will have seen, in some quiet little church, a monument erected by faithful companions in arms to the memory of Colonel A, Major B, Captains C, D and E, Lieutenants F and G, Ensigns H, I and J, seven non-commissioned officers, and one hundred and thirty rank and file, who fell in the discharge of their duty on the memorable day.

The story of Nobody is the story of the rank and file
of the earth. They bear their share of the battle;
they have their part in the victory; they fall; they
leave no name but in the mass. The march of the
proudest of us, leads to the dusty way by which they
go. O! Let us think of them this year at the Christmas fire, and not forget them when it is burnt out.

THE SEVEN POOR TRAVELLERS

[1854]

THE SEVEN POOR TRAVELLERS

IN THREE CHAPTERS

CHAPTER I

IN THE OLD CITY OF ROCHESTER

STRICTLY speaking, there were only six Poor Travellers; but, being a Traveller myself, though an idle one, and being withal as poor as I hope to be, I brought the number up to seven. This word of explanation is due at once, for what says the inscription over the quaint old door?

RICHARD WATTS, ESQ.
by his Will, dated 22 Aug. 1579,
founded this Charity
for Six poor Travellers,
who not being ROGUES, OR PROCTORS,
May receive gratis for one Night,
Lodging, Entertainment,
and Fourpence each.

It was in the ancient little city of Rochester in Kent, of all the good days in the year upon a Christmas-eve, that I stood reading this inscription over the quaint old door in question. I had been wandering about the neighbouring Cathedral, and had seen the tomb of Richard Watts, with the effigy of worthy

Master Richard starting out of it like a ship's figure-head; and I had felt that I could do no less, as I gave the Verger his fee, than inquire the way to Watts's Charity. The way being very short and very plain, I had come prosperously to the inscription and the quaint old door.

'Now,' said I to myself, as I looked at the knocker, 'I know I am not a Proctor; I wonder whether I am a Rogue!'

Upon the whole, though Conscience reproduced two or three pretty faces which might have had smaller attraction for a moral Goliath than they had had for me, who am but a Tom Thumb in that way, I came to the conclusion that I was not a Rogue. So, beginning to regard the establishment as in some sort my property, bequeathed to me and divers co-legatees, share and share alike, by the Worshipful Master Richard Watts, I stepped backward into the road to survey my inheritance.

I found it to be a clean white house, of a staid and venerable air, with the quaint old door already three times mentioned (an arched door), choice, little, long, low lattice-windows, and a roof of three gables. The silent High Street of Rochester is full of gables, with old beams and timbers carved into strange faces. It is oddly garnished with a queer old clock that projects over the pavement out of a grave red-brick building, as if Time carried on business there, and hung out his sign. Sooth to say, he did an active stroke of work in Rochester, in the old days of the Romans, and the Saxons, and the Normans; and down to the times of King John, when the rugged castle—I will not undertake to say how many hundreds of years old then—was abandoned to the centuries of weather which have so defaced the dark apertures in its walls, that the

ruin looks as if the rooks and daws had pecked its
eyes out.

I was very well pleased, both with my property and
its situation. While I was yet surveying it with
growing content, I spied at one of the upper lattices
which stood open, a decent body, of a wholesome matronly appearance, whose eyes I caught inquiringly
addressed to mine. They said so plainly, 'Do you wish
to see the house?' that I answered aloud, 'Yes, if you
please.' And within a minute the old door opened,
and I bent my head, and went down two steps into the
entry.

'This,' said the matronly presence, ushering me into
a low room on the right, 'is where the travellers sit by
the fire, and cook what bits of suppers they buy with
their fourpences.'

'O! Then they have no Entertainment?' said I.
For the inscription over the outer door was still running in my head, and I was mentally repeating, in a
kind of tune, 'Lodging, entertainment, and fourpence each.'

'They have a fire provided for 'em,' returned the
matron,—a mighty civil person, not, as I could make
out, overpaid; 'and these cooking utensils. And this
what 's painted on a board is the rules for their
behaviour. They have their fourpences when they
get their tickets from the steward over the way,—for
I don't admit 'em myself, they must get their tickets
first, and sometimes one buys a rasher of bacon, and
another a herring, and another a pound of potatoes,
or what not. Sometimes two or three of 'em will club
their fourpences together, and make a supper that
way. But not much of anything is to be got for
fourpence, at present, when provisions is so dear.'

'True indeed,' I remarked. I had been looking

about the room, admiring its snug fireside at the upper end, its glimpse of the street through the low mullioned window, and its beams overhead. 'It is very comfortable,' said I.

'Ill-conwenient,' observed the matronly presence.

I liked to hear her say so; for it showed a commendable anxiety to execute in no niggardly spirit the intentions of Master Richard Watts. But the room was really so well adapted to its purpose that I protested, quite enthusiastically, against her disparagement.

'Nay, ma'am,' said I, 'I am sure it is warm in winter and cool in summer. It has a look of homely welcome and soothing rest. It has a remarkably cosy fireside, the very blink of which, gleaming out into the street upon a winter night, is enough to warm all Rochester's heart. And as to the convenience of the six Poor Travellers—'

'I don't mean them,' returned the presence. 'I speak of its being an ill-conwenience to myself and my daughter, having no other room to sit in of a night.'

This was true enough, but there was another quaint room of corresponding dimensions on the opposite side of the entry: so I stepped across to it, through the open doors of both rooms, and asked what this chamber was for.

'This,' returned the presence, 'is the Board Room. Where the gentlemen meet when they come here.'

Let me see. I had counted from the street six upper windows besides these on the ground-story. Making a perplexed calculation in my mind, I rejoined, 'Then the six Poor Travellers sleep upstairs?'

My new friend shook her head. 'They sleep,' she answered, 'in two little outer galleries at the back, where their beds has always been, ever since the

Charity was founded. It being so very ill-conwenient to me as things is at present, the gentlemen are going to take off a bit of the back yard, and make a slip of a room for 'em there, to sit in before they go to bed.'

'And then the six Poor Travellers,' said I, 'will be entirely out of the house?'

'Entirely out of the house,' assented the presence, comfortably smoothing her hands. 'Which is considered much better for all parties, and much more conwenient.'

I had been a little startled, in the Cathedral, by the emphasis with which the effigy of Master Richard Watts was bursting out of his tomb; but I began to think, now, that it might be expected to come across the High Street some stormy night, and make a disturbance here.

Howbeit, I kept my thoughts to myself, and accompanied the presence to the little galleries at the back. I found them on a tiny scale, like the galleries in old inn-yards; and they were very clean. While I was looking at them, the matron gave me to understand that the prescribed number of Poor Travellers were forthcoming every night from year's end to year's end; and that the beds were always occupied. My questions upon this, and her replies, brought us back to the Board Room so essential to the dignity of 'the gentlemen,' where she showed me the printed accounts of the Charity hanging up by the window. From them I gathered that the greater part of the property bequeathed by the Worshipful Master Richard Watts for the maintenance of this foundation was, at the period of his death, mere marshland; but that, in course of time, it had been reclaimed and built upon, and was very considerably increased in value. I found, too, that about a thirtieth part of the annual

revenue was now expended on the purposes com-
memorated in the inscription over the door; the rest
being handsomely laid out in Chancery, law expenses,
collectorship, receivership, poundage, and other appendages of management, highly complimentary to
the importance of the six Poor Travellers.   In
short, I made the not entirely new discovery that it
may be said of an establishment like this, in dear old
England, as of the fat oyster in the American story,
that it takes a good many men to swallow it whole.

'And pray, ma'am,' said I, sensible that the blank-
ness of my face began to brighten as the thought
occurred to me, 'could one see these Travellers?'

'Well!' she returned dubiously, 'no!'

'Not to-night, for instance!' said I.

'Well!' she returned more positively, 'no.   Nobody
ever asked to see them, and nobody ever did see them.'

As I am not easily baulked in a design when I am
set upon it, I urged to the good lady that this was
Christmas-eve; that Christmas comes but once a year,
—which is unhappily too true, for when it begins to
stay with us the whole year round we shall make this
earth a very different place; that I was possessed by
the desire to treat the Travellers to a supper and a
temperate glass of hot Wassail; that the voice of
Fame had been heard in that land, declaring my
ability to make hot Wassail; that if I were permitted
to hold the feast, I should be found conformable to
reason, sobriety, and good hours; in a word, that I
could be merry and wise myself, and had been even
known at a pinch to keep others so, although I was
decorated with no badge or medal, and was not a
Brother, Orator, Apostle, Saint, or Prophet of any
denomination whatever.   In the end I prevailed, to
my great joy.   It was settled that at nine o'clock
that night a Turkey and a piece of Roast Beef should

smoke upon the board; and that I, faint and un-worthy minister for once of Master Richard Watts, should preside as the Christmas-supper host of the six Poor Travellers.

I went back to my inn to give the necessary direc-tions for the Turkey and Roast Beef, and, during the remainder of the day, could settle to nothing for thinking of the Poor Travellers. When the wind blew hard against the windows,—it was a cold day, with dark gusts of sleet alternating with periods of wild brightness, as if the year were dying fitfully,— I pictured them advancing towards their resting-place along various cold roads, and felt delighted to think how little they foresaw the supper that awaited them. I painted their portraits in my mind, and in-dulged in little heightening touches. I made them footsore; I made them weary; I made them carry packs and bundles; I made them stop by finger-posts and milestones, leaning on their bent sticks, and look-ing wistfully at what was written there; I made them lose their way; and filled their five wits with appre-hensions of lying out all night, and being frozen to death. I took up my hat, and went out, climbed to the top of the Old Castle, and looked over the windy hills that slope down to the Medway, almost believing that I could descry some of my Travellers in the dis-tance. After it fell dark, and the Cathedral bell was heard in the invisible steeple—quite a bower of frosty rime when I had last seen it—striking five, six, seven, I became so full of my Travellers that I could eat no dinner, and felt constrained to watch them still in the red coals of my fire. They were all arrived by this time, I thought, had got their tickets, and were gone in.—There my pleasure was dashed by the re-flection that probably some Travellers had come too late and were shut out.

After the Cathedral bell had struck eight, I could smell a delicious savour of Turkey and Roast Beef rising to the window of my adjoining bedroom, which looked down into the inn-yard just where the lights of the kitchen reddened a massive fragment of the Castle Wall. It was high time to make the Wassail now; therefore I had up the materials (which, together with their proportions and combinations, I must decline to impart, as the only secret of my own I was ever known to keep), and made a glorious jorum. Not in a bowl; for a bowl anywhere but on a shelf is a low superstition, fraught with cooling and slopping; but in a brown earthenware pitcher, tenderly suffocated, when full, with a coarse cloth. It being now upon the stroke of nine, I set out for Watts's Charity, carrying my brown beauty in my arms. I would trust Ben, the waiter, with untold gold; but there are strings in the human heart which must never be sounded by another, and drinks that I make myself are those strings in mine.

The Travellers were all assembled, the cloth was laid, and Ben brought a great billet of wood, and had laid it artfully on the top of the fire, so that a touch or two of the poker after supper should make a roaring blaze. Having deposited my brown beauty in a red nook of the hearth, inside the fender, where she soon began to sing like an ethereal cricket, diffusing at the same time odours as of ripe vineyards, spice forests, and orange groves,—I say, having stationed my beauty in a place of security and improvement, I introduced myself to my guests by shaking hands all round, and giving them a hearty welcome.

I found the party to be thus composed. Firstly, myself. Secondly, a very decent man indeed, with

his right arm in a sling, who had a certain clean, agreeable smell of wood about him, from which I judged him to have something to do with shipbuilding. Thirdly, a little sailor-boy, a mere child, with a profusion of rich dark brown hair, and deep womanly-looking eyes. Fourthly, a shabby-genteel personage in a threadbare black suit, and apparently in very bad circumstances, with a dry, suspicious look; the absent buttons on his waistcoat eked out with red tape; and a bundle of extraordinarily tattered papers sticking out of an inner breast-pocket. Fifthly, a foreigner by birth, but an Englishman in speech, who carried his pipe in the band of his hat, and lost no time in telling me, in an easy, simple, engaging way, that he was a watchmaker from Geneva, and travelled all about the Continent, mostly on foot, working as a journeyman, and seeing new countries,—possibly (I thought) also smuggling a watch or so, now and then. Sixthly, a little widow, who had been very pretty and was still very young, but whose beauty had been wrecked in some great misfortune, and whose manner was remarkably timid, scared, and solitary. Seventhly and lastly, a Traveller of a kind familiar to my boyhood, but now almost obsolete,—a Book-Pedler, who had a quantity of Pamphlets and Numbers with him, and who presently boasted that he could repeat more verses in an evening than he could sell in a twelvemonth.

All these I have mentioned in the order in which they sat at table. I presided, and the matronly presence faced me. We were not long in taking our places, for the supper had arrived with me, in the following procession:

Myself with the pitcher.
Ben with Beer.
Inattentive Boy with hot plates. Inattentive Boy
with hot plates.
THE TURKEY.
Female carrying sauces to be heated on the spot.
THE BEEF.
Man with Tray on his head, containing Vegetables
and Sundries.
Volunteer Hostler from Hotel, grinning,
And rendering no assistance.

As we passed along the High Street, comet-like,
we left a long tail of fragrance behind us which
caused the public to stop, sniffing in wonder. We
had previously left at the corner of the inn-yard a
wall-eyed young man connected with the Fly department, and well accustomed to the sound of a railway
whistle which Ben always carries in his pocket, whose
instructions were, so soon as he should hear the
whistle blown, to dash into the kitchen, seize the hot
plum-pudding and mince-pies, and speed with them
to Watts's Charity, where they would be received (he
was further instructed) by the sauce-female, who
would be provided with brandy in a blue state of
combustion.

All these arrangements were executed in the most
exact and punctual manner. I never saw a finer
turkey, finer beef, or greater prodigality of sauce
and gravy; and my Travellers did wonderful justice
to everything set before them. It made my heart
rejoice to observe how their wind and frost hardened
faces softened in the clatter of plates and knives and
forks, and mellowed in the fire and supper heat.
While their hats and caps and wrappers, hanging
up, a few small bundles on the ground in a corner,

and in another corner three or four old walking-sticks, worn down at the end to mere fringe, linked this snug interior with the bleak outside in a golden chain.

When supper was done, and my brown beauty had been elevated on the table, there was a general requisition to me to 'take the corner'; which suggested to me comfortably enough how much my friends here made of a fire,—for when had *I* ever thought so highly of the corner, since the days when I connected it with Jack Horner? However, as I declined, Ben, whose touch on all convivial instruments is perfect, drew the table apart, and instructing my Travellers to open right and left on either side of me, and form round the fire, closed up the centre with myself and my chair, and preserved the order we had kept at table. He had already, in a tranquil manner, boxed the ears of the inattentive boys until they had been by imperceptible degrees boxed out of the room; and he now rapidly skirmished the sauce-female into the High Street, disappeared, and softly closed the door.

This was the time for bringing the poker to bear on the billet of wood. I tapped it three times, like an enchanted talisman, and a brilliant host of merry-makers burst out of it, and sported off by the chimney,—rushing up the middle in a fiery country dance, and never coming down again. Meanwhile, by their sparkling light, which threw our lamp into the shade, I filled the glasses, and gave my Travellers, CHRIST-MAS!—CHRISTMAS-EVE, my friends, when the shepherds, who were Poor Travellers, too, in their way, heard the Angels sing, 'On earth, peace. Good-will towards men!'

I don't know who was the first among us to think that we ought to take hands as we sat, in deference to the toast, or whether any one of us anticipated the

others, but at any rate we all did it. We then drank to the memory of the good Master Richard Watts. And I wish his Ghost may never have had worse usage under that roof than it had from us.

It was the witching time for Story-telling. 'Our whole life, Travellers,' said I, 'is a story more or less intelligible,—generally less; but we shall read it by a clearer light when it is ended. I, for one, am so divided this night between fact and fiction, that I scarce know which is which. Shall I beguile the time by telling you a story as we sit here?'

They all answered, yes. I had little to tell them, but I was bound by my own proposal. Therefore, after looking for awhile at the spiral column of smoke wreathing up from my brown beauty, through which I could have almost sworn I saw the effigy of Master Richard Watts less startled than usual, I fired away.

CHAPTER II

THE STORY OF RICHARD DOUBLEDICK

In the year one thousand seven hundred and ninety-nine, a relative of mine came limping down, on foot, to this town of Chatham. I call it this town, because if anybody present knows to a nicety where Rochester ends and Chatham begins, it is more than I do. He was a poor traveller, with not a farthing in his pocket. He sat by the fire in this very room, and he slept one night in a bed that will be occupied to-night by some one here.

My relative came down to Chatham to enlist in a cavalry regiment, if a cavalry regiment would have him; if not, to take King George's shilling from any

corporal or sergeant who would put a bunch of ribbons in his hat. His object was to get shot; but he thought he might as well ride to death as be at the trouble of walking.

My relative's Christian name was Richard, but he was better known as Dick. He dropped his own surname on the road down, and took up that of Doubledick. He was passed as Richard Doubledick; age, twenty-two; height, five foot ten; native place, Exmouth, which he had never been near in his life. There was no cavalry in Chatham when he limped over the bridge here with half a shoe to his dusty feet, so he enlisted into a regiment of the line, and was glad to get drunk and forget all about it.

You are to know that this relative of mine had gone wrong, and run wild. His heart was in the right place, but it was sealed up. He had been betrothed to a good and beautiful girl, whom he had loved better than she—or perhaps even he—believed; but in an evil hour he had given her cause to say to him solemnly, 'Richard, I will never marry another man. I will live single for your sake, but Mary Marshall's lips'—her name was Mary Marshall—'never address another word to you on earth. Go, Richard! Heaven forgive you!' This finished him. This brought him down to Chatham. This made him Private Richard Doubledick, with a determination to be shot.

There was not a more dissipated and reckless soldier in Chatham barracks, in the year one thousand seven hundred and ninety-nine, than Private Richard Doubledick. He associated with the dregs of every regiment; he was as seldom sober as he could be, and was constantly under punishment. It became clear to the whole barracks that Private Richard Doubledick would very soon be flogged.

Now the Captain of Richard Doubledick's company was a young gentleman not above five years his senior, whose eyes had an expression in them which affected Private Richard Doubledick in a very remarkable way. They were bright, handsome, dark eyes,—what are called laughing eyes generally, and, when serious, rather steady than severe,—but they were the only eyes now left in his narrowed world that Private Richard Doubledick could not stand. Unabashed by evil report and punishment, defiant of everything else and everybody else, he had but to know that those eyes looked at him for a moment, and he felt ashamed. He could not so much as salute Captain Taunton in the street like any other officer. He was reproached and confused,—troubled by the mere possibility of the captain's looking at him. In his worst moments, he would rather turn back, and go any distance out of his way, than encounter those two handsome, dark, bright eyes.

One day, when Private Richard Doubledick came out of the Black hole, where he had been passing the last eight-and-forty hours, and in which retreat he spent a good deal of his time, he was ordered to betake himself to Captain Taunton's quarters. In the stale and squalid state of a man just out of the Black hole, he had less fancy than ever for being seen by the Captain; but he was not so mad yet as to disobey orders, and consequently went up to the terrace overlooking the parade-ground, where the officers' quarters were; twisting and breaking in his hands, as he went along, a bit of the straw that had formed the decorative furniture of the Black hole.

'Come in!' cried the Captain, when he knocked with his knuckles at the door. Private Richard Doubledick pulled off his cap, took a stride forward, and

felt very conscious that he stood in the light of the dark, bright eyes.

There was a silent pause. Private Richard Doubledick had put the straw in his mouth, and was gradually doubling it up into his windpipe and choking himself.

'Doubledick,' said the Captain, 'do you know where you are going to?'

'To the Devil, sir?' faltered Doubledick.

'Yes,' returned the Captain. 'And very fast.'

Private Richard Doubledick turned the straw of the Black hole in his mouth, and made a miserable salute of acquiescence.

'Doubledick,' said the Captain, 'since I entered his Majesty's service, a boy of seventeen, I have been pained to see many men of promise going that road; but I have never been so pained to see a man determined to make the shameful journey as I have been, ever since you joined the regiment, to see you.'

Private Richard Doubledick began to find a film stealing over the floor at which he looked; also to find the legs of the Captain's breakfast-table turning crooked, as if he saw them through water.

'I am only a common soldier, sir,' said he. 'It signifies very little what such a poor brute comes to.'

'You are a man,' returned the Captain, with grave indignation, 'of education and superior advantages; and if you say that, meaning what you say, you have sunk lower than I had believed. How low that must be, I leave you to consider, knowing what I know of your disgrace, and seeing what I see.'

'I hope to get shot soon, sir,' said Private Richard Doubledick; 'and then the regiment and the world together will be rid of me.'

The legs of the table were becoming very crooked. Doubledick, looking up to steady his vision, met the eyes that had so strong an influence over him. He put his hand before his own eyes, and the breast of his disgrace-jacket swelled as if it would fly asunder.

'I would rather,' said the young Captain, 'see this in you, Doubledick, than I would see five thousand guineas counted out upon this table for a gift to my good mother. Have you a mother?'

'I am thankful to say she is dead, sir.'

'If your praises,' returned the Captain, 'were sounded from mouth to mouth through the whole regiment, through the whole army, through the whole country, you would wish she had lived to say, with pride and joy, "He is my son!"'

'Spare me, sir,' said Doubledick. 'She would never have heard any good of me. She would never have had any pride and joy in owning herself my mother. Love and compassion she might have had, and would have always had, I know; but not—Spare me, sir! I am a broken wretch, quite at your mercy!' And he turned his face to the wall, and stretched out his imploring hand.

'My friend—' began the Captain.

'God bless you, sir,' sobbed Private Richard Doubledick.

'You are at the crisis of your fate. Hold your course unchanged a little longer, and you know what must happen. *I* know even better than you can imagine, that, after that has happened, you are lost. No man who could shed those tears could bear those marks.'

'I fully believe it, sir,' in a low, shivering voice said Private Richard Doubledick.

'But a man in any station can do his duty,' said the young Captain, 'and, in doing it, can earn his

own respect, even if his case should be so very unfortunate and so very rare that he can earn no other man's. A common soldier, poor brute though you called him just now, has this advantage in the stormy times we live in, that he always does his duty before a host of sympathising witnesses. Do you doubt that he may so do it as to be extolled through a whole regiment, through a whole army, through a whole country? Turn while you may yet retrieve the past, and try.'

'I will! I ask for only one witness, sir,' cried Richard, with a bursting heart.

'I understand you. I will be a watchful and a faithful one.'

I have heard from Private Richard Doubledick's own lips, that he dropped down upon his knee, kissed that officer's hand, arose, and went out of the light of the dark, bright eyes, an altered man.

In that year, one thousand seven hundred and ninety-nine, the French were in Egypt, in Italy, in Germany, where not? Napoleon Bonaparte had likewise begun to stir against us in India, and most men could read the signs of the great troubles that were coming on. In the very next year, when we formed an alliance with Austria against him, Captain Taunton's regiment was on service in India. And there was not a finer non-commissioned officer in it,—no, nor in the whole line—than Corporal Richard Doubledick.

In eighteen hundred and one, the Indian army were on the coast of Egypt. Next year was the year of the proclamation of the short peace, and they were recalled. It had then become well known to thousands of men, that wherever Captain Taunton, with the dark, bright eyes, led, there, close to him, ever at his side, firm as a rock, true as the sun, and brave

as Mars, would be certain to be found, while life beat in their hearts, that famous soldier, Sergeant Richard Doubledick.

Eighteen hundred and five, besides being the great year of Trafalgar, was a year of hard fighting in India. That year saw such wonders done by a Sergeant-Major, who cut his way single-handed through a solid mass of men, recovered the colours of his regiment, which had been seized from the hand of a poor boy shot through the heart, and rescued his wounded Captain, who was down, and in a very jungle of horses' hoofs and sabres,—saw such wonders done, I say, by this brave Sergeant-Major, that he **was** specially made the bearer of the colours he had won; and Ensign Richard Doubledick had risen from the ranks.

Sorely cut up in every battle, but always reinforced by the bravest of men,—for the fame of following the old colours, shot through and through, which Ensign Richard Doubledick had saved, inspired all breasts, —this regiment fought its way through the Peninsular war, up to the investment of Badajos in eighteen hundred and twelve. Again and again it had been cheered through the British ranks until the tears had sprung into men's eyes at the mere hearing of the mighty British voice, so exultant in their valour; and there was not a drummer-boy but knew the legend, that wherever the two friends, Major Taunton, with the dark, bright eyes, and Ensign Richard Doubledick, who was devoted to him, were seen to go, there the boldest spirits in the English army became wild to follow.

One day, at Badajos,—not in the great storming, but in repelling a hot sally of the besieged upon our men at work in the trenches, who had given way,— the two officers found themselves hurrying forward,

face to face, against a party of French infantry, who made a stand. There was an officer at their head, encouraging his men,—a courageous, handsome, gallant officer of five-and-thirty, whom Doubledick saw hurriedly, almost momentarily, but saw well. He particularly noticed this officer waving his sword, and rallying his men with an eager and excited cry, when they fired in obedience to his gesture, and Major Taunton dropped.

It was over in ten minutes more, and Doubledick returned to the spot where he had laid the best friend man ever had on a coat spread upon the wet clay. Major Taunton's uniform was opened at the breast, and on his shirt were three little spots of blood.

'Dear Doubledick,' said he, 'I am dying.'

'For the love of Heaven, no!' exclaimed the other, kneeling down beside him, and passing his arm round his neck to raise his head. 'Taunton! My preserver, my guardian angel, my witness! Dearest, truest, kindest of human beings! Taunton! For God's sake!'

The bright, dark eyes—so very, very dark now, in the pale face—smiled upon him; and the hand he had kissed thirteen years ago laid itself fondly on his breast.

'Write to my mother. You will see Home again. Tell her how we became friends. It will comfort her, as it comforts me.'

He spoke no more, but faintly signed for a moment towards his hair as it fluttered in the wind. The Ensign understood him. He smiled again when he saw that, and, gently turning his face over on the supporting arm as if for rest, died, with his hand upon the breast in which he had revived a soul.

No dry eye looked on Ensign Richard Doubledick that melancholy day. He buried his friend on the

field, and became a lone, bereaved man. Beyond his duty he appeared to have but two remaining cares in life,—one, to preserve the little packet of hair he was to give to Taunton's mother; the other, to encounter that French officer who had rallied the men under whose fire Taunton fell. A new legend now began to circulate among our troops; and it was, that when he and the French officer came face to face once more, there would be weeping in France.

The war went on—and through it went the exact picture of the French officer on the one side, and the bodily reality upon the other—until the Battle of Toulouse was fought. In the returns sent home appeared these words: 'Severely wounded, but not dangerously, Lieutenant Richard Doubledick.'

At Midsummer-time, in the year eighteen hundred and fourteen, Lieutenant Richard Doubledick, now a browned soldier, seven-and-thirty years of age, came home to England invalided. He brought the hair with him, near his heart. Many a French officer had he seen since that day; many a dreadful night, in searching with men and lanterns for his wounded, had he relieved French officers lying disabled; but the mental picture and the reality had never come together.

Though he was weak and suffered pain, he lost not an hour in getting down to Frome in Somersetshire, where Taunton's mother lived. In the sweet, compassionate words that naturally present themselves to the mind to-night, 'he was the only son of his mother, and she was a widow.'

It was a Sunday evening, and the lady sat at her quiet garden-window, reading the Bible; reading to herself, in a trembling voice, that very passage in it, as I have heard him tell. He heard the words: 'Young man, I say unto thee, arise!'

He had to pass the window; and the bright, dark eyes of his debased time seemed to look at him. Her heart told her who he was; she came to the door quickly, and fell upon his neck.

'He saved me from ruin, made me a human creature, won me from infamy and shame. O, God for ever bless him! As He will, He will!'

'He will!' the lady answered. 'I know he is in Heaven!' Then she piteously cried, 'But O, my darling boy, my darling boy!'

Never from the hour when Private Richard Double-dick enlisted at Chatham had the Private, Corporal, Sergeant, Sergeant-Major, Ensign, or Lieutenant breathed his right name, or the name of Mary Mar-shall, or a word of the story of his life, into any ear except his reclaimer's. That previous scene in his existence was closed. He had firmly resolved that his expiation should be to live unknown; to disturb no more the peace that had long grown over his old offences; to let it be revealed, when he was dead, that he had striven and suffered, and had never forgotten; and then, if they could forgive him and believe him— well, it would be time enough—time enough!

But that night, remembering the words he had cherished for two years, 'Tell her how we became friends. It will comfort her, as it comforts me,' he related everything. It gradually seemed to him as if in his maturity he had recovered a mother; it gradu-ally seemed to her as if in her bereavement she had found a son. During his stay in England, the quiet garden into which he had slowly and painfully crept, a stranger, became the boundary of his home; when he was able to rejoin his regiment in the spring, he left the garden, thinking was this indeed the first time he had ever turned his face towards the old colours with a woman's blessing!

He followed them—so ragged, so scarred and pierced now, that they would scarcely hold together —to Quatre Bras and Ligny. He stood beside them, in an awful stillness of many men, shadowy through the mist and drizzle of a wet June forenoon, on the field of Waterloo. And down to that hour the picture in his mind of the French officer had never been compared with the reality.

The famous regiment was in action early in the battle, and received its first check in many an eventful year, when he was seen to fall. But it swept on to avenge him, and left behind it no such creature in the world of consciousness as Lieutenant Richard Doubledick.

Through pits of mire, and pools of rain; along deep ditches, once roads, that were pounded and ploughed to pieces by artillery, heavy waggons, tramp of men and horses, and the struggle of every wheeled thing that could carry wounded soldiers; jolted among the dying and the dead, so disfigured by blood and mud as to be hardly recognisable for humanity; undisturbed by the moaning of men and the shrieking of horses, which, newly taken from the peaceful pursuits of life, could not endure the sight of the stragglers lying by the wayside, never to resume their toilsome journey; dead, as to any sentient life that was in it, and yet alive,—the form that had been Lieutenant Richard Doubledick, with whose praises England rang, was conveyed to Brussels. There it was tenderly laid down in hospital; and there it lay, week after week, through the long, bright summer days, until the harvest, spared by war, had ripened and was gathered in.

Over and over again the sun rose and set upon the crowded city; over and over again the moonlight

nights were quiet on the plains of Waterloo: and all
that time was a blank to what had been Lieutenant
Richard Doubledick.   Rejoicing troops marched into
Brussels, and marched out; brothers and fathers,
sisters, mothers, and wives, came thronging thither,
drew their lots of joy or agony, and departed; so
many times a day the bells rang; so many times the
shadows of the great buildings changed; so many
lights sprang up at dusk; so many feet passed here
and there upon the pavements; so many hours of
sleep and cooler air of night succeeded: indifferent to
all, a marble face lay on a bed, like the face of a re-
cumbent statue on the tomb of Lieutenant Richard
Doubledick.

Slowly labouring, at last, through a long, heavy
dream of confused time and place, presenting faint
glimpses of army surgeons whom he knew, and of
faces that had been familiar to his youth,—dearest
and kindest among them, Mary Marshall's, with a
solicitude upon it more like reality than anything he
could discern,—Lieutenant Richard Doubledick came
back to life.   To the beautiful life of a calm autumn
evening sunset, to the peaceful life of a fresh, quiet
room with a large window standing open; a balcony
beyond, in which were moving leaves and sweet-
smelling flowers; beyond, again, the clear sky, with
the sun full in his sight, pouring its golden radiance
on his bed.

It was so tranquil and so lovely that he thought
he had passed into another world.   And he said in a
faint voice, 'Taunton, are you near me?'

A face bent over him.   Not his, his mother's.

'I came to nurse you.   We have nursed you many
weeks.   You were moved here long ago.   Do you
remember nothing?'

'Nothing.'

The lady kissed his cheek, and held his hand, sooth-ing him.

'Where is the regiment? What has happened? Let me call you mother. What has happened, mother?'

'A great victory, dear. The war is over, and the regiment was the bravest in the field.'

His eyes kindled, his lips trembled, he sobbed, and the tears ran down his face. He was very weak, too weak to move his hand.

'Was it dark just now?' he asked presently.

'No.'

'It was only dark to me? Something passed away, like a black shadow. But as it went, and the sun—O the blessed sun, how beautiful it is!—touched my face, I thought I saw a light white cloud pass out at the door. Was there nothing that went out?'

She shook her head, and in a little while he fell asleep, she still holding his hand, and soothing him.

From that time, he recovered. Slowly, for he had been desperately wounded in the head, and had been shot in the body, but making some little advance every day. When he had gained sufficient strength to con-verse as he lay in bed, he soon began to remark that Mrs. Taunton always brought him back to his own history. Then he recalled his preserver's dying words, and thought, 'It comforts her.'

One day he awoke out of a sleep, refreshed, and asked her to read to him. But the curtain of the bed, softening the light, which she always drew back when he awoke, that she might see him from her table at the bedside where she sat at work, was held un-drawn; and a woman's voice spoke, which was not hers.

'Can you bear to see a stranger?' it said softly. 'Will you like to see a stranger?'

'Stranger!' he repeated. The voice awoke old memories, before the days of Private Richard Doubledick.

'A stranger now, but not a stranger once,' it said in tones that thrilled him. 'Richard, dear Richard, lost through so many years, my name—'

He cried out her name, 'Mary,' and she held him in her arms, and his head lay on her bosom.

'I am not breaking a rash vow, Richard. These are not Mary Marshall's lips that speak. I have another name.'

She was married.

'I have another name, Richard. Did you ever hear it?'

'Never!'

He looked into her face, so pensively beautiful, and wondered at the smile upon it through her tears.

'Think again, Richard. Are you sure you never heard my altered name?'

'Never!'

'Don't move your head to look at me, dear Richard. Let it lie here, while I tell my story. I loved a generous, noble man; loved him with my whole heart; loved him for years and years; loved him faithfully, devotedly; loved him with no hope of return; loved him, knowing nothing of his highest qualities—not even knowing that he was alive. He was a brave soldier. He was honoured and beloved by thousands of thousands, when the mother of his dear friend found me, and showed me that in all his triumphs he had never forgotten me. He was wounded in a great battle. He was brought, dying, here, into Brussels. I came to watch and tend him, as I would

have joyfully gone, with such a purpose, to the dreariest ends of the earth. When he knew no one else, he knew me. When he suffered most, he bore his sufferings barely murmuring, content to rest his head where yours rests now. When he lay at the point of death, he married me, that he might call me Wife before he died. And the name, my dear love, that I took on that forgotten night—'

'I know it now!' he sobbed. 'The shadowy remembrance strengthens. It is come back. I thank Heaven that my mind is quite restored! My Mary, kiss me; lull this weary head to rest, or I shall die of gratitude. His parting words were fulfilled. I see Home again!'

Well! They were happy. It was a long recovery, but they were happy through it all. The snow had melted on the ground, and the birds were singing in the leafless thickets of the early spring, when those three were first able to ride out together, and when people flocked about the open carriage to cheer and congratulate Captain Richard Doubledick.

But even then it became necessary for the Captain, instead of returning to England, to complete his recovery in the climate of Southern France. They found a spot upon the Rhône, within a ride of the old town of Avignon, and within view of its broken bridge, which was all they could desire; they lived there, together, six months; then returned to England. Mrs. Taunton, growing old after three years— though not so old as that her bright, dark eyes were dimmed—and remembering that her strength had been benefited by the change, resolved to go back for a year to those parts. So she went with a faithful servant, who had often carried her son in his arms; and she was to be rejoined and escorted home, at the year's end, by Captain Richard Doubledick.

She wrote regularly to her children (as she called them now), and they to her. She went to the neighbourhood of Aix; and there, in their own château near the farmer's house she rented, she grew into intimacy with a family belonging to that part of France. The intimacy began in her often meeting among the vineyards a pretty child, a girl with a most compassionate heart, who was never tired of listening to the solitary English lady's stories of her poor son and the cruel wars. The family were as gentle as the child, and at length she came to know them so well that she accepted their invitation to pass the last month of her residence abroad under their roof. All this intelligence she wrote home, piecemeal as it came about, from time to time; and at last enclosed a polite note, from the head of the château, soliciting, on the occasion of his approaching mission to that neighbourhood, the honour of the company of cet homme si justement célèbre, Monsieur le Capitaine Richard Doubledick.

Captain Doubledick, now a hardy, handsome man in the full vigour of life, broader across the chest and shoulders than he had ever been before, despatched a courteous reply, and followed it in person. Travelling through all that extent of country after three years of Peace, he blessed the better days on which the world had fallen. The corn was golden, not drenched in unnatural red; was bound in sheaves for food, not trodden underfoot by men in mortal fight. The smoke rose up from peaceful hearths, not blazing ruins. The carts were laden with the fair fruits of the earth, not with wounds and death. To him who had so often seen the terrible reverse, these things were beautiful indeed; and they brought him in a softened spirit to the old château near Aix upon a deep blue evening.

It was a large château of the genuine old ghostly kind, with round towers, and extinguishers, and a high leaden roof, and more windows than Aladdin's Palace. The lattice blinds were all thrown open after the heat of the day, and there were glimpses of rambling walls and corridors within. Then there were immense out-buildings fallen into partial decay, masses of dark trees, terrace-gardens, balustrades; tanks of water, too weak to play and too dirty to work; statues, weeds, and thickets of iron railing that seemed to have overgrown themselves like the shrubberies, and to have branched out in all manner of wild shapes. The entrance doors stood open, as doors often do in that country when the heat of the day is past; and the Captain saw no bell or knocker, and walked in.

He walked into a lofty stone hall, refreshingly cool and gloomy after the glare of a Southern day's travel. Extending along the four sides of this hall was a gallery, leading to suites of rooms; and it was lighted from the top. Still no bell was to be seen.

'Faith,' said the Captain halting, ashamed of the clanking of his boots, 'this is a ghostly beginning!'

He started back, and felt his face turn white. In the gallery, looking down at him, stood the French officer—the officer whose picture he had carried in his mind so long and so far. Compared with the original, at last—in every lineament how like it was!

He moved, and disappeared, and Captain Richard Doubledick heard his steps coming quickly down into the hall. He entered through an archway. There was a bright, sudden look upon his face, much such a look as it had worn in that fatal moment.

Monsieur le Capitaine Richard Doubledick? Enchanted to receive him! A thousand apologies! The servants were all out in the air. There was a little

fête among them in the garden. In effect, it was the fête day of my daughter, the little cherished and protected of Madame Taunton.

He was so gracious and so frank that Monsieur le Capitaine Richard Doubledick could not withhold his hand. 'It is the hand of a brave Englishman,' said the French officer, retaining it while he spoke. 'I could respect a brave Englishman, even as my foe, how much more as my friend! I also am a soldier!'

'He has not remembered me, as I have remembered him; he did not take such note of my face, that day, as I took of his,' thought Captain Richard Doubledick. 'How shall I tell him?'

The French officer conducted his guest into a garden and presented him to his wife, an engaging and beautiful woman, sitting with Mrs. Taunton in a whimsical old-fashioned pavilion. His daughter, her fair young face beaming with joy, came running to embrace him; and there was a boy-baby to tumble down among the orange trees on the broad steps, in making for his father's legs. A multitude of children visitors were dancing to sprightly music; and all the servants and peasants about the château were dancing too. It was a scene of innocent happiness that might have been invented for the climax of the scenes of peace which had soothed the Captain's journey.

He looked on, greatly troubled in his mind, until a resounding bell rang, and the French officer begged to show him his rooms. They went upstairs into the gallery from which the officer had looked down; and Monsieur le Capitaine Richard Doubledick was cordially welcomed to a grand outer chamber, and a smaller one within, all clocks and draperies, and hearths, and brazen dogs, and tiles, and cool devices, and elegance, and vastness.

'You were at Waterloo,' said the French officer.

'I was,' said Captain Richard Doubledick. 'And at Badajos.'

Left alone with the sound of his own stern voice in his ears, he sat down to consider, What shall I do, and how shall I tell him? At that time, unhappily, many deplorable duels had been fought between English and French officers, arising out of the recent war; and these duels, and how to avoid this officer's hospitality, were the uppermost thought in Captain Richard Doubledick's mind.

He was thinking, and letting the time run out in which he should have dressed for dinner, when Mrs. Taunton spoke to him outside the door, asking if he could give her the letter he had brought from Mary. 'His mother, above all,' the Captain thought. 'How shall I tell *her?*'

'You will form a friendship with your host, I hope,' said Mrs. Taunton, whom he hurriedly admitted, 'that will last for life. He is so true-hearted and so generous, Richard, that you can hardly fail to esteem one another. If He had been spared,' she kissed (not without tears) the locket in which she wore his hair, 'he would have appreciated him with his own magnanimity, and would have been truly happy that the evil days were past which made such a man his enemy.'

She left the room; and the Captain walked, first to one window, whence he could see the dancing in the garden, then to another, whence he could see the smiling prospect and the peaceful vineyards.

'Spirit of my departed friend,' said he, 'is it through thee these better thoughts are rising in my mind? Is it thou who hast shown me, all the way I have been drawn to meet this man, the blessings of the altered time? Is it thou who hast sent thy stricken

mother to me, to stay my angry hand? Is it from thee the whisper comes, that this man did his duty as thou didst,—and as I did, through thy guidance, which has wholly saved me here on earth,—and that he did no more?'

He sat down, with his head buried in his hands, and, when he rose up, made the second strong resolution of his life,—that neither to the French officer, nor to the mother of his departed friend, nor to any soul, while either of the two was living, would he breathe what only he knew. And when he touched that French officer's glass with his own, that day at dinner, he secretly forgave him in the name of the Divine Forgiver of injuries.

Here I ended my story as the first Poor Traveller. But, if I had told it now, I could have added that the time has since come when the son of Major Richard Doubledick, and the son of that French officer, friends as their fathers were before them, fought side by side in one cause, with their respective nations, like long-divided brothers whom the better times have brought together, fast united.

CHAPTER III

THE ROAD

My story being finished, and the Wassail too, we broke up as the Cathedral bell struck Twelve. I did not take leave of my travellers that night; for it had come into my head to reappear, in conjunction with some hot coffee, at seven in the morning.

As I passed along the High Street, I heard the Waits at a distance, and struck off to find them.

They were playing near one of the old gates of the City, at the corner of a wonderfully quaint row of red-brick tenements, which the clarionet obligingly informed me were inhabited by the Minor-Canons. They had odd little porches over the doors, like sounding-boards over old pulpits; and I thought I should like to see one of the Minor-Canons come out upon his top step, and favour us with a little Christmas discourse about the poor scholars of Rochester; taking for his text the words of his Master relative to the devouring of Widows' houses.

The clarionet was so communicative, and my inclinations were (as they generally are) of so vagabond a tendency, that I accompanied the Waits across an open green called the Vines, and assisted—in the French sense—at the performance of two waltzes, two polkas, and three Irish melodies, before I thought of my inn any more.   However, I returned to it then, and found a fiddle in the kitchen, and Ben, the wall-eyed young man, and two chambermaids, circling round the great deal table with the utmost animation.

I had a very bad night.   It cannot have been owing to the turkey or the beef,—and the Wassail is out of the question,—but in every endeavour that I made to get to sleep I failed most dismally.   I was never asleep; and in whatsoever unreasonable direction my mind rambled, the effigy of Master Richard Watts perpetually embarrassed it.

In a word, I only got out of the Worshipful Master Richard Watts's way by getting out of bed in the dark at six o'clock, and tumbling, as my custom is, into all the cold water that could be accumulated for the purpose.   The outer air was dull and cold enough in the street, when I came down there; and the one candle in our supper-room at Watts's Charity looked as pale in the burning as if it had had a bad night

too. But my Travellers had all slept soundly, and they took to the hot coffee, and the piles of bread-and-butter, which Ben had arranged like deals in a timber-yard, as kindly as I could desire.

While it was yet scarcely daylight, we all came out into the street together, and there shook hands. The widow took the little sailor towards Chatham, where he was to find a steamboat for Sheerness; the lawyer, with an extremely knowing look, went his own way, without committing himself by announcing his intentions; two more struck off by the cathedral and old castle for Maidstone; and the book-pedler accompanied me over the bridge. As for me, I was going to walk by Cobham Woods, as far upon my way to London as I fancied.

When I came to the stile and footpath by which I was to diverge from the main road, I bade farewell to my last remaining Poor Traveller, and pursued my way alone. And now the mists began to rise in the most beautiful manner, and the sun to shine; and as I went on through the bracing air, seeing the hoar-frost sparkle everywhere, I felt as if all Nature shared in the joy of the great Birthday.

Going through the woods, the softness of my tread upon the mossy ground and among the brown leaves enhanced the Christmas sacredness by which I felt surrounded. As the whitened stems environed me, I thought how the Founder of the time had never raised his benignant hand, save to bless and heal, except in the case of one unconscious tree. By Cobham Hall, I came to the village, and the churchyard where the dead had been quietly buried, 'in the sure and certain hope' which Christmas-time inspired. What children could I see at play, and not be loving of, recalling who had loved them! No garden that I passed was out of unison with the day, for I remem-

bered that the tomb was in a garden, and that 'she, supposing him to be the gardener,' had said, 'Sir, if thou have borne him hence, tell me where thou hast laid him, and I will take him away.' In time, the distant river with the ships came full in view, and with it pictures of the poor fishermen, mending their nets, who arose and followed him,—of the teaching of the people from a ship pushed off a little way from shore, by reason of the multitude,—of a majestic figure walking on the water, in the loneliness of night. My very shadow on the ground was eloquent of Christmas; for did not the people lay their sick where the mere shadows of the men who had heard and seen him might fall as they passed along?

Thus Christmas begirt me, far and near, until I had come to Blackheath, and had walked down the long vista of gnarled old trees in Greenwich Park, and was being steam-rattled through the mists now closing in once more, towards the lights of London. Brightly they shone, but not so brightly as my own fire, and the brighter faces around it, when we came together to celebrate the day. And there I told of worthy Master Richard Watts, and of my supper with the Six Poor Travellers who were neither Rogues nor Proctors, and from that hour to this I have never seen one of them again.

THE HOLLY-TREE

[1855]

THE HOLLY-TREE

THREE BRANCHES

FIRST BRANCH

MYSELF

1 HAVE kept one secret in the course of my life. 1 am a bashful man. Nobody would suppose it, nobody ever does suppose it, nobody ever did suppose it, but I am naturally a bashful man. This is the secret which I have never breathed until now.

I might greatly move the reader by some account of the innumerable places I have not been to, the innumerable people I have not called upon or received, the innumerable social evasions I have been guilty of, solely because I am by original constitution and character a bashful man. But I will leave the reader unmoved, and proceed with the object before me.

That object is to give a plain account of my travels and discoveries in the Holly-Tree Inn; in which place of good entertainment for man and beast I was once snowed up.

It happened in the memorable year when I parted for ever from Angela Leath, whom I was shortly to have married, on making the discovery that she preferred my bosom friend. From our school-days I had freely admitted Edwin, in my own mind, to be far superior to myself; and, though I was grievously wounded at heart, I felt the preference to be natural.

and tried to forgive them both. It was under these circumstances that I resolved to go to America—on my way to the Devil.

Communicating my discovery neither to Angela nor to Edwin, but resolving to write each of them an affecting letter conveying my blessing and forgiveness, which the steam-tender for shore should carry to the post when I myself should be bound for the New World, far beyond recall,—I say, locking up my grief in my own breast, and consoling myself as I could with the prospect of being generous, I quietly left all I held dear, and started on the desolate journey I have mentioned.

The dead winter-time was in full dreariness when I left my chambers for ever, at five o'clock in the morning. I had shaved by candle-light, of course, and was miserably cold, and experienced that general all-pervading sensation of getting up to be hanged which I have usually found inseparable from untimely rising under such circumstances.

How well I remember the forlorn aspect of Fleet Street when I came out of the Temple! The street-lamps flickered in the gusty north-east wind, as if the very gas were contorted with cold; the white-topped houses; the bleak, star-lighted sky; the market people and other early stragglers, trotting to circulate their almost frozen blood; the hospitable light and warmth of the few coffee-shops and public-houses that were open for such customers; the hard, dry, frosty rime with which the air was charged (the wind had already beaten it into every crevice), and which lashed my face like a steel whip.

It wanted nine days to the end of the month, and end of the year. The Post-office packet for the United States was to depart from Liverpool, weather permitting, on the first of the ensuing month, and

I had the intervening time on my hands. I had taken this into consideration, and had resolved to make a visit to a certain spot (which I need not name) on the farther borders of Yorkshire. It was endeared to me by my having first seen Angela at a farmhouse in that place, and my melancholy was gratified by the idea of taking a wintry leave of it before my expatriation. I ought to explain, that, to avoid being sought out before my resolution should have been rendered irrevocable by being carried into full effect, I had written to Angela overnight, in my usual manner, lamenting that urgent business, of which she should know all particulars by and by—took me unexpectedly away from her for a week or ten days.

There was no Northern Railway at that time, and in its place there were stage-coaches; which I occasionally find myself, in common with some other people, affecting to lament now, but which everybody dreaded as a very serious penance then. I had secured the box-seat on the fastest of these, and my business in Fleet Street was to get into a cab with my portmanteau, so to make the best of my way to the Peacock at Islington, where I was to join this coach. But when one of our Temple watchmen, who carried my portmanteau into Fleet Street for me, told me about the huge blocks of ice that had for some days past been floating in the river, having closed up in the night, and made a walk from the Temple Gardens over to the Surrey shore, I began to ask myself the question, whether the box-seat would not be likely to put a sudden and a frosty end to my unhappiness. I was heart-broken, it is true, and yet I was not quite so far gone as to wish to be frozen to death.

When I got up to the Peacock,—where I found everybody drinking hot purl, in self-preservation,—I asked if there were an inside seat to spare. I then

discovered that, inside or out, I was the only passenger. This gave me a still livelier idea of the great inclemency of the weather, since that coach always loaded particularly well. However, I took a little purl (which I found uncommonly good), and got into the coach. When I was seated, they built me up with straw to the waist, and, conscious of making a rather ridiculous appearance, I began my journey.

It was still dark when we left the Peacock. For a little while, pale, uncertain ghosts of houses and trees appeared and vanished, and then it was hard, black, frozen day. People were lighting their fires; smoke was mounting straight up high into the rarefied air; and we were rattling for Highgate Archway over the hardest ground I have ever heard the ring of iron shoes on. As we got into the country, everything seemed to have grown old and grey. The roads, the trees, thatched roofs of cottages and homesteads, the ricks in farmers' yards. Out-door work was abandoned, horse-troughs at roadside inns were frozen hard, no stragglers lounged about, doors were close shut, little turnpike houses had blazing fires inside, and children (even turnpike people have children, and seem to like them) rubbed the frost from the little panes of glass with their chubby arms, that their bright eyes might catch a glimpse of the solitary coach going by. I don't know when the snow began to set in; but I know that we were changing horses somewhere when I heard the guard remark, 'That the old lady up in the sky was picking her geese pretty hard to-day.' Then, indeed, I found the white down falling fast and thick.

The lonely day wore on, and I dozed it out, as a lonely traveller does. I was warm and valiant after eating and drinking,—particularly after dinner; cold and depressed at all other times. I was always be-

wildered as to time and place, and always more or less out of my senses. The coach and horses seemed to execute in chorus Auld Lang Syne, without a moment's intermission. They kept the time and tune with the greatest regularity, and rose into the swell at the beginning of the Refrain, with a precision that worried me to death. While we changed horses, the guard and coachman went stumping up and down the road, printing off their shoes in the snow, and poured so much liquid consolation into themselves without being any the worse for it, that I began to confound them, as it darkened again, with two great white casks standing on end. Our horses tumbled down in solitary places, and we got them up,—which was the pleasantest variety *I* had, for it warmed me. And it snowed and snowed, and still it snowed, and never left off snowing. All night long we went on in this manner. Thus we came round the clock, upon the Great North Road, to the performance of Auld Lang Syne all day again. And it snowed and snowed, and still it snowed, and never left off snowing.

I forget now where we were at noon on the second day, and where we ought to have been; but I know that we were scores of miles behindhand; and that our case was growing worse every hour. The drift was becoming prodigiously deep; landmarks were getting snowed out; the road and the fields were all one; instead of having fences and hedge-rows to guide us, we went crunching on over an unbroken surface of ghastly white that might sink beneath us at any moment and drop us down a whole hillside. Still the coachman and guard—who kept together on the box, always in council, and looking well about them—made out the track with astonishing sagacity.

When we came in sight of a town, it looked, to my

fancy, like a large drawing on a slate, with abundance of slate-pencil expended on the churches and houses where the snow lay thickest. When we came within a town, and found the church clocks all stopped, the dial-faces choked with snow, and the inn-signs blotted out, it seemed as if the whole place were overgrown with white moss. As to the coach, it was a mere snowball; similarly, the men and boys who ran along beside us to the town's end, turning our clogged wheels and encouraging our horses, were men and boys of snow; and the bleak, wild solitude to which they at last dismissed us was a snowy Sahara. One would have thought this enough: notwithstanding which, I pledge my word that it snowed, and snowed, and still it snowed, and never left off snowing.

We performed Auld Lang Syne the whole day; seeing nothing out of towns and villages, but the track of stoats, hares, and foxes, and sometimes of birds. At nine o'clock at night, on a Yorkshire moor, a cheerful burst from our horn, and a welcome sound of talking, with a glimmering and moving about of lanterns, roused me from my drowsy state. I found that we were going to change.

They helped me out, and I said to a waiter, whose bare head became as white as King Lear's in a single minute, 'What Inn is this?'

'The Holly-Tree, sir,' said he.

'Upon my word, I believe,' said I, apologetically, to the guard and coachman, 'that I must stop here.'

Now the landlord, and the landlady, and the ostler, and the postboy, and all the stable authorities, had already asked the coachman, to the wide-eyed interest of all the rest of the establishment, if he meant to go on. The coachman had already replied, 'Yes, he'd take her through it,'—meaning by Her the coach,—

'if so be as George would stand by him.' George was the guard, and he had already sworn that he *would* stand by him. So the helpers were already getting the horses out.

My declaring myself beaten, after this parley, was not an announcement without preparation. Indeed, but for the way to the announcement being smoothed by the parley, I more than doubt whether, as an innately bashful man, I should have had the confidence to make it. As it was, it received the approval even of the guard and coachman. Therefore, with many confirmations of my inclining, and many remarks from one bystander to another, that the gentleman could go for'ard by the mail to-morrow, whereas to-night he would only be froze, and where was the good of a gentleman being froze,—ah, let alone buried alive (which latter clause was added by a humorous helper as a joke at my expense, and was extremely well received), I saw my portmanteau got out stiff, like a frozen body; did the handsome thing by the guard and coachman; wished them good-night and a prosperous journey; and, a little ashamed of myself, after all, for leaving them to fight it out alone, followed the landlord, landlady, and waiter of the Holly-Tree upstairs.

I thought I had never seen such a large room as that into which they showed me. It had five windows, with dark red curtains that would have absorbed the light of a general illumination; and there were complications of drapery at the top of the curtains, that went wandering about the wall in a most extraordinary manner. I asked for a smaller room, and they told me there was no smaller room. They could screen me in, however, the landlord said. They brought a great old japanned screen, with natives

(Japanese, I suppose) engaged in a variety of idiotic pursuits all over it; and left me roasting whole before an immense fire.

My bedroom was some quarter of a mile off, up a great staircase at the end of a long gallery; and nobody knows what a misery this is to a bashful man who would rather not meet people on the stairs. It was the grimmest room I have ever had the nightmare in; and all the furniture, from the four posts of the bed to the two old silver candlesticks, was tall, high-shouldered, and spindle-waisted. Below, in my sitting-room, if I looked round my screen, the wind rushed at me like a mad bull; if I stuck to my arm-chair, the fire scorched me to the colour of a new brick. The chimney-piece was very high, and there was a bad glass—what I may call a wavy glass—above it, which, when I stood up, just showed me my anterior phrenological developments,—and these never look well, in any subject, cut short off at the eyebrow. If I stood with my back to the fire, a gloomy vault of darkness above and beyond the screen insisted on being looked at; and, in its dim remoteness, the drapery of the ten curtains of the five windows went twisting and creeping about, like a nest of gigantic worms.

I suppose that what I observe in myself must be observed by some other men of similar character in *themselves;* therefore I am emboldened to mention, that, when I travel, I never arrive at a place but I immediately want to go away from it. Before I had finished my supper of broiled fowl and mulled port, I had impressed upon the waiter in detail my arrangements for departure in the morning. Breakfast and bill at eight. Fly at nine. Two horses, or, if needful, even four.

Tired though I was, the night appeared about a week long. In oases of nightmare, I thought of

Angela, and felt more depressed than ever by the reflection that I was on the shortest road to Gretna
Green.   What had *I* to do with Gretna Green.   I
was not going *that* way to the Devil, but by the
American route, I remarked in my bitterness.

In the morning I found that it was snowing still,
that it had snowed all night, and that I was snowed
up.   Nothing could get out of that spot on the moor,
or could come at it, until the road had been cut out
by labourers from the market-town.   When they
might cut their way to the Holly-Tree nobody could
tell me.

It was now Christmas-eve.   I should have had a
dismal Christmas-time of it anywhere, and consequently that did not so much matter; still, being
snowed up was like dying of frost, a thing I had not
bargained for.   I felt very lonely.   Yet I could no
more have proposed to the landlord and landlady to
admit me to their society (though I should have liked
it very much) than I could have asked them to present
me with a piece of plate.   Here my great secret, the
real bashfulness of my character, is to be observed.
Like most bashful men, I judge of other people as
if they were bashful too.   Besides being far too
shamefaced to make the proposal myself, I really had
a delicate misgiving that it would be in the last degree
disconcerting to them.

Trying to settle down, therefore, in my solitude, I
first of all asked what books there were in the house.
The waiter brought me a *Book of Roads,* two or three
old Newspapers, a little Song-Book, terminating in
a collection of Toasts and Sentiments, a little Jest-
Book, an odd volume of *Peregrine Pickle,* and the
Sentimental Journey.   I knew every word of the two
last already, but I read them through again, then tried
to hum all the songs (Auld Lang Syne was among

them); went entirely through the jokes,—in which I found a fund of melancholy adapted to my state of mind; proposed all the toasts, enunciated all the sentiments, and mastered the papers. The latter had nothing in them but stock advertisements, a meeting about a country rate, and a highway robbery. As I am a greedy reader, I could not make this supply hold out until night; it was exhausted by tea-time. Being then entirely cast upon my own resources, I got through an hour in considering what to do next. Ultimately, it came into my head (from which I was anxious by any means to exclude Angela and Edwin), that I would endeavour to recall my experience of Inns, and would try how long it lasted me. I stirred the fire, moved my chair a little to one side of the screen,—not daring to go far, for I knew the wind was waiting to make a rush at me, I could hear it growling,—and began.

My first impressions of an Inn dated from the Nursery; consequently I went back to the Nursery for a starting-point, and found myself at the knee of a sallow woman with a fishy eye, an aquiline nose, and a green gown, whose specialty was a dismal narrative of a landlord by the roadside, whose visitors unaccountably disappeared for many years, until it was discovered that the pursuit of his life had been to convert them into pies. For the better devotion of himself to this branch of industry, he had constructed a secret door behind the head of the bed; and when the visitor (oppressed with pie) had fallen asleep, this wicked landlord would look softly in with a lamp in one hand and a knife in the other, would cut his throat, and would make him into pies; for which purpose he had coppers, underneath a trap-door, always boiling; and rolled out his pastry in the dead of the night. Yet even he was not insensible to the stings of

conscience, for he never went to sleep without being
heard to mutter, 'Too much pepper!' which was
eventually the cause of his being brought to justice.
I had no sooner disposed of this criminal than there
started up another of the same period, whose profession was originally housebreaking; in the pursuit
of which art he had had his right ear chopped off one
night, as he was burglariously getting in at a window,
by a brave and lovely servant-maid (whom the aqui-
line-nosed woman, though not at all answering the
description, always mysteriously implied to be herself). After several years, this brave and lovely
servant-maid was married to the landlord of a country
Inn; which landlord had this remarkable character-
istic, that he always wore a silk nightcap, and never
would on any consideration take it off. At last, one
night, when he was fast asleep, the brave and lovely
woman lifted up his silk nightcap on the right side,
and found that he had no ear there; upon which she
sagaciously perceived that he was the clipped housebreaker, who had married her with the intention of
putting her to death. She immediately heated the
poker and terminated his career, for which she was
taken to King George upon his throne, and received
the compliments of royalty on her great discretion
and valour. This same narrator, who had a Ghoulish
pleasure, I have long been persuaded, in terrifying
me to the utmost confines of my reason, had another authentic anecdote within her own experience,
founded, I now believe, upon *Raymond and Agnes,
or the Bleeding Nun.* She said it happened to her
brother-in-law, who was immensely rich,—which my
father was not; and immensely tall,—which my father
was not. It was always a point with this Ghoul to
present my dearest relations and friends to my youthful mind under circumstances of disparaging con-

trast. The brother-in-law was riding once through a forest on a magnificent horse (we had no magnificent horse at our house), attended by a favourite and valuable Newfoundland dog (we had no dog), when he found himself benighted, and came to an Inn. A dark woman opened the door, and he asked her if he could have a bed there. She answered yes, and put his horse in the stable, and took him into a room where there were two dark men. While he was at supper, a parrot in the room began to talk, saying, 'Blood, blood! Wipe up the blood!' Upon which one of the dark men wrung the parrot's neck, and said he was fond of roasted parrots, and he meant to have this one for breakfast in the morning. After eating and drinking heartily, the immensely rich, tall brother-in-law went up to bed; but he was rather vexed, because they had shut his dog in the stable, saying that they never allowed dogs in the house. He sat very quiet for more than an hour, thinking and thinking, when, just as his candle was burning out, he heard a scratch at the door. He opened the door, and there was the Newfoundland dog! The dog came softly in, smelt about him, went straight to some straw in the corner which the dark men had said covered apples, tore the straw away, and disclosed two sheets steeped in blood. Just at that moment the candle went out, and the brother-in-law, looking through a chink in the door, saw the two dark men stealing upstairs; one armed with a dagger that long (about five feet); the other carrying a chopper, a sack, and a spade. Having no remembrance of the close of this adventure, I suppose my faculties to have been always so frozen with terror at this stage of it, that the power of listening stagnated within me for some quarter of an hour.

These barbarous stories carried me, sitting there on

the Holly-Tree hearth, to the Roadside Inn, renowned
in my time in a sixpenny book with a folding plate,
representing in a central compartment of oval form
the portrait of Jonathan Bradford, and in four corner
compartments four incidents of the tragedy with
which the name is associated,—coloured with a hand at
once so free and economical, that the bloom of Jonathan's complexion passed without any pause into the
breeches of the ostler, and, smearing itself off into
the next division, became rum in a bottle. Then I
remembered how the landlord was found at the murdered traveller's bedside, with his own knife at his
feet, and blood upon his hand; how he was hanged for
the murder, notwithstanding his protestation that he
had indeed come there to kill the traveller for his sad-
dle-bags, but had been stricken motionless on finding
him already slain; and how the ostler, years afterwards, owned the deed. By this time I had made
myself quite uncomfortable. I stirred the fire, and
stood with my back to it as long as I could bear the
heat, looking up at the darkness beyond the screen,
and at the wormy curtains creeping in and creeping
out, like the worms in the ballad of Alonzo the Brave
and the Fair Imogene.

There was an Inn in the cathedral town where I
went to school, which had pleasanter recollections
about it than any of these. I took it next. It was
the Inn where friends used to put up, and where we
used to go to see parents, and to have salmon and
fowls, and be tipped. It had an ecclesiastical sign,—
the Mitre,—and a bar that seemed to be the next best
thing to a bishopric, it was so snug. I loved the landlord's youngest daughter to distraction,—but let that
pass. It was in this Inn that I was cried over by my
rosy little sister, because I had acquired a black eye

in a fight. And though she had been, that Holly-Tree night, for many a long year where all tears are dried, the Mitre softened me yet.

'To be continued to-morrow,' said I, when I took my candle to go to bed. But my bed took it upon itself to continue the train of thought that night. It carried me away, like the enchanted carpet, to a distant place (though still in England), and there, alighting from a stage-coach at another Inn in the snow, as I had actually done some years before, I repeated in my sleep a curious experience I had really had here. More than a year before I made the journey in the course of which I put up at that Inn, I had lost a very near and dear friend by death. Every night since, at home or away from home, I had dreamed of that friend; sometimes as still living; sometimes as returning from the world of shadows to comfort me; always as being beautiful, placid, and happy, never in association with any approach to fear or distress. It was at a lonely Inn in a wide moorland place, that I halted to pass the night. When I had looked from my bedroom window over the waste of snow on which the moon was shining, I sat down by my fire to write a letter. I had always, until that hour, kept it within my own breast that I dreamed every night of the dear lost one. But in the letter that I wrote I recorded the circumstance, and added that I felt much interested in proving whether the subject of my dream would still be faithful to me, travel-tired, and in that remote place. No. I lost the beloved figure of my vision in parting with the secret. My sleep has never looked upon it since, in sixteen years, but once. I was in Italy, and awoke (or seemed to awake), the well-remembered voice distinctly in my ears, conversing with it. I entreated it, as it rose above my bed and soared up to the vaulted

roof of the old room, to answer me a question I had asked touching the Future Life. My hands were still outstretched towards it as it vanished, when I heard a bell ringing by the garden wall, and a voice in the deep stillness of the night calling on all good Christians to pray for the souls of the dead; it being All Souls' Eve.

To return to the Holly-Tree. When I awoke next day, it was freezing hard, and the lowering sky threatened more snow. My breakfast cleared away, I drew my chair into its former place, and, with the fire getting so much the better of the landscape that I sat in twilight, resumed my Inn remembrances.

That was a good Inn down in Wiltshire where I put up once, in the days of the hard Wiltshire ale, and before all beer was bitterness. It was on the skirts of Salisbury Plain, and the midnight wind that rattled my lattice window came moaning at me from Stonehenge. There was a hanger-on at that establishment (a supernaturally preserved Druid I believe him to have been, and to be still), with long white hair, and a flinty blue eye always looking afar off; who claimed to have been a shepherd, and who seemed to be ever watching for the reappearance, on the verge of the horizon, of some ghostly flock of sheep that had been mutton for many ages. He was a man with a weird belief in him that no one could count the stones of Stonehenge twice, and make the same number of them; likewise, that any one who counted them three times nine times, and then stood in the centre and said, 'I dare!' would behold a tremendous apparition, and be stricken dead. He pretended to have seen a bustard (I suspect him to have been familiar with the dodo), in manner following: He was out upon the plain at the close of a late autumn day, when he dimly discerned, going on before him at a

curious, fitfully bounding pace, what he at first supposed to be a gig-umbrella that had been blown from some conveyance, but what he presently believed to be a lean dwarf man upon a little pony. Having followed this object for some distance without gaining on it, and having called to it many times without receiving any answer, he pursued it for miles and miles, when, at length coming up with it, he discovered it to be the last bustard in Great Britain, degenerated into a wingless state, and running along the ground. Resolved to capture him or perish in the attempt, he closed with the bustard; but the bustard, who had formed a counter-resolution that he should do neither, threw him, stunned him, and was last seen making off due west. This weird man, at that stage of metempsychosis, may have been a sleep-walker or an enthusiast or a robber; but I awoke one night to find him in the dark at my bedside, repeating the Athanasian Creed in a terrific voice. I paid my bill next day, and retired from the county with all possible precipitation.

That was not a commonplace story which worked itself out at a little Inn in Switzerland, while I was staying there. It was a very homely place, in a village of one narrow, zigzag street, among mountains, and you went in at the main door through the cow-house, and among the mules and the dogs and the fowls, before ascending a great bare staircase to the rooms; which were all of unpainted wood, without plastering or papering,—like rough packing-cases. Outside there was nothing but the straggling street, a little toy church with a copper-coloured steeple, a pine forest, a torrent, mists, and mountain-sides. A young man belonging to this Inn had disappeared eight weeks before (it was winter-time), and was supposed to have had some undiscovered love affair, and

to have gone for a soldier. He had got up in the night, and dropped into the village street from the loft in which he slept with another man; and he had done it so quietly, that his companion and fellow-labourer had heard no movement when he was awakened in the morning, and they said, 'Louis, where is Henri?' They looked for him high and low, in vain, and gave him up. Now, outside this Inn, there stood, as there stood outside every dwelling in the village, a stack of firewood; but the stack belonging to the Inn was higher than any of the rest, because the Inn was the richest house, and burnt the most fuel. It began to be noticed, while they were looking high and low, that a Bantam cock, part of the live stock of the Inn, put himself wonderfully out of his way to get to the top of this wood-stack; and that he would stay there for hours and hours, crowing, until he appeared in danger of splitting himself. Five weeks went on,—six weeks,—and still this terrible Bantam, neglecting his domestic affairs, was always on the top of the wood-stack, crowing the very eyes out of his head. By this time it was perceived that Louis had become inspired with a violent animosity towards the terrible Bantam, and one morning he was seen by a woman, who sat nursing her goître at a little window in a gleam of sun, to catch up a rough billet of wood, with a great oath, hurl it at the terrible Bantam crowing on the wood-stack, and bring him down dead. Hereupon the woman, with a sudden light in her mind, stole round to the back of the wood-stack, and, being a good climber, as all those women are, climbed up, and soon was seen upon the summit, screaming, looking down the hollow within, and crying, 'Seize Louis, the murderer! Ring the church bell! Here is the body!' I saw the murderer that day, and I saw him as I sat by my fire at the Holly-Tree Inn, and I

see him now, lying shackled with cords on the stable litter, among the mild eyes and the smoking breath of the cows, waiting to be taken away by the police, and stared at by the fearful village. A heavy animal,—the dullest animal in the stables,—with a stupid head, and a lumpish face devoid of any trace of sensibility, who had been, within the knowledge of the murdered youth, an embezzler of certain small moneys belonging to his master, and who had taken this hopeful mode of putting a possible accuser out of his way. All of which he confessed next day, like a sulky wretch who couldn't be troubled any more, now that they had got hold of him, and meant to make an end of him. I saw him once again, on the day of my departure from the Inn. In that Canton the headsman still does his office with a sword; and I came upon this murderer sitting bound to a chair, with his eyes bandaged, on a scaffold in a little market-place. In that instant, a great sword (loaded with quicksilver in the thick part of the blade) swept round him like a gust of wind or fire, and there was no such creature in the world. My wonder was, not that he was so suddenly despatched, but that any head was left unreaped, within a radius of fifty yards of that tremendous sickle.

That was a good Inn, too, with the kind, cheerful landlady and the honest landlord, where I lived in the shadow of Mont Blanc, and where one of the apartments has a zoological papering on the walls, not so accurately joined but that the elephant occasionally rejoices in a tiger's hind legs and tail, while the lion puts on a trunk and tusks, and the bear, moulting as it were, appears as to portions of himself like a leopard. I made several American friends at that Inn, who all called Mont Blanc Mount Blank,—except one good-humoured gentleman, of a very sociable nature,

who became on such intimate terms with it that he
spoke of it familiarly as 'Blank'; observing, at breakfast, 'Blank looks pretty tall this morning'; or considerably doubting in the courtyard in the evening,
whether there warn't some go-ahead naters in our
country, sir, that would make out the top of Blank
in a couple of hours from first start—now!

Once I passed a fortnight at an Inn in the North
of England, where I was haunted by the ghost of a
tremendous pie. It was a Yorkshire pie, like a
fort,—an abandoned fort with nothing in it; but the
waiter had a fixed idea that it was a point of ceremony
at every meal to put the pie on the table. After some
days I tried to hint, in several delicate ways, that I
considered the pie done with; as, for example, by
emptying fag-ends of glasses of wine into it; putting
cheese-plates and spoons into it, as into a basket;
putting wine-bottles into it, as into a cooler; but always in vain, the pie being invariably cleaned out
again and brought up as before. At last, beginning
to be doubtful whether I was not the victim of a
spectral illusion, and whether my health and spirits
might not sink under the horrors of an imaginary
pie, I cut a triangle out of it, fully as large as the
musical instrument of that name in a powerful orchestra. Human prevision could not have foreseen
the result—but the waiter mended the pie. With
some effectual species of cement, he adroitly fitted
the triangle in again, and I paid my reckoning and
fled.

The Holly-Tree was getting rather dismal. I
made an overland expedition beyond the screen, and
penetrated as far as the fourth window. Here I was
driven back by stress of weather. Arrived at my
winter-quarters once more, I made up the fire, and
took another Inn.

It was in the remotest part of Cornwall. A great annual Miners' Feast was being holden at the Inn, when I and my travelling companions presented ourselves at night among the wild crowd that were dancing before it by torchlight. We had had a breakdown in the dark, on a stony morass some miles away; and I had the honour of leading one of the unharnessed post-horses. If any lady or gentleman, on perusal of the present lines, will take any very tall post-horse with his traces hanging about his legs, and will conduct him by the bearing-rein into the heart of a country dance of a hundred and fifty couples, that lady or gentleman will then, and only then, form an adequate idea of the extent to which that post-horse will tread on his conductor's toes. Over and above which, the post-horse, finding three hundred people whirling about him, will probably rear, and also lash out with his hind legs, in a manner incompatible with dignity or self-respect on his conductor's part. With such little drawbacks on my usually impressive aspect, I appeared at this Cornish Inn, to the unutterable wonder of the Cornish Miners. It was full, and twenty times full, and nobody could be received but the post-horse,—though to get rid of that noble animal was something. While my fellow-travellers and I were discussing how to pass the night and so much of the next day as must intervene before the jovial blacksmith and the jovial wheelwright would be in a condition to go out on the morass and mend the coach, an honest man stepped forth from the crowd and proposed his unlet floor of two rooms, with supper of eggs and bacon, ale and punch. We joyfully accompanied him home to the strangest of clean houses, where we were well entertained to the satisfaction of all parties. But the novel feature of the entertainment was, that our host was a chair-maker, and that

the chairs assigned to us were mere frames, altogether
without bottoms of any sort; so that we passed the
evening on perches.   Nor was this the absurdest consequence; for when we unbent at supper, and any one
of us gave way to laughter, he forgot the peculiarity
of his position, and instantly disappeared.   I myself,
doubled up into an attitude from which self-extrica-
tion was impossible, was taken out of my frame, like a
clown in a comic pantomime who has tumbled into a
tub, five times by the taper's light during the eggs
and bacon.

The Holly-Tree was fast reviving within me a sense
of loneliness.   I began to feel conscious that my subject would never carry on until I was dug out.   I
might be a week here,—weeks!

There was a story with a singular idea in it, connected with an Inn I once passed a night at in a picturesque old town on the Welsh border.   In a large
double-bedded room of this Inn there had been a suicide committed by poison, in one bed, while a tired
traveller slept unconscious in the other.   After that
time, the suicide bed was never used, but the other
constantly was; the disused bedstead remaining in the
room empty, though as to all other respects in its old
state.   The story ran, that whosoever slept in this
room, though never so entire a stranger, from never
so far off, was invariably observed to come down in
the morning with an impression that he smelt Lauda-
num, and that his mind always turned upon the subject of suicide; to which, whatever kind of man he
might be, he was certain to make some reference if
he conversed with any one.   This went on for years,
until it at length induced the landlord to take the disused bedstead down, and bodily burn it,—bed, hang-
ings, and all.   The strange influence (this was the
story) now changed to a fainter one, but never

changed afterwards. The occupant of that room, with occasional but very rare exceptions, would come down in the morning, trying to recall a forgotten dream he had had in the night. The landlord, on his mentioning his perplexity, would suggest various common-place subjects, not one of which, as he very well knew, was the true subject. But the moment the landlord suggested 'Poison,' the traveller started, and cried, 'Yes!' He never failed to accept that suggestion, and he never recalled any more of the dream.

This reminiscence brought the Welsh Inns in general before me; with the women in their round hats, and the harpers with their white beards (venerable, but humbugs, I am afraid), playing outside the door while I took my dinner. The transition was natural to the Highland Inns, with the oatmeal bannocks, the honey, the venison steaks, the trout from the loch, the whisky, and perhaps (having the materials so temptingly at hand) the Athol brose. Once was I coming south from the Scottish Highlands in hot haste, hoping to change quickly at the station at the bottom of a certain wild historical glen, when these eyes did with mortification see the landlord come out with a telescope and sweep the whole prospect for the horses; which horses were away picking up their own living, and did not heave in sight under four hours. Having thought of the loch-trout, I was taken by quick association to the Anglers' Inns of England (I have assisted at innumerable feats of angling by lying in the bottom of the boat, whole summer days, doing nothing with the greatest perseverance; which I have generally found to be as effectual towards the taking of fish as the finest tackle and the utmost science), and to the pleasant white, clean, flower-pot-decorated bedrooms of those inns, overlooking the river, and the ferry, and the green ait,

and the church-spire, and the country bridge; and to
the peerless Emma with the bright eyes and the pretty
smile, who waited, bless her! with a natural grace
that would have converted Blue-Beard. Casting my
eyes upon my Holly-Tree fire, I next discerned
among the glowing coals the pictures of a score or
more of those wonderful English posting-inns which
we are all so sorry to have lost, which were so large
and so comfortable, and which were such monuments
of British submission to rapacity and extortion. He
who would see these houses pining away, let him
walk from Basingstoke, or even Windsor, to London,
by way of Hounslow, and moralise on their perishing
remains; the stables crumbling to dust; unsettled
labourers and wanderers bivouacking in the out-
houses; grass growing in the yards; the rooms, where
erst so many hundred beds of down were made up,
let off to Irish lodgers at eighteenpence a week; a
little ill-looking beer-shop shrinking in the tap of
former days, burning coach-house gates for firewood,
having one of its two windows bunged up, as if it
had received punishment in a fight with the Railroad;
a low, bandy-legged, brick-making bulldog standing
in the doorway. What could I next see in my fire
so naturally as the new railway-house of these times
near the dismal country station; with nothing particular on draught but cold air and damp, nothing
worth mentioning in the larder but new mortar, and
no business doing beyond a conceited affectation of
luggage in the hall? Then I came to the Inns of
Paris, with the pretty apartment of four pieces up
one hundred and seventy-five waxed stairs, the privilege of ringing the bell all day long without influ-
encing anybody's mind or body but your own, and the
not-too-much-for-dinner, considering the price. Next
to the provincial Inns of France, with the great

church-tower rising above the courtyard, the horse-
bells jingling merrily up and down the street beyond,
and the clocks of all descriptions in all the rooms,
which are never right, unless taken at the precise
minute when, by getting exactly twelve hours too fast
or too slow, they unintentionally become so. Away
I went, next, to the lesser roadside Inns of Italy;
where all the dirty clothes in the house (not in wear)
are always lying in your anteroom; where the mosqui-
toes make a raisin pudding of your face in summer,
and the cold bites it blue in winter; where you get
what you can, and forget what you can't; where I
should again like to be boiling my tea in a pocket-
handkerchief dumpling, for want of a teapot. So to
the old palace Inns and old monastery Inns, in towns
and cities of the same bright country; with their massive quadrangular staircases, whence you may look
from among clustering pillars high into the blue vault
of heaven; with their stately banqueting rooms, and
vast refectories; with their labyrinths of ghostly bed-
chambers, and their glimpses into gorgeous streets
that have no appearance of reality or possibility. So
to the close little Inns of the Malaria districts, with
their pale attendants, and their peculiar smell of never
letting in the air. So to the immense fantastic Inns
of Venice, with the cry of the gondolier below, as he
skims the corner; the grip of the watery odours on one
particular little bit of the bridge of your nose (which
is never released while you stay there) ; and the great
bell of St. Mark's Cathedral tolling midnight. Next
I put up for a minute at the restless Inns upon the
Rhine, where your going to bed, no matter at what
hour, appears to be the tocsin for everybody else's
getting up; and where, in the table-d'hôte room at
the end of the long table (with several Towers of
Babel on it at the other end, all made of white plates),

one knot of stoutish men, entirely dressed in jewels
and dirt, and having nothing else upon them, *will*
remain all night, clinking glasses, and singing about
the river that flows, and the grape that grows, and
Rhine wine that beguiles, and Rhine woman that
smiles and hi drink drink my friend and ho drink
drink my brother, and all the rest of it. I departed
thence, as a matter of course, to other German Inns,
where all the eatables are soddened down to the same
flavour, and where the mind is disturbed by the apparition of hot puddings, and boiled cherries, sweet and
slab, at awfully unexpected periods of the repast.
After a draught of sparkling beer from a foaming
glass jug, and a glance of recognition through the
windows of the student beer-houses at Heidelberg and
elsewhere, I put out to sea for the Inns of America,
with their four hundred beds apiece, and their eight
or nine hundred ladies and gentlemen at dinner every
day. Again I stood in the bar-rooms thereof, taking
my evening cobbler, julep, sling, or cocktail. Again
I listened to my friend the General,—whom I had
known for five minutes, in the course of which period
he had made me intimate for life with two Majors,
who again had made me intimate for life with three
Colonels, who again had made me brother to twenty-
two civilians,—again, I say, I listened to my friend
the General, leisurely expounding the resources of the
establishment, as to gentlemen's morning-room, sir;
ladies' morning-room, sir; gentlemen's evening-room,
sir; ladies' evening-room, sir; ladies' and gentlemen's
evening reuniting-room, sir; music-room, sir; reading-
room, sir; over four hundred sleeping-rooms, sir; and
the entire planned and finited within twelve calendar
months from the first clearing off of the old encum-
brances on the plot, at a cost of five hundred thousand
dollars, sir. Again I found, as to my individual way

of thinking, that the greater, the more gorgeous, and the more dollarous the establishment was, the less desirable it was. Nevertheless, again I drank my cobbler, julep, sling, or cocktail, in all good-will, to my friend the General, and my friends the Majors, Colonels, and civilians all; full well knowing that, whatever little motes my beamy eyes may have descried in theirs, they belong to a kind, generous, large-hearted, and great people.

I had been going on lately at a quick pace to keep my solitude out of my mind; but here I broke down for good, and gave up the subject. What was I to do? What was to become of me? Into what extremity was I submissively to sink? Supposing that, like Baron Trenck, I looked out for a mouse or spider, and found one, and beguiled my imprisonment by training it? Even that might be dangerous with a view to the future. I might be so far gone when the road did come to be cut through the snow, that, on my way forth, I might burst into tears, and beseech, like the prisoner who was released in his old age from the Bastille, to be taken back again to the five windows, the ten curtains, and the sinuous drapery.

A desperate idea came into my head. Under any other circumstances I should have rejected it; but, in the strait at which I was, I held it fast. Could I so far overcome the inherent bashfulness which withheld me from the landlord's table and the company I might find there, as to call up the Boots, and ask him to take a chair,—and something in a liquid form,—and talk to me? I could. I would. I did.

SECOND BRANCH

THE BOOTS

WHERE had he been in his time? he repeated, when I asked him the question. Lord, he had been everywhere! And what had he been? Bless you, he had been everything you could mention a'most!

Seen a good deal? Why, of course he had. I should say so, he could assure me, if I only knew about a twentieth part of what had come in *his* way. Why, it would be easier for him, he expected, to tell what he hadn't seen than what he had. Ah! A deal, it would.

What was the curiousest thing he had seen? Well! He didn't know. He couldn't momently name what was the curiousest thing he had seen,—unless it was a Unicorn,—and he see *him* once at a Fair. But supposing a young gentleman not eight year old was to run away with a fine young woman of seven, might I think *that* a queer start? Certainly. Then that was a start as he himself had had his blessed eyes on, and he had cleaned the shoes they run away in—and they was so little that he couldn't get his hand into 'em.

Master Harry Walmers' father, you see, he lived at the Elmses, down away by Shooter's Hill there, six or seven miles from Lunnon. He was a gentleman of spirit, and good-looking, and held his head up when he walked, and had what you may call Fire about him. He wrote poetry, and he rode, and he ran, and he cricketed, and he danced, and he acted, and he done it all equally beautiful. He was uncommon proud of Master Harry as was his only child; but he didn't spoil him neither. He was a gentleman that

had a will of his own and a eye of his own, and that
would be minded. Consequently, though he made
quite a companion of the fine bright boy, and was
delighted to see him so fond of reading his fairy books,
and was never tired of hearing him say my name is
Norval, or hearing him sing his songs about Young
May Moons is beaming love, and When he as adores
thee has left but the name, and that; still he kept the
command over the child, and the child *was* a child, and
it 's to be wished more of 'em was!

How did Boots happen to know all this? Why,
through being under-gardener.   Of course he couldn't
be under-gardener, and be always about, in the sum-
mer-time, near the windows on the lawn, a mowing,
and sweeping, and weeding, and pruning, and this
and that, without getting acquainted with the ways
of the family.   Even supposing Master Harry hadn't
come to him one morning early, and said, 'Cobbs, how
should you spell Norah, if you was asked?' and then
began cutting it in print all over the fence.

He couldn't say he had taken particular notice of
children before that; but really it was pretty to see
them two mites a going about the place together, deep
in love.   And the courage of the boy! Bless your
soul, he 'd have throwed off his little hat, and tucked
up his little sleeves, and gone in at a Lion, he would,
if they had happened to meet one, and she had been
frightened of him.   One day he stops, along with
her, where Boots was hoeing weeds in the gravel, and
says, speaking up, 'Cobbs,' he says, 'I like *you*.' 'Do
you, sir? I 'm proud to hear it.' 'Yes, I do, Cobbs.
Why do I like you, do you think, Cobbs?' 'Don't
know, Master Harry, I am sure.' 'Because Norah
likes you, Cobbs.' 'Indeed, sir? That 's very gratifying.' 'Gratifying, Cobbs? It 's better than millions of the brightest diamonds to be liked by Norah.'

'Certainly, sir.' 'You 're going away, ain't you, Cobbs?' 'Yes, sir.' 'Would you like another situation, Cobbs?' 'Well, sir, I shouldn't object, if it was a good 'un.' 'Then, Cobbs,' says he, 'you shall be our Head Gardener when we are married.' And he tucks her, in her little sky-blue mantle, under his arm, and walks away.

Boots could assure me that it was better than a picter, and equal to a play, to see them babies, with their long, bright, curling hair, their sparkling eyes, and their beautiful light tread, a rambling about the garden, deep in love. Boots was of opinion that the birds believed they was birds, and kept up with 'em, singing to please 'em. Sometimes they would creep under the Tulip-tree, and would sit there with their arms round one another's necks, and their soft cheeks touching, a reading about the Prince and the Dragon, and the good and bad enchanters, and the king's fair daughter. Sometimes he would hear them planning about having a house in a forest, keeping bees and a cow, and living entirely on milk and honey. Once he came upon them by the pond, and heard Master Harry say, 'Adorable Norah, kiss me, and say you love me to distraction, or I 'll jump in head-foremost.' And Boots made no question he would have done it if she hadn't complied. On the whole, Boots said it had a tendency to make him feel as if he was in love himself—only he didn't exactly know who with.

'Cobbs,' said Master Harry, one evening, when Cobbs was watering the flowers, 'I am going on a visit, this present Midsummer, to my grandmamma's at York.'

'Are you indeed, sir? I hope you 'll have a pleasant time. I am going into Yorkshire myself, when I leave here.'

'Are you going to your grandmamma's, Cobbs?'

'No, sir. I haven't got such a thing.'

'Not as a grandmamma, Cobbs?'

'No, sir.'

The boy looked on at the watering of the flowers for a little while, and then said, 'I shall be very glad indeed to go, Cobbs,—Norah's going.'

'You 'll be all right then, sir,' says Cobbs, 'with your beautiful sweetheart by your side.'

'Cobbs,' returned the boy, flushing, 'I never let anybody joke about it, when I can prevent them.'

'It wasn't a joke, sir,' says Cobbs, with humility,—'wasn't so meant.'

'I am glad of that, Cobbs, because I like you, you know, and you 're going to live with us.—Cobbs!'

'Sir.'

'What do you think my grandmamma gives me when I go down there?'

'I couldn't so much as make a guess, sir.'

'A Bank of England five-pound note, Cobbs.'

'Whew!' says Cobbs, 'that 's a spanking sum of money, Master Harry.'

'A person could do a good deal with such a sum of money as that,—couldn't a person, Cobbs?'

'I believe you, sir!'

'Cobbs,' said the boy, 'I 'll tell you a secret. At Norah's house, they have been joking her about me, and pretending to laugh at our being engaged,—pretending to make game of it, Cobbs!'

'Such, sir,' says Cobbs, 'is the depravity of human natur.'

The boy, looking exactly like his father, stood for a few minutes with his glowing face towards the sunset, and then departed with, 'Good-night, Cobbs. I 'm going in.'

If I was to ask Boots how it happened that he was a going to leave that place just at that present time,

well, he couldn't rightly answer me. He did suppose he might have stayed there till now if he had been anyways inclined. But, you see, he was younger then, and he wanted change. That's what he wanted,—change. Mr. Walmers, he said to him when he gave him notice of his intentions to leave, 'Cobbs,' he says, 'have you anything to complain of? I make the inquiry because if I find that any of my people really has anythink to complain of, I wish to make it right if I can.' 'No, sir,' says Cobbs; 'thanking you, sir, I find myself as well sitiwated here as I could hope to be anywheres. The truth is, sir, that I'm a going to seek my fortun'.' 'O, indeed, Cobbs!' he says; 'I hope you may find it.' And Boots could assure me—which he did, touching his hair with his bootjack, as a salute in the way of his present calling—that he hadn't found it yet.

Well, sir! Boots left the Elmses when his time was up, and Master Harry, he went down to the old lady's at York, which old lady would have given that child the teeth out of her head (if she had had any), she was so wrapped up in him. What does that Infant do,—for Infant you may call him and be within the mark,—but cut away from that old lady's with his Norah, on a expedition to go to Gretna Green and be married!

Sir, Boots was at this identical Holly-Tree Inn (having left it several times since to better himself, but always come back through one thing or another), when, one summer afternoon, the coach drives up, and out of the coach gets them two children. The Guard says to our Governor, 'I don't quite make out these little passengers, but the young gentleman's words was, that they was to be brought here.' The young gentleman gets out; hands his lady out; gives the Guard something for himself; says to our Governor,

'We 're to stop here to-night, please. Sitting-room
and two bed-rooms will be required. Chops and
cherry-pudding for two!' and tucks her, in her little
sky-blue mantle, under his arm, and walks into the
house much bolder than Brass.

Boots leaves me to judge what the amazement of
that establishment was, when these two tiny creatures
all alone by themselves was marched into the Angel,—
much more so, when he, who had seen them without
their seeing him, give the Governor his views of the
expedition they was upon. 'Cobbs,' says the Governor, 'if this is so, I must set off myself to York, and
quiet their friends' minds. In which case you must
keep your eye upon 'em, and humour 'em, till I come
back. But before I take these measures, Cobbs, I
should wish you to find from themselves whether your
opinion is correct.' 'Sir, to you,' says Cobbs, 'that
shall be done directly.'

So Boots goes upstairs to the Angel, and there he
finds Master Harry on a e-normous sofa,—immense
at any time, but looking like the Great Bed of Ware,
compared with him,—a drying the eyes of Miss Norah
with his pocket-hankecher. Their little legs was entirely off the ground, of course, and it really is not
possible for Boots to express to me how small them
children looked.

'It 's Cobbs! It 's Cobbs!' cried Master Harry, and
comes running to him, and catching hold of his hand.
Miss Norah comes running to him on t' other side
and catching hold of his t' other hand, and they both
jump for joy.

'I see you getting out, sir,' says Cobbs. 'I
thought it was you. I thought I couldn't be mistaken
in your height and figure. What 's the object of
your journey, sir? Matrimonial?'

'We are going to be married, Cobbs, at Gretna

Green,' returned the boy. 'We have run away on purpose. Norah has been in rather low spirits, Cobbs; but she 'll be happy, now we have found you to be our friend.'

'Thank you, sir, and thank *you,* miss,' says Cobbs, 'for your good opinion. *Did* you bring any luggage with you, sir?'

If I will believe Boots when he gives me his word and honour upon it, the lady had got a parasol, a smelling-bottle, a round and a half of cold buttered toast, eight peppermint drops, and a hair-brush,— seemingly a doll's. The gentleman had got about half a dozen yards of string, a knife, three or four sheets of writing-paper folded up surprisingly small, a orange, and a Chaney mug with his name upon it.

'What may be the exact natur of your plans, sir?' says Cobbs.

'To go on,' replied the boy,—which the courage of that boy was something wonderful!—'in the morning, and be married to-morrow.'

'Just so, sir,' says Cobbs. 'Would it meet your views, sir, if I was to accompany you?'

When Cobbs said this, they both jumped for joy again, and cried out, 'Oh, yes, yes, Cobbs! Yes!'

'Well, sir,' says Cobbs. 'If you will excuse my having the freedom to give an opinion, what I should recommend would be this. I 'm acquainted with a pony, sir, which, put in a pheayton that I could borrow, would take you and Mrs. Harry Walmers, Junior (myself driving, if you approved,) to the end of your journey in a very short space of time. I am not altogether sure, sir, that this pony will be at liberty to-morrow, but even if you had to wait over to-morrow for him, it might be worth your while. As to the small account here, sir, in case you was to find yourself running at all short, that don't signify; be-

cause I'm a part proprietor of this inn, and it could stand over.'

Boots assures me that when they clapped their hands, and jumped for joy again, and called him 'Good Cobbs!' and 'Dear Cobbs!' and bent across him to kiss one another in the delight of their confiding hearts, he felt himself the meanest rascal for deceiving 'em that ever was born.

'Is there anything you want just at present, sir?' says Cobbs, mortally ashamed of himself.

'We should like some cakes after dinner,' answered Master Harry, folding his arms, putting out one leg, and looking straight at him, 'and two apples,—and jam. With dinner we should like to have toast-and-water. But Norah has always been accustomed to half a glass of currant wine at dessert. And so have I.'

'It shall be ordered at the bar, sir,' says Cobbs; and away he went.

Boots has the feeling as fresh upon him at this minute of speaking as he had then, that he would far rather have had it out in half a dozen rounds with the Governor than have combined with him; and that he wished with all his heart there was any impossible place where those two babies could make an impossible marriage, and live impossibly happy ever afterwards. However, as it couldn't be, he went into the Governor's plans, and the Governor set off for York in half an hour.

The way in which the women of that house—without exception—every one of 'em—married *and* single —took to that boy when they heard the story, Boots considers surprising. It was as much as he could do to keep 'em from dashing into the room and kissing him. They climbed up all sorts of places, at the risk of their lives, to look at him through a pane of glass.

They was seven deep at the keyhole. They was out of their minds about him and his bold spirit.

In the evening, Boots went into the room to see how the runaway couple was getting on. The gentleman was on the window-seat, supporting the lady in his arms. She had tears upon her face, and was lying, very tired and half asleep, with her head upon his shoulder.

'Mrs. Harry Walmers, Junior, fatigued, sir?' says Cobbs.

'Yes, she is tired, Cobbs; but she is not used to be away from home, and she has been in low spirits again. Cobbs, do you think you could bring a biffin, please?'

'I ask your pardon, sir,' says Cobbs. 'What was it you—?'

'I think a Norfolk biffin would rouse her, Cobbs. She is very fond of them.'

Boots withdrew in search of the required restorative, and, when he brought it in, the gentleman handed it to the lady, and fed her with a spoon, and took a little himself; the lady being heavy with sleep, and rather cross. 'What should you think, sir,' says Cobbs, 'of a chamber candlestick?' The gentleman approved; the chambermaid went first, up the great staircase; the lady, in her sky-blue mantle, followed, gallantly escorted by the gentleman; the gentleman embraced her at her door, and retired to his own apartment, where Boots softly locked him up.

Boots couldn't but feel with increased acuteness what a base deceiver he was, when they consulted him at breakfast (they had ordered sweet milk-and-water and toast and currant jelly, overnight) about the pony. It really was as much as he could do, he don't mind confessing to me, to look them two young things in the face, and think what a wicked old father of

lies he had grown up to be.   Howsomever, he went
on a lying like a Trojan about the pony.   He told
'em that it did so unfort'nately happen that the pony
was half clipped, you see, and that he couldn't be taken
out in that state, for fear it should strike to his inside.
But that he 'd be finished clipping in the course of the
day, and that to-morrow morning at eight o'clock the
pheayton would be ready.   Boots's view of the whole
case, looking back on it in my room, is, that Mrs.
Harry Walmers, Junior, was beginning to give in.
She hadn't had her hair curled when she went to bed,
and she didn't seem quite up to brushing it herself,
and its getting in her eyes put her out.   But nothing
put out Master Harry.   He sat behind his breakfast-
cup, a tearing away at the jelly, as if he had been his
own father.

After breakfast, Boots is inclined to consider that
they drawed soldiers,—at least, he knows that many
such was found in the fireplace, all on horseback.   In
the course of the morning, Master Harry rang the
bell,—it was surprising how that there boy did carry
on,—and said, in a sprightly way, 'Cobbs, is there
any good walks in this neighbourhood?'

'Yes, sir,' says Cobbs.   'There 's Love Lane.'

'Get out with you, Cobbs!'—that was that there
boy's expression,—'you 're joking.'

'Begging your pardon, sir,' says Cobbs, 'there really
is Love Lane.   And a pleasant walk it is, and proud
shall I be to show it to yourself and Mrs. Harry
Walmers, Junior.'

'Norah, dear,' said Master Harry, 'this is curious.
We really ought to see Love Lane.   Put on your
bonnet, my sweetest darling, and we will go there with
Cobbs.'

Boots leaves me to judge what a Beast he felt himself to be, when that young pair told him, as they all

three jogged along together, that they had made up their minds to give him two thousand guineas a year as head-gardener, on accounts of his being so true a friend to 'em. Boots could have wished at the moment that the earth would have opened and swallowed him up, he felt so mean, with their beaming eyes a looking at him, and believing him. Well, sir, he turned the conversation as well as he could, and he took 'em down Love Lane to the water-meadows, and there Master Harry would have drowned himself in half a moment more, a getting out a water-lily for her,—but nothing daunted that boy. Well, sir, they was tired out. All being so new and strange to 'em, they was tired as tired could be. And they laid down on a bank of daisies, like the children in the wood, leastways meadows, and fell asleep.

Boots don't know—perhaps I do,—but never mind, it don't signify either way—why it made a man fit to make a fool of himself to see them two pretty babies a lying there in the clear, still, sunny day, not dreaming half so hard when they was asleep as they done when they was awake. But, Lord! when you come to think of yourself, you know, and what a game you have been up to ever since you was in your own cradle, and what a poor sort of a chap you are, and how it's always either Yesterday with you, or else To-morrow, and never To-day, that 's where it is!

Well, sir, they woke up at last, and then one thing was getting pretty clear to Boots, namely, that Mrs. Harry Walmerses, Junior's, temper was on the move. When Master Harry took her round the waist, she said he 'teased her so'; and when he says, 'Norah, my young May Moon, your Harry tease you?' she tells him, 'Yes; and I want to go home!'

A biled fowl, and baked bread-and-butter pudding, brought Mrs. Walmers up a little; but Boots could

have wished, he must privately own to me, to have seen her more sensible of the woice of love, and less abandoning of herself to currants. However, Master Harry, he kept up, and his noble heart was as fond as ever. Mrs. Walmers turned very sleepy about dusk, and began to cry. Therefore, Mrs. Walmers went off to bed as per yesterday; and Master Harry ditto repeated.

About eleven or twelve at night comes back the Governor in a chaise, along with Mr. Walmers and a elderly lady. Mr. Walmers looks amused and very serious, both at once, and says to our missis, 'We are much indebted to you, ma'am, for your kind care of our little children, which we can never sufficiently acknowledge. Pray, ma'am, where is my boy?' Our missis says, 'Cobbs has the dear child in charge, sir. Cobbs, show Forty!' Then he says to Cobbs, 'Ah, Cobbs, I am glad to see *you!* I understood you was here!' And Cobbs says, 'Yes, sir. Your most obedient, sir.'

I may be surprised to hear Boots say it, perhaps; but Boots assures me that his heart beat like a hammer, going upstairs. 'I beg your pardon, sir,' says he, while unlocking the door; 'I hope you are not angry with Master Harry. For Master Harry is a fine boy, sir, and will do you credit and honour.' And Boots signifies to me, that, if the fine boy's father had contradicted him in the daring state of mind in which he then was, he thinks he should have 'fetched him a crack,' and taken the consequences.

But Mr. Walmers only says, 'No, Cobbs. No, my good fellow. Thank you!' And, the door being opened, goes in.

Boots goes in too, holding the light, and he sees Mr. Walmers go up to the bedside, bend gently down, and kiss the little sleeping face. Then he stands look-

ing at it for a minute, looking wonderfully like it
(they do say he ran away with Mrs. Walmers); and
then he gently shakes the little shoulder.

'Harry, my dear boy! Harry!'

Master Harry starts up and looks at him. Looks
at Cobbs too. Such is the honour of that mite, that
he looks at Cobbs, to see whether he has brought him
into trouble.

'I am not angry, my child. I only want you to
dress yourself and come home.'

'Yes, pa.'

Master Harry dresses himself quickly. His breast
begins to swell when he has nearly finished, and it
swells more and more as he stands, at last, a looking
at his father: his father standing a looking at him, the
quiet image of him.

'Please may I'—the spirit of that little creatur, and
the way he kept his rising tears down!—'please, dear
pa—may I—kiss Norah before I go?'

'You may, my child.'

So he takes Master Harry in his hand, and Boots
leads the way with the candle, and they come to that
other bedroom, where the elderly lady is seated by the
bed, and poor little Mrs. Harry Walmers, Junior, is
fast asleep. There the father lifts the child up to
the pillow, and he lays his little face down for an
instant by the little warm face of poor unconscious
little Mrs. Harry Walmers, Junior, and gently draws
it to him,—a sight so touching to the chambermaids
who are peeping through the door, that one of them
calls out, 'It's a shame to part 'em!' But this chambermaid was always, as Boots informs me, a soft-
hearted one. Not that there was any harm in that
girl. Far from it.

Finally, Boots says, that's all about it. Mr.
Walmers drove away in the chaise, having hold of

Master Harry's hand. The elderly lady and Mrs. Harry Walmers, Junior, that was never to be (she married a Captain long afterwards, and died in India), went off next day. In conclusion, Boots put it to me whether I hold with him in two opinions: firstly, that there are not many couples on their way to be married who are half as innocent of guile as those two children; secondly, that it would be a jolly good thing for a great many couples on their way to be married, if they could only be stopped in time, and brought back separately.

THIRD BRANCH

THE BILL

I HAD been snowed up a whole week. The time had hung so lightly on my hands, that I should have been in great doubt of the fact but for a piece of documentary evidence that lay upon my table.

The road had been dug out of the snow on the previous day, and the document in question was my bill. It testified emphatically to my having eaten and drunk, and warmed myself, and slept among the sheltering branches of the Holly-Tree, seven days and nights.

I had yesterday allowed the road twenty-four hours to improve itself, finding that I required that additional margin of time for the completion of my task. I had ordered my Bill to be upon the table, and a chaise to be at the door, 'at eight o'clock to-morrow evening.' It was eight o'clock to-morrow evening when I buckled up my travelling writing-desk in its leather case, paid my Bill, and got on my warm coats

and wrappers. Of course, no time now remained for my travelling on to add a frozen tear to the icicles which were doubtless hanging plentifully about the farmhouse where I had first seen Angela. What I had to do was to get across to Liverpool by the shortest open road, there to meet my heavy baggage and embark. It was quite enough to do, and I had not an hour too much time to do it in.

I had taken leave of all my Holly-Tree friends— almost, for the time being, of my bashfulness too— and was standing for half a minute at the Inn door watching the ostler as he took another turn at the cord which tied my portmanteau on the chaise, when I saw lamps coming down towards the Holly-Tree. The road was so padded with snow that no wheels were audible; but all of us who were standing at the Inn door saw lamps coming on, and at a lively rate too, between the walls of snow that had been heaped up on either side of the track. The chambermaid instantly divined how the case stood, and called to the ostler, 'Tom, this is a Gretna job!' The ostler, knowing that her sex instinctively scented a marriage, or anything in that direction, rushed up the yard bawling, 'Next four out!' and in a moment the whole establishment was thrown into commotion.

I had a melancholy interest in seeing the happy man who loved and was beloved; and therefore, instead of driving off at once, I remained at the Inn door when the fugitives drove up. A bright-eyed fellow, muffled in a mantle, jumped out so briskly that he almost overthrew me. He turned to apologise, and, by Heaven, it was Edwin!

'Charley!' said he, recoiling. 'Gracious powers, what do you do here?'

'Edwin,' said I, recoiling, 'gracious powers, what do

you do here?' I struck my forehead as I said it, and an insupportable blaze of light seemed to shoot before my eyes.

He hurried me into the little parlour (always kept with a slow fire in it and no poker), where posting company waited while their horses were putting to, and, shutting the door, said:

'Charley, forgive me!'

'Edwin!' I returned. 'Was this well? When I loved her so dearly! When I had garnered up my heart so long!' I could say no more.

He was shocked when he saw how moved I was, and made the cruel observation, that he had not thought I should have taken it so much to heart.

I looked at him. I reproached him no more. But I looked at him.

'My dear, dear Charley,' said he, 'don't think ill of me, I beseech you! I know you have a right to my utmost confidence, and, believe me, you have ever had it until now. I abhor secrecy. Its meanness is intolerable to me. But I and my dear girl have observed it for your sake.'

He and his dear girl! It steeled me.

'You have observed it for my sake, sir?' said I, wondering how his frank face could face it out so.

'Yes!—and Angela's,' said he.

I found the room reeling round in an uncertain way, like a labouring humming-top. 'Explain yourself,' said I, holding on by one hand to an arm-chair.

'Dear old darling Charley!' returned Edwin, in his cordial manner, 'consider! When you were going on so happily with Angela, why should I compromise you with the old gentleman by making you a party to our engagement, and (after he had declined my proposals) to our secret intention? Surely it was better that you should be able honourably to say, "He never took

counsel with me, never told me, never breathed a word of it." If Angela suspected it, and showed me all the favour and support she could—God bless her for a precious creature and a priceless wife—I couldn't help that. Neither I nor Emmeline ever told her, any more than we told you. And for the same good reason, Charley; trust me, for the same good reason, and no other upon earth!'

Emmeline was Angela's cousin. Lived with her. Had been brought up with her. Was her father's ward. Had property.

'Emmeline is in the chaise, my dear Edwin!' said I, embracing him with the greatest affection.

'My good fellow!' said he, 'do you suppose I should be going to Gretna Green without her?'

I ran out with Edwin, I opened the chaise door, I took Emmeline in my arms, I folded her to my heart. She was wrapped in soft white fur, like the snowy landscape: but was warm, and young, and lovely. I put their leaders to with my own hands, I gave the boys a five-pound note apiece, I cheered them as they drove away, I drove the other way myself as hard as I could pelt.

I never went to Liverpool, I never went to America, I went straight back to London, and I married Angela. I have never until this time, even to her, disclosed the secret of my character, and the mistrust and the mistaken journey into which it led me. When she, and they, and our eight children and their seven— I mean Edwin's and Emmeline's, whose eldest girl is old enough now to wear white for herself, and to look very like her mother in it—come to read these pages, as of course they will, I shall hardly fail to be found out at last. Never mind! I can bear it. I began at the Holly-Tree, by idle accident, to associate the Christmas-time of year with human interest, and with

some inquiry into, and some care for, the lives of those by whom I find myself surrounded. I hope that I am none the worse for it, and that no one near me or afar off is the worse for it. And I say, May the green Holly-Tree flourish, striking its roots deep into our English ground, and having its germinating qualities carried by the birds of Heaven all over the world!

THE WRECK OF THE
GOLDEN MARY

[1856]

THE WRECK OF THE GOLDEN MARY

THE WRECK

I was apprenticed to the Sea when I was twelve years old, and I have encountered a great deal of rough weather, both literal and metaphorical. It has always been my opinion since I first possessed such a thing as an opinion, that the man who knows only one subject is next tiresome to the man who knows no subject. Therefore, in the course of my life I have taught myself whatever I could, and although I am not an educated man, I am able, I am thankful to say, to have an intelligent interest in most things.

A person might suppose, from reading the above, that I am in the habit of holding forth about number one. That is not the case. Just as if I was to come into a room among strangers, and must either be introduced or introduce myself, so I have taken the liberty of passing these few remarks, simply and plainly that it may be known who and what I am. I will add no more of the sort than that my name is William George Ravender, that I was born at Penrith half a year after my own father was drowned, and that I am on the second day of this present blessed Christmas week of one thousand eight hundred and fifty-six, fifty-six years of age.

When the rumour first went flying up and down that there was gold in California—which, as most people know, was before it was discovered in the British colony of Australia—I was in the West Indies, trading among the Islands. Being in command and likewise part-owner of a smart schooner, I had my work cut out for me, and I was doing it. Consequently, gold in California was no business of mine.

But, by the time when I came home to England again, the thing was as clear as your hand held up before you at noonday. There was Californian gold in the museums and in the goldsmiths' shops, and the very first time I went upon 'Change, I met a friend of mine (a seafaring man like myself), with a California nugget hanging to his watch-chain. I handled it. It was as like a peeled walnut with bits unevenly broken off here and there, and then electrotyped all over, as ever I saw anything in my life.

I am a single man (she was too good for this world and for me, and she died six weeks before our marriage-day), so when I am ashore, I live in my house at Poplar. My house at Poplar is taken care of and kept ship-shape by an old lady who was my mother's maid before I was born. She is as handsome and as upright as any old lady in the world. She is as fond of me as if she had ever had an only son, and I was he. Well do I know wherever I sail that she never lays down her head at night without having said, 'Merciful Lord! bless and preserve William George Ravender, and send him safe home, through Christ our Saviour!' I have thought of it in many a dangerous moment, when it has done me no harm, I am sure.

In my house at Poplar, along with this old lady, I lived quiet for the best part of a year: having had a long spell of it among the Islands, and having (which was very uncommon in me) taken the fever rather badly. At last, being strong and hearty, and having read every book I could lay hold of, right out, I was walking down Leadenhall Street in the City of Lon-

don, thinking of turning-to again, when I met what I call Smithick and Watersby of Liverpool. I chanced to lift up my eyes from looking in at a ship's chronometer in a window, and I saw him bearing down upon me, head on.

It is, personally, neither Smithick, nor Watersby, that I here mention, nor was I ever acquainted with any man of either of those names, nor do I think that there has been any one of either of those names in that Liverpool House for years back. But, it is in reality the House itself that I refer to; and a wiser merchant or a truer gentleman never stepped.

'My dear Captain Ravender,' says he. 'Of all the men on earth, I wanted to see you most. I was on my way to you.'

'Well!' says I. 'That looks as if you *were* to see me, don't it?' With that I put my arm in his, and we walked on towards the Royal Exchange, and when we got there, walked up and down at the back of it where the Clock-Tower is. We walked an hour and more, for he had much to say to me. He had a scheme for chartering a new ship of their own to take out a cargo to the diggers and emigrants in California, and to buy and bring back gold. Into the particulars of that scheme I will not enter, and I have no right to enter. All I say of it is, that it was a very original one, a very fine one, a very sound one, and a very lucrative one beyond doubt.

He imparted it to me as freely as if I had been a part of himself. After doing so, he made me the handsomest sharing offer that ever was made to me, boy or man—or I believe to any other captain in the Merchant Navy—and he took this round turn to finish with:

'Ravender, you are well aware that the lawlessness of that coast and country at present, is as special as

the circumstances in which it is placed. Crews of vessels outward-bound, desert as soon as they make the land; crews of vessels homeward-bound, ship at enormous wages, with the express intention of murdering the captain and seizing the gold freight; no man can trust another, and the devil seems let loose. Now,' says he, 'you know my opinion of you, and you know I am only expressing it, and with no singularity, when I tell you that you are almost the only man on whose integrity, discretion, and energy—' etc., etc. For, I don't want to repeat what he said, though I was and am sensible of it.

Notwithstanding my being, as I have mentioned, quite ready for a voyage, still I had some doubts of this voyage. Of course I knew, without being told, that there were peculiar difficulties and dangers in it, a long way over and above those which attend all voyages. It must not be supposed that I was afraid to face them; but, in my opinion a man has no manly motive or sustainment in his own breast for facing dangers, unless he has well considered what they are, and is able quietly to say to himself, 'None of these perils can now take me by surprise; I shall know what to do for the best in any of them; all the rest lies in the higher and greater hands to which I humbly commit myself.' On this principle I have so attentively considered (regarding it as my duty) all the hazards I have ever been able to think of, in the ordinary way of storm, shipwreck, and fire at sea, that I hope I should be prepared to do, in any of those cases, whatever could be done, to save the lives intrusted to my charge.

As I was thoughtful, my good friend proposed that he should leave me to walk there as long as I liked, and that I should dine with him by and by at his club in Pall Mall. I accepted the invitation and I

walked up and down there, quarter-deck fashion, a matter of a couple of hours; now and then looking up at the weathercock as I might have looked up aloft; and now and then taking a look into Cornhill, as I might have taken a look over the side.

All dinner-time, and all after dinner-time, we talked it over again. I gave him my views of his plan, and he very much approved of the same. I told him I had nearly decided, but not quite. 'Well, well,' says he, 'come down to Liverpool to-morrow with me, and see the Golden Mary.' I liked the name (her name was Mary, and she was golden, if golden stands for good), so I began to feel that it was almost done when I said I would go to Liverpool. On the next morning but one we were on board the Golden Mary. I might have known, from his asking me to come down and see her, what she was. I declare her to have been the completest and most exquisite Beauty that ever I set my eyes upon.

We had inspected every timber in her, and had come back to the gangway to go ashore from the dock-basin when I put out my hand to my friend. 'Touch upon it,' says I, 'and touch heartily. I take command of this ship, and I am hers and yours, if I can get John Steadiman for my chief mate.'

John Steadiman had sailed with me four voyages. The first voyage John was third mate out to China, and came home second. The other three voyages he was my first officer. At this time of chartering the Golden Mary, he was aged thirty-two. A brisk, bright, blue-eyed fellow, a very neat figure and rather under the middle size, never out of the way and never in it, a face that pleased everybody and that all children took to, a habit of going about singing as cheerily as a blackbird, and a perfect sailor.

We were in one of those Liverpool hackney-

coaches in less than a minute, and we cruised about
in her upwards of three hours, looking for John.
John had come home from Van Diemen's Land barely
a month before, and I had heard of him as taking a
frisk in Liverpool. We asked after him, among many
other places, at the two boarding-houses he was fond-
est of, and we found he had had a week's spell at
each of them; but, he had gone here and gone there,
and had set off 'to lay out on the main-to'-gallant-
yard of the highest Welsh mountain' (so he had told
the people of the house), and where he might be
then, or when he might come back, nobody could tell
us.   But it was surprising, to be sure, to see how every
face brightened the moment there was mention made
of the name of Mr. Steadiman.

We were taken aback at meeting with no better
luck, and we had wore ship and put her head for my
friends, when as we were jogging through the streets,
I clap my eyes on John himself coming out of a toyshop! He was carrying a little boy, and conducting
two uncommon pretty women to their coach, and he
told me afterwards that he had never in his life seen
one of the three before, but that he was so taken with
them on looking in at the toyshop while they were
buying the child a cranky Noah's Ark, very much
down by the head, that he had gone in and asked the
ladies' permission to treat him to a tolerably correct
Cutter there was in the window, in order that such a
handsome boy might not grow up with a lubberly idea
of naval architecture.

We stood off and on until the ladies' coachman began to give way, and then we hailed John. On his
coming aboard of us, I told him, very gravely, what
I had said to my friend. It struck him, as he said
himself, amidships. He was quite shaken by it.
'Captain Ravender,' were John Steadiman's words,

'such an opinion from you is true commendation, and I 'll sail round the world with you for twenty years if you hoist the signal, and stand by you for ever!' And now indeed I felt that it was done, and that the Golden Mary was afloat.

Grass never grew yet under the feet of Smithick and Watersby. The riggers were out of that ship in a fortnight's time, and we had begun taking in cargo. John was always aboard, seeing everything stowed with his own eyes; and whenever I went aboard myself early or late, whether he was below in the hold, or on deck at the hatchway, or overhauling his cabin, nailing up pictures in it of the Blush Roses of England, the Blue Belles of Scotland, and the female Shamrock of Ireland: of a certainty I heard John singing like a blackbird.

We had room for twenty passengers. Our sailing advertisement was no sooner out, than we might have taken these twenty times over. In entering our men, I and John (both together) picked them, and we entered none but good hands—as good as were to be found in that port. And so, in a good ship of the best build, well owned, well arranged, well officered, well manned, well found in all respects, we parted with our pilot at a quarter past four o'clock in the afternoon of the seventh of March, one thousand eight hundred and fifty-one, and stood with a fair wind out to sea.

It may be easily believed that up to that time I had had no leisure to be intimate with my passengers. The most of them were then in their berths sea-sick: however, in going among them, telling them what was good for them, persuading them not to be there, but to come up on deck and feel the breeze, and in rousing them with a joke, or a comfortable word, I made acquaintance with them, perhaps, in a more

friendly and confidential way from the first, than I might have done at the cabin table.

Of my passengers, I need only particularise, just at present, a bright-eyed, blooming young wife who was going out to join her husband in California, taking with her their only child, a little girl of three years old, whom he had never seen; a sedate young woman in black, some five years older (about thirty as I should say), who was going out to join a brother; and an old gentleman, a good deal like a hawk if his eyes had been better and not so red, who was always talking, morning, noon, and night, about the gold discovery.   But, whether he was making the voyage, thinking his old arms could dig for gold, or whether his speculation was to buy it, or to barter for it, or to cheat for it, or to snatch it anyhow from other people, was his secret.   He kept his secret.

These three and the child were the soonest well. The child was a most engaging child, to be sure, and very fond of me: though I am bound to admit that John Steadiman and I were borne on her pretty little books in reverse order, and that he was captain there, and I was mate.   It was beautiful to watch her with John, and it was beautiful to watch John with her. Few would have thought it possible, to see John playing at bo-peep round the mast, that he was the man who had caught up an iron bar and struck a Malay and a Maltese dead, as they were gliding with their knives down the cabin stair aboard the barque Old England, when the captain lay ill in his cot, off Saugar Point.   But he was; and give him his back against a bulwark, he would have done the same by half a dozen of them.   The name of the young mother was Mrs. Atherfield, the name of the young lady in black was Miss Coleshaw, and the name of the old gentleman was Mr. Rarx.

As the child had a quantity of shining fair hair, clustering in curls all about her face, and as her name was Lucy, Steadiman gave her the name of the Golden Lucy. So, we had the Golden Lucy and the Golden Mary; and John kept up the idea to that extent as he and the child went playing about the decks, that I believe she used to think the ship was alive somehow—a sister or companion, going to the same place as herself. She liked to be by the wheel, and in fine weather, I have often stood by the man whose trick it was at the wheel, only to hear her, sitting near my feet, talking to the ship. Never had a child such a doll before, I suppose; but she made a doll of the Golden Mary, and used to dress her up by tying ribbons and little bits of finery to the belaying-pins; and nobody ever moved them, unless it was to save them from being blown away.

Of course I took charge of the two young women, and I called them 'my dear,' and they never minded, knowing that whatever I said was said in a fatherly and protecting spirit. I gave them their places on each side of me at dinner, Mrs. Atherfield on my right and Miss Coleshaw on my left; and I directed the unmarried lady to serve out the breakfast, and the married lady to serve out the tea. Likewise I said to my black steward in their presence, 'Tom Snow, these two ladies are equally the mistresses of this house, and do you obey their orders equally'; at which Tom laughed, and they all laughed.

Old Mr. Rarx was not a pleasant man to look at, nor yet to talk to, or to be with, for no one could help seeing that he was a sordid and selfish character, and that he had warped further and further out of the straight with time. Not but what he was on his best behaviour with us, as everybody was; for we had no bickering among us, for'ard or aft. I only mean to

say, he was not the man one would have chosen for a messmate.   If choice there had been, one might even have gone a few points out of one's course, to say, 'No! Not him!'   But, there was one curious inconsistency in Mr. Rarx.   That was, that he took an astonishing interest in the child.   He looked, and I may add, he was, one of the last of men to care at all for a child, or to care much for any human creature. Still, he went so far as to be habitually uneasy, if the child was long on deck, out of his sight.   He was always afraid of her falling overboard, or falling down a hatchway, or of a block or what not coming down upon her from the rigging in the working of the ship, or of her getting some hurt or other.   He used to look at her and touch her, as if she were something precious to him.   He was always solicitous about her not injuring her health, and constantly entreated her mother to be careful of it.   This was so much the more curious, because the child did not like him, but used to shrink away from him, and would not even put out her hand to him without coaxing from others.   I believe that every soul on board frequently noticed this, and not one of us understood it.   However, it was such a plain fact, that John Steadiman said more than once when old Mr. Rarx was not within earshot, that if the Golden Mary felt a tenderness for the dear old gentleman she carried in her lap, she must be bitterly jealous of the Golden Lucy.

Before I go any further with this narrative, I will state that our ship was a barque of three hundred tons, carrying a crew of eighteen men, a second mate in addition to John, a carpenter, an armourer or smith, and two apprentices (one a Scotch boy, poor little fellow).   We had three boats; the Long-boat, capable of carrying twenty-five men; the Cutter, capable of carrying fifteen; and the Surf-boat, capable

of carrying ten. I put down the capacity of these boats according to the numbers they were really meant to hold.

We had tastes of bad weather and head-winds, of course; but, on the whole we had as fine a run as any reasonable man could expect, for sixty days. I then began to enter two remarks in the ship's Log and in my Journal; first, that there was an unusual and amazing quantity of ice; second, that the nights were most wonderfully dark, in spite of the ice.

For five days and a half, it seemed quite useless and hopeless to alter the ship's course so as to stand out of the way of this ice. I made what southing I could; but, all that time, we were beset by it. Mrs. Atherfield after standing by me on deck once, looking for some time in an awed manner at the great bergs that surrounded us, said in a whisper, 'O! Captain Ravender, it looks as if the whole solid earth had changed into ice, and broken up!' I said to her, laughing, 'I don't wonder that it does, to your inexperienced eyes, my dear.' But I had never seen a twentieth part of the quantity, and, in reality, I was pretty much of her opinion.

However, at two P.M. on the afternoon of the sixth day, that is to say, when we were sixty-six days out, John Steadiman who had gone aloft, sang out from the top, that the sea was clear ahead. Before four P.M. a strong breeze springing up right astern, we were in open water at sunset. The breeze then freshening into half a gale of wind, and the Golden Mary being a very fast sailer, we went before the wind merrily, all night.

I had thought it impossible that it could be darker than it had been, until the sun, moon, and stars should fall out of the Heavens, and Time should be destroyed; but, it had been next to light, in comparison

with what it was now. The darkness was so profound, that looking into it was painful and oppressive—like looking, without a ray of light, into a dense black bandage put as close before the eyes as it could be, without touching them. I doubled the look-out, and John and I stood in the bow side-by-side, never leaving it all night. Yet I should no more have known that he was near me when he was silent, without putting out my arm and touching him, than I should if he had turned in and been fast asleep below. We were not so much looking out, all of us, as listening to the utmost, both with our eyes and ears.

Next day, I found that the mercury in the barometer, which had risen steadily since we cleared the ice, remained steady. I had had very good observations, with now and then the interruption of a day or so, since our departure. I got the sun at noon, and found that we were in Lat. 58° S., Long. 60° W., off New South Shetland; in the neighbourhood of Cape Horn. We were sixty-seven days out, that day. The ship's reckoning was accurately worked and made up. The ship did her duty admirably, all on board were well, and all hands were as smart, efficient, and contented, as it was possible to be.

When the night came on again as dark as before, it was the eighth night I had been on deck. Nor had I taken more than a very little sleep in the day-time, my station being always near the helm, and often at it, while we were among the ice. Few but those who have tried it can imagine the difficulty and pain of only keeping the eyes open—physically open—under such circumstances, in such darkness. They get struck by the darkness, and blinded by the darkness. They make patterns in it, and they flash in it, as if they had gone out of your head to look at you. On the turn of midnight, John Steadiman, who was alert

and fresh (for I had always made him turn in by day), said to me, 'Captain Ravender, I entreat of you to go below. I am sure you can hardly stand, and your voice is getting weak, sir. Go below, and take a little rest. I'll call you if a block chafes.' I said to John in answer, 'Well, well, John! Let us wait till the turn of one o'clock, before we talk about that.' I had just had one of the ship's lanterns held up, that I might see how the night went by my watch, and it was then twenty minutes after twelve.

At five minutes before one, John sang out to the boy to bring the lantern again, and when I told him once more what the time was, entreated and prayed of me to go below. 'Captain Ravender,' says he, 'all's well; we can't afford to have you laid up for a single hour; and I respectfully and earnestly beg of you to go below.' The end of it was, that I agreed to do so, on the understanding that if I failed to come up of my own accord within three hours, I was to be punctually called. Having settled that, I left John in charge. But I called him to me once afterwards, to ask him a question. I had been to look at the barometer, and had seen the mercury still perfectly steady, and had come up the companion again to take a last look about me—if I can use such a word in reference to such darkness—when I thought that the waves, as the Golden Mary parted them and shook them off, had a hollow sound in them; something that I fancied was a rather unusual reverberation. I was standing by the quarter-deck rail on the starboard side, when I called John aft to me, and bade him listen. He did so with the greatest attention. Turning to me he then said, 'Rely upon it, Captain Ravender, you have been without rest too long, and the novelty is only in the state of your sense of hearing.' I thought so too by that time, and I think so now,

though I can never know for absolute certain in this world, whether it was or not.

When I left John Steadiman in charge, the ship was still going at a great rate through the water. The wind still blew right astern. Though she was making great way, she was under shortened sail, and had no more than she could easily carry. All was snug, and nothing complained. There was a pretty sea running, but not a very high sea neither, nor at all a confused one.

I turned in, as we seamen say, all standing. The meaning of that is, I did not pull my clothes off— no, not even so much as my coat: though I did my shoes, for my feet were badly swelled with the deck. There was a little swing-lamp alight in my cabin. I thought, as I looked at it before shutting my eyes, that I was so tired of darkness, and troubled by darkness, that I could have gone to sleep best in the midst of a million of flaming gas-lights. That was the last thought I had before I went off, except the prevailing thought that I should not be able to get to sleep at all.

I dreamed that I was back at Penrith again, and was trying to get round the church, which had altered its shape very much since I last saw it, and was cloven all down the middle of the steeple in a most singular manner. Why I wanted to get round the church I don't know; but I was as anxious to do it as if my life depended on it. Indeed, I believe it did in the dream. For all that, I could not get round the church. I was still trying, when I came against it with a violent shock, and was flung out of my cot against the ship's side. Shrieks and a terrific outcry struck me far harder than the bruising timbers, and amidst sounds of grinding and crashing, and a heavy rushing and breaking of water—sounds I understood too well—I made my way on deck. It was not an easy thing to

do, for the ship heeled over frightfully, and was beating in a furious manner.

I could not see the men as I went forward, but I
could hear that they were hauling in sail, in disorder.
I had my trumpet in my hand, and, after directing
and encouraging them in this till it was done, I hailed
first John Steadiman, and then my second mate, Mr.
William Rames. Both answered clearly and steadily.
Now, I had practised them and all my crew, as I have
ever made it a custom to practise all who sail with
me, to take certain stations and wait my orders, in
case of any unexpected crisis. When my voice was
heard hailing, and their voices were heard answering,
I was aware, through all the noises of the ship and
sea, and all the crying of the passengers below, that
there was a pause. 'Are you ready, Rames?'—'Ay,
ay, sir!'—'Then light up, for God's sake!' In a moment he and another were burning blue-lights, and
the ship and all on board seemed to be enclosed in a
mist of light, under a great black dome.

The light shone up so high that I could see the
huge Iceberg upon which we had struck, cloven at
the top and down the middle, exactly like Penrith
Church in my dream. At the same moment I could
see the watch last relieved, crowding up and down on
deck; I could see Mrs. Atherfield and Miss Coleshaw
thrown about on the top of the companion as they
struggled to bring the child up from below; I could
see that the masts were going with the shock and the
beating of the ship; I could see the frightful breach
stove in on the starboard side, half the length of the
vessel, and the sheathing and timbers spirting up; I
could see that the Cutter was disabled, in a wreck of
broken fragments: and I could see every eye turned
upon me. It is my belief that if there had been ten
thousand eyes there, I should have seen them all, with

their different looks.   And all this in a moment.   But you must consider what a moment.

I saw the men, as they looked at me, fall towards their appointed stations, like good men and true.   If she had not righted, they could have done very little there or anywhere but die—not that it is little for a man to die at his post—I mean they could have done nothing to save the passengers and themselves.   Happily, however, the violence of the shock with which we had so determinedly borne down direct on that fatal Iceberg, as if it had been our destination instead of our destruction, had so smashed and pounded the ship that she got off in this same instant and righted.   I did not want the carpenter to tell me she was filling and going down; I could see and hear that.   I gave Rames the word to lower the Long-boat and the Surf-boat, and I myself told off the men for each duty. Not one hung back, or came before the other.   I now whispered to John Steadiman, 'John, I stand at the gangway here, to see every soul on board safe over the side.   You shall have the next post of honour, and shall be the last but one to leave the ship.   Bring up the passengers, and range them behind me; and put what provision and water you can get at, in the boats. Cast your eye for'ard, John, and you 'll see you have not a moment to lose.'

My noble fellows got the boats over the side as orderly as I ever saw boats lowered with any sea running, and, when they were launched, two or three of the nearest men in them as they held on, rising and falling with the swell, called out, looking up at me, 'Captain Ravender, if anything goes wrong with us, and you are saved, remember we stood by you!'— 'We 'll all stand by one another ashore, yet, please God, my lads!' says I.   'Hold on bravely, and be tender with the women.'

The women were an example to us. They trembled very much, but they were quiet and perfectly collected. 'Kiss me, Captain Ravender,' says Mrs. Atherfield, 'and God in heaven bless you, you good man!' 'My dear,' says I, 'those words are better for me than a life-boat,' I held her child in my arms till she was in the boat, and then kissed the child and handed her safe down. I now said to the people in her, 'You have got your freight, my lads, all but me, and I am not coming yet awhile. Pull away from the ship, and keep off!'

That was the Long-boat. Old Mr. Rarx was one of her complement, and he was the only passenger who had greatly misbehaved since the ship struck. Others had been a little wild, which was not to be wondered at, and not very blamable; but, he had made a lamentation and uproar which it was dangerous for the people to hear, as there is always contagion in weakness and selfishness. His incessant cry had been that he must not be separated from the child, that he couldn't see the child, and that he and the child must go together. He had even tried to wrest the child out of my arms, that he might keep her in his. 'Mr. Rarx,' said I to him when it came to that, 'I have a loaded pistol in my pocket; and if you don't stand out of the gangway, and keep perfectly quiet, I shall shoot you through the heart, if you have got one.' Says he, 'You won't do murder, Captain Ravender!' 'No, sir,' says I, 'I won't murder forty-four people to humour you, but I'll shoot you to save them.' After that he was quiet, and stood shivering a little way off, until I named him to go over the side.

The Long-boat being cast off, the Surf-boat was soon filled. There only remained aboard the Golden Mary, John Mullion the man who had kept on burning the blue-lights (and who had lighted every new

one at every old one before it went out, as quietly
as if he had been at an illumination); John Steadiman; and myself.   I hurried those two into the Surf-
boat, called to them to keep off, and waited with a
grateful and relieved heart for the Long-boat to come
and take me in, if she could.   I looked at my watch,
and it showed me, by the blue-light, ten minutes past
two.   They lost no time.   As soon as she was near
enough, I swung myself into her, and called to the
men, 'With a will, lads!   She's reeling!'   We were
not an inch too far out of the inner vortex of her
going down, when, by the blue-light which John Mullion still burnt in the bow of the Surf-boat, we saw
her lurch, and plunge to the bottom head-foremost.
The child cried, weeping wildly, 'O the dear Golden
Mary!   O look at her!   Save her!   Save the poor
Golden Mary!'   And then the light burnt out, and
the black dome seemed to come down upon us.

I suppose if we had all stood a-top of a mountain,
and seen the whole remainder of the world sink away
from under us, we could hardly have felt more shocked
and solitary than we did when we knew we were alone
on the wide ocean, and that the beautiful ship in which
most of us had been securely asleep within half an
hour was gone forever.   There was an awful silence
in our boat, and such a kind of palsy on the rowers
and the man at the rudder, that I felt they were
scarcely keeping her before the sea.   I spoke out then,
and said, 'Let every one here thank the Lord for our
preservation!'   All the voices answered (even the
child's), 'We thank the Lord!'   I then said the Lord's
Prayer, and all hands said it after me with a solemn
murmuring.   Then I gave the word, 'Cheerily, O
men, Cheerily!' and I felt that they were handling
the boat again as a boat ought to be handled.

The Surf-boat now burnt another blue-light to

show us where they were, and we made for her, and laid ourselves as nearly alongside of her as we dared. I had always kept my boats with a coil or two of good stout stuff in each of them, so both boats had a rope at hand. We made a shift, with much labour and trouble, to get near enough to one another to divide the blue-lights (they were no use after that night, for the sea-water soon got at them), and to get a tow-rope out between us. All night long we kept together, sometimes obliged to cast off the rope, and sometimes getting it out again, and all of us wearying for the morning—which appeared so long in coming that old Mr. Rarx screamed out, in spite of his fears of me, 'The world is drawing to an end, and the sun will never rise any more!'

When the day broke, I found that we were all huddled together in a miserable manner. We were deep in the water; being, as I found on mustering, thirty-one in number, or at least six too many. In the Surf-boat they were fourteen in number, being at least four too many. The first thing I did, was to get myself passed to the rudder—which I took from that time—and to get Mrs. Atherfield, her child, and Miss Coleshaw, passed on to sit next me. As to old Mr. Rarx, I put him in the bow, as far from us as I could. And I put some of the best men near us in order that if I should drop there might be a skilful hand ready to take the helm.

The sea moderating as the sun came up, though the sky was cloudy and wild, we spoke the other boat, to know what stores they had, and to overhaul what we had. I had a compass in my pocket, a small telescope, a double-barrelled pistol, a knife, and a fire-box and matches. Most of my men had knives, and some had a little tobacco: some, a pipe as well. We had a mug among us, and an iron spoon. As to

provisions, there were in my boat two bags of biscuit, one piece of raw beef, one piece of raw pork, a bag of coffee, roasted but not ground (thrown in, I imagine, by mistake, for something else), two small casks of water, and about half-a-gallon of rum in a keg. The Surf-boat, having rather more rum than we, and fewer to drink it, gave us, as I estimated, another quart into our keg. In return, we gave them three double handfuls of coffee, tied up in a piece of a handkerchief; they reported that they had aboard besides, a bag of biscuit, a piece of beef, a small cask of water, a small box of lemons, and a Dutch cheese. It took a long time to make these exchanges, and they were not made without risk to both parties; the sea running quite high enough to make our approaching near to one another very hazardous. In the bundle with the coffee, I conveyed to John Steadiman (who had a ship's compass with him), a paper written in pencil, and torn from my pocket-book, containing the course I meant to steer, in the hope of making land, or being picked up by some vessel—I say in the hope, though I had little hope of either deliverance. I then sang out to him, so as all might hear, that if we two boats could live or die together, we would; but, that if we should be parted by the weather, and join company no more, they should have our prayers and blessings, and we asked for theirs. We then gave them three cheers, which they returned, and I saw the men's heads droop in both boats as they fell to their oars again.

These arrangements had occupied the general attention advantageously for all, though (as I expressed in the last sentence) they ended in a sorrowful feeling. I now said a few words to my fellow-voyagers on the subject of the small stock of food on which our lives depended if they were preserved from the

great deep, and on the rigid necessity of our eking it out in the most frugal manner. One and all replied that whatever allowance I thought best to lay down should be strictly kept to. We made a pair of scales out of a thin strap of iron-plating and some twine, and I got together for weights such of the heaviest buttons among us as I calculated made up some fraction over two ounces. This was the allowance of solid food served out once a-day to each, from that time to the end; with the addition of a coffee-berry, or sometimes half a one, when the weather was very fair, for breakfast. We had nothing else whatever, but half a pint of water each per day, and sometimes, when we were coldest and weakest, a teaspoonful of rum each, served out as a dram. I know how learnedly it can be shown that rum is poison, but I also know that in this case, as in all similar cases I have ever read of—which are numerous—no words can express the comfort and support derived from it. Nor have I the least doubt that it saved the lives of far more than half our number. Having mentioned half a pint of water as our daily allowance, I ought to observe that sometimes we had less, and sometimes we had more; for much rain fell, and we caught it in a canvas stretched for the purpose.

Thus, at that tempestuous time of the year, and in that tempestuous part of the world, we shipwrecked people rose and fell with the waves. It is not my intention to relate (if I can avoid it) such circumstances appertaining to our doleful condition as have been better told in many other narratives of the kind than I can be expected to tell them. I will only note, in so many passing words, that day after day and night after night, we received the sea upon our backs to prevent it from swamping the boat; that one party was always kept baling, and that every hat and cap

among us soon got worn out, though patched up fifty times, as the only vessels we had for that service; that another party lay down in the bottom of the boat, while a third rowed; and that we were soon all in boils and blisters and rags.

The other boat was a source of such anxious interest to all of us that I used to wonder whether, if we were saved, the time could ever come when the survivors in this boat of ours could be at all indifferent to the fortunes of the survivors in that. We got out a tow-rope whenever the weather permitted, but that did not often happen, and how we two parties kept within the same horizon, as we did, He, who mercifully permitted it to be so for our consolation, only knows. I never shall forget the looks with which, when the morning light came, we used to gaze about us over the stormy waters, for the other boat. We once parted company for seventy-two hours, and we believed them to have gone down, as they did us. The joy on both sides when we came within view of one another again, had something in a manner Divine in it; each was so forgetful of individual suffering, in tears of delight and sympathy for the people in the other boat.

I have been wanting to get round to the individual or personal part of my subject, as I call it, and the foregoing incident puts me in the right way. The patience and good disposition aboard of us, was wonderful. I was not surprised by it in the women; for all men born of women know what great qualities they will show when men will fail; but, I own I was a little surprised by it in some of the men. Among one-and-thirty people assembled at the best of times, there will usually, I should say, be two or three uncertain tempers. I knew that I had more than one rough temper with me among my own people, for I

had chosen those for the Longboat that I might have them under my eye. But, they softened under their misery, and were as considerate of the ladies, and as compassionate of the child, as the best among us, or among men—they could not have been more so. I heard scarcely any complaining. The party lying down would moan a good deal in their sleep, and I would often notice a man—not always the same man, it is to be understood, but nearly all of them at one time or other—sitting moaning at his oar, or in his place, as he looked mistily over the sea. When it happened to be long before I could catch his eye, he would go on moaning all the time in the dismallest manner; but, when our looks met, he would brighten and leave off. I almost always got the impression that he did not know what sound he had been making, but that he thought he had been humming a tune.

Our sufferings from cold and wet were far greater than our sufferings from hunger. We managed to keep the child warm; but, I doubt if any one else among us ever was warm for five minutes together; and the shivering, and the chattering of teeth, were sad to hear. The child cried a little at first for her lost playfellow, the Golden Mary; but hardly ever whimpered afterwards; and when the state of the weather made it possible, she used now and then to be held up in the arms of some of us, to look over the sea for John Steadiman's boat. I see the golden hair and the innocent face now, between me and the driving clouds, like an angel going to fly away.

It had happened on the second day, towards night, that Mrs. Atherfield, in getting Little Lucy to sleep, sang her a song. She had a soft, melodious voice, and, when she had finished it, our people up and begged for another. She sang them another, and after it had fallen dark ended with the Evening Hymn.

From that time, whenever anything could be heard
above the sea and wind, and while she had any voice
left, nothing would serve the people but that she
should sing at sunset. She always did, and always
ended with the Evening Hymn. We mostly took
up the last line, and shed tears when it was done, but
not miserably. We had a prayer night and morning,
also, when the weather allowed of it.

Twelve nights and eleven days we had been driving in the boat, when old Mr. Rarx began to be deliri-
ous, and to cry out to me to throw the gold overboard
or it would sink us, and we should all be lost. For
days past the child had been declining, and that was
the great cause of his wildness. He had been over
and over again shrieking out to me to give her all the
remaining meat, to give her all the remaining rum,
to save her at any cost, or we should all be ruined. At
this time, she lay in her mother's arms at my feet.
One of her little hands was almost always creeping
about her mother's neck or chin. I had watched the
wasting of the little hand, and I knew it was nearly
over.

The old man's cries were so discordant with the
mother's love and submission, that I called out to him
in an angry voice, unless he held his peace on the instant, I would order him to be knocked on the head
and thrown overboard. He was mute then, until the
child died, very peacefully, an hour afterwards:
which was known to all in the boat by the mother's
breaking out into lamentations for the first time since
the wreck—for, she had great fortitude and constancy, though she was a little, gentle woman. Old
Mr. Rarx then became quite ungovernable, tearing
what rags he had on him, raging in imprecations, and
calling to me that if I had thrown the gold overboard

(always the gold with him!) I might have saved the child. 'And now,' says he, in a terrible voice, 'we shall founder, and all go to the Devil, for our sins will sink us, when we have no innocent child to bear us up!' We so discovered with amazement, that this old wretch had only cared for the life of the pretty little creature dear to all of us, because of the influence he superstitiously hoped she might have in preserving him! Altogether it was too much for the smith or armourer, who was sitting next the old man, to bear. He took him by the throat and rolled him under the thwarts, where he lay still enough for hours afterwards.

All that thirteenth night, Miss Coleshaw, lying across my knees as I kept the helm, comforted and supported the poor mother. Her child, covered with a pea-jacket of mine, lay in her lap. It troubled me all night to think that there was no Prayer-Book among us, and that I could remember but very few of the exact words of the burial service. When I stood up at broad day, all knew what was going to be done, and I noticed that my poor fellows made the motion of uncovering their heads, though their heads had been stark bare to the sky and sea for many a weary hour. There was a long heavy swell on, but otherwise it was a fair morning, and there were broad fields of sunlight on the waves in the east. I said no more than this: 'I am the Resurrection and the Life, saith the Lord. He raised the daughter of Jairus the ruler, and said she was not dead but slept. He raised the widow's son. He arose Himself, and was seen of many. He loved little children, saying, Suffer them to come unto Me and rebuke them not, for of such is the kingdom of heaven. In His name, my friends, and committed to His merciful goodness!' With

those words I laid my rough face softly on the placid little forehead, and buried the Golden Lucy in the grave of the Golden Mary.

Having had it on my mind to relate the end of this dear little child, I have omitted something from its exact place, which I will supply here. It will come quite as well here as anywhere else.

Foreseeing that if the boat lived through the stormy weather, the time must come, and soon come, when we should have absolutely no morsel to eat, I had one momentous point often in my thoughts. Although I had, years before that, fully satisfied myself that the instances in which human beings in the last distress have fed upon each other, are exceedingly few, and have very seldom indeed (if ever) occurred when the people in distress, however dreadful their extremity, have been accustomed to moderate forbearance and restraint; I say, though I had long before quite satisfied my mind on this topic, I felt doubtful whether there might not have been in former cases some harm and danger from keeping it out of sight and pretending not to think of it. I felt doubtful whether some minds, growing weak with fasting and exposure and having such a terrific idea to dwell upon in secret, might not magnify it until it got to have an awful attraction about it. This was not a new thought of mine, for it had grown out of my reading. However, it came over me stronger than it had ever done before—as it had reason for doing—in the boat, and on the fourth day I decided that I would bring out into the light that unformed fear which must have been more or less darkly in every brain among us. Therefore, as a means of beguiling the time and inspiring hope, I gave them the best summary in my power of Bligh's voyage of more than three thousand miles, in an open boat, after the Mutiny of the

Bounty, and of the wonderful preservation of that boat's crew. They listened throughout with great interest, and I concluded by telling them, that, in my opinion, the happiest circumstance in the whole narrative was, that Bligh, who was no delicate man either, had solemnly placed it on record therein that he was sure and certain that under no conceivable circumstances whatever would that emaciated party, who had gone through all the pains of famine, have preyed on one another. I cannot describe the visible relief which this spread through the boat, and how the tears stood in every eye. From that time I was as well convinced as Bligh himself that there was no danger, and that this phantom, at any rate, did not haunt us.

Now, it was a part of Bligh's experience that when the people in his boat were most cast down, nothing did them so much good as hearing a story told by one of their number. When I mentioned that, I saw that it struck the general attention as much as it did my own, for I had not thought of it until I came to it in my summary. This was on the day after Mrs. Atherfield first sang to us. I proposed that, whenever the weather would permit, we should have a story two hours after dinner (I always issued the allowance I have mentioned at one o'clock, and called it by that name), as well as our song at sunset. The proposal was received with a cheerful satisfaction that warmed my heart within me; and I do not say too much when I say that those two periods in the four-and-twenty hours were expected with positive pleasure, and were really enjoyed by all hands. Spectres as we soon were in our bodily wasting, our imaginations did not perish like the gross flesh upon our bones. Music and Adventure, two of the great gifts of Providence to mankind, could charm us long after that was lost.

The wind was almost always against us after the

second day; and for many days together we could not nearly hold our own. We had all varieties of bad weather. We had rain, hail, snow, wind, mist, thunder and lightning. Still the boats lived through the heavy seas, and still we perishing people rose and fell with the great waves.

Sixteen nights and fifteen days, twenty nights and nineteen days, twenty-four nights and twenty-three days. So the time went on. Disheartening as I knew that our progress, or want of progress, must be, I never deceived them as to my calculations of it. In the first place, I felt that we were all too near eternity for deceit; in the second place, I knew that if I failed, or died, the man who followed me must have a knowledge of the true state of things to begin upon. When I told them at noon, what I reckoned we had made or lost, they generally received what I said in a tranquil and resigned manner, and always gratefully towards me. It was not unusual at any time of the day for some one to burst out weeping loudly without any new cause; and, when the burst was over, to calm down a little better than before. I had seen exactly the same thing in a house of mourning.

During the whole of this time, old Mr. Rarx had had his fits of calling out to me to throw the gold (always the gold!) overboard, and of heaping violent reproaches upon me for not having saved the child; but now, the food being all gone, and I having nothing left to serve out but a bit of coffee-berry now and then, he began to be too weak to do this, and consequently fell silent. Mrs. Atherfield and Miss Coleshaw generally lay, each with an arm across one of my knees, and her head upon it. They never complained at all. Up to the time of her child's death, Mrs. Atherfield had bound up her own beautiful hair every day; and I took particular notice that this was

always before she sang her song at night, when every one looked at her. But she never did it after the loss of her darling; and it would have been now all tangled with dirt and wet, but that Miss Coleshaw was careful of it long after she was herself, and would sometimes smooth it down with her weak, thin hands.

We were past mustering a story now; but one day, at about this period, I reverted to the superstition of old Mr. Rarx, concerning the Golden Lucy, and told them that nothing vanished from the eye of God, though much might pass away from the eyes of men. 'We were all of us,' says I, 'children once; and our baby feet have strolled in green woods ashore; and our baby hands have gathered flowers in gardens, where the birds were singing. The children that we were, are not lost to the great knowledge of our Creator. Those innocent creatures will appear with us before Him, and plead for us. What we were in the best time of our generous youth will arise and go with us too. The purest part of our lives will not desert us at the pass to which all of us here present are gliding. What we were then, will be as much in existence before Him, as what we are now.' They were no less comforted by this consideration, than I was myself; and Miss Coleshaw, drawing my ear nearer to her lips, said, 'Captain Ravender, I was on my way to marry a disgraced and broken man, whom I dearly loved when he was honourable and good. Your words seem to have come out of my own poor heart.' She pressed my hand upon it, smiling.

Twenty-seven nights and twenty-six days. We were in no want of rain-water, but we had nothing else. And yet, even now, I never turned my eyes upon a waking face but it tried to brighten before

mine.   O, what a thing it is, in a time of danger and in the presence of death, the shining of a face upon a face!   I have heard it broached that orders should be given in great new ships by electric telegraph.   I admire machinery as much as any man, and am as thankful to it as any man can be for what it does for us.   But it will never be a substitute for the face of a man, with his soul in it, encouraging another man to be brave and true.   Never try it for that.   It will break down like a straw.

I now began to remark certain changes in myself which I did not like.   They caused me much disquiet. I often saw the Golden Lucy in the air above the boat.   I often saw her I have spoken of before, sitting beside me.   I saw the Golden Mary go down, as she really had gone down, twenty times in a day. And yet the sea was mostly, to my thinking, not sea neither, but moving country and extraordinary mountainous regions, the like of which have never been beheld.   I felt it time to leave my last words regarding John Steadiman, in case any lips should last out to repeat them to any living ears.   I said that John had told me (as he had on deck) that he had sung out 'Breakers ahead!' the instant they were audible, and had tried to wear ship, but she struck before it could be done.   (His cry, I dare say, had made my dream.) I said that the circumstances were altogether without warning, and out of any course that could have been guarded against; that the same loss would have happened if I had been in charge; and that John was not to blame, but from first to last had done his duty nobly, like the man he was.   I tried to write it down in my pocket-book, but could make no words, though I knew what the words were that I wanted to make. When it had come to that, her hands—though she was dead so long—laid me down gently in the bottom of

the boat, and she and the Golden Lucy swung me to sleep.

All that follows, was written by John Steadiman, Chief Mate:

On the twenty-sixth day after the foundering of the Golden Mary at sea, I, John Steadiman, was sitting in my place in the stern-sheets of the Surf-boat, with just sense enough left in me to steer—that is to say, with my eyes strained, wide-awake, over the bows of the boat, and my brains fast asleep and dreaming —when I was roused upon a sudden by our second mate, Mr. William Rames.

'Let me take a spell in your place,' says he. 'And look you out for the Long-boat astern. The last time she rose on the crest of a wave, I thought I made out a signal flying aboard her.'

We shifted our places, clumsily and slowly enough, for we were both of us weak and dazed with wet, cold, and hunger. I waited some time, watching the heavy rollers astern, before the Long-boat rose a-top of one of them at the same time with us. At last, she was heaved up for a moment well in view, and there, sure enough, was the signal flying aboard of her—a strip of rag of some sort, rigged to an oar, and hoisted in her bows.

'What does it mean?' says Rames to me in a quavering, trembling sort of voice. 'Do they signal a sail in sight?'

'Hush, for God's sake!' says I, clapping my hand over his mouth. 'Don't let the people hear you. They'll all go mad together if we mislead them about that signal. Wait a bit, till I have another look at it.'

I held on by him, for he had set me all of a tremble

with his notion of a sail in sight, and watched for the Long-boat again.   Up she rose on the top of another roller.   I made out the signal clearly, that second time, and saw that it was rigged half-mast high.

'Rames,' says I, 'it's a signal of distress.   Pass the word forward to keep her before the sea, and no more.   We must get the Long-boat within hailing distance of us, as soon as possible.'

I dropped down into my old place at the tiller without another word—for the thought went through me like a knife that something had happened to Captain Ravender.   I should consider myself unworthy to write another line of this statement, if I had not made up my mind to speak the truth, the whole truth, and nothing but the truth—and I must, therefore, confess plainly that now, for the first time, my heart sank within me.   This weakness on my part was produced in some degree, as I take it, by the exhausting effects of previous anxiety and grief.

Our provisions—if I may give that name to what we had left—were reduced to the rind of one lemon and about a couple of handsfull of coffee-berries. Besides these great distresses, caused by the death, the danger, and the suffering among my crew and passengers, I had had a little distress of my own to shake me still more, in the death of the child whom I had got to be very fond of on the voyage out—so fond that I was secretly a little jealous of her being taken in the Long-boat instead of mine when the ship foundered. It used to be a great comfort to me, and I think to those with me also, after we had seen the last of the Golden Mary, to see the Golden Lucy, held up by the men in the Long-boat, when the weather allowed it, as the best and brightest sight they had to show. She looked, at the distance we saw her from, almost like a little white bird in the air.   To miss her for

the first time, when the weather lulled a little again, and we all looked out for our white bird and looked in vain, was a sore disappointment. To see the men's heads bowed down and the captain's hand pointing into the sea when we hailed the Long-boat, a few days after, gave me as heavy a shock and as sharp a pang of heartache to bear as ever I remember suffering in all my life. I only mention these things to show that if I did give way a little at first, under the dread that our captain was lost to us, it was not without having been a good deal shaken beforehand by more trials of one sort or another than often fall to one man's share.

I had got over the choking in my throat with the help of a drop of water, and had steadied my mind again so as to be prepared against the worst, when I heard the hail (Lord help the poor fellows, how weak it sounded!) —

'Surf-boat, ahoy!'

I looked up, and there were our companions in misfortune tossing abreast of us; not so near that we could make out the features of any of them, but near enough, with some exertion for people in our condition, to make their voices heard in the intervals when the wind was weakest.

I answered the hail, and waited a bit, and heard nothing, and then sung out the captain's name. The voice that replied did not sound like his; the words that reached us were:

'Chief-mate wanted on board!'

Every man of my crew knew what that meant as well as I did. As second officer in command, there could be but one reason for wanting me on board the Long-boat. A groan went all round us, and my men looked darkly in each other's faces, and whispered under their breaths:

'The captain is dead!'

I commanded them to be silent, and not to make too sure of bad news, at such a pass as things had now come to with us. Then, hailing the Long-boat, I signified that I was ready to go on board when the weather would let me—stopped a bit to draw a good long breath—and then called out as loud as I could the dreadful question:

'Is the captain dead?'

The black figures of three or four men in the after-part of the Long-boat all stooped down together as my voice reached them. They were lost to view for about a minute; then appeared again—one man among them was held up on his feet by the rest, and he hailed back the blessed words (a very faint hope went a very long way with people in our desperate situation): 'Not yet!'

The relief felt by me, and by all with me, when we knew that our captain, though unfitted for duty, was not lost to us, it is not in words—at least, not in such words as a man like me can command—to express. I did my best to cheer the men by telling them what a good sign it was that we were not as badly off yet as we had feared; and then communicated what instructions I had to give, to William Rames, who was to be left in command in my place when I took charge of the Long-boat. After that, there was nothing to be done, but to wait for the chance of the wind dropping at sunset, and the sea going down afterwards, so as to enable our weak crews to lay the two boats alongside of each other, without undue risk—or, to put it plainer, without saddling ourselves with the necessity for any extraordinary exertion of strength or skill. Both the one and the other had now been starved out of us for days and days to-gether.

At sunset the wind suddenly dropped, but the sea, which had been running high for so long a time past, took hours after that before it showed any signs of getting to rest. The moon was shining, the sky was wonderfully clear, and it could not have been, according to my calculations, far off midnight, when the long, slow, regular swell of the calming ocean fairly set in, and I took the responsibility of lessening the distance between the Long-boat and ourselves.

It was, I dare say, a delusion of mine; but I thought I had never seen the moon shine so white and ghastly anywhere, either at sea or on land, as she shone that night while we were approaching our companions in misery. When there was not much more than a boat's length between us, and the white light streamed cold and clear over all our faces, both crews rested on their oars with one great shudder, and stared over the gunwale of either boat, panic-stricken at the first sight of each other.

'Any lives lost among you?' I asked, in the midst of that frightful silence.

The men in the Long-boat huddled together like sheep at the sound of my voice.

'None yet, but the child, thanks be to God!' answered one among them.

And at the sound of his voice, all my men shrank together like the men in the Long-boat. I was afraid to let the horror produced by our first meeting at close quarters after the dreadful changes that wet, cold, and famine had produced, last one moment longer than could be helped; so, without giving time for any more questions and answers, I commanded the men to lay the two boats close alongside of each other. When I rose up and committed the tiller to the hands of Rames, all my poor fellows raised their white faces imploringly to mine. 'Don't leave us, sir,' they said,

'don't leave us.' 'I leave you,' says I, 'under the command and the guidance of Mr. William Rames, as good a sailor as I am, and as trusty and kind a man as ever stepped. Do your duty by him, as you have done it by me; and remember to the last, that while there is life there is hope. God bless and help you all!' With those words I collected what strength I had left, and caught at two arms that were held out to me, and so got from the stern-sheets of one boat into the stern-sheets of the other.

'Mind where you step, sir,' whispered one of the men who had helped me into the Long-boat. I looked down as he spoke. Three figures were huddled up below me, with the moonshine falling on them in ragged streaks through the gaps between the men standing or sitting above them. The first face I made out was the face of Miss Coleshaw; her eyes were wide open and fixed on me. She seemed still to keep her senses, and, by the alternate parting and closing of her lips, to be trying to speak, but I could not hear that she uttered a single word. On her shoulder rested the head of Mrs. Atherfield. The mother of our poor little Golden Lucy must, I think, have been dreaming of the child she had lost; for there was a faint smile just ruffling the white stillness of her face, when I first saw it turned upward, with peaceful closed eyes towards the heavens. From her, I looked down a little, and there, with his head on her lap, and with one of her hands resting tenderly on his cheek—there lay the Captain, to whose help and guidance, up to this miserable time, we had never looked in vain,—there, worn out at last in our service, and for our sakes, lay the best and bravest man of all our company. I stole my hand in gently through his clothes and laid it on his heart, and felt a little feeble warmth over it, though my cold dulled touch could

not detect even the faintest beating.   The two men
in the stern-sheets with me, noticing what I was doing
—knowing I loved him like a brother—and seeing,
I suppose, more distress in my face than I myself was
conscious of its showing, lost command over themselves
altogether, and burst into a piteous moaning, sobbing
lamentation over him.   One of the two drew aside a
jacket from his feet, and showed me that they were
bare, except where a wet, ragged strip of stocking still
clung to one of them.   When the ship struck the
Iceberg, he had run on deck leaving his shoes in his
cabin.   All through the voyage in the boat his feet
had been unprotected; and not a soul had discovered
it until he dropped!   As long as he could keep his
eyes open, the very look of them had cheered the men,
and comforted and upheld the women.   Not one
living creature in the boat, with any sense about him,
but had felt the good influence of that brave man in
one way or another.   Not one but had heard him,
over and over again, give the credit to others which
was due only to himself; praising this man for
patience, and thanking that man for help, when the
patience and the help had really and truly, as to the
best part of both, come only from him.   All this, and
much more, I heard pouring confusedly from the
men's lips while they crouched down, sobbing and crying over their commander, and wrapping the jacket
as warmly and tenderly as they could over his cold
feet.   It went to my heart to check them; but I knew
that if this lamenting spirit spread any further, all
chance of keeping alight any last sparks of hope and
resolution among the boat's company would be lost for
ever.   Accordingly I sent them to their places, spoke
a few encouraging words to the men forward, promising to serve out, when the morning came, as much as
I dared, of any eatable thing left in the lockers; called

to Rames, in my old boat, to keep as near us as he safely could; drew the garments and coverings of the two poor suffering women more closely about them; and, with a secret prayer to be directed for the best in bearing the awful responsibility now laid on my shoulders, took my Captain's vacant place at the helm of the Long-boat.

This, as well as I can tell it, is the full and true account of how I came to be placed in charge of the lost passengers and crew of the Golden Mary, on the morning of the twenty-seventh day after the ship struck the Iceberg, and foundered at sea.

THE PERILS OF CERTAIN ENGLISH PRISONERS

[1857]

THE PERILS OF CERTAIN ENGLISH PRISONERS

IN TWO CHAPTERS

CHAPTER I

THE ISLAND OF SILVER-STORE

IT was in the year of our Lord one thousand seven hundred and forty-four, that I, Gill Davis to command, His Mark, having then the honour to be a private in the Royal Marines, stood a-leaning over the bulwarks of the armed sloop Christopher Columbus, in the South American waters off the Mosquito shore.

My lady remarks to me, before I go any further, that there is no such christian-name as Gill, and that her confident opinion is, that the name given to me in the baptism wherein I was made, etc., was Gilbert. She is certain to be right, but I never heard of it. I was a foundling child, picked up somewhere or another, and I always understood my christian-name to be Gill. It is true that I was called Gills when employed at Snorridge Bottom betwixt Chatham and Maidstone to frighten birds; but that had nothing to do with the Baptism wherein I was made, etc., and wherein a number of things were promised for me by somebody, who let me alone ever afterwards as to performing any of them, and who, I consider, must have been the Beadle. Such name of Gills was entirely owing to my cheeks, or gills, which at that time of life were of a raspy description.

My lady stops me again, before I go any further, by laughing exactly in her old way and waving the feather of her pen at me. That action on her part calls to my mind as I look at her hand with the rings on it—Well! I won't! To be sure it will come in, in its own place. But it's always strange to me, noticing the quiet hand, and noticing it (as I have done, you know, so many times) a-fondling children and grandchildren asleep, to think that when blood and honour were up—there! I won't! not at present!— Scratch it out.

She won't scratch it out, and quite honourable; because we have made an understanding that everything is to be taken down, and that nothing that is once taken down shall be scratched out. I have the great misfortune not to be able to read and write, and I am speaking my true and faithful account of those Adventures, and my lady is writing it, word for word.

I say, there I was, a-leaning over the bulwarks of the sloop Christopher Columbus in the South American waters off the Mosquito shore: a subject of his Gracious Majesty King George of England, and a private in the Royal Marines.

In those climates, you don't want to do much. I was doing nothing. I was thinking of the shepherd (my father, I wonder?) on the hill-sides by Snorridge Bottom, with a long staff, and with a rough white coat in all weathers all the year round, who used to let me lie in a corner of his hut by night, and who used to let me go about with him and his sheep by day when I could get nothing else to do, and who used to give me so little of his victuals and so much of his staff, that I ran away from him—which was what he wanted all along, I expect—to be knocked about the world in

preference to Snorridge Bottom. I had been knocked about the world for nine-and-twenty years in all, when I stood looking along those bright blue South American Waters. Looking after the shepherd, I may say. Watching him in a half-waking dream, with my eyes half-shut, as he, and his flock of sheep, and his two dogs, seemed to move away from the ship's side, far away over the blue water, and go right down into the sky.

'It's rising out of the water, steady,' a voice said close to me. I had been thinking on so, that it like woke me with a start, though it was no stranger voice than the voice of Harry Charker, my own comrade.

'What's rising out of the water, steady?' I asked my comrade.

'What?' says he. 'The Island.'

'O! The Island!' says I, turning my eyes towards it. 'True. I forgot the Island.'

'Forgot the port you're going to? That's odd, ain't it?'

'It is odd,' says I.

'And odd,' he said, slowly considering with himself, 'ain't even. Is it, Gill?'

He had always a remark just like that to make, and seldom another. As soon as he had brought a thing round to what it was not, he was satisfied. He was one of the best of men, and, in a certain sort of a way, one with the least to say for himself. I qualify it, because, besides being able to read and write like a Quarter-master, he had always one most excellent idea in his mind. That was, Duty. Upon my soul, I don't believe, though I admire learning beyond everything, that he could have got a better idea out of all the books in the world, if he had learnt them every word, and been the cleverest of scholars.

My comrade and I had been quartered in Jamaica,

and from there we had been drafted off to the British settlement of Belize, lying away West and North of the Mosquito coast.   At Belize there had been great alarm of one cruel gang of pirates (there were always more pirates than enough in those Caribbean Seas), and as they got the better of our English cruisers by running into out-of-the-way creeks and shallows, and taking the land when they were hotly pressed, the governor of Belize had received orders from home to keep a sharp look-out for them along shore.   Now, there was an armed sloop came once a-year from Port Royal, Jamaica, to the Island, laden with all manner of necessaries, to eat, and to drink, and to wear, and to use in various ways; and it was aboard of that sloop which had touched at Belize, that I was a-standing, leaning over the bulwarks.

The Island was occupied by a very small English colony.   It had been given the name of Silver-Store. The reason of its being so called, was, that the English colony owned and worked a silver mine over on the mainland, in Honduras, and used this Island as a safe and convenient place to store their silver in, until it was annually fetched away by the sloop.   It was brought down from the mine to the coast on the backs of mules, attended by friendly Indians and guarded by white men; from thence it was conveyed over to Silver-Store, when the weather was fair, in the canoes of that country; from Silver-Store, it was carried to Jamaica by the armed sloop once a-year, as I have already mentioned; from Jamaica, it went, of course, all over the world.

How I came to be aboard the armed sloop, is easily told.   Four-and-twenty marines under command of a lieutenant—that officer's name was Linderwood—had been told off at Belize, to proceed to Silver-Store, in aid of boats and seamen stationed there for the chase

of the Pirates. The Island was considered a good post of observation against the pirates, both by land and sea; neither the pirate ship nor yet her boats had been seen by any of us, but they had been so much heard of, that the reinforcement was sent. Of that party, I was one. It included a corporal and a sergeant. Charker was corporal, and the sergeant's name was Drooce. He was the most tyrannical non-commissioned officer in His Majesty's service.

The night came on, soon after I had had the foregoing words with Charker. All the wonderful bright colours went out of the sea and sky in a few minutes, and all the stars in the Heavens seemed to shine out together, and to look down at themselves in the sea, over one another's shoulders, millions deep. Next morning, we cast anchor off the Island. There was a snug harbour within a little reef; there was a sandy beach; there were cocoa-nut trees with high straight stems, quite bare, and foliage at the top like plumes of magnificent green feathers; there were all the objects that are usually seen in those parts, and I am not going to describe them, having something else to tell about.

Great rejoicings, to be sure, were made on our arrival. All the flags in the place were hoisted, all the guns in the place were fired, and all the people in the place came down to look at us. One of those Sambo fellows—they call those natives Sambos, when they are half-negro and half-Indian—had come off outside the reef, to pilot us in, and remained on board after we had let go our anchor. He was called Christian George King, and was fonder of all hands than anybody else was. Now, I confess, for myself, that on that first day, if I had been captain of the Christopher Columbus, instead of private in the Royal Marines, I should have kicked Christian George King—who was

no more a Christian than he was a King or a George —over the side, without exactly knowing why, except that it was the right thing to do.

But, I must likewise confess, that I was not in a particularly pleasant humour, when I stood under arms that morning, aboard the Christopher Columbus in the harbour of the Island of Silver-Store. I had had a hard life, and the life of the English on the Island seemed too easy and too gay to please me. 'Here you are,' I thought to myself, 'good scholars and good livers; able to read what you like, able to write what you like, able to eat and drink what you like, and spend what you like, and do what you like; and much *you* care for a poor, ignorant Private in the Royal Marines! Yet it 's hard, too, I think, that you should have all the halfpence, and I all the kicks; you all the smooth, and I all the rough; you all the oil, and I all the vinegar.' It was as envious a thing to think as might be, let alone its being nonsensical; but, I thought it. I took it so much amiss, that, when a very beautiful young English lady came aboard, I grunted to myself, 'Ah! *you* have got a lover, I 'll be bound!' As if there was any new offence to me in that, if she had!

She was sister to the captain of our sloop, who had been in a poor way for some time, and who was so ill then that he was obliged to be carried ashore. She was the child of a military officer, and had come out there with her sister, who was married to one of the owners of the silver-mine, and who had three children with her. It was easy to see that she was the light and spirit of the Island. After I had got a good look at her, I grunted to myself again, in an even worse state of mind than before, 'I 'll be damned, if I don't hate him, whoever he is!'

My officer, Lieutenant Linderwood, was as ill as the

captain of the sloop, and was carried ashore, too. They were both young men of about my age, who had been delicate in the West India climate.   I even took *that* in bad part.   I thought I was much fitter for the work than they were, and that if all of us had our deserts, I should be both of them rolled into one.   (It may be imagined what sort of an officer of marines I should have made, without the power of reading a written order.   And as to any knowledge how to command the sloop—Lord! I should have sunk her in a quarter of an hour!)

However, such were my reflections; and when we men were ashore and dismissed, I strolled about the place along with Charker, making my observations in a similar spirit.

It was a pretty place: in all its arrangements partly South American and partly English, and very agreeable to look at on that account, being like a bit of home that had got chipped off and had floated away to that spot, accommodating itself to circumstances as it drifted along.   The huts of the Sambos, to the number of five-and-twenty, perhaps, were down by the beach to the left of the anchorage.   On the right was a sort of barrack, with a South American Flag and the Union Jack, flying from the same staff, where the little English colony could all come together, if they saw occasion.   It was a walled square of building, with a sort of pleasure-ground inside, and inside that again a sunken block like a powder magazine, with a little square trench round it, and steps down to the door.   Charker and I were looking in at the gate, which was not guarded; and I had said to Charker, in reference to the bit like a powder magazine, 'That's where they keep the silver you see'; and Charker had said to me, after thinking it over, 'And silver ain't gold.   Is it, Gill?' when the beautiful young English

lady I had been so bilious about, looked out of a door, or a window—at all events looked out, from under a bright awning. She no sooner saw us two in uniform, than she came out so quickly that she was still putting on her broad Mexican hat of plaited straw when we saluted.

'Would you like to come in,' she said, 'and see the place? It is rather a curious place.'

We thanked the young lady, and said we didn't wish to be troublesome; but, she said it could be no trouble to an English soldier's daughter, to show English soldiers how their countrymen and countrywomen fared, so far away from England; and consequently we saluted again, and went in. Then, as we stood in the shade, she showed us (being as affable as beautiful), how the different families lived in their separate houses, and how there was a general house for stores, and a general reading-room, and a general room for music and dancing, and a room for Church; and how there were other houses on the rising ground called the Signal Hill, where they lived in the hotter weather.

'Your officer has been carried up there,' she said, 'and my brother, too, for the better air. At present, our few residents are dispersed over both spots: deducting, that is to say, such of our number as are always going to, or coming from, or staying at, the Mine.'

('*He* is among one of those parties,' I thought, 'and I wish somebody would knock his head off.')

'Some of our married ladies live here,' she said, 'during at least half the year, as lonely as widows, with their children.'

'Many children here, ma'am?'

'Seventeen. There are thirteen married ladies, and there are eight like me.'

There were not eight like her—there was not one like her—in the world. She meant single.

'Which, with about thirty Englishmen of various degrees,' said the young lady, 'form the little colony now on the Island. I don't count the sailors, for they don't belong to us. Nor the soldiers,' she gave us a gracious smile when she spoke of the soldiers, 'for the same reason.'

'Nor the Sambos, ma'am,' said I.

'No.'

'Under your favour, and with your leave, ma'am,' said I, 'are they trustworthy?'

'Perfectly! We are all very kind to them, and they are very grateful to us.'

'Indeed, ma'am? Now—Christian George King—?'

'Very much attached to us all. Would die for us.'

She was, as in my uneducated way I have observed very beautiful women almost always to be, so composed, that her composure gave great weight to what she said, and I believed it.

Then, she pointed out to us the building like a powder magazine, and explained to us in what manner the silver was brought from the mine, and was brought over from the mainland, and was stored there. The Christopher Columbus would have a rich lading, she said, for there had been a great yield that year, a much richer yield than usual, and there was a chest of jewels besides the silver.

When we had looked about us, and were getting sheepish, through fearing we were troublesome, she turned us over to a young woman, English born but West India bred, who served her as her maid. This young woman was the widow of a non-commissioned officer in a regiment of the line. She had got married and widowed at St. Vincent, with only a few

months between the two events. She was a little saucy woman, with a bright pair of eyes, rather a neat little foot and figure, and rather a neat little turned-up nose. The sort of young woman, I considered at the time, who appeared to invite you to give her a kiss, and who would have slapped your face if you accepted the invitation.

I couldn't make out her name at first; for, when she gave it in answer to my inquiry, it sounded like Beltot, which didn't sound right. But, when we became better acquainted—which was while Charker and I were drinking sugar-cane sangaree, which she made in a most excellent manner—I found that her Christian name was Isabella, which they shortened into Bell, and that the name of the deceased non-commissioned officer was Tott. Being the kind of neat little woman it was natural to make a toy of—I never saw a woman so like a toy in my life—she had got the plaything name of Belltott. In short, she had no other name on the island. Even Mr. Commissioner Pordage (and *he* was a grave one!) formally addressed her as Mrs. Belltott. But, I shall come to Mr. Commissioner Pordage presently.

The name of the captain of the sloop was Captain Maryon, and therefore it was no news to hear from Mrs. Belltott, that his sister, the beautiful unmarried young English lady, was Miss Maryon. The novelty was, that her Christian name was Marion too. Marion Maryon. Many a time I have run off those two names in my thoughts, like a bit of verse. Oh many, and many, and many a time!

We saw out all the drink that was produced, like good men and true, and then took our leaves, and went down to the beach. The weather was beautiful; the wind steady, low, and gentle; the island, a picture; the sea, a picture; the sky, a picture. In that country

there are two rainy seasons in the year. One sets in at about our English Midsummer; the other, about a fortnight after our English Michaelmas. It was the beginning of August at that time; the first of these rainy seasons was well over; and everything was in its most beautiful growth, and had its loveliest look upon it.

'They enjoy themselves here,' I says to Charker, turning surly again. 'This is better than private-soldiering.'

We had come down to the beach, to be friendly with the boat's-crew who were camped and hutted there; and we were approaching towards their quarters over the sand, when Christian George King comes up from the landing-place at a wolf's-trot, crying, 'Yup, So-Jeer!'—which was that Sambo Pilot's barbarous way of saying, Hallo, Soldier! I have stated myself to be a man of no learning, and, if I entertain prejudices, I hope allowance may be made. I will now confess to one. It may be a right one or it may be a wrong one; but, I never did like Natives, except in the form of oysters.

So, when Christian George King, who was individually unpleasant to me besides, comes a trotting along the sand, clucking, 'Yup, So-Jeer!' I had a thundering good mind to let fly at him with my right. I certainly should have done it, but that it would have exposed me to reprimand.

'Yup, So-Jeer!' says he. 'Bad job.'

'What do you mean?' says I.

'Yup, So-Jeer!' says he, 'Ship Leakee.'

'Ship leaky?' says I.

'Iss,' says he, with a nod that looked as if it was jerked out of him by a most violent hiccup—which is the way with those savages.

I cast my eyes at Charker, and we both heard the

pumps going aboard the sloop, and saw the signal run up, 'Come on board; hands wanted from the shore.' In no time some of the sloop's liberty-men were already running down to the water's edge, and the party of seamen, under orders against the Pirates, were putting off to the Columbus in two boats.

'O Christian George King sar berry sorry!' says that Sambo vagabond, then. 'Christian George King cry, English fashion!' His English fashion of crying was to screw his black knuckles into his eyes, howl like a dog, and roll himself on his back on the sand. It was trying not to kick him, but I gave Charker the word, 'Double-quick, Harry!' and we got down to the water's edge, and got on board the sloop.

By some means or other, she had sprung such a leak, that no pumping would keep her free; and what between the two fears that she would go down in the harbour, and that, even if she did not, all the supplies she had brought for the little colony would be destroyed by the sea-water as it rose in her, there was great confusion. In the midst of it, Captain Maryon was heard hailing from the beach. He had been carried down in his hammock, and looked very bad; but he insisted on being stood there on his feet; and I saw him, myself, come off in the boat, sitting upright in the stern-sheets, as if nothing was wrong with him.

A quick sort of council was held, and Captain Maryon soon resolved that we must all fall to work to get the cargo out, and that when that was done, the guns and heavy matters must be got out, and that the sloop must be hauled ashore, and careened, and the leak stopped. We were all mustered (the Pirate-Chace party volunteering), and told off into parties, with so many hours of spell and so many hours of relief, and we all went at it with a will. Christian

George King was entered one of the party in which I worked, at his own request, and he went at it with as good a will as any of the rest. He went at it with so much heartiness, to say the truth, that he rose in my good opinion almost as fast as the water rose in the ship. Which was fast enough, and faster.

Mr. Commissioner Pordage kept in a red-and-black japanned box, like a family lump-sugar box, some document or other, which some Sambo chief or other had got drunk and spilt some ink over (as well as I could understand the matter), and by that means had given up lawful possession of the Island. Through having hold of this box, Mr. Pordage got his title of Commissioner. He was styled Consul too, and spoke of himself as 'Government.'

He was a stiff-jointed, high-nosed old gentleman, without an ounce of fat on him, of a very angry temper and a very yellow complexion. Mrs. Commissioner Pordage, making allowance for difference of sex, was much the same. Mr. Kitten, a small, youngish, bald, botanical and mineralogical gentleman, also connected with the mine—but everybody there was that, more or less—was sometimes called by Mr. Commissioner Pordage, his Vice-commissioner, and sometimes his Deputy-consul. Or sometimes he spoke of Mr. Kitten, merely as being 'under Government.'

The beach was beginning to be a lively scene with the preparations for careening the sloop, and, with cargo, and spars, and rigging, and water-casks, dotted about it, and with temporary quarters for the men rising up there out of such sails and odds and ends as could be best set on one side to make them, when Mr. Commissioner Pordage comes down in a high fluster, and asks for Captain Maryon. The

Captain, ill as he was, was slung in his hammock betwixt two trees, that he might direct; and he raised his head, and answered for himself.

'Captain Maryon,' cries Mr. Commissioner Pordage, 'this is not official. This is not regular.'

'Sir,' says the Captain, 'it hath been arranged with the clerk and supercargo, that you should be communicated with, and requested to render any little assistance that may lie in your power. I am quite certain that hath been duly done.'

'Captain Maryon,' replies Mr. Commissioner Pordage, 'there hath been no written correspondence. No documents have passed, no memoranda have been made, no minutes have been made, no entries and counter-entries appear in the official muniments. This is indecent. I call upon you, sir, to desist, until all is regular, or Government will take this up.'

'Sir,' says Captain Maryon, chafing a little, as he looked out of his hammock; 'between the chances of Government taking this up, and my ship taking herself down, I much prefer to trust myself to the former.'

'You do, sir?' cries Mr. Commissioner Pordage.

'I do, sir,' says Captain Maryon, lying down again.

'Then, Mr. Kitten,' says the Commissioner, 'send up instantly for my Diplomatic coat.'

He was dressed in a linen suit at that moment; but, Mr. Kitten started off himself and brought down the Diplomatic coat, which was a blue cloth one, gold-laced, and with a crown on the button.

'Now, Mr. Kitten,' says Pordage, 'I instruct you, as Vice-commissioner, and Deputy-consul of this place, to demand of Captain Maryon, of the sloop Christopher Columbus, whether he drives me to the act of putting this coat on?'

'Mr. Pordage,' says Captain Maryon, looking out

of his hammock again, 'as I can hear what you say, I can answer it without troubling the gentleman. I should be sorry that you should be at the pains of putting on too hot a coat on my account; but, otherwise, you may put it on hind-side before, or inside-out, or with your legs in the sleeves, or your head in the skirts, for any objection that I have to offer to your thoroughly pleasing yourself.'

'Very good, Captain Maryon,' says Pordage, in a tremendous passion. 'Very good, sir. Be the consequences on your own head! Mr. Kitten, as it has come to this, help me on with it.'

When he had given that order, he walked off in the coat, and all our names were taken, and I was afterwards told that Mr. Kitten wrote from his dictation more than a bushel of large paper on the subject, which cost more before it was done with, than ever could be calculated, and which only got done with after all, by being lost.

Our work went on merrily, nevertheless, and the Christopher Columbus, hauled up, lay helpless on her side like a great fish out of water. While she was in that state, there was a feast, or a ball, or an entertainment, or more properly all three together, given us in honour of the ship, and the ship's company, and the other visitors. At that assembly, I believe, I saw all the inhabitants then upon the Island, without any exception. I took no particular notice of more than a few, but I found it very agreeable in that little corner of the world to see the children, who were of all ages, and mostly very pretty—as they mostly are. There was one handsome elderly lady, with very dark eyes and gray hair, that I inquired about. I was told that her name was Mrs. Venning; and her married daughter, a fair, slight thing, was pointed out to me by the name of Fanny Fisher. Quite a child she

looked, with a little copy of herself holding to her dress; and her husband, just come back from the mine, exceeding proud of her. They were a good-looking set of people on the whole, but I didn't like them. I was out of sorts; in conversation with Charker, I found fault with all of them. I said of Mrs. Venning, she was proud; of Mrs. Fisher, she was a delicate little baby-fool. What did I think of this one? Why, he was a fine gentleman. What did I say to that one? Why, she was a fine lady. What could you expect them to be (I asked Charker), nursed in that climate, with the tropical night shining for them, musical instruments playing to them, great trees bending over them, soft lamps lighting them, fire-flies sparkling in among them, bright flowers and birds brought into existence to please their eyes, delicious drinks to be had for the pouring out, delicious fruit to be got for the picking, and every one dancing and murmuring happily in the scented air, with the sea breaking low on the reef for a pleasant chorus.

'Fine gentlemen and fine ladies, Harry?' I says to Charker. 'Yes, I think so! Dolls! Dolls! Not the sort of stuff for wear, that comes of poor private soldiering in the Royal Marines!'

However, I could not gainsay that they were very hospitable people, and that they treated us uncommonly well. Every man of us was at the entertainment, and Mrs. Belltott had more partners than she could dance with: though she danced all night, too. As to Jack (whether of the Christopher Columbus, or of the Pirate pursuit party, it made no difference), he danced with his brother Jack, danced with himself, danced with the moon, the stars, the trees, the prospect, anything. I didn't greatly take to the chief-officer of that party, with his bright eyes, brown face, and easy figure. I didn't much like his way when he first

happened to come where we were, with Miss Maryon on his arm. 'O, Captain Carton,' she says, 'here are two friends of mine!' He says, 'Indeed? These two Marines?'—meaning Charker and self. 'Yes,' says she, 'I showed these two friends of mine when they first came, all the wonders of Silver-Store.' He gave us a laughing look, and says he, 'You are in luck, men. I would be disrated and go before the mast to-morrow, to be shown the way upward again by such a guide. You are in luck, men.' When we had saluted, and he and the lady had waltzed away, I said, 'You are a pretty fellow, too, to talk of luck. You may go to the Devil!'

Mr. Commissioner Pordage and Mrs. Commissioner, showed among the company on that occasion like the King and Queen of a much Greater Britain than Great Britain. Only two other circumstances in that jovial night made much separate impression on me. One was this. A man in our draft of marines, named Tom Packer, a wild, unsteady young fellow, but the son of a respectable shipwright in Portsmouth Yard, and a good scholar who had been well brought up, comes to me after a spell of dancing, and takes me aside by the elbow, and says, swearing angrily:

'Gill Davis, I hope I may not be the death of Sergeant Drooce one day!'

Now, I knew Drooce had always borne particularly hard on this man, and I knew this man to be of a very hot temper: so, I said:

'Tut, nonsense! don't talk so to me! If there's a man in the corps who scorns the name of an assassin, that man and Tom Packer are one.'

Tom wipes his head, being in a mortal sweat, and says he:

'I hope so, but I can't answer for myself when he lords it over me, as he has just now done, before a woman.

I tell you what, Gill! Mark my words! It will go hard with Sergeant Drooce, if ever we are in an engagement together, and he has to look to me to save him. Let him say a prayer then, if he knows one, for it's all over with him, and he is on his Death-bed. Mark my words!'

I did mark his words, and very soon afterwards, too, as will shortly be taken down.

The other circumstance that I noticed at that ball, was, the gaiety and attachment of Christian George King. The innocent spirits that Sambo Pilot was in, and the impossibility he found himself under of showing all the little colony, but especially the ladies and children, how fond he was of them, how devoted to them, and how faithful to them for life and death, for present, future, and everlasting, made a great impression on me. If ever a man, Sambo or no Sambo, was trustful and trusted, to what may be called quite an infantine and sweetly beautiful extent, surely, I thought that morning when I did at last lie down to rest, it was that Sambo Pilot, Christian George King.

This may account for my dreaming of him. He stuck in my sleep, cornerwise, and I couldn't get him out. He was always flitting about me, dancing round me, and peeping in over my hammock, though I woke and dozed off again fifty times. At last, when I opened my eyes, there he really was, looking in at the open side of the little dark hut; which was made of leaves, and had Charker's hammock slung in it as well as mine.

'So-Jeer!' says he, in a sort of a low croak. 'Yup!'

'Hallo!' says I, starting up. 'What? You *are* there, are you?'

'Iss,' says he. 'Christian George King got news.'

'What news has he got?'

'Pirates out!'

I was on my feet in a second. So was Charker. We were both aware that Captain Carton, in command of the boats, constantly watched the mainland for a secret signal, though, of course, it was not known to such as us what the signal was.

Christian George King had vanished before we touched the ground. But, the word was already passing from hut to hut to turn out quietly, and we knew that the nimble barbarian had got hold of the truth, or something near it.

In a space among the trees behind the encampment of us visitors, naval and military, was a snugly-screened spot, where we kept the stores that were in use, and did our cookery. The word was passed to assemble here. It was very quickly given, and was given (so far as we were concerned) by Sergeant Drooce, who was as good in a soldier point of view, as he was bad in a tyrannical one. We were ordered to drop into this space, quietly, behind the trees, one by one. As we assembled here, the seamen assembled too. Within ten minutes, as I should estimate, we were all here, except the usual guard upon the beach. The beach (we could see it through the wood) looked as it always had done in the hottest time of the day. The guard were in the shadow of the sloop's hull, and nothing was moving but the sea, and that moved very faintly. Work had always been knocked off at that hour, until the sun grew less fierce, and the sea-breeze rose; so that its being holiday with us, made no difference, just then, in the look of the place. But I may mention that it was a holiday, and the first we had had since our hard work began. Last night's ball had been given, on the leak's being repaired, and the careening done. The worst of the work was over,

and to-morrow we were to begin to get the sloop afloat again.

We marines were now drawn up here under arms. The chase-party were drawn up separate. The men of the Columbus were drawn up separate. The officers stepped out into the midst of the three parties, and spoke so as all might hear. Captain Carton was the officer in command, and he had a spy-glass in his hand. His coxswain stood by him with another spy-glass, and with a slate on which he seemed to have been taking down signals.

'Now, men!' says Captain Carton; 'I have to let you know, for your satisfaction: Firstly, that there are ten pirate boats, strongly manned and armed, lying hidden up a creek yonder on the coast, under the overhanging branches of the dense trees. Secondly, that they will certainly come out this night when the moon rises, on a pillaging and murdering expedition, of which some part of the mainland is the object. Thirdly—don't cheer, men!—that we will give chase, and, if we can get at them, rid the world of them, please God!'

Nobody spoke, that I heard, and nobody moved, that I saw. Yet there was a kind of ring, as if every man answered and approved with the best blood that was inside of him.

'Sir,' says Captain Maryon, 'I beg to volunteer on this service, with my boats. My people volunteer, to the ship's boys.'

'In His Majesty's name and service,' the other answers, touching his hat, 'I accept your aid with pleasure. Lieutenant Linderwood, how will you divide your men?'

I was ashamed—I give it out to be written down as large and plain as possible—I was heart and soul ashamed of my thoughts of those two sick officers,

Captain Maryon and Lieutenant Linderwood, when I saw them, then and there. The spirit in those two gentlemen beat down their illness (and very ill I knew them to be) like Saint George beating down the Dragon. Pain and weakness, want of ease and want of rest, had no more place in their minds than fear itself. Meaning now to express for my lady to write down, exactly what I felt then and there, I felt this: 'You two brave fellows that I had been so grudgeful of, I know that if you were dying you would put it off to get up and do your best, and then you would be so modest that in lying down again to die, you would hardly say, "I did it!" '

It did me good. It really did me good.

But, to go back to where I broke off. Says Captain Carton to Lieutenant Linderwood, 'Sir, how will you divide your men? There is not room for all; and a few men should, in any case, be left here.'

There was some debate about it. At last, it was resolved to leave eight Marines and four seamen on the Island, besides the sloop's two boys. And because it was considered that the friendly Sambos would only want to be commanded in case of any danger (though none at all was apprehended there), the officers were in favour of leaving the two non-commissioned officers, Drooce and Charker. It was a heavy disappointment to them, just as my being one of the left was a heavy disappointment to me—then, but not soon afterwards. We men drew lots for it, and I drew 'Island.' So did Tom Packer. So, of course, did four more of our rank and file.

When this was settled, verbal instructions were given to all hands to keep the intended expedition secret, in order that the women and children might not be alarmed, or the expedition put in a difficulty by more volunteers. The assembly was to be on that

same spot at sunset. Every man was to keep up an appearance, meanwhile, of occupying himself in his usual way. That is to say, every man excepting four old trusty seamen, who were appointed, with an officer, to see to the arms and ammunition, and to muffle the rullocks of the boats, and to make everything as trim and swift and silent as it could be made.

The Sambo Pilot had been present all the while, in case of his being wanted, and had said to the officer in command, five hundred times over if he had said it once, that Christian George King would stay with the So-Jeers, and take care of the booffer ladies and the booffer childs—booffer being that native's expression for beautiful. He was now asked a few questions concerning the putting off of the boats, and in particular whether there was any way of embarking at the back of the Island: which Captain Carton would have half liked to do, and then have dropped round in its shadow and slanted across to the main. But, 'No,' says Christian George King. 'No, no, no! Told you so, ten time. No, no, no! All reef, all rock, all swim, all drown!' Striking out as he said it, like a swimmer gone mad, and turning over on his back on dry land, and spluttering himself to death, in a manner that made him quite an exhibition.

The sun went down, after appearing to be a long time about it, and the assembly was called. Every man answered to his name, of course, and was at his post. It was not yet black dark, and the roll was only just gone through, when up comes Mr. Commissioner Pordage with his Diplomatic coat on.

'Captain Carton,' says he, 'Sir, what is this?'

'This, Mr. Commissioner' (he was very short with him), 'is an expedition against the Pirates. It is a secret expedition, so please to keep it a secret.'

'Sir,' says Commissioner Pordage, 'I trust there is going to be no unnecessary cruelty committed?'

'Sir,' returns the officer, 'I trust not.'

'That is not enough, sir,' cries Commissioner Pordage, getting wroth. 'Captain Carton, I give you notice. Government requires you to treat the enemy with great delicacy, consideration, clemency, and forbearance.'

'Sir,' says Captain Carton, 'I am an English officer, commanding English Men, and I hope I am not likely to disappoint the Government's just expectations. But, I presume you know that these villains under their black flag have despoiled our countrymen of their property, burnt their homes, barbarously murdered them and their little children, and worse than murdered their wives and daughters?'

'Perhaps I do, Captain Carton,' answers Pordage, waving his hand with dignity; 'perhaps I do not. It is not customary, sir, for Government to commit itself.'

'It matters very little, Mr. Pordage, whether or no. Believing that I hold my commission by the allowance of God, and not that I have received it direct from the Devil, I shall certainly use it, with all avoidance of unnecessary suffering and with all merciful swiftness of execution, to exterminate these people from the face of the earth. Let me recommend you to go home, sir, and to keep out of the night-air.'

Never another syllable did that officer say to the Commissioner, but turned away to his men. The Commissioner buttoned his Diplomatic coat to the chin, said, 'Mr. Kitten, attend me!' gasped, half choked himself, and took himself off.

It now fell very dark, indeed. I have seldom, if ever, seen it darker, nor yet so dark. The moon was

not due until one in the morning, and it was but a little after nine when our men lay down where they were mustered. It was pretended that they were to take a nap, but everybody knew that no nap was to be got under the circumstances. Though all were very quiet, there was a restlessness among the people; much what I have seen among the people on a race-course, when the bell has rung for the saddling for a great race with large stakes on it.

At ten, they put off; only one boat putting off at a time; another following in five minutes; both then lying on their oars until another followed. Ahead of all, paddling his own outlandish little canoe without a sound, went the Sambo pilot, to take them safely outside the reef. No light was shown but once, and that was in the commanding officer's own hand. I lighted the dark lantern for him, and he took it from me when he embarked. They had blue lights and such like with them, but kept themselves as dark as Murder.

The expedition got away with wonderful quietness, and Christian George King soon came back dancing with joy.

'Yup, So-Jeer,' says he to myself in a very objectionable kind of convulsions, 'Christian George King sar berry glad. Pirates all be blown a-pieces. Yup! Yup!'

My reply to that cannibal was, 'However glad you may be, hold your noise, and don't dance jigs and slap your knees about it, for I can't bear to see you do it.'

I was on duty then; we twelve who were left being divided into four watches of three each, three hours' spell. I was relieved at twelve. A little before that time, I had challenged, and Miss Maryon and Mrs. Belltott had come in.

'Good Davis,' says Miss Maryon, 'what is the matter? Where is my brother?'

I told her what was the matter, and where her brother was.

'O Heaven help him!' says she, clasping her hands and looking up—she was close in front of me, and she looked most lovely to be sure; 'he is not sufficiently recovered, not strong enough for such strife!'

'If you had seen him, miss,' I told her, 'as I saw him when he volunteered, you would have known that his spirit is strong enough for any strife. It will bear his body, miss, to wherever duty calls him. It will always bear him to an honourable life, or a brave death.'

'Heaven bless you!' says she, touching my arm. 'I know it. Heaven bless you!'

Mrs. Belltott surprised me by trembling and saying nothing. They were still standing looking towards the sea and listening, after the relief had come round. It continuing very dark, I asked to be allowed to take them back. Miss Maryon thanked me, and she put her arm in mine, and I did take them back. I have now got to make a confession that will appear singular. After I had left them, I laid myself down on my face on the beach, and cried for the first time since I had frightened birds as a boy at Snorridge Bottom, to think what a poor, ignorant, low-placed, private soldier I was.

It was only for half a minute or so. A man can't at all times be quite master of himself, and it was only for half a minute or so. Then I up and went to my hut, and turned into my hammock, and fell asleep with wet eyelashes, and a sore, sore heart. Just as I had often done when I was a child, and had been worse used than usual.

I slept (as a child under those circumstances might)

very sound, and yet very sore at heart all through my sleep. I was awoke by the words, 'He is a determined man.' I had sprung out of my hammock, and had seized my firelock, and was standing on the ground, saying the words myself. 'He is a determined man.' But, the curiosity of my state was, that I seemed to be repeating them after somebody, and to have been wonderfully startled by hearing them.

As soon as I came to myself, I went out of the hut, and away to where the guard was. Charker challenged:

'Who goes there?'

'A friend.'

'Not Gill?' says he, as he shouldered his piece.

'Gill,' says I.

'Why, what the deuce do you do out of your hammock?' says he.

'Too hot for sleep,' says I; 'is all right?'

'Right!' says Charker, 'yes, yes; all 's right enough here; what should be wrong here? It 's the boats that we want to know of. Except for fire-flies twinkling about, and the lonesome splashes of great creatures as they drop into the water, there 's nothing going on here to ease a man's mind from the boats.'

The moon was above the sea, and had risen, I should say, some half an hour. As Charker spoke, with his face towards the sea, I, looking landward, suddenly laid my right hand on his breast, and said, 'Don't move. Don't turn. Don't raise your voice! You never saw a Maltese face here?'

'No. What do you mean?' he asks, staring at me.

'Nor yet an English face, with one eye and a patch across the nose?'

'No. What ails you? What do you mean?'

I had seen both, looking at us round the stem of a cocoa-nut tree, where the moon struck them. I had

seen that Sambo Pilot, with one hand laid on the stem of the tree, drawing them back into the heavy shadow. I had seen their naked cutlasses twinkle and shine, like bits of the moonshine in the water that had got blown ashore among the trees by the light wind. I had seen it all, in a moment. And I saw in a moment (as any man would), that the signalled move of the pirates on the mainland was a plot and a feint; that the leak had been made to disable the sloop; that the boats had been tempted away, to leave the Island unprotected; that the pirates had landed by some secreted way at the back; and that Christian George King was a double-dyed traitor, and a most infernal villain.

I considered, still all in one and the same moment, that Charker was a brave man, but not quick with his head; and that Sergeant Drooce, with a much better head was close by. All I said to Charker was, 'I am afraid we are betrayed. Turn your back full to the moonlight on the sea, and cover the stem of the cocoanut tree which will then be right before you, at the height of a man's heart. Are you right?'

'I am right,' says Charker, turning instantly, and falling into the position with a nerve of iron; 'and right ain't left. Is it, Gill?'

A few seconds brought me to Sergeant Drooce's hut. He was fast asleep, and being a heavy sleeper, I had to lay my hands upon him to rouse him. The instant I touched him he came rolling out of his hammock, and upon me like a tiger. And a tiger he was, except that he knew what he was up to, in his utmost heat, as well as any man.

I had to struggle with him pretty hard to bring him to his senses, panting all the while (for he gave me a breather), 'Sergeant, I am Gill Davis! Treachery! Pirates on the Island!'

The last words brought him round, and he took his hands off. 'I have seen two of them within this minute,' said I. And so I told him what I had told Harry Charker.

His soldierly, though tyrannical, head was clear in an instant. He didn't waste one word, even of surprise. 'Order the guard,' says he, 'to draw off quietly into the Fort.' (They called the enclosure I have before mentioned, the Fort, though it was not much of that.) 'Then get you to the Fort, as quick as you can, rouse up every soul there, and fasten the gate. I will bring in all those who are up at the Signal Hill. If we are surrounded before we can join you, you must make a sally and cut us out if you can. The word among our men is, "Women and children!"'

He burst away, like fire going before the wind over dry reeds. He roused up the seven men who were off duty, and had them bursting away with him, before they knew they were not asleep. I reported orders to Charker, and ran to the Fort, as I have never run at any other time in all my life: no, not even in a dream.

The gate was not fast, and had no good fastening: only a double wooden bar, a poor chain, and a bad lock. Those, I secured as well as they could be secured in a few seconds by one pair of hands, and so ran to that part of the building where Miss Maryon lived. I called to her loudly by her name until she answered. I then called loudly all the names I knew —Mrs. Macey (Miss Maryon's married sister), Mr. Macey, Mrs. Venning, Mr. and Mrs. Fisher, even Mr. and Mrs. Pordage. Then I called out, 'All you gentlemen here, get up and defend the place! We are caught in a trap. Pirates have landed. We are attacked!'

At the terrible word 'Pirates!'—for, those villains had done such deeds in those seas as never can be told in writing, and can scarcely be so much as thought of—cries and screams rose up from every part of the place. Quickly lights moved about from window to window, and the cries moved about with them, and men, women, and children came flying down into the square. I remarked to myself, even then, what a number of things I seemed to see at once. I noticed Mrs. Macey coming towards me, carrying all her three children together. I noticed Mr. Pordage in the greatest terror, in vain trying to get on his Diplomatic coat; and Mr. Kitten respectfully tying his pocket-handkerchief over Mrs. Pordage's nightcap. I noticed Mrs. Belltott run out screaming, and shrink upon the ground near me, and cover her face in her hands, and lie all of a bundle, shivering. But, what I noticed with the greatest pleasure was, the determined eyes with which those men of the Mine that I had thought fine gentlemen, came round me with what arms they had: to the full as cool and resolute as I could be, for my life—ay, and for my soul, too, into the bargain!

The chief person being Mr. Macey, I told him how the three men of the guard would be at the gate directly, if they were not already there, and how Sergeant Drooce and the other seven were gone to bring in the outlying part of the people of Silver-Store. I next urged him, for the love of all who were dear to him, to trust no Sambo, and, above all, if he could get any good chance at Christian George King, not to lose it, but to put him out of the world.

'I will follow your advice to the letter, Davis,' says he; 'what next?'

My answer was, 'I think, sir, I would recommend

you next, to order down such heavy furniture and lumber as can be moved, and make a barricade within the gate.'

'That's good again,' says he: 'will you see it done?'

'I'll willingly help to do it,' says I, 'unless or until my superior, Sergeant Drooce, gives me other orders.'

He shook me by the hand, and having told off some of his companions to help me, bestirred himself to look to the arms and ammunition. A proper, quick, brave, steady, ready gentleman!

One of their three little children was deaf and dumb. Miss Maryon had been from the first with all the children, soothing them, and dressing them (poor little things, they had been brought out of their beds), and making them believe that it was a game of play, so that some of them were now even laughing. I had been working hard with the others at the barricade, and had got up a pretty good breastwork within the gate. Drooce and the seven had come back, bringing in the people from the Signal Hill, and had worked along with us: but, I had not so much as spoken a word to Drooce, nor had Drooce so much as spoken a word to me, for we were both too busy. The breastwork was now finished, and I found Miss Maryon at my side, with a child in her arms. Her dark hair was fastened round her head with a band. She had a quantity of it, and it looked even richer and more precious, put up hastily out of her way, than I had seen it look when it was carefully arranged. She was very pale, but extraordinarily quiet and still.

'Dear good Davis,' said she, 'I have been waiting to speak one word to you.'

I turned to her directly. If I had received a musket-ball in the heart, and she had stood there, I almost believe I should have turned to her before I dropped.

'This pretty little creature,' said she, kissing the child in her arms, who was playing with her hair and trying to pull it down, 'cannot hear what we say—can hear nothing. I trust you so much, and have such great confidence in you, that I want you to make me a promise.'

'What is it, Miss?'

'That if we are defeated, and you are absolutely sure of my being taken, you will kill me.'

'I shall not be alive to do it, Miss. I shall have died in your defence before it comes to that. They must step across my body to lay a hand on you.'

'But, if you are alive, you brave soldier.' How she looked at me! 'And if you cannot save me from the Pirates, living, you will save me, dead. Tell me so.'

Well! I told her I would do that at the last, if all else failed. She took my hand—my rough, coarse hand—and put it to her lips. She put it to the child's lips, and the child kissed it. I believe I had the strength of half a dozen men in me, from that moment, until the fight was over.

All this time, Mr. Commissioner Pordage had been wanting to make a Proclamation to the Pirates to lay down their arms and go away; and everybody had been hustling him about and tumbling over him, while he was calling for pen and ink to write it with. Mrs. Pordage, too, had some curious ideas about the British respectability of her nightcap (which had as many frills to it, growing in layers one inside another, as if it was a white vegetable of the artichoke sort), and she wouldn't take the nightcap off, and would be angry when it got crushed by the other ladies who were handing things about, and, in short, she gave as much trouble as her husband did. But, as we were now forming for the defence of the place, they were both poked out of the way with no ceremony. The

children and ladies were got into the little trench which surrounded the silver-house (we were afraid of leaving them in any of the light buildings, lest they should be set on fire), and we made the best disposition we could. There was a pretty good store, in point of amount, of tolerable swords and cutlasses. Those were issued. There were, also, perhaps a score or so of spare muskets. Those were brought out. To my astonishment, little Mrs. Fisher that I had taken for a doll and a baby, was not only very active in that service, but volunteered to load the spare arms.

'For, I understand it well,' says she, cheerfully, without a shake in her voice.

'I am a soldier's daughter and a sailor's sister, and I understand it too,' says Miss Maryon, just in the same way.

Steady and busy behind where I stood, those two beautiful and delicate young women fell to handling the guns, hammering the flints, looking to the locks, and quietly directing others to pass up powder and bullets from hand to hand, as unflinching as the best of tried soldiers.

Sergeant Drooce had brought in word that the pirates were very strong in numbers—over a hundred was his estimate—and that they were not, even then, all landed; for, he had seen them in a very good position on the further side of the Signal Hill, evidently waiting for the rest of their men to come up. In the present pause, the first we had had since the alarm, he was telling this over again to Mr. Macey, when Mr. Macey suddenly cried out: 'The signal! Nobody has thought of the signal!'

We knew of no signal, so we could not have thought of it.

'What signal may you mean, sir?' says Sergeant Drooce, looking sharp at him.

'There is a pile of wood upon the Signal Hill. If it could be lighted—which never has been done yet—it would be a signal of distress to the mainland.'

Charker cries, directly: 'Sergeant Drooce, dispatch me on that duty. Give me the two men who were on guard with me to-night, and I 'll light the fire, if it can be done.'

'And if it can't, Corporal—' Mr. Macey strikes in.

'Look at these ladies and children, sir!' says Charker. 'I 'd sooner *light myself,* than not try any chance to save them.'

We gave him a Hurrah!—it burst from us, come of it what might—and he got his two men, and was let out at the gate, and crept away. I had no sooner come back to my place from being one of the party to handle the gate, than Miss Maryon said in a low voice behind me:

'Davis, will you look at this powder? This is not right.'

I turned my head. Christian George King again, and treachery again! Sea-water had been conveyed into the magazine, and every grain of powder was spoiled!

'Stay a moment,' said Sergeant Drooce, when I had told him, without causing a movement in a muscle of his face: 'look to your pouch, my lad. You Tom Packer, look to your pouch, confound you! Look to your pouches, all you Marines.'

The same artful savage had got at them, somehow or another, and the cartridges were all unserviceable. 'Hum!' says the Sergeant. 'Look to your loading, men. You are right so far?'

Yes; we were right so far.

'Well, my lads and gentlemen all,' says the Sergeant, 'this will be a hand-to-hand affair, and so much the better.'

He treated himself to a pinch of snuff, and stood up, square-shouldered and broad-chested, in the light of the moon—which was now very bright—as cool as if he was waiting for a play to begin. He stood quiet, and we all stood quiet, for a matter of something like half an hour. I took notice from such whispered talk as there was, how little we that the silver did not belong to, thought about it, and how much the people that it did belong to, thought about it. At the end of the half-hour, it was reported from the gate that Charker and the two were falling back on us, pursued by about a dozen.

'Sally! Gate-party, under Gill Davis,' says the Sergeant, 'and bring 'em in! Like men, now!'

We were not long about it, and we brought them in. 'Don't take me,' says Charker, holding me round the neck, and stumbling down at my feet when the gate was fast, 'don't take me near the ladies or the children, Gill. They had better not see Death, till it can't be helped. They'll see it soon enough.'

'Harry!' I answered, holding up his head. 'Comrade!'

He was cut to pieces. The signal had been secured by the first pirate party that landed; his hair was all singed off, and his face was blackened with the running pitch from a torch.

He made no complaint of pain, or of anything. 'Good-bye, old chap,' was all he said, with a smile. 'I've got my death. And Death ain't life. Is it, Gill?'

Having helped to lay his poor body on one side, I went back to my post. Sergeant Drooce looked at me, with his eyebrows a little lifted. I nodded. 'Close up here, men and gentlemen all!' said the Sergeant. 'A place too many, in the line.'

The Pirates were so close upon us at this time, that

the foremost of them were already before the gate. More and more came up with a great noise, and shouting loudly. When we believed from the sound that they were all there, we gave three English cheers. The poor little children joined, and were so fully convinced of our being at play, that they enjoyed the noise, and were heard clapping their hands in the silence that followed.

Our disposition was this, beginning with the rear. Mrs. Venning, holding her daughter's child in her arms, sat on the steps of the little square trench surrounding the silver-house, encouraging and directing those women and children as she might have done in the happiest and easiest time of her life. Then, there was an armed line, under Mr. Macey, across the width of the enclosure, facing that way and having their backs towards the gate, in order that they might watch the walls and prevent our being taken by surprise. Then there was a space of eight or ten feet deep, in which the spare arms were, and in which Miss Maryon and Mrs. Fisher, their hands and dresses blackened with the spoilt gunpowder, worked on their knees, tying such things as knives, old bayonets, and spearheads, to the muzzles of the useless muskets. Then, there was a second armed line, under Sergeant Drooce, also across the width of the enclosure, but facing the gate. Then came the breastwork we had made, with a zig-zag way through it for me and my little party to hold good in retreating, as long as we could, when we were driven from the gate. We all knew that it was impossible to hold the place long, and that our only hope was in the timely discovery of the plot by the boats, and in their coming back.

I and my men were now thrown forward to the gate. From a spy-hole, I could see the whole crowd of Pirates. There were Malays among them, Dutch,

Maltese, Greeks, Sambos, Negroes, and Convict Englishmen from the West India Islands; among the last,
him with the one eye and the patch across the nose.
There were some Portuguese, too, and a few Span-
iards. The captain was a Portuguese; a little man
with very large ear-rings under a very broad hat, and
a great bright shawl twisted about his shoulders.
They were all strongly armed, but like a boarding
party, with pikes, swords, cutlasses, and axes. I
noticed a good many pistols, but not a gun of any
kind among them. This gave me to understand that
they had considered that a continued roll of musketry
might perhaps have been heard on the mainland; also
that for the reason that fire would be seen from the
mainland they would not set the Fort in flames and
roast us alive; which was one of their favourite ways
of carrying on. I looked about for Christian George
King, and if I had seen him I am much mistaken if
he would not have received my one round of ball-
cartridge in his head. But, no Christian George
King was visible.

A sort of a wild Portuguese demon, who seemed
either fierce-mad or fierce-drunk—but, they all seemed
one or the other—came forward with the black flag,
and gave it a wave or two. After that, the Portuguese captain called out in shrill English, 'I say you!
English fools! Open the gate! Surrender!'

As we kept close and quiet, he said something to
his men which I didn't understand, and when he had
said it, the one-eyed English rascal with the patch
(who had stepped out when he began), said it again
in English. It was only this. 'Boys of the black
flag, this is to be quickly done. Take all the prisoners you can. If they don't yield, kill the children
to make them. Forward!' Then, they all came on

at the gate, and, in another half minute were smashing and splitting it in.

We struck at them through the gaps and shivers, and we dropped many of them, too; but, their very weight would have carried such a gate, if they had been unarmed. I soon found Sergeant Drooce at my side, forming us six remaining marines in line—Tom Packer next to me—and ordering us to fall back three paces, and, as they broke in, to give them our one little volley at short distance. 'Then,' says he, 'receive them behind your breastwork on the bayonet, and at least let every man of you pin one of the cursed cockchafers through the body.'

We checked them by our fire, slight as it was, and we checked them at the breastwork. However, they broke over it like swarms of devils—they were, really and truly, more devils than men—and then it was hand to hand, indeed.

We clubbed our muskets and laid about us; even then, those two ladies—always behind me—were steady and ready with the arms. I had a lot of Maltese and Malays upon me, and, but for a broadsword that Miss Maryon's own hand put in mine, should have got my end from them. But, was that all? No. I saw a heap of banded dark hair and a white dress come thrice between me and them, under my own raised right arm, which each time might have destroyed the wearer of the white dress; and each time one of the lot went down, struck dead.

Drooce was armed with a broadsword, too, and did such things with it, that there was a cry, in half a dozen languages, of 'Kill that sergeant!' as I knew, by the cry being raised in English, and taken up in other tongues. I had received a severe cut across the left arm a few moments before, and should have

known nothing of it, except supposing that somebody had struck me a smart blow, if I had not felt weak, and seen myself covered with spouting blood, and, at the same instant of time, seen Miss Maryon tearing her dress and binding it with Mrs. Fisher's help round the wound. They called to Tom Packer, who was scouring by, to stop and guard me for one minute, while I was bound, or I should bleed to death in trying to defend myself. Tom stopped directly, with a good sabre in his hand.

In that same moment—all things seem to happen in that same moment, at such a time—half a dozen had rushed howling at Sergeant Drooce. The Sergeant, stepping back against the wall, stopped one howl for ever with such a terrible blow, and waited for the rest to come on, with such a wonderfully unmoved face, that they stopped and looked at him.

'See him now!' cried Tom Packer. 'Now, when I could cut him out! Gill! Did I tell you to mark my words?'

I implored Tom Packer in the Lord's name, as well as I could in my faintness, to go to the Sergeant's aid.

'I hate and detest him,' says Tom, moodily wavering. 'Still, he is a brave man.' Then he calls out, 'Sergeant Drooce, Sergeant Drooce! Tell me you have driven me too hard, and are sorry for it.'

The Sergeant, without turning his eyes from his assailants, which would have been instant death to him, answers:

'No. I won't.'

'Sergeant Drooce!' cries Tom, in a kind of an agony. 'I have passed my word that I would never save you from Death, if I could, but would leave you to die. Tell me you have driven me too hard and are sorry for it, and that shall go for nothing.'

One of the group laid the Sergeant's bald bare head open. The Sergeant laid him dead.

'I tell you,' says the Sergeant, breathing a little short, and waiting for the next attack, 'no. I won't. If you are not man enough to strike for a fellow-soldier because he wants help, and because of nothing else, I 'll go into the other world and look for a better man.'

Tom swept upon them, and cut him out. Tom and he fought their way through another knot of them, and sent them flying, and came over to where I was beginning again to feel, with inexpressible joy, that I had got a sword in my hand.

They had hardly come to us, when I heard, above all the other noises, a tremendous cry of women's voices. I also saw Miss Maryon, with quite a new face, suddenly clap her two hands over Mrs. Fisher's eyes. I looked towards the silver-house, and saw Mrs. Venning—standing upright on the top of the steps of the trench, with her gray hair and her dark eyes—hide her daughter's child behind her, among the folds of her dress, strike a pirate with her other hand, and fall, shot by his pistol.

The cry arose again, and there was a terrible and confusing rush of the women into the midst of the struggle. In another moment, something came tumbling down upon me that I thought was the wall. It was a heap of Sambos who had come over the wall; and of four men who clung to my legs like serpents, one who clung to my right leg was Christian George King.

'Yup, So-Jeer,' says he, 'Christian George King sar berry glad So-Jeer a prisoner. Christian George King been waiting for So-Jeer sech long time. Yup, yup!'

What could I do, with five-and-twenty of them on

me, but be tied hand and foot? So, I was tied hand and foot. It was all over now—boats not come back —all lost! When I was fast bound and was put up against the wall, the one-eyed English convict came up with the Portuguese Captain, to have a look at me.

'See!' says he. 'Here's the determined man! If you had slept sounder, last night, you'd have slept your soundest last night, my determined man.'

The Portuguese Captain laughed in a cool way, and with the flat of his cutlass, hit me crosswise, as if I was the bough of a tree that he played with: first on the face, and then across the chest and the wounded arm. I looked him steady in the face without tumbling while he looked at me, I am happy to say; but, when they went away, I fell, and lay there.

The sun was up, when I was roused and told to come down to the beach and be embarked. I was full of aches and pains, and could not at first remember; but, I remembered quite soon enough. The killed were lying about all over the place, and the Pirates were burying their dead, and taking away their wounded on hastily-made litters, to the back of the Island. As for us prisoners, some of their boats had come round to the usual harbour, to carry us off. We looked a wretched few, I thought, when I got down there; still, it was another sign that we had fought well, and made the enemy suffer.

The Portuguese Captain had all the women already embarked in the boat he himself commanded, which was just putting off when I got down. Miss Maryon sat on one side of him, and gave me a moment's look, as full of quiet courage, and pity, and confidence, as if it had been an hour long. On the other side of him was poor little Mrs. Fisher, weeping for her child and her mother. I was shoved into the same boat with Drooce and Packer, and the remainder of our party

of marines: of whom we had lost two privates, besides Charker, my poor, brave comrade. We all made a melancholy passage, under the hot sun over to the mainland. There, we landed in a solitary place, and were mustered on the sea sand. Mr. and Mrs. Macey and their children were amongst us, Mr. and Mrs. Pordage, Mr. Kitten, Mr. Fisher, and Mrs. Belltott. We mustered only fourteen men, fifteen women, and seven children. Those were all that remained of the English who had lain down to sleep last night, unsuspecting and happy, on the Island of Silver-Store.

[The second chapter, which was not written by Dickens, describes the Prisoners (twenty-two women and children) taken into the interior by the Pirate Captain, who makes them the material guarantee for the precious metal and jewels left on the island; declaring that, if the latter be wrested by English ships from the pirates in charge, he will murder the captives. From their 'Prison in the Woods,' however (this being the title of the second chapter), they escape by means of rafts down the river; and the sequel is told in a third and concluding chapter by Dickens.]

CHAPTER III

THE RAFTS ON THE RIVER

WE contrived to keep afloat all that night, and, the stream running strong with us, to glide a long way down the river. But, we found the night to be a dangerous time for such navigation, on account of the eddies and rapids, and it was therefore settled next day that in future we would bring-to at sunset, and encamp on the shore. As we knew of no boats that the Pirates possessed, up at the Prison in the Woods,

we settled always to encamp on the opposite side of
the stream, so as to have the breadth of the river between our sleep and them. Our opinion was, that if
they were acquainted with any near way by land to
the mouth of this river, they would come up it in
force, and retake us or kill us, according as they could;
but that if that was not the case, and if the river
ran by none of their secret stations, we might escape.

When I say we settled this or that, I do not mean
that we planned anything with any confidence as to
what might happen an hour hence. So much had happened in one night, and such great changes had been
violently and suddenly made in the fortunes of many
among us, that we had got better used to uncertainty,
in a little while, than I dare say most people do in
the course of their lives.

The difficulties we soon got into, through the off-
settings and point-currents of the stream, made the
likelihood of our being drowned, alone—to say nothing of our being retaken—as broad and plain as the
sun at noonday to all of us. But, we all worked hard
at managing the rafts, under the direction of the
seamen (of our own skill, I think we never could have
prevented them from oversetting), and we also worked
hard at making good the defects in their first hasty
construction—which the water soon found out. While
we humbly resigned ourselves to going down, if it
was the will of Our Father that was in Heaven, we
humbly made up our minds, that we would all do the
best that was in us.

And so we held on, gliding with the stream. It
drove us to this bank, and it drove us to that bank,
and it turned us, and whirled us; but yet it carried
us on. Sometimes much too slowly; sometimes much
too fast, but yet it carried us on.

My little deaf and dumb boy slumbered a good

deal now, and that was the case with all the children.
They caused very little trouble to any one.   They
seemed, in my eyes, to get more like one another, not
only in quiet manner, but in the face, too.   The motion of the raft was usually so much the same, the
scene was usually so much the same, the sound of the
soft wash and ripple of the water was usually so much
the same, that they were made drowsy, as they might
have been by the constant playing of one tune.   Even
on the grown people, who worked hard and felt anxiety, the same things produced something of the same
effect.   Every day was so like the other, that I soon
lost count of the days, myself, and had to ask Miss
Maryon, for instance, whether this was the third or
fourth?   Miss Maryon had a pocket-book and pencil,
and she kept the log; that is to say, she entered up a
clear little journal of the time, and of the distances
our seamen thought we had made, each night.

So, as I say, we kept afloat and glided on.   All
day long, and every day, the water, and the woods,
and sky; all day long, and every day, the constant
watching of both sides of the river, and far ahead at
every bold turn and sweep it made, for any signs of
Pirate-boats, or Pirate-dwellings.   So, as I say, we
kept afloat and glided on.   The days melting themselves together to that degree, that I could hardly
believe my ears when I asked, 'How many, now,
Miss?' and she answered, 'Seven.'

To be sure, poor Mr. Pordage had, by about now,
got his Diplomatic coat into such a state as never was
seen.   What with the mud of the river, what with
the water of the river, what with the sun, and the
dews, and the tearing boughs, and the thickets, it
hung about him in discoloured shreds like a mop.
The sun had touched him a bit.   He had taken to
always polishing one particular button, which just

held on to his left wrist, and to always calling for stationery. I suppose that man called for pens, ink, and paper, tape, and sealing-wax, upwards of one thousand times in four-and-twenty hours. He had an idea that we should never get out of that river unless we were written out of it in a formal Memorandum; and the more we laboured at navigating the rafts, the more he ordered us not to touch them at our peril, and the more he sat and roared for stationery.

Mrs. Pordage, similarly, persisted in wearing her night-cap. I doubt if any one but ourselves who had seen the progress of that article of dress, could by this time have told what it was meant for. It had got so limp and ragged that she couldn't see out of her eyes for it. It was so dirty, that whether it was vegetable matter out of a swamp, or weeds out of the river, or an old porter's-knot from England, I don't think any new spectator could have said. Yet, this unfortunate old woman had a notion that it was not only vastly genteel, but that it was the correct thing as to propriety. And she really did carry herself over the other ladies who had no night-caps, and who were forced to tie up their hair how they could, in a superior manner that was perfectly amazing.

I don't know what she looked like, sitting in that blessed nightcap, on a log of wood, outside the hut or cabin upon our raft. She would have rather resembled a fortune-teller in one of the picture-books that used to be in the shop windows in my boyhood, except for her stateliness. But, Lord bless my heart, the dignity with which she sat and moped, with her head in that bundle of tatters, was like nothing else in the world! She was not on speaking terms with more than three of the ladies. Some of them had,

what she called, 'taken precedence' of her—in getting into, or out of, that miserable little shelter!—and others had not called to pay their respects, or something of that kind. So, there she sat, in her own state and ceremony, while her husband sat on the same log of wood, ordering us one and all to let the raft go to the bottom, and to bring him stationery.

What with this noise on the part of Mr. Commissioner Pordage, and what with the cries of Sergeant Drooce on the raft astern (which were sometimes more than Tom Packer could silence), we often made our slow way down the river, anything but quietly. Yet, that it was of great importance that no ears should be able to hear us from the woods on the banks, could not be doubted. We were looked for, to a certainty, and we might be retaken at any moment. It was an anxious time: it was, indeed, indeed, an anxious time.

On the seventh night of our voyage on the rafts, we made fast, as usual, on the opposite side of the river to that from which we had started, in as dark a place as we could pick out. Our little encampment was soon made, and supper was eaten, and the children fell asleep. The watch was set, and everything made orderly for the night. Such a starlight night, with such blue in the sky, and such black in the places of heavy shade on the banks of the great stream!

Those two ladies, Miss Maryon and Mrs. Fisher, had always kept near me since the night of the attack. Mr. Fisher, who was untiring in the work of our raft, had said to me:

'My dear little childless wife has grown so attached to you, Davis, and you are such a gentle fellow, as well as such a determined one'; our party had adopted

that last expression from the one-eyed English pirate, and I repeat what Mr. Fisher said, only because he said it; 'that it takes a load off my mind to leave her in your charge.'

I said to him: 'Your lady is in far better charge than mine, sir, having Miss Maryon to take care of her; but, you may rely upon it, that I will guard them both—faithful and true.'

Says he: 'I do rely upon it, Davis, and I heartily wish all the silver on our old Island was yours.'

That seventh starlight night, as I have said, we made our camp, and got our supper, and set our watch, and the children fell asleep. It was solemn and beautiful in those wild and solitary parts, to see them, every night before they lay down, kneeling under the bright sky, saying their little prayers at women's laps. At that time we men all uncovered, and mostly kept at a distance. When the innocent creatures rose up, we murmured 'Amen!' all together. For, though we had not heard what they said, we knew it must be good for us.

At that time, too, as was only natural, those poor mothers in our company, whose children had been killed, shed many tears. I thought the sight seemed to console them while it made them cry; but, whether I was right or wrong in that, they wept very much. On this seventh night, Mrs. Fisher had cried for her lost darling until she cried herself asleep. She was lying on a little couch of leaves and such-like (I made the best little couch I could for them every night), and Miss Maryon had covered her, and sat by her, holding her hand. The stars looked down upon them. As for me, I guarded them.

'Davis!' says Miss Maryon. (I am not going to say what a voice she had. I couldn't if I tried.)

'I am here, Miss.'

'The river sounds as if it were swollen to-night.'

'We all think, Miss, that we are coming near the sea.'

'Do you believe now, we shall escape?'

'I do now, Miss, really believe it.' I had always said I did; but, I had in my own mind been doubtful.

'How glad you will be, my good Davis, to see England again!'

I have another confession to make that will appear singular. When she said these words, something rose in my throat; and the stars I looked away at, seemed to break into sparkles that fell down my face and burnt it.

'England is not much to me, Miss, except as a name.'

'O, so true an Englishman should not say that!— Are you not well to-night, Davis?' Very kindly, and with a quick change.

'Quite well, Miss.'

'Are you sure? Your voice sounds altered in my hearing.'

'No, Miss, I am a stronger man than ever. But, England is nothing to me.'

Miss Maryon sat silent for so long a while, that I believed she had done speaking to me for one time. However, she had not; for by and by she said in a distinct, clear tone:

'No, good friend; you must not say that England is nothing to you. It is to be much to you, yet— everything to you. You have to take back to England the good name you have earned here, and the gratitude and attachment and respect you have won here: and you have to make some good English girl very happy and proud, by marrying her; and I shall one day see her, I hope, and make her happier and prouder still, by telling her what noble services her

husband's were in South America, and what a noble friend he was to me there.'

Though she spoke these kinds words in a cheering manner, she spoke them compassionately. I said nothing. It will appear to be another strange confession, that I paced to and fro, within call, all that night, a most unhappy man, reproaching myself all the night long. 'You are as ignorant as any man alive; you are as obscure as any man alive; you are as poor as any man alive; you are no better than the mud under your foot.' That was the way in which I went on against myself until the morning.

With the day, came the day's labour. What I should have done without the labour, I don't know. We were afloat again at the usual hour, and were again making our way down the river. It was broader, and clearer of obstructions than it had been, and it seemed to flow faster. This was one of Drooce's quiet days; Mr. Pordage, besides being sulky, had almost lost his voice; and we made good way, and with little noise.

There was always a seaman forward on the raft, keeping a bright look-out. Suddenly, in the full heat of the day, when the children were slumbering, and the very trees and reeds appeared to be slumbering, this man—it was Short—holds up his hand, and cries with great caution: 'Avast! Voices ahead!'

We held on against the stream as soon as we could bring her up, and the other raft followed suit. At first, Mr. Macey, Mr. Fisher, and myself, could hear nothing; though both the seamen aboard of us agreed that they could hear voices and oars. After a little pause, however, we united in thinking that we *could* hear the sound of voices, and the dip of oars. But, you can hear a long way in those countries, and there

was a bend of the river before us, and nothing was to be seen except such waters and such banks as we were now in the eight day (and might, for the matter of our feelings, have been in the eightieth), of having seen with anxious eyes.

It was soon decided to put a man ashore, who should creep through the wood, see what was coming, and warn the rafts. The rafts in the meantime to keep the middle of the stream. The man to be put ashore, and not to swim ashore, as the first thing could be more quickly done than the second. The raft conveying him, to get back into mid-stream, and to hold on along with the other, as well as it could, until signalled by the man. In case of danger, the man to shift for himself until it should be safe to take him on board again. I volunteered to be the man.

We knew that the voices and oars must come up slowly against the stream; and our seamen knew, by the set of the stream, under which bank they would come. I was put ashore accordingly. The raft got off well, and I broke into the wood.

Steaming hot it was, and a tearing place to get through. So much the better for me, since it was something to contend against and do. I cut off the bend of the river, at a great saving of space, came to the water's edge again, and hid myself, and waited. I could now hear the dip of the oars very distinctly; the voices had ceased.

The sound came on in a regular tune, and as I lay hidden, I fancied the tune so played to be, 'Chris'en—George—King! Chris'en—George—King! Chris'en—George—King!' over and over again, always the same, with the pauses always at the same places. I had likewise time to make up my mind that if these were the Pirates, I could and would (barring my be-

ing shot) swim off to my raft, in spite of my wound, the moment I had given the alarm, and hold my old post by Miss Maryon.

'Chris'en—George—-King! Chris'en — George — King! Chris'en—George—King!' coming up, now, very near.

I took a look at the branches about me, to see where a shower of bullets would be most likely to do me least hurt; and I took a look back at the track I had made in forcing my way in; and now I was wholly prepared and fully ready for them.

'Chris'en—George—King! Chris'en—George—King! Chris'en—George—King!' Here they were!

Who were they? The barbarous Pirates, scum of all nations, headed by such men as the hideous little Portuguese monkey, and the one-eyed English convict with the gash across his face, that ought to have gashed his wicked head off? The worst men in the world picked out from the worst, to do the cruellest and most atrocious deeds that ever stained it? The howling, murdering, black-flag waving, mad, and drunken crowd of devils that had overcome us by numbers and by treachery? No. These were English men in English boats—good blue-jackets and red-coats—marines that I knew myself, and sailors that knew our seamen! At the helm of the first boat, Captain Carton, eager and steady. At the helm of the second boat, Captain Maryon, brave and bold. At the helm of the third boat, an old seaman, with determination carved into his watchful face, like the figure-head of a ship. Every man doubly and trebly armed from head to foot. Every man lying-to at his work, with a will that had all his heart and soul in it. Every man looking out for any trace of friend or enemy, and burning to be the first to do good or avenge evil. Every man with his face on fire when

he saw me, his countryman who had been taken prisoner, and hailed me with a cheer, as Captain Carton's boat ran in and took me on board.

I reported, 'All escaped, sir! All well, all safe, all here!'

God bless me—and God bless them—what a cheer! It turned me weak, as I was passed on from hand to hand to the stern of the boat: every hand patting me or grasping me in some way or other, in the moment of my going by.

'Hold up, my brave fellow,' says Captain Carton, clapping me on the shoulder like a friend, and giving me a flask. 'Put your lips to that, and they'll be red again. Now, boys, give way!'

The banks flew by us as if the mightiest stream that ever ran was with us; and so it was, I am sure, meaning the stream to those men's ardour and spirit. The banks flew by us, and we came in sight of the rafts—the banks flew by us, and we came alongside of the rafts—the banks stopped; and there was a tumult of laughing and crying, and kissing and shaking of hands, and catching up of children and setting of them down again, and a wild hurry of thankfulness and joy that melted every one and softened all hearts.

I had taken notice, in Captain Carton's boat, that there was a curious and quite new sort of fitting on board. It was a kind of a little bower made of flowers, and it was set up behind the captain, and betwixt him and the rudder. Not only was this arbour, so to call it, neatly made of flowers, but it was ornamented in a singular way. Some of the men had taken the ribbons and buckles off their hats, and hung them among the flowers; others had made festoons and streamers of their handkerchiefs, and hung them there; others had intermixed such trifles as bits of glass and shining fragments of lockets and to-

bacco-boxes with the flowers; so that altogether it was a very bright and lively object in the sunshine. But why there, or what for, I did not understand.

Now, as soon as the first bewilderment was over, Captain Carton gave the order to land for the present. But this boat of his, with two hands left in her, immediately put off again when the men were out of her, and kept off, some yards from the shore. As she floated there, with the two hands gently backing water to keep her from going down the stream, this pretty little arbour attracted many eyes. None of the boat's crew, however, had anything to say about it, except that it was the captain's fancy.

The captain—with the women and children clustering round him, and the men of all ranks grouped outside them, and all listening—stood telling how the Expedition, deceived by its bad intelligence, had chased the light Pirate boats all that fatal night, and had still followed in their wake next day, and had never suspected until many hours too late that the great Pirate body had drawn off in the darkness when the chase began, and shot over to the Island. He stood telling how the Expedition, supposing the whole array of armed boats to be ahead of it, got tempted into shallows and went aground; but not without having its revenge upon the two decoy-boats, both of which it had come up with, overhand, and sent to the bottom with all on board. He stood telling how the Expedition, fearing then that the case stood as it did, got afloat again, by great exertion, after the loss of four more tides, and returned to the Island, where they found the sloop scuttled and the treasure gone. He stood telling how my officer, Lieutenant Linderwood, was left upon the Island, with as strong a force as could be got together hurriedly from the mainland, and how the three boats we saw before us

were manned and armed and had come away, exploring the coast and inlets, in search of any tidings of us. He stood telling all this, with his face to the river; and, as he stood telling it, the little arbour of flowers floated in the sunshine before all the faces there.

Leaning on Captain Carton's shoulder, between him and Miss Maryon, was Mrs. Fisher, her head drooping on her arm. She asked him, without raising it, when he had told so much, whether he had found her mother?

'Be comforted! She lies,' said the Captain gently, 'under the cocoa-nut trees on the beach.'

'And my child, Captain Carton, did you find my child, too? Does my darling rest with my mother?'

'No. Your pretty child sleeps,' said the Captain, 'under a shade of flowers.'

His voice shook; but there was something in it that struck all the hearers. At that moment there sprung from the arbour in his boat a little creature, clapping her hands and stretching out her arms, and crying, 'Dear papa! Dear mamma! I am not killed. I am saved. I am coming to kiss you. Take me to them, take me to them, good, kind sailors!'

Nobody who saw that scene has ever forgotten it, I am sure, or ever will forget it. The child had kept quite still, where her brave grandmamma had put her (first whispering in her ear, 'Whatever happens to me, do not stir, my dear!'), and had remained quiet until the fort was deserted; she had then crept out of the trench, and gone into her mother's house; and there, alone on the solitary Island, in her mother's room, and asleep on her mother's bed, the Captain had found her. Nothing could induce her to be parted from him after he

took her up in his arms, and he had brought her away with him, and the men had made the bower for her. To see those men now, was a sight. The joy of the women was beautiful; the joy of those women who had lost their own children, was quite sacred and divine; but, the ecstasies of Captain Carton's boat's crew, when their pet was restored to her parents, were wonderful for the tenderness they showed in the midst of roughness. As the Captain stood with the child in his arms, and the child's own little arms now clinging round his neck, now round her father's, now round her mother's, now round some one who pressed up to kiss her, the boat's crew shook hands with one another, waved their hats over their heads, laughed, sang, cried, danced—and all among themselves, without wanting to interfere with anybody—in a manner never to be represented. At last, I saw the coxswain and another, two very hard-faced men, with grizzled heads, who had been the heartiest of the hearty all along, close with one another, get each of them the other's head under his arm, and pommel away at it with his fist as hard as he could, in his excess of joy.

When we had well rested and refreshed ourselves —and very glad we were to have some of the heartening things to eat and drink that had come up in the boats—we recommenced our voyage down the river: rafts, and boats, and all. I said to myself, it was a very different kind of voyage now, from what it had been; and I fell into my proper place and station among my fellow-soldiers.

But, when we halted for the night, I found that Miss Maryon had spoken to Captain Carton concerning me. For, the Captain came straight up to me, and says he, 'My brave fellow, you have been Miss Maryon's body-guard all along, and you shall

remain so. Nobody shall supersede you in the distinction and pleasure of protecting that young lady.' I thanked his honour in the fittest words I could find, and that night I was placed on my old post of watching the place where she slept. More than once in the night, I saw Captain Carton come out into the air, and stroll about there, to see that all was well. I have now this other singular confession to make, that I saw him with a heavy heart. Yes; I saw him with a heavy, heavy heart.

In the day-time, I had the like post in Captain Carton's boat. I had a special station of my own, behind Miss Maryon, and no hands but hers ever touched my wound. (It has been healed these many long years; but, no other hands have ever touched it.) Mr. Pordage was kept tolerably quiet now, with pen and ink, and began to pick up his senses a little. Seated in the second boat, he made documents with Mr. Kitten, pretty well all day; and he generally handed in a Protest about something whenever we stopped. The Captain, however, made so very light of these papers, that it grew into a saying among the men, when one of them wanted a match for his pipe, 'Hand us over a Protest, Jack!' As to Mrs. Pordage, she still wore the nightcap, and she now had cut all the ladies on account of her not having been formally and separately rescued by Captain Carton before anybody else. The end of Mr. Pordage, to bring to an end all I know about him, was, that he got great compliments at home for his conduct on these trying occasions, and that he died of yellow jaundice, a Governor and a K.C.B.

Sergeant Drooce had fallen from a high fever into a low one. Tom Packer—the only man who could have pulled the Sergeant through it—kept hospital aboard the old raft, and Mrs. Belltott, as brisk as

ever again (but the spirit of that little woman, when things tried it, was not equal to appearances), was head-nurse under his directions. Before we got down to the Mosquito coast, the joke had been made by one of our men, that we should see her gazetted Mrs. Tom Packer, *vice* Belltott exchanged.

When we reached the coast, we got native boats as substitutes for the rafts; and we rowed along under the land; and in that beautiful climate, and upon that beautiful water, the blooming days were like enchantment. Ah! They were running away, faster than any sea or river, and there was no tide to bring them back. We were coming very near the settlement where the people of Silver-Store were to be left, and from which we Marines were under orders to return to Belize.

Captain Carton had, in the boat by him, a curious long-barrelled Spanish gun, and he had said to Miss Maryon one day that it was the best of guns, and had turned his head to me, and said:

'Gill Davis, load her fresh with a couple of slugs, against a chance of showing how good she is.'

So, I had discharged the gun over the sea, and had loaded her, according to orders, and there it had lain at the Captain's feet, convenient to the Captain's hand.

The last day but one of our journey was an uncommonly hot day. We started very early; but, there was no cool air on the sea as the day got on, and by noon the heat was really hard to bear, considering that there were women and children to bear it. Now, we happened to open, just at that time, a very pleasant little cove or bay, where there was a deep shade from a great growth of trees. Now, the Captain, therefore, made the signal to the other boats to follow him in and lie by a while.

The men who were off duty went ashore, and lay down, but were ordered, for caution's sake, not to stray, and to keep within view. The others rested on their oars, and dozed. Awnings had been made of one thing and another, in all the boats, and the passengers found it cooler to be under them in the shade, when there was room enough, than to be in the thick woods. So, the passengers were all afloat, and mostly sleeping. I kept my post behind Miss Maryon, and she was on Captain Carton's right in the boat, and Mrs. Fisher sat on her right again. The Captain had Mrs. Fisher's daughter on his knee. He and the two ladies were talking about the Pirates, and were talking softly; partly, because people do talk softly under such indolent circumstances, and partly because the little girl had gone off asleep.

I think I have before given it out for my Lady to write down, that Captain Carton had a fine bright eye of his own. All at once, he darted me a side look, as much as to say, 'Steady—don't take on—I see something!'—and gave the child into her mother's arms. That eye of his was so easy to understand, that I obeyed it by not so much as looking either to the right or to the left out of a corner of my own, or changing my attitude the least trifle. The Captain went on talking in the same mild and easy way; but began—with his arms resting across his knees, and his head a little hanging forward, as if the heat were rather too much for him—began to play with the Spanish gun.

'They had laid their plans, you see,' says the Captain, taking up the Spanish gun across his knees, and looking, lazily, at the inlaying on the stock, 'with a great deal of art; and the corrupt or blundering local authorities were so easily deceived'; he ran his left hand idly along the barrel, but I saw, with my breath

held, that he covered the action of cocking the gun with his right—'so easily deceived, that they summoned us to come out into the trap. But my intention as to future operations—' In a flash the Spanish gun was at his bright eye, and he fired.

All started up; innumerable echoes repeated the sound of the discharge; a cloud of bright-coloured birds flew out of the woods screaming; a handful of leaves were scattered in the place where the shot had struck; a crackling of branches was heard; and some lithe but heavy creature sprang into the air, and fell forward, head down, over the muddy bank.

'What is it?' cries Captain Maryon from his boat. All silent then, but the echoes rolling away.

'It is a Traitor and a Spy,' said Captain Carton, handing me the gun to load again. 'And I think the other name of the animal is Christian George King!'

Shot through the heart. Some of the people ran round to the spot, and drew him out, with the slime and wet trickling down his face; but his face itself would never stir any more to the end of time.

'Leave him hanging to that tree,' cried Captain Carton; his boat's crew giving way, and he leaping ashore. 'But first into this wood, every man in his place. And boats! Out of gunshot!'

It was a quick change, well meant and well made, though it ended in disappointment. No Pirates were there; no one but the Spy was found. It was supposed that the Pirates, unable to retake us, and expecting a great attack upon them to be the consequence of our escape, had made from the ruins in the Forest, taken to their ship along with the Treasure, and left the Spy to pick up what intelligence he could. In the evening we went away, and he was left hanging to the tree, all alone, with the red sun making a kind of a dead sunset on his black face.

Next day, we gained the settlement on the Mosquito coast for which we were bound. Having stayed there to refresh seven days, and having been much commended, and highly spoken of, and finely entertained, we Marines stood under orders to march from the Town-Gate (it was neither much of a town nor much of a gate), at five in the morning.

My officer had joined us before then. When we turned out at the gate, all the people were there; in the front of them all those who had been our fellow-prisoners, and all the seamen.

'Davis,' says Lieutenant Linderwood. 'Stand out, my friend!'

I stood out from the ranks, and Miss Maryon and Captain Carton came up to me.

'Dear Davis,' says Miss Maryon, while the tears fell fast down her face, 'your grateful friends, in most unwillingly taking leave of you, ask the favour that, while you bear away with you their affectionate remembrance, which nothing can ever impair, you will also take this purse of money—far more valuable to you, we all know, for the deep attachment and thankfulness with which it is offered, than for its own contents, though we hope those may prove useful to you, too, in after life.'

I got out, in answer, that I thankfully accepted the attachment and affection, but not the money. Captain Carton looked at me very attentively, and stepped back, and moved away. I made him my bow as he stepped back, to thank him for being so delicate.

'No, miss,' said I, 'I think it would break my heart to accept of money. But, if you could condescend to give to a man so ignorant and common as myself, any little thing you have worn—such as a bit of ribbon—'

She took a ring from her finger, and put it in my hand. And she rested her hand in mine, while she said these words:

'The brave gentlemen of old—but not one of them was braver, or had a nobler nature than you—took such gifts from ladies, and did all their good actions for the givers' sakes. If you will do yours for mine, I shall think with pride that I continue to have some share in the life of a gallant and generous man.'

For the second time in my life she kissed my hand. I made so bold, for the first time, as to kiss hers; and I tied the ring at my breast, and I fell back to my place.

Then, the horse-litter went out at the gate with Sergeant Drooce in it; and the horse-litter went out at the gate with Mrs. Belltott in it; and Lieutenant Linderwood gave the word of command, 'Quick march!' and, cheered and cried for, we went out of the gate too, marching along the level plain towards the serene blue sky, as if we were marching straight to Heaven.

When I have added here that the Pirate scheme was blown to shivers, by the Pirate-ship which had the Treasure on board being so vigorously attacked by one of His Majesty's cruisers, among the West India Keys, and being so swiftly boarded and carried, that nobody suspected anything about the scheme until three-fourths of the Pirates were killed, and the other fourth were in irons, and the Treasure was recovered; I come to the last singular confession I have got to make.

It is this. I well knew what an immense and hopeless distance there was between me and Miss Maryon; I well knew that I was no fitter company for her than I was for the angels; I well knew that she was as

high above my reach as the sky over my head; and yet I loved her. What put it in my low heart to be so daring, or whether such a thing ever happened before or since, as that a man so uninstructed and obscure as myself got his unhappy thoughts lifted up to such a height, while knowing very well how presumptuous and impossible to be realised they were, I am unable to say; still, the suffering to me was just as great as if I had been a gentleman. I suffered agony— agony. I suffered hard, and I suffered long. I thought of her last words to me, however, and I never disgraced them. If it had not been for those dear words, I think I should have lost myself in despair and recklessness.

The ring will be found lying on my heart, of course, and will be laid with me wherever I am laid. I am getting on in years now, though I am able and hearty. I was recommended for promotion, and everything was done to reward me that could be done; but my total want of all learning stood in my way, and I found myself so completely out of the road to it, that I could not conquer any learning, though I tried. I was long in the service, and I respected it, and was respected in it, and the service is dear to me at this present hour.

At this present hour, when I give this out to my Lady to be written down, all my old pain has softened away, and I am as happy as a man can be, at this present fine old country-house of Admiral Sir George Carton, Baronet. It was my Lady Carton who herself sought me out, over a great many miles of the wide world, and found me in Hospital wounded, and brought me here. It is my Lady Carton who writes down my words. My Lady was Miss Maryon. And now, that I conclude what I had to

tell, I see my Lady's honoured grey hair droop over
her face, as she leans a little lower at her desk; and
I fervently thank her for being so tender as I see
she is, towards the past pain and trouble of her poor,
old, faithful, humble soldier.

GOING INTO SOCIETY

[1858]

GOING INTO SOCIETY

At one period of its reverses, the House fell into the occupation of a Showman. He was found registered as its occupier, on the parish books of the time when he rented the House, and there was therefore no need of any clue to his name. But, he himself was less easy to be found; for, he had led a wandering life, and settled people had lost sight of him, and people who plumed themselves on being respectable were shy of admitting that they had ever known anything of him. At last, among the marsh lands near the river's level, that lie about Deptford and the neighbouring market-gardens, a Grizzled Personage in velveteen, with a face so cut up by varieties of weather that he looked as if he had been tattooed, was found smoking a pipe at the door of a wooden house on wheels. The wooden house was laid up in ordinary for the winter, near the mouth of a muddy creek; and everything near it, the foggy river, the misty marshes, and the steaming market-gardens, smoked in company with the grizzled man. In the midst of this smoking party, the funnel-chimney of the wooden house on wheels was not remiss, but took its pipe with the rest in a companionable manner.

On being asked if it were he who had once rented the House to Let, Grizzled Velveteen looked surprised, and said yes. Then his name was Magsman? That was it, Toby Magsman—which lawfully christened Robert; but called in the line, from a infant, Toby. There was nothing agin Toby Magsman, he

271

believed? If there was suspicion of such—mention it!

There was no suspicion of such, he might rest assured. But, some inquiries were making about that House, and would he object to say why he left it?

Not at all; why should he? He left it, along of a Dwarf.

Along of a Dwarf?

Mr. Magsman repeated, deliberately and emphatically, Along of a Dwarf.

Might it be compatible with Mr. Magsman's inclination and convenience to enter, as a favour, into a few particulars?

Mr. Magsman entered into the following particulars.

It was a long time ago, to begin with;—afore lotteries and a deal more was done away with. Mr. Magsman was looking about for a good pitch, and he see that house, and he says to himself, 'I'll have you, if you're to be had. If money'll get you, I'll have you.'

The neighbours cut up rough, and made complaints; but Mr. Magsman don't know what they *would* have had. It was a lovely thing. First of all, there was the canvass, representin the picter of the Giant, in Spanish trunks and a ruff, who was himself half the heighth of the house, and was run up with a line and pulley to a pole on the roof, so that his Ed was coeval with the parapet. Then, there was the canvass, representin the picter of the Albina lady, showing her white air to the Army and Navy in correct uniform. Then, there was the canvass, representin the picter of the Wild Indian a scalpin a member of some foreign nation. Then, there was the canvass, representin the picter of a child of a British Planter, seized by two Boa Constrictors—not that

we never had no child, nor no Constrictors neither.
Similarly, there was the canvass, representin the picter of the Wild Ass of the Prairies—not that *we*
never had no wild asses, nor wouldn't have had 'em at
a gift.   Last, there was the canvass, representin the
picter of the Dwarf, and like him too (considerin),
with George the Fourth in such a state of astonishment at him as His Majesty couldn't with his utmost
politeness and stoutness express.   The front of the
House was so covered with canvasses, that there wasn't
a spark of daylight ever visible on that side.   'MAGS-
MAN'S AMUSEMENTS,' fifteen foot long by two foot
high, ran over the front door and parlour winders.
The passage was a Arbour of green baize and garden-
stuff.   A barrel-organ performed there unceasing.
And as to respectability,—if threepence ain't respectable, what is?

But, the Dwarf is the principal article at present,
and he was worth the money.   He was wrote up as
MAJOR TPSCHOFFKI, OF THE IMPERIAL BULGRADER-
IAN BRIGADE.   Nobody couldn't pronounce the name,
and it never was intended anybody should.   The public always turned it, as a regular rule, into Chopski.
In the line he was called Chops; partly on that account, and partly because his real name, if he ever
had any real name (which was very dubious), was
Stakes.

He was a un-common small man, he really was.
Certainly not so small as he was made out to be, but
where *is* your Dwarf as is?   He was a most uncommon small man, with a most uncommon large Ed;
and what he had inside that Ed, nobody never knowed
but himself; even supposin himself to have ever took
stock of it, which it would have been a stiff job for
even him to do.

The kindest little man as never growed!   Spirited,

but not proud. When he travelled with the Spotted Baby—though he knowed himself to be a nat'ral Dwarf, and knowed the Baby's spots to be put upon him artificial, he nursed that Baby like a mother. You never heerd him give a ill-name to a Giant. He *did* allow himself to break out into strong language respectin the Fat Lady from Norfolk; but that was an affair of the 'art; and when a man's 'art has been trifled with by a lady, and the preference giv to a Indian, he ain't master of his actions.

He was always in love, of course; every human nat'ral phenomenon is. And he was always in love with a large woman; *I* never knowed the Dwarf as could be got to love a small one. Which helps to keep 'em the Curiosities they are.

One sing'ler idea he had in that Ed of his, which must have meant something, or it wouldn't have been there. It was always his opinion that he was entitled to property. He never would put his name to anything. He had been taught to write, by the young man without arms, who got his living with his toes (quite a writing master *he* was, and taught scores in the line), but Chops would have starved to death, afore he 'd have gained a bit of bread by putting his hand to a paper. This is the more curious to bear in mind, because HE had no property, nor hope of property, except his house and a sarser. When I say his house, I mean the box, painted and got up outside like a reg'lar six-roomer, that he used to creep into, with a diamond ring (or quite as good to look at) on his forefinger, and ring a little bell out of what the Public believed to be the Drawing-room winder. And when I say a sarser, I mean a Chaney sarser in which he made a collection for himself at the end of every Entertainment. His cue for that, he took from me; 'Ladies and gentlemen, the little

man will now walk three times round the Cairawan, and retire behind the curtain.' When he said anything important, in private life, he mostly wound it up with this form of words, and they was generally the last thing he said to me at night afore he went to bed.

He had what I consider a fine mind—a poetic mind. His ideas respectin his property never come upon him so strong as when he sat upon a barrel-organ and had the handle turned. Arter the wibration had run through him a little time, he would screech out, 'Toby, I feel my property coming—grind away! I'm counting my guineas by thousands, Toby—grind away! Toby, I shall be a man of fortun! I feel the Mint a jingling in me, Toby, and I'm swelling out into the Bank of England!' Such is the influence of music on a poetic mind. Not that he was partial to any other music but a barrel-organ; on the contrairy, hated it.

He had a kind of a everlasting grudge agin the Public: which is a thing you may notice in many phenomenons that get their living out of it. What riled him most in the nater of his occupation was, that it kep him out of Society. He was continiwally saying, 'Toby, my ambition is, to go into Society. The curse of my position towards the Public is, that it keeps me hout of Society. This don't signify to a low beast of a Indian; he an't formed for Society. This don't signify to a Spotted Baby; *he* an't formed for Society.—I am.'

Nobody never could make out what Chops done with his money. He had a good salary, down on the drum every Saturday as the day come round, besides having the run of his teeth—and he was a Woodpecker to eat—but all Dwarfs are. The sarser was a little income, bringing him in so many halfpence

that he 'd carry 'em for a week together, tied up in a pocket-handkercher. And yet he never had money. And it couldn't be the Fat Lady from Norfolk, as was once supposed; because it stands to reason that when you have a animosity towards a Indian, which makes you grind your teeth at him to his face, and which can hardly hold you from Goosing him audible when he 's going through his War-Dance—it stands to reason you wouldn't under them circumstances deprive yourself, to support that Indian in the lap of luxury.

Most unexpected, the mystery come out one day at Egham Races. The Public was shy of bein pulled in, and Chops was ringin his little bell out of his drawing-room winder, and was snarlin to me over his shoulder as he kneeled down with his legs out at the back-door—for he couldn't be shoved into his house without kneeling down, and the premises wouldn't accommodate his legs—was snarlin, 'Here 's a precious Public for you; why the Devil don't they tumble up?' when a man in the crowd holds up a carrier-pigeon, and cries out, 'If there 's any person here as has got a ticket, the Lottery 's just drawed, and the number as has come up for the great prize is three, seven, forty-two! Three, seven, forty-two!' I was givin the man to the Furies myself, for calling off the Public's attention—for the Public will turn away, at any time, to look at anything in preference to the thing showed 'em; and if you doubt it, get 'em together for any indiwidual purpose on the face of the earth, and send only two people in late, and see if the whole company an't far more interested in takin particular notice of them two than of you—I say, I wasn't best pleased with the man for callin out, and wasn't blessin him in my own mind, when I see Chops's little bell fly out of winder at a old lady, and he gets up and kicks

his box over, exposin the whole secret, and he catches
hold of the calves of my legs and he says to me,
'Carry me into the wan, Toby, and throw a pail of
water over me or I 'm a dead man, for I 've come into
my property!'

Twelve thousand odd hundred pound, was Chops's
winnins. He had bought a half-ticket for the twenty-
five thousand prize, and it had come up. The first
use he made of his property, was, to offer to fight
the Wild Indian for five hundred pound a side, him
with a poisoned darnin-needle and the Indian with a
club; but the Indian being in want of backers to that
amount, it went no further.

Arter he had been mad for a week—in a state of
mind, in short, in which, if I had let him sit on the
organ for only two minutes, I believe he would have
bust—but we kep the organ from him—Mr. Chops
come round, and behaved liberal and beautiful to all.
He then sent for a young man he knowed, as had a
wery genteel appearance and was a Bonnet at a gam-
ing-booth (most respectable brought up, father havin
been imminent in the livery stable line but unfort'nate
in a commercial crisis, through paintin a old gray,
ginger-bay, and sellin him with a Pedigree), and Mr.
Chops said to this Bonnet, who said his name was
Normandy, which it wasn't:

'Normandy, I 'm a goin into Society. Will you
go with me?'

Says Normandy: 'Do I understand you, Mr.
Chops, to hintimate that the 'ole of the expenses of
that move will be borne by yourself?'

'Correct,' says Mr. Chops. 'And you shall have a
Princely allowance too.'

The Bonnet lifted Mr. Chops upon a chair, to
shake hands with him, and replied in poetry, with
his eyes seemingly full of tears:

'My boat is on the shore,
And my bark is on the sea,
And I do not ask for more,
But I 'll Go:—along with thee.'

They went into Society, in a chay and four grays with silk jackets. They took lodgings in Pall Mall, London, and they blazed away.

In consequence of a note that was brought to Bartlemy Fair in the autumn of next year by a servant, most wonderful got up in milk-white cords and tops, I cleaned myself and went to Pall Mall, one evening appinted. The gentlemen was at their wine arter dinner, and Mr. Chops's eyes was more fixed in that Ed of his than I thought good for him. There was three of 'em (in company, I mean), and I knowed the third well. When last met, he had on a white Roman shirt, and a bishop's mitre covered with leopard-skin, and played the clarionet all wrong, in a band at a Wild Beast Show.

This gent took on not to know me, and Mr. Chops said: 'Gentlemen, this is a old friend of former days': and Normandy looked at me through a eye-glass, and said, 'Magsman, glad to see you!'—which I 'll take my oath he wasn't. Mr. Chops, to git him convenient to the table, had his chair on a throne (much of the form of George the Fourth's in the canvass), but he hardly appeared to me to be King there in any other pint of view, for his two gentlemen ordered about like Emperors. They was all dressed like May-Day—gorgeous!—and as to Wine, they swam in all sorts.

I made the round of the bottles, first separate (to say I had done it), and then mixed 'em all together (to say I had done it), and then tried two of 'em as half-and-half, and then t' other two. Altogether, I passed a pleasin evenin, but with a tendency to feel

muddled, until I considered it good manners to get up and say, 'Mr. Chops, the best of friends must part, I thank you for the wariety of foreign drains you have stood so 'ansome, I looks towards you in red wine, and I takes my leave.'   Mr. Chops replied, 'If you 'll just hitch me out of this over your right arm, Magsman, and carry me downstairs, I 'll see you out.'   I said I couldn't think of such a thing, but he would have it, so I lifted him off his throne.   He smelt strong of Maideary, and I couldn't help thinking as I carried him down that it was like carrying a large bottle full of wine, with a rayther ugly stopper, a good deal out of proportion.

When I set him on the door-mat in the hall, he kep me close to him by holding on to my coat-collar, and he whispers:

'I ain't 'appy, Magsman.'

'What 's on your mind, Mr. Chops?'

'They don't use me well.   They an't grateful to me.   They puts me on the mantel-piece when I won't have in more Champagne-wine, and they locks me in the sideboard when I won't give up my property.'

'Get rid of 'em, Mr. Chops.'

'I can't.   We 're in Society together, and what would Society say?'

'Come out of Society!' says I.

'I can't.   You don't know what you 're talking about.   When you have once gone into Society, you mustn't come out of it.'

'Then if you 'll excuse the freedom, Mr. Chops,' were my remark, shaking my head grave, 'I think it 's a pity you ever went in.'

Mr. Chops shook that deep Ed of his, to a surprisin extent, and slapped it half a dozen times with his hand, and with more Wice than I thought were in him.   Then, he says, 'You 're a good fellow, but

you don't understand. Good night, go along. Magsman, the little man will now walk three times round the Cairawan, and retire behind the curtain.' The last I see of him on that occasion was his tryin, on the extremest werge of insensibility, to climb up the stairs, one by one, with his hands and knees. They 'd have been much too steep for him, if he had been sober; but he wouldn't be helped.

It warn't long after that, that I read in the newspaper of Mr. Chops's being presented at court. It was printed, 'It will be recollected'—and I 've noticed in my life, that it is sure to be printed that it *will* be recollected, whenever it won't—'that Mr. Chops is the individual of small stature, whose brilliant success in the last State Lottery attracted so much attention.' Well, I says to myself, Such is Life! He has been and done it in earnest at last! He has astonished George the Fourth!

(On account of which, I had that canvass new-painted, him with a bag of money in his hand, a presentin it to George the Fourth, and a lady in Ostrich Feathers fallin in love with him in a bag-wig, sword, and buckles correct.)

I took the House as is the subject of present inquiries—though not the honour of bein acquainted—and I run Magsman's Amusements in it thirteen months—sometimes one thing, sometimes another, sometimes nothin particular, but always all the canvasses outside. One night, when we had played the last company out, which was a shy company, through its raining Heavens hard, I was takin a pipe in the one pair back along with the young man with the toes, which I had taken on for a month (though he never drawed—except on paper), and I heard a kickin at the street door. 'Halloa!' I says to the young man, 'what 's up!' He rubs his eyebrows with his toes, and

he says, 'I can't imagine, Mr. Magsman'—which he never could imagine nothin, and was monotonous company.

The noise not leavin off, I laid down my pipe, and I took up a candle, and I went down and opened the door. I looked out into the street; but nothin could I see, and nothin was I aware of, until I turned round quick, because some creetur run between my legs into the passage. There was Mr. Chops!

'Magsman,' he says, 'take me, on the old terms, and you 've got me; if it 's done, say done!'

I was all of a maze, but I said, 'Done, sir.'

'Done to your done, and double done!' says he. 'Have you got a bit of supper in the house?'

Bearin in mind them sparklin warieties of foreign drains as we 'd guzzled away at in Pall Mall, I was ashamed to offer him cold sassages and gin-and-water; but he took 'em both and took 'em free; havin a chair for his table, and sittin down at it on a stool, like hold times. I, all of a maze all the while.

It was arter he had made a clean sweep of the sassages (beef, and to the best of my calculations two pound and a quarter), that the wisdom as was in that little man began to come out of him like perspiration.

'Magsman,' he says, 'look upon me! You see afore you, One as has both gone into Society and come out.'

'O! You *are* out of it, Mr. Chops? How did you get out, sir?'

'SOLD OUT!' says he. You never saw the like of the wisdom as his Ed expressed, when he made use of them two words.

'My friend Magsman, I 'll impart to you a discovery I 've made. It 's wallable; it 's cost twelve thousand five hundred pound; it may do you good in life.—

The secret of this matter is, that it ain't so much that a person goes into Society, as that Society goes into a person.'

Not exactly keeping up with his meanin, I shook my head, put on a deep look, and said, 'You 're right there, Mr. Chops.'

'Magsman,' he says, twitchin me by the leg, 'Society has gone into me, to the tune of every penny of my property.'

I felt that I went pale, and though nat'rally a bold speaker, I couldn't hardly say, 'Where 's Normandy?'

'Bolted.   With the plate,' said Mr. Chops.

'And t' other one?' meaning him as formerly wore the bishop's mitre.

'Bolted.   With the jewels,' said Mr. Chops.

I sat down and looked at him, and he stood up and looked at me.

'Magsman,' he says, and he seemed to myself to get wiser as he got hoarser; 'Society, taken in the lump, is all dwarfs.   At the court of St. James's, they was all a doing my old business—all a goin three times round the Cairawan, in the hold court-suits and properties.   Elsewheres, they was most of 'em ringin their little bells out of make-believes.   Everywheres, the sarser was a goin round.   Magsman, the sarser is the uniwersal Institution!'

I perceived, you understand, that he was soured by his misfortunes, and I felt for Mr. Chops.

'As to Fat Ladies,' says he, giving his head a tremendious one agin the wall, 'there 's lots of *them* in Society, and worse than the original.   *Hers* was a outrage upon Taste—simply a outrage upon Taste—awakenin contempt—carryin its own punishment in the form of a Indian!'   Here he giv himself another tremendious one.   'But *theirs,* Magsman, *theirs* is

mercenary outrages. Lay in Cashmeer shawls, buy bracelets, strew 'em and a lot of 'andsome fans and things about your rooms, let it be known that you give away like water to all as come to admire, and the Fat Ladies that don't exhibit for so much down upon the drum, will come from all the pints of the compass to flock about you, whatever you are. They'll drill holes in your 'art, Magsman, like a Cullender. And when you've no more left to give, they'll laugh at you to your face, and leave you to have your bones picked dry by Wulturs, like the dead Wild Ass of the Prairies that you deserve to be!' Here he giv himself the most tremendious one of all, and dropped.

I thought he was gone. His Ed was so heavy, and he knocked it so hard, and he fell so stoney, and the sassagerial disturbance in him must have been so immense, that I thought he was gone. But, he soon come round with care, and he sat up on the floor, and he said to me, with wisdom comin out of his eyes, if ever it come:

'Magsman! The most material difference between the two states of existence through which your unappy friend has passed'; he reached out his poor little hand, and his tears dropped down on the moustachio which it was a credit to him to have done his best to grow, but it is not in mortals to command success,— 'the difference is this. When I was out of Society, I was paid light for being seen. When I went into Society, I paid heavy for being seen. I prefer the former, even if I wasn't forced upon it. Give me out through the trumpet, in the hold way, to-morrow.'

Arter that, he slid into the line again as easy as if he had been iled all over. But the organ was kep from him, and no allusions was ever made, when a company was in, to his property. He got wiser every

day; his views of Society and the Public was luminous, bewilderin, awful; and his Ed got bigger and bigger as his Wisdom expanded it.

He took well, and pulled 'em in most excellent for nine weeks. At the expiration of that period, when his Ed was a sight, he expressed one evenin, the last Company havin been turned out, and the door shut, a wish to have a little music.

'Mr. Chops,' I said (I never dropped the 'Mr.' with him; the world might do it, but not me) ; 'Mr. Chops, are you sure as you are in a state of mind and body to sit upon the organ?'

His answer was this: 'Toby, when next met with on the tramp, I forgive her and the Indian. And I am.'

It was with fear and trembling that I began to turn the handle; but he sat like a lamb. It will be my belief to my dying day, that I see his Ed expand as he sat; you may therefore judge how great his thoughts was. He sat out all the changes, and then he come off.

'Toby,' he says, with a quiet smile, 'the little man will now walk three times round the Cairawan, and retire behind the curtain.'

When we called him in the morning, we found him gone into a much better Society than mine or Pall Mall's. I giv Mr. Chops as comfortable a funeral as lay in my power, followed myself as Chief, and had the George the Fourth canvass carried first, in the form of a banner. But, the House was so dismal arterwards, that I giv it up, and took to the Wan again.

'I don't triumph,' said Jarber, folding up the second manuscript, and looking hard at Trottle. 'I

don't triumph over this worthy creature. I merely ask him if he is satisfied now?'

'How can he be anything else?' I said, answering for Trottle, who sat obstinately silent. 'This time, Jarber, you have not only read us a delightfully amusing story, but you have also answered the question about the House. Of course it stands empty now. Who would think of taking it after it had been turned into a caravan?' I looked at Trottle, as I said those last words, and Jarber waved his hand indulgently in the same direction.

'Let this excellent person speak,' said Jarber. 'You were about to say, my good man—?'

'I only wished to ask, sir,' said Trottle doggedly, 'if you could kindly oblige me with a date or two in connection with that last story?'

'A date!' repeated Jarber. 'What does the man want with dates!'

'I should be glad to know, with great respect,' persisted Trottle, 'if the person named Magsman was the last tenant who lived in the House. It's my opinion —if I may be excused for giving it—that he most decidedly was not.'

With those words, Trottle made a low bow, and quietly left the room.

There is no denying that Jarber, when we were left together, looked sadly discomposed. He had evidently forgotten to inquire about dates; and, in spite of his magnificent talk about his series of discoveries, it was quite as plain that the two stories he had just read, had really and truly exhausted his present stock. I thought myself bound, in common gratitude, to help him out of his embarrassment by a timely suggestion. So I proposed that he should come to tea again, on the next Monday evening, the thirteenth,

and should make such inquiries in the meantime, as might enable him to dispose triumphantly of Trottle's objection.

He gallantly kissed my hand, made a neat little speech of acknowledgment, and took his leave. For the rest of the week I would not encourage Trottle by allowing him to refer to the House at all. I suspected he was making his own inquiries about dates, but I put no questions to him.

On Monday evening, the thirteenth, that dear unfortunate Jarber came, punctual to the appointed time. He looked so terribly harassed, that he was really quite a spectacle of feebleness and fatigue. I saw, at a glance, that the question of dates had gone against him, that Mr. Magsman had not been the last tenant of the House, and that the reason of its emptiness was still to seek.

'What I have gone through,' said Jarber, 'words are not eloquent enough to tell. O Sophonisba, I have begun another series of discoveries! Accept the last two as stories laid on your shrine; and wait to blame me for leaving your curiosity unappeased, until you have heard Number Three.'

Number Three looked like a very short manuscript, and I said as much. Jarber explained to me that we were to have some poetry this time. In the course of his investigations he had stepped into the Circulating Library, to seek for information on the one important subject. All the Library-people knew about the House was, that a female relative of the last tenant, as they believed, had, just after that tenant left, sent a little manuscript poem to them which she described as referring to events that had actually passed in the House; and which she wanted the proprietor of the Library to publish. She had written no address on her letter; and the proprietor had kept the manu-

script ready to be given back to her (the publishing of poems not being in his line) when she might call for it. She had never called for it; and the poem had been lent to Jarber, at his express request, to read to me.

Before he began, I rang the bell for Trottle; being determined to have him present at the new reading, as a wholesome check on his obstinacy. To my surprise Peggy answered the bell, and told me that Trottle had stepped out without saying where. I instantly felt the strongest possible conviction that he was at his old tricks: and that his stepping out in the evening, without leave, meant—Philandering.

Controlling myself on my visitor's account, I dismissed Peggy, stifled my indignation, and prepared, as politely as might be, to listen to Jarber.

CHRISTMAS STORIES
FROM
'ALL THE YEAR ROUND

THE HAUNTED HOUSE

[1859]

THE HAUNTED HOUSE

IN TWO CHAPTERS [1]

THE MORTALS IN THE HOUSE

UNDER none of the accredited ghostly circumstances, and environed by none of the conventional ghostly surroundings, did I first make acquaintance with the house which is the subject of this Christmas piece. I saw it in the daylight, with the sun upon it. There was no wind, no rain, no lightning, no thunder, no awful or unwonted circumstance, of any kind, to heighten its effect. More than that: I had come to it direct from a railway station: it was not more than a mile distant from the railway station; and, as I stood outside the house, looking back upon the way I had come, I could see the goods train running smoothly along the embankment in the valley. I will not say that everything was utterly commonplace, because I doubt if anything can be that, except to utterly commonplace people—and there my vanity steps in; but, I will take it on myself to say that anybody might see the house as I saw it, any fine autumn morning.

The manner of my lighting on it was this.

I was travelling towards London out of the North, intending to stop by the way, to look at the house. My health required a temporary residence in the country; and a friend of mine who knew that, and who

293

had happened to drive past the house, had written to me to suggest it as a likely place. I had got into the train at midnight, and had fallen asleep, and had woke up and had sat looking out of window at the brilliant Northern Lights in the sky, and had fallen asleep again, and had woke up again to find the night gone, with the usual discontented conviction on me that I hadn't been to sleep at all;—upon which question, in the first imbecility of that condition, I am ashamed to believe that I would have done wager by battle with the man who sat opposite me. That opposite man had had, through the night—as that opposite man always has—several legs too many, and all of them too long. In addition to this unreasonable conduct (which was only to be expected of him), he had had a pencil and a pocket-book, and had been perpetually listening and taking notes. It had appeared to me that these aggravating notes related to the jolts and bumps of the carriage, and I should have resigned myself to his taking them, under a general supposition that he was in the civil-engineering way of life, if he had not sat staring straight over my head whenever he listened. He was a goggle-eyed gentleman of a perplexed aspect, and his demeanour became unbearable.

It was a cold, dead morning (the sun not being up yet), and when I had out-watched the paling light of the fires of the iron country, and the curtain of heavy smoke that hung at once between me and the stars and between me and the day, I turned to my fellow-traveller and said:

'I *beg* your pardon, sir, but do you observe anything particular in me?' For, really, he appeared to be taking down, either my travelling-cap or my hair, with a minuteness that was a liberty.

The goggle-eyed gentleman withdrew his eyes from

behind me, as if the back of the carriage were a hundred miles off, and said, with a lofty look of compassion for my insignificance:

'In you, sir?—B.'

'B, sir?' said I, growing warm.

'I have nothing to do with you, sir,' returned the
gentleman; 'pray let me listen—O.'

He enunciated this vowel after a pause, and noted
it down.

At first I was alarmed, for an Express lunatic and
no communication with the guard, is a serious position.   The thought came to my relief that the gentleman might be what is popularly called a Rapper:
one of a sect for (some of) whom I have the highest
respect, but whom I don't believe in.   I was going
to ask him the question, when he took the bread out
of my mouth.

'You will excuse me,' said the gentleman contemp-
tuously, 'if I am too much in advance of common
humanity to trouble myself at all about it.   I have
passed the night—as indeed I pass the whole of my
time now—in spiritual intercourse.'

'O!' said I, somewhat snappishly.

'The conferences of the night began,' continued
the gentleman, turning several leaves of his note-book,
'with this message: "Evil communications corrupt
good manners." '

'Sound,' said I; 'but, absolutely new?'

'New from spirits,' returned the gentleman.

I could only repeat my rather snappish 'O!' and ask
if I might be favoured with the last communication.

' "A bird in the hand," ' said the gentleman, reading his last entry with great solemnity, ' "is worth
two in the Bosh." '

'Truly I am of the same opinion,' said I; 'but
shouldn't it be Bush?'

'It came to me, Bosh,' returned the gentleman.

The gentleman then informed me that the spirit of Socrates had delivered this special revelation in the course of the night. 'My friend, I hope you are pretty well. There are two in this railway carriage. How do you do? There are seventeen thousand four hundred and seventy-nine spirits here, but you cannot see them. Pythagoras is here. He is not at liberty to mention it, but hopes you like travelling.' Galileo likewise had dropped in, with this scientific intelligence. 'I am glad to see you, *amico. Come sta?* Water will freeze when it is cold enough. *Addio!*' In the course of the night, also, the following phenomena had occurred. Bishop Butler had insisted on spelling his name, 'Bubler,' for which offence against orthography and good manners he had been dismissed as out of temper. John Milton (suspected of wilful mystification) had repudiated the authorship of Paradise Lost, and had introduced, as joint authors of that poem, two Unknown gentlemen, respectively named Grungers and Scadgingtone. And Prince Arthur, nephew of King John of England, had described himself as tolerably comfortable in the seventh circle, where he was learning to paint on velvet, under the direction of Mrs. Trimmer and Mary Queen of Scots.

If this should meet the eye of the gentleman who favoured me with these disclosures, I trust he will excuse my confessing that the sight of the rising sun, and the contemplation of the magnificent Order of the vast Universe, made me impatient of them. In a word, I was so impatient of them, that I was mightily glad to get out at the next station, and to exchange these clouds and vapours for the free air of Heaven.

By that time it was a beautiful morning. As I walked away among such leaves as had already fallen

from the golden, brown, and russet trees; and as I looked around me on the wonders of Creation, and thought of the steady, unchanging, and harmonious laws by which they are sustained; the gentleman's spiritual intercourse seemed to me as poor a piece of journey-work as ever this world saw. In which heathen state of mind, I came within view of the house, and stopped to examine it attentively.

It was a solitary house, standing in a sadly neglected garden: a pretty even square of some two acres. It was a house of about the time of George the Second; as stiff, as cold, as formal, and in as bad taste, as could possibly be desired by the most loyal admirer of the whole quartett of Georges. It was uninhabited, but had, within a year or two, been cheaply repaired to render it habitable; I say cheaply, because the work had been done in a surface manner, and was already decaying as to the paint and plaster, though the colours were fresh. A lop-sided board drooped over the garden wall, announcing that it was 'to let on very reasonable terms, well furnished.' It was much too closely and heavily shadowed by trees, and, in particular, there were six tall poplars before the front windows, which were excessively melancholy, and the site of which had been extremely ill chosen.

It was easy to see that it was an avoided house—a house that was shunned by the village, to which my eye was guided by a church spire some half a mile off —a house that nobody would take. And the natural inference was, that it had the reputation of being a haunted house.

No period within the four-and-twenty hours of day and night is so solemn to me, as the early morning. In the summer time, I often rise very early, and repair to my room to do a day's work before breakfast, and I am always on those occasions deeply im-

pressed by the stillness and solitude around me.   Besides that there is something awful in the being surrounded by familiar faces asleep—in the knowledge
that those who are dearest to us and to whom we are
dearest, are profoundly unconscious of us, in an im-
passive state, anticipative of that mysterious condition to which we are all tending—the stopped life,
the broken threads of yesterday, the deserted seat, the
closed book, the unfinished but abandoned occupation,
all are images of Death.   The tranquillity of the
hour is the tranquillity of Death.   The colour and
the chill have the same association.   Even a certain
air that familiar household objects take upon them
when they first emerge from the shadows of the night
into the morning, of being newer, and as they used
to be long ago, has its counterpart in the subsidence
of the worn face of maturity or age, in death, into
the old youthful look.   Moreover, I once saw the
apparition of my father, at this hour.   He was alive
and well, and nothing ever came of it, but I saw him
in the daylight, sitting with his back towards me, on
a seat that stood beside my bed.   His head was resting on his hand, and whether he was slumbering or
grieving, I could not discern.   Amazed to see him
there, I sat up, moved my position, leaned out of
bed, and watched him.   As he did not move, I spoke
to him more than once.   As he did not move then, I
became alarmed and laid my hand upon his shoulder,
as I thought—and there was no such thing.

For all these reasons, and for others less easily and
briefly statable, I find the early morning to be my
most ghostly time.   Any house would be more or less
haunted, to me, in the early morning; and a haunted
house could scarcely address me to greater advantage than then.

I walked on into the village, with the desertion of

this house upon my mind, and I found the landlord of the little inn, sanding his door-step. I bespoke breakfast, and broached the subject of the house.

'Is it haunted?' I asked.

The landlord looked at me, shook his head and answered, 'I say nothing.'

'Then it *is* haunted?'

'Well!' cried the landlord, in an outburst of frankness that had the appearance of desperation—'I wouldn't sleep in it.'

'Why not?'

'If I wanted to have all the bells in a house ring, with nobody to ring 'em; and all the doors in a house bang, with nobody to bang 'em; and all sorts of feet treading about, with no feet there; why, then,' said the landlord, 'I 'd sleep in that house.'

'Is anything seen there?'

The landlord looked at me again, and then, with his former appearance of desperation, called down his stableyard for 'Ikey!'

The call produced a high-shouldered young fellow, with a round red face, a short crop of sandy hair, a very broad humorous mouth, a turned-up nose, and a great sleeved waistcoat of purple bars, with mother-of-pearl buttons, that seemed to be growing upon him, and to be in a fair way—if it were not pruned—of covering his head and overrunning his boots.

'This gentleman wants to know,' said the landlord, 'if anything 's seen at the Poplars.'

' 'Ooded woman with a howl,' said Ikey, in a state of great freshness.

'Do you mean a cry?'

'I mean a bird, sir.'

'A hooded woman with an owl. Dear me! Did you ever see her?'

'I seen the howl.'

'Never the woman?'

'Not so plain as the howl, but they always keeps together.'

· 'Has anybody ever seen the woman as plainly as the owl?'

'Lord bless you, sir! Lots.'

'Who?'

'Lord bless you, sir! Lots.'

'The general-dealer opposite, for instance, who is opening his shop?'

'Perkins? Bless you, Perkins wouldn't go a-nigh the place. No!' observed the young man, with considerable feeling; 'he an't overwise, an't Perkins, but he an't such a fool as *that*.'

(Here, the landlord murmured his confidence in Perkins's knowing better.)

'Who is—or who was—the hooded woman with the owl? Do you know?'

'Well!' said Ikey, holding up his cap with one hand while he scratched his head with the other, 'they say, in general, that she was murdered, and the howl he 'ooted the while.'

This very concise summary of the facts was all I could learn, except that a young man, as hearty and likely a young man as ever I see, had been took with fits and held down in 'em, after seeing the hooded woman. Also, that a personage, dimly described as 'a hold chap, a sort of one-eyed tramp, answering to the name of Joby, unless you challenged him as Greenwood, and then he said, "Why not? and even if so, mind your own business,"' had encountered the hooded woman, a matter of five or six times. But, I was not materially assisted by these witnesses: inasmuch as the first was in California, and the last was, as Ikey said (and he was confirmed by the landlord), Anywheres.

Now, although I regard with a hushed and solemn fear, the mysteries, between which and this state of existence is interposed the barrier of the great trial and change that fall on all the things that live; and although I have not the audacity to pretend that I know anything of them; I can no more reconcile the mere banging of doors, ringing of bells, creaking of boards, and such-like insignificances, with the majestic beauty and pervading analogy of all the Divine rules that I am permitted to understand, than I had been able, a little while before, to yoke the spiritual intercourse of my fellow-traveller to the chariot of the rising sun.   Moreover, I had lived in two haunted houses—both abroad.   In one of these, an old Italian palace, which bore the reputation of being very badly haunted indeed, and which had recently been twice abandoned on that account, I lived eight months, most tranquilly and pleasantly: notwithstanding that the house had a score of mysterious bedrooms, which were never used, and possessed, in one large room in which I sat reading, times out of number at all hours, and next to which I slept, a haunted chamber of the first pretensions.   I gently hinted these considerations to the landlord.   And as to this particular house having a bad name, I reasoned with him, Why how many things had bad names undeservedly, and how easy it was to give bad names, and did he not think that if he and I were persistently to whisper in the village that any weird-looking, old drunken tinker of the neighbourhood had sold himself to the Devil, he would come in time to be suspected of that commercial venture!   All this wise talk was perfectly ineffective with the landlord, I am bound to confess, and was as dead a failure as ever I made in my life.

To cut this part of the story short, I was piqued about the haunted house, and was already half re-

solved to take it. So, after breakfast, I got the keys from Perkins's brother-in-law (a whip and harness maker, who keeps the Post Office, and is under submission to a most rigorous wife of the Doubly Seceding Little Emmanuel persuasion), and went up to the house, attended by my landlord and by Ikey.

Within, I found it, as I had expected, transcendently dismal. The slowly changing shadows waved on it from the heavy trees were doleful in the last degree; the house was ill-placed, ill-built, ill-planned, and ill-fitted. It was damp, it was not free from dry rot, there was a flavour of rats in it, and it was the gloomy victim of that indescribable decay which settles on all the work of man's hands whenever it is not turned to man's account. The kitchens and offices were too large, and too remote from each other. Above stairs and below, waste tracts of passage intervened between patches of fertility represented by rooms; and there was a mouldy old well with a green growth upon it, hiding like a murderous trap, near the bottom of the back-stairs, under the double row of bells. One of these bells was labelled, on a black ground in faded white letters, MASTER B. This, they told me, was the bell that rang the most.

'Who was Master B.?' I asked. 'Is it known what he did while the owl hooted?'

'Rang the bell,' said Ikey.

I was rather struck by the prompt dexterity with which this young man pitched his fur cap at the bell, and rang it himself. It was a loud, unpleasant bell, and made a very disagreeable sound. The other bells were inscribed according to the names of the rooms to which their wires were conducted: as 'Picture Room,' 'Double Room,' 'Clock Room,' and the like. Following Master B.'s bell to its source, I found that young gentleman to have had but indifferent third-class accommodation in a triangular cabin under the cock-loft, with a corner fireplace which Master B. must have been exceedingly small if he were ever able to warm himself at, and a corner chimney-piece like a pyramidal staircase to the ceiling for Tom Thumb. The papering of one side of the room had dropped down bodily, with fragments of plaster adhering to it, and almost blocked up the door. It appeared that Master B., in his spiritual condition, always made a point of pulling the paper down. Neither the land-lord nor Ikey could suggest why he made such a fool of himself.

Except that the house had an immensely large ram-bling loft at top, I made no other discoveries. It was moderately well furnished, but sparely. Some of the furniture—say, a third—was as old as the house; the rest was of various periods within the last half cen-tury. I was referred to a corn-chandler in the market-place of the county town to treat for the house. I went that day, and I took it for six months.

It was just the middle of October when I moved in with my maiden sister (I venture to call her eight-and-thirty, she is so very handsome, sensible, and en-gaging). We took with us, a deaf stable-man, my bloodhound Turk, two women servants, and a young person called an Odd Girl. I have reason to record of the attendant last enumerated, who was one of the Saint Lawrence's Union Female Orphans, that she was a fatal mistake and a disastrous engagement.

The year was dying early, the leaves were falling fast, it was a raw cold day when we took possession, and the gloom of the house was most depressing. The cook (an amiable woman, but of a weak turn of intellect) burst into tears on beholding the kitchen, and requested that her silver watch might be deliv-ered over to her sister (2 Tuppintock's Gardens,

Liggs's Walk, Clapham Rise), in the event of anything happening to her from the damp. Streaker,
the housemaid, feigned cheerfulness, but was the
greater martyr. The Odd Girl, who had never been
in the country, alone was pleased, and made arrangements for sowing an acorn in the garden outside the
scullery window, and rearing an oak.

We went, before dark, through all the natural—as
opposed to supernatural—miseries incidental to our
state. Dispiriting reports ascended (like the smoke)
from the basement in volumes, and descended from the
upper rooms. There was no rolling-pin, there was no
salamander (which failed to surprise me, for I don't
know what it is), there was nothing in the house, what
there was, was broken, the last people must have lived
like pigs, what could the meaning of the landlord be?
Through these distresses, the Odd Girl was cheerful
and exemplary. But within four hours after dark
we had got into a supernatural groove, and the Odd
Girl had seen 'Eyes,' and was in hysterics.

My sister and I had agreed to keep the haunting
strictly to ourselves, and my impression was, and still
is, that I had not left Ikey, when he helped to unload
the cart, alone with the women, or any one of them,
for one minute. Nevertheless, as I say, the Odd Girl
had 'seen Eyes' (no other explanation could ever be
drawn from her), before nine, and by ten o'clock had
had as much vinegar applied to her as would pickle
a handsome salmon.

I leave a discerning public to judge of my feelings,
when, under these untoward circumstances, at about
half-past ten o'clock Master B.'s bell began to ring
in a most infuriated manner, and Turk howled until
the house resounded with his lamentations!

I hope I may never again be in a state of mind so
unchristian as the mental frame in which I lived for

some weeks, respecting the memory of Master **B.**
Whether his bell was rung by rats, or mice, or bats, or
wind, or what other accidental vibration, or sometimes
by one cause, sometimes another, and sometimes by
collusion, I don't know; but, certain it is, that it did
ring two nights out of three, until I conceived the
happy idea of twisting Master **B.**'s neck—in other
words, breaking his bell short off—and silencing that
young gentleman, as to my experience and belief, for
ever.

But, by that time, the Odd Girl had developed
such improving powers of catalepsy, that she had
become a shining example of that very inconvenient
disorder. She would stiffen, like a Guy Fawkes en-
dowed with unreason, on the most irrelevant occasions.
I would address the servants in a lucid manner, pointing out to them that I had painted Master **B.**'s room
and balked the paper, and taken Master **B.**'s bell away
and balked the ringing, and if they could suppose
that that confounded boy had lived and died, to clothe
himself with no better behaviour than would most
unquestionably have brought him and the sharpest
particles of a birch-broom into close acquaintance in
the present imperfect state of existence, could they
also suppose a mere poor human being, such as I was,
capable by those contemptible means of counteracting
and limiting the powers of the disembodied spirits of
the dead, or of any spirits?—I say I would become
emphatic and cogent, not to say rather complacent, in
such an address, when it would all go for nothing by
reason of the Odd Girl's suddenly stiffening from
the toes upward, and glaring among us like a
parochial petrifaction.

Streaker, the housemaid, too, had an attribute of a
most discomfiting nature. I am unable to say
whether she was of an unusually lymphatic tempera-

ment, or what else was the matter with her, but this young woman became a mere Distillery for the production of the largest and most transparent tears I ever met with. Combined with these characteristics, was a peculiar tenacity of hold in those specimens, so that they didn't fall, but hung upon her face and nose. In this condition, and mildly and deplorably shaking her head, her silence would throw me more heavily than the Admirable Crichton could have done in a verbal disputation for a purse of money. Cook, likewise, always covered me with confusion as with a garment, by neatly winding up the session with the protest that the Ouse was wearing her out, and by meekly repeating her last wishes regarding her silver watch.

As to our nightly life, the contagion of suspicion and fear was among us, and there is no such contagion under the sky. Hooded woman? According to the accounts, we were in a perfect Convent of hooded women. Noises? With that contagion downstairs, I myself have sat in the dismal parlour, listening, until I have heard so many and such strange noises, that they would have chilled my blood if I had not warmed it by dashing out to make discoveries. Try this in bed, in the dead of the night; try this at your own comfortable fireside, in the life of the night. You can fill any house with noises, if you will, until you have a noise for every nerve in your nervous system.

I repeat; the contagion of suspicion and fear was among us, and there is no such contagion under the sky. The women (their noses in a chronic state of excoriation from smelling-salts) were always primed and loaded for a swoon, and ready to go off with hair-triggers. The two elder detached the Odd Girl on all expeditions that were considered doubly haz-

ardous, and she always established the reputation of
such adventures by coming back cataleptic. If Cook
or Streaker went overhead after dark, we knew we
should presently hear a bump on the ceiling; and this
took place so constantly, that it was as if a fighting
man were engaged to go about the house, administering a touch of his art which I believe is called The
Auctioneer, to every domestic he met with.

It was in vain to do anything. It was in vain to
be frightened, for the moment in one's own person,
by a real owl, and then to show the owl. It was in
vain to discover, by striking an accidental discord on
the piano, that Turk always howled at particular
notes and combinations. It was in vain to be a Rhad-
amanthus with the bells, and if an unfortunate bell
rang without leave, to have it down inexorably and
silence it. It was in vain to fire up chimneys, let
torches down the well, charge furiously into suspected
rooms and recesses. We changed servants, and it was
no better. The new set ran away, and a third set
came, and it was no better. At last, our comfortable
housekeeping got to be so disorganised and wretched,
that I one night dejectedly said to my sister: 'Patty,
I begin to despair of our getting people to go on with
us here, and I think we must give this up.'

My sister, who is a woman of immense spirit, replied, 'No, John, don't give it up. Don't be beaten,
John. There is another way.'

'And what is that?' said I.

'John,' returned my sister, 'if we are not to be driven
out of this house, and that for no reason whatever that
is apparent to you or me, we must help ourselves and
take the house wholly and solely into our own hands.'

'But, the servants,' said I.

'Have no servants,' said my sister, boldly.

Like most people in my grade of life, I had never

thought of the possibility of going on without those faithful obstructions. The notion was so new to me when suggested, that I looked very doubtful.

'We know they come here to be frightened and infect one another, and we know they are frightened and do infect one another,' said my sister.

'With the exception of Bottles,' I observed, in a meditative tone.

(The deaf stable-man. I kept him in my service, and still keep him, as a phenomenon of moroseness not to be matched in England.)

'To be sure, John,' assented my sister; 'except Bottles. And what does that go to prove? Bottles talks to nobody, and hears nobody unless he is absolutely roared at, and what alarm has Bottles ever given, or taken! None.'

This was perfectly true; the individual in question having retired, every night at ten o'clock, to his bed over the coach-house, with no other company than a pitchfork and a pail of water. That the pail of water would have been over me, and the pitchfork through me, if I had put myself without announcement in Bottles's way after that minute, I had deposited in my own mind as a fact worth remembering. Neither had Bottles ever taken the least notice of any of our many uproars. An imperturbable and speechless man, he had sat at his supper, with Streaker present in a swoon, and the Odd Girl marble, and had only put another potato in his cheek, or profited by the general misery to help himself to beefsteak pie.

'And so,' continued my sister, 'I exempt Bottles. And considering, John, that the house is too large, and perhaps too lonely, to be kept well in hand by Bottles, you, and me, I propose that we cast about among our friends for a certain selected number of the most reliable and willing—form a Society here for

three months—wait upon ourselves and one another—
live cheerfully and socially—and see what happens.'

I was so charmed with my sister, that I embraced
her on the spot, and went into her plan with the greatest ardour.

We were then in the third week of November; but,
we took our measures so vigorously, and were so well
seconded by the friends in whom we confided, that
there was still a week of the month unexpired, when
our party all came down together merrily, and mustered in the haunted house.

I will mention, in this place, two small changes
that I made while my sister and I were yet alone.   It
occurring to me as not improbable that Turk howled
in the house at night, partly because he wanted to get
out of it, I stationed him in his kennel outside, but
unchained; and I seriously warned the village that
any man who came in his way must not expect to leave
him without a rip in his own throat.   I then casually
asked Ikey if he were a judge of a gun?   On his saying, 'Yes, sir, I knows a good gun when I sees her,'
I begged the favour of his stepping up to the house
and looking at mine.

'*She's* a true one, sir,' said Ikey, after inspecting a
double-barrelled rifle that I bought in New York a
few years ago.   'No mistake about *her,* sir.'

'Ikey,' said I, 'don't mention it; I have seen something in this house.'

'No, sir?' he whispered, greedily opening his eyes.
' 'Oooded lady, sir?'

'Don't be frightened,' said I.   'It was a figure
rather like you.'

'Lord, sir?'

'Ikey!' said I, shaking hands with him warmly: I
may say affectionately; 'if there is any truth in these
ghost-stories, the greatest service I can do you, is, to

fire at that figure. And I promise you, by Heaven and earth, I will do it with this gun if I see it again!'

The young man thanked me, and took his leave with some little precipitation, after declining a glass of liquor. I imparted my secret to him, because I had never quite forgotten his throwing his cap at the bell; because I had, on another occasion, noticed something very like a fur cap, lying not far from the bell, one night when it had burst out ringing; and because I had remarked that we were at our ghostliest whenever he came up in the evening to comfort the servants. Let me do Ikey no injustice. He was afraid of the house, and believed in its being haunted; and yet he would play false on the haunting side, so surely as he got an opportunity. The Odd Girl's case was exactly similar. She went about the house in a state of real terror, and yet lied monstrously and wilfully, and invented many of the alarms she spread, and made many of the sounds we heard. I had had my eye on the two, and I know it. It is not necessary for me, here, to account for this preposterous state of mind; I content myself with remarking that it is familiarly known to every intelligent man who has had fair medical, legal, or other watchful experience; that it is as well established and as common a state of mind as any with which observers are acquainted; and that it is one of the first elements, above all others, rationally to be suspected in, and strictly looked for, and separated from, any question of this kind.

To return to our party. The first thing we did when we were all assembled, was, to draw lots for bedrooms. That done, and every bedroom, and, indeed, the whole house, having been minutely examined by the whole body, we allotted the various household duties, as if we had been on a gipsy party, or a yachting party, or a hunting party, or were shipwrecked.

I then recounted the floating rumours concerning the hooded lady, the owl and Master B.: with others, still more filmy, which had floated about during our occupation, relative to some ridiculous old ghost of the female gender who went up and down, carrying the ghost of a round table; and also to an impalpable Jackass, whom nobody was ever able to catch. Some of these ideas I really believe our people below had communicated to one another in some diseased way, without conveying them in words. We then gravely called one another to witness, that we were not there to be deceived, or to deceive—which we considered pretty much the same thing—and that, with a serious sense of responsibility, we would be strictly true to one another, and would strictly follow out the truth. The understanding was established, that any one who heard unusual noises in the night, and who wished to trace them, should knock at my door; lastly, that on Twelfth Night, the last night of holy Christmas, all our individual experiences since that then present hour of our coming together in the haunted house, should be brought to light for the good of all; and that we would hold our peace on the subject till then, unless on some remarkable provocation to break silence.

We were, in number and in character, as follows:

First—to get my sister and myself out of the way—there were we two. In the drawing of lots, my sister drew her own room, and I drew Master B.'s. Next, there was our first cousin John Herschel, so called after the great astronomer: than whom I suppose a better man at a telescope does not breathe. With him, was his wife: a charming creature to whom he had been married in the previous spring. I thought it (under the circumstances) rather imprudent to bring her, because there is no knowing what even a false alarm may do at such a time; but I suppose

he knew his own business best, and I must say that if she had been *my* wife, I never could have left her endearing and bright face behind. They drew the Clock Room. Alfred Starling, an uncommonly agreeable young fellow of eight-and-twenty for whom I have the greatest liking, was in the Double Room; mine, usually, and designated by that name from having a dressing-room within it, with two large and cumbersome windows, which no wedges *I* was ever able to make, would keep from shaking, in any weather, wind or no wind. Alfred is a young fellow who pretends to be 'fast' (another word for loose, as I understand the term), but who is much too good and sensible for that nonsense, and who would have distinguished himself before now, if his father had not unfortunately left him a small independence of two hundred a year, on the strength of which his only occupation in life has been to spend six. I am in hopes, however, that his Banker may break, or that he may enter into some speculation guaranteed to pay twenty per cent.; for, I am convinced that if he could only be ruined, his fortune is made. Belinda Bates, bosom friend of my sister, and a most intellectual, amiable, and delightful girl, got the Picture Room. She has a fine genius for poetry, combined with real business earnestness, and 'goes in'- —to use an expression of Alfred's—for Woman's mission, Woman's rights, Woman's wrongs, and everything that is woman's with a capital W, or is not and ought to be, or is and ought not to be. 'Most praiseworthy, my dear, and Heaven prosper you!' I whispered to her on the first night of my taking leave of her at the Picture-Room door, 'but don't overdo it. And in respect of the great necessity there is, my darling, for more employments being within the reach of Woman than our civilisation has as yet assigned to

her, don't fly at the unfortunate men, even those men who are at first sight in your way, as if they were the natural oppressors of your sex; for, trust me, Belinda, they do sometimes spend their wages among wives and daughters, sisters, mothers, aunts, and grandmothers; and the play is, really, not *all* Wolf and Red Riding-Hood, but has other parts in it.' However, I digress.

Belinda, as I have mentioned, occupied the Picture Room. We had but three other chambers: the Corner Room, the Cupboard Room, and the Garden Room. My old friend, Jack Governor, 'slung his hammock,' as he called it, in the Corner Room. I have always regarded Jack as the finest-looking sailor that ever sailed. He is gray now, but as handsome as he was a quarter of a century ago—nay, handsomer. A portly, cheery, well-built figure of a broad-shouldered man, with a frank smile, a brilliant dark eye, and a rich dark eyebrow. I remember those under darker hair, and they look all the better for their silver setting. He has been wherever his Union namesake flies, has Jack, and I have met old ship-mates of his, away in the Mediterranean and on the other side of the Atlantic, who have beamed and brightened at the casual mention of his name, and have cried, 'You know Jack Governor? Then you know a prince of men!' That he is! And so unmistakably a naval officer, that if you were to meet him coming out of an Esquimaux snow-hut in seal's skin, you would be vaguely persuaded he was in full naval uniform.

Jack once had that bright clear eye of his on my sister; but, it fell out that he married another lady and took her to South America, where she died. This was a dozen years ago or more. He brought down with him to our haunted house a little cask of salt beef; for, he is always convinced that all salt beef not

of his own pickling, is mere carrion, and invariably, when he goes to London, packs a piece in his portmanteau. He had also volunteered to bring with him one 'Nat Beaver,' an old comrade of his, captain of a merchantman. Mr. Beaver, with a thick-set, wooden face and figure, and apparently as hard as a block all over, proved to be an intelligent man, with a world of watery experiences in him, and great practical knowledge. At times, there was a curious nervousness about him, apparently the lingering result of some old illness; but, it seldom lasted many minutes. He got the Cupboard Room, and lay there next to Mr. Undery, my friend and solicitor: who came down, in an amateur capacity, 'to go through with it,' as he said, and who plays whist better than the whole Law List, from the red cover at the beginning to the red cover at the end.

I never was happier in my life, and I believe it was the universal feeling among us. Jack Governor, always a man of wonderful resources, was Chief Cook, and made some of the best dishes I ever ate, including unapproachable curries. My sister was pastrycook and confectioner. Starling and I were Cook's Mate, turn and turn about, and on special occasions the chief cook 'pressed' Mr. Beaver. We had a great deal of out-door sport and exercise, but nothing was neglected within, and there was no ill-humour or misunderstanding among us, and our evenings were so delightful that we had at least one good reason for being reluctant to go to bed.

We had a few night alarms in the beginning. On the first night, I was knocked up by Jack with a most wonderful ship's lantern in his hand, like the gills of some monster of the deep, who informed me that he 'was going aloft to the main truck,' to have the weathercock down. It was a stormy night and I remon-

strated; but Jack called my attention to its making a sound like a cry of despair, and said somebody would be 'hailing a ghost' presently, if it wasn't done. So, up to the top of the house, where I could hardly stand for the wind, we went, accompanied by Mr. Beaver; and there Jack, lantern and all, with Mr. Beaver after him, swarmed up to the top of the cupola, some two dozen feet above the chimneys, and stood upon nothing particular, coolly knocking the weathercock off, until they both got into such good spirits with the wind and the height, that I thought they would never come down. Another night, they turned out again, and had a chimney-cowl off. Another night, they cut a sobbing and gulping water-pipe away. Another night, they found out something else. On several occasions, they both, in the coolest manner, simultaneously dropped out of their respective bedroom windows, hand over hand by their counterpanes, to 'overhaul' something mysterious in the garden.

The engagement among us was faithfully kept, and nobody revealed anything. All we knew was, if any one's room were haunted, no one looked the worse for it.

THE GHOST IN MASTER B.'S ROOM

WHEN I established myself in the triangular garret which had gained so distinguished a reputation, my thoughts naturally turned to Master B. My speculations about him were uneasy and manifold. Whether his Christian name was Benjamin, Bissextile (from his having been born in Leap Year), Bartholomew, or Bill. Whether the initial letter belonged to his family name, and that was Baxter, Black, Brown, Barker, Buggins, Baker, or Bird. Whether he was a foundling, and had been baptized B. Whether he was a lion-hearted boy, and B. was short for Briton, or for Bull. Whether he could possibly have been kith and kin to an illustrious lady who brightened my own childhood, and had come of the blood of the brilliant Mother Bunch?

With these profitless meditations I tormented myself much. I also carried the mysterious letter into the appearance and pursuits of the deceased; wondering whether he dressed in Blue, wore Boots (he couldn't have been Bald), was a boy of Brains, liked Books, was good at Bowling, had any skill as a Boxer, even in his Buoyant Boyhood Bathed from a Bathing-machine at Bognor, Bangor, Bournemouth, Brighton, or Broadstairs, like a Bounding Billiard Ball?

So, from the first, I was haunted by the letter B.

It was not long before I remarked that I never by any hazard had a dream of Master B., or of anything belonging to him. But, the instant I awoke from sleep, at whatever hour of the night, my thoughts took him up, and roamed away, trying to attach his initial letter to something that would fit it and keep it quiet.

For six nights, I had been worried thus in Master B.'s room, when I began to perceive that things were going wrong.

The first appearance that presented itself was early in the morning when it was but just daylight and no more. I was standing shaving at my glass, when I suddenly discovered, to my consternation and amazement, that I was shaving—not myself—I am fifty—but a boy. Apparently Master B.!

I trembled and looked over my shoulder; nothing there. I looked again in the glass, and distinctly saw the features and expression of a boy, who was shaving, not to get rid of a beard, but to get one. Extremely

troubled in my mind, I took a few turns in the room, and went back to the looking-glass, resolved to steady my hand and complete the operation in which I had been disturbed. Opening my eyes, which I had shut while recovering my firmness, I now met in the glass, looking straight at me, the eyes of a young man of four or five and twenty. Terrified by this new ghost, I closed my eyes, and made a strong effort to recover myself. Opening them again, I saw, shaving his cheek in the glass, my father, who has long been dead. Nay, I even saw my grandfather, too, whom I never did see in my life.

Although naturally much affected by these remarkable visitations, I determined to keep my secret, until the time agreed upon for the present general disclosure. Agitated by a multitude of curious thoughts, I retired to my room, that night, prepared to encounter some new experience of a spectral character. Nor was my preparation needless, for, waking from an uneasy sleep at exactly two o'clock in the morning, what were my feelings to find that I was sharing my bed with the skeleton of Master B.!

I sprang up, and the skeleton sprang up also. I then heard a plaintive voice saying, 'Where am I? What is become of me?' and, looking hard in that direction, perceived the ghost of Master B.

The young spectre was dressed in an obsolete fashion: or rather, was not so much dressed as put into a case of inferior pepper-and-salt cloth, made horrible by means of shining buttons. I observed that these buttons went, in a double row, over each shoulder of the young ghost, and appeared to descend his back. He wore a frill round his neck. His right hand (which I distinctly noticed to be inky) was laid upon his stomach; connecting this action with some feeble pimples on his countenance, and his general air of

nausea, I concluded this ghost to be the ghost of a boy who had habitually taken a great deal too much medicine.

'Where am I?' said the little spectre, in a pathetic voice. 'And why was I born in the Calomel days, and why did I have all that Calomel given me?'

I replied, with sincere earnestness, that upon my soul I couldn't tell him.

'Where is my little sister,' said the ghost, 'and where my angelic little wife, and where is the boy I went to school with?'

I entreated the phantom to be comforted, and above all things to take heart respecting the loss of the boy he went to school with. I represented to him that probably that boy never did, within human experience, come out well, when discovered. I urged that I myself had, in later life, turned up several boys whom I went to school with, and none of them had at all answered. I expressed my humble belief that that boy never did answer. I represented that he was a mythic character, a delusion, and a snare. I recounted how, the last time I found him, I found him at a dinner party behind a wall of white cravat, with an inconclusive opinion on every possible subject, and a power of silent boredom absolutely Titanic. I related how, on the strength of our having been together at 'Old Doylance's,' he had asked himself to breakfast with me (a social offence of the largest magnitude); how, fanning my weak embers of belief in Doylance's boys, I had let him in; and how, he had proved to be a fearful wanderer about the earth, pursuing the race of Adam with inexplicable notions concerning the currency, and with a proposition that the Bank of England should, on pain of being abolished, instantly strike off and circulate, God knows how many thousand millions of ten-and-sixpenny notes.

The ghost heard me in silence, and with a fixed stare. 'Barber!' it apostrophised me when I had finished.

'Barber?' I repeated—for I am not of that profession.

'Condemned,' said the ghost, 'to shave a constant change of customers—now, me—now, a young man—now, thyself as thou art—now, thy father—now, thy grandfather; condemned, too, to lie down with a skeleton every night, and to rise with it every morning—'

(I shuddered on hearing this dismal announcement.)

'Barber! Pursue me!'

I had felt, even before the words were uttered, that I was under a spell to pursue the phantom. I immediately did so, and was in Master B.'s room no longer.

Most people know what long and fatiguing night journeys had been forced upon the witches who used to confess, and who, no doubt, told the exact truth —particularly as they were always assisted with leading questions, and the Torture was always ready. I asseverate that, during my occupation of Master B.'s room, I was taken by the ghost that haunted it, on expeditions fully as long and wild as any of those. Assuredly, I was presented to no shabby old man with a goat's horns and tail (something between Pan and an old clothesman), holding conventional receptions, as stupid as those of real life and less decent; but, I came upon other things which appeared to me to have more meaning.

Confident that I speak the truth and shall be believed, I declare without hesitation that I followed the ghost, in the first instance on a broom-stick, and afterwards on a rocking-horse. The very smell of the animal's paint—especially when I brought it out, by

making him warm—I am ready to swear to. I followed the ghost, afterwards, in a hackney coach; an institution with the peculiar smell of which the present generation is unacquainted, but to which I am again ready to swear as a combination of stable, dog with the mange, and very old bellows. (In this, I appeal to previous generations to confirm or refute me.) I pursued the phantom, on a headless donkey: at least, upon a donkey who was so interested in the state of his stomach that his head was always down there, investigating it; on ponies, expressly born to kick up behind; on roundabouts and swings, from fairs; in the first cab—another forgotten institution where the fare regularly got into bed, and was tucked up with the driver.

Not to trouble you with a detailed account of all my travels in pursuit of the ghost of Master B., which were longer and more wonderful than those of Sinbad the Sailor, I will confine myself to one experience from which you may judge of many.

I was marvellously changed. I was myself, yet not myself. I was conscious of something within me, which has been the same all through my life, and which I have always recognised under all its phases and varieties as never altering, and yet I was not the I who had gone to bed in Master B.'s room. I had the smoothest of faces and the shortest of legs, and I had taken another creature like myself, also with the smoothest of faces and the shortest of legs, behind a door, and was confiding to him a proposition of the most astounding nature.

This proposition was, that we should have a Seraglio.

The other creature assented warmly. He had no notion of respectability, neither had I. It was the custom of the East, it was the way of the good

Caliph Haroun Alraschid (let me have the corrupted name again for once, it is so scented with sweet memories!), the usage was highly laudable, and most worthy of imitation. 'O, yes! Let us,' said the other creature with a jump, 'have a Seraglio.'

It was not because we entertained the faintest doubts of the meritorious character of the Oriental establishment we proposed to import, that we perceived it must be kept a secret from Miss Griffin. It was because we knew Miss Griffin to be bereft of human sympathies, and incapable of appreciating the greatness of the great Haroun. Mystery impenetrably shrouded from Miss Griffin then, let us entrust it to Miss Bule.

We were ten in Miss Griffin's establishment by Hampstead Ponds; eight ladies and two gentlemen. Miss Bule, whom I judge to have attained the ripe age of eight or nine, took the lead in society. I opened the subject to her in the course of the day, and proposed that she should become the Favourite.

Miss Bule, after struggling with the diffidence so natural to, and charming in, her adorable sex, expressed herself as flattered by the idea, but wished to know how it was proposed to provide for Miss Pipson? Miss Bule—who was understood to have vowed towards that young lady, a friendship, halves, and no secrets, until death, on the Church Service and Lessons complete in two volumes with case and lock— Miss Bule said she could not, as the friend of Pipson, disguise from herself, or me, that Pipson was not one of the common.

Now, Miss Pipson, having curly light hair and blue eyes (which was my idea of anything mortal and feminine that was called Fair), I promptly replied that I regarded Miss Pipson in the light of a Fair Circassian.

'And what then?' Miss Bule pensively asked.

I replied that she must be inveigled by a Merchant, brought to me veiled, and purchased as a slave.

[The other creature had already fallen into the second male place in the State, and was set apart for Grand Vizier. He afterwards resisted this disposal of events, but had his hair pulled until he yielded.]

'Shall I not be jealous?' Miss Bule inquired, casting down her eyes.

'Zobeide, no,' I replied; 'you will ever be the favourite Sultana; the first place in my heart, and on my throne, will be ever yours.'

Miss Bule, upon that assurance, consented to propound the idea to her seven beautiful companions. It occurring to me, in the course of the same day, that we knew we could trust a grinning and good-natured soul called Tabby, who was the serving drudge of the house, and had no more figure than one of the beds, and upon whose face there was always more or less black-lead, I slipped into Miss Bule's hand after supper, a little note to that effect: dwelling on the black-lead as being in a manner deposited by the finger of Providence, pointing Tabby out for Mesrour, the celebrated chief of the Blacks of the Hareem.

There were difficulties in the formation of the desired institution, as there are in all combinations. The other creature showed himself of a low character, and, when defeated in aspiring to the throne, pretended to have conscientious scruples about prostrating himself before the Caliph; wouldn't call him Commander of the Faithful; spoke of him slightingly and inconsistently as a mere 'chap'; said he, the other creature, 'wouldn't play'—Play!—and was otherwise coarse and offensive. This meanness of disposition was, however, put down by the general indignation of an united Seraglio, and I became blessed in the

smiles of eight of the fairest of the daughters of men.

The smiles could only be bestowed when Miss Griffin was looking another way, and only then in a very wary manner, for there was a legend among the followers of the Prophet that she saw with a little round ornament in the middle of the pattern on the back of her shawl. But every day after dinner, for an hour, we were all together, and then the Favourite and the rest of the Royal Hareem competed who should most beguile the leisure of the Serene Haroun reposing from the cares of State—which were generally, as in most affairs of State, of an arithmetical character, the Commander of the Faithful being a fearful boggler at a sum.

On these occasions, the devoted Mesrour, chief of the Blacks of the Hareem, was always in attendance (Miss Griffin usually ringing for that officer, at the same time, with great vehemence), but never acquitted himself in a manner worthy of his historical reputation. In the first place, his bringing a broom into the Divan of the Caliph, even when Haroun wore on his shoulders the red robe of anger (Miss Pipson's pelisse), though it might be got over for the moment, was never to be quite satisfactorily accounted for. In the second place, his breaking out into grinning exclamations of 'Lork you pretties!' was neither Eastern nor respectful. In the third place, when specially instructed to say 'Bismillah!' he always said 'Hallelujah!' This officer, unlike his class, was too good-humoured altogether, kept his mouth open far too wide, expressed approbation to an incongruous extent, and even once—it was on the occasion of the purchase of the Fair Circassian for five hundred thousand purses of gold, and cheap, too—embraced the Slave, the Favourite, and the Caliph, all round. (Parenthetically let me say God bless Mesrour, and

may there have been sons and daughters on that tender bosom, softening many a hard day since!)

Miss Griffin was a model of propriety, and I am at
a loss to imagine what the feelings of the virtuous
woman would have been, if she had known, when she
paraded up and down the Hampstead Road two and
two, that she was walking with a stately step at the
head of Polygamy and Mohammedanism.   I believe
that a mysterious and terrible joy with which the contemplation of Miss Griffin, in this unconscious state,
inspired us, and a grim sense prevalent among us that
there was a dreadful power in our knowledge of what
Miss Griffin (who knew all things that could be learnt
out of book) didn't know, were the mainspring of the
preservation of our secret.   It was wonderfully kept,
but was once upon the verge of self-betrayal.   The
danger and escape occurred upon a Sunday.   We
were all ten ranged in a conspicuous part of the gallery at church, with Miss Griffin at our head—as we
were every Sunday—advertising the establishment in
an unsecular sort of way—when the description of Solomon in his domestic glory happened to be read.   The
moment that monarch was thus referred to, conscience
whispered me, 'Thou, too, Haroun!'   The officiating
minister had a cast in his eye, and it assisted conscience by giving him the appearance of reading personally at me.   A crimson blush, attended by a fearful perspiration, suffused my features.   The Grand
Vizier became more dead than alive, and the whole
Seraglio reddened as if the sunset of Bagdad shone
direct upon their lovely faces.   At this portentous
time the awful Griffin rose, and balefully surveyed
the children of Islam.   My own impression was, that
Church and State had entered into a conspiracy with
Miss Griffin to expose us, and that we should all be
put into white sheets, and exhibited in the centre aisle.

But, so Westerly—if I may be allowed the expression as opposite to Eastern associations—was Miss Griffin's sense of rectitude, that she merely suspected Apples, and we were saved.

I have called the Seraglio, united. Upon the question, solely, whether the Commander of the Faithful durst exercise a right of kissing in that sanctuary of the palace, were its peerless inmates divided. Zobeide asserted a counter-right in the Favourite to scratch, and the fair Circassian put her face, for refuge, into a green baize bag, originally designed for books. On the other hand, a young antelope of transcendent beauty from the fruitful plains of Camden Town (whence she had been brought, by traders, in the half-yearly caravan that crossed the intermediate desert after the holidays), held more liberal opinions, but stipulated for limiting the benefit of them to that dog, and son of a dog, the Grand Vizier—who had no rights, and was not in question. At length, the difficulty was compromised by the installation of a very youthful slave as Deputy. She, raised upon a stool, officially received upon her cheeks the salutes intended by the gracious Haroun for other Sultanas, and was privately rewarded from the coffers of the Ladies of the Hareem.

And now it was, at the full height of enjoyment of my bliss, that I became heavily troubled. I began to think of my mother, and what she would say to my taking home at Midsummer eight of the most beautiful of the daughters of men, but all unexpected. I thought of the number of beds we made up at our house, of my father's income, and of the baker, and my despondency redoubled. The Seraglio and malicious Vizier, divining the cause of their Lord's unhappiness, did their utmost to augment it. They professed unbounded fidelity, and declared that they

would live and die with him.   Reduced to the utmost
wretchedness by these protestations of attachment, I
lay awake, for hours at a time, ruminating on my
frightful lot.   In my despair, I think I might have
taken an early opportunity of falling on my knees
before Miss Griffin, avowing my resemblance to Solomon, and praying to be dealt with according to the
outraged laws of my country, if an unthought-of
means of escape had not opened before me.

One day, we were out walking, two and two—on
which occasion the Vizier had his usual instructions
to take note of the boy at the turnpike, and if he pro-
fanely gazed (which he always did) at the beauties
of the Hareem, to have him bow-strung in the course
of the night—and it happened that our hearts were
veiled in gloom.   An unaccountable action on the
part of the antelope had plunged the State into disgrace.   That charmer, on the representation that the
previous day was her birthday, and that vast treasures had been sent in a hamper for its celebration
(both baseless assertions), had secretly but most press-
ingly invited thirty-five neighbouring princes and
princesses to a ball and supper: with a special stipu-
lation that they were 'not to be fetched till twelve.'
This wandering of the antelope's fancy, led to the surprising arrival at Miss Griffin's door, in divers equi-
pages and under various escorts, of a great company
in full dress, who were deposited on the top step in
a flush of high expectancy, and who were dismissed
in tears.   At the beginning of the double knocks
attendant on these ceremonies, the antelope had retired
to a back attic, and bolted herself in; and at every
new arrival, Miss Griffin had gone so much more and
more distracted, that at last she had been seen to tear
her front.   Ultimate capitulation on the part of the
offender had been followed by solitude in the linen-

closet, bread and water and a lecture to all of vindictive length, in which Miss Griffin had used expressions: Firstly, 'I believe you all of you knew of it'; Secondly, 'Every one of you is as wicked as another'; Thirdly, 'A pack of little wretches.'

Under these circumstances, we were walking drearily along; and I especially, with my Moosulmaun responsibilities heavy on me, was in a very low state of mind; when a strange man accosted Miss Griffin, and, after walking on at her side for a little while and talking with her, looked at me. Supposing him to be a minion of the law, and that my hour was come, I instantly ran away, with the general purpose of making for Egypt.

The whole Seraglio cried out, when they saw me making off as fast as my legs would carry me (I had an impression that the first turning on the left, and round by the public-house, would be the shortest way to the Pyramids), Miss Griffin screamed after me, the faithless Vizier ran after me, and the boy at the turnpike dodged me into a corner, like a sheep, and cut me off. Nobody scolded me when I was taken and brought back; Miss Griffin only said with a stunning gentleness, This was very curious! Why had I run away when the gentleman looked at me?

If I had had any breath to answer with, I dare say I should have made no answer; having no breath, I certainly made none. Miss Griffin and the strange man took me between them, and walked me back to the palace in a sort of state; but not at all (as I couldn't help feeling, with astonishment) in culprit state.

When we got there, we went into a room by ourselves, and Miss Griffin called in to her assistance, Mesrour, chief of the dusky guards of the Hareem. Mesrour, on being whispered to, began to shed tears.

'Bless you, my precious!' said that officer, turning to me; 'your Pa 's took bitter bad!'

I asked, with a fluttered heart, 'Is he very ill?'

'Lord temper the wind to you, my lamb!' said the good Mesrour, kneeling down, that I might have a comforting shoulder for my head to rest on, 'your Pa 's dead!'

Haroun Alraschid took to flight at the words; the Seraglio vanished; from that moment, I never again saw one of the eight of the fairest of the daughters of men.

I was taken home, and there was Debt at home as well as Death, and we had a sale there. My own little bed was so superciliously looked upon by a Power unknown to me, hazily called 'The Trade,' that a brass coal-scuttle, a roasting-jack, and a bird-cage, were obliged to be put into it to make a Lot of it, and then it went for a song. So I heard mentioned, and I wondered what song, and thought what a dismal song it must have been to sing!

Then, I was sent to a great, cold, bare, school of big boys; where everything to eat and wear was thick and clumpy, without being enough; where everybody, large and small, was cruel; where the boys knew all about the sale, before I got there, and asked me what I had fetched, and who had bought me, and hooted at me. 'Going, going, gone!' I never whispered in that wretched place that I had been Haroun, or had had a Seraglio: for, I knew that if I mentioned my reverses, I should be so worried, that I should have to drown myself in the muddy pond near the playground, which looked like the beer.

Ah me, ah me! No other ghost has haunted the boy's room, my friends, since I have occupied it, than the ghost of my own childhood, the ghost of my own innocence, the ghost of my own airy belief. Many

a time have I pursued the phantom: never with this man's stride of mine to come up with it, never with these man's hands of mine to touch it, never more to this man's heart of mine to hold it in its purity. And here you see me working out, as cheerfully and thankfully as I may, my doom of shaving in the glass a constant change of customers, and of lying down and rising up with the skeleton allotted to me for my mortal companion.

A MESSAGE FROM THE SEA

[1860]

A MESSAGE FROM THE SEA

CHAPTER I

THE VILLAGE

'AND a mighty sing'lar and pretty place it is, as ever I saw in all the days of my life!' said Captain Jorgan, looking up at it.

Captain Jorgan had to look high to look at it, for the village was built sheer up the face of a steep and lofty cliff. There was no road in it, there was no wheeled vehicle in it, there was not a level yard in it. From the sea-beach to the cliff-top two irregular rows of white houses, placed opposite to one another, and twisting here and there, and there and here, rose, like the sides of a long succession of stages of crooked ladders, and you climbed up the village or climbed down the village by the staves between, some six feet wide or so, and made of sharp irregular stones. The old pack-saddle, long laid aside in most parts of England as one of the appendages of its infancy, flourished here intact. Strings of pack-horses and pack-donkeys toiled slowly up the staves of the ladders, bearing fish, and coal, and such other cargo as was unshipping at the pier from the dancing fleet of village boats, and from two or three little coasting traders. As the beasts of burden ascended laden, or descended light, they got so lost at intervals in the floating clouds of village smoke, that they seemed to dive down some of the village chimneys, and come to

the surface again far off, high above others. No
two houses in the village were alike, in chimney, size,
shape, door, window, gable, roof-tree, anything. The
sides of the ladders were musical with water, running
clear and bright. The staves were musical with the
clattering feet of the pack-horses and pack-donkeys,
and the voices of the fishermen urging them up, mingled with the voices of the fishermen's wives and their
many children. The pier was musical with the wash of
the sea, the creaking of capstans and windlasses, and the
airy fluttering of little vanes and sails. The rough,
sea-bleached boulders of which the pier was made, and
the whiter boulders of the shore, were brown with drying nets. The red-brown cliffs, richly wooded to their
extremest verge, had their softened and beautiful
forms reflected in the bluest water, under the clear
North Devonshire sky of a November day without a
cloud. The village itself was so steeped in autumnal
foliage, from the houses lying on the pier to the topmost round of the topmost ladder, that one might have
fancied it was out a bird's-nesting, and was (as indeed
it was) a wonderful climber. And mentioning birds,
the place was not without some music from them too;
for the rook was very busy on the higher levels, and
the gull with his flapping wings was fishing in the
bay, and the lusty little robin was hopping among the
great stone blocks and iron rings of the break-water,
fearless in the faith of his ancestors, and the Children
in the Wood.

Thus it came to pass that Captain Jorgan, sitting
balancing himself on the pier-wall, struck his leg with
his open hand, as some men do when they are pleased
—and as he always did when he was pleased—and
said,—

'A mighty sing'lar and pretty place it is, as ever I
saw in all the days of my life!'

Captain Jorgan had not been through the village, but had come down to the pier by a winding side-road, to have a preliminary look at it from the level of his own natural element. He had seen many things and places, and had stowed them all away in a shrewd intellect and a vigorous memory. He was an American born, was Captain Jorgan,—a New-Englander, —but he was a citizen of the world, and a combination of most of the best qualities of most of its best countries.

For Captain Jorgan to sit anywhere in his long-skirted blue coat and blue trousers, without holding converse with everybody within speaking distance, was a sheer impossibility. So the captain fell to talking with the fishermen, and to asking them knowing questions about the fishery, and the tides, and the currents, and the race of water off that point yonder, and what you kept in your eye, and got into a line with what else when you ran into the little harbour; and other nautical profundities. Among the men who exchanged ideas with the captain, was a young fellow, who exactly hit his fancy,—a young fisherman of two or three and twenty, in the rough sea-dress of his craft, with a brown face, dark curling hair, and bright, modest eyes under his Sou'wester hat, and with a frank, but simple and retiring manner, which the captain found uncommonly taking. 'I'd bet a thousand dollars,' said the captain to himself, 'that your father was an honest man!'

'Might you be married now?' asked the captain, when he had had some talk with his new acquaintance.

'Not yet.'

'Going to be?' said the captain.

'I hope so.'

The captain's keen glance followed the slightest possible turn of the dark eye, and the slightest possible

tilt of the Sou'wester hat.   The captain then slapped
both his legs, and said to himself,—

'Never knew such a good thing in all my life!
There's his sweetheart looking over the wall!'

There was a very pretty girl looking over the wall,
from a little platform of cottage, vine, and fuchsia;
and she certainly did not look as if the presence of
this young fisherman in the landscape made it any
the less sunny and hopeful for her.

Captain Jorgan, having doubled himself up to
laugh with that hearty good-nature which is quite
exultant in the innocent happiness of other people,
had undoubled himself, and was going to start a new
subject, when there appeared coming down the lower
ladders of stones, a man whom he hailed as 'Tom Pettifer, Ho!'   Tom Pettifer, Ho, responded with alacrity, and in speedy course descended on the pier.

'Afraid of a sunstroke in England in November,
Tom, that you wear your tropical hat, strongly paid
outside and paper-lined inside, here?' said the captain,
eyeing it.

'It's as well to be on the safe side, sir,' replied Tom.

'Safe side!' repeated the captain, laughing.   'You'd
guard against a sun-stroke, with that old hat, in an
Ice Pack.   Wa'al!   What have you made out at the
Postoffice?'

'It *is* the Post-office, sir.'

'What's the Post-office?' said the captain.

'The name, sir.   The name keeps the Post-office.'

'A coincidence!' said the captain.   'A lucky hit!
Show me where it is.   Good-bye, shipmates, for the
present!   I shall come and have another look at you,
afore I leave, this afternoon.'

This was addressed to all there, but especially the
young fisherman; so all there acknowledged it, but
especially the young fisherman.   '*He's* a sailor!' said

one to another, as they looked after the captain, moving away. That he was; and so outspeaking was the sailor in him, that although his dress had nothing nautical about it, with the single exception of its colour, but was a suit of shore-going shape and form, too long in the sleeves and too short in the legs, and too unaccommodating everywhere, terminating earthward in a pair of Wellington boots, and surmounted by a tall, stiff hat, which no mortal could have worn at sea in any wind under heaven; nevertheless, a glimpse of his sagacious, weather-beaten face, or his strong, brown hand, would have established the captain's calling. Whereas Mr. Pettifer—a man of a certain plump neatness, with a curly whisker, and elaborately nautical in a jacket, and shoes, and all things correspondent—looked no more like a seaman, beside Captain Jorgan, than he looked like a sea-serpent.

The two climbed high up the village,—which had the most arbitrary turns and twists in it, so that the cobbler's house came dead across the ladder, and to have held a reasonable course, you must have gone through his house, and through him too, as he sat at his work between two little windows, with one eye microscopically on the geological formation of that part of Devonshire, and the other telescopically on the open sea,—the two climbed high up the village, and stopped before a quaint little house, on which was painted, 'MRS. RAYBROCK, DRAPER'; and also 'POST-OFFICE.' Before it, ran a rill of murmuring water, and access to it was gained by a little plank-bridge.

'Here's the name,' said Captain Jorgan, 'sure enough. You can come in if you like, Tom.'

The captain opened the door, and passed into an odd little shop, about six feet high, with a great variety of beams and bumps in the ceiling, and, besides

the principal window giving on the ladder of stones, a purblind little window of a single pane of glass, peeping out of an abutting corner at the sun-lighted ocean, and winking at its brightness.

'How do you do, ma'am?' said the captain. 'I am very glad to see you. I have come a long way to see you.'

'*Have* you, sir? Then I am sure I am very glad to see *you,* though I don't know you from Adam.'

Thus a comely, elderly woman, short of stature, plump of form, sparkling and dark of eye, who, perfectly clean and neat herself, stood in the midst of her perfectly clean and neat arrangements, and surveyed Captain Jorgan with smiling curiosity. 'Ah! but you are a sailor, sir,' she added, almost immediately, and with a slight movement of her hands, that was not very unlike wringing them; 'then you are heartily welcome.'

'Thank 'ee, ma'am,' said the captain, 'I don't know what it is, I am sure, that brings out the salt in me, but everybody seems to see it on the crown of my hat and the collar of my coat. Yes, ma'am, I am in that way of life.'

'And the other gentleman, too,' said Mrs. Raybrock.

'Well now, ma'am,' said the captain, glancing shrewdly at the other gentleman, 'you are that nigh right, that he goes to sea,—if that makes him a sailor. This is my steward, ma'am, Tom Pettifer; he's been a'most all trades you could name, in the course of his life,—would have bought all your chairs and tables once, if you had wished to sell 'em,—but now he's my steward. My name's Jorgan, and I'm a shipowner, and I sail my own and my partners' ships, and have done so this five-and-twenty year. According

to custom I am called Captain Jorgan, but I am no more a captain, bless your heart! than you are.'

'Perhaps you 'll come into my parlour, sir, and take a chair?' said Mrs. Raybrock.

'Ex-actly what I was going to propose myself, ma'am. After you.'

Thus replying, and enjoining Tom to give an eye to the shop, Captain Jorgan followed Mrs. Raybrock into the little, low back-room,—decorated with divers plants in pots, tea-trays, old china teapots, and punch-bowls,—which was at once the private sitting-room of the Raybrock family and the inner cabinet of the post-office of the village of Steepways.

'Now, ma'am,' said the captain, 'it don't signify a cent to you where I was born, except—' But here the shadow of some one entering fell upon the captain's figure, and he broke off to double himself up, slap both his legs, and ejaculate, 'Never knew such a thing in all my life! Here he is again! How are you?'

These words referred to the young fellow who had so taken Captain Jorgan's fancy down at the pier. To make it all quite complete he came in accompanied by the sweetheart whom the captain had detected looking over the wall. A prettier sweetheart the sun could not have shone upon that shining day. As she stood before the captain, with her rosy lips just parted in surprise, her brown eyes a little wider open than was usual from the same cause, and her breathing a little quickened by the ascent (and possibly by some mysterious hurry and flurry at the parlour door, in which the captain had observed her face to be for a moment totally eclipsed by the Sou'wester hat), she looked so charming, that the captain felt himself under a moral obligation to slap both his legs again.

She was very simply dressed, with no other ornament than an autumnal flower in her bosom. She wore neither hat nor bonnet, but merely a scarf or kerchief, folded squarely back over the head, to keep the sun off,—according to a fashion that may be sometimes seen in the more genial parts of England as well as of Italy, and which is probably the first fashion of head-dress that came into the world when grasses and leaves went out.

'In my country,' said the captain, rising to give her his chair, and dexterously sliding it close to another chair on which the young fisherman must necessarily establish himself,—'in my country we should call Devonshire beauty first-rate!'

Whenever a frank manner is offensive, it is because it is strained or feigned; for there may be quite as much intolerable affectation in plainness as in mincing nicety. All that the captain said and did was honestly according to his nature; and his nature was open nature and good nature; therefore, when he paid this little compliment, and expressed with a sparkle or two of his knowing eye, 'I see how it is, and nothing could be better,' he had established a delicate confidence on that subject with the family.

'I was saying to your worthy mother,' said the captain to the young man, after again introducing himself by name and occupation,—'I was saying to your mother (and you 're very like her) that it didn't signify where I was born, except that I was raised on question-asking ground, where the babies as soon as ever they come into the world, inquire of their mothers, "Neow, how old may *you* be, and wa'at air you a goin' to name me?"—which is a fact.' Here he slapped his leg. 'Such being the case, I may be excused for asking if your name 's Alfred?'

'Yes, sir, my name is Alfred,' returned the young man.

'I am not a conjurer,' pursued the captain, 'and don't think me so, or I shall right soon undeceive you. Likewise don't think, if you please, though I *do* come from that country of the babies, that I am asking questions for question-asking's sake, for I am not. Somebody belonging to you went to sea?'

'My elder brother, Hugh,' returned the young man. He said it in an altered and lower voice, and glanced at his mother, who raised her hands hurriedly, and put them together across her black gown, and looked eagerly at the visitor.

'No! For God's sake, don't think that!' said the captain, in a solemn way; 'I bring no good tidings of him.'

There was a silence, and the mother turned her face to the fire and put her hand between it and her eyes. The young fisherman slightly motioned toward the window, and the captain, looking in that direction, saw a young widow, sitting at a neighbouring window across a little garden, engaged in needlework, with a young child sleeping on her bosom. The silence continued until the captain asked of Alfred,—

'How long is it since it happened?'

'He shipped for his last voyage better than three years ago.'

'Ship struck upon some reef or rock, as I take it,' said the captain, 'and all hands lost?'

'Yes.'

'Wa'al!' said the captain, after a shorter silence, 'Here I sit who may come to the same end, like enough. He holds the seas in the hollow of His hand. We must all strike somewhere and go down. Our comfort, then, for ourselves and one another is to have

done our duty. I'd wager your brother did his!'

'He did!' answered the young fisherman. 'If ever man strove faithfully on all occasions to do his duty, my brother did. My brother was not a quick man (anything but that), but he was a faithful, true, and just man. We were the sons of only a small trades-man in this country, sir; yet our father was as watch-ful of his good name as if he had been a king.'

'A precious sight more so, I hope,—bearing in mind the general run of that class of crittur,' said the captain. 'But I interrupt.'

'My brother considered that our father left the good name to us, to keep clear and true.'

'Your brother considered right,' said the captain; 'and you couldn't take care of a better legacy. But again I interrupt.'

'No; for I have nothing more to say. We know that Hugh lived well for the good name, and we feel certain that he died well for the good name. And now it has come into my keeping. And that's all.'

'Well spoken!' cried the captain. 'Well spoken, young man! Concerning the manner of your broth-er's death,'—by this time the captain had released the hand he had shaken, and sat with his own broad, brown hands spread out on his knees, and spoke aside, —'concerning the manner of your brother's death, it may be that I have some information to give you; though it may not be, for I am far from sure. Can we have a little talk alone?'

The young man rose; but not before the captain's quick eye had noticed that, on the pretty sweetheart's turning to the window to greet the young widow with a nod and a wave of the hand, the young widow had held up to her the needlework on which she was en-gaged, with a patient and pleasant smile. So the captain said, being on his legs,—

'What might she be making now?'

'What is Margaret making, Kitty?' asked the young fisherman,—with one of his arms apparently mislaid somewhere.

As Kitty only blushed in reply, the captain doubled himself up as far as he could, standing, and said, with a slap of his leg,—

'In my country we should call it wedding-clothes. Fact! We should, I do assure you.'

But it seemed to strike the captain in another light too; for his laugh was not a long one, and he added, in quite a gentle tone,—

'And it's very pretty, my dear, to see her—poor young thing, with her fatherless child upon her bosom—giving up her thoughts to your home and your happiness. It's very pretty, my dear, and it's very good. May your marriage be more prosperous than hers, and be a comfort to her too. May the blessed sun see you all happy together, in possession of the good name, long after I have done ploughing the great salt field that is never sown!'

Kitty answered very earnestly, 'O! Thank you, sir, with all my heart!' And, in her loving little way, kissed her hand to him, and possibly by implication to the young fisherman, too, as the latter held the parlour-door open for the captain to pass out.

CHAPTER II

THE MONEY

'THE stairs are very narrow, sir,' said Alfred Raybrock to Captain Jorgan.

'Like my cabin-stairs,' returned the captain, 'on many a voyage.'

'And they are rather inconvenient for the head.'

'If my head can't take care of itself by this time, after all the knocking about the world it has had,' replied the captain, as unconcernedly as if he had no connection with it, 'it's not worth looking after.'

Thus they came into the young fisherman's bed-room, which was as perfectly neat and clean as the shop and parlour below; though it was but a little place, with a sliding window, and a phrenological ceiling expressive of all the peculiarities of the house-roof. Here the captain sat down on the foot of the bed, and glancing at a dreadful libel on Kitty which ornamented the wall,—the production of some wandering limner, whom the captain secretly admired as having studied portraiture from the figure-heads of ships,—motioned to the young man to take the rush-chair on the other side of the small, round table. That done, the captain put his hand in the deep breast-pocket of his long-skirted blue coat, and took out of it a strong square case-bottle,—not a large bottle but such as may be seen in any ordinary ship's medicine-chest. Setting this bottle on the table without removing his hand from it, Captain Jorgan then spake as follows:—

'In my last voyage homeward-bound,' said the captain, 'and that's the voyage off of which I now come straight, I encountered such weather off the Horn as is not very often met with, even there. I have rounded that stormy Cape pretty often, and I believe I first beat about there in the identical storms that blew the Devil's horns and tail off, and led to the horns being worked up into toothpicks for the plantation overseers in my country, who may be seen (if you travel down South, or away West, fur enough) picking their teeth with 'em, while the whips, made of the tail, flog hard. In this last voyage, homeward-

bound for Liverpool from South America, I say to you, my young friend, it blew. Whole measures! No half measures, nor making believe to blow; it blew! Now I warn't blown clean out of the water into the sky,—though I expected to be even that,— but I was blown clean out of my course; and when at last it fell calm, it fell dead calm, and a strong current set one way, day and night, night and day, and I drifted—drifted—drifted—out of all the ordinary tracks and courses of ships, and drifted yet, and yet drifted. It behooves a man who takes charge of fellow-critturs' lives, never to rest from making himself master of his calling. I never did rest, and consequently I knew pretty well ('specially looking over the side in the dead calm of that strong current) what dangers to expect, and what precautions to take against 'em. In short, we were driving head on to an island. There was no island in the chart, and, therefore, you may say it was ill-manners in the island to be there; I don't dispute its bad breeding, but there it was. Thanks be to Heaven, I was as ready for the island as the island was ready for me. I made it out myself from the masthead, and I got enough way upon her in good time to keep her off. I ordered a boat to be lowered and manned, and went in that boat myself to explore the island. There was a reef outside it, and, floating in a corner of the smooth water within the reef, was a heap of sea-weed, and entangled in that sea-weed was this bottle.'

Here the captain took his hand from the bottle for a moment, that the young fisherman might direct a wondering glance at it; and then replaced his hand and went on:—

'If ever you come—or even if ever you don't come —to a desert place, use your eyes and your spy-glass well; for the smallest thing you see may prove of use

to you, and may have some information or some warning in it.   That's the principle on which I came to see this bottle.   I picked up the bottle and ran the boat alongside the island, and made fast and went ashore armed, with a part of my boat's crew.   We found that every scrap of vegetation on the island (I give it you as my opinion, but scant and scrubby at the best of times) had been consumed by fire.   As we were making our way, cautiously and toilsomely, over the pulverised embers, one of my people sank into the earth breast-high.   He turned pale, and "Haul me out smart, shipmates," says he, "for my feet are among bones."   We soon got him on his legs again, and then we dug up the spot, and we found that the man was right, and that his feet had been among bones.   More than that, they were human bones; though whether the remains of one man, or of two or three men, what with calcination and ashes, and what with a poor practical knowledge of anatomy, I can't undertake to say.   We examined the whole island and made out nothing else, save and except that, from its opposite side, I sighted a considerable tract of land, which land I was able to identify, and according to the bearings of which (not to trouble you with my log) I took a fresh departure.   When I got aboard again I opened the bottle, which was oil-skin-covered as you see, and glass-stoppered as you see.   Inside of it,' pursued the captain, suiting his action to his words, 'I found this little crumpled, folded paper, just as you see.   Outside of it was written, as you see, these words: *"Whoever finds this, is solemnly entreated by the dead to convey it unread to Alfred Raybrock, Steepways, North Devon, England."*   A sacred charge,' said the captain, concluding his narrative, 'and, Alfred Raybrock, there it is!'

'This is my poor brother's writing!'

'I suppose so,' said Captain Jorgan. 'I'll take a look out of this little window while you read it.'

'Pray no, sir! I should be hurt. My brother couldn't know it would fall into such hands as yours.'

The captain sat down again on the foot of the bed, and the young man opened the folded paper with a trembling hand, and spread it on the table. The ragged paper, evidently creased and torn both before and after being written on, was much blotted and stained, and the ink had faded and run, and many words were wanting. What the captain and the young fisherman made out together, after much re-reading and much humouring of the folds of the paper, is given on the next page.

The young fisherman had become more and more agitated as the writing had become clearer to him. He now left it lying before the captain, over whose shoulder he had been reading it, and dropping into his former seat, leaned forward on the table and laid his face in his hands.

'What, man,' urged the captain, 'don't give in! Be up and doing *like* a man!'

'It is selfish, I know,—but doing what, doing what?' cried the young fisherman, in complete despair, and stamping his sea-boot on the ground.

'Doing what?' returned the captain. 'Something! I'd go down to the little breakwater below yonder, and take a wrench at one of the salt-rusted iron rings there, and either wrench it up by the roots or wrench my teeth out of my head, sooner than I'd do nothing. Nothing!' ejaculated the captain. 'Any fool or fainting heart can do *that,* and nothing can come of nothing,—which was pretended to be found out, I believe,

by one of them Latin critters,' said the captain with the deepest disdain; 'as if Adam hadn't found it out, afore ever he so much as named the beasts!'

Yet the captain saw, in spite of his bold words, that there was some greater reason than he yet understood for the young man's distress.   And he eyed him with a sympathising curiosity.

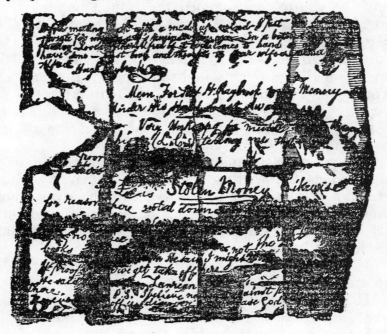

'Come, come!' continued the captain.   'Speak out. What is it, boy!'

'You have seen how beautiful she is, sir,' said the young man, looking up for the moment, with a flushed face and rumpled hair.

'Did any man ever say she warn't beautiful?' retorted the captain.   'If so, go and lick him.'

The young man laughed fretfully in spite of himself, and said,

'It 's not that, it 's not that.'

'Wa'al, then, what is it?' said the captain in a more soothing tone.

The young fisherman mournfully composed himself to tell the captain what it was, and began: 'We were to have been married next Monday week—'

'Were to have been!' interrupted Captain Jorgan. 'And are to be? Hey?'

Young Raybrock shook his head, and traced out with his forefinger the words, *'poor father's five hundred pounds,'* in the written paper.

'Go along,' said the captain. 'Five hundred pounds? Yes?'

'That sum of money,' pursued the young fisherman, entering with the greatest earnestness on his demonstration, while the captain eyed him with equal earnestness, 'was all my late father possessed. When he died, he owed no man more than he left means to pay, but he had been able to lay by only five hundred pounds.'

'Five hundred pounds,' repeated the captain. 'Yes?'

'In his lifetime, years before, he had expressly laid the money aside to leave to my mother,—like to settle upon her, if I make myself understood.'

'Yes?'

'He had risked it once—my father put down in writing at that time, respecting the money—and was resolved never to risk it again.'

'Not a spec'lator,' said the captain. 'My country wouldn't have suited him. Yes?'

'My mother has never touched the money till now. And now it was to have been laid out, this very next week, in buying me a handsome share in our neighbouring fishery here, to settle me in life with Kitty.'

The captain's face fell, and he passed and repassed

his sun-browned right hand over his thin hair, in a discomfited manner.

'Kitty's father has no more than enough to live on, even in the sparing way in which we live about here. He is a kind of bailiff or steward of manor rights here, and they are not much, and it is but a poor little office. He was better off once, and Kitty must never marry to mere drudgery and hard living.'

The captain still sat stroking his thin hair, and looking at the young fisherman.

'I am as certain that my father had no knowledge that any one was wronged as to this money, or that any restitution ought to be made, as I am certain that the sun now shines. But, after this solemn warning from my brother's grave in the sea, that the money is Stolen Money,' said Young Raybrock, forcing himself to the utterance of the words, 'can I doubt it? Can I touch it?'

'About not doubting, I ain't so sure,' observed the captain; 'but about not touching—no—I don't think you can.'

'See then,' said Young Raybrock, 'why I am so grieved. Think of Kitty. Think what I have got to tell her!'

His heart quite failed him again when he had come round to that, and he once more beat his sea-boot softly on the floor. But not for long; he soon began again, in a quietly resolute tone.

'However! Enough of that! You spoke some brave words to me just now, Captain Jorgan, and they shall not be spoken in vain. I have got to do something. What I have got to do, before all other things, is to trace out the meaning of this paper, for the sake of the Good Name that has no one else to put it right. And still for the sake of the Good Name, and my father's memory, not a word of this

writing must be breathed to my mother, or to Kitty, or to any human creature. You agree in this?'

'I don't know what they 'll think of us below,' said the captain, 'but for certain I can't oppose it. Now, as to tracing. How will you do?'

They both, as by consent, bent over the paper again, and again carefully puzzled out the whole of the writing.

'I make out that this would stand, if all the writing was here, "Inquire among the old men living there, for"—some one. Most like, you 'll go to this village named here?' said the captain, musing, with his finger on the name.

'Yes! And Mr. Tregarthen is a Cornishman, and —to be sure!—comes from Lanrean.'

'Does he?' said the captain quietly. 'As I ain't acquainted with him, who may *he* be?'

'Mr. Tregarthen is Kitty's father.'

'Ay, ay!' cried the captain. 'Now you speak! Tregarthen knows this village of Lanrean, then?'

'Beyond all doubt he does. I have often heard him mention it, as being his native place. He knows it well.'

'Stop half a moment,' said the captain. 'We want a name here. You could ask Tregarthen (or if you couldn't I could) what names of old men he remembers in his time in those diggings? Hey?'

'I can go straight to his cottage, and ask him now.'

'Take me with you,' said the captain, rising in a solid way that had a most comfortable reliability in it, 'and just a word more first. I have knocked about harder than you, and have got along further than you. I have had, all my sea-going life long, to keep my wits polished bright with acid and friction, like the brass cases of the ship's instruments. I 'll keep you company on this expedition. Now you don't live by

talking any more than I do. Clench that hand of yours in this hand of mine, and that's a speech on both sides.'

Captain Jorgan took command of the expedition with that hearty shake. He at once refolded the paper exactly as before, replaced it in the bottle, put the stopper in, put the oilskin over the stopper, confided the whole to Young Raybrock's keeping, and led the way downstairs.

But it was harder navigation below-stairs than above. The instant they set foot in the parlour the quick, womanly eye detected that there was something wrong. Kitty exclaimed, frightened, as she ran to her lover's side, 'Alfred! What's the matter?' Mrs. Raybrock cried out to the captain, 'Gracious! what have you done to my son to change him like this all in a minute?' And the young widow—who was there with her work upon her arm—was at first so agitated that she frightened the little girl she held in her hand, who hid her face in her mother's skirts and screamed. The captain, conscious of being held responsible for this domestic change, contemplated it with quite a guilty expression of countenance, and looked to the young fisherman to come to his rescue.

'Kitty, darling,' said Young Raybrock, 'Kitty, dearest love, I must go away to Lanrean, and I don't know where else or how much further, this very day. Worse than that—our marriage, Kitty, must be put off, and I don't know for how long.'

Kitty stared at him, in doubt and wonder and in anger, and pushed him from her with her hand.

'Put off?' cried Mrs. Raybrock. 'The marriage put off? And you going to Lanrean! Why, in the name of the dear Lord?'

'Mother dear, I can't say why; I must not say why. It would be dishonourable and undutiful to say why.'

'Dishonourable and undutiful?' returned the dame. 'And is there nothing dishonourable or undutiful in the boy's breaking the heart of his own plighted love, and his mother's heart too, for the sake of the dark secrets and counsels of a wicked stranger? Why did you ever come here?' she apostrophised the innocent captain. 'Who wanted you? Where did you come from? Why couldn't you rest in your own bad place, wherever it is, instead of disturbing the peace of quiet unoffending folk like us?'

'And what?' sobbed the poor little Kitty, 'have I ever done to you, you hard and cruel captain, that you should come and serve me so?'

And then they both began to weep most pitifully, while the captain could only look from the one to the other, and lay hold of himself by the coat collar.

'Margaret,' said the poor young fisherman, on his knees at Kitty's feet, while Kitty kept both her hands before her tearful face, to shut out the traitor from her view,—but kept her fingers wide asunder and looked at him all the time,—'Margaret, you have suffered so much, so uncomplainingly, and are always so careful and considerate! Do take my part, for poor Hugh's sake!'

The quiet Margaret was not appealed to in vain. 'I will, Alfred,' she returned, 'and I do. I wish this gentleman had never come near us'; whereupon the captain laid hold of himself the tighter; 'but I take your part for all that. I am sure you have some strong reason and some sufficient reason for what you do, strange as it is, and even for not saying why you do it, strange as that is. And, Kitty darling, you are bound to think so more than any one, for true love believes everything, and bears everything, and trusts everything. And, mother dear, you are bound to think so too, for you know you have been blest with

good sons, whose word was always as good as their oath, and who were brought up in as true a sense of honour as any gentleman in this land. And I am sure you have no more call, mother, to doubt your living son than to doubt your dead son; and for the sake of the dear dead, I stand up for the dear living.'

'Wa'al now,' the captain struck in, with enthusiasm, 'this I say, That whether your opinions flatter me or not, you are a young woman of sense, and spirit, and feeling; and I'd sooner have you by my side, in the hour of danger, than a good half of the men I've ever fallen in with—or fallen out with, ayther.'

Margaret did not return the captain's compliment, or appear fully to reciprocate his good opinion, but she applied herself to the consolation of Kitty, and of Kitty's mother-in-law that was to have been next Monday week, and soon restored the parlour to a quiet condition.

'Kitty, my darling,' said the young fisherman, 'I must go to your father to entreat him still to trust me in spite of this wretched change and mystery, and to ask him for some directions concerning Lanrean. Will you come home? Will you come with me, Kitty?'

Kitty answered not a word, but rose sobbing, with the end of her simple head-dress at her eyes. Captain Jorgan followed the lovers out, quite sheepishly, pausing in the shop to give an instruction to Mr. Pettifer.

'Here, Tom!' said the captain, in a low voice. 'Here's something in your line. Here's an old lady poorly and low in spirits. Cheer her up a bit, Tom. Cheer 'em all up.'

Mr. Pettifer, with a brisk nod of intelligence, immediately assumed his steward face, and went with his quiet, helpful, steward step into the parlour, where the captain had the great satisfaction of seeing him,

through the glass door, take the child in his arms (who offered no objection), and bend over Mrs. Raybrock, administering soft words of consolation.

'Though what he finds to say, unless he's telling her that 't 'll soon be over, or that most people is so at first, or that it 'll do her good afterward, I cannot imaginate!' was the captain's reflection as he followed the lovers.

He had not far to follow them, since it was but a short descent down the stony ways to the cottage of Kitty's father. But short as the distance was, it was long enough to enable the captain to observe that he was fast becoming the village Ogre; for there was not a woman standing working at her door, or a fisherman coming up or going down, who saw Young Raybrock unhappy and little Kitty in tears, but he or she instantly darted a suspicious and indignant glance at the captain, as the foreigner who must somehow be responsible for this unusual spectacle. Consequently, when they came into Tregarthen's little garden,—which formed the platform from which the captain had seen Kitty peeping over the wall,—the captain brought to, and stood off and on at the gate, while Kitty hurried to hide her tears in her own room, and Alfred spoke with her father, who was working in the garden. He was a rather infirm man, but could scarcely be called old yet, with an agreeable face and a promising air of making the best of things. The conversation began on his side with great cheerfulness and good humour, but soon became distrustful, and soon angry. That was the captain's cue for striking both into the conversation and the garden.

'Morning, sir!' said Captain Jorgan. 'How do you do?'

'The gentleman I am going away with,' said the young fisherman to Tregarthen.

'O!' returned Kitty's father, surveying the unfortunate captain with a look of extreme disfavour. 'I confess that I can't say I am glad to see you.'

'No,' said the captain, 'and, to admit the truth, that seems to be the general opinion in these parts. But don't be hasty; you may think better of me by and by.'

'I hope so,' observed Tregarthen.

'Wa'al, *I* hope so,' observed the captain, quite at his ease; 'more than that, I believe so,—though you don't. Now, Mr. Tregarthen, you don't want to exchange words of mistrust with me; and if you did, you couldn't, because I wouldn't. You and I are old enough to know better than to judge against experience from surfaces and appearances; and if you haven't lived to find out the evil and injustice of such judgments, you are a lucky man.'

The other seemed to shrink under this remark, and replied, 'Sir, I *have* lived to feel it deeply.'

'Wa'al,' said the captain, mollified, 'then I 've made a good cast without knowing it. Now, Tregarthen, there stands the lover of your only child, and here stand I who know his secret. I warrant it a righteous secret, and none of his making, though bound to be of his keeping. I want to help him out with it, and tewwards that end we ask you to favour us with the names of two or three old residents in the village of Lanrean. As I am taking out my pocket-book and pencil to put the names down, I may as well observe to you that this, wrote atop of the first page here, is my name and address: "Silas Jonas Jorgan, Salem, Massachusetts, United States." If ever you take it in your head to run over any morning, I shall be glad to welcome you. Now, what may be the spelling of these said names?'

'There was an elderly man,' said Tregarthen, 'named David Polreath. He may be dead.'

'Wa'al,' said the captain, cheerfully, 'if Polreath's dead and buried, and can be made of any service to us, Polreath won't object to our digging of him up. Polreath's down, anyhow.'

'There was another named Penrewen. I don't know his Christian name.'

'Never mind his Chris'en name,' said the captain. 'Penrewen, for short.'

'There was another named John Tredgear.'

'And a pleasant-sounding name, too,' said the captain; 'John Tredgear's booked.'

'I can recall no other except old Parvis.'

'One of old Parvis's fam'ly I reckon,' said the captain, 'kept a dry-goods store in New York city, and realised a handsome competency by burning his house to ashes. Same name, anyhow. David Polreath, Unchris'en Penrewen, John Tredgear, and old Arson Parvis.'

'I cannot recall any others at the moment.'

'Thank 'ee,' said the captain. 'And so, Tregarthen, hoping for your good opinion yet, and likewise for the fair Devonshire Flower's, your daughter's, I give you my hand, sir, and wish you good day.'

Young Raybrock accompanied him disconsolately; for there was no Kitty at the window when he looked up, no Kitty in the garden when he shut the gate, no Kitty gazing after them along the stony ways when they began to climb back.

'Now I tell you what,' said the captain. 'Not being at present calc'lated to promote harmony in your family, I won't come in. You go and get your dinner at home, and I'll get mine at the little hotel. Let our hour of meeting be two o'clock, and you'll find me smoking a cigar in the sun afore the hotel door   Tell Tom Pettifer, my steward, to consider himself on duty, and to look after your people till we come back;

you 'll find he 'll have made himself useful to 'em already, and will be quite acceptable.'

All was done as Captain Jorgan directed. Punctually at two o'clock the young fisherman appeared with his knapsack at his back; and punctually at two o'clock the captain jerked away the last feather-end of his cigar.

'Let me carry your baggage, Captain Jorgan; I can easily take it with mine.'

'Thank 'ee,' said the captain. 'I 'll carry it myself. It 's only a comb.'

They climbed out of the village, and paused among the trees and fern on the summit of the hill above, to take breath, and to look down at the beautiful sea. Suddenly the captain gave his leg a resounding slap, and cried, 'Never knew such a right thing in all my life!'—and ran away.

The cause of this abrupt retirement on the part of the captain was little Kitty among the trees. The captain went out of sight and waited, and kept out of sight and waited, until it occurred to him to beguile the time with another cigar. He lighted it, and smoked it out, and still he was out of sight and waiting. He stole within sight at last, and saw the lovers, with their arms entwined and their bent heads touching, moving slowly among the trees. It was the golden time of the afternoon then, and the captain said to himself, 'Golden sun, golden sea, golden sails, golden leaves, golden love, golden youth,—a golden state of things altogether!'

Nevertheless the captain found it necessary to hail his young companion before going out of sight again. In a few moments more he came up and they began their journey.

'That still young woman with the fatherless child,' said Captain Jorgan, as they fell into step, 'didn't

throw her words away; but good honest words are never thrown away.   And now that I am conveying you off from that tender little thing that loves, and relies, and hopes, I feel just as if I was the snarling crittur in the picters, with the tight legs, the long nose, and the feather in his cap, the tips of whose moustaches get up nearer to his eyes the wickeder he gets.'

The young fisherman knew nothing of Mephistopheles; but he smiled when the captain stopped to double himself up and slap his leg, and they went along in right good-fellowship.

NOTE.—The third and fourth chapters of this Christmas number were not by Dickens. After the first and second he did not resume the pen until the chapter entitled the 'Restitution,' here numbered as the fifth. For the two intervening chapters the reader is referred to the number as republished in the volume of the *Nine Christmas numbers of all the Year Round.*

CHAPTER V

THE RESTITUTION

CAPTAIN JORGAN, up and out betimes, had put the whole village of Lanrean under an amicable cross-examination, and was returning to the King Arthur's Arms to breakfast, none the wiser for his trouble, when he beheld the young fisherman advancing to meet him, accompanied by a stranger.   A glance at the stranger assured the captain that he could be no other than the Seafaring Man; and the captain was about to hail him as a fellow-craftsman, when the two stood still and silent before the captain, and the captain stood still, silent, and wondering before them.

'Why, what's this?' cried the captain, when at last he broke the silence.   'You two are alike.   You two are much alike!   What's this?'

Not a word was answered on the other side, until

after the seafaring brother had got hold of the captain's right hand, and the fisherman brother had got hold of the captain's left hand; and if ever the captain had had his fill of hand-shaking, from his birth to that hour, he had it then. And presently up and spoke the two brothers, one at a time, two at a time, two dozen at a time for the bewilderment into which they plunged the captain, until he gradually had Hugh Raybrock's deliverance made clear to him, and also unravelled the fact that the person referred to in the half-obliterated paper was Tregarthen himself.

'Formerly, dear Captain Jorgan,' said Alfred, 'of Lanrean, you recollect? Kitty and her father came to live at Steepways after Hugh shipped on his last voyage.'

'Ay, ay!' cried the captain, fetching a breath. '*Now* you have me in tow. Then your brother here don't know his sister-in-law that is to be so much as by name?'

'Never saw her; never heard of her!'

'Ay, ay, ay!' cried the captain. 'Why then we every one go back together—paper, writer, and all— and take Tregarthen into the secret we kept from him?'

'Surely,' said Alfred, 'we can't help it now. We must go through with our duty.'

'Not a doubt,' returned the captain. 'Give me an arm apiece, and let us set this ship-shape.'

So walking up and down in the shrill wind on the wild moor, while the neglected breakfast cooled within, the captain and the brothers settled their course of action.

It was that they should all proceed by the quickest means they could secure to Barnstaple, and there look over the father's books and papers in the lawyer's keeping; as Hugh had proposed to himself to do if

ever he reached home. That, enlightened or unenlightened, they should then return to Steepways and go straight to Mr. Tregarthen, and tell him all they knew, and see what came of it, and act accordingly. Lastly, that when they got there they should enter the village with all precautions against Hugh's being recognised by any chance; and that to the captain should be consigned the task of preparing his wife and mother for his restoration to this life.

'For you see,' quoth Captain Jorgan, touching the last head, 'it requires caution any way, great joys being as dangerous as great griefs, if not more dangerous, as being more uncommon (and therefore less provided against) in this round world of ours. And besides, I should like to free my name with the ladies, and take you home again at your brightest and luckiest; so don't let 's throw away a chance of success.'

The captain was highly lauded by the brothers for his kind interest and foresight.

'And now stop!' said the captain, coming to a standstill, and looking from one brother to the other, with quite a new rigging of wrinkles about each eye; 'you are of opinion,' to the elder, 'that you are ra'ather slow?'

'I assure you I am very slow,' said the honest Hugh.

'Wa'al,' replied the captain, 'I assure *you* that to the best of my belief I am ra'ather smart. Now a slow man ain't good at quick business, is he?'

That was clear to both.

'You,' said the captain, turning to the younger brother, 'are a little in love; ain't you?'

'Not a little, Captain Jorgan.'

'Much or little, you 're sort preoccupied; ain't you?'

It was impossible to be denied.

'And a sort preoccupied man ain't good at quick business, is he?' said the captain.

Equally clear on all sides.

'Now,' said the captain, 'I ain't in love myself, and I 've made many a smart run across the ocean, and I should like to carry on and go ahead with this affair of yours and make a run slick through it. Shall I try? Will you hand it over to me?'

They were both delighted to do so, and thanked him heartily.

'Good,' said the captain, taking out his watch. 'This is half-past eight A.M., Friday morning. I 'll jot that down, and we 'll compute how many hours we 've been out when we run into your mother's post-office. There! The entry 's made, and now we go ahead.'

They went ahead so well that before the Barnstaple lawyer's office was open next morning, the captain was sitting whistling on the step of the door, waiting for the clerk to come down the street with his key and open it. But instead of the clerk there came the master, with whom the captain fraternised on the spot to an extent that utterly confounded him.

As he personally knew both Hugh and Alfred, there was no difficulty in obtaining immediate access to such of the father's papers as were in his keeping. These were chiefly old letters and cash accounts; from which the captain, with a shrewdness and despatch that left the lawyer far behind, established with perfect clearness, by noon, the following particulars:—

That one Lawrence Clissold had borrowed of the deceased, at a time when he was a thriving young tradesman in the town of Barnstaple, the sum of five hundred pounds. That he had borrowed it on the written statement that it was to be laid out in further-ance of a speculation which he expected would raise him to independence; he being, at the time of writing

that letter, no more than a clerk in the house of Dringworth Brothers, America Square, London. That the
money was borrowed for a stipulated period; but that,
when the term was out, the aforesaid speculation
failed, and Clissold was without means of repayment.
That, hereupon, he had written to his creditor, in no
very persuasive terms, vaguely requesting further
time. That the creditor had refused this concession,
declaring that he could not afford delay. That Clissold then paid the debt, accompanying the remittance
of the money with an angry letter describing it as
having been advanced by a relative to save him from
ruin. That, in acknowledging the receipt, Raybrock had cautioned Clissold to seek to borrow money
of him no more, as he would never so risk money
again.

Before the lawyer the captain said never a word
in reference to these discoveries. But when the papers
had been put back in their box, and he and his two
companions were well out of the office, his right leg
suffered for it, and he said,—

'So far this run's begun with a fair wind and a
prosperous; for don't you see that all this agrees with
that dutiful trust in his father maintained by the slow
member of the Raybrock family?'

Whether the brothers had seen it before or no, they
saw it now. Not that the captain gave them much
time to contemplate the state of things at their ease,
for he instantly whipped them into a chaise again, and
bore them off to Steepways. Although the afternoon was but just beginning to decline when they
reached it, and it was broad daylight, still they had
no difficulty, by dint of muffling the returned sailor
up, and ascending the village rather than descending
it, in reaching Tregarthen's cottage unobserved.

Kitty was not visible, and they surprised Tregarthen sitting writing in the small bay-window of his little room.

'Sir,' said the captain, instantly shaking hands with him, pen and all, 'I 'm glad to see you, sir. How do you do, sir? I told you you 'd think better of me by and by, and I congratulate you on going to do it.'

Here the captain's eye fell on Tom Pettifer Ho, engaged in preparing some cookery at the fire.

'That critter,' said the captain, smiting his leg, 'is a born steward, and never ought to have been in any other way of life. Stop where you are, Tom, and make yourself useful. Now, Tregarthen, I 'm going to try a chair.'

Accordingly the captain drew one close to him, and went on:—

'This loving member of the Raybrock family you know, sir. This slow member of the same family you don't know, sir. Wa'al, these two are brothers,— fact! Hugh 's come to life again, and here he stands. Now see here, my friend! You don't want to be told that he was cast away, but you do want to be told (for there 's a purpose in it) that he was cast away with another man. That man by name was Lawrence Clissold.'

At the mention of this name Tregarthen started and changed colour. 'What 's the matter?' said the captain.

'He was a fellow-clerk of mine thirty—five-and-thirty—years ago.'

'True,' said the captain, immediately catching at the clew: 'Dringworth Brothers, America Square, London City.'

The other started again, nodded, and said, 'That was the house.'

'Now,' pursued the captain, 'between those two

men cast away there arose a mystery concerning the
round sum of five hundred pound.'

Again Tregarthen started, changing colour.
Again the captain said, 'What's the matter?'

As Tregarthen only answered, 'Please to go on,'
the captain recounted, very tersely and plainly, the
nature of Clissold's wanderings on the barren island,
as he had condensed them in his mind from the seafaring man. Tregarthen became greatly agitated
during this recital, and at length exclaimed,—

'Clissold was the man who ruined me! I have suspected it for many a long year, and now I know it.'

'And how,' said the captain, drawing his chair still
closer to Tregarthen, and clapping his hand upon his
shoulder,—'how may you know it?'

'When we were fellow-clerks,' replied Tregarthen,
'in that London house, it was one of my duties to
enter daily in a certain book an account of the sums
received that day by the firm, and afterward paid
into the bankers.' One memorable day,—a Wednesday, the black day of my life,—among the sums I so
entered was one of five hundred pounds.'

'I begin to make it out,' said the captain. 'Yes?'

'It was one of Clissold's duties to copy from this
entry a memorandum of the sums which the clerk
employed to go to the bankers' paid in there. It was
my duty to hand the money to Clissold; it was Clissold's to hand it to the clerk, with that memorandum
of his writing. On that Wednesday I entered a sum
of five hundred pounds received. I handed that sum,
as I handed the other sums in the day's entry, to Clissold. I was absolutely certain of it at the time; I have
been absolutely certain of it ever since. A sum of
five hundred pounds was afterward found by the
house to have been that day wanting from the bag,
from Clissold's memorandum, and from the entries in

my book. Clissold, being questioned, stood upon his perfect clearness in the matter, and emphatically declared that he asked no better than to be tested by "Tregarthen's book." My book was examined, and the entry of five hundred pounds was not there.'

'How not there,' said the captain, 'when you made it yourself?'

Tregarthen continued:—

'I was then questioned. Had I made the entry? Certainly I had. The house produced my book, and it was not there. I could not deny my book; I could not deny my writing. I knew there must be forgery by some one; but the writing was wonderfully like mine, and I could impeach no one if the house could not. I was required to pay the money back. I did so; and I left the house, almost broken-hearted, rather than remain there,—even if I could have done so,—with a dark shadow of suspicion always on me. I returned to my native place, Lanrean, and remained there, clerk to a mine, until I was appointed to my little post here.'

'I well remember,' said the captain, 'that I told you that if you had no experience of ill judgments on deceiving appearances, you were a lucky man. You went hurt at that, and I see why. I 'm sorry.'

'Thus it is,' said Tregarthen. 'Of my own innocence I have of course been sure; it has been at once my comfort and my trial. Of Clissold I have always had suspicions almost amounting to certainty; but they have never been confirmed until now. For my daughter's sake and for my own I have carried this subject in my own heart, as the only secret of my life, and have long believed that it would die with me.'

'Wa'al, my good sir,' said the captain cordially, 'the present question is, and will be long, I hope, concerning living, and not dying. Now, here are our

two honest friends, the loving Raybrock and the slow. Here they stand, agreed on one point, on which I 'd back 'em round the world, and right across it from north to south, and then again from east to west, and through it, from your deepest Cornish mine to China. It is, that they will never use this same so-often-mentioned sum of money, and that restitution of it must be made to you. These two, the loving member and the slow, for the sake of the right and of their father's memory, will have it ready for you to-morrow. Take it, and ease their minds and mine, and end a most unfort'nate transaction.'

Tregarthen took the captain by the hand, and gave his hand to each of the young men, but positively and finally answered No. He said, they trusted to his word, and he was glad of it, and at rest in his mind; but there was no proof, and the money must remain as it was. All were very earnest over this; and earnestness in men, when they are right and true, is so impressive, that Mr. Pettifer deserted his cookery and looked on quite moved.

'And so,' said the captain, 'so we come—as that lawyer-crittur over yonder where we were this morning might—to mere proof; do we? We must have it; must we? How? From this Clissold's wanderings, and from what you say, it ain't hard to make out that there was a neat forgery of your writing committed by the too smart rowdy that was grease and ashes when I made his acquaintance, and a substitution of a forged leaf in your book for a real and true leaf torn out. Now was that real and true leaf then and there destroyed? No,—for says he, in his drunken way, he slipped it into a crack in his own desk, because you came into the office before there was time to burn it, and could never get back to it arterwards. Wait a bit. Where is that desk now?

Do you consider it likely to be in America Square, London City?'

Tregarthen shook his head.

'The house has not, for years, transacted business in that place. I have heard of it, and read of it, as removed, enlarged, every way altered. Things alter so fast in these times.'

'You think so,' returned the captain, with compassion; 'but you should come over and see *me* afore you talk about *that.* Wa'al, now. This desk, this paper,—this paper, this desk,' said the captain, ruminating and walking about, and looking, in his uneasy abstraction, into Mr. Pettifer's hat on a table, among other things. 'This desk, this paper,—this paper, this desk,' the captain continued, musing and roaming about the room, 'I'd give—'

However, he gave nothing, but took up his steward's hat instead, and stood looking into it, as if he had just come into church. After that he roamed again, and again said, 'This desk, belonging to this house of Dringworth Brothers, America Square, London City—'

Mr. Pettifer, still strangely moved, and now more moved than before, cut the captain off as he backed across the room, and bespake him thus:—

'Captain Jorgan, I have been wishful to engage your attention, but I couldn't do it. I am unwilling to interrupt Captain Jorgan, but I must do it. *I* know something about that house.'

The captain stood stock-still and looked at him,— with his (Mr. Pettifer's) hat under his arm.

'You're aware,' pursued his steward, 'that I was once in the broking business, Captain Jorgan?'

'I was aware,' said the captain, 'that you had failed in that calling, and in half the businesses going, Tom.'

'Not quite so, Captain Jorgan; but I failed in the

broking business. I was partners with my brother, sir. There was a sale of old office furniture at Dring-worth Brothers' when the house was moved from America Square, and me and my brother made what we call in the trade a Deal there, sir. And I'll make bold to say, sir, that the only thing I ever had from my brother, or from any relation,—for my relations have mostly taken property from me instead of giving me any,—was an old desk we bought at that same sale, with a crack in it. My brother wouldn't have given me even that, when we broke partnership, if it had been worth anything.'

'Where is that desk now?' said the captain.

'Well, Captain Jorgan,' replied the steward, 'I couldn't say for certain where it is now; but when I saw it last,—which was last time we were outward bound,—it was at a very nice lady's at Wapping, along with a little chest of mine which was detained for a small matter of a bill owing.'

The captain, instead of paying that rapt attention to his steward which was rendered by the other three persons present, went to Church again, in respect of the steward's hat. And a most especially agitated and memorable face the captain produced from it, after a short pause.

'Now, Tom,' said the captain, 'I spoke to you, when we first came here, respecting your constitutional weakness on the subject of sunstroke.'

'You did, sir.'

'Will my slow friend,' said the captain, 'lend me his arm, or I shall sink right back'ards into this blessed steward's cookery? Now, Tom,' pursued the captain, when the required assistance was given, 'on your oath as a steward, didn't you take that desk to pieces to make a better one of it, and put it together fresh,— or something of the kind?'

'On my oath I did, sir,' replied the steward.

'And by the blessing of Heaven, my friends, one and all,' cried the captain, radiant with joy,—'of the Heaven that put it into this Tom Pettifer's head to take so much care of his head against the bright sun, —he lined his hat with the original leaf in Tregarthen's writing,—and here it is!'

With that the captain, to the utter destruction of Mr. Pettifer's favourite hat, produced the book-leaf, very much worn, but still legible, and gave both his legs such tremendous slaps that they were heard far off in the bay, and never accounted for.

'A quarter past five P.M.,' said the captain, pulling out his watch, 'and that's thirty-three hours and a quarter in all, and a pritty run!'

How they were all overpowered with delight and triumph; how the money was restored, then and there, to Tregarthen; how Tregarthen, then and there, gave it all to his daughter; how the captain undertook to go to Dringworth Brothers and reëstablish the reputation of their forgotten old clerk; how Kitty came in, and was nearly torn to pieces, and the marriage was re-appointed, needs not to be told. Nor how she and the young fisherman went home to the post-office to prepare the way for the captain's coming, by declaring him to be the mightiest of men, who had made all their fortunes,—and then dutifully withdrew together, in order that he might have the domestic coast entirely to himself. How he availed himself of it is all that remains to tell.

Deeply delighted with his trust, and putting his heart into it, he raised the latch of the post-office parlour where Mrs. Raybrock and the young widow sat, and said,—

'May I come in?'

'Sure you may, Captain Jorgan!' replied the old

lady. 'And good reason you have to be free of the house, though you have not been too well used in it by some who ought to have known better. I ask your pardon.'

'No you don't, ma'am,' said the captain, 'for I won't let you. Wa'al, to be sure!'

By this time he had taken a chair on the hearth between them.

'Never felt such an evil spirit in the whole course of my life! There! I tell you! I could a'most have cut my own connection. Like the dealer in my country, away West, who when he had let himself be outdone in a bargain, said to himself, "Now I tell you what! I 'll never speak to you again." And he never did, but joined a settlement of oysters, and translated the multiplication table into their language, —which is a fact than can be proved. If you doubt it, mention it to any oyster you come across, and see if he 'll have the face to contradict it.'

He took the child from her mother's lap and set it on his knee.

'Not a bit afraid of me now, you see. Knows I am fond of small people. I have a child, and she 's a girl, and I sing to her sometimes.'

'What do you sing?' asked Margaret.

'Not a long song, my dear.

> Silas Jorgan
> Played the organ.

That 's about all. And sometimes I tell her stories, —stories of sailors supposed to be lost, and recovered after all hope was abandoned.' Here the captain musingly went back to his song,—

> Silas Jorgan
> Played the organ;

repeating it with his eyes on the fire, as he softly danced the child on his knee. For he felt that Margaret had stopped working.

'Yes,' said the captain, still looking at the fire, 'I make up stories and tell 'em to that child. Stories of shipwreck on desert islands, and long delay in getting back to civilised lands. It is to stories the like of that, mostly, that

> Silas Jorgan
> Plays the organ.'

There was no light in the room but the light of the fire; for the shades of night were on the village, and the stars had begun to peep out of the sky one by one, as the houses of the village peeped out from among the foliage when the night departed. The captain felt that Margaret's eyes were upon him, and thought it discreetest to keep his own eyes on the fire.

'Yes; I make 'em up,' said the captain. 'I make up stories of brothers brought together by the good providence of GOD,—of sons brought back to mothers, husbands brought back to wives, fathers raised from the deep, for little children like herself.'

Margaret's touch was on his arm, and he could not choose but look round now. Next moment her hand moved imploringly to his breast, and she was on her knees before him,—supporting the mother, who was also kneeling.

'What's the matter?' said the captain. 'What's the matter?

> Silas Jorgan
> Played the——'

Their looks and tears were too much for him, and he could not finish the song, short as it was.

'Mistress Margaret, you have borne ill fortune well. Could you bear good fortune equally well, if it was to come?'

'I hope so. I thankfully and humbly and earnestly hope so!'

'Wa'al, my dear,' said the captain, 'p'rhaps it has come. He's—don't be frightened—shall I say the word—'

'Alive?'

'Yes!'

The thanks they fervently addressed to Heaven were again too much for the captain, who openly took out his handkerchief and dried his eyes.

'He's no further off,' resumed the captain, 'than my country. Indeed, he's no further off than his own native country. To tell you the truth, he's no further off than Falmouth. Indeed, I doubt if he's quite so fur. Indeed, if you was sure you could bear it nicely, and I was to do no more than whistle for him—'

The captain's trust was discharged. A rush came, and they were all together again.

This was a fine opportunity for Tom Pettifer to appear with a tumbler of cold water, and he presently appeared with it, and administered it to the ladies; at the same time soothing them, and composing their dresses, exactly as if they had been passengers crossing the Channel. The extent to which the captain slapped his legs, when Mr. Pettifer acquitted himself of this act of stewardship, could have been thoroughly appreciated by no one but himself; inasmuch as he must have slapped them black and blue, and they must have smarted tremendously.

He couldn't stay for the wedding, having a few appointments to keep at the irreconcilable distance of about four thousand miles. So next morning all the

village cheered him up to the level ground above, and there he shook hands with a complete Census of its population, and invited the whole, without exception, to come and stay several months with him at Salem, Mass., U. S. And there as he stood on the spot where he had seen that little golden picture of love and parting, and from which he could that morning contemplate another golden picture with a vista of golden years in it, little Kitty put her arms around his neck, and kissed him on both his bronzed cheeks, and laid her pretty face upon his storm-beaten breast, in sight of all,—ashamed to have called such a noble captain names. And there the captain waved his hat over his head three final times; and there he was last seen, going away accompanied by Tom Pettifer Ho, and carrying his hands in his pockets. And there, before that ground was softened with the fallen leaves of three more summers, a rosy little boy took his first unsteady run to a fair young mother's breast, and the name of that infant fisherman was Jorgan Raybrock.

TOM TIDDLER'S GROUND

[1861]

TOM TIDDLER'S GROUND

IN THREE CHAPTERS [1]

I

PICKING UP SOOT AND CINDERS

'AND why Tom Tiddler's ground?' asked the Traveller.

'Because he scatters halfpence to Tramps and such-like,' returned the Landlord, 'and of course they pick 'em up. And this being done on his own land (which it *is* his own land, you observe, and were his family's before him), why it is but regarding the halfpence as gold and silver, and turning the ownership of the property a bit round your finger, and there you have the name of the children's game complete. And it's appropriate too,' said the Landlord, with his favourite action of stooping a little, to look across the table out of window at vacancy, under the window-blind which was half drawn down. 'Leastwise it has been so considered by many gentlemen which have partook of chops and tea in the present humble parlour.'

The Traveller was partaking of chops and tea in the present humble parlour, and the Landlord's shot was fired obliquely at him.

'And you call him a Hermit?' said the Traveller.

'They call him such,' returned the Landlord, evading personal responsibility; 'he is in general so considered.'

'What *is* a Hermit?' asked the Traveller.

377

'What is it?' repeated the Landlord, drawing his hand across his chin.

'Yes, what is it?'

The Landlord stooped again, to get a more comprehensive view of vacancy under the window-blind, and—with an asphyxiated appearance on him as one unaccustomed to definition—made no answer.

'I'll tell you what I suppose it to be,' said the Traveller. 'An abominably dirty thing.'

'Mr. Mopes is dirty, it cannot be denied,' said the Landlord.

'Intolerably conceited.'

'Mr. Mopes is vain of the life he leads, some do say,' replied the Landlord, as another concession.

'A slothful, unsavoury, nasty reversal of the laws of human nature,' said the Traveller; 'and for the sake of God's working world and its wholesomeness, both moral and physical, I would put the thing on the treadmill (if I had my way) wherever I found it; whether on a pillar, or in a hole; whether on Tom Tiddler's ground, or the Pope of Rome's ground, or a Hindoo fakeer's ground, or any other ground.'

'I don't know about putting Mr. Mopes on the treadmill,' said the Landlord, shaking his head very seriously. 'There ain't a doubt but what he has got landed property.'

'How far may it be to this said Tom Tiddler's ground?' asked the Traveller.

'Put it at five mile,' returned the Landlord.

'Well! When I have done my breakfast,' said the Traveller, 'I'll go there. I came over here this morning, to find it out and see it.'

'Many does,' observed the Landlord.

The conversation passed, in the Midsummer weather of no remote year of grace, down among the pleasant dales and trout-streams of a green English county.

No matter what county. Enough that you may hunt
there, shoot there, fish there, traverse long grass-
grown Roman roads there, open ancient barrows
there, see many a square mile of richly cultivated land
there, and hold Arcadian talk with a bold peasantry,
their country's pride, who will tell you (if you want
to know) how pastoral housekeeping is done on nine
shillings a week.

Mr. Traveller sat at his breakfast in the little
sanded parlour of the Peal of Bells village alehouse,
with the dew and dust of an early walk upon his
shoes—an early walk by road and meadow and cop-
pice, that had sprinkled him bountifully with little
blades of grass, and scraps of new hay, and with
leaves both young and old, and with other such fragrant tokens of the freshness and wealth of summer.
The window through which the landlord had concentrated his gaze upon vacancy was shaded, because the
morning sun was hot and bright on the village street.
The village street was like most other village streets:
wide for its height, silent for its size, and drowsy
in the dullest degree. The quietest little dwellings
with the largest of window-shutters (to shut up Nothing as carefully as if it were the Mint, or the Bank
of England), had called in the Doctor's house so suddenly, that his brass door-plate and three stories stood
among them as conspicuous and different as the Doctor himself in his broadcloth, among the smock-frocks
of his patients. The village residences seemed to
have gone to law with a similar absence of consideration, for a score of weak little lath-and-plaster cabins
clung in confusion about the Attorney's red-brick
house, which, with glaring doorsteps and a most terrific scraper, seemed to serve all manner of ejectments
upon them. They were as various as labourers—
high-shouldered, wry-necked, one-eyed, goggle-eyed,

squinting, bow-legged, knock-kneed, rheumatic, crazy. Some of the small tradesmen's houses, such as the crockery-shop and the harness-maker's, had a Cyclops window in the middle of the gable, within an inch or two of its apex, suggesting that some forlorn rural Prentice must wriggle himself into that apartment horizontally, when he retired to rest, after the manner of the worm. So bountiful in its abundance was the surrounding country, and so lean and scant the village, that one might have thought the village had sown and planted everything it once possessed, to convert the same into crops. This would account for the bareness of the little shops, the bareness of the few boards and trestles designed for market purposes in a corner of the street, the bareness of the obsolete Inn and Inn Yard, with the ominous inscription 'Excise Office' not yet faded out from the gateway, as indicating the very last thing that poverty could get rid of. This would also account for the determined abandonment of the village by one stray dog, fast lessening in the perspective where the white posts and the pond were, and would explain his conduct on the hypothesis that he was going (through the act of suicide) to convert himself into manure, and become a part proprietor in turnips or mangold-wurzel.

Mr. Traveller having finished his breakfast and paid his moderate score, walked out to the threshold of the Peal of Bells, and, thence directed by the pointing finger of his host, betook himself towards the ruined hermitage of Mr. Mopes the hermit.

For, Mr. Mopes, by suffering everything about him to go to ruin, and by dressing himself in a blanket and skewer, and by steeping himself in soot and grease and other nastiness, had acquired great renown in all that country-side—far greater renown than he could ever have won for himself, if his career

had been that of any ordinary Christian, or decent Hottentot. He had even blanketed and skewered and sooted and greased himself, into the London papers. And it was curious to find, as Mr. Traveller found by stopping for a new direction at this farmhouse or at that cottage as he went along, with how much accuracy the morbid Mopes had counted on the weakness of his neighbours to embellish him. A mist of home-brewed marvel and romance surrounded Mopes, in which (as in all fogs) the real proportions of the real object were extravagantly heightened. He had murdered his beautiful beloved in a fit of jealousy and was doing penance; he had made a vow under the influence of grief; he had made a vow under the influence of a fatal accident; he had made a vow under the influence of religion; he had made a vow under the influence of drink; he had made a vow under the influence of disappointment; he had never made any vow, but 'had got led into it' by the possession of a mighty and most awful secret; he was enormously rich, he was stupendously charitable, he was profoundly learned, he saw spectres, he knew and could do all kinds of wonders. Some said he went out every night, and was met by terrified wayfarers stalking along dark roads, others said he never went out, some knew his penance to be nearly expired, others had positive information that his seclusion was not a penance at all, and would never expire but with himself. Even, as to the easy facts of how old he was, or how long he had held verminous occupation of his blanket and skewer, no consistent information was to be got, from those who must know if they would. He was represented as being all the ages between five-and-twenty and sixty, and as having been a hermit seven years, twelve, twenty, thirty,—though twenty, on the whole, appeared the favourite term.

'Well, well!' said Mr. Traveller. 'At any rate, let us see what a real live Hermit looks like.'

So, Mr. Traveller went on, and on, and on, until he came to Tom Tiddler's ground.

It was a nook in a rustic by-road, which the genius of Mopes had laid waste as completely, as if he had been born an Emperor and a Conqueror. Its centre object was a dwelling-house, sufficiently substantial, all the window-glass of which had been long ago abolished by the surprising genius of Mopes, and all the windows of which were barred across with rough-split logs of trees nailed over them on the outside. A rickyard, hip-high in vegetable rankness and ruin, contained outbuildings, from which the thatch had lightly fluttered away, on all the winds of all the seasons of the year, and from which the planks and beams had heavily dropped and rotted. The frosts and damps of winter, and the heats of summer, had warped what wreck remained, so that not a post or a board retained the position it was meant to hold, but everything was twisted from its purpose, like its owner, and degraded and debased. In this homestead of the sluggard, behind the ruined hedge, and sinking away among the ruined grass and the nettles, were the last perishing fragments of certain ricks: which had gradually mildewed and collapsed, until they looked like mounds of rotten honeycomb, or dirty sponge. Tom Tiddler's ground could even show its ruined water; for, there was a slimy pond into which a tree or two had fallen—one soppy trunk and branches lay across it then—which in its accumulation of stagnant weed, and in its black decomposition, and in all its foulness and filth, was almost comforting, regarded as the only water that could have reflected the shameful place without seeming polluted by that low office.

Mr. Traveller looked all around him on Tim Tiddler's ground, and his glance at last encountered a dusky Tinker lying among the weeds and rank grass, in the shade of the dwelling-house. A rough walking-staff lay on the ground by his side, and his head rested on a small wallet. He met Mr. Traveller's eye without lifting up his head, merely depressing his chin a little (for he was lying on his back) to get a better view of him.

'Good day!' said Mr. Traveller.

'Same to you, if you like it,' returned the Tinker.

'Don't *you* like it? It's a very fine day.'

'I ain't partickler in weather,' returned the Tinker, with a yawn.

Mr. Traveller had walked up to where he lay, and was looking down at him. 'This is a curious place,' said Mr. Traveller.

'Ay, I suppose so!' returned the Tinker. 'Tom Tiddler's ground, they call this.'

'Are you well acquainted with it?'

'Never saw it afore to-day,' said the Tinker, with another yawn, 'and don't care if I never see it again. There was a man here just now, told me what it was called. If you want to see Tom himself, you must go in at that gate.' He faintly indicated with his chin a little mean ruin of a wooden gate at the side of the house.

'Have you seen Tom?'

'No, and I ain't partickler to see him. I can see a dirty man anywhere.'

'He does not live in the house, then?' said Mr. Traveller, casting his eyes upon the house anew.

'The man said,' returned the Tinker, rather irritably,—'him as was here just now,—"this what you're a lying on, mate, is Tom Tiddler's ground. And if you want to see Tom," he says, "you must go

in at that gate." The man come out at that gate himself, and he ought to know.'

'Certainly,' said Mr. Traveller.

'Though, perhaps,' exclaimed the Tinker, so struck by the brightness of his own idea, that it had the electric effect upon him of causing him to lift up his head an inch or so, 'perhaps he was a liar! He told some rum'uns—him as was here just now, did about this place of Tom's. He says—him as was here just now—"When Tom shut up the house, mate, to go to rack, the beds was left, all made, like as if somebody was a-going to sleep in every bed. And if you was to walk through the bedrooms now, you'd see the ragged mouldy bedclothes a heaving and a heaving like seas. And a heaving and a heaving with what?" he says. "Why, with the rats under 'em." '

'I wish I had seen that man,' Mr. Traveller remarked.

'You'd have been welcome to see him instead of me seeing him,' growled the Tinker; 'for he was a long-winded one.'

Not without a sense of injury in the remembrance, the Tinker gloomily closed his eyes. Mr. Traveller, deeming the Tinker a short-winded one, from whom no further breath of information was to be derived, betook himself to the gate.

Swung upon its rusty hinges, it admitted him into a yard in which there was nothing to be seen but an outhouse attached to the ruined building, with a barred window in it. As there were traces of many recent footsteps under this window, and as it was a low window, and unglazed, Mr. Traveller made bold to peep within the bars. And there to be sure, he had a real live Hermit before him, and could judge how the real dead Hermits used to look.

He was lying on a bank of soot and cinders, on the floor, in front of a rusty fireplace. There was nothing else in the dark little kitchen, or scullery, or whatever his den had been originally used as, but a table with a litter of old bottles on it. A rat made a clatter among these bottles, jumped down, and ran over the real live Hermit on his way to his hole, or the man in *his* hole would not have been so easily discernible. Tickled in the face by the rat's tail, the owner of Tom Tiddler's ground opened his eyes, saw Mr. Traveller, started up, and sprang to the window.

'Humph!' thought Mr. Traveller, retiring a pace or two from the bars. 'A compound of Newgate, Bedlam, a Debtors' Prison in the worst time, a chimney-sweep, a mudlark, and the Noble Savage! A nice old family, the Hermit family. Hah!'

Mr. Traveller thought this, as he silently confronted the sooty object in the blanket and skewer (in sober truth it wore nothing else), with the matted hair and the staring eyes. Further, Mr. Traveller thought, as the eye surveyed him with a very obvious curiosity in ascertaining the effect they produced, 'Vanity, vanity, vanity! Verily, all is vanity!'

'What is your name, sir, and where do you come from?' asked Mr. Mopes the Hermit—with an air of authority, but in the ordinary human speech of one who has been to school.

Mr. Traveller answered the inquiries.

'Did you come here, sir, to see *me?*'

'I did. I heard of you, and I came to see you.—I know you like to be seen.' Mr. Traveller coolly threw the last words in, as a matter of course, to forestall an affectation of resentment or objection that he saw rising beneath the grease and grime of the face. They had their effect.

'So,' said the Hermit, after a momentary silence,

unclasping the bars by which he had previously held, and seating himself behind them on the ledge of the window, with his bare legs and feet crouched up, 'you know I like to be seen?'

Mr. Traveller looked about him for something to sit on, and, observing a billet of wood in a corner, brought it near the window. Deliberately seating himself upon it, he answered, 'Just so.'

Each looked at the other, and each appeared to take some pains to get the measure of the other.

'Then you have come to ask me why I lead this life,' said the Hermit, frowning in a stormy manner. 'I never tell that to any human being. I will not be asked that.'

'Certainly you will not be asked that by me,' said Mr. Traveller, 'for I have not the slightest desire to know.'

'You are an uncouth man,' said Mr. Mopes the Hermit.

'You are another,' said Mr. Traveller.

The Hermit, who was plainly in the habit of over-awing his visitors with the novelty of his filth and his blanket and skewer, glared at his present visitor in some discomfiture and surprise: as if he had taken aim at him with a sure gun, and his piece had missed fire.

'Why do you come here at all?' he asked, after a pause.

'Upon my life,' said Mr. Traveller, 'I was made to ask myself that very question only a few minutes ago—by a Tinker too.'

As he glanced towards the gate in saying it, the Hermit glanced in that direction likewise.

'Yes. He is lying on his back in the sunlight out-side,' said Mr. Traveller, as if he had been asked con-

cerning the man, 'and he won't come in; for he says—
and really very reasonably—"What should I come in
for? I can see a dirty man anywhere." '

'You are an insolent person. Go away from my
premises. Go!' said the Hermit, in an imperious and
angry tone.

'Come, come!' returned Mr. Traveller, quite undisturbed. 'This is a little too much. You are not going to call yourself clean? Look at your legs. And
as to these being your premises:—they are in far too
disgraceful a condition to claim any privilege of ownership, or anything else.'

The Hermit bounced down from his window-ledge,
and cast himself on his bed of soot and cinders.

'I am not going,' said Mr. Traveller, glancing in
after him; 'you won't get rid of me in that way. You
had better come and talk.'

'I won't talk,' said the Hermit, flouncing round to
get his back towards the window.

'Then I will,' said Mr. Traveller. 'Why should
you take it ill that I have no curiosity to know why
you live this highly absurd and highly indecent life?
When I contemplate a man in a state of disease,
surely there is no moral obligation on me to be anxious to know how he took it.'

After a short silence, the Hermit bounced up again,
and came back to the barred window.

'What? You are not gone?' he said, affecting to
have supposed that he was.

'Nor going,' Mr. Traveller replied; 'I design to
pass this summer day here.'

'How dare you come, sir, upon my premises—' the
Hermit was returning, when his visitor interrupted
him.

'Really, you know, you must *not* talk about your

premises. I cannot allow such a place as this to be dignified with the name of premises.'

'How dare you,' said the Hermit, shaking his bars, 'come in at my gate, to taunt me with being in a diseased state?'

'Why, Lord bless my soul,' returned the other, very composedly, 'you have not the face to say that you are in a wholesome state? Do allow me again to call your attention to your legs. Scrape yourself any-where—with anything—and then tell me you are in a wholesome state. The fact is, Mr. Mopes, that you are not only a Nuisance—'

'A Nuisance?' repeated the Hermit, fiercely.

'What is a place in this obscene state of dilapida-tion but a Nuisance? What is a man in your obscene state of dilapidation but a Nuisance? Then, as you very well know, you cannot do without an audience, and your audience is a Nuisance. You attract all the disreputable vagabonds and prowlers within ten miles around, by exhibiting yourself to them in that objec-tionable blanket, and by throwing copper money among them, and giving them drink out of those very dirty jars and bottles that I see in there (their stom-achs need be strong!); and in short,' said Mr. Travel-ler, summing up in a quietly and comfortably settled manner, 'you are a Nuisance, and this kennel is a Nuisance, and the audience that you cannot possibly dispense with is a Nuisance, and the Nui-sance is not merely a local Nuisance, because it is a general Nuisance to know that there *can be* such a Nuisance left in civilisation so very long after its time.'

'Will you go away? I have a gun in here,' said the Hermit.

'Pooh!'

'I *have!*'

'Now, I put it to you. Did I say you had not? And as to going away, didn't I say I am not going away? You have made me forget where I was. I now remember that I was remarking on your conduct being a Nuisance. Moreover, it is in the last and lowest degree inconsequent foolishness and weakness.'

'Weakness?' echoed the Hermit.

'Weakness,' said Mr. Traveller, with his former comfortably settled final air.

'I weak, you fool?' cried the Hermit, 'I, who have held to my purpose, and my diet, and my only bed there, all these years?'

'The more the years, the weaker you,' returned Mr. Traveller. 'Though the years are not so many as folks say, and as you willingly take credit for. The crust upon your face is thick and dark, Mr. Mopes, but I can see enough of you through it, to see that you are still a young man.'

'Inconsequent foolishness is lunacy, I suppose?' said the Hermit.

'I suppose it is very like it,' answered Mr. Traveller.

'Do I converse like a lunatic?'

'One of us two must have a strong presumption against him of being one, whether or no. Either the clean and decorously clad man, or the dirty and indecorously clad man. I don't say which.'

'Why, you self-sufficient bear,' said the Hermit, 'not a day passes but I am justified in my purpose by the conversations I hold here; not a day passes but I am shown, by everything I hear and see here, how right and strong I am in holding my purpose.'

Mr. Traveller, lounging easily on his billet of wood, took out a pocket pipe and began to fill it. 'Now, that a man,' he said, appealing to the summer sky as he did so, 'that a man—even behind bars, in a blanket and skewer—should tell me that he can see, from day

to day, any orders or conditions of men, women, or children, who can by any possibility teach him that it is anything but the miserablest drivelling for a human creature to quarrel with his social nature—not to go so far as to say, to renounce his common human decency, for that is an extreme case; or who can teach him that he can in any wise separate himself from his kind and the habits of his kind, without becoming a deteriorated spectacle calculated to give the Devil (and perhaps the monkeys) pleasure,—is something wonderful! I repeat,' said Mr. Traveller, beginning to smoke, 'the unreasoning hardihood of it is something wonderful—even in a man with the dirt upon him an inch or two thick—behind bars—in a blanket and skewer!'

The Hermit looked at him irresolutely, and retired to his soot and cinders and lay down, and got up again and came to the bars, and again looked at him irresolutely, and finally said with sharpness: 'I don't like tobacco.'

'I don't like dirt,' rejoined Mr. Traveller; 'tobacco is an excellent disinfectant. We shall both be the better for my pipe. It is my intention to sit here through this summer day, until that blessed summer sun sinks low in the west, and to show you what a poor creature you are, through the lips of every chance wayfarer who may come in at your gate.'

'What do you mean?' inquired the Hermit, with a furious air.

'I mean that yonder is your gate, and there are you, and here am I; I mean that I know it to be a moral impossibility that any person can stray in at that gate from any point of the compass, with any sort of experience, gained at first hand, or derived from another, that can confute me and justify you.'

'You are an arrogant and boastful hero,' said the Hermit. 'You think yourself profoundly wise.'

'Bah!' returned Mr. Traveller, quietly smoking. 'There is little wisdom in knowing that every man must be up and doing, and that all mankind are made dependent on one another'

'You have companions outside,' said the Hermit. 'I am not to be imposed upon by your assumed confidence in the people who may enter.'

'A depraved distrust,' returned the visitor, compassionately raising his eyebrows, 'of course belongs to your state. I can't help that.'

'Do you mean to tell me you have no confederates?'

'I mean to tell you nothing but what I have told you. What I have told you is, that it is a moral impossibility that any son or daughter of Adam can stand on this ground that I put my foot on, or on any ground that mortal treads, and gainsay the healthy tenure on which we hold our existence.'

'Which is,' sneered the Hermit, 'according to you—'

'Which is,' returned the other, 'according to Eternal Providence, that we must arise and wash our faces and do our gregarious work and act and re-act on one another, leaving only the idiot and the palsied to sit blinking in the corner. Come!' apostrophising the gate. 'Open Sesame! Show his eyes and grieve his heart! I don't care who comes, for I know what must come of it!'

With that, he faced round a little on his billet of wood towards the gate; and Mr. Mopes, the Hermit, after two or three ridiculous bounces of indecision at his bed and back again, submitted to what he could not help himself against, and coiled himself on his window-ledge, holding to his bars and looking out rather anxiously.

VI

PICKING UP MISS KIMMEENS

THE day was by this time waning, when the gate
again opened, and, with the brilliant golden light that
streamed from the declining sun and touched the very
bars of the sooty creature's den, there passed in a little
child; a little girl with beautiful bright hair. She
wore a plain straw hat, had a door-key in her hand,
and tripped towards Mr. Traveller as if she were
pleased to see him and were going to repose some
childish confidence in him, when she caught sight of
the figure behind the bars, and started back in terror.

'Don't be alarmed, darling!' said Mr. Traveller,
taking her by the hand.

'Oh, but I don't like it!' urged the shrinking child;
'it's dreadful.'

'Well! I don't like it either,' said Mr. Traveller.

'Who has put it there?' asked the little girl. 'Does
it bite?'

'No,—only barks. But can't you make up your
mind to see it, my dear?' For she was covering her
eyes.

'O no, no, no!' returned the child. 'I cannot bear
to look at it!'

Mr. Traveller turned his head towards his friend
in there, as much as to ask him how he liked that instance of his success, and then took the child out at the
still open gate, and stood talking to her for some half
an hour in the mellow sunlight. At length he returned, encouraging her as she held his arm with both
her hands; and laying his protecting hand upon her
head and smoothing her pretty hair, he addressed his
friend behind the bars as follows:

Miss Pupford's establishment for six young ladies of tender years, is an establishment of a compact nature, an establishment in miniature, quite a pocket establishment. Miss Pupford, Miss Pupford's assistant with the Parisian accent, Miss Pupford's cook, and Miss Pupford's housemaid, complete what Miss Pupford calls the educational and domestic staff of her Lilliputian College.

Miss Pupford is one of the most amiable of her sex; it necessarily follows that she possesses a sweet temper, and would own to the possession of a great deal of sentiment if she considered it quite reconcilable with her duty to parents. Deeming it not in the bond, Miss Pupford keeps it as far out of sight as she can—which (God bless her!) is not very far.

Miss Pupford's assistant with the Parisian accent, may be regarded as in some sort an inspired lady, for she never conversed with a Parisian, and she was never out of England—except once in the pleasure-boat Lively, in the foreign waters that ebb and flow two miles off Margate at high water. Even under those geographically favourable circumstances for the acquisition of the French language in its utmost politeness and purity, Miss Pupford's assistant did not fully profit by the opportunity; for the pleasure-boat, Lively, so strongly asserted its title to its name on that occasion, that she was reduced to the condition of lying in the bottom of the boat pickling in brine—as if she were being salted down for the use of the Navy —undergoing at the same time great mental alarm, corporeal distress, and clear-starching derangement.

When Miss Pupford and her assistant first foregathered, is not known to men, or pupils. But, it was long ago. A belief would have established itself among pupils that the two once went to school together, were it not for the difficulty and audacity of

imagining Miss Pupford born without mittens, and
without a front, and without a bit of gold wire among
her front teeth, and without little dabs of powder on
her neat little face and nose.   Indeed, whenever Miss
Pupford gives a little lecture on the mythology of the
misguided heathens (always carefully excluding
Cupid from recognition), and tells how Minerva
sprang, perfectly equipped, from the brain of Jupiter, she is half supposed to hint, 'So I myself came
into the world, completely up in Pinnock, Magnall,
Tables, and the use of the Globes.'

Howbeit, Miss Pupford and Miss Pupford's assistant are old, old friends.   And it is thought by
pupils that, after pupils are gone to bed, they even
call one another by their christian names in the quiet
little parlour.   For, once upon a time on a thunderous
afternoon, when Miss Pupford fainted away without
notice, Miss Pupford's assistant (never heard, before
or since, to address her otherwise than as Miss Pupford) ran to her, crying out 'My dearest Euphemia!'
And Euphemia is Miss Pupford's christian name on
the sampler (date picked out) hanging up in the
College-hall, where the two peacocks, terrified to death
by some German text that is waddling down hill after
them out of a cottage, are scuttling away to hide their
profiles in two immense bean-stalks growing out of
flower-pots.

Also, there is a notion latent among pupils, that Miss
Pupford was once in love, and that the beloved object
still moves upon this ball.   Also, that he is a public
character, and a personage of vast consequence.
Also, that Miss Pupford's assistant knows all about
it.   For, sometimes of an afternoon when Miss Pupford has been reading the paper through her little
gold eye-glass (it is necessary to read it on the spot,
as the boy calls for it, with ill-conditioned punctu-

ality, in an hour), she has become agitated, and
has said to her assistant 'G!' Then Miss Pupford's
assistant has gone to Miss Pupford, and Miss Pupford has pointed out, with her eye-glass, G in the
paper, and then Miss Pupford's assistant has read
about G, and has shown sympathy. So stimulated
has the pupil-mind been in its time to curiosity on the
subject of G, that once, under temporary circumstances favourable to the bold sally, one fearless pupil
did actually obtain possession of the paper, and range
all over it in search of G, who had been discovered
therein by Miss Pupford not ten minutes before.
But no G could be identified, except one capital offender who had been executed in a state of great
hardihood, and it was not to be supposed that Miss
Pupford could ever have loved *him*. Besides, he
couldn't be always being executed. Besides, he got
into the paper again, alive, within a month.

On the whole, it is suspected by the pupil-mind that
G is a short, chubby old gentleman, with little black
sealing-wax boots up to his knees, whom a sharply
observant pupil, Miss Linx, when she once went to
Tunbridge Wells with Miss Pupford for the holidays,
reported on her return (privately and confidentially)
to have seen come capering up to Miss Pupford on
the Promenade, and to have detected in the act of
squeezing Miss Pupford's hand, and to have heard
pronounce the words, 'Cruel Euphemia, ever thine!'—
or something like that. Miss Linx hazarded a guess
that he might be House of Commons, or Money
Market, or Court Circular, or Fashionable Move-
ments; which would account for his getting into the
paper so often. But, it was fatally objected by the
pupil-mind, that none of those notabilities could possibly be spelt with a G.

There are other occasions, closely watched and per-

fectly comprehended by the pupil-mind, when Miss
Pupford imparts with mystery to her assistant that
there is special excitement in the morning paper.
These occasions are, when Miss Pupford finds an old
pupil coming out under the head Births, or Marriages.   Affectionate tears are invariably seen in Miss
Pupford's meek little eyes when this is the case; and
the pupil-mind, perceiving that its order has distinguished itself—though the fact is never mentioned by
Miss Pupford—becomes elevated, and feels that it
likewise is reserved for greatness.

Miss Pupford's assistant with the Parisian accent
has a little more bone than Miss Pupford, but is of
the same trim, orderly, diminutive cast, and, from long
contemplation, admiration, and imitation of Miss
Pupford, has grown like her.   Being entirely devoted
to Miss Pupford, and having a pretty talent for
pencil-drawing, she once made a portrait of that lady:
which was so instantly identified and hailed by the
pupils, that it was done on stone at five shillings.
Surely the softest and milkiest stone that ever was
quarried, received that likeness of Miss Pupford!
The lines of her placid little nose are so undecided in
it that strangers to the work of art are observed to be
exceedingly perplexed as to where the nose goes to,
and involuntarily feel their own noses in a discon-
certed manner.   Miss Pupford being represented in a
state of dejection at an open window, ruminating over
a bowl of gold fish, the pupil-mind has settled that
the bowl was presented by G, and that he wreathed
the bowl with flowers of soul, and that Miss Pupford
is depicted as waiting for him on a memorable occasion when he was behind his time.

The approach of the last Midsummer holidays had
a particular interest for the pupil-mind, by reason of
its knowing that Miss Pupford was bidden, on the

second day of these holidays, to the nuptials of a former pupil. As it was impossible to conceal the fact —so extensive were the dress-making preparations— Miss Pupford openly announced it. But, she held it due to parents to make the announcement with an air of gentle melancholy, as if marriage were (as indeed it exceptionally has been) rather a calamity. With an air of softened resignation and pity, therefore, Miss Pupford went on with her preparations: and meanwhile no pupil ever went upstairs, or came down, without peeping in at the door of Miss Pupford's bedroom (when Miss Pupford wasn't there), and bringing back some surprising intelligence concerning the bonnet.

The extensive preparations being completed on the day before the holidays, an unanimous entreaty was preferred to Miss Pupford by the pupil-mind—finding expression through Miss Pupford's assistant— that she would deign to appear in all her splendour. Miss Pupford consenting, presented a lovely spectacle. And although the oldest pupil was barely thirteen, every one of the six became in two minutes perfect in the shape, cut, colour, price, and quality, of every article Miss Pupford wore.

Thus delightfully ushered in, the holidays began. Five of the six pupils kissed little Kitty Kimmeens twenty times over (round total, one hundred times, for she was very popular), and so went home. Miss Kitty Kimmeens remained behind, for her relations and friends were all in India, far away. A self-helpful, steady little child is Miss Kitty Kimmeens: a dimpled child too, and a loving.

So, the great marriage-day came, and Miss Pupford, quite as much fluttered as any bride could be (G! thought Miss Kitty Kimmeens), went away, splendid to behold, in the carriage that was sent for

her. But not Miss Pupford only went away; for Miss Pupford's assistant went away with her, on a dutiful visit to an aged uncle—though surely the venerable gentleman couldn't live in the gallery of the church where the marriage was to be, thought Miss Kitty Kimmeens—and yet Miss Pupford's assistant had let out that she was going there. Where the cook was going, didn't appear, but she generally conveyed to Miss Kimmeens that she was bound, rather against her will, on a pilgrimage to perform some pious office that rendered new ribbons necessary to her best bonnet, and also sandals to her shoes.

'So you see,' said the housemaid, when they were all gone, 'there's nobody left in the house but you and me, Miss Kimmeens.'

'Nobody else,' said Miss Kitty Kimmeens, shaking her curls a little sadly. 'Nobody!'

'And you wouldn't like your Bella to go too; would you, Miss Kimmeens?' said the housemaid. (She being Bella.)

'N—no,' answered little Miss Kimmeens.

'Your poor Bella is forced to stay with you, whether she likes it or not; ain't she, Miss Kimmeens?'

'*Don't* you like it?' inquired Kitty.

'Why, you're such a darling, Miss, that it would be unkind of your Bella to make objections. Yet my brother-in-law has been took unexpected bad by this morning's post. And your poor Bella is much attached to him, letting alone her favourite sister, Miss Kimmeens.'

'Is he very ill?' asked little Kitty.

'Your poor Bella has her fears so, Miss Kimmeens,' returned the housemaid, with her apron at her eyes. 'It was but his inside, it is true, but it might mount, and the doctor said that if it mounted he wouldn't answer.' Here the housemaid was so overcome that

Kitty administered the only comfort she had ready: which was a kiss.

'If it hadn't been for disappointing Cook, dear Miss Kimmeens,' said the housemaid, 'your Bella would have asked her to stay with you. For Cook is sweet company, Miss Kimmeens, much more so than your own poor Bella.'

'But you are very nice, Bella.'

'Your Bella could wish to be so, Miss Kimmeens,' returned the housemaid, 'but she knows full well that it do not lay in her power this day.'

With which despondent conviction, the housemaid drew a heavy sigh, and shook her head, and dropped it on one side.

'If it had been anyways right to disappoint Cook,' she pursued, in a contemplative and abstracted manner, 'it might have been so easy done! I could have got to my brother-in-law's, and had the best part of the day there, and got back, long before our ladies come home at night, and neither the one nor the other of them need never have known it. Not that Miss Pupford would at all object, but that it might put her out, being tender-hearted. Hows'ever, your own poor Bella, Miss Kimmeens,' said the housemaid, rousing herself, 'is forced to stay with you, and you 're a precious love, if not a liberty.'

'Bella,' said little Kitty, after a short silence.

'Call your own poor Bella, *your* Bella, dear,' the housemaid besought her.

'My Bella, then.'

'Bless your considerate heart!' said the housemaid.

'If you would not mind leaving me, I should not mind being left. I am not afraid to stay in the house alone. And you need not be uneasy on my account, for I would be very careful to do no harm.'

'O! As to harm, you more than sweetest, if not a

liberty,' exclaimed the housemaid, in a rapture, 'your Bella could trust you anywhere, being so steady, and so answerable. The oldest head in this house (me and Cook says), but for its bright hair, is Miss Kimmeens. But no, I will not leave you; for you would think your Bella unkind.'

'But if you are my Bella, you *must* go,' returned the child.

'Must I?' said the housemaid, rising, on the whole with alacrity. 'What must be, must be, Miss Kimmeens. Your own poor Bella acts according, though unwilling. But go or stay, your own poor Bella loves you, Miss Kimmeens.'

It was certainly go, and not stay, for within five minutes Miss Kimmeens's own poor Bella—so much improved in point of spirits as to have grown almost sanguine on the subject of her brother-in-law—went her way, in apparel that seemed to have been expressly prepared for some festive occasion. Such are the changes of this fleeting world, and so short-sighted are we poor mortals!

When the house door closed with a bang and a shake, it seemed to Miss Kimmeens to be a very heavy house door, shutting her up in a wilderness of a house. But, Miss Kimmeens being, as before stated, of a self-reliant and methodical character, presently began to parcel out the long summer-day before her.

And first she thought she would go all over the house, to make quite sure that nobody with a great-coat on and a carving-knife in it, had got under one of the beds or into one of the cupboards. Not that she had ever before been troubled by the image of anybody armed with a great-coat and a carving-knife, but that it seemed to have been shaken into existence by the shake and the bang of the great street door, reverberating through the solitary house. So,

little Miss Kimmeens looked under the five empty
beds of the five departed pupils, and looked under
her own bed, and looked under Miss Pupford's bed,
and looked under Miss Pupford's assistant's bed.
And when she had done this, and was making the tour
of the cupboards, the disagreeable thought came into
her young head, What a very alarming thing it would
be to find somebody with a mask on, like Guy Fawkes,
hiding bolt upright in a corner and pretending not to
be alive!   However, Miss Kimmeens having finished
her inspection without making any such uncomfortable discovery, sat down in her tidy little manner to
needlework, and began stitching away at a great
rate.

The silence all about her soon grew very oppressive, and the more so because of the odd inconsistency
that the more silent it was, the more noises there were.
The noise of her own needle and thread as she stitched,
was infinitely louder in her ears than the stitching of
all the six pupils, and of Miss Pupford, and of Miss
Pupford's assistant, all stitching away at once on a
highly emulative afternoon.   Then, the school-room
clock conducted itself in a way in which it had never
conducted itself before—fell lame, somehow, and yet
persisted in running on as hard and loud as it could:
the consequence of which behaviour was, that it staggered among the minutes in a state of the greatest
confusion, and knocked them about in all directions
without appearing to get on with its regular work.
Perhaps this alarmed the stairs: but be that as it
might, they began to creak in a most unusual manner,
and then the furniture began to crack, and then poor
little Miss Kimmeens, not liking the furtive aspect of
things in general, began to sing as she stitched.   But,
it was not her own voice that she heard—it was somebody else making believe to be Kitty, and singing

excessively flat, without any heart—so as that would never mend matters, she left off again.

By and by, the stitching became so palpable a failure that Miss Kitty Kimmeens folded her work neatly and put it away in its box, and gave it up. Then the question arose about reading. But no; the book that was so delightful when there was somebody she loved for her eyes to fall on when they rose from the page, had not more heart in it than her own singing now. The book went to its shelf as the needlework had gone to its box, and, since something *must* be done—thought the child, 'I 'll go put my room to rights.'

She shared her room with her dearest little friend among the other five pupils, and why then should she now conceive a lurking dread of the little friend's bedstead? But she did. There was a stealthy air about its innocent white curtains, and there were even dark hints of a dead girl lying under the coverlet. The great want of human company, the great need of a human face, began now to express itself in the facility with which the furniture put on strange exaggerated resemblances to human looks. A chair with a menacing frown was horribly out of temper in a corner; a most vicious chest of drawers snarled at her from between the windows. It was no relief to escape from those monsters to the looking-glass, for the reflection said, 'What? Is that you all alone there? How you stare!' And the background was all a great void stare as well.

The day dragged on, dragging Kitty with it very slowly by the hair of her head, until it was time to eat. There were good provisions in the pantry, but their right flavour and relish had evaporated with the five pupils, and Miss Pupford, and Miss Pupford's assistant, and the cook and housemaid. Where was the

use of laying the cloth symmetrically for one small
guest, who had gone on ever since the morning growing smaller and smaller, while the empty house had
gone on swelling larger and larger? The very Grace
came out wrong, for who were 'we' who were going
to receive and be thankful? So, Miss Kimmeens was
not thankful, and found herself taking her dinner
in very slovenly style—gobbling it up, in short, rather
after the manner of the lower animals, not to particularise the pigs.

But, this was by no means the worst of the change
wrought out in the naturally loving and cheery little
creature as the solitary day wore on. She began to
brood and be suspicious. She discovered that she
was full of wrongs and injuries. All the people she
knew, got tainted by her lonely thoughts and turned
bad.

It was all very well for Papa, a widower in India,
to send her home to be educated, and to pay a handsome round sum every year for her to Miss Pupford,
and to write charming letters to his darling little
daughter; but what did he care for her being left by
herself, when he was (as no doubt he always was)
enjoying himself in company from morning till night?
Perhaps he only sent her here, after all, to get her
out of the way. It looked like it—looked like it to-
day, that is, for she had never dreamed of such a
thing before.

And this old pupil who was being married. It was
insupportably conceited and selfish in the old pupil to
be married. She was very vain, and very glad to
show off; but it was highly probable that she wasn't
pretty; and even if she were pretty (which Miss Kimmeens now totally denied), she had no business to be
married; and, even if marriage were conceded, she had
no business to ask Miss Pupford to her wedding.

As to Miss Pupford, she was too old to go to any wedding. She ought to know that. She had much better attend to her business. She had thought she looked nice in the morning, but she didn't look nice. She was a stupid old thing. G was another stupid old thing. Miss Pupford's assistant was another. They were all stupid old things together.

More than that: it began to be obvious that this was a plot. They had said to one another, 'Never mind Kitty; you get off, and I 'll get off; and we 'll leave Kitty to look after herself. Who cares for *her?*' To be sure they were right in that question; for who *did* care for her, a poor little lonely thing against whom they all planned and plotted? Nobody, nobody! Here Kitty sobbed.

At all other times she was the pet of the whole house, and loved her five companions in return with a child's tenderest and most ingenuous attachment; but now, the five companions put on ugly colours, and appeared for the first time under a sullen cloud. There they were, all at their homes that day, being made much of, being taken out, being spoilt and made disagreeable, and caring nothing for her. It was like their artful selfishness always to tell her when they came back, under pretence of confidence and friendship, all those details about where they had been, and what they had done and seen, and how often they had said, 'O! If we had only darling little Kitty here!' Here indeed! I dare say! When they came back after the holidays, they were used to being received by Kitty, and to saying that coming to Kitty was like coming to another home. Very well then, why did they go away? If they meant it, why did they go away? Let them answer that. But they didn't mean it, and couldn't answer that, and they didn't tell the truth, and people who didn't tell the

truth were hateful.   When they came back next time,
they should be received in a new manner; they should
be avoided and shunned.

And there, the while she sat all alone revolving how
ill she was used, and how much better she was than
the people who were not alone, the wedding breakfast
was going on: no question of it!   With a nasty great
bride-cake, and with those ridiculous orange-flowers,
and with that conceited bride, and that hideous bridegroom, and those heartless bridesmaids, and Miss
Pupford stuck up at the table!   They thought they
were enjoying themselves, but it would come home to
them one day to have thought so.   They would all
be dead in a few years, let them enjoy themselves
ever so much.   It was a religious comfort to know
that.

It was such a comfort to know it, that little Miss
Kitty Kimmeens suddenly sprang from the chair in
which she had been musing in a corner, and cried out,
'O those envious thoughts are not mine, O this wicked
creature isn't me! Help me, somebody! I go wrong,
alone by my weak self! Help me, anybody!'

'—Miss Kimmeens is not a professed philosopher,
sir,' said Mr. Traveller, presenting her at the barred
window, and smoothing her shining hair, 'but I appre-
hend there was some tincture of philosophy in her
words, and in the prompt action with which she followed them.   That action was, to emerge from her
unnatural solitude, and look abroad for wholesome
sympathy, to bestow and to receive.   Her footsteps
strayed to this gate, bringing her here by chance, as
an opposite contrast to you.   The child came out, sir.
If you have the wisdom to learn from a child (but I
doubt it, for that requires more wisdom than one in
your condition would seem to possess), you cannot

do better than imitate the child, and come out too—
from that very demoralising hutch of yours.'

VII

PICKING UP THE TINKER

IT was now sunset.   The Hermit had betaken himself
to his bed of cinders half an hour ago, and lying on
it in his blanket and skewer with his back to the window, took not the smallest heed of the appeal addressed to him.

All that had been said for the last two hours, had
been said to a tinkling accompaniment performed by
the Tinker, who had got to work upon some villager's
pot or kettle, and was working briskly outside.   This
music still continuing, seemed to put it into Mr. Traveller's mind to have another word or two with the
Tinker.   So, holding Miss Kimmeens (with whom
he was now on the most friendly terms) by the hand,
he went out at the gate to where the Tinker was seated
at his work on the patch of grass on the opposite side
of the road, with his wallet of tools open before him,
and his little fire smoking.

'I am glad to see you employed,' said Mr. Traveller.

'I am glad to *be* employed,' returned the Tinker,
looking up as he put the finishing touches to his job.
'But why are you glad?'

'I thought you were a lazy fellow when I saw you
this morning.'

'I was only disgusted,' said the Tinker.

'Do you mean with the fine weather?'

'With the fine weather?' repeated the Tinker, staring.

'You told me you were not particular as to weather, and I thought—'

'Ha, ha! How should such as me get on, if we *was* particular as to weather? We must take it as it comes, and make the best of it. There 's something good in all weathers. If it don't happen to be good for my work to-day, it 's good for some other man's to-day, and will come round to me to-morrow. We must all live.'

'Pray shake hands,' said Mr. Traveller.

'Take care, sir,' was the Tinker's caution, as he reached up his hand in surprise; 'the black comes off.'

'I am glad of it,' said Mr. Traveller. 'I have been for several hours among other black that does not come off.'

'You are speaking of Tom in there?'

'Yes.'

'Well now,' said the Tinker, blowing the dust off his job: which was finished. 'Ain't it enough to disgust a pig, if he could give his mind to it?'

'If he could give his mind to it,' returned the other, smiling, 'the probability is that he wouldn't be a pig.'

'There you clench the nail,' returned the Tinker. 'Then what 's to be said for Tom?'

'Truly, very little.'

'Truly nothing you mean, sir,' said the Tinker, as he put away his tools.

'A better answer, and (I freely acknowledge) my meaning. I infer that he was the cause of your disgust?'

'Why, look 'ee here, sir,' said the Tinker, rising to his feet, and wiping his face on the corner of his black apron energetically; 'I leave you to judge!—I ask you!—Last night I has a job that needs to be done in the night, and I works all night. Well, there 's

nothing in that. But this morning I comes along this road here, looking for a sunny and soft spot to sleep in, and I sees this desolation and ruination. I've lived myself in desolation and ruination; I knows many a fellow-creetur that's forced to live life long in desolation and ruination; and I sits me down and takes pity on it, as I casts my eyes about. Then comes up the long-winded one as I told you of, from that gate, and spins himself out like a silkworm concerning the Donkey (if my Donkey at home will excuse me) as has made it all—made it of his own choice! And tells me, if you please, of his likewise choosing to go ragged and naked, and grimy—maskerading, mountebanking, in what is the real hard lot of thousands and thousands! Why, then I say it's a unbearable and nonsensical piece of inconsistency, and I'm disgusted. I'm ashamed and disgusted!'

'I wish you would come and look at him,' said Mr. Traveller, clapping the Tinker on the shoulder.

'Not I, sir,' he rejoined. '*I* ain't a going to flatter him up by looking at him!'

'But he is asleep.'

'Are you sure he is asleep?' asked the Tinker, with an unwilling air, as he shouldered his wallet.

'Sure.'

'Then I'll look at him for a quarter of a minute,' said the Tinker, 'since you so much wish it; but not a moment longer.'

They all three went back across the road; and, through the barred window, by the dying glow of the sunset coming in at the gate—which the child held open for its admission—he could be pretty clearly discerned lying on his bed.

'You see him?' asked Mr. Traveller.

'Yes,' returned the Tinker, 'and he's worse than I thought him.'

Mr. Traveller then whispered in few words what he had done since morning; and asked the Tinker what he thought of that?

'I think,' returned the Tinker, as he turned from the window, 'that you 've wasted a day on him.'

'I think so too; though not, I hope, upon myself. Do you happen to be going anywhere near the Peal of Bells?'

'That 's my direct way, sir,' said the Tinker.

'I invite you to supper there. And as I learn from this young lady that she goes some three-quarters of a mile in the same direction, we will drop her on the road, and we will spare time to keep her company at her garden gate until her own Bella comes home.'

So, Mr. Traveller, and the child, and the Tinker, went along very amicably in the sweet-scented evening; and the moral with which the Tinker dismissed the subject was, that he said in his trade that metal that rotted for want of use, had better be left to rot, and couldn't rot too soon, considering how much true metal rotted from over-use and hard service.

SOMEBODY'S LUGGAGE

[1862]

SOMEBODY'S LUGGAGE

IN FOUR CHAPTERS

CHAPTER I

HIS LEAVING IT TILL CALLED FOR

THE writer of these humble lines being a Waiter, and having come of a family of Waiters, and owning at the present time five brothers who are all Waiters, and likewise an only sister who is a Waitress, would wish to offer a few words respecting his calling; first having the pleasure of hereby in a friendly manner offering the Dedication of the same unto JOSEPH, much respected Head Waiter at the Slamjam Coffeehouse, London, E.C., than which a individual more eminently deserving of the name of man, or a more amenable honour to his own head and heart, whether considered in the light of a Waiter or regarded as a human being, do not exist.

In case confusion should arise in the public mind (which it is open to confusion on many subjects) respecting what is meant or implied by the term Waiter, the present humble lines would wish to offer an explanation. It may not be generally known that the person as goes out to wait is *not* a Waiter. It may not be generally known that the hand as is called in extra, at the Freemasons' Tavern, or the London, or the Albion, or otherwise, is *not* a Waiter. Such hands may be took on for Public Dinners by the bushel

(and you may know them by their breathing with difficulty when in attendance, and taking away the bottle
ere yet it is half out) ; but such are *not* Waiters.　For
you cannot lay down the tailoring, or the shoemaking,
or the brokering, or the green-grocering, or the pic-
torial-periodicalling, or the second-hand wardrobe, or
the small fancy businesses,—you cannot lay down those
lines of life at your will and pleasure by the half-day
or evening, and take up Waitering.　You may suppose you can, but you cannot; or you may go so far
as to say you do, but you do not.　Nor yet can you
lay down the gentleman's-service when stimulated by
prolonged incompatibility on the part of Cooks (and
here it may be remarked that Cooking and Incompatibility will be mostly found united), and take up Waitering.　It has been ascertained that what a gentleman
will sit meek under, at home, he will not bear out of
doors, at the Slamjam or any similar establishment.
Then, what is the inference to be drawn respecting
true Waitering?　You must be bred to it.　You must
be born to it.

　Would you know how born to it, Fair Reader,—if
of the adorable female sex?　Then learn from the
biographical experience of one that is a Waiter in
the sixty-first year of his age.

　You were conveyed,—ere yet your dawning powers
were otherwise developed than to harbour vacancy in
your inside,—you were conveyed, by surreptitious
means, into a pantry adjoining the Admiral Nelson,
Civic and General Dining-Rooms, there to receive
by stealth that healthful sustenance which is the pride
and boast of the British female constitution.　Your
mother was married to your father (himself a distant
Waiter) in the profoundest secrecy; for a Waitress
known to be married would ruin the best of businesses,
—it is the same as on the stage.　Hence your being

smuggled into the pantry, and that—to add to the infliction—by an unwilling grandmother. Under the combined influence of the smells of roast and boiled, and soup, and gas, and malt liquors, you partook of your earliest nourishment; your unwilling grandmother sitting prepared to catch you when your mother was called and dropped you; your grandmother's shawl ever ready to stifle your natural complainings; your innocent mind surrounded by uncongenial cruets, dirty plates, dish-covers, and cold gravy; your mother calling down the pipe for veals and porks, instead of soothing you with nursery rhymes. Under these untoward circumstances you were early weaned. Your unwilling grandmother, ever growing more unwilling as your food assimilated less, then contracted habits of shaking you till your system curdled, and your food would not assimilate at all. At length she was no longer spared, and could have been thankfully spared much sooner. When your brothers began to appear in succession, your mother retired, left off her smart dressing (she had previously been a smart dresser), and her dark ringlets (which had previously been flowing), and haunted your father late of nights, lying in wait for him, through all weathers, up the shabby court which led to the back door of the Royal Old Dust-Bin (said to have been so named by George the Fourth), where your father was Head. But the Dust-Bin was going down then, and your father took but little,—excepting from a liquid point of view. Your mother's object in those visits was of a housekeeping character, and you was set on to whistle your father out. Sometimes he came out, but generally not. Come or not come, however, all that part of his existence which was unconnected with open Waitering was kept a close secret, and was acknowledged by your mother to be a close secret, and you and your

mother flitted about the court, close secrets both of you, and would scarcely have confessed under torture that you knew your father, or that your father had any name than Dick (which wasn't his name, though he was never known by any other), or that he had kith or kin or chick or child. Perhaps the attraction of this mystery, combined with your father's having a damp compartment to himself, behind a leaky cistern, at the Dust-Bin,—a sort of a cellar compartment, with a sink in it, and a smell, and a plate-rack, and a bottle-rack, and three windows that didn't match each other or anything else, and no daylight,—caused your young mind to feel convinced that you must grow up to be a Waiter too; but you did feel convinced of it, and so did all your brothers, down to your sister. Every one of you felt convinced that you was born to the Waitering. At this stage of your career, what was your feelings one day when your father came home to your mother in open broad daylight,—of itself an act of Madness on the part of a Waiter,—and took to his bed (leastwise, your mother and family's bed), with the statement that his eyes were devilled kidneys. Physicians being in vain, your father expired, after repeating at intervals for a day and a night, when gleams of reason and old business fitfully illuminated his being, 'Two and two is five. And three is sixpence.' Interred in the parochial department of the neighbouring churchyard, and accompanied to the grave by as many Waiters of long standing as could spare the morning time from their soiled glasses (namely, one), your bereaved form was attired in a white neckankecher, and you was took on from motives of benevolence at The George and Gridiron, theatrical and supper. Here, supporting nature on what you found in the plates (which was as it happened, and but too often

thoughtlessly, immersed in mustard), and on what you found in the glasses (which rarely went beyond driblets and lemon), by night you dropped asleep standing, till you was cuffed awake, and by day was set to polishing every individual article in the coffee-room. Your couch being sawdust; your counterpane being ashes of cigars. Here, frequently hiding a heavy heart under the smart tie of your white neck-ankecher (or correctly speaking lower down and more to the left), you picked up the rudiments of knowledge from an extra, by the name of Bishops, and by calling plate-washer, and gradually elevating your mind with chalk on the back of the corner-box partition, until such time as you used the inkstand when it was out of hand, attained to manhood, and to be the Waiter that you find yourself.

I could wish here to offer a few respectful words on behalf of the calling so long the calling of myself and family, and the public interest in which is but too often very limited. We are not generally understood. No, we are not. Allowance enough is not made for us. For, say that we ever show a little drooping listlessness of spirits, or what might be termed indifference or apathy. Put it to yourself what would your own state of mind be, if you was one of an enormous family every member of which except you was always greedy, and in a hurry. Put it to yourself that you was regularly replete with animal food at the slack hours of one in the day and again at nine P.M., and that the repleter you was, the more voracious all your fellow-creatures came in. Put it to yourself that it was your business, when your digestion was well on, to take a personal interest and sympathy in a hundred gentlemen fresh and fresh (say, for the sake of argument, only a hundred), whose imaginations was given up to grease and fat

and gravy and melted butter, and abandoned to questioning you about cuts of this, and dishes of that,—each of 'em going on as if him and you and the bill of fare was alone in the world. Then look what you are expected to know. You are never out, but they seem to think you regularly attend everywhere. 'What's this, Christopher, that I hear about the smashed Excursion Train?'—'How are they doing at the Italian Opera, Christopher?'—'Christopher, what are the real particulars of this business at the Yorkshire Bank?' Similarly a ministry gives me more trouble than it gives the Queen. As to Lord Palmerston, the constant and wearing connection into which I have been brought with his lordship during the last few years is deserving of a pension. Then look at the Hypocrites we are made, and the lies (white, I hope) that are forced upon us! Why must a sedentary-pursuited Waiter be considered to be a judge of horseflesh, and to have a most tremenjous interest in horse-training and racing? Yet it would be half our little incomes out of our pockets if we didn't take on to have those sporting tastes. It is the same (inconceivable why!) with Farming. Shooting, equally so. I am sure that so regular as the months of August, September, and October come round, I am ashamed of myself in my own private bosom for the way in which I make believe to care whether or not the grouse is strong on the wing (much their wings, or drumsticks either, signifies to me, uncooked!), and whether the partridges is plentiful among the turnips, and whether the pheasants is shy or bold, or anything else you please to mention. Yet you may see me, or any other Waiter of my standing, holding on by the back of the box, and leaning over a gentleman with his purse out and his bill before him, discussing these points in a confidential tone of

voice, as if my happiness in life entirely depended on 'em.

I have mentioned our little incomes. Look at the most unreasonable point of all, and the point on which the greatest injustice is done us! Whether it is owing to our always carrying so much change in our right-hand trousers-pocket, and so many halfpence in our coat-tails, or whether it is human nature (which I were loth to believe), what is meant by the everlasting fable that Head Waiters is rich? How did that fable get into circulation? Who first put it about, and what are the facts to establish the unblushing statement? Come forth, thou slanderer, and refer the public to the Waiter's will in Doctors' Commons supporting thy malignant hiss! Yet this is so commonly dwelt upon—especially by the screws who give Waiters the least—that denial is vain; and we are obliged, for our credit's sake, to carry our heads as if we were going into a business, when of the two we are much more likely to go into a union. There was formerly a screw as frequented the Slamjam ere yet the present writer had quitted that establishment on a question of tea-ing his assistant staff out of his own pocket, which screw carried the taunt to its bitterest height. Never soaring above threepence, and as often as not grovelling on the earth a penny lower, he yet represented the present writer as a large holder of Consols, a lender of money on mortgage, a Capitalist. He has been overheard to dilate to other customers on the allegation that the present writer put out thousands of pounds at interest in Distilleries and Breweries. 'Well, Christopher,' he would say (having grovelled his lowest on the earth, half a moment before), 'looking out for a House to open, eh? Can't find a business to be disposed of on a scale as is up to your resources, humph?' To such a dizzy precipice of

falsehood has this misrepresentation taken wing, that
the well-known and highly-respected OLD CHARLES,
long eminent at the West Country Hotel, and by
some considered the Father of the Waitering, found
himself under the obligation to fall into it through
so many years that his own wife (for he had an unbeknown old lady in that capacity towards himself) believed it! And what was the consequence? When
he was borne to his grave on the shoulders of six picked
Waiters, with six more for change, six more acting as
pall-bearers, all keeping step in a pouring shower
without a dry eye visible, and a concourse only inferior
to Royalty, his pantry and lodgings was equally ran-
sacked high and low for property, and none was
found! How could it be found, when, beyond his
last monthly collection of walking-sticks, umbrellas,
and pocket-handkerchiefs (which happened to have
been not yet disposed of, though he had ever been
through life punctual in clearing off his collections by
the month), there was no property existing? Such,
however, is the force of this universal libel, that the
widow of Old Charles, at the present hour an inmate
of the Almshouses of the Cork-Cutters' Company, in
Blue Anchor Road (identified sitting at the door of
one of 'em, in a clean cap and a Windsor arm-chair,
only last Monday), expects John's hoarded wealth to
be found hourly! Nay, ere yet he had succumbed to
the grisly dart, and when his portrait was painted in
oils life-size, by subscription of the frequenters of the
West Country, to hang over the coffee-room chimney-
piece, there were not wanting those who contended
that what is termed the accessories of such a portrait
ought to be the Bank of England out of window, and
a strong-box on the table. And but for better-regu-
lated minds contending for a bottle and screw and the

attitude of drawing,—and carrying their point,—it would have been so handed down to posterity.

I am now brought to the title of the present remarks. Having, I hope without offence to any quarter, offered such observations as I felt it my duty to offer, in a free country which has ever dominated the seas, on the general subject, I will now proceed to wait on the particular question.

At a momentous period of my life, when I was off, so far as concerned notice given, with a House that shall be nameless,—for the question on which I took my departing stand was a fixed charge for waiters, and no House as commits itself to that eminently Un-English act of more than foolishness and baseness shall be advertised by me,—I repeat, at a momentous crisis, when I was off with a House too mean for mention, and not yet on with that to which I have ever since had the honour of being attached in the capacity of Head,[1] I was casting about what to do next. Then it were that proposals were made to me on behalf of my present establishment. Stipulations were necessary on my part, emendations were necessary on my part: in the end, ratifications ensued on both sides, and I entered on a new career.

We are a bed business, and a coffee-room business. We are not a general dining business, nor do we wish it. In consequence, when diners drop in, we know what to give 'em as will keep 'em away another time. We are a Private Room or Family business also; but Coffee-room principal. Me and the Directory and the Writing Materials and cetrer occupy a place to ourselves—a place fended off up a step or two at the end of the Coffee-room, in what I call the good old-

---

[1] Its name and address at length, with other full particulars, all editorially struck out.

fashioned style. The good old-fashioned style is, that whatever you want, down to a wafer, you must be olely and solely dependent on the Head Waiter for. You must put yourself a new-born Child into his hands. There is no other way in which a business untinged with Continental Vice can be conducted. (It were bootless to add, that if languages is required to be jabbered and English is not good enough, both families and gentlemen had better go somewhere else.)

When I began to settle down in this right-principled and well-conducted House, I noticed, under the bed in No. 24 B (which it is up a angle off the staircase, and usually put off upon the lowly-minded), a heap of things in a corner. I asked our Head Chambermaid in the course of the day,

'What are them things in 24 B?'

To which she answered with a careless air,

'Somebody's Luggage.'

Regarding her with a eye not free from severity, I says,

'Whose Luggage?'

Evading my eye, she replied,

'Lor! How should I know!'

—Being, it may be right to mention, a female of some pertness, though acquainted with her business.

A Head Waiter must be either Head or Tail. He must be at one extremity or the other of the social scale. He cannot be at the waist of it, or anywhere else but the extremities. It is for him to decide which of the extremities.

On the eventful occasion under consideration, I gave Mrs. Pratchett so distinctly to understand my decision, that I broke her spirit as towards myself, then and there, and for good. Let not inconsistency be suspected on account of my mentioning Mrs. Pratchett as 'Mrs.,' and having formerly remarked

that a waitress must not be married. Readers are respectfully requested to notice that Mrs. Pratchett was not a waitress, but a chambermaid. Now a chambermaid *may* be married; if Head, generally is married,—or says so. It comes to the same thing as expressing what is customary. (N.B. Mr. Pratchett is in Australia, and his address there is 'the Bush.')

Having took Mrs. Pratchett down as many pegs as was essential to the future happiness of all parties, I requested her to explain herself.

'For instance,' I says, to give her a little encouragement, 'who is Somebody?'

'I give you my sacred honour, Mr. Christopher,' answers Pratchett, 'that I haven't the faintest notion.'

But for the manner in which she settled her capstrings, I should have doubted this; but in respect of positiveness it was hardly to be discriminated from an affidavit.

'Then you never saw him?' I followed her up with.

'Nor yet,' said Mrs. Pratchett, shutting her eyes and making as if she had just took a pill of unusual circumference,—which gave a remarkable force to her denial,—'nor yet any servant in this house. All have been changed, Mr. Christopher, within five year, and Somebody left his Luggage here before then.'

Inquiry of Miss Martin yielded (in the language of the Bard of A. 1), 'confirmation strong.' So it had really and truly happened. Miss Martin is the young lady at the bar as makes out our bills; and though higher than I could wish considering her station, is perfectly well-behaved.

Farther investigations led to the disclosure that there was a bill against this Luggage to the amount of two sixteen six. The luggage had been lying under the bedstead of 24 B over six year. The bedstead is a four-poster, with a deal of old hanging and val-

ance, and is, as I once said, probably connected with more than 24 Bs,—which I remember my hearers was pleased to laugh at, at the time.

I don't know why,—when DO we know why?—but this Luggage laid heavy on my mind. I fell a wondering about Somebody, and what he had got and been up to. I couldn't satisfy my thoughts why he should leave so much Luggage against so small a bill. For I had the Luggage out within a day or two and turned it over, and the following were the items:—A black portmanteau, a black bag, a desk, a dressing-case, a brown-paper parcel, a hat-box, and an umbrella strapped to a walking-stick. It was all very dusty and fluey. I had our porter up to get under the bed and fetch it out; and though he habitually wallows in dust,—swims in it from morning to night, and wears a close-fitting waitscoat with black calimanco sleeves for the purpose,—it made him sneeze again, and his throat was that hot with it that it was obliged to be cooled with a drink of Allsopp's draft.

The Luggage so got the better of me, that instead of having it put back when it was well dusted and washed with a wet cloth,—previous to which it was so covered with feathers that you might have thought it was turning into poultry, and would by and by begin to Lay,—I say, instead of having it put back, I had it carried into one of my places downstairs. There from time to time I stared at it and stared at it, till it seemed to grow big and grow little, and come forward at me and retreat again, and go through all manner of performances resembling intoxication. When this had lasted weeks,—I may say months, and not be far out,—I one day thought of asking Miss Martin for the particulars of the Two sixteen six total. She was so obliging as to extract it from the

books,—it dating before her time,—and here follows
a true copy:

Coffee-Room.

1856.	No. 4.	£	s.	d.
Feb. 2d, Pen and Paper		0	0	6
Port Negus		0	2	0
Ditto		0	2	0
Pen and Paper		0	0	6
Tumbler broken		0	2	6
Brandy		0	2	0
Pen and paper		0	0	6
Anchovy toast		0	2	6
Pen and paper		0	0	6
Bed		0	3	0
Feb. 3d, Pen and paper		0	0	6
Breakfast		0	2	6
" Broiled ham . .		0	2	0
" Eggs . . .		0	1	0
" Watercresses . .		0	1	0
Breakfast—Shrimps . . .		0	1	0
Pen and paper		0	0	6
Blotting-paper		0	0	6
Messenger to Paternoster Row and back		0	1	6
Again, when No Answer . .		0	1	6
Brandy 2s., Devilled Pork chop 2s.		0	4	0
Pens and paper		0	1	0
Messenger to Albemarle Street and back		0	1	0
Again (detained), when No Answer		0	1	6
Carried forward .		1	15	6

		£	s	d
Brought forward .		£1	15	6
Salt-cellar broken		0	3	6
Large Liqueur-glass Orange Brandy		0	1	6
Dinner, Soup, Fish, Joint, and bird		0	7	6
Bottle old East India Brown		0	8	0
Pen and paper		0	0	6
		£2	16	6

Mem.: January 1st, 1857. He went out after dinner, directing Luggage to be ready when he called for it. Never called.

So far from throwing a light upon the subject, this bill appeared to me, if I may so express my doubts, to involve it in a yet more lurid halo. Speculating it over with the Mistress, she informed me that the luggage had been advertised in the Master's time as being to be sold after such and such a day to pay expenses, but no farther steps had been taken. (I may here remark, that the Mistress is a widow in her fourth year. The Master was possessed of one of those unfortunate constitutions in which Spirits turn to Water, and rises in the ill-starred Victim.)

My speculating it over, not then only, but repeatedly, sometimes with the Mistress, sometimes with one, sometimes with another, led up to the Mistress's saying to me,—whether at first in a joke or in earnest, or half joke and half earnest, it matters not:

'Christopher, I am going to make you a handsome offer.'

(If this should meet her eye—a lovely blue,—may she not take it ill my mentioning that if I had been eight or ten year younger, I would have done as much by her! That is, I would have made her a offer. It

is for others than me to denominate it a handsome one.)

'Christopher, I am going to make you a handsome offer.'

'Put a name to it, ma'am.'

'Look here, Christopher. Run over the articles of Somebody's Luggage. You 've got it all by heart, I know.'

'A black portmanteau, ma'am, a black bag, a desk, a dressing-case, a brown-paper parcel, a hat-box, and an umbrella strapped to a walking-stick.'

'All just as they were left. Nothing opened, nothing tampered with.'

'You are right, ma'am. All locked but the brown-paper parcel, and that sealed.'

The Mistress was leaning on Miss Martin's desk at the bar-window, and she taps the open book that lays upon the desk,—she has a pretty-made hand to be sure,—and bobs her head over it and laughs.

'Come,' says she, 'Christopher. Pay me Somebody's bill, and you shall have Somebody's Luggage.'

I rather took to the idea from the first moment; but,

'It mayn't be worth the money,' I objected, seeming to hold back.

'That 's a Lottery,' says the Mistress, folding her arms upon the book,—it ain't her hands alone that 's pretty made, the observation extends right up her arms. Won't you venture two pound sixteen shillings and sixpence in the Lottery? Why, there 's no blanks!' says the Mistress, laughing and bobbing her head again, 'you *must* win. If you lose, you must win! All prizes in this Lottery! Draw a blank, and remember, Gentlemen-Sportsmen, you 'll still be entitled to a black portmanteau, a black bag, a desk, a dressing-case, a sheet of brown paper, a hat-box, and an umbrella strapped to a walking-stick!'

To make short of it, Miss Martin come round me, and Mrs. Pratchett come round me, and the Mistress she was completely round me already, and all the women in the house come round me, and if it had been Sixteen two instead of Two sixteen, I should have thought myself well out of it. For what can you do when they do come round you?

So I paid the money—down— and such a laughing as there was among 'em! But I turned the tables on 'em regularly, when I said:

'My family-name is Blue-Beard. I'm going to open Somebody's Luggage all alone in the Secret Chamber, and not a female eye catches sight of the contents!'

Whether I thought proper to have the firmness to keep to this, don't signify, or whether any female eye, and if any, how many, was really present when the opening of the Luggage came off. Somebody's Luggage is the question at present: Nobody's eyes, nor yet noses.

What I still look at most, in connection with that Luggage, is the extraordinary quantity of writing-paper, and all written on! And not our paper neither, —not the paper charged in the bill, for we know our paper,—so he must have been always at it. And he had crumpled up this writing of his, everywhere, in every part and parcel of his luggage. There was writing in his dressing-case, writing in his boots, writing among his shaving-tackle, writing in his hat-box, writing folded away down among the very whalebones of his umbrella.

His clothes wasn't bad, what there was of 'em. His dressing-case was poor,—not a particle of silver stopper,—bottle apertures with nothing in 'em, like empty little dog-kennels,—and a most searching description of tooth-powder diffusing itself around, as

under a deluded mistake that all the chinks in the fittings was divisions in teeth. His clothes I parted with, well enough, to a second-hand dealer not far from St. Clement's Danes, in the Strand,—him as the officers in the Army mostly dispose of their uniforms to, when hard pressed with debts of honour, if I may judge from their coats and epaulets diversifying the window with their backs towards the public. The same party bought in one lot the portmanteau, the bag, the desk, the dressing-case, the hat-box, the umbrella, strap and walking-stick. On my remarking that I should have thought those articles not quite in his line, he said: 'No more ith a man'th grandmother, Mithter Chrithtopher; but if any man will bring hith grandmother here, and offer her at a fair trifle below what the 'll feth with good luck when the 'th thcoured and turned —I 'll buy her!'

These transactions brought me home, and, indeed, more than home, for they left a goodish profit on the original investment. And now there remained the writings; and the writings I particular wish to bring under the candid attention of the reader.

I wish to do so without postponement, for this reason. This is to say, namely, viz. *i.e.,* as follows, thus:—Before I proceed to recount the mental sufferings of which I became the prey in consequence of the writings, and before following up that harrowing tale with a statement of the wonderful and impressive catastrophe, as thrilling in its nature as unlooked for in any other capacity, which crowned the ole and filled the cup of unexpectedness to overflowing, the writings themselves ought to stand forth to view. Therefore it is that they now come next. One word to introduce them, and I lay down my pen (I hope, my unassuming pen) until I take it up to trace the gloomy sequel of a mind with something on it.

He was a smeary writer, and wrote a dreadful bad hand. Utterly regardless of ink, he lavished it on every undeserving object,—on his clothes, his desk, his hat, the handle of his tooth-brush, his umbrella. Ink was found freely on the coffee-room carpet by No. 4 table, and two blots was on his restless couch. A reference to the document I have given entire will show that on the morning of the third of February, eighteen fifty-six, he procured his no less than fifth pen and paper. To whatever deplorable act of ungovernable composition he immolated those materials obtained from the bar, there is no doubt that the fatal deed was committed in bed, and that it left its evidences but too plainly, long afterwards, upon the pillow-case.

He had put no Heading to any of his writings. Alas! Was he likely to have a Heading without a Head, and where was *his* Head when he took such things into it? In some cases, such as his Boots, he would appear to have hid the writings; thereby involving his style in greater obscurity. But his boots was at least pairs,—and no two of his writings can put in any claim to be so regarded. Here follows (not to give more specimens) what was found in—

CHAPTER II

HIS BOOTS

'Eh! well then, Monsieur Mutuel! What do I know, what can I say? I assure you that he calls himself Monsieur The Englishman.'

'Pardon. But I think it is impossible,' said Monsieur Mutuel,—a spectacled, snuffy, stooping old gentleman in carpet shoes and a cloth cap with a peaked

shade, a loose blue frock-coat reaching to his heels, a large limp white shirt-frill, and cravat to correspond, —that is to say, white was the natural colour of his linen on Sundays, but it toned down with the week.

'It is,' repeated Monsieur Mutuel, his amiable old walnut-shell countenance very walnut-shelly indeed as he smiled and blinked in the bright morning sunlight,—'it is, my cherished Madame Bouclet, I think, impossible!'

'Hey!' (with a little vexed cry and a great many tosses of her head.) 'But it is not impossible that you are a Pig!' retorted Madame Bouclet, a compact little woman of thirty-five or so. 'See then,—look there,—read! "On the second floor Monsieur L'Anglais." Is it not so?'

'It is so,' said Monsieur Mutuel.

'Good. Continue your morning walk. Get out!' Madame Bouclet dismissed him with a lively snap of her fingers.

The morning walk of Monsieur Mutuel was in the brightest patch that the sun made in the Grande Place of a dull old fortified French town. The manner of his morning walk was with his hands crossed behind him; an umbrella, in figure the express image of himself, always in one hand; a snuff-box in the other. Thus, with the shuffling gait of the Elephant (who really does deal with the very worst trousers-maker employed by the Zoological world, and who appeared to have recommended him to Monsieur Mutuel), the old gentleman sunned himself daily when sun was to be had—of course, at the same time sunning a red ribbon at his button-hole; for was he not an ancient Frenchman?

Being told by one of the angelic sex to continue his morning walk and get out, Monsieur Mutuel laughed a walnut-shell laugh, pulled off his cap at

arm's length with the hand that contained his snuff-box, kept it off for a considerable period after he had parted from Madame Bouclet, and continued his morning walk and got out, like a man of gallantry as he was.

The documentary evidence to which Madame Bouclet had referred Monsieur Mutuel was the list of her lodgers, sweetly written forth by her own Nephew and Bookkeeper, who held the pen of an Angel, and posted up at the side of her gateway, for the information of the Police: 'Au second, M. L'Anglais, Propriétaire.' On the second floor, Mr. The Englishman, man of property. So it stood; nothing could be plainer.

Madame Bouclet now traced the line with her fore-finger, as it were to confirm and settle herself in her parting snap at Monsieur Mutuel, and so placing her right hand on her hip with a defiant air, as if nothing should ever tempt her to unsnap that snap, strolled out into the Place to glance up at the windows of Mr. The Englishman. That worthy happening to be looking out of window at the moment, Madame Bouclet gave him a graceful salutation with her head, looked to the right and looked to the left to account to him for her being there, considered for a moment, like one who accounted to herself for somebody she had expected not being there, and reëntered her own gateway. Madame Bouclet let all her house giving on the Place in furnished flats or floors, and lived up the yard behind in company with Monsieur Bouclet her husband (great at billiards), an inherited brew-ing business, several fowls, two carts, a nephew, a little dog in a big kennel, a grape-vine, a counting-house, four horses, a married sister (with a share in the brew-ing business), the husband and two children of the married sister, a parrot, a drum (performed on by the

little boy of the married sister), two billeted soldiers, a quantity of pigeons, a fife (played by the nephew in a ravishing manner), several domestics and supernumeraries, a perpetual flavour of coffee and soup, a terrific range of artificial rocks and wooden precipices at least four feet high, a small fountain, and half a dozen large sunflowers.

Now the Englishman, in taking his Appartement, —or, as one might say on our side of the Channel, his set of chambers,—had given his name, correct to the letter, LANGLEY. But as he had a British way of not opening his mouth very wide on foreign soil, except at meals, the Brewery had been able to make nothing of it but L'Anglais. So Mr. The Englishman he had become and he remained.

'Never saw such a people!' muttered Mr. The Englishman, as he now looked out of window. 'Never did, in my life!'

This was true enough, for he had never before been out of his own country,—a right little island, a tight little island, a bright little island, a show-fight little island, and full of merit of all sorts; but not the whole round world.

'These chaps,' said Mr. The Englishman to himself, as his eye rolled over the Place, sprinkled with military here and there, 'are no more like soldiers—' Nothing being sufficiently strong for the end of his sentence, he left it unended.

This again (from the point of view of his experience) was strictly correct; for though there was a great agglomeration of soldiers in the town and neighbouring country, you might have held a grand Review and Field-day of them every one, and looked in vain among them all for a soldier choking behind his foolish stock, or a soldier lamed by his ill-fitting shoes, or a soldier deprived of the use of his limbs by straps

and buttons, or a soldier elaborately forced to be self-helpless in all the small affairs of life. A swarm of brisk, bright, active, bustling, handy, odd, skirmishing fellows, able to turn cleverly at anything, from a siege to soup, from great guns to needles and thread, from the broadsword exercise to slicing an onion, from making war to making omelets, was all you would have found.

What a swarm! From the Great Place under the eye of Mr. The Englishman, where a few awkward squads from the last conscription were doing the goose-step—some members of those squads still as to their bodies, in the chrysalis peasant-state of Blouse, and only military butterflies as to their regimentally-clothed legs—from the Great Place, away outside the fortifications, and away for miles along the dusty roads, soldiers swarmed. All day long, upon the grass-grown ramparts of the town, practising soldiers trumpeted and bugled; all day long, down in angles of dry trenches, practising soldiers drummed and drummed. Every forenoon, soldiers burst out of the great barracks into the sandy gymnasium-ground hard by, and flew over the wooden horse, and hung on to flying ropes, and dangled upside-down between parallel bars, and shot themselves off wooden platforms,—splashes, sparks, coruscations, showers of soldiers. At every corner of the town-wall, every guard-house, every gate-way, every sentry-box, every drawbridge, every reedy ditch, and rushy dike, soldiers, soldiers, soldiers. And the town being pretty well all wall, guard-house, gateway, sentry-box, drawbridge, reedy ditch, and rushy dike, the town was pretty well all soldiers.

What would the sleepy old town have been without the soldiers, seeing that even with them it had so overslept itself as to have slept its echoes hoarse, its defen-

sive bars and locks and bolts and chains all rusty, and its ditches stagnant! From the days when VAUBAN engineered it to that perplexing extent that to look at it was like being knocked on the head with it, the stranger becoming stunned and stertorous under the shock of its incomprehensibility,—from the days when VAUBAN made it the express incorporation of every substantive and adjective in the art of military engineering, and not only twisted you into it and twisted you out of it, to the right, to the left, opposite, under here, over there, in the dark, in the dirt, by the gateway, archway, covered way, dry way, wet way, fosse, portcullis, drawbridge, sluice, squat tower, pierced wall, and heavy battery, but likewise took a fortifying dive under the neighbouring country, and came to the surface three or four miles off, blowing out incomprehensible mounds and batteries among the quiet crops of chicory and beet-root,—from those days to these the town had been asleep, and dust and rust and must had settled on its drowsy Arsenals and Magazines, and grass had grown up in its silent streets.

On market-days alone, its Great Place suddenly leaped out of bed. On market-days, some friendly enchanter struck his staff upon the stones of the Great Place, and instantly arose the liveliest booths and stalls, and sittings and standings, and a pleasant hum of chaffering and huckstering from many hundreds of tongues, and a pleasant, though peculiar, blending of colours,—white caps, blue blouses, and green vegetables,—and at last the Knight destined for the adventure seemed to have come in earnest, and all the Vaubanois sprang up awake. And now, by long, low-lying avenues of trees, jolting in white-hooded donkey-cart, and on donkey-back, and in tumbril and wagon, and cart and cabriolet, and afoot with barrow and burden,—and along the dikes and ditches and

canals, in little peak-prowed country-boats,—came peasant-men and women in flocks and crowds, bringing articles for sale. And here you had boots and shoes, and sweetmeats and stuffs to wear, and here (in the cool shade of the Town-hall) you had milk and cream and butter and cheese, and here you had fruits and onions and carrots, and all things needful for your soup, and here you had poultry and flowers and protesting pigs, and here new shovels, axes, spades, and bill-hooks for your farming work, and here huge mounds of bread, and here your unground grain in sacks, and here your children's dolls, and here the cake-seller, announcing his wares by beat and roll of drum. And hark! fanfaronade of trumpets, and here into the Great Place, resplendent in an open carriage, with four gorgeously-attired servitors up behind, playing horns, drums, and cymbals, rolled 'the Daughter of a Physician' in massive golden chains and ear-rings, and blue-feathered hat, shaded from the admiring sun by two immense umbrellas of artificial roses, to dispense (from motives of philanthropy) that small and pleasant dose which had cured so many thousands! Toothache, earache, headache, heartache, stomachache, debility, nervousness, fits, fainting, fever, ague, all equally cured by the small and pleasant dose of the great Physician's great daughter! The process was this,—she, the Daughter of a Physician, proprietess of the superb equipage you now admired with its confirmatory blasts of trumpet, drum, and cymbal, told you so: On the first day after taking the small and pleasant dose, you would feel no particular influence beyond a most harmonious sensation of indescribable and irresistible joy; on the second day you would be so astonishingly better that you would think yourself changed into somebody else; on the third day you would be entirely

free from your disorder, whatever its nature and however long you had had it, and would seek out the
Physician's Daughter to throw yourself at her feet,
kiss the hem of her garment, and buy as many more
of the small and pleasant doses as by the sale of all
your few effects you could obtain; but she would be
inaccessible,—gone for herbs to the Pyramids of
Egypt,—and you would be (though cured) reduced
to despair! Thus would the Physician's Daughter
drive her trade (and briskly too), and thus would the
buying and selling and mingling of tongues and colours continue, until the changing sunlight, leaving the
Physician's Daughter in the shadow of high roofs,
admonished her to jolt out westward, with a departing effect of gleam and glitter on the splendid equipage and brazen blast. And now the enchanter
struck his staff upon the stones of the Great Place
once more, and down went the booths, the sittings
and standings, and vanished the merchandise, and
with it the barrows, donkeys, donkey-carts, and
tumbrils, and all other things on wheels and feet, except the slow scavengers with unwieldy carts and
meagre horses clearing up the rubbish, assisted by
the sleek town pigeons, better plumped out than on
non-market days. While there was yet an hour or
two to wane before the autumn sunset, the loiterer
outside town-gate and drawbridge, and postern and
double-ditch, would see the last white-hooded cart lessening in the avenue of lengthening shadows of trees,
or the last country boat, paddled by the last market-
woman on her way home, showing black upon the
reddening, long, low, narrow dike between him and
the mill; and as the paddle-parted scum and weed
closed over the boat's track, he might be comfortably
sure that its sluggish rest would be troubled no more
until next market-day.

As it was not one of the Great Place's days for getting out of bed, when Mr. The Englishman looked down at the young soldiers practising the goose-step there, his mind was left at liberty to take a military turn.

'These fellows are billeted everywhere about,' said he; 'and to see them lighting the people's fires, boiling the people's pots, minding the people's babies, rocking the people's cradles, washing the people's greens, and making themselves generally useful, in every sort of unmilitary way, is most ridiculous! Never saw such a set of fellows,—never did in my life!'

All perfectly true again. Was there not Private Valentine in that very house, acting as sole housemaid, valet, cook, steward, and nurse, in the family of his captain, Monsieur le Capitaine de la Cour,—cleaning the floors, making the beds, doing the marketing, dressing the captain, dressing the dinners, dressing the salads, and dressing the baby, all with equal readiness? Or, to put him aside, he being in loyal attendance on his Chief, was there not Private Hyppolite, billeted at the Perfumer's two hundred yards off, who, when not on duty, volunteered to keep shop while the fair Perfumeress stepped out to speak to a neighbour or so, and laughingly sold soap with his war-sword girded on him? Was there not Emile, billeted at the Clock-maker's, perpetually turning to of an evening with his coat off, winding up the stock? Was there not Eugène, billeted at the Tinman's, cultivating, pipe in mouth, a garden four feet square, for the Tinman, in the little court behind the shop, and extorting the fruits of the earth from the same, on his knees, with the sweat of his brow? Not to multiply examples, was there not Baptiste, billeted on the poor Water-carrier, at that very instant sitting

on the pavement in the sunlight, with his martial legs asunder, and one of the Water-carrier's spare pails between them, which (to the delight and glory of the heart of the Water-carrier coming across the Place from the fountain, yoked and burdened) he was painting bright-green outside and bright-red within? Or, to go no farther than the Barber's at the very next door, was there not Corporal Théophile—

'No,' said Mr. The Englishman, glancing down at the Barber's, he is not there at present.   There's the child, though.'

A mere mite of a girl stood on the steps of the Barber's shop, looking across the Place. A mere baby, one might call her, dressed in the close white linen cap which small French country children wear (like the children in Dutch pictures), and in a frock of homespun blue, that had no shape except where it was tied round her little fat throat.   So that, being naturally short and round all over, she looked, behind, as if she had been cut off at her natural waist, and had had her head neatly fitted on it.

'There's the child, though.'

To judge from the way in which the dimpled hand was rubbing the eyes, the eyes had been closed in a nap, and were newly opened.   But they seemed to be looking so intently across the Place, that the Englishman looked in the same direction.

'O!' said he presently.   'I thought as much.   The Corporal's there.'

The Corporal, a smart figure of a man of thirty, perhaps a thought under the middle size, but very neatly made,—a sunburnt Corporal with a brown peaked beard,—faced about at the moment, addressing voluble words of instruction to the squad in hand. Nothing was amiss or awry about the Corporal.   A lithe and nimble Corporal, quite complete, from the

sparkling dark eyes under his knowing uniform cap to his sparkling white gaiters. The very image and presentment of a Corporal of his country's army, in the line of his shoulders, the line of his waist, the broadest line of his Bloomer trousers, and their narrowest line at the calf of his leg.

Mr. The Englishman looked on, and the child looked on, and the Corporal looked on (but the last-named at his men), until the drill ended a few minutes afterwards, and the military sprinkling dried up directly, and was gone. Then said Mr. The Englishman to himself, 'Look here! By George!' And the Corporal, dancing towards the Barber's with his arms wide open, caught up the child, held her over his head in a flying attitude, caught her down again, kissed her, and made off with her into the Barber's house.

Now Mr. The Englishman had had a quarrel with his erring and disobedient and disowned daughter, and there was a child in that case too. Had not his daughter been a child, and had she not taken angel-flights above his head as this child had flown above the Corporal's?'

'He's a'—National Participled—'fool!' said the Englishman, and shut his window.

But the windows of the house of Memory, and the windows of the house of Mercy, are not so easily closed as windows of glass and wood. They fly open unexpectedly; they rattle in the night; they must be nailed up. Mr. The Englishman had tried nailing them, but had not driven the nails quite home. So he passed but a disturbed evening and a worse night.

By nature a good-tempered man? No; very little gentleness, confounding the quality with weakness. Fierce and wrathful when crossed? Very, and stupendously unreasonable. Moody? Exceedingly so. Vindictive? Well; he *had* had scowling thoughts

that he would formally curse his daughter, as he had
seen it done on the stage.   But remembering that the
real Heaven is some paces removed from the mock
one in the great chandelier of the Theatre, he had
given that up.

And he had come abroad to be rid of his repudiated
daughter for the rest of his life.   And here he was.

At bottom, it was for this reason, more than for any
other, that Mr. The Englishman took it extremely ill
that Corporal Thèophile should be so devoted to little
Bebelle, the child at the Barber's shop.   In an unlucky moment he had chanced to say to himself, 'Why,
confound the fellow, he is not her father!'   There was
a sharp sting in the speech which ran into him suddenly, and put him in a worse mood.   So he had National Participled the unconscious Corporal with most
hearty emphasis, and had made up his mind to think
no more about such a mountebank.

But it came to pass that the Corporal was not to
be dismissed.   If he had known the most delicate
fibres of the Englishman's mind, instead of knowing
nothing on earth about him, and if he had been the
most obstinate Corporal in the Grand Army of
France, instead of being the most obliging, he could
not have planted himself with more determined immovability plump in the midst of all the Englishman's thoughts.   Not only so, but he seemed to be
always in his view.   Mr. The Englishman had but
to look out of window, to look upon the Corporal
with little Bebelle.   He had but to go for a walk, and
there was the Corporal walking with Bebelle.   He had
but to come home again, disgusted, and the Corporal
and Bebelle were at home before him.   If he looked
out at his back windows early in the morning, the
Corporal was in the Barber's back yard, washing and
dressing and brushing Bebelle.   If he took refuge

at his front windows, the Corporal brought his breakfast out into the Place, and shared it there with Bebelle. Always Corporal and always Bebelle. Never Corporal without Bebelle. Never Bebelle without Corporal.

Mr. The Englishman was not particularly strong in the French language as a means of oral communication, though he read it very well. It is with languages as with people,—when you only know them by sight, you are apt to mistake them; you must be on speaking terms before you can be said to have established an acquaintance.

For this reason, Mr. The Englishman had to gird up his loins considerably before he could bring himself to the point of exchanging ideas with Madame Bouclet on the subject of this Corporal and this Bebelle. But Madame Bouclet looking in apologetically one morning to remark, that, O Heaven! she was in a state of desolation because the lamp-maker had not sent home that lamp confided to him to repair, but that truly he was a lamp-maker against whom the whole world shrieked out, Mr. The Englishman seized the occasion.

'Madame, that baby—'

'Pardon, monsieur. That lamp.'

'No, no, that little girl.'

'But, pardon!' said Madame Bouclet, angling for a clew, 'one cannot light a little girl, or send her to be repaired?'

'The little girl—at the house of the barber.'

'Ah-h-h!' cried Madame Bouclet, suddenly catching the idea with her delicate little line and rod. 'Little Bebelle? Yes, yes, yes! And her friend the Corporal? Yes, yes, yes, yes! So genteel of him,—is it not?'

'He is not—?'

'Not at all; not at all!   He is not one of her relations.   Not at all!'

'Why, then, he—'

'Perfectly!' cried Madame Bouclet, 'you are right,
monsieur.   It is so genteel of him.   The less relation, the more genteel.   As you say.'

'Is she—?'

'The child of the barber?'   Madame Bouclet
whisked up her skilful little line and rod again.   'Not
at all, not at all!   She is the child of—in a word, of
no one.'

'The wife of the barber, then—?'

'Indubitably.   As you say.   The wife of the barber receives a small stipend to take care of her.   So
much by the month.   Eh, then!   It is without doubt
very little, for we are all poor here.'

'You are not poor, madame.'

'As to my lodgers,' replied Madame Bouclet, with
a smiling and a gracious bend of her head, 'no.   As to
all things else, so-so.'

'You flatter me, madame.'

'Monsieur, it is you who flatter me in living here.'

Certain fishy gasps on Mr. The Englishman's part,
denoting that he was about to resume his subject under difficulties, Madame Bouclet observed him closely,
and whisked up her delicate line and rod again with
triumphant success.

'O no, monsieur, certainly not.   The wife of the
barber is not cruel to the poor child, but she is careless.   Her health is delicate, and she sits all day, looking out at window.   Consequently, when the Corporal first came, the poor little Bebelle was much
neglected.'

'It is a curious—' began Mr. The Englishman.

'Name?   That Bebelle?   Again you are right,
monsieur.   But it is a playful name for Gabrielle.'

'And so the child is a mere fancy of the Corporal's?' said Mr. The Englishman, in a gruffly disparaging tone of voice.

'Eh, well!' returned Madame Bouclet, with a pleading shrug: 'one must love something. Human nature is weak.'

('Devilish weak,' muttered the Englishman, in his own language.)

'And the Corporal,' pursued Madame Bouclet, 'being billeted at the barber's,—where he will probably remain a long time, for he is attached to the General, —and finding the poor unowned child in need of being loved, and finding himself in need of loving,— why, there you have it all, you see!'

Mr. The Englishman accepted this interpretation of the matter with an indifferent grace, and observed to himself, in an injured manner, when he was again alone: 'I shouldn't mind it so much, if these people were not such a'—National Participled—'sentimental people!'

There was a Cemetery outside the town, and it happened ill for the reputation of the Vaubanois, in this sentimental connection, that he took a walk there that same afternoon. To be sure there were some wonderful things in it (from the Englishman's point of view), and of a certainty in all Britain you would have found nothing like it. Not to mention the fanciful flourishes of hearts and crosses in wood and iron, that were planted all over the place, making it look very like a Firework-ground, where a most splendid pyrotechnic display might be expected after dark, there were so many wreaths upon the graves, embroidered, as it might be, 'To my mother,' 'To my daughter,' 'To my father,' 'To my brother,' 'To my sister,' 'To my friend,' and those many wreaths were in so many stages of elaboration and decay, from the

wreath of yesterday, all fresh colour and bright beads, to the wreath of last year, a poor mouldering wisp of straw! There were so many little gardens and grottoes made upon graves, in so many tastes, with plants and shells and plaster figures and porcelain pitchers, and so many odds and ends! There were so many tributes of remembrance hanging up, not to be discriminated by the closest inspection from little round waiters, whereon were depicted in glowing hues either a lady or a gentleman with a white pocket-handkerchief out of all proportion, leaning, in a state of the most faultless mourning and most profound affliction, on the most architectural and gorgeous urn! There were so many surviving wives who had put their names on the tombs of their deceased husbands, with a blank for the date of their own departure from this weary world; and there were so many surviving husbands who had rendered the same homage to their deceased wives; and out of the number there must have been so many who had long ago married again! In fine, there was so much in the place that would have seemed mere frippery to a stranger, save for the consideration that the lightest paper flower that lay upon the poorest heap of earth was never touched by a rude hand, but perished there, a sacred thing!

'Nothing of the solemnity of Death here,' Mr. The Englishman had been going to say, when this last consideration touched him with a mild appeal, and on the whole he walked out without saying it. 'But these people are,' he insisted, by way of compensation, when he was well outside the gate, 'they are so'— Participled—'sentimental!'

His way back lay by the military gymnasium-ground. And there he passed the Corporal glibly instructing young soldiers how to swing themselves over rapid and deep water-courses on their way to

Glory, by means of a rope, and himself deftly plunging off a platform, and flying a hundred feet or two, as an encouragement to them to begin. And there he also passed, perched on a crowning eminence (probably by the Corporal's careful hands), the small Bebelle, with her round eyes wide open, surveying the proceeding like a wonderful sort of blue and white bird.

'If that child was to die,' this was his reflection as he turned his back and went his way,—'and it would almost serve the fellow right for making such a fool of himself,—I suppose we should have *him* sticking up a wreath and a waiter in that fantastic burying-ground.'

Nevertheless, after another early morning or two of looking out of window, he strolled down into the Place, when the Corporal and Bebelle were walking there, and touching his hat to the Corporal (an immense achievement), wished him Good-day.

'Good-day, monsieur.'

'This is a rather pretty child you have here,' said Mr. The Englishman, taking her chin in his hand, and looking down into her astonished blue eyes.

'Monsieur, she is a very pretty child,' returned the Corporal, with a stress on his polite correction of the phrase.

'And good?' said the Englishman.

'And very good. Poor little thing!'

'Hah!' The Englishman stooped down and patted her cheek, not without awkwardness, as if he were going too far in his conciliation. 'And what is this medal round your neck, my little one?'

Bebelle having no other reply on her lips than her chubby right fist, the Corporal offered his services as interpreter.

'Monsieur demands, what is this, Bebelle?'

'It is the Holy Virgin,' said Bebelle.

'And who gave it you?' asked the Englishman.

'Théophile.'

'And who is Théophile?'

Bebelle broke into a laugh, laughed merrily and heartily, clapped her chubby hands, and beat her little feet on the stone pavement of the Place.

'He doesn't know Théophile! Why, he doesn't know any one! He doesn't know anything!' Then, sensible of a small solecism in her manners, Bebelle twisted her right hand in a leg of the Corporal's Bloomer trousers, and, laying her cheek against the place, kissed it.

'Monsieur Théophile, I believe?' said the Englishman to the Corporal.

'It is I, monsieur.'

'Permit me.' Mr. The Englishman shook him heartily by the hand and turned away. But he took it mighty ill that old Monsieur Mutuel in his patch of sunlight, upon whom he came as he turned, should pull off his cap to him with a look of pleased approval. And he muttered, in his own tongue, as he returned the salutation, 'Well, walnut-shell! And what business is it of *yours?*'

Mr. The Englishman went on for many weeks passing but disturbed evenings and worse nights, and constantly experiencing that those aforesaid windows in the houses of Memory and Mercy rattled after dark, and that he had very imperfectly nailed them up. Likewise, he went on for many weeks daily improving the acquaintance of the Corporal and Bebelle. That is to say, he took Bebelle by the chin, and the Corporal by the hand, and offered Bebelle sous and the Corporal cigars, and even got the length of changing pipes with the Corporal and kissing Bebelle. But he did it all in a shamefaced way, and always

took it extremely ill that Monsieur Mutuel in his patch of sunlight should note what he did. Whenever that seemed to be the case, he always growled in his own tongue, 'There you are again, walnut-shell! What business is it of *yours?*'

In a word, it had become the occupation of Mr. The Englishman's life to look after the Corporal and little Bebelle, and to resent old Monsieur Mutuel's looking after *him.* An occupation only varied by a fire in the town one windy night, and much passing of water-buckets from hand to hand (in which the Englishman rendered good service), and much beating of drums,— when all of a sudden the Corporal disappeared.

Next, all of a sudden, Bebelle disappeared.

She had been visible a few days later than the Corporal,—sadly deteriorated as to washing and brushing,—but she had not spoken when addressed by Mr. The Englishman, and had looked scared and had run away. And now it would seem that she had run away for good. And there lay the Great Place under the windows, bare and barren.

In his shamefaced and constrained way, Mr. The Englishman asked no question of any one, but watched from his front windows, and watched from his back windows, and lingered about the Place, and peeped in at the Barber's shop, and did all this and much more with a whistling and tune-humming pretence of not missing anything, until one afternoon when Monsieur Mutuel's patch of sunlight was in shadow, and when, according to all rule and precedent, he had no right whatever to bring his red ribbon out of doors, behold here he was, advancing with his cap already in his hand twelve paces off!

Mr. The Englishman had got as far into his usual objurgation as, 'What bu—si—' when he checked himself.

'Ah, it is sad, it is sad! Hélas, it is unhappy, it is sad!' Thus old Monsieur Mutuel, shaking his gray head.

'What busin—at least, I would say, what do you mean, Monsieur Mutuel?'

'Our Corporal. Hélas, our dear Corporal!'

'What has happened to him?'

'You have not heard?'

'No.'

'At the fire. But he was so brave, so ready. Ah, too brave, too ready!'

'May the Devil carry you away!' the Englishman broke in impatiently; 'I beg your pardon,—I mean me,—I am not accustomed to speak French,—go on, will you?'

'And a falling beam—'

"Good God!' exclaimed the Englishman. 'It was a private soldier who was killed?'

'No. A Corporal, the same Corporal, our dear Corporal. Beloved by all his comrades. The funeral ceremony was touching,—penetrating. Monsieur The Englishman, your eyes fill with tears.'

'What bu—si—'

'Monsieur The Englishman, I honour those emotions. I salute you with profound respect. I will not obtrude myself upon your noble heart.'

Monsieur Mutuel,—a gentleman in every thread of his cloudy linen, under whose wrinkled hand every grain in the quarter of an ounce of poor snuff in his poor little tin box became a gentleman's property,— Monsieur Mutuel passed on, with his cap in his hand.

'I little thought,' said the Englishman, after walking for several minutes, and more than once blowing his nose, 'when I was looking round that cemetery— I 'll go there!'

Straight he went there, and when he came within

the gate he paused, considering whether he should ask at the lodge for some direction to the grave. But he was less than ever in a mood for asking questions, and he thought, 'I shall see something on it to know it by.'

In search of the Corporal's grave he went softly on, up this walk and down that, peering in, among the crosses and hearts and columns and obelisks and tombstones, for a recently disturbed spot. It troubled him now to think how many dead there were in the cemetery,—he had not thought them a tenth part so numerous before,—and after he had walked and sought for some time, he said to himself, as he struck down a new vista of tombs, 'I might suppose that every one was dead but I.'

Not every one. A live child was lying on the ground asleep. Truly he had found something on the Corporal's grave to know it by, and the something was Bebelle.

With such a loving will had the dead soldier's comrades worked at his resting-place, that it was already a neat garden. On the green turf of the garden Bebelle lay sleeping, with her cheek touching it. A plain, unpainted little wooden Cross was planted in the turf, and her short arm embraced this little Cross, as it had many a time embraced the Corporal's neck. They had put a tiny flag (the flag of France) at his head, and a laurel garland.

Mr. The Englishman took off his hat, and stood for a while silent. Then, covering his head again, he bent down on one knee, and softly roused the child.

'Bebelle! My little one!'

Opening her eyes, on which the tears were still wet, Bebelle was at first frightened; but seeing who it was, she suffered him to take her in his arms, looking steadfastly at him.

'You must not lie here, my little one. You must come with me.'

'No, no. I can't leave Théophile. I want the good dear Théophile.'

'We will go and seek him, Bebelle. We will go and look for him in England. We will go and look for him at my daughter's, Bebelle.'

'Shall we find him there?'

'We shall find the best part of him there. Come with me, poor forlorn little one. Heaven is my witness,' said the Englishman, in a low voice, as, before he rose, he touched the turf above the gentle Corporal's breast, 'that I thankfully accept this trust!'

It was a long way for the child to have come unaided. She was soon asleep again, with her embrace transferred to the Englishman's neck. He looked at her worn shoes, and her galled feet, and her tired face, and believed that she had come there every day.

He was leaving the grave with the slumbering Bebelle in his arms, when he stopped, looked wistfully down at it, and looked wistfully at the other graves around. 'It is the innocent custom of the people,' said Mr. The Englishman, with hesitation. 'I think I should like to do it. No one sees.'

Careful not to wake Bebelle as he went, he repaired to the lodge where such little tokens of remembrance were sold, and bought two wreaths. One, blue and white and glistening silver, 'To my friend'; one of a soberer red and black and yellow, 'To my friend.' With these he went back to the grave, and so down on one knee again. Touching the child's lips with the brighter wreath, he guided her hand to hang it on the Cross; then hung his own wreath there. After all, the wreaths were not far out of keeping with the little garden. To my friend. To my friend.

Mr. The Englishman took it very ill when he

looked round a street corner into the Great Place, carrying Bebelle in his arms, that old Mutuel should be there airing his red ribbon.   He took a world of pains to dodge the worthy Mutuel, and devoted a surprising amount of time and trouble to skulking into his own lodging like a man pursued by Justice. Safely arrived there at last, he made Bebelle's toilet with as accurate a remembrance as he could bring to bear upon that work of the way in which he had often seen the poor Corporal make it, and having given her to eat and drink, laid her down on his own bed.   Then he slipped out into the barber's shop, and after a brief interview with the barber's wife, and a brief recourse to his purse and card-case, came back again with the whole of Bebelle's personal property in such a very little bundle that it was quite lost under his arm.

As it was irreconcilable with his whole course and character that he should carry Bebelle off in state, or receive any compliments or congratulations on that feat, he devoted the next day to getting his two portmanteaus out of the house by artfulness and stealth, and to comporting himself in every particular as if he were going to run away,—except, indeed, that he paid his few debts in the town, and prepared a letter to leave for Madame Bouclet, enclosing a sufficient sum of money in lieu of notice.   A railway train would come through at midnight, and by that train he would take away Bebelle to look for Théophile in England and at his forgiven daughter's.

At midnight, on a moonlight night, Mr. The Englishman came creeping forth like a harmless assassin, with Bebelle on his breast instead of a dagger.   Quiet the Great Place, and quiet the never-stirring streets; closed the cafés; huddled together motionless their billiard-balls; drowsy the guard or

sentinel on duty here and there; lulled for the time, by sleep, even the insatiate appetite of the Office of Town-dues.

Mr. The Englishman left the Place behind, and left the streets behind, and left the civilian-inhabited town behind, and descended down among the military works of Vauban, hemming all in. As the shadow of the first heavy arch and postern fell upon him and was left behind, as the shadow of the second heavy arch and postern fell upon him and was left behind, as his hollow tramp over the first drawbridge was succeeded by a gentler sound, as his hollow tramp over the second drawbridge was succeeded by a gentler sound, as he overcame the stagnant ditches one by one, and passed out where the flowing waters were and where the moonlight, so the dark shades and the hollow sounds and the unwholesomely locked currents of his soul were vanquished and set free. See to it, Vaubans of your own hearts, who gird them in with triple walls and ditches, and with bolt and chain and bar and lifted bridge,—raze those fortifications, and lay them level with the all-absorbing dust, before the night cometh when no hand can work!

All went prosperously, and he got into an empty carriage in the train, where he could lay Bebelle on the seat over against him, as on a couch, and cover her from head to foot with his mantle. He had just drawn himself up from perfecting this arrangement, and had just leaned back in his own seat contemplating it with great satisfaction, when he became aware of a curious appearance at the open carriage window, —a ghostly little tin box floating up in the moonlight, and hovering there.

He leaned forward, and put out his head. Down among the rails and wheels and ashes, Monsieur Mutuel, red ribbon and all!

'Excuse me, Monsieur The Englishman,' said Monsieur Mutuel, holding up his box at arm's length, the carriage being so high and he so low; 'but I shall reverence the little box for ever, if your so generous hand will take a pinch from it at parting.'

Mr. The Englishman reached out of the window before complying, and—without asking the old fellow what business it was of his—shook hands and said, 'Adieu! God bless you!'

'And, Mr. The Englishman, God bless *you!*' cried Madame Bouclet, who was also there among the rails and wheels and ashes. 'And God will bless you in the happiness of the protected child now with you. And God will bless you in your own child at home. And God will bless you in your own remembrances. And this from me!'

He had barely time to catch a bouquet from her hand, when the train was flying through the night. Round the paper that enfolded it was bravely written (doubtless by the nephew who held the pen of an Angel), 'Homage to the friend of the friendless.'

'Not bad people, Bebelle!' said Mr. The Englishman, softly drawing the mantle a little from her sleeping face, that he might kiss it, 'though they are so—'

Too 'sentimental' himself at the moment to be able to get out that word, he added nothing but a sob, and travelled for some miles, through the moonlight, with his hand before his eyes.

CHAPTER III

HIS BROWN-PAPER PARCEL

My works are well known. I am a young man in the Art line. You have seen my works many a time, though it's fifty thousand to one if you have seen me. You say you don't want to see me? You say your interest is in my works, and not in me? Don't be too sure about that. Stop a bit.

Let us have it down in black and white at the first go off, so that there may be no unpleasantness or wrangling afterwards. And this is looked over by a friend of mine, a ticket writer, that is up to literature. I am a young man in the Art line—in the Fine-Art line. You have seen my works over and over again, and you have been curious about me, and you think you have seen me. Now, as a safe rule, you never have seen me, and you never do see me, and you never will see me. I think that's plainly put—and it's what knocks me over.

If there's a blighted public character going, I am the party.

It has been remarked by a certain (or an uncertain) philosopher, that the world knows nothing of its greatest men. He might have put it plainer if he had thrown his eye in my direction. He might have put it, that while the world knows something of them that apparently go in and win, it knows nothing of them that really go in and don't win. There it is again in another form—and that's what knocks me over.

Not that it's only myself that suffers from injustice, but that I am more alive to my own injuries than to any other man's. Being, as I have mentioned, in

the Fine-Art line, and not the Philanthropic line, I openly admit it. As to company in injury, I have company enough. Who are you passing every day at your Competitive Excruciations? The fortunate candidates whose heads and livers you have turned upside down for life? Not you. You are really passing the Crammers and Coaches. If your principle is right, why don't you turn out to-morrow morning with the keys of your cities on velvet cushions, your musicians playing, and your flags flying, and read addresses to the Crammers and Coaches on your bended knees, beseeching them to come out and govern you? Then, again, as to your public business of all sorts, your Financial statements and your Budgets; the Public knows much, truly, about the real doers of all that! Your Nobles and Right Honourables are first-rate men? Yes, and so is a goose a first-rate bird. But I 'l' tell you this about the goose;—you 'll find his natural flavour disappointing, without stuffing.

Perhaps I am soured by not being popular? But suppose I AM popular. Suppose my works never fail to attract. Suppose that, whether they are exhibited by natural light or by artificial, they inevitably draw the public. Then no doubt they are preserved in some Collection? No, they are not; they are not preserved in any Collection. Copyright? No, nor yet copyright. Anyhow they must be somewhere? Wrong again, for they are often nowhere.

Says you, 'At all events, you are in a moody state of mind, my friend.' My answer is, I have described myself as a public character with a blight upon him—which fully accounts for the curdling of the milk in *that* cocoa-nut.

Those that are acquainted with London are aware of a locality on the Surrey side of the river Thames, called the Obelisk, or, more generally, the Obstacle.

Those that are not acquainted with London will also be aware of it, now that I have named it. My lodging is not far from that locality. I am a young man of that easy dispositon, that I lie abed till it 's absolutely necessary to get up and earn something, and then I lie abed again till I have spent it.

It was on an occasion when I had had to turn to with a view to victuals, that I found myself walking along the Waterloo Road, one evening after dark, accompanied by an acquaintance and fellow-lodger in the gas-fitting way of life. He is very good company, having worked at the theatres, and, indeed, he has a theatrical turn himself, and wishes to be brought out in the character of Othello; but whether on account of his regular work always blacking his face and hands more or less, I cannot say.

'Tom,' he says, 'what a mystery hangs over you!'

'Yes, Mr. Click'—the rest of the house generally give him his name, as being first, front, carpeted all over, his own furniture, and if not mahogany, an out-and-out imitation—'yes, Mr. Click, a mystery does hang over me.'

'Makes you low, you see, don't it?' says he, eyeing me sideways.

"Why, yes, Mr. Click, there are circumstances connected with it that have,' I yielded to a sigh, 'a lowering effect.'

'Gives you a touch of the misanthrope too, don't it?' says he. 'Well, I 'll tell you what. If I was you, I 'd shake it off.'

'If I was you, I would, Mr. Click; but, if you was me, you wouldn't.'

'Ah!' says he, 'there 's something in that.'

When we had walked a little further, he took it up again by touching me on the chest.

'You see, Tom, it seems to me as if, in the words

of the poet who wrote the domestic drama of The Stranger, you had a silent sorrow there.'

'I have, Mr. Click.'

'I hope, Tom,' lowering his voice in a friendly way, 'it isn't coining, or smashing?'

'No, Mr. Click. Don't be uneasy.'

'Nor yet forg—' Mr. Click checked himself, and added, 'counterfeiting anything, for instance?'

'No, Mr. Click. I am lawfully in the Art line— Fine-Art line—but I can say no more.'

'Ah! Under a species of star? A kind of malignant spell? A sort of a gloomy destiny? A cankerworm pegging away at your vitals in secret, as well as I make it out?' said Mr. Click, eyeing me with some admiration.

I told Mr. Click that was about it, if we came to particulars; and I thought he appeared rather proud of me.

Our conversation had brought us to a crowd of people, the greater part struggling for a front place from which to see something on the pavement, which proved to be various designs executed in coloured chalks on the pavement stones, lighted by two candles stuck in mud sconces. The subjects consisted of a fine fresh salmon's head and shoulders, supposed to have been recently sent home from the fishmonger's; a moonlight night at sea (in a circle); dead game; scroll-work; the head of a hoary hermit engaged in devout contemplation; the head of a pointer smoking a pipe; and a cherubim, his flesh creased as in infancy, going on a horizontal errand against the wind. All these subjects appeared to me to be exquisitely done.

On his knees on one side of this gallery, a shabby person of modest appearance who shivered dreadfully (though it wasn't at all cold), was engaged in blowing the chalk-dust off the moon, toning the outline

of the back of the hermit's head with a bit of leather, and fattening the down-stroke of a letter or two in the writing.   I have forgotten to mention that writing formed a part of the composition, and that it also— as it appeared to me—was exquisitely done.   It ran as follows, in fine round characters: 'An honest man is the noblest work of God.   1 2 3 4 5 6 7 8 9 0.   £ s. d. Employment in an office is humbly requested.   Honour the Queen.   Hunger is a 0 9 8 7 6 5 4 3 2 1 sharp thorn.   Chip chop, cherry chop, fol de rol de ri do. Astronomy and mathematics.   I do this to support my family.'

Murmurs of admiration at the exceeding beauty of this performance went about among the crowd.   The artist, having finished his touching (and having spoilt those places), took his seat on the pavement, with his knees crouched up very nigh his chin; and half-pence began to rattle in.

'A pity to see a man of that talent brought so low; ain't it?' said one of the crowd to me.

'What he might have done in the coach-painting, or house-decorating!' said another man, who took up the first speaker because I did not.

'Why, he writes—alone—like the Lord Chancellor!' said another man.

'Better,' said another.   'I know *his* writing.   *He* couldn't support his family this way.'

Then, a woman noticed the natural fluffiness of the hermit's hair, and another woman, her friend, mentioned of the salmon's gills that you could almost see him gasp.   Then, an elderly country gentleman stepped forward and asked the modest man how he executed his work?   And the modest man took some scraps of brown paper with colours in 'em out of his pockets, and showed them.   Then a fair-complexioned donkey, with sandy hair and spectacles, asked

if the hermit was a portrait? To which the modest
man, casting a sorrowful glance upon it, replied that
it was, to a certain extent, a recollection of his father.
This caused a boy to yelp out, 'Is the Pinter a smoking the pipe your mother?' who was immediately
shoved out of view by a sympathetic carpenter with
his basket of tools at his back.

At every fresh question or remark the crowd leaned
forward more eagerly, and dropped the halfpence
more freely, and the modest man gathered them up
more meekly. At last, another elderly gentleman
came to the front, and gave the artist his card, to
come to his office to-morrow and get some copying to
do. The card was accompanied by sixpence, and the
artist was profoundly grateful, and, before he put the
card in his hat, read it several times by the light of his
candles to fix the address well in his mind, in case he
should lose it. The crowd was deeply interested by
this last incident, and a man in the second row with
a gruff voice growled to the artist, 'You 've got a
chance in life now, ain't you?' The artist answered
(sniffing in a very low-spirited way, however), 'I 'm
thankful to hope so.' Upon which there was a general chorus of '*You* are all right,' and the halfpence
slackened very decidedly.

I felt myself pulled away by the arm, and Mr.
Click and I stood alone at the corner of the next
crossing.

'Why, Tom,' said Mr. Click, 'what a horrid expression of face you 've got!'

'Have I?' says I.

'Have you?' says Mr. Click. 'Why, you looked
as if you would have his blood.'

'Whose blood?'

'The artist's.'

'The artist's?' I repeated. And I laughed, fran-

tically, wildly, gloomily, incoherently, disagreeably. I am sensible that I did. I know I did.

Mr. Click stared at me in a scared sort of a way, but said nothing until we had walked a street's length. He then stopped short, and said, with excitement on the part of his forefinger:

'Thomas, I find it necessary to be plain with you. I don't like the envious man. I have identified the canker-worm that's pegging away at *your* vitals, and it's envy, Thomas.'

'Is it?' says I.

'Yes, it is,' says he. 'Thomas, beware of envy. It is the green-eyed monster which never did and never will improve each shining hour, but quite the reverse. I dread the envious man, Thomas. I confess that I am afraid of the envious man, when he is so envious as you are. Whilst you contemplated the works of a gifted rival, and whilst you heard that rival's praises, and especially whilst you met his humble glance as he put that card away, your countenance was so malevolent as to be terrific. Thomas, I have heard of the envy of them that follows the Fine-Arts line, but I never believed it could be what yours is. I wish you well, but I take my leave of you. And if you should ever get into trouble through knifeing—or say, garotting—a brother artist, as I believe you will, don't call me to character, Thomas, or I shall be forced to injure your case.'

Mr. Click parted from me with those words, and we broke off our acquaintance.

I became enamoured. Her name was Henrietta. Contending with my easy disposition, I frequently got up to go after her. She also dwelt in the neighbourhood of the Obstacle, and I did fondly hope that no other would interpose in the way of our union.

To say that Henrietta was volatile is but to say

that she was woman. To say that she was in the bonnet-trimming is feebly to express the taste which reigned predominant in her own.

She consented to walk with me. Let me do her the justice to say that she did so upon trial. 'I am not,' said Henrietta, 'as yet prepared to regard you, Thomas, in any other light than as a friend; but as a friend I am willing to walk with you, on the understanding that softer sentiments may flow.'

We walked.

Under the influence of Henrietta's beguilements, I now got out of bed daily. I pursued my calling with an industry before unknown, and it cannot fail to have been observed at that period, by those most familiar with the streets of London, that there was a larger supply. But hold! The time is not yet come!

One evening in October I was walking with Henrietta, enjoying the cool breezes wafted over Vauxhall Bridge. After several slow turns, Henrietta gaped frequently (so inseparable from woman is the love of excitement), and said, 'Let's go home by Grosvenor Place, Piccadilly, and Waterloo'—localities, I may state for the information of the stranger and the foreigner, well known in London, and the last a Bridge.

'No. Not by Piccadilly, Henrietta,' said I.

'And why not Piccadilly, for goodness' sake?' said Henrietta.

Could I tell her? Could I confess to the gloomy presentiment that overshadowed me? Could I make myself intelligible to her? No.

'I don't like Piccadilly, Henrietta.'

'But I do,' said she. 'It's dark now, and the long rows of lamps in Piccadilly after dark are beautiful. I *will* go to Piccadilly!'

Of course we went. It was a pleasant night, and there were numbers of people in the streets. It was

a brisk night, but not too cold, and not damp. Let me darkly observe, it was the best of all nights—FOR THE PURPOSE.

As we passed the garden wall of the Royal Palace, going up Grosvenor Place, Henrietta murmured:

'I wish I was a Queen!'

'Why so, Henrietta?'

'I would make *you* Something,' said she, and crossed her two hands on my arm, and turned away her head.

Judging from this that the softer sentiments alluded to above had begun to flow, I adapted my conduct to that belief. Thus happily we passed on into the detested thoroughfare of Piccadilly. On the right of that thoroughfare is a row of trees, the railing of the Green Park, and a fine broad eligible piece of pavement.

'Oh my!' cried Henrietta presently. 'There's been an accident!'

I looked to the left, and said, 'Where, Henrietta?'

'Not there, stupid!' said she. 'Over by the Park railings. Where the crowd is. Oh no, it's not an accident, it's something else to look at! What's them lights?'

She referred to two lights twinkling low amongst the legs of the assemblage: two candles on the pavement.

'Oh, do come along!' cried Henrietta, skipping across the road with me. I hung back, but in vain. 'Do let's look!'

Again, designs upon the pavement. Centre compartment, Mount Vesuvius going it (in a circle), supported by four oval compartments, severally representing a ship in heavy weather, a shoulder of mutton attended by two cucumbers, a golden harvest with distant cottage of proprietor, and a knife and fork after

nature; above the centre compartment a bunch of grapes, and over the whole a rainbow. The whole, as it appeared to me, exquisitely done.

The person in attendance on these works of art was in all respects, shabbiness excepted, unlike the former personage. His whole appearance and manner denoted briskness. Though threadbare, he expressed to the crowd that poverty had not subdued his spirit, or tinged with any sense of shame this honest effort to turn his talents to some account. The writing which formed a part of his composition was conceived in a similarly cheerful tone. It breathed the following sentiments: 'The writer is poor, but not despondent. To a British 1 2 3 4 5 6 7 8 9 0 Public he £ s. d. appeals. Honour to our brave Army! And also 0 9 8 7 6 5 4 3 2 1 to our gallant Navy. BRITONS STRIKE the A B C D E F G writer in common chalks would be grateful for any suitable employment HOME! HURRAH!' The whole of this writing appeared to me to be exquisitely done.

But this man, in one respect like the last, though seemingly hard at it with a great show of brown paper and rubbers, was only really fattening the down-stroke of a letter here and there, or blowing the loose chalk off the rainbow, or toning the outside edge of the shoulder of mutton. Though he did this with the greatest confidence, he did it (as it struck me) in so ignorant a manner, and so spoilt everything he touched, that when he began upon the purple smoke from the chimney of the distant cottage of the proprietor of the golden harvest (which smoke was beautifully soft), I found myself saying aloud, without considering of it:

'Let that alone, will you?'

'Halloa!' said the man next me in the crowd, jerking me roughly from him with his elbow, 'why didn't

you send a telegram? If we had known you was coming, we'd have provided something better for you. You understand the man's work better than he does himself, don't you? Have you made your will? You 're too clever to live long.'

'Don't be hard upon the gentleman, sir,' said the person in attendance on the works of art, with a twinkle in his eye as he looked at me; 'he may chance to be an artist himself. If so, sir, he will have a fellow-feeling with me, sir, when I'—he adapted his action to his words as he went on, and gave a smart slap of his hands between each touch, working himself all the time about and about the composition—'when I lighten the bloom of my grapes—shade off the orange in my rainbow—dot the i of my Britons—throw a yellow light into my cow-cum-*ber*—insinuate another morsel of fat into my shoulder of mutton—dart another zigzag flash of lightning at my ship in distress!'

He seemed to do this so neatly, and was so nimble about it, that the halfpence came flying in.

'Thanks, generous public, thanks!' said the professor. 'You will stimulate me to further exertions. My name will be found in the list of British Painters yet. I shall do better than this, with encouragement. I shall indeed.'

'You never can do better than that bunch of grapes,' said Henrietta. 'Oh, Thomas, them grapes!'

'Not better than *that,* lady? I hope for the time when I shall paint anything but your own bright eyes and lips equal to life.'

'(Thomas, did you ever?) But it must take a long time, sir,' said Henrietta, blushing, 'to paint equal to that.'

'I was prenticed to it, miss,' said the young man, smartly touching up the composition—'prenticed to

it in the caves of Spain and Portingale, ever so long and two year over.'

There was a laugh from the crowd; and a new man who had worked himself in next me, said, 'He's a smart chap, too; ain't he?'

'And what a eye!' exclaimed Henrietta softly.

'Ah! He need have a eye,' said the man.

'Ah! He just need,' was murmured among the crowd.

'He couldn't come that 'ere burning mountain without a eye,' said the man. He had got himself accepted as an authority, somehow, and everybody looked at his finger as it pointed out Vesuvius. 'To come that effect in a general illumination would require a eye; but to come it with two dips—why, it's enough to blind him!'

That impostor, pretending not to have heard what was said, now winked to any extent with both eyes at once, as if the strain upon his sight was too much, and threw back his long hair—it was very long—as if to cool his fevered brow. I was watching him doing it, when Henrietta suddenly whispered, 'Oh, Thomas, how horrid you look!' and pulled me out by the arm.

Remembering Mr. Click's words, I was confused when I retorted, 'What do you mean by horrid?'

'Oh gracious! Why, you looked,' said Henrietta, 'as if you would have his blood.'

I was going to answer, 'So I would, for twopence—from his nose,' when I checked myself and remained silent.

We returned home in silence. Every step of the way, the softer sentiments that had flowed, ebbed twenty mile an hour. Adapting my conduct to the ebbing, as I had done to the flowing, I let my arm drop limp, so as she could scarcely keep hold of it, and I wished her such a cold good night at parting,

that I keep within the bounds of truth when I characterise it as a Rasper.

In the course of the next day I received the following document:

'Henrietta informs Thomas that my eyes are open to you. I must ever wish you well, but walking and us is separated by an unfarmable abyss. One so malignant to superiority—Oh that look at him!—can never never conduct   HENRIETTA
P.S.—To the altar.'

Yielding to the easiness of my disposition, I went to bed for a week, after receiving this letter. During the whole of such time, London was bereft of the usual fruits of my labour. When I resumed it, I found that Henrietta was married to the artist of Piccadilly.

Did I say to the artist? What fell words were those, expressive of what a galling hollowness, of what a bitter mockery! I—I—I—am the artist. I was the real artist of Piccadilly, I was the real artist of the Waterloo Road, I am the only artist of all those pavement-subjects which daily and nightly arouse your admiration. I do 'em, and I let 'em out. The man you behold with the papers of chalks and the rubbers, touching up the down-strokes of the writing and shading off the salmon, the man you give the credit to, the man you give the money to, hires—yes! and I live to tell it!—hires those works of art of me, and brings nothing to 'em but the candles.

Such is genius in a commercial country. I am not up to the shivering, I am not up to the liveliness, I am not up to the wanting-employment-in-an-office move; I am only up to originating and executing the work. In consequence of which you never see me; you think

you see me when you see somebody else, and that somebody else is a mere Commercial character. The one seen by self and Mr. Click in the Waterloo Road can only write a single word, and that I taught him, and it's MULTIPLICATION—which you may see him execute upside down, because he can't do it the natural way. The one seen by self and Henrietta by the Green Park railings can just smear into existence the two ends of a rainbow, with his cuff and a rubber— if very hard put upon making a show—but he could no more come the arch of the rainbow, to save his life, than he could come the moonlight, fish, volcano, ship- wreck, mutton, hermit, or any of my most celebrated effects.

To conclude as I began: if there's a blighted public character going, I am the party. And often as you have seen, do see, and will see, my Works, it's fifty thousand to one if you'll ever see me, unless, when the candles are burnt down and the Commercial character is gone, you should happen to notice a neglected young man perseveringly rubbing out the last traces of the pictures, so that nobody can renew the same. That's me.

CHAPTER IV

HIS WONDERFUL END.

IT will have been, ere now, perceived that I sold the foregoing writings. From the fact of their being printed in these pages, inference will, ere now, have been drawn by the reader (may I add, the gentle reader?) that I sold them to One who never yet—[1]

Having parted with the writings on most satis-

---

[1] The remainder of this complimentary sentence editorially struck out.

factory terms,—for, in opening negotiations with the present Journal, was I not placing myself in the hands of One of whom it may be said, in the words of Another,[1]—I resumed my usual functions. But I too soon discovered that peace of mind had fled from a brow which, up to that time, Time had merely took the hair off, leaving an unruffled expanse within.

It were superfluous to veil it,—the brow to which I allude is my own.

Yes, over that brow uneasiness gathered like the sable wing of the fabled bird, as—as no doubt will be easily identified by all right-minded individuals. If not, I am unable, on the spur of the moment, to enter into particulars of him. The reflection that the writings must now inevitably get into print, and that He might yet live and meet with them, sat like the Hag of Night upon my jaded form. The elasticity of my spirits departed. Fruitless was the Bottle, whether Wine or Medicine. I had recourse to both, and the effect of both upon my system was witheringly lowering.

In this state of depression, into which I subsided when I first began to revolve what could I ever say if He—the unknown—was to appear in the Coffee-room and demand reparation, I one forenoon in this last November received a turn that appeared to be given me by the finger of Fate and Conscience, hand in hand. I was alone in the Coffee-room, and had just poked the fire into a blaze, and was standing with my back to it, trying whether heat would penetrate with soothing influence to the Voice within, when a young man in a cap, of an intelligent countenance, though requiring his hair cut, stood before me.

'Mr. Christopher, the Head Waiter?'

'The same.'

---

[1] The remainder of this complimentary sentence editorially struck out.

The young man shook his hair out of his vision,—
which it impeded,—took a packet from his breast, and
handing it over to me, said, with his eye (or did I
dream?) fixed with a lambent meaning on me, 'THE
PROOFS.'

Although I smelt my coat-tails singeing at the fire,
I had not the power to withdraw them.   The young
man put the packet in my faltering grasp, and repeated,—let me do him the justice to add, with
civility:

'THE PROOFS.   A. Y. R.'

With those words he departed.

A. Y. R.?   And You Remember.   Was that his
meaning?   At Your Risk.   Were the letters short
for *that* reminder?   Anticipate Your Retribution.
Did they stand for *that warning?*   Out-dacious
Youth Repent?   But no; for that, a O was happily
wanting, and the vowel here was a A.

I opened the packet, and found that its contents
were the foregoing writings printed just as the reader
(may I add the discerning reader?) peruses them.
In vain was the reassuring whisper,—A. Y. R., All
the Year Round,—it could not cancel the Proofs.
Too appropriate name.   The Proofs of my having
sold the Writings.

My wretchedness daily increased.   I had not
thought of the risk I ran, and the defying publicity I
put my head into, until all was done, and all was in
print.   Give up the money to be off the bargain and
prevent the publication, I could not.   My family was
down in the world, Christmas was coming on, a brother
in the hospital and a sister in the rheumatics could not
be entirely neglected.   And it was not only ins in the
family that had told on the resources of one unaided
Waitering; outs were not wanting.   A brother out of

a situation, and another brother out of money to meet
an acceptance, and another brother out of his mind,
and another brother out at New York (not the same,
though it might appear so), had really and truly
brought me to a stand till I could turn myself round.
I got worse and worse in my meditations, constantly
reflecting 'The Proofs,' and reflecting that when
Christmas drew nearer, and the Proofs were pub-
lished, there could be no safety from hour to hour but
that He might confront me in the Coffee-room,
and in the face of day and his country demand his
rights.

The impressive and unlooked-for catastrophe towards which I dimly pointed the reader (shall I add,
the highly intellectual reader?) in my first remarks
now rapidly approaches.

It was November still, but the last echoes of the
Guy Foxes had long ceased to reverberate. We was
slack,—several joints under our average mark, and
wine, of course, proportionate. So slack had we become at last, that Beds Nos. 26, 27, 28, and 31, having took their six o'clock dinners, and dozed over
their respective pints, had drove away in their respective Hansoms for their respective Night Mail-trains
and left us empty.

I had took the evening paper to No. 6 table,—
which is warm and most to be preferred,—and, lost
in the all-absorbing topics of the day, had dropped into a slumber. I was recalled to consciousness by the
well-known intimation, 'Waiter!' and replying, 'Sir!'
found a gentleman standing at No. 4 table. The
reader (shall I add, the observant reader?) will please
to notice the locality of the gentleman,—*at No. 4
table*.

He had one of the new-fangled uncollapsable bags

in his hand (which I am against, for I don't see why you shouldn't collapse, while you are about it, as your fathers collapsed before you), and he said:

'I want to dine, waiter. I shall sleep here to-night.'

'Very good, sir. What will you take for dinner, sir?'

'Soup, bit of codfish, oyster sauce, and the joint.'

'Thank you, sir.'

I rang the chambermaid's bell; and Mrs. Pratchett marched in, according to custom, demurely carrying a lighted flat candle before her, as if she was one of a long public procession, all the other members of which was invisible.

In the meanwhile the gentleman had gone up to the mantelpiece, right in front of the fire, and had laid his forehead against the mantelpiece (which it is a low one, and brought him into the attitude of leap-frog), and had heaved a tremenjous sigh. His hair was long and lightish; and when he laid his forehead against the mantelpiece, his hair all fell in a dusty fluff together over his eyes; and when he now turned round and lifted up his head again, it all fell in a dusty fluff together over his ears. This give him a wild ap-pearance, similar to a blasted heath.

'O! The chambermaid. Ah!' He was turning something in his mind. 'To be sure. Yes. I won't go upstairs now, if you will take my bag. It will be enough for the present to know my number.—Can you give me 24 B?'

(O Conscience, what a Adder art thou!)

Mrs. Pratchett allotted him the room, and took his bag to it. He then went back before the fire, and fell a biting his nails.

'Waiter!' biting between the words, 'give me,' bite,

'pen and paper; and in five minutes,' bite, 'let me have, if you please,' bite, 'a,' bite, 'Messenger.'

Unmindful of his waning soup, he wrote and sent off six notes before he touched his dinner. Three were City; three West-End. The City letters were to Cornhill, Ludgate Hill, and Farringdon Street. The West-End letters were to Great Marlborough Street, New Burlington Street, and Piccadilly. Everybody was systematically denied at every one of the six places, and there was not a vestige of any answer. Our light porter whispered to me, when he came back with that report, 'All Booksellers.'

But before then he had declared off his dinner, and his bottle of wine. He now—mark the concurrence with the document formerly given in full!—knocked a plate of biscuits off the table with his agitated elber (but without breakage), and demanded boiling brandy-and-water.

Now fully convinced that it was Himself, I perspired with the utmost freedom. When he became flushed with the heated stimulant referred to, he again demanded pen and paper, and passed the succeeding two hours in producing a manuscript which he put in the fire when completed. He then went up to bed, attended by Mrs. Pratchett. Mrs. Pratchett (who was aware of my emotions) told me, on coming down, that she had noticed his eye rolling into every corner of the passages and staircase, as if in search of his Luggage, and that, looking back as she shut the door of 24 B, she perceived him with his coat already thrown off immersing himself bodily under the bedstead, like a chimley-sweep before the application of machinery.

The next day—I forbear the horrors of that night —was a very foggy day in our part of London, inso-

much that it was necessary to light the Coffee-room gas. We was still alone, and no feverish words of mine can do justice to the fitfulness of his appearance as he sat at No. 4 table, increased by there being something wrong with the meter.

Having again ordered his dinner, he went out, and was out for the best part of two hours. Inquiring on his return whether any of the answers had arrived, and receiving an unqualified negative, his instant call was for mulligatawny, the cayenne pepper, and orange brandy.

Feeling that the mortal struggle was now at hand, I also felt that I must be equal to him, and with that view resolved that whatever he took I would take. Behind my partition, but keeping my eye on him over the curtain, I therefore operated on Mulligatawny, Cayenne Pepper, and Orange Brandy. And at a later period of the day, when he again said, 'Orange Brandy,' I said so too, in a lower tone, to George, my Second Lieutenant (my First was absent on leave), who acts between me and the bar.

Throughout that awful day he walked about the Coffee-room continually. Often he came close up to my partition, and then his eye rolled within, too evidently in search of any signs of his Luggage. Half-past six came, and I laid his cloth. He ordered a bottle of Old Brown. I likewise ordered a bottle of Old Brown. He drank his. I drank mine (as nearly as my duties would permit) glass for glass against his. He topped with coffee and a small glass. I topped with coffee and a small glass. He dozed. I dozed. At last, 'Waiter!'—and he ordered his bill. The moment was now at hand when we two must be locked in the deadly grapple.

Swift as the arrow from the bow, I had formed my resolution; in other words, I had hammered it out be-

tween nine and nine. It was, that I would be the first to open up the subject with a full acknowledgment, and would offer any gradual settlement within my power. He paid his bill (doing what was right by attendance) with his eye rolling about him to the last for any tokens of his Luggage. One only time our gaze then met, with the lustrous fixedness (I believe I am correct in imputing that character to it?) of the well-known Basilisk. The decisive moment had arrived.

With a tolerable steady hand, though with humility, I laid The Proofs before him.

'Gracious Heavens!' he cries out, leaping up, and catching hold of his hair. 'What's this? Print!'

'Sir,' I replied, in a calming voice, and bending forward, 'I humbly acknowledge to being the unfortunate cause of it. But I hope, sir, that when you have heard the circumstances explained, and the innocence of my intentions—'

To my amazement, I was stopped short by his catching me in both his arms, and pressing me to his breastbone; where I must confess to my face (and particular, nose) having undergone some temporary vexation from his wearing his coat buttoned high up, and his buttons being uncommon hard.

'Ha, ha, ha!' he cries, releasing me with a wild laugh, and grasping my hand. 'What is your name, my Benefactor?'

'My name, sir' (I was crumpled, and puzzled to make him out), 'is Christopher; and I hope, sir, that, as such, when you've heard my ex—'

'In print!' he exclaims again, dashing the proofs over and over as if he was bathing in them. 'In print!! O Christopher! Philanthropist! Nothing can recompense you,—but what sum of money would be acceptable to you?'

I had drawn a step back from him, or I should have suffered from his buttons again.

'Sir, I assure you, I have been already well paid, and—'

'No, no, Christopher! Don't talk like that! What sum of money would be acceptable to you, Christopher? Would you find twenty pounds acceptable, Christopher?'

However great my surprise, I naturally found words to say, 'Sir, I am not aware that the man was ever yet born without more than the average amount of water on the brain as would *not* find twenty pounds acceptable. But—extremely obliged to you, sir, I 'm sure'; for he had tumbled it out of his purse and crammed it in my hand in two bank-notes; 'but I could wish to know, sir, if not intruding, how I have merited this liberality?'

'Know then, my Christopher,' he says, 'that from boyhood's hour I have unremittingly and unavailingly endeavoured to get into print. Know, Christopher, that all the Booksellers alive—and several dead— have refused to put me into print. Know, Christopher, that I have written unprinted Reams. But they shall be read to you, my friend and brother. You sometimes have a holiday?'

Seeing the great danger I was in, I had the presence of mind to answer, 'Never!' To make it more final, I added, 'Never! Not from the cradle to the grave.'

'Well,' says he, thinking no more about that, and chuckling at his proofs again. 'But I am in print! The first flight of ambition emanating from my father's lowly cot is realised at length! The golden bow,'—he was getting on,—'struck by the magic hand, has emitted a complete and perfect sound! When did this happen, my Christopher?'

'Which happen, sir?'

'This,' he held it out at arm's length to admire it,—
'this Per-rint.'

When I had given him my detailed account of it,
he grasped me by the hand again, and said:

'Dear Christopher, it should be gratifying to you
to know that you are an instrument in the hands of
Destiny. Because you *are*.'

A passing Something of a melancholy cast put it
into my head to shake it, and to say, 'Perhaps we all
are.'

'I don't mean that,' he answered; 'I don't take
that wide range; I confine myself to the special case.
Observe me well, my Christopher! Hopeless of getting rid, through any effort of my own, of any of the
manuscripts among my Luggage,—all of which, send
them where I would, were always coming back to
me,—it is now some seven years since I left that Luggage here, on the desperate chance, either that the
too, too faithful manuscripts would come back to me
no more, or that some one less accursed than I might
give them to the world. You follow me, my Christopher?'

'Pretty well, sir.' I followed him so far as to judge
that he had a weak head, and that the Orange, the
Boiling, and Old Brown combined was beginning to
tell. (The Old Brown, being heady, is best adapted
to seasoned cases.)

'Years elapsed, and those compositions slumbered
in dust. At length, Destiny, choosing her agent from
all mankind, sent You here, Christopher, and lo! the
Casket was burst asunder, and the Giant was free!'

He made hay of his hair after he said this, and he
stood a-tiptoe.

'But,' he reminded himself in a state of excitement,
'we must sit up all night, my Christopher. I must

correct these Proofs for the press. Fill all the ink-stands, and bring me several new pens.'

He smeared himself and he smeared the Proofs, the night through, to that degree that when Sol gave him warning to depart (in a four-wheeler), few could have said which was them, and which was him, and which was blots. His last instructions was, that I should instantly run and take his corrections to the office of the present Journal. I did so. They most likely will not appear in print, for I noticed a message being brought round from Beauford Printing House, while I was a throwing this concluding statement on paper, that the ole resources of that establishment was unable to make out what they meant. Upon which a certain gentleman in company, as I will not more particularly name,—but of whom it will be sufficient to remark, standing on the broad basis of a wave-girt isle, that whether we regard him in the light of,—[1] laughed, and put the corrections in the fire.

[1] The remainder of this complimentary parenthesis editorially struck out.